Chevrons Locked: The Unofficial and Unauthorized Oral History of Stargate SG-1, The First 25 Years

By Ed Gross
Foreword by Brad Wright

Previous Books by Edward Gross

Voices from Krypton: The Complete, Unauthorized Oral History of Superman
(Nacelle Books)

The Fifty-Year Mission: The Complete Oral History of Star Trek: The First 25 Years
(Thomas Dunne Books)

The Fifty-Year Mission: The Next 25 Years, from The Next Generation to J.J. Abrams
(Thomas Dunne Books)

Slayers & Vampires: The Complete Oral History of Buffy & Angel
(Tor Books)

So Say We All: The Complete Oral History of Battlestar Galactica
(Tor Books)

Nobody Does It Better: The Complete Oral History of James Bond
(Forge Books)

Secrets of the Force: The Complete Oral History of Star Wars
(St. Martin's Press)

They Shouldn't Have Killed His Dog: The Complete Oral History of Gun Fu, John Wick and the New Age of Action Films
(St. Martin's Press)

Above & Below: A 35th Anniversary Beauty and the Beast Companion
(Bearmanor Media)

All in This Together: The Unofficial Story of High School Musical
(ECW)

Rocky: The Complete Guide
(DK Books)

Spider-Man: Confidential
(Hyperion)

To my wife and fellow empty-nester, Eileen.
Let's take a trip through a Stargate and see where it takes us

ISBN 978-1-7373801-8-4

ACKNOWLEDGMENTS

Normally acknowledgements are saved until the end of these kinds of books, but that just didn't feel right in this case, because, quite frankly, *Chevrons Locked* would never have happened without these people.

And there are quite a number of people to thank for making this project a reality, starting with Brad Wright, who opened so many doors for me to make contact with others involved with the show. And who, over the course of our *many* zoom conversations, has become a friend- an unexpected but very welcome bonus.

Thanks also to Jonathan Glassner, Robert C. Cooper, Joseph Mallozzi, Paul Mullie, Peter Deluise, John G. Lenic, Ben Browder, Richard Hudolin, Thomas P. Vitale and the fine folks behind Gatecon for the sometimes repeated and often rushed interviews.

Special heartfelt thanks to both Darren Sumner, the founder of GateWorld.net and keeper of the flame; and David Read, who is doing such a spectacular job creating an interview archive of the *Stargate* cast and crew streaming on his *Dial the Gate* YouTube channel; not only for their advice and incredible support every step of the way, but for being interviewed and giving me access to their interview archives, which played so important a role in this book's creation. I'll be eternally grateful.

To Brian Volk-Weiss for his support and genuine enthusiasm for this project and my work in general, and for making me feel like a part of the Nacelle family.

And, finally, to my good friend and frequent collaborator, Mark A. Altman, who introduced me to the oral history format. I missed you this time out, sir!

TABLE OF CHEVRONS

FOREWORD
Brad Wright kicks things off

ONCE MORE INTO THE GATE...
How this book came to be

DRAMATIS PERSONAE
The voices you'll "hear" in Chevrons Locked

CHEVRON I: STARGATE: THE MOVIE,
FROM BIG SCREEN TO SHOWTIME
"It's not 'door to heaven' ... it's *Stargate!*"

CHEVRON II: THEY ARE FAMILY
The Cast of **Stargate SG-1**
"Despite the fact you've been a terrific pain in the ass for the last five years,
I may have grown to admire you. A little. I think."

CHEVRON III: THE EVOLUTION OF STARGATE SG-1
"You don't understand. This book may contain knowledge of the universe.
I mean, this is meaning-of-life stuff."

CHEVRON IV: SPIN-OFFS, ENDINGS AND LEGACIES
"You are the Fifth Race. Your role is clear. If there is any hope in preserving the future,
it lies with you and your people."

CHEVRON V: STARGATE SG-1 EPISODE GUIDE
"That's why we've come all this way. Why we had to endure all that singing.
Get rid of the last bad guy, then there's ... cake."

FOREWORD

25 years ago, *Stargate SG-1* aired on Showtime in the United States for the first time. It was most definitely not acclaimed by critics. In retrospect, it's hard to argue with them. But fortunately, our fans stuck with us and our show became something I'm deeply proud of. "Children of the Gods" marked the beginning of a three-series television franchise that ran for 17 seasons, 354 episodes and two DVD movies. A damn good run, by any measure.

And it all started with *SG-1*.

When Ed first contacted me about his book, he asked me if I would chat with him for an hour or two about *Stargate*. That's how he structured this book, like an oral history. That first zoom call we covered, oh, five percent of what he had hoped to get from me. So, I offered to talk again the following week. And again, the week after. I don't know how many times we talked over the course of the last year, but that may be because we only talked about *Stargate* about half the time. Ed and I are about the same age and got along so well, we found ourselves talking about everything under the sun. One writer to another. When another hour or two had flown by and he still hadn't got everything he wanted from me, we booked another zoom call. It was fun.

This book only covers *SG-1*, so I doubt we're done yet.

As Ed would attest, I don't remember everything about all those years on *Stargate*. Some of it's a blur, either because my nose was so close to the grindstone or because I had handed over the showrunning reins for a season. Fortunately, I introduced Ed to other people on the show who I knew would remember far more. I had to laugh at myself more than once for failing to remember who wrote or directed or starred-in what, or in which season, but Ed helped me along.

My memory of specific things from all those years ago may be lacking, but my memory of the experience as a whole is very much intact. It was a hell of a ride.

I get too much credit for *Stargate*. I shouldn't name names, because it'll just get me into trouble, but I have to share credit with Jon Glassner, who got the ball rolling with me and taught me so much; Rob Cooper, who became my co-showrunner and whose enormous talent raised the bar higher each season; Joe Mallozzi and Paul Mullie, who brought fresh blood and creativity from season 4 onwards, along with Carl Binder, with whom I first worked over 33 years ago on my very first show. Martin Gero, who came later, is currently taking over the television world. So much credit belongs to our incredible cast who stayed with us for so many seasons and whose names you already know.

Our core of directors — Martin Wood, Peter Deluise and Andy Mikita — made our show better each season, beautifully shot by DPs Peter Woeste and Jim Menard. John Smith and John Lenic were the line-producers who ran our well-run machine along with Michael Greenberg, RDA's producing partner. Our original Production designer, Richard Hudolin, followed by Bridget McGuire and James Robbins, designed our incredible sets over the years and Thom Wells built them. James Tichenor and Krista McLean made our visual effects more incredible each year. Set Decorator/sculptor/golf buddy extraordinaire, Mark Davidson, was there for the whole damn ride. So were editors Brad Rines and Rick Martin. Everyone at MGM was incredibly supportive throughout our long run, but I have to thank MGM president of television, John Symes, for trusting me in the first place, along with Hank Cohen and Charlie Cohen.

Finally, I have to mention our composer Joel Goldsmith, whose incredible music elevated our show to heights unreachable without him. May he rest in peace.

It was a helluva team.

There are dozens more I should mention but I know for a fact at least some of those names will come out in these pages. as they should be! A series like *Stargate* demands an enormous team. What made our team unique was how long so many of us stuck around and stuck together. We were like a family. I hope you get a sense of that through Ed's book.

That's what I remember of *Stargate* most fondly.

Brad Wright
January 2023

ONCE MORE INTO THE GATE...

With all due respect to my parents, I consider myself a child of filmed science fiction, the imagination of my childhood and adolescence nurtured by the allegorical storytelling of the original *Star Trek*, as well as the brilliance of Hollywood's first multi-film saga in the genre — predating George Lucas' *Star Wars* or Peter Jackson's *Lord of the Rings* trilogy — *Planet of the Apes*.

Now I'm not going to spend one minute pretending I recognized what *Trek* was allegorizing (I was six when the show debuted in 1966) or the racial undertones of *Apes* (instead, I was caught up in the oh-so-cool fact that there were talking monkeys and some great storytelling over five films), but I knew in both instances that there was something special there.

And as the '60s morphed into the '70s, I looked for something to complement *Trek* and *Apes*, but never quite found it. There was 1973's *The Starlost*, a Canadian production created by Harlan Ellison that was just godawful; 1974's TV version of *Planet of the Apes*, which played like *The Fugitive* with monkeys; 1975's *Space: 1999*, about a chunk of the moon with a base on it flying around the galaxy and getting into all sorts of adventures (seriously); 1977's *The Fantastic Journey*, which played like *The Fugitive* with people from the past, present and future seeking a way home; 1977's *Logan's Run*, from the feature film, which played like …. *The Fugitive* with the title character being chased by a former "Sandman" enforcement officer; 1978's *Battlestar Galactica*, which (sort of) played like *The Fugitive* in space, with the Cylons pursuing the remnants of humanity, and it went on from there.

Obviously as time continued to unfold, the genre would continue to expand on both the big screen (hello, *Star Wars*!) and small, one of the big phenomenons being TV shows based on feature films. These included *Alien Nation, Blue Thunder, Buffy the Vampire Slayer, Highlander: The Series, Honey, I Shrunk the Kids; Starman, RoboCop, The Young Indiana Jones Chronicles* and a little oddity called *Stargate*.

And I was aboard for many of them, particularly *Stargate*, hence the eventual writing of the book you're holding in your hands or have stored on your tablet, *Chevrons Locked*.

Stargate (1994) was the creation of filmmakers Roland Emmerich and Dean Devlin, starring Kurt Russell and James Spader. It grossed nearly $200 million, almost quadrupling its $55 million budget, but it's *true* success would be its adaptation to television. That's the medium where writers/executive producers Brad Wright and Jonathan Glassner, guiding forces on Showtime's revival of the classic anthology series *The Outer Limits*, individually lobbied MGM to allow them to produce a series based on *Stargate*, believing that at its core it had the perfect story-generating machine.

In the end, the studio suggested that they develop the TV version together, and from nearly the outset, the duo was given an extraordinary opportunity that no other television series has had before *or* since: the initial 44-episode commitment from the Showtime cable network became 88. And while these days it's a given that the vast majority of shows are offered full season commitments from streaming services, where the average "season" consists of maybe six to 10 episodes, it's important to bear in mind that Wright and Glassner were given the green light to produce no less than 22 episodes a year. *Guaranteed.*

It didn't stop there. In its sixth season, *Stargate SG-1* shifted from Showtime to the Sci-Fi Channel with the show running a total of 10 seasons, producing 214 episodes and a pair of original made-for-DVD movies. On top of that, it spawned the spin-off series *Stargate Atlantis, which ran* for five seasons between 2004 and 2009; and two seasons of *Stargate Universe* between 2009 and 2011. The production of the first few seasons of *Atlantis* were done concurrently with *SG-1*, meaning that the shows' creatives were responsible for 40 hours of television a year.

From the outside looking in, the basic concept of *Stargate* might seem relatively simple: a device of alien construct provides a means of transportation from here to other worlds within the Milky Way Galaxy. But it's actually much deeper than that. The show follows a team of four, consisting of two members of the Air Force, an archeologist/linguist and an alien who has sworn to aid them, stepping through the Stargate on missions of discovery and adventure, while ultimately providing some illumination on who we are and what our place is in the universe, with some laughs along the way.

Not a bad way to spend an hour, is it?

Especially when your guides, beyond the shows' writers and crewmembers, include people like Richard Dean Anderson, Amanda Tapping, Michel Shanks, Christopher Judge, Don S. Davis, Ben Browder, Claudia Black, Beau Bridges, Corin Jemic and a plethora of recurring guest stars who help bring the *Stargate* universe to life.

Chevrons Locked: The Unofficial and Unauthorized Oral History of Stargate SG-1, The First 25 Years, is a behind the scenes look at the making of the show that presents the personal views of cast and crew in their own words, reminiscent of sitting down with several dozen of your closest friends for a casual conversation about *SG-1*. Memories may vary, but in the end, you should get a sense of how these people and the wonderful world they created came to be.

I genuinely hope you enjoy the journey as much as I did.

Edward Gross
January 2023

DRAMATIS PERSONAE:
The Voices You'll "Hear" in *Chevrons Locked*

Cath-Anne Ambrose: Script coordinator, *SG-1*.
Tony Amendola: Actor, "Master Bra'tac," *SG-1*.
Richard Dean Anderson: Actor, "Jack O'Neill," *SG-1* and the spin-offs.
Erick Avari: Actor, "Kasuf"
Claudia Black: Actor, "Vala Mal Doran," *SG-1*.
Beau Bridges: Actor, "Major General Hank Landry," *SG-1* and *Stargate: Atlantis*.
Ben Browder: Actor, "Lieutenant Colonel Cameron Mitchell," *SG-1*.
Morris Chapdelaine: Puppeteer, *SG-1* and *Stargate Atlantis*.
Robert C. Cooper: Writer/co-executive producer and a director of *SG-1*, and
co-creator/co-executive producer/director of *Stargate Atlantis* and *Stargate Universe*.
Ronny Cox: Actor, "Senator/Vice President Robert Kinsey," *SG-1*.
Patrick Currie: Actor, "Eamon" and "Chaka"
Peter Deluise: Writer/director/creative consultant, *SG-1* and producer/director of
Stargate Atlantis and director *Stargate: Universe*.
Dean Devlin: Co-writer/producer, *Stargate* feature film.
Don S. Davis: Actor, "George S. Hammond," *SG-1*
Roland Emmerich: Co-writer/director, *Stargate* (from production notes)
Jonathan Glassner: Co-developer/executive producer, *SG-1*.
Allan Gowen: Gatecon founder, part owner/organizer and staging coordinator.
Michael Greenburg: Executive producer, *SG-1*.
Holger Gross: Production designer, *Stargate* feature film (from production notes)
Elizabeth Hoffman: Actress, "Catherine Langford"
Richard Hudolin: Production designer, *SG-1*.
Christopher Judge: Actor, "Teal'c," *SG-1*.
John G. Lenic: Producer, *SG-1*
Joseph Mallozzi: Executive producer, *SG-1, Stargate: Atlantis, Stargate: Universe*
Joel Michael: Producer, *Stargate* (from production notes)
Andy Mikita: Director, *SG-1*
Paul Mullie: Executive producer, *SG-1, Stargate Atlantis, Stargate Universe*
Corin Nemec: Actor, "Jonas Quinn," *SG-1*
Jeff Okun: Visual effects supervisor, *Stargate* feature film (from production notes)
Richard Pasco: Gatecon
David Read: Host, *Dial the Gate* YouTube Channel
Frynn Rogers: Gatecon
Kurt Russell: Actor, "Jack O'Neil," *Stargate* (from production notes)
Oliver Scholl: Conceptual designer, *Stargate* feature film (from production notes)
Michael Shanks: Actor, "Daniel Jackson," *SG-1*

Cliff Simon: Actor, "Baal," *SG-1*
N. John Smith: Line producer/executive producer, *SG-1*
James Spader: Actor, "Daniel Jackson," *Stargate* (from production notes)
Darren Sumner: Founder, GateWorld.net
Amanda Tapping: Actor, "Samantha Carter," *SG-1*
James Tichenor: Visual effects supervisor, *SG-1*
Thomas P. Vitale: Former EVP Programming at Syfy Channel and Chiller Networks
Peter Williams: Actor, "Apophis," *SG-1*
Martin Wood: Director, *SG-1*
Brad Wright: Co-developer/executive producer *SG-1*

CHEVRON I: STARGATE: THE MOVIE, FROM BIG SCREEN TO SHOWTIME

"It's not 'door to heaven' … it's **Stargate**!"

One of the greatest complaints about movies and many TV shows — and one repeated so often that it itself has fallen to the level of cliché — is the adage that there are no new ideas in Hollywood. That the studios have become so mired in exploiting titles it already owns, that fresh concepts are largely ignored.

For instance, three of the movies released in 1994 – Body Snatchers, The Getaway *and* Wes Craven's New Nightmare *– were remakes, a dozen were sequels —* Naked Gun 33 1/3: The Final Insult, Major League II, Beverly Hills Cop III *and* The Next Karate Kid *among them–, two –* Car 54, Where Are You? *and* Maverick *— were adaptations of TV shows, and one was an adaptation of two TV shows and a sequel wrapped up in one —* Star Trek: Generations, *which famously brought together William Shatner's Captain James T. Kirk and Patrick Stewart's Captain Jean Luc Picard).*

In that 1994 mix of big screen arrivals, an original that caught the attention of moviegoers was the sci-fi adventure Stargate, *created by director Roland Emmerich who co-wrote the script with producer Dean Devlin. The duo would go on to create alien invasion flick* Independence Day *and the first American version of* Godzilla.

ROLAND EMMERICH (co-writer/director, **Stargate**): When I was in film school, there was a wave of theories about aliens visiting Earth thousands of years ago and being responsible for the pyramids and such. It wasn't so much that I believed in the theories, but I always thought the idea could be the basis for a fantastic adventure movie.

DEAN DEVLIN (co-writer/producer, **Stargate**): Roland told me about a concept he had for a film set inside the Great Pyramids of Egypt. I told him about an idea I had for a kind of desert epic in outer space. We decided to combine the two and *Stargate* was born.

Here's how MGM describes the plot of the original film: "Set against the wondrous backdrop of the Great Pyramids of Giza, Stargate tells the story of two very different men who join forces to unravel the mystery of a curious artifact which could reveal the origin of civilization. A tough-minded military man, Colonel Jack O'Neil (Kurt Russell) heads a top-secret team investigating a mysterious artifact unearthed at Giza. Daniel Jackson (James Spader) is a brilliant Egyptologist whose scientific curiosity clashes with O'Neil's secret agenda. But it is Jackson who identifies the object as a stargate — a portal to another world. O'Neil leads Jackson and a reconnaissance team through the Stargate, which transports them millions of light years from Earth where they are stranded on a strange and alien planet. When the enigmatic ruler of this extraordinary world discovers that the doorway to Earth can be reopened, he devises a deadly plot. Racing against time, O'Neil and Jackson must overcome Ra if they are to save Earth and find a way back home."

The clash between the military and scientific communities' ambitions for the Stargate are brought to life through the film's two main characters: Special Forces Colonel Jack O'Neil and brilliant young Egyptologist Daniel Jackson. For O'Neil, the Stargate represents the fulfillment of a personal as well as professional mission; for Jackson it is the culmination of a life's work.

JOEL MICHAEL (producer, **Stargate**): The Stargate is the object of conflict because it has the capability of satisfying two very different objectives. O'Neil has his own clandestine plan, while Jackson understands that he has discovered something quite magnificent ... and wonderful.

DEAN DEVLIN: They each have their own agenda of what they want to accomplish when they go through the Stargate, and they're at opposite ends of the spectrum. One of the things this film is about is the two sides learning to respect one another and ultimately working together toward a single goal.

KURT RUSSELL (actor, "Jack O'Neil"): O'Neil is drawn to this mission because he has, in his own estimation, nothing left to live for. That makes him mysterious ... and certainly dangerous.

JAMES SPADER (actor, "Daniel Jackson"): I think Daniel is something of an island, an outsider. He's become frustrated by the world around him and then, all of a sudden, this door opens up that is ... perfect.

KURT RUSSELL: What drew me to it was Roland has a clear vision, and the producers were equally enthusiastic about it. It made me feel as if they could achieve what they were setting out to do. They cared a lot, and it was infectious.

JAMES SPADER: The script was unlike anything I had ever done or even considered doing. Then I met Roland and found him to be tremendously excited about this. He and the producers made it seem like it was going to be a fascinating journey, and I wanted to go on it. So, I did. And I'm glad I did.

DEAN DEVILIN: Kurt's ideas for his character were right on the money, and James can identify a line that's not right and knows just how to change it to make it work.

ROLAND EMMERICH: They are both extremely talented actors, but their styles and approach to their work couldn't be more different. James examines his role from an intellectual point of view, while Kurt is more emotional, going straight to the heart of the character. Ironically, their parts were similar in that way, so the relationship between them worked perfectly.

KURT RUSSELL: *Stargate* is a great journey, but in the end, it is a very human story. That is to say, simply, that you can travel to the other end of the universe, but whatever life form you encounter, you are still going to have to deal with your own humanity.

JAMES SPADER: My character spent his life studying entire civilizations spanning centuries. The breadth of one lifetime is meaningless to him. I think what he discovers in the course of the story is the value of that one life and that every culture is made up of millions of single lifetimes.

Stargate transports audiences to the city of Nagada on the planet Abydos, millions of light years from Earth. However, its culture is steeped in an ancient and earthbound civilization. It was this notion that would, in many ways, eventually serve as a launching point for what would become the Stargate SG-1 *television series — though that show's co-developers and executive producers, Brad Wright and Jonathan Glassner, extrapolated from the film's set-up.*

DEAN DEVLIN: One of the leaps we asked the audience to accept is that Egyptian culture didn't evolve but was actually a legacy — an imitation of something that had been there before. We needed to juxtapose a very primitive society with what could have been the inspiration for ancient Egyptian art and culture. To do that, our creative team had to design a world that would have the style of ancient Egypt, yet seem high-tech.

BRAD WRIGHT (co-developer/executive producer, **Stargate SG-1**): There was this race of beings that look just like us, that have been around for over a million years. And they were quite a dominant, quite wonderful race of people who explored the Milky Way and went on to explore other galaxies. And we called them the Ancients or the Gate Builders. They had a series of these devices called Stargates that they use to travel from civilization to civilization. What a Stargate does is open a stable wormhole. It's like a conduit from one planet to another. It's a shimmering pool of water that you walk into and it demolecularize you and you appear on the other side and you're intact. And then it shuts off. When we first discovered the Stargate, it was in the feature film *Stargate*. The Earth Stargate was dug up from the sands of Egypt near Cairo. So, in the show we were going to try and use it again. The intrepid Air Force Special Forces step through the Stargate for the first time and encounter what we call on the television series the Goa'uld. This is a race of beings that have taken human populations to their worlds, acted as their gods and enslaved the population. Over the course of *Stargate SG-1*, which was our first television series, we came up against the Goa'uld and we helped free the oppressed and made alliances. These teams, which we call SG teams, the leading of which is SG-1, explored and eventually freed the Milky Way of these bad guys called Goa'uld.

The movie version of Stargate was greeted by middling reviews upon its release, but was financially successful with nearly $200 million global gross — not bad considering its $55 million budget. With a profit margin like that, Devlin and Emmerich were understandably confident that they would be able to continue the story in their hoped-for big screen trilogy. But that wasn't in the cards, much to their disappointment.

By all reports, MGM wasn't considering any sort of future for Stargate on the big screen, the studio's focus being on television at that time, particularly dipping into their library for IPs that could be newly exploited. There was the small screen adaptation (1988-1994) of the theatrical hit, In the Heat of the Night *(1967), starring Carroll O'Connor (post-Archie Bunker) and Howard Rollins; the primetime remake of sixties daytime gothic horror sensation* Dark Shadows *(1991); an animated series* James Bond, Jr. *(1991-1994), and their biggest hit of the time, an updated version of the sci-fi anthology ,* The Outer Limits *(1960's), which aired on the Showtime cable network. There were also plans for a series based (in name only) on the Poltergeist films, which became* Poltergeist: The Legacy *(1996 to 1999).*

The primary reason that Stargate even entered the corporate zeitgeist was concern that writer/producers Wright and Jonathan Glassner remain with the highly successful The Outer Limits, *for which they served as executive producers. Both men had separately come to John Symes, the president of MGM at the time, with the notion of turning* Stargate *into a weekly series.*

PETER DELUISE (writer/director/creative consultant, **Stargate SG-1**): Jonathan Glassner and Brad Wright were running *The Outer Limits*, which was an anthology show, and everyone there was a writer/producer. There were quite a lot of them; each one of those people on that show were ultimately qualified showrunners in their own right — they could have *easily* all run their own show if they wanted to, but they were all working together as a group. And each one of them had to take their own episodes through prep, shooting and then post. So, what happened was *Stargate* came out and Jonathan and Brad, independently of each other, recognized that it was the perfect setup for a series. There's this expression in writing called *The Door in*, which means, what is the door into this story and how do we get there? It's not just the inciting incident, although it can be that. And the Stargate itself was, in fact, a doorway to another world where you didn't have to spend excruciating amounts of money on the spaceship ride over to it. So, they both recognized that it was the perfect device for a series and they each approached MGM with the idea of making a show based on the movie.

BRAD WRIGHT: I remember walking out of the movie thinking: *That wasn't great, but that Stargate is one of the best storytelling devices I've seen since the Enterprise on Star Trek.* I mean, it's a story-making machine. And the other thing is that I think one of the reasons *Stargate* was successful was that it featured people from the here and now. And the only reason we had access to space was due to this magical device that allows you to do it.

ROBERT C. COOPER (co-executive producer, **Stargate SG-1**): I liked the movie, although I didn't know that I immediately said, "Oh, *there's* a television series I would want to work on for 17 seasons." As it turned out, back in the day, when you were doing a more episodic show, *Stargate* proved itself to be a brilliant engine. Today, I really look for a great character to get me started that I can follow through the show. The movie had that, too. At the end of the day, Jack O'Neil is a guy who is a little bit *Lethal Weapon*; his son had died, and he was willing to throw everything out the window. And Daniel Jackson's a passionate, headstrong archaeology nerd. Those were great characters. But at the core, it also had a great engine, it had a device, like the starship *Enterprise*, which could take you anywhere you wanted to go this week and get you into trouble.

JONATHAN GLASSNER (co-developer/executive producer, **Stargate SG-1**): What fascinated me about the movie was really quite simple. It was in a day when television was still very episodic and not very serialized. Each episode had to stand alone, and this giant gate that could take you to another planet lent itself really well to being episodic. It was a great way to do a new story with new characters every week on new adventures every week while keeping ongoing arcs for the continuing characters. *That's* what struck me when I saw the film. It was just the perfect venue to do a show.

ROBERT C. COOPER: I just recently watched an interview with Dean Devlin, which I thought was great. He looked back on it and explained some of the challenges they had, what their hopes and dreams were for it and how it maybe fell short. Basically, I agree with his point of view on it, but thought that it was a brilliant idea. Maybe not 100% realized to its full potential. It was interesting to hear him come full circle. Originally, he was quite bitter and angry at the show, and maybe a little critical of it. Frankly, in the early seasons it was probably deserved, but he has developed, at least, an understanding and respect for what we did after that.

ANDY MIKITA (director, **Stargate SG-1**): I was a big fan of the original *Stargate* movie. The whole concept was just so cool. The fact that it was present day, was part of the US Air Force, had Egyptian mythologies and how everything was tied in with future, present, past, was just so intriguing. That was one of the big draws for me initially and I love that about *SG-1*.

BRAD WRIGHT: When I saw the movie, I objected to this one thing only, which was that the first two obstacles that they ran into became the entire story. Obstacle one, how do we get home? Obstacle two, how do they figure out what they're saying? So, the language and the way to get home became their two biggest obstacles. The other thing I *did* like was the sarcophagus, because it was a get out of jail free card, which we ended up basically doing over and over again ourselves. The sarcophagus is a device the Goa'uld use to quickly heal injuries and can even bring people who have recently died back to life. I also liked Kurt Russell's character, though he was a little humorless for me, but I thought James Spader was interesting and the scope was wonderful and huge. It was sci-fi and I *love* sci-fi.

PETER DELUISE: Dean Devlin had other things in mind for *Stargate*. They thought that they were going to shoot a trilogy of that story. To hear them talk about it, that's what their plan was. But MGM thought there would be more money in television, I guess. I mean, why would you try to make *less* money? And I think MGM said a series sounded like a good idea; let's do that.

DAVID READ (host YouTube channel, **Dial the Gate**): MGM recognized that a lot of these sci-fi stories — especially when you have a device like a "ring" that will take you anywhere in the galaxy —would serve itself better as an hour-long TV series to really get into those existential social issues like *Star Trek* did and other series attempted to do. Even Dean Devlin admitted to me on *Dial the Gate* that you can't do 350 plus hours of product if something isn't really working.

DEAN DEVLIN: The original plan was to do three movies, and so there were going to be three major addresses for the Stargate. And that's why we needed the nine [chevrons]. Parts two and three would have also used seven-chevron addresses, but with a different chevron lighting on the Stargate to travel to a different planet. We had big plans for it, but we never got to explore it. There are two different places on Earth that are famous for pyramids. One was an Egyptian, and our second was going to be a Mayan culture. And then the third was going to tie in almost every mystery that we've ever had on Earth! Whether it was Bigfoot or the Yeti — we were going to tie everything together into a larger mythology. And it was going to be so much fun. It was going to be so wild. But we never got to go there. We never got to explore it.

ROBERT C. COOPER: Dean Devlin recounted in this interview I read, which I had not really heard before, that MGM basically said to him, "We want to make a TV show," and he was, like, "Okay, great. Let's do that," and they said, "No, we don't want you to do it." If that had been me, I would have been bitter, too.

JONATHAN GLASSNER: When Brad and I were gearing up to do *Stargate*, Dean Devlin and Roland Emmerich were saying some bad things about it to the press. Cut to 20 or 25 years later, I get a call from my agent, who said, "Dean Devlin wants to meet you," and I'm, like, "Why?" "He read your script" — it was another script– a script that he and I are still trying to sell, by the way, "and he loved it and wants to talk to you about it." And I said, "He's going to punk me," because there was *such* bad stuff said about us. So, I went in and actually he had read a different script than the one we're working on together now, and he said, "Do you have any other ideas?" And so, I pitched him this idea and the whole time I'm thinking, "He's making me do this as an exercise, just to screw with me." But after I finished the pitch, he said, "I love this. Let's take it out."

While we've been trying to do this, he ended up asking me to run *The Outpost*, and I worked with him on that for four years. And we *have* had a *Stargate* conversation. He has not watched the show. He *did* watch the pilot and when he saw the nudity, it pissed him off and he turned it off. But we really hit it off, which is kind of ironic.

DEAN DEVLIN: The film was made entirely independently. MGM agreed to re-lease the film when no one else would release it, because no one believed in the movie. And the *week before* the movie opened, the people who had financed it — which was a group out of France — were so sure that they had a bomb, that they sold the movie to MGM for $5 million. So then, MGM owned *Stargate*. Roland and I went in to meet with them to talk about the series, and they said, "Oh, we don't really want you guys involved." It was a very painful thing for a long time, because you're watching someone else raise your children. It was very hard. But many years later it was obvious to me that, even though I had not been watching the show, that they must have been doing something right, because you don't get to live that long, you don't get to have that many fans and you don't get that kind of passion unless you've done a really good show.

DARREN SUMNER (creator, GateWorld.net): The two-hour premiere episode of *SG-1*, "Children of the Gods," certainly means to pick up where the movie had left off. It is one year later, Daniel Jackson is alive and well and living on Abydos, and the Stargate is in mothballs at the bottom of a military installation deep inside Cheyenne Mountain (not Creek Mountain, as in the movie — but that's a detail for us nitpickers). When the gate activates and an alien who looks a lot like Ra steps through, O'Neill is reactivated once again to finish the mission he'd thought was a success. There are a few changes — some subtle (Sha'uri becomes the easier-to-pronounce Sha're) and some not so subtle (Ra's species is not extinct but thriving, and they don't look like Roswell Greys). But the move to a weekly format worked. And it just made sense. The Stargate has 39 symbols on it, with millions of possible combinations, so it's only logical that one gate can go to many different places.

DAVID READ: The biggest change from movie to TV was probably the villain. If you look at the *Stargate* novels by Bill McKay, which Dean Devlin considers canon to his universe, they were really going to go in a different direction with the villains. It was Brad and Jonathan's genius idea to make them parasitical and to invent the Jaffa; the Jaffa were not a thing in the feature film. There's a line in "Children of the Gods" that there were no creatures like this on Abydos, which is their nod to say that this is a completely original species. Part of that was that Ra came from a dying race, but in the television series that's not the case. The Goa'uld are everywhere. Fans have tried to reverse engineer that idea to explain it, but there are things that are just not compatible.

For production reasons, every other Stargate out there doesn't have its own symbols; the symbols are standardized throughout the Stargate network to make it compliant, budget wise, with the TV series. They can't come up with a set of 40 new symbols for the dial home device in every episode; certain things had to be adapted to make the show work. At the same time, why *not* make the chevrons glow instead of being solid black? There were little things that Brad and Jonathan took advantage of that increased the quality of a series that would eventually turn into 10 seasons, with seven more seasons of spinoffs.

Brad Wright was born on May 2, 1961, in Toronto, Ontario, Canada. Growing up, he was a fan of the Apollo space program as well as military history, both of which would ultimately come into play as part of his writing life.

BRAD WRIGHT: I'm literally a child of the Apollo program. I was eight years old when Neil Armstrong walked on the moon and I was, like, "Wow, we can do that!" And I actually expected to be able to do it later in my life. Also, one of the very first novels I ever read as a young boy was called *Run Silent, Run Deep*, a World War II submarine yarn by Edward Beach. It was just riveting to me, and I loved the real drama of war and the built-in nature of that drama, because everything is life and death. Most shows — medical dramas, cop dramas — are that, too, because there is built-in drama in those worlds. So, I just started ravenously reading military fiction, and then all of the Asimov and Heinlein I could get my hands on. Right through my teen years I was loving all of this, but I'm Canadian and Canadians didn't make science fiction. It was just too expensive. There *was* one show called *Starlost*, but that was brutally bad. Harlan Ellison created it, but they just did not have the money to do whatever the hell they were trying to do with it.

In his twenties, Wright decided to give acting a try and became part of a six-member ensemble theater company (where he would meet his future wife) that he describes as "social action theater," touring high schools with one of the first plays on AIDS and having about a dozen shows in their repertoire. Coincidentally, he also co-wrote those plays.

BRAD WRIGHT: I actually wrote three plays in high school that we produced, so I was writing them at 15. *That's* where the writing thing came in. But I had this idea in my head that I was also an actor, which was dumb, and I thought I could do both. And for a while I did in my 20s, and then I realized that I was never going to succeed as an actor. When my wife and I got pregnant, I was in my late 20s. I wrote a pair of spec screenplays, both of which were science-fiction. They were ideas that I had been playing around with in my head, and both of them got into the hands of producers relatively quickly. They didn't get made, but they made people say, "You should check this guy out; he's pretty good."

He began writing for Canadian television, notably two episodes of The Adventures of Black Beauty *in 1990, two episodes of vampire drama* Forever Knight *in 1992, a pair of episodes of* Northwood *in 1993, and then got what was really his first big break with the 1990 to 1994 drama series,* Neon Rider.

BRAD WRIGHT: We were two weeks away from our first child being born when I got a job offer to be junior story editor on the show. The producer, Mary Kahn, told me to get on a plane and get there after the baby was born. In the meantime, I was sent a script they wanted me to look at, which arrived when the birth was very close, and we were getting very close to a gigantic change. Well, the script was *terrible*. Truly terrible writing, but the story was kind of good. When I wasn't packing and making dinner, and whatever you're doing when babies are getting ready to be born, I rewrote the script over a weekend. I made it pretty much as good as I could make that story and kept all the characters, and I sent it back to FedEx (this was pre-email). So, it took me a couple of days to get a response, and at this point we're about to go to the hospital when I get a call from Mary Kahn and she goes, "Dear, I have good news and bad news." I said, 'What's the bad news?' "The bad news is we didn't want you to rewrite the bloody script. We just wanted you to read it." And I went, "Oh, shit, I thought I should just fix it up." And she said, "You did. That's the good news. Have your baby, thanks for already doing some work before you even received a contract. Sign your contract and send it back." So, I stuck around with the baby for a while when I had no idea what a story editor was. I had no idea about *any* of it. There was just one executive story editor on the show, Aubrey Solomon, a lovely guy. And he just taught me everything. Then we rewrote and wrote the rest of the season. It was great.

I ended up being a co-producer on the show and was doing a lot more than that — casting, editing and was almost a showrunner at that point, but I didn't know any better. I met Carl Binder on the second season of that show; we were the writers together and I brought him aboard *Stargate*.

In 1994, the year Neon Rider *ended, Wright wrote two episodes of* Madison, *one of* Highlander: The Series *and three of* The Odyssey. *When that show ended, he had a deal with Aaron Spelling for a solo pilot at NBC titled* Charm, *which was essentially* The Matrix, *but it didn't end up going into production — much to his relief.*

BRAD WRIGHT: It was ahead of its time in terms of what you could do with CG in television, but I didn't know any better. The only thing I had carved out in this contract is that if it went forward, I had to be allowed to write a script for Showtime's *The Outer Limits*, because that was a dream gig for me. It was an anthology, *and* it was science-fiction. Well, I ended up on *The Outer Limits* for four years. My door into it was that they read a sample of mine and the showrunner, Michael Cassutt said, "Oh, this is great. Let's take a meeting." To be honest, though, for them to take advantage of Canadian content rules, to use an American director they *had* to have a Canadian writer, so they were basically just giving a Canadian writer a script and then rewriting it. But they would have preferred not to do that.

I had two pitches for two stories ready to go. I showed up and said I had a meeting with Michael Cassutt, and they said, "No you don't. He got fired this morning." I just stood there, and they said, "Well, Richard's here, he's the executive producer of the show. I guess he'll take the meeting." So, I'm pitching my idea to the executive producer, Richard Barton Lewis, and his phone did not stop ringing. It took me a good hour to get through a 15-minute pitch, because he would take the call and then say, "Okay, keep going." I finished the pitch and thought, "I don't have a hope in hell of getting this job." But they gave me a freelance assignment, which I wrote, and they liked, so I got a staff offer. And I became for them a bit of a writing machine. They had all these dead scripts that they didn't think were going anywhere and that the studio didn't like, and I just basically fixed them — like I did with the very first script I ever did. I just took them and rewrote them. So that season I wrote a chunk of scripts that don't have my name on them, and a giant chunk that does.

Wright began as a writer on The Outer Limits *and quickly advanced to executive story consultant. From there, he became a supervising producer and, then, co-executive producer. At that point he developed a strong relationship with MGM and* Outer Limits *Executive Producer Jonathan Glassner, with whom he worked well.*

JONATHAN GLASSNER: I will say one of the things that the previous showrunner on *The Outer Limits* had done right was hire Brad. He was one of the few elements that I kept. He was probably the only writer on the show that I *didn't* have to rewrite. So, I kept moving him up and teaching him the ropes of running a show and eventually he was rewriting half the episodes and I was rewriting the other half. We ended up just kind of splitting the episodes and he ended up co-executive producer.

BRAD WRIGHT: In 1996, MGM also asked me to take a look at their pilot script for *Poltergeist: The Legacy.* I read the script and was, like, "Guys, my advice is to get out of prep and go on hiatus," and they said they couldn't, they'd miss their date. I said, "Well, you're in trouble." But they needed me to do an emergency rewrite, and, in a week, a two-hour pilot got turned around. I gave it back to the director of the pilot and I ended up with a writing credit on it, which I didn't expect or want. Just this weird week. But I didn't stay involved with *Poltergeist* at all. Honestly, ghosts and that stuff are not at all my thing; I don't relate to it at all. I enjoy vampire movies and zombie movies, but I would be the first to die facing the zombie horde, telling them that the laws of thermodynamics preclude their existence. I mean, it just makes no sense at all. But I did the pilot, because they needed me to do it, but I would not have been able to succeed on that show.

At the same time, I knew I would have continued with *The Outer Limits* forever. It was the most fun you can have. Your actors are always on their best behavior, because they're there for, like, a week to 10 days. And they're there to have fun. I got to work with Steven Weber on his very first directing assignment, which is stressful for a writer/ producer, because he's never directed before. And so, you have to really kind of have their back in that respect. But I worked with Catherine O'Hara. I worked with so many great actors and, again, it was like doing 22 little movies every year. It was also probably the most stressful time creatively, because you can't say, "Okay, we'll just hold that for next week." You *have* to get your shots. You have to get *everything*, and we would get into holes and sometimes I would do rewrites on the spot to simplify the afternoon's work just so that you could get the show done. In any case, after *Poltergeist* I went back to *The Outer Limits.* Now on that show, Jonathan Glassner and I were very successful when he directed and I wrote. Some of my favorite episodes were that partnership.

Jonathan Glassner was born in Roanoke, Virginia. When he was a teenager, he, like Brad

Wright, decided to become an actor, doing so in regional theater performances throughout the state. He began as a theater major when he enrolled at Northwestern University, but it wasn't long before he realized that there was something else he'd rather be doing.

JONATHAN GLASSNER: I wanted to be a director and I started taking all of these directing classes, thinking I would just graduate and become a director — you know, a naïve college kid. One of the speakers who came and spoke at the school was Bob Thompson, who used to be the staff director on the TV version of *The Paper Chase*. He said, "If you want to become a director in television, episodic television in particular, the fastest way to get there is to be a writer." It might not be true anymore, but it was back then for sure, because it's really hard to find directors unless they have film, and how do they have film unless they've made a movie or something? Back in those days it was *really* expensive to make something. The best way was to be in the position where you could hire yourself and move up the ranks so that you could hire yourself as a director. That's basically what my plan was, but that didn't happen for a very long time because I ended up loving writing and showrunning. I sold my first script to *Alfred Hitchcock Presents* — the remake in the '80s — and they liked it so much that they gave me a blind commitment for two more. From there, I went off and just kept going. I haven't *not* worked for more than maybe four months since then.

From there I worked my way up at Stephen J. Cannell's company and ended up running the last season of *21 Jump Street*; I was 26 when I became a showrunner and was kind of in over my head a little bit and went on and did a bunch of other failed shows. Spent two years on *Street Justice* with Carl Weathers, and then I worked with Lee Rich, one of the founders of Lorimar Productions, who was the back-then cliché of the cigar-smoking producer. And he said, "Kid, way back I produced a show called *Rat Patrol*. And I want to do a science fiction version." Well, I thought that was the stupidest idea ever, but I came back and pitched an idea that had almost nothing to do with *Rat Patrol*, and they loved it. *And* they bought it. *And* we sold it. We made a pilot called *Island City* and that pilot ran so many times that I actually got checks for profit participation. Well, that suddenly made me a science fiction writer, and everybody was calling me for science fiction projects, and I ultimately went on *The Outer Limits*.

I originally went on it as a writer consultant, but then they fired the showrunner and asked me to take it over. I hadn't moved my wife up to Vancouver and the deal was that I was going to go up there for a year to straighten it out, and then come home and run it from home like they were trying to do before. But I quickly learned that you can't do that with a show like this because it was an anthology, and every episode was like doing a little movie. Every week, new cast, new sets, new wardrobe and, because it was science fiction, new creatures and visual effects. And we were looking at 22 of them a year, which was insane.

They kept offering me more and more money to keep staying with the show, which was hard to say no to. But eventually, after the third season, I told them, "That's it. This is not a negotiation. You can offer me a billion dollars, but I'm not staying. My wife is in L.A., my family is in L.A., my wife's family is in L.A. This is just too hard for us." And she was *miserable*. At that point the president of MGM came to me and said, "We have this title and a commitment from Showtime for 22 episodes of a new series. It's yours if you want it, *if* you'll stay for another three years." I said, "Probably still no, but let me think about it." I remember struggling with it and I came back to him and said, "You have this movie in your library, *Stargate*, that would make a better series than a movie. If you let me do that, then I'll stay." And he said, "I don't think we can do that, but let me think about it and get back to you."

BRAD WRIGHT: It was during the second season of *The Outer Limits* that the movie version of *Stargate* was released. When I saw it, my reaction was, "Man, this would be a better series than it ever was a movie." I liked the movie, but it had the potential of being a *great* series. So I went to Hank Cohen, the vice president of MGM Television, and said, "I have a spin for a *Stargate* series I would like you to hear."

JONATHAN GLASSNER: About two weeks later, John Symes called me, and he said, "*Stargate* is yours if you want it, but there's a catch. Brad Wright has talked about the same thing."

BRAD WRIGHT: I didn't know at the time that Jonathan Glassner had gone to John Symes with the same statement, and, of course, MGM was way ahead of us. John said, "We already thought of that, but we would like you guys to do it together." So that partnership came out of having successfully worked together on *The Outer Limits*, and John Symes' desire not to piss off either one of us. He also thought that together we were a good team.

When looking back at the history of Stargate, *one cannot underestimate the impact that the Showtime cable network has had on it. Back in 1993, the channel struck a production and licensing deal with MGM that gave Showtime — at that time trying its best to compete with HBO — exclusive premium TV rights to theatrical films from MGM Pictures, United Artists and Goldwyn Films, as well as original series created by MGM TV.*

THOMAS P. VITALE (former EVP Programming at Syfy Channel and Chiller Network): At the time, HBO was the number one pay cable network with the most number of subscribers, and Showtime was looking for a strategy to catch up to HBO by focusing on different types of programing. One of Showtime's programming initiatives was to air original science fiction programming. To that end, Showtime partnered with MGM to produce three genre shows based on MGM brands. The first was the new *Outer Limits*, which launched in March 1995; the second was *Poltergeist: The Legacy*, which launched in April 1996; and the third was *Stargate SG-1*, which launched in July 1997.

JONATHAN GLASSNER: John Symes, who was the president of MGM TV at the time, was a brilliant businessman and he had made a deal with Showtime. I don't know all the particulars of it, but basically what it was, was that they could have access to the MGM library of movies and, I think, some old TV shows to air on Showtime, but they had to give him a commitment for a full season of a series. Back then they didn't order 13 and then a back nine; it would always end up at 22. That became *The Outer Limits*, which did so well for them, that he leveraged it. He just kept saying, "Well, if you want two more years of *The Outer Limits*, you've got to give me one more commitment." And Showtime was happy with everything that MGM was providing them, so they were happy to do it.

THOMAS P. VITALE: But Showtime didn't pay the full cost for any of these shows, so MGM had to devise a creative financing plan to get these shows produced. So, in addition to the fees paid by Showtime, these three series were financed with multiple other revenue sources as well. As Canadian productions, the shows took advantage of the various Canadian production incentives available, which generally made up about 30% of the budget. In addition, MGM sold the shows internationally, which brought in healthy fees. But, still, there wasn't quite enough money, so MGM also sold the series into broadcast syndication following the Showtime premiere window. Therefore, financing came from four sources: 1) Canadian financial incentives – pretty standard, 2) International sales, also standard, 3 & 4) Simultaneous dual sale in the U.S. –not standard at the time. What does that mean in layman's terms? Basically, these shows were sold twice in the U.S. for different telecast "windows." More specifically, each September following Showtime's premiere of a full season of one of those shows, they would air around the U.S. in local station syndication, usually on Saturday afternoons or evenings on one of the independent TV stations in most markets around the country.

So, specifically, the first season of *Stargate SG-1,* which launched on a weekly basis on Showtime in July 1997, would air on free broadcast stations for a year starting in September 1998. In September 1999, episodes would be back on Showtime, along with original episodes of season three, while season two episodes would be off Showtime and would air on broadcast stations. The scenario was complicated for viewers who didn't always know where to catch different episodes, but it made sense for MGM, Showtime and the local stations. Ultimately, MGM was able to close the gap in its financing for these shows, stations were able to air high-quality programs that very few people had seen, since Showtime was subscribed in only about 15 to 20% of U.S. homes. And Showtime was able to get quality shows at an affordable price, and additionally, Showtime could have its original programming exposed across the country on local stations to viewers who, if they got hooked on the three series, would hopefully then subscribe to Showtime, increasing Showtime's subscriber base and revenue."

When MGM broached the idea of a Stargate *television series with Showtime, there was, before a single word of it had been written, a guarantee for a 22-episode first season, which expanded to 44 episodes once the actual pilot was delivered. Then, in March 1998, MGM and Showtime extended their deal, and the* SG-1 *guarantee expanded to 88 episodes — which was unprecedented.*

JONATHAN GLASSNER: That kind of order is very handy when you're producing a science-fiction show, because you can amortize a lot of this stuff over the first 44 episodes. So, we were able to build massive sets and spend a lot of money, because we could amortize it. If you think about the Stargate room, where the gate was, that was two-stories tall. It was *huge*, right with the gate in it. And that was just one of our sets. We had to build worlds all the time.

DAVID READ: There is a terrific story Brad tells about pitching *Stargate* as a series to the executives at Showtime in the parking garage, because someone pulled the fire alarm. So, they're out there and the executive is still, like, "Okay, keep going."

BRAD WRIGHT: Jonathan and I are sitting with Jerry Offsay of Showtime and Poncho Mansfield, his right-hand man. John Symes and Hank Cohen are there, too. Jon and I had spent part of the summer developing our concept of what *Stargate* should be. I had this whole sort of intro of it, having a sense of the Mercury Astronauts, sort of like *The Right Stuff* with that early NASA quality. That's why it was small teams walking through a stargate, dipping our foot in the water. Jon did his spiel. I was in the middle of mine and the fire alarm goes off. Jerry Offsay, a lovely man, turns to his assistant and says, "What's the fine if we don't leave?" And she says, "Sir, we have to leave. I'm sorry." I go downstairs with him, and we go into the area we're supposed to go. Jerry's about six-five and I am not, and we're all kind of clumped together and I'm looking pretty much right up his nose. He looks down at me and says, "Okay, go on." So, I finished my part of the pitch, the alarm stopped, and I just kept going. We head back upstairs. Jerry goes, "I got it. It's great." So, Jonathan and I looked at each other wondering if that was a good or bad thing. Poncho leans over to me and says, "You did good."

Then the other *Stargate* shoe dropped: they wanted us to continue doing *The Outer Limits* as well. So, for the first two years after launching the show, we were also writers/producers on *The Outer* Limits. One of the big saving graces was the fact that *Stargate* eventually became a well-oiled machine, and guys like Rob Cooper, Carl Binder, Paul Mullie and Joe Mallozzi could eventually run with their own episodes, which meant I didn't have to be on top of everything. But with *The Outer Limits*, if you were the writer/producer of an episode, it was like doing a pilot — you were doing a little movie every time. So, trying to do that while at the same time launching *Stargate* was pretty tough. In those days, I was walking around with two sets of headphones and forgetting what meeting we were in. But how much fun is that? I'll tell you: it was terrific fun.

JONATHAN GLASSNER: At the same time, we very quickly learned that if we were to continue doing that — working on both shows concurrently — we would have ended up dead. We'd just done too many shows, so we let Sammy [Sam Egan] take over on *The Outer Limits* and both of us just stayed on *Stargate*.

BRAD WRIGHT: I remember saying to John Symes, "Honestly, we need to pay more attention to *Stargate*. We can't do this anymore. *Stargate* is a show that deserves more attention, and I think it's showing that we're not devoting enough time and energy to it." He said, "Well, I think you're doing great, but okay." He didn't think MGM was going to let us out of it, but they did, so we stepped away after the first two seasons of trying to do both shows at the same time. But because we were in the same studio, during those two seasons we had two offices and would go back and forth. *Outer Limits* would be on one stage, *Stargate* on another and it was crazy. You'd walk into the wrong stage and say, "Oops, sorry." Then *Poltergeist* got shot on the same lot, so there was a time when we were shooting *Stargate SG-1*, *Poltergeist* and *The Outer Limits* on the same lot, and I was involved with all three shows.

Once Glassner and Wright were told that they would be able to produce the TV version of Stargate, *the development process of the adaptation began, with the concepts of the Goa'uld and the Jaffa being among the first things created. The Goa'uld, of which Ra was one, are a dominant species in the Milky Way Galaxy and have been for thousands of years. They are serpent parasites that forcibly take human hosts and fill them with an unquenchable thirst for power and worship. Many worlds have been enslaved by them, their inhabitants serving as hosts, soldiers, miners and personal slaves. And the Jaffa are the Goa'uld's slaves, consisting of humans from countless worlds, most of whom have been implanted with larval Goa'uld symbiotes.*

BRAD WRIGHT: I don't remember all of the details, but we were working on *The Outer Limits* together and basically stealing time to work on *Stargate*; we were slipping away at lunch to talk about it. Like I said, a big thing I wanted was elements of *The Right Stuff*, which was one of my favorite films. I wanted it to have that feel, I wanted the teams to have that feel — the five astronauts about to go into the unknown. So early NASA was what I wanted Stargate Command to feel like. We don't know what's out there, we're going to go and have that sort of mission quality and to have mission experts. We wanted there to be an alien, and that came in the form of the Jaffa, Teal'c, although the symbiote sounded like a better idea than it ended up on screen. I don't know who came up with that, to be honest. But we riffed very well together, so all of that back and forth helped us to build up the concept.

JONATHAN GLASSNER: Fortunately, by that point we had a shorthand since we had done 66 episodes of *The Outer Limits* together. We sat in the MGM offices and wandered around the lot and talked about the movie. One of the things that was really important to us was being true to the movie, because we knew it had a big fan base and we didn't want to piss them off. So we said, "Well, what's left open? What are the holes? We knew they'd left Abydos behind them and closed off the gate. Can we re-open it? Why did it only go one place in the movie when there's all those symbols and all the combinations you could possibly make of them? Why don't we think of the gate as an old-fashioned dialer on a telephone that can send you all kinds of places?" *That* was a big deal to us. What was Ra, which was never really defined in the movie? What species was he? Who were the people that worked for him when we made the Jaffa? Where is Abydos, why is it primitive? We kind of latched onto the idea — without saying it out loud; it was in the back of our heads that the world was populated by this same species that is all over the universe, which is why a lot of them look like us. A lot of the planets where people look like us don't speak English. And that's why everything looked Egyptian – because that's what the culture looked like here at the time, which led us to start saying there are other cultures that also came. So, we played with the whole idea of aliens visiting Earth.

BRAD WRIGHT: When we were developing the series, my struggle was still with the question — which was one of my struggles with the movie — "How are we going to have people who understand English?" Jon said, "Well, it works for *Star Trek,* and it worked for every other show. Audiences just accept it." Well, that bothers me. I regret the decision, but Jon won the argument. It was my complaint about the movie, too, but he gotta throw that in my face as to why you *shouldn't* worry about it: every episode would have to have that component of explanation. *Star Trek* had the universal translator. We should have just stolen it or maybe it was an effect of going through the stargate. Just *some* sort of rationale.

JONATHAN GLASSNER: In the movie something is up with Ra, but you don't know what it is because they never really explain it. He's clearly human, but his eyes glow and he talks funny. So, we were saying, "Why is that? How can we explain that?" And that's when we came up with the Goa'uld. Brad and I also realized that that was a really rich thing for drama down the line, because it's two people or two beings in one body and they don't agree. There was definitely fun to be had, and it immediately gave us the idea that Sha're – Daniel Jackson's Abydonian wife – becomes taken over by one of them.

BRAD WRIGHT: We started writing the pilot, basically handing the script back and forth. And I *will* say this: When we finished it, I had some issues with it. I had issues with the teaser, because I didn't like not meeting any of our regular cast in it. I wanted to restructure it, but I was the only one who thought that. Everybody else liked it, so I lost that argument.

CHEVRON II: THEY ARE FAMILY

The Cast of *Stargate SG-1*

"Despite the fact you've been a terrific pain in the ass for the last five years, I may have grown to admire you. A little. I think."

The heart of any successful television series is its ensemble of characters and whether those characters (and the actors who bring them to life) connect with each other and the audience. This is particularly true when it comes to the science-fiction genre — consider the bridge crew of any Star Trek *series, the triumvirate of Han, Leia and Luke in* Star Wars *and the SG-1 team in* Stargate.

Ask any fan, cast or crew member of Stargate *why the show endures, and it invariably comes back to the family of cast/characters. In the case of SG-1, that family consists of Richard Dean Anderson as Colonel Jack O'Neill, Michael Shanks as Egyptologist Daniel Jackson, Amanda Tapping as astrophysicist Captain Samantha ``Sam" Carter, Christopher Judge as the Jaffa, Teal'c, who elects to become a member of the team; and Don S. Davis as Lieutenant General George Hammond. Eventually joining were Corin Nemec as humanoid alien Jonas Quinn (who had a recurring role in Seasons 5 and 7 and was a main cast member in Season 6), Ben Browder as Lieutenant Colonel Cameron ``Cam" Mitchell (Seasons 9 and 10), Beau Bridges as Major General Henry "Hank" Landry (Seasons 9 and 10) and Claudia Black as alien con artist Vala Mal Doran (recurring in Seasons 8 and 9, main cast in season 10).*

BRAD WRIGHT: Originally, we came up with a loose concept of the series as a whole, Stargate Command and individual teams. And I remember when John Symes said, "What have you guys got so far, I know it's early?" We said we want O'Neill and Daniel and a woman scientist to be on the team with another person from the film that was Kawalsky. He ended up dying in the second episode, and that's why Teal'c joined us on SG-1. His joining was kind of a strange decision, to be honest, because he was an alien and we immediately trusted him and immediately got him to join us, but we wanted that element. John's response was, "So, it's like a team?" and I said, "Yes, there are nine teams and this is SG-1. Our team has that designation." John nodded and later, after the meeting, I said to him, "I don't think SG-1 makes sense, because it's Stargate One. We should come up with something else." And he went, "Really? Is that what you have to say, Bradley?" — he called me Bradley — and I went, "Yeah, why?" And he said, "I was going to surprise you with this," and then he opened a spread in *Variety* magazine that says, "*Stargate SG-1* Premiering Soon." I responded, "Oh. It's starting to grow on me." I mean, it was just literally a throwaway during a pitch conversation.

Things evolved from there. We knew that we could go to another Goa'uld and we knew that we would have an arc with Apophis and that at the end of the season, we wanted the bad guys to find a way to find Earth. *And* we would have to find a way to stop them. As for the details of who came up with what, I have no memory of this. Jonathan might even remember more than me, because, again, 300 episodes is a large number.

JONATHAN GLASSNER: People ask me, "Why do you think *Stargate* was so successful?" I've done writing seminars on that subject and my answer is always, it's about the characters, not the plot. Don't think about the plot, because if you don't have good characters living that plot, it's not going to be a success. The audience has to want to invite those people into their living room every week. And if they *don't* want to, it's not going to speak to them.

BRAD WRIGHT: In some ways, in retrospect, the casting process was incredibly painless. If you think about it, we threw out an ad across the country and we got a cast almost painlessly. Talk about natural chemistry — they were great for 10 years. How rare is *that*? And the chemistry between the people actually created chemistry between the characters.

DAVID READ: When you talk with the cast of *Stargate SG-1*, you get the sense that they really recognize that what they had then was lightning in a bottle and continue to consider it as such to this day. That works through the fan interactions and through any time that they mention the work that they did. They really get that what they were part of was something that shouldn't under normal circumstances exist.

BRAD WRIGHT: The actors and the characters matured in real time of the show. I mean, Daniel, my God, he goes through *such* a journey, including an ascension, and becomes practically immortal and then human again. And then I don't remember everything. But the bonds between all of them never wavered. And that's the one rule we never broke: when they rarely disagreed, or were angry, with each other and disappointed with each other, they still had each other's backs like nobody's business. It's one of the reasons fans love this show — they know those characters would never let them down. And so, if anything, those bonds just got deeper and deeper and deeper, culminating in the final episode before the DVD movies, "Unending." It's a brilliant hour of TV, where they basically all age together and go through more time in one episode than all of their time before. The bonds get deeper and their connections become even more meaningful.

And each of them had their connection. The O'Neill and Teal'c bond was incredibly powerful and continued to grow. Chris Judge as an actor got better and better and just grew over the course of the episodes, allowing us to give him more to do as an actor to explore. Amanda Tapping, oh my God, she became incredibly three-dimensional as a character through the show, but she was always a strong actor from day one. The stuff that we would give her to say and expect her to nail … a poor person having to carry all of that science mumbo jumbo. And it just went on from there.

ROBERT C. COOPER: We had this team of four people and the dynamic is like having four friends and you're always out with those four friends. But then when you get together with just one of them, that dynamic changes and your relationship with them changes. There's always that feeling of, "Who am I the most friends with?" or "What relationship do I have with them?" So it was always interesting to split the team up, and it's one of the reasons why there's that whole rule of four in writing that sort of mythology about characters and pairing them up differently. When you do, it's always a different chemistry or dynamic that emerges and four just creates that perfect symmetry in that way. That was really seminal. The "Carter-O'Neill-ship" was a good example. Prior to that it felt a little military cold, until we got to an episode that *was* cold, "Solitudes," but you know what I mean.

DAVID READ: The impression I got from what I observed by visiting the sets is that there was definitely a closeness between a lot of the cast members of *Stargate: Atlantis* — they all respected each other and enjoyed working together very much. But it was a different temperature than the *SG-1* cast; a different energy. I got the impression going from the *SG-1* set to the *Atlantis* set, that it was much more than they were there to do a job on *SG-1*. The *Atlantis* cast did the job well and enjoyed it, but it was much more of a job whereas with *SG-1*, it was a family.

MICHAEL SHANKS (actor, "Daniel Jackson"): It's very rare that you get people who work so often, so many hours a day, that actually after so many years still like one another, because we know way too much information about each other. It's amazing that the chemistry and the original dynamic that sparked in an audition room so many years ago has managed to remain consistent and bonded us as a family. It's just a wonderful experience to share with those people.

BRAD WRIGHT: They were always very open to things. The trust factor takes time, so I can't count Season 1, because Michael and Amanda and Christopher were all new and basically just doing whatever they thought they were told to do, but eventually people would say, "I just don't understand why I'm doing that when I can do *this*." I remember one instance where Michael basically added a whole bunch to a scene and I went, "You know what? That's all good, meaty stuff and I'll put it in, but, honestly, you're asking me to type the subtext. So write it, shoot it, say it, but then we're going to go into the editing room and we're going to see." And I called him in and said, "Do you really think it needs to be there?" He said, "No, but thank you for letting me say it, because it's how I got my performance to that point." We'd shot it in such a way that we could cut it.

DAVID READ: The thing about Brad Wright is that at his core he's a playwright. He can put two people in a room together and you are duct taped to that television set. You hang off of every word. At least I do. There's just something about setting Brad loose on those characters, sticking them in a room and just letting them talk. And the caliber of the cast, they would interpret the documents in such a way that they would make you just laugh so hard. And Brad was so receptive to Rick and others, particularly Rick, because he's very off the cuff for making line suggestions and just making a meal out of anything presented to him. As fans, it was a gift to watch so much of that. And to see it again, years later, in rewatches, it holds up exactly the same.

BRAD WRIGHT: I have a huge respect for the process, too. Some people really need to know every beat going in. Beau Bridges would come in and say, "This moment just doesn't quite feel like Landry the way I see him," and he would ask me, "Can you justify why I'm doing this?" And if I couldn't, I'd say, "No, you're right. Let's change it. I apologize. I should have made that better." He was excellent at just *knowing*. Such a professional; unbelievably so. When you wrote a scene for him and he would say, "Brad, I just have these questions," they were very specific. Some actors don't really know they're going to object to something until the day. They read it, it makes sense to them at the moment, they learn the lines and they get in the moment and go, "That's not working. I can't get to this." That's when, if I'm on the stage and it comes up during rehearsal, I'll go, "You're right" and we'll do a rewrite or a change, or just sometimes it's as simple as cutting the offensive line out of the moment where they go, "Oh, okay. Now I don't feel like I'm arguing two different points." Or, "Why don't we just give this line to so and so and then the point still comes across…" And *that's* how you solve it.

I don't think it's humility. Sometimes you just have to acknowledge that something that you had in your head or put on the page, isn't necessarily going to work on the stage the way you had it in your mind. And actors should be able to make it work for themselves, otherwise it will feel disingenuous. I'm not one of those people who says, "No it has to be letter perfect." Never have been. I try to make it so that you can say the line letter perfectly and it'll be great. I try every time, but I don't always succeed. And I think I got better at it over the years. Even on *Travelers*, Eric McCormack's from the theater, so you don't change the words in the play. It's been work-shopped a hundred times, the dialogue's been said before the play was published in various ways. In film and television, sometimes you wrote the scene two days earlier, so you can't be too precious.

Great example: I'm on the stage and it's a young actor and they think they're getting the gist of it. This is for *Stargate Universe*, so forgive me for jumping all over the place. But Jamil Walker Smith, who played Greer, was doing a scene from the episode "Twin Destinies." When Lou Diamond Phillips' character says, "I have a good mind to take you people by force," Greer's line was, "Good luck with that." Instead, he said, "I'd like to see you try" on take one, and on take two I said, "Is it really the same?" He said it was and I said it's more words, but it's much, much weaker. It's a passive voice. "Good luck with that" is explosive, it's stronger. Don't think that we don't put some thought into this shit. And it's only on an occasion like that where I will step in, because most really good actors are aware of their own power and the power of language and say, "Oh, that is a stronger line. I'm going to say the stronger version, of course."

Even with Chris. I said, "You know what, dude? Stop saying 'indeed' every second line. I'm going to have to keep cutting them out." Sometimes it's just a tick, too, in the way people will add the word "okay" before a sentence. I would say, "You're using the word 'okay' to launch yourself into the next thought, because you don't know the line well enough. Just go into the next thought, because I'm having to pull them out in editing." Then sometimes I'll hear a line of dialogue in a read through that is just a word salad. Somebody like Amanda will try to make it work and I'll go over to them and I'll say, "I am so sorry for this horrible line of dialogue I've written for you. Please allow me to fix it for the next draft." And I'll go back to my office and I'll take a shitty line and make it a better line for them, if I can. And as an actor gets more and more honed in their craft, there's nothing like acting to make you better. They start becoming aware of how to deliver a line stronger, how to maybe cut a little bit out and make it better for their character.

And when that happens, when you're editing, you see the line, but the script supervisor has changed the line from what it was to what was said. And if you're a good team and you're on it, that doesn't happen that much. Quite often it's a very minor thing and I don't care. I might not even notice. Or I'll say, "Oh, that's better. Thanks." You care about the end results. I have said to Rick [Richard Dean Anderson] on a couple of occasions, "Please just try it the scripted way." And he would do it, but he wouldn't do it wholeheartedly enough for me to be able to use it. It had nothing to do with him being half-assed. He could only do genuine things and he couldn't even say it if it didn't feel real. He needed it to be real for him to be able to say it. Real to him, whatever that meant. And as long as there was an element of wryness, he would be bang on.

One other point I'd like to make is that the relationships between the characters just got more mature and the connections deeper, but we never went into the territory of animus between them. There's *maybe* a moment in "Unnatural Selection" where there's a character who was a non-human, a humanoid Replicator who was basically this innocent young person who believed in us and wanted us to save him. He was like Pinocchio, and we used his burgeoning humanity, if you want to call it that, against him in order to win and as they're leaving Jonas and Carter both go, "That wasn't cool, we should not have done that," and O'Neill goes, "It was the right thing to do and you know it." Like, shut up. O'Neill knows what they did. Basically having to rely on his dark side, on his own personal dark side, to save their collective asses.

When it comes to the cast you may notice, which isn't the same for the majority of television shows, that there was never a "gag" or "blooper" reel for Stargate SG-1. *The reason for that is that Wright has never been a believer in them, for two reasons. First, actors began making mistakes on purpose, which isn't so "hilarious" when you consider that it took $100,000 a day to shoot* SG-1.

BRAD WRIGHT: "That whole setup that took three and a half minutes cost us this much money for your little joke, so knock it off." And, two, when an actor forgets a line and says "shit," to me it's like airing their dirty laundry. It's revealing their ineptitude for a laugh and it's not fair. They were either up all night or getting in makeup at 6am. And now, given a giant long line of technobabble that they had to spout out on day one, or it's the end of a 12-hour day and they've said this line 500 times and it's just not there anymore, to make a gag reel of somebody swearing because they couldn't remember their lines just feels unfair to me. The one that we did, in "Solitudes" where Amanda says, "I'm stuck in an ice cave with MacGyver for God's sake, like, build a helicopter or something." So, she had this whole comedy rant and that was, I think, out of her nervousness of basically doing a two hander with the star of the show, and that was a bit of a self-defense mechanism of just trying to define the relationship a little bit. And I think it was encouraged by [writer/director] Martin Wood. And it was after that where I said, "Hey, let's not do that anymore."

RICHARD DEAN ANDERSON (JACK O'NEILL)

By the time he joined Stargate SG-1, *Richard Dean Anderson had already become a television icon thanks to his 1985 to 1992 starring turn in* MacGyver. *That success set him up for life in terms of clout in Hollywood and allowed his character to enter the popular vernacular as both a noun and a verb.*

He was born January 23, 1950 in Minneapolis, Minnesota, the oldest of four sons. In his youth he dreamt of becoming a professional hockey player, which ended when he broke both of his arms. Interest shifted to such subjects as music, art, acting and the possibility of becoming a jazz musician. He ended up studying acting at St. Cloud State University and, then, Ohio University, though he dropped out before graduation.

RICHARD DEAN ANDERSON: I wanted to race cars when I was a kid. My dad turned me on to Formula One and I've been a fan of it ever since, but it was too expensive. We didn't have money and I didn't know how to do it back in Minnesota. So I adapted to the environment and wanted to ski at the Olympics, but my knees were shot so I couldn't do that. At one point I was really interested in still trying to support the forest and trees and stuff. I wanted to be not like Smokey Bear, but someone similar to him, just because I like the woods and the mountains and that kind of stuff. Anything I could do to work and have a living, I wanted to do something like a forest ranger. At one point in junior high school we had to put together a project where you had to list three things you thought you wanted to be and write a treatise on each one. My three were dentist, motel manager and the third one I can't remember.

After his junior year in high school, back in 1967, when he was 17-years-old, his life was seriously impacted by a bicycle *trip to Alaska.*

RICHARD DEAN ANDERSON: I started out from Minneapolis, my home, and rode up through North Dakota, Saskatchewan and Alberta all the way up to Skagway, Alaska. We then took boats down to Juneau and then Prince Rupert and eventually down to Victoria and then straight across. There were three of us that started out and after about, I think, a month, we all wanted to see different parts. I chose to go up to Dawson Creek and to Mile Zero, the Alcan Highway. My buddies went different directions. It's through the Canadian Rockies, which is a little rough on a 10-speed bike. I learned to survive elements of the wild that I didn't know that I could. Actually, I was ill-prepared for it, so I didn't know that I would have to. I had 900 miles to go along the Alcan Highway to White Horse alone. I ended up having to camp just off the side of the road where there's nothing but brush. It was a dirt road.

These are things that *did* change me. In fact, I awoke to the sound of what I'm sure were Grizzly Bears crashing through the woods around me and I'm in a mosquito mesh tent. Hearing that, I ended up having to change myself. Literally. Moments like that would happen too often, so I had to develop some kind of meditation, which I didn't even know that's what it was at the time, but I had to somehow give off "don't hurt me vibes." Finally, I made it to White Horse. So it was three months, two of which I was alone, because the guys wanted to see other parts of Canada. I made it across trans-Canada and home again for my senior year in high school. Basically, just spending that much time alone, doing something like riding a bicycle for endless miles, there would be something wrong with you if you didn't discover something about yourself. You'd have to be kind of callous. I wasn't out there to self-explore, but I was forced to do it, because of my situation. So I developed a survival instinct, if that means anything, about how to take care of myself. All while riding a 10-speed Schwinn.

Following his trip, he moved to North Hollywood, then New York City and, finally, to Los Angeles, where his jobs included handling whales for a marine mammal show, serving as a musician in a medieval dinner theater and, finally, as a juggler and street mime. Quite a mix, representing, as he put it, one of the happiest times of his life. From 1976 to 1981 he played Dr. Jeff Webber (his first role) on the daytime soap opera General Hospital. *After that he scored a guest starring part on* The Facts of Life, *followed by regular roles on* Seven Brides for Seven Brothers *and* Emerald Point N.A.S. *Seven years of* MacGyver *were next, playing Angus MacGyver, a spy with an innate ability to use whatever is at his disposable to get out of virtually any situation. The series was followed by a pair of TV movies — 1994's* MacGyver: Lost Treasure of Atlantis *and* MacGyver: Trail to Doomsday *— which he produced, having learned a great deal during the making of the series. He would also star in the 1995 sci-fi western series* Legend.

RICHARD DEAN ANDERSON: The whole thing about the concept behind *MacGyver* was kind of based in methodical logical problem solving. It's seeing a problem, looking around and seeing some potential possible solutions, gathering them, putting them together and seeing if it works. It was really hard, arduous work to put *MacGyver* together, because there was so much to the technical aspects of it and having to think ahead, which just taxes me terribly. There were different producers I worked with as well, which brought its own challenges.

One of them was Michael Greenburg, who had been an executive producer of sports for ABC and NBC. He made the shift over to working on films when he was being asked to become a producer on MacGyver *for a "couple of months," but stayed there for years until the end of the run and into the TV movie follow-ups. His association with Anderson would carry over to* Stargate SG-1.

MICHAEL GREENBURG (executive producer, **Stargate SG-1**): *MacGyver* was a great show. It's an iconic television show, and Rick made it what it was. His on-camera persona was television's answer to Harrison Ford. I mean, he really made it what it is. Without his personality, I don't think it would have been as iconic as it ended up being. I met him on *MacGyver* and the first day I was on the set, I went to his dressing room [and] introduced myself. I think Henry Winkler [who was producing] may have been there, too. We immediately hit it off, because the first thing I wanted to do was to get rid of all the voiceovers on the show. I just thought that was more indicative of a radio show. I think I said at the time, "We're doing a film. Let the pictures do the talking. I don't know why the character has to talk so much." That was the one thing that stood out in the tapes that they'd sent me. Back then it was tapes, not DVD's. I think he got up and gave me a big hug, and said "This is going to be great, because, yeah, I don't want to do that anymore either!" So I think that's when we first hit it off, over the concept of where to take the show from that point. But it wasn't me. It was a collective creative environment with Steve Downing and John Rich and Henry Winkler, all the way down through our writing staff. Everybody got in sync and that's how we were able to sustain seven years. And the two movies that we shot in London.

JONATHAN GLASSNER: John Symes, who was brilliant and I miss him — he's still alive, but he works in other fields — called and said, "Now, don't jump down my throat until you think about this for a minute. What do you think of Richard Dean Anderson as Jack O'Neill?" We were both, like, "Are you kidding? We'd love him to play O'Neill." John said, "He wants to meet with you before he agrees to do it."

MICHAEL GREENBURG: I got a phone call from John Symes. John was our executive at Paramount on *MacGyver*. He went over to become president of MGM and he called saying that they were making *Stargate* the movie into a television show, would we be interested? I'd seen the film. I think Rick's first reaction was he didn't see how he could do that character. But then Symes said, "What if I told you it was a 44-episode commitment?" Then I said "Yeah, well then, that's definitely something to think about!" Rick looked at the movie, and [had] a couple of creative sessions with John and Brad and Jonathan, who showed Rick that he would have the ability to stretch the character, and make it more like he is. Not quite as stretched as *Legend*, but at least he had room to work.

RICHARD DEAN ANDERSON: I'd worked for John Symes during the *MacGyver* days over at Paramount. He'd since moved over to MGM and apparently Brad Wright and Jonathan Glassner came up with a concept to make a series out of the movie *Stargate*. John just called me and said, "Look, I want you to do this role." And *that* was my audition. John knew what he was talking about; the show was on the air for 10 years.

JONATHAN GLASSNER: We met with him and Rick said, "I don't want Jack to be this depressing guy that he was in the movie. He's got to have a sense of humor, or I won't do it." We said, "That's how we both write anyway. We can't help but write with a sense of humor, so that's not a problem." And that generated a much different tone for the show than it had been in the movie.

DAVID READ: If you look at the pilot, "Children of the Gods," Rick is largely playing the Kurt Russell character in terms of attitude. It's been a year since O'Neill's son's death and he's figuring out how to cope with his existence now. Daniel gave him back his purpose, the Abydonian people have given him back his purpose. Now there's *not* going to be a suicide, Sara and he have split, so what's next for him? The only thing to do for him to move forward is to give him a greater purpose. SG-1, the unit, the team — Daniel, Sam, Teal'c — provide him with that purpose. If you look at the show, you can see that the approach Rick took was clever in that he buries the grief of the death of his son through humor. I think most fans would agree with that interpretation. The product that we get from that is fantastic, and when the villains or one of his allies occasionally taps into that pain, he will, based on the situation, often explode or get very serious. And you can tell that that was kind of Rick's idea: "I'm going to use the excuse of humor to cover up this deep wound that will never heal." There's a moment in season six when a Replicator who's invaded his mind plays the moments of Charlie's accidental death and Jack says, "Don't go there ever again," and the Replicator says "That will be your punishment every time you disobey me." His pain is always there.

PETER DELUISE: Richard Dean Anderson saw what Kurt Russell had done in the movie and he was, like, "I can't do that. Not only can I not do that, I don't *want* to do it." You know, being so serious. And he begins with, "I'm going to commit suicide because my son just died is a *terrible* way to start." And Brad Wright said, "Look, I've got it covered. You don't have to do what Kurt Russell did. You and I, we'll be the only ones who know this, but Kurt Russell is playing Colonel O'Neil, spelled with one "l." And you are playing Colonel O'Neill, spelled with two "l's." And Richard Dean Anderson said, "Can we do that?" So, if you look very carefully, Kurt's character is with one "l" and Richard's is with two "l's." It's just saying that Richard could make the part his own.

BRAD WRIGHT: The concept for the show was pretty much what we intended and what we pitched. The one big thing that changed happened when Rick was cast. When he saw the film he said, "I can't do what Kurt did," and after he read the script for the TV show, he said, "But I *can* do *this*; this is something I could do." It's a line I'd written in the pilot when Teal'c says, "I have nowhere to go," and O'Neill says, "You can stay at my place." *That*, to him, was the character. That, to him, is what he thought O'Neill was. *Yes*, he was running and shooting an alien weapon and helping people escape, but he needed the line "You can stay at my place" for it to be the Jack O'Neill he wanted to play. Just a lighter touch at certain moments. Part of it comes down to the fact that I think Rick is a better actor than he thinks he is. He feels he needs a lighter touch so that he's not too self-important and can be a little bit self-effacing in that way. In part, it's his personality; it's who he is. I think it's embarrassing for him to try and do a dramatic scene and fall short in terms of how good he wants to be. So the humor gives a sort of built-in disclaimer, but, frankly, he's naturally funny.

RICHARD DEAN ANDERSON: I remember the first table reading we had. We were all just meeting and we sat at this long table in a conference room and had a read-through before we even started. I don't know if I can call them antics, maybe it's nervous energy. Maybe it's just my absolute desire or need to make sure that people have a good time and that there's an understanding that I think things shouldn't be taken so seriously. I certainly don't take myself that seriously. There are times that I don't know what's going to come out of my mouth, which kind of leads me to believe that I really don't know what's going on in my head. My sense of humor tends to be irreverent, sarcastic, at times cynical. But the character, and I guess my general approach, had to have some humor in it. Some levity to it. It worked out. People were happy with what they saw in the pilot and I have played it ever since. My fellow cast members had to endure not just my eccentricities, but I guess my appreciation for the absurd as well.

BRAD WRIGHT: Rick's humor clicked with me, because I can't help myself either. The more dramatic the situation, the more I want to put a joke in and it's for almost exactly the same reason. Additionally, it adds a dynamic and level of humor to a scene that ultimately makes *Stargate*, *Stargate*. There's elements of that in *Star Trek*, too, obviously, but they kind of had an on and off switch. They would do "Balance of Terror" and then "The Trouble with Tribbles" — I can't believe I remember the titles of those episodes. But *Stargate* had that naturally; that banter between Daniel and Jack. That dynamic was the core of the show for us, at least at the beginning.

PETER DELUISE: It was interesting to watch Richard as O'Neill become more and more lighthearted, and his job as the leader was to corral the experts. That's one of the things that I always felt Shatner as Kirk did so well on *Star Trek* in that he had experts and would use whatever information they would give him — as leaders tend to do, and they then move forward with a strategy or plan. I've seen him do that. Plus, Richard Dean Anderson's character's knowledge of anything other than military was quite limited. He represented every man's point of view. So what was suggested was, "I don't understand what you're saying, because you're saying a lot of technobabble." So, naturally, O'Neill is going to go, "Huh?" Or, "Can you just dumb it down a little bit?" or "Daniel, speak English. Carter, *please!*" We started it very sophisticated and almost immediately O'Neill would say, "*Please.*" That was the shorthand for just dumb it down, and then they would simplify it for him *and* the audience.

RICHARD DEAN ANDERSON: At that point in my career when *Stargate* came around, I was wise enough to make sure that I got to have more creative input than

I did prior with *MacGyver*, so I became executive producer and that allowed me to make some decisions. I didn't want to be the focus; when I had done *MacGyver*, I knew what it was like to carry a show and I just didn't want to. And thankfully we had an impeccable cast where we kind of created a camaraderie and a kind of rhythm to our characters that fit really well to each other. So I didn't have to carry anything.

JOSEPH MALLOZZI (executive producer, **Stargate SG-1**): Rick was the lead of the show and it survived as long as it did because of him. He had a certain sense of humor, which I loved, which really became his character, but also kind of seeped into *everything*. The show's tone always kind of skirted that line. It always had an underlying sense of humor, which really appeals to sci-fi fans, but for some reason not executives, who tend to like the grimmer stuff. But I think that sense of humor is so key and Rick embraces that — to the point where the fandom began using the term "Dumb Jack," in that he would basically either be clueless or tend to be clueless about stuff. I've always been a firm believer in humor going a long way in allowing fans to connect with characters and shows.

JONATHAN GLASSNER: What we discovered was that not only Rick, but the rest of the cast as well — especially Michael Shanks and Rick — had a really amazing sense of comic timing. And the more you gave them, the more they played it so that it affected the show. All the people you end up working with affect the show and it evolves into something that you never really thought it would.

BRAD WRIGHT: One of the reasons I say Rick is better than he thinks he is, is that when he's in a scene, he's kind of incapable of being ingenuine. He's either him or he's not him and he won't do it unless it feels like him. He will change it until it is, which is where the slightly sardonic part comes from. When you're acting opposite your lead character, it just grounds everything and grounds everyone. So scenes with the highfalutin sci-fi talk seem more grounded because of it. And that's *amazing*. People say, "What is that star factor? Why is one person just a good working actor and somebody else is a star?" And it's different for everybody, but for Rick it's that. It's just a charm and it's so natural. Even when he's mean, when he's angry in character, it feels real.

I wrote an episode, which was a tough one, which was Daniel's return in season seven called "Abyss." I was asking Rick to do scenes which were way more dramatic than anything he'd ever done. But because it was scenes with Michael — two-handers, just them with an intimate camera — it's some of their best work. It's just a charm that's so natural.

DAVID READ: Rick is so much more of a comedic creature, and he provided subtext to Jack O'Neill going from a person who had lost his child and done God knows what in the Cold War, to coming out the other end as this kind of sarcastic individual who emerged after all of those years. It allowed him to play this level of humor that brought the show to life in so many ways that the Kurt Russell version just couldn't have. Rick's contribution to this franchise from that standpoint alone cannot be overstated.

MICHAEL SHANKS: When I first met Richard, he was a very private person, but once you get inside and spend so much time around him, you realize he's like the biggest kid. He's someone who has been through the wars and has all the wisdom of that, but at the same time he's like an eight-year-old kid just busting to get out. If it wasn't for the social propriety making him do these certain things, I think you'd see this whack job running around doing anything for a joke. That sense of humor we share, both on and off the set ... we seem to be on a level playing field regarding a lot of different things. Our strongest bond is not only joking with each other off camera, but working with each other. We are always keeping each other laughing. Whenever we were working together, there was rarely a serious moment.

ROBERT C. COOPER: First and foremost, Richard Dean Anderson is a big per-sonality and he came into it with, I think, an understanding of what made the character of O'Neill appealing. He's extremely astute at forwarding his own TV Q — how to protect his character, what he can do best as an actor. He wanted to separate himself from Kurt Russell. It was also important to him to create chemistry and a dynamic with the Daniel character, because that was another aspect of the movie that I think was important to carry forward.

PETER DELUISE: I always thought Richard Dean Anderson was amazing, but I also knew what his strengths were. He and his production partner, Michael Green-burg, learned from a book called *Adventures in the Screen Trade*, the William Goldman book. And one of the things that William Goldman explains is that a hero never talks about himself. I think Goldman uses an example like Steve McQueen in *The Great Escape*, and how he wants to be separate and he never talks about anybody else. He's just his own guy. That's heroic, and you never asked questions. That was the other one. You don't talk about anybody else; you let them talk about you. And you don't ask questions.

Michael Greenberg was functioning as Richard Dean Anderson's production partner, because Richard had producer credit but he couldn't exercise it. What he did was he hired Michael Greenburg as his quality control guy, his go to guy. Greenberg would be looking out for Richard Dean Anderson and say things like, "This shouldn't be his line, somebody else should be talking about that. So make that somebody else's line."

DAVID READ: He notoriously does *not* like to talk about the acting process, he just kind of does it and it comes to life. That's not what he's in it for. But the fact of the matter is that when you give him a serious script, and you really back him into a corner and force him to "act," he will fight his way out of it, creating something absolutely magical in the process. He has earned every bit of success he has had from that. I'm not a big *MacGyver* fan, and the little bit of *MacGyver* that I've seen, I don't recall that much humor. It's, like, "Your talent is being wasted on this."

PETER DELUISE: As good as Richard is, and I'm not speaking out of school because a lot of people know this already, he had a two-finger rule. Two-fingers are if you held up your two fingers to a script on Richard Dean Anderson's dialogue, and if it ran longer than a two-finger space, it was too long. It's like two fingers of Scotch. As a result, O'Neill's responses were short and he could say them in one breath. Not a lot of people know that, because when you watch the show, it all seems very natural. But if he had more than that to say, if he had too much, he would start to say it and somebody would interrupt or provide some info and he would finish it off at the end. But, again, it was never more than a two-finger space at a time, which I always thought was amazing. And it didn't even occur to me until I started writing for him, and then I was told and I was, like, "Oh, I didn't realize it could only be a two-finger space."

JOHN G. LENIC (producer, **Stargate SG-1**): Brad or any of the other writers would write some of these big, long speeches for him at times and Michael would go, "No, we need to shorten that thing. Saying that much is going to be boring" or, "It's not action-based." Richard was always about making sure the episodes were moving forward and being driven by action of some sort.

BRAD WRIGHT: This is another funny story about Rick. When Rick ran into Kurt Russell and said, "I'm doing the TV version of *Stargate*," he went, "Oh, really?" This is season two, three and we're clicking along. It's summer. Everything's great. Kurt Russell's shooting on the lot in another movie, and he's in cowboy make-up for something to do with Vegas. I can't remember the name. It's a heist movie. He walks over and he says, "Is it okay if I just see the set and say hi?" So we're down on the stage and he goes, "Man, this is as good as ours. It's smaller, but it's pretty cool for TV. It's amazing. Good for you. I can't believe this turned into a series. When they handed me that script I read it and threw it across the room." He told us, and I think even Dean Devlin has told this story, so I don't mind saying it, "and then they told me how much I was going to get paid for it and I went across the room and picked it up."

I didn't ask him at the time, because it would have been inappropriate, but I asked our casting person to contact his manager and say we'll give $10,000 to the charity of his choice for him to do a scene where he gets in a uniform and is in an elevator. The doors open and standing on the other side of the doors is Rick, who says, "Hi, Jack." Kurt goes, "Hi, Jack," and they cross paths as the doors close again. I just pitched it like that. And his manager said, "Not in a million years." I don't even think they took it to him. It would have been good for us and do absolutely nothing for him. I should have asked him, I should have been more forceful. I should have had the balls to ask him personally, although he probably would have said, "Sure, ask my manager." It's not like I didn't think of it. That's my point.

Shifting the subject back to Richard Dean Anderson, Wright points to a moment early on in season two when it's believed that Daniel has died aboard an alien ship. But then Daniel comes through the Stargate and he and O'Neill embrace.

BRAD WRIGHT: They hug each other and, for some reason, Rick ad-libs the line, "Space Monkey." Like a term of endearment, which I don't think he ever intended for it to be in the final episode. I have no idea why he said it. We just kind of said, "Why don't we just leave it in?" And so we did. It's an ad-lib moment, as was not uncommon in seasons one and two, but he learned to trust us eventually. Early on I would say, "Feel free to use the typewritten pages as an alternative, too." I would write a joke and he would write another joke that was very similar to that joke. In his mind it would be him making it his own, but I'm, like, "Yeah, but it's not as good. If You're going to make it your own, make it better." I'm totally always open to that. And we hashed that out and he got it, but we actually had a bit of an argument in the trailer, because it was leading to everybody wanting to make up their own dialogue. It was like, "No, we have reasons for these words."

RICHARD DEAN ANDERSON: What I brought to the table reads of the scripts was the attitude that everything was potentially a setup for a funny line, which doesn't make writers and producers very happy. Their stuff is gold … well, maybe not gold. Maybe brass. But in their eyes, they're "God's words." I don't mean to say that, either. In any case, these table reads are the first time we're seeing the script. To me, those are just little seeds for going somewhere else. So during these table reads I'd be ad-libbing on what was a fresh script. Most of it was getting laughs, some didn't, but it didn't matter, because I wasn't reading the words the way they were written. So Brad took me aside and took me into his office like the principal and said, "You know, you're not doing the writers a great service by doing what you're doing in those rehearsals. Every one of us works hard to write the script and when we first hear them, you guys read them. We'd actually like to hear the words." He basically chastised the hell out of me, which I deserved. And I told him so. And it occurred to me that I should be showing some more respect for the writers, who, to this day, I respect the most out of the whole process.

BRAD WRIGHT: My view was, "This doesn't have to be letter perfect, but tell me the changes you want to make. I will put it in the script and then we'll do it together. I will happily make all the changes you want, but sometimes there's information that I have to get across as the storyteller that you're cutting out in your version of the speech," because Rick never, ever made his speeches longer. It was a snip. And, again, it was a good lesson. We were better writers for it when we realized, "Too many words, let's make it shorter." After that, it was great. He realized he could trust us. I think people who have been big stars are always wary of putting their fate in other people's hands. But he was my guide.

RICHARD DEAN ANDERSON: So it was a very important conversation that we had, because the improv that I would bring to the table, I no longer brought to the table reads. I would be on set during rehearsals; they gave me too much time before we shot, which was the problem. Generally speaking, I never wrote any of the funnies down for myself, but I did show respect for the writers. If I found something during rehearsals and set ups, I'd take it to Brad, Mr. Cooper … somebody, just to let them know what was coming and to see if they were okay with it. For the most part they were, but there was a balance there. I let a lot of things go that were gems; just gold.

AMANDA TAPPING (actress, "Samantha Carter"): Rick really paved the way to make the show a lot more accessible, because of his sense of humor. Even in the most-dire situation, he ended it with a funny line, which was usually ad libbed by him. The hardest part was keeping a straight face.

BRAD WRIGHT: It was a very successful one-star show. He was the title card. And you can't do this without him, basically. Name another television star who basically carried the whole show on their back to that extent, other than maybe Tom Selleck from the same era. And at a time when you were getting a 30 share when you aired. But like I said, he eventually trusted us with the character and I found his voice. He adapted to what I was trying to do with him and it ended up being a great partnership, because he was always a producer. And I had no problems with him being an executive producer. He *knew* how to use it.

MICHAEL SHANKS (DANIEL JACKSON)

Long before he stepped through a Stargate, Michael Garrett Shanks wrestled with whether or not he should step into the hockey rink as a professional player — at least that was the temptation when he was 16. Born December 15, 1970 in Vancouver, British Columbia, he spent his school years playing hockey and rugby, became a member of the Student Council and joined his school's theater group, which also provided him with the opportunity to direct. Ultimately deciding that a career in hockey was not *the way to go, he attended the University of British Columbia, where he studied business. Being done in by calculus, he switched to studying theater — when he was* this *close to a business degree — and graduated in 1994 with a degree in Fine Arts.*

He spent two years at Ontario's Stratford Festival and then began scoring television roles on Highlander: The Series *and the TV movies* A Family Divided *and* The Call of the Wild: Dog of the Yukon. *His role as Daniel Jackson on* Stargate SG-1 *would commence with the series premiere in 1997. In between his stint on that show, he could be seen in two episodes of* The Outer Limits, Andromeda, 24 *and* Eureka *as well as about a dozen TV movies.*

BRAD WRIGHT: One of the things we wanted to do was honor the feature so that the fans knew that this was a continuation of Daniel Jackson's story. We might have been smart *not* to do that, but we liked the continuity of it.

MICHAEL SHANKS: My story is that I auditioned [for the show]. Rick was gracious enough to come to the screen test that we had in LA and he read with everybody. I was actually told afterwards that I was the second choice by most people; that they went around the room and everybody else was going towards the other guy. Brad was the one who said, "No, Michael's the guy." After a certain amount of convincing, they trusted Brad to make that decision. I was kind of almost *not* chosen for the part.

BRAD WRIGHT: For Daniel, there were people we had narrowed the search down to. Rick did scenes with Michael and the other two candidates, and, for me, Michael Shanks was Daniel hands down. Trouble was, and what MGM was a little concerned about, that he was very young. I think he was 26 at the time and it just seemed to lack a little bit of credibility that this character knew these languages and was as smart as he was at such a young age. But I said, "I promise you one thing: he *will* get older. So Daniel is a wunderkind and the character's a bit different," and nobody batted an eye at it. He was terrific. And his performance evolved quite wonderfully from kind of an impression of James Spader to his own Daniel.

MICHAEL SHANKS: James Spader is a pretty darn good actor, so when the opportunity came I went, "Oh, boy, I don't know if I can do the job that he did," but I also ripped off his performance completely. So in one way it was a crutch, but in another way it was a terror, so I guess it balanced itself out. And how did I do? Well, given that I had over 200 hours to play the character, then, yes, I would say I did a better job than he did in his two.

JONATHAN GLASSNER: We found Michael pretty early in the process. We auditioned a bunch of actors for that and, I'm telling you, there were 10 good choices. But what Michael had that the others didn't is that he looked a little bit like Spader, and he had that comic timing that he brought out in the reading, even on lines that weren't all that funny. He did well. And, let's face it, he's a great looking guy, which is always a value, because he could be a romantic lead as we went on. He was the easiest role to cast, frankly. The only debate about him, again, was that because he looked a little bit like Spader, we worried that people would think we were trying to find a lookalike. But then, of course, when he came in he didn't look anything like him; he had just kind of put on the glasses and done himself up to make himself as much like Spader as he could.

ROBERT C. COOPER: I think Michael would admit that he started with a little bit more of an impersonation of Spader, but quickly settled into his own interpretation of the character.

JOSEPH MALLOZZI: He is such a phenomenal actor and brought such passion to the character. In many ways, I think he was our eyes into the character for a lot of the audience in that he was kind of the outsider, not the military guy and was almost like a fish out of water. And yet his enthusiasm in exploration and discovery was very much what resonated with sci-fi fandom in general. Michael was so great at really connecting with the audience on that level.

RICHARD DEAN ANDERSON: As an actor, I don't get that deep. Michael does. He's a fine, studied actor. First thing I saw him do in Vancouver was *Hamlet* and he was *really* good. Come on, let's face it, if you're really objective and you look at all the regulars on the show, Michael's the only one that really knew what he was doing as an actor. I mean, Amanda was good, but is more of a comedian and she's got that down. Michael knows what he's doing. I'm so jealous, I'm getting all teary. Not really.

JOSEPH MALLOZZI: Michael left the show after the fifth season and came back the following year, and that would be a conversation to have with him, but I know he felt his character was being minimized. I didn't see it, but he had the talk with Brad and decided that he wanted to part ways with the production, but Brad left the door open for guest spots. And then, when Rick decided to really minimize his presence, the decision was made to bring Michael back to kind of maintain that core and keep the original spirit of the show alive.

BRAD WRIGHT: This is more about James Spader than Michael, but in season six the Sci-Fi Channel is taking over. We fly down to meet the executive and he says, "I love the show and what you're doing, but we need to do something splashy, and I have it for you. I want you to do this: Bring James Spader into the show." And I went, "James Spader played Daniel." "Yeah, as a scientist or something." I said, "First of all, if James Spader's career is at the point where he's going to come and do a guest spot in a spinoff series of his own feature, not even as his original character, we're going to have to have a suicide watch at his trailer. Second, he won't do it and I'm not even going to ask him to do it." He said, "Well, he could be any one of these characters; just change the names," and I said, "I'm sorry that we're starting off this way. I don't think that's a good idea, it would cost a lot of money." Finally, he said, "If you don't like it, I don't want you to embrace it." No problem there.

RICHARD DEAN ANDERSON: When we were shooting the pilot and I heard Michael's dialogue, I thought at the time, "What the *hell* is he talking about?" Actually he said a lot of things where I said, "What the hell is he talking about?" Even today.

MICHAEL SHANKS: I was reading some swath of expository mumbo jumbo, and I rattled it off in one take and sort of sat there, feeling prideful, like, "Yeah, I did that." And Rick came up and said, "Well done, well done. You know you're screwed, right?" I said, "What do you mean?" He goes, "You showed them you could do it. They're going to keep making you do it." He said, "I have this little rule; call it the rule of thumb. Any passage of dialogue that's longer than my thumb on the page, I won't say it." He spent the entire first season, even when he was completely capable of doing it, screwing up any line that was longer than his thumb. They tried to get him to do some other stuff and, no freaking way. Sure enough, what ended up happening was that Amanda and I became these sleep-deprived dimwits, because we'd have to go home and learn six pages of exposition. He was absolutely right.

PETER DELUISE: What was nice about Michael's Daniel Jackson character is because Carter was military, she could not offer what we call the "moral center." Many people felt that Daniel Jackson was the moral center of the group. If something was military, it fell to O'Neill. This was set up in the movie in that Kurt Russell brought the bomb to Abydos, just in case. And he was about to commit suicide, because his son had just died. And then Daniel Jackson goes, "Hey, we can't blow these people up. It's not their fault that this happened." So that was handed over to us from the movie, that relationship. Plus, because he was civilian and *not* military, Daniel was going to be at odds with O'Neill all the time. O'Neill's job was to carry out military assignments with military precision and discipline, and, of course, Daniel Jackson was there to argue the humanity of how that was wrong.

MICHAEL SHANKS: When I left the show at the end of Season 5, it's one of those things where you make the decision and it's a job you move on from. I've moved on from many of them. But when you make that choice, there are a lot of other people that are on board for that decision-making process as well. Leaving and coming back felt like two chapters. It truly does. I knew at the time how I felt, that it was time to go at that point when I left. When I came back, it was a different environment. It felt really good to be back on the show and it felt really good to tell the stories that we were telling at that time. There was a little bit more wiggle room. It was nice to have that break. For Christopher and Amanda, who didn't get the chance to have that time away, they suffered more fatigue the further we went along. And for me, I was a lot fresher when I came back. It was nice, but it does feel like there are two separate stories there. Two separate series.

I guess there was a strong reaction from a lot of people [after season five] that weren't happy with the fact that that character had stepped out of the realm of being a regular on the show. And they let their feelings be known. It's great to get that kind of expression, because you realize that regardless of what you think you may have accomplished, you've touched a chord with a lot of people who are very reverential to the character that has been created on the show that's going away. And it comes with a sudden wake up call and realization that there is a bit of responsibility that goes with playing a character on television. You find that your fans will, at the end of the day, make you or break you. Apparently a lot of fans out there are very supportive of the work that I've done in the show, which is fantastic.

AMANDA TAPPING (SAMANTHA CARTER)

Although she was born August 28, 1965 in Rochford, Essex, England, Amanda Tapping and her family made the move to Ontario, Canada when she was only three-years-old. She later attended North Toronto High School, where she received awards in dramatic arts and environmental science. Yet despite being encouraged by her parents to pursue a career in science, she felt an unyielding pull towards the world of acting. As a result, she studied drama as well as environmental science when she attended the North Toronto Collegiate Institute, but when she graduated in 1984, she shifted over to the University of Windsor School of Dramatic Arts in Windsor, Ontario.

AMANDA TAPPING: After four years of theater school, I graduated only to find myself woefully unprepared for the *business* of acting. I had great stage experiences and vowed I would never prostitute myself. I started doing more theater and I co-founded a comedy troupe in Toronto called Random Acts, which did sketch comedy with a real feminist ideology. I still firmly believe that if you want people to listen, they've got to be laughing as well. But I started getting commercials and then bigger parts on shows like *Forever Knight, Goosebumps, Due South, Kung Fu: The Legend Continues, The X-Files, The Outer Limits* and *Millennium*. It was sort of a natural progression over the years that I got to this point, but I guess it was something I always wanted to do. The real change happened when I was cast as Samantha Carter.

JONATHAN GLASSNER: I insisted that we have a female lead. And, of course, as soon as I said that, the studio wanted her to be this sexy girl that walks around in tutus all the time. Brad and I had to fight that. When we did the casting, they wanted all the people that *they* picked; these girls in low-cut outfits that came in being sexy. We insisted that Amanda be one of the final choices. They didn't want her because of that, even though she was clearly the best actress. But she didn't play what they were looking for.

BRAD WRIGHT: For us at the beginning, Carter was a super genius — in fact, probably too much of one. What an incredible job Amanda did, considering the burden we placed on her to be a super genius, also fabulous soldier in a woman who was superhuman.

JONATHAN GLASSNER: The other girls would come in with push-up bras and they were selling the sexy aspect of it. In those days, there were a lot of actors, both male and female, who got by on their looks more than their acting. The other ones were all that. Amanda was already an accomplished actress in Canada; she didn't *have* to do *Stargate*. She also had great timing. And the great thing about her was that you believe she could be a soldier. You take those women selling their sexiness and dress them in a uniform, she can say she's a soldier, but she's not. Amanda you could buy in the role. On top of that, she could do all the science jargon. She knew what it meant.

AMANDA TAPPING: I have to say, and I've said this before, the moment I read the script, or actually the moment I read the sides for the audition, I was, like, "This is a really cool character. Oh my God, I really want to play this." I just loved her strength and her integrity and her being kind of ballsy. When I was cast, I really dove deep into astrophysics and the idea of being in the military. I trained with a Navy SEAL to learn about the hierarchy in the military and not just how to wear the uniform, but what the mentality was. The character was in the Air Force, but Navy SEALS and I also really studied the astrophysics of it. So, for me, that was an intellectual approach into the character, the emotional part of it. The writing then allowed me to dive into who this woman was beneath that. And then I had 10 years to play with her, which was awesome.

BRAD WRIGHT: The choice for Carter was between Amanda Tapping and another actor, and Amanda was playing the scene way too serious. But between reads, she was naturally hilarious and was bantering with Rick and so they wanted to bring her back for another read of another scene.

JONATHAN GLASSNER: As soon as we had the callbacks, they saw her do all that stuff. Then we did a chemistry test with all the people we thought were going to be in the finals. She and Rick hit it off, so she had a slam dunk and we won that battle, thankfully, because she was so good. But we had to fight for her in the room, which was frustrating.

BRAD WRIGHT: I had gone to Amanda privately and I said, "You know that side of yourself that you're showing with Rick after the scene is over? *That's* good. Let that bubble through. Even if you have to add levity a little bit, let it come through, because Carter has to have that. Carter can't just be this boring scientist woman; it'll kill us." And she did. The second reading she nailed it and, in fact, threw Rick off a little bit, who did, like, a double take to the audience and smiled. From that point on, Amanda was Carter. It was done.

ROBERT C. COOPER: I think Amanda did an amazing job. In fact, a lot of the issues with her character of maybe not being as fully fleshed out was on us as the writers. I have to go back and look at when I really felt her character became who Carter eventually was on the show, but it wasn't right away. It was certainly more like seasons three or four. The difficulty was, here's this woman in this unit and what do we do with her to make her different from being just another soldier? Sometimes I think you overcompensate for that and make the stories all about the fact that she's a woman instead of the fact that she's just very smart or a great soldier.

AMANDA TAPPING: Carter started out so young and I think she felt very much like a woman in a man's world, always feeling that she needed to prove herself. Personally, I wasn't fond of playing that dynamic, because it's sort of tiring to keep bringing up the gender war. The writers, to their great credit, really fleshed her out and gave her a lot less of a didactic message. So once it was established that she was an integral part of the team, they slowly started to introduce a sense of humor to her, as she was probably the most uptight of all the characters on the show — except for maybe Teal'c.

BRAD WRIGHT: Hanging a lantern on the fact that she was the only woman in the room wasn't helpful. There's an episode, "Singularity," where she won't leave Cassandra, a girl who's going to blow up because there's a bomb on her. Carter won't leave her and doesn't think it's going to happen. She thinks it was the Stargate that caused the problem, so taking her away would solve the problem and the girl would be fine. But that was an early debate in the series about her womanhood, really. Why would she do that? She's a soldier and Jack gave her an order. Maybe this was exactly what Robert's talking about; too much of that. But the character needed something really defining that wasn't her military skill or her brain. She needed to have a completely emotional response to something to make her more three-dimensional in the moment, and male or female. Maybe Daniel would have made the same decision. It was her humanity, not necessarily her womanness, and I just remembered that argument very, very vividly. It's very effective and a great scene, but I haven't seen it in years. Rob may have a point on that, but again, the beauty of the evolution of a show is that a three-dimensional person rebuilds itself eventually.

ROBERT C. COOPER: In my original pitch for "First Commandment," it was not her ex-fiancé. At the time I took the suggestion and thought, "Yeah, it makes it more interesting if it's personal." That was a writing choice that I thought made sense, but it also defined her in a way that was a mistake. Looking back, I wouldn't do it again. Bottom line is that when you're defining a female character *as* the female character, it's problematic. Look, Carter became a very strong, powerful character and regardless of gender, I'm quite proud of what Amanda did with it. It just was a growing period for her.

AMANDA TAPPING: After the pilot, when I found out that I was going to continue with the role, I spoke to them just about the writing of her. Not trying to write a woman, but just writing her as a person. I said, "Write her as a guy and I'll just bring an inherent femininity to it, but I don't think she needs to be written as a woman. And especially as an angry feminist." That was sort of the biggest thing we dealt with. They would talk to us at the beginning of the seasons to see what we wanted to see happen to our characters. What *haven't* we explored? So they were very amenable to us talking to them about things that we wanted to see, which was great. So kudos to them.

JOSEPH MALLOZZI: I can't tell you the number of female fans who have reached out to say, "I went into a career in science or aeronautics because of Samantha Carte." And that's always kind of heartening and I love that fact. Amanda was amazing and is a lot like Samantha Carter in that she's super genuine and kind. One of my favorite stories is when my aunt came to visit the set one day and we were watching as they did a scene. As soon as she finished, Amanda came over and introduced herself to my aunt. It was just a small thing, but for years afterwards, to this day, my aunt says, "How's Amanda doing?" Amanda just brought that warmth, which a lot of fandom responded to.

AMANDA TAPPING: Over the course of time, the writers obviously wrote to each of us, to how we were playing the characters. They wrote Michael the way he was playing Daniel, Rick the way he was playing O'Neill and how Chris was playing Teal'c.

It became more organized and then in later seasons it was, "How do I find a new way into this character? How do I keep her interesting? How do I keep it vibrating inside of me to make it feel real and not feel staid and boring?" It was interesting every year to find a new challenge, a new way to play her, a new angle on her. Often at the beginning of the season, it was just a matter of walking around in the army boots and sort of feeling that physicality of her again. But what a gift that character was. The whole show was a huge gift.

PETER DELUISE: Amanda Tapping as Carter was, without question, the workhorse. She did all the heavy-lifting as far as I'm concerned — which is a bit of hyperbole, because I know that Michael Shanks as Daniel would step in to handle all that exposition. But Amanda Tapping is another very talented actor and also *very* funny. She was actually quite funny before she started on the show and, of course, didn't get to show that in the beginning. Slowly but surely they let that out and it became a little bit funnier and more balanced. So here she is, super smart and all about science, and Amanda Tapping actually put in the work and understood what she was saying. She absolutely understood the scientific concepts that she was putting forward, the physics she was explaining. She would not just spout that stuff off. And if somebody had a problem with the way she was describing it, she could back it up. She was, like, "No, I looked this up. What I'm saying is actually right."

AMANDA TAPPING: Carter is just so comfortable in her own skin. I think that she came into her own as a woman, which as a woman, happens to you when you hit your 30s and you say, "Wait a sec, I'm not that scared kid I was at 20." I think that that naturally evolved for her, too. She was a lot more familial in a sort of touchy sense with her co-workers and I think that what the writers had done is flesh out that dynamic that all four of us have as actors and friends. As we went on the series, I liked her. Not that I didn't like her in the beginning, but I wasn't fond of her. Carter was one of those women you just wanted to tell to shut up, but it became interesting to hear what she has to say.

DAVID READ: Amanda Tapping is one of the most genuine people I've ever met in my life. She has gone on to be one of the most prominent directors in the industry, particularly in Canada, and has earned every single iota of it. And she has a memory that is extraordinary — she'll meet someone years later and remember who they are. You will never meet someone more grateful for the opportunities that she's been given or aware of what it is that *Stargate* has given her career. That moved on into *Sanctuary* and into other guest roles and now finally into directing, which is what she always wanted to do. Her genuine nature is *not* something you always get when you're in a show for 10 years and sucked into doing all the technobabble that she had to do.

BRAD WRIGHT: Technobabble! I did an episode with Brent Spiner on *The Outer Limits* and I asked him, "How did you pull the part of Data off on *Star Trek: The Next Generation*? I mean, the stuff that you had to learn and rattle off..." He couldn't go "ummm" as Data, because he is a robot. He had to be perfect. What he taught me then, and what I passed on to every actor I've ever had to hand a boatload of technobabble to, was say the words out loud when you're learning them. As soon as you do that, the ridiculousness of what you're saying becomes really obvious, because it's technical. And it's harder to do. And so, if you say it out loud, you get used to what it sounds like and the ridiculousness of what it sounds like. That was great advice to pass on.

RICHARD DEAN ANDERSON: There was a dynamic on the show that really worked. First of all, they had enough sense to give Michael and Amanda all of the dialogue, the main dialogue, and I was relegated to the reactionary, "What?" Which kind of helped the dynamic along, but there was no way we could do it any other way. I couldn't memorize that dialogue to save my life and she could.

BRAD WRIGHT: There was a deep but strictly under the surface connection between Carter and O'Neill, because the military would never have allowed any actual relationship. It would have been inappropriate. And if they would, if they did fall in love, they would have been separated. Just as a sideline to this conversation, I was lucky enough to spend a night on an aircraft carrier, the Carl Vinson out at sea. And there was a woman who was in charge of all the enlisted people — there's a lot of young women on the ship as well as young men — and she said, "A good portion of my job every day is to try to stop the young men and women onboard this ship from having sex with each other in corners." And it's because, she says, they can't have romance. You can't fall in love with somebody, because when there's an emergency and your duty is to go fight the fire on the deck, but you're more worried about the person you have a crush on in another compartment, you have to do your duty first. That dynamic is all through *Stargate*. You know they care about each other deeply, but duty was always first. So the little looks between Carter and O'Neill and that she would put his head on her shoulder occasionally, and when they forgot who they were, we were able to do that. But we never crossed the line. We never *ever* crossed the line.

AMANDA TAPPING: I think now Jack and Sam are together. I don't know if they're married; I actually don't know if they would get married, but I think that for sure they're together. Sam probably goes off and does her missions and Jack is probably quite happily retired. And when she comes back from her missions, they're together. She comes back to the cabin and he's got dinner made and the laundry is done and the place is clean. There's hospital corners on the bed, tucked in properly. Oh, *and* fresh fish.

BRAD WRIGHT: Robert did a page one rewrite on season one's "There but for the Grace of God." They're about to die in this alternate reality — it's not even our reality — and Carter and O'Neill kiss each other before he goes off to die in battle. And the Air Force went, "Absolutely not!" And we said, "Okay, it's an alternate reality. What if she's Dr. Carter, not Major Carter?" And they went, "Oh, that's fine." Just because we wanted the kiss; we wanted in an alternate reality to insinuate that in another time, another place, they would have had a relationship.

One of the most important things to happen to Tapping during the course of production of Stargate SG-1 *was the opportunity she was given to direct the season seven episode of the show, "Resurrection." That gig would ultimately lead to her helming episodes of* Sanctuary *(which she also starred in),* Primeval: New World, Continuum, Olympus, Dark Matter, X Company, The Magicians, Van Helsing, Travelers *(nine episodes!),* Supernatural, Siren, The 100, Motherland: Fort Salem, The Flash, Batwoman, Chilling Adventures of Sabrina *and* First Kill. *It should be noted that her approach on "Resurrection" stood out from other episodes of the series, established in the opening scene in which police officers mill around a crime scene, followed by a detective writing in his notebook with one foot resting on the bumper of a car. For a moment, it seemed as though the viewer had accidentally turned on* Law & Order, *until Carter appeared on screen.*

AMANDA TAPPING: That whole shot was written to be very high and wide-angle. It seemed to beg for a crane shot, but I didn't want to do a typical crane shot. Instead, what I did was have a lot of extras and foreground movement and have the scene just look really active so that your eyes are never resting in one place. Shooting that scene was very complicated and it took a long time to set up. That's the kind of thing I did a lot of, things that pushed the envelope in terms of what the producers maybe thought I could do. Directing is all about preparation, having a strong vision and having answers on the top of your head when you're asked a thousand questions a day. For me, it was all about putting my own stamp on *Stargate.*

When it comes to the character of Samantha Carter and herself as an actress and person, Tapping has come to some distinct conclusions.

AMANDA TAPPING: There are so many new fans coming to *Stargate* and I hope with Amanda Carter they see the strength and integrity and the desire to push boundaries. What I loved about Sam was there wasn't a shrillness to her, there wasn't a harsh aspect to her, even though she probably had to fight really hard in a man's world. But she didn't choose that route. She chose to just be and live in the environment that she was in. To prove herself by being who she was without always waving the flag, "I'm a woman and I'm just as good." I think that that will eventually change for girls where they don't have to do that, but that you can just prove yourself now, prove your self-worth as a young woman without having to stand on a soap box. I hope that that's the case and that there will just be no need for it at all whatsoever.

As to myself, you're just an actor on a show who lucked into a great gig. The fact that the gig continued for as long as it did and that you have been given the privilege to be able to do what you love to do for a living for as long as you've been able to do it — well, as soon as you start taking that for granted, you're in trouble. I've always said to my friends and family, "As soon as I start taking any of this for granted, just kick me in the ass, because then I really don't deserve it."

CHRISTOPHER JUDGE (TEAL'C)

He's not an alien, he only plays one on TV — or did, for over a decade as the Jaffa, Teal'c, on Stargate SG-1. *In our world, Douglas Christopher Judge was born on October 13, 1964 in Los Angeles, California. Believing that sports could result in a path leading to acting, he became an All-L.A. City football player at Carson High School, graduating in 1982 with a scholarship to the University of Oregon. From 1982 to 1985 he played defensive back and safety for the Ducks and was named Newcomer of the Year. In his senior year he won a contest that led to him hosting the FOX KLSR Morning Show, which in turn led to his getting an agent and making the move to Los Angeles.*

Prior to Stargate SG-1, *he made appearances on such television series as* Neon Rider, MacGyver, 21 Jump Street, Booker, Sirens *(in a recurring role) and* The Fresh Prince of Bel-Air, *as well as films (either big screen, for television or direct-to-DVD) like* Bird on a Wire, Cadence *and* House Party 2.

CHRISTOPHER JUDGE: Young men in their lives want to be policemen, firemen, athletes, doctors ... real world stuff. I had an uncle who was in show business, so I was familiar with the world. Show business was never put forth as something that was penetrable to people. [But] I remember exactly the moment where I said this is what I want to do. I was probably six or seven years old and I watched the movie *Sounder*. It was about a boy whose dad had gone to prison and his best friend was his dog, Sounder. Then, at the end of the movie, Sounder passes away and I was devastated for whatever reason. I said, "That's what I want to do. I want to make people feel like I feel right now." And it's never wavered.

And he was ready when the opportunity presented itself — in a situation that was purely coincidental — for him to audition for the part of Teal'c on Stargate SG-1.

CHRISTOPHER JUDGE: I was visiting my best friend from high school and his roommate was an actor. He was running lines, getting ready for an audition. I just happened to be there and it sounded interesting. He went to his room to change or whatever and I looked at the sides and was, like, "Wow!" I immediately called my agent and said, "Have you heard of this *Stargate*?" "Oh, yeah, we've heard." I said, "Get me an audition or I'm leaving the agency." It was just material I hadn't seen before. It was different. It was well-written and smart. Within that week that was my first tape audition. I rewatched the movie before my audition, but there was really no clue how to play a Jaffa, because they didn't really speak.

BRAD WRIGHT: Chris Judge walked in and he was particularly buff that day and wearing a tight T-shirt, and Rick goes, "Why didn't you go to the gym first? Don't you care?" Chris laughed his head off in that Chris Judge way, which is very wonderful and very, very contagious. Jon and I looked at each other and instantly knew that he was perfect for the role.

RICHARD DEAN ANDERSON: Chris came in to audition and all he did, literally, was walk onto the stage in a T-shirt, I believe, and he was just coming from the gym. He just stood there, they told him he had the job and they literally sent 10 other guys home.

JONATHAN GLASSNER: We needed a big guy who looked unique and didn't just look like every other big guy out there. I'll never forget sitting in the theater where we were doing auditions with Brad, and Chris walked in the room. He just had this look that made you kind of go, "Whoa, he *is* an alien!" He's a very unique looking guy, because he's a combination of ethnicities, so it makes him have a distinctive look. Thankfully as soon as he opened his mouth there Teal'c was. To be honest, though, he was the only one I was unsure of in the beginning, because I'd had bad experiences with casting big buff guys and their acting ability. Usually God gives you one or the other, but he turned out to be great.

CHRISTOPHER JUDGE: One of the greatest pieces of advice I ever got as an actor was from James Earl Jones when I had a spot on his show, *Gabriel's Fire*. I was playing this robber and I was very big, very broad. One of the A.D.s says to me, "Mr. Jones would like to have lunch with you." So I had lunch with him and he said, "You're okay," which is what every actor wants to hear. Then he told me, "Don't ever move unless you have to." I live by that to this day — maybe too much. I wanted to be as minimalist with Teal'c as possible. Even in the beginning, during the pilot, I was talking to Brad and Jonathan and we were discussing how much he should know about Goa'uld technology and how much he should speak. I said, "I really don't think he should talk much, because then everything he says is important."

ROBERT C. COOPER: Chris Judge had to do a lot with a little, and that's a talent, too. Just an amazing ability to create sympathy and pathos and humor and all those things with just a look or an expression or silence. *That* takes courage. And he obviously had a physical presence that ate the screen up, but I think his character took a while to become three-dimensional and really kind of get that stoicism. He wasn't given a lot of material to work with early on. He had his backstory with the lack of trust, but I don't think we wrote very well for him for some time.

CHRISTOPHER JUDGE: Knowing that we had 44 episodes, one of the things we talked about was not bringing him along too quickly. It was really great fortune to be able to bring his evolution almost in real time.

JOSEPH MALLOZZI: Chris did, obviously, a remarkable job as Teal'c, even though he was the polar opposite of the solemn character. Teal'c is very much also kind of a fish out of water. And what Chris did over time was kind of imbue him with a sense of humor as well that I think the Teal'c character was totally oblivious to, but which the fans loved. That sense of humor allowed the fans to connect with Teal'c as well, just because he was such an outsider. So capable as a warrior, yet so clueless in certain respects in dealing with and adjusting to life on Earth. Each of those actors brought something special to their roles.

BRAD WRIGHT: Teal'c was not somebody who made random observations on humanity. He just wasn't that guy. He was just simply a Jaffa. He had an incredibly powerful sense of right and wrong and loyalty. He was almost the opposite of Spock; he was our window into the world we *didn't* know. It was, like, "Who are all these Goa'uld and why do they do what they do?" He knew *everything* and was our inside guy on all of that stuff. And we just wanted him to be alone and fighting for what's right. The whole "I die free" thing was a big deal for that character.

JOSEPH MALLOZZI: What was interesting was the way that characters like Spock and Teal'c are able to comment on truths in a way that really only children are able to do and get right. And because we, as adults, have gotten kind of accustomed to seeing the world in a certain way, the ridiculous aspects of the world become sort of mundane to us, whereas to a child or an alien they are bizarre.

PETER DELUISE: Chris is a talented actor with an amazing speaking voice, which he's been using in voiceover work and currently in video games, in things like *God of*

War. And what was great is that his character becomes a turncoat, like Worf, if you will, because an enemy is brought into our fold and we move past that and onto the next thing. Taking an alien and making him a part of your team just makes really good sense. He was different from everybody else and he could do fish out of water against Earth culture, which is ripe for comedy. Somebody might say, "It could be a booby trap" and he's, like, "Booby?" And, of course, for anything involving the Goa'uld, he was your go-to guy; he would help us understand in a way that would make sense. It's not like you could look it up on Wikipedia.

JONATHAN GLASSNER: One of the first things we said when we were developing the show is that we wanted an alien character, just because it makes things more interesting. It gives you a perspective on other things on other worlds without having to go there. So you have a character who can say, "Yes, I've met the Asgard." It also gave us a way to explore the Jaffa.

BRAD WRIGHT: He wasn't out in the world. He wasn't hanging out at the Dairy Freeze. He was at the base and didn't have as much of a life. *Which* we explored later and you had to give him one, and then he ended up having to go home again. Great scene in that episode where a guy's running away and he picks up a soup can, throws it 200 yards and the can hits the guy in the back of the head. CG, obviously, but it was such a great moment. I love that. Chris was funny, too, because he's a big, strong guy. I would go on two or three golf trips a year with Chris, who could hit 300 yards. Rarely in the direction he wanted to, but no problem. So here's this gigantic guy, but if a squirrel runs by, he freaks out.

Judge remained a part of SG-1 right through the end, though interestingly he feels that for much of it Teal'c was oftentimes an "observer," which he attributes to his own "laziness." That seemed to change beginning in season nine with the new team dynamic made by the departure of Richard Dean Anderson and the addition of cast members Ben Browder and Claudia Black.

CHRISTOPHER JUDGE: I actually enjoyed playing Teal'c as the observer. Oftentimes I wouldn't really have to read the scripts [*laughs*]. My work ethic had to change, because there was no telling who was going to adlib something to you. So there was no such thing as not knowing what's going on in the scene, what preceded it, and what comes after it, because somebody was going to adlib something. You always had to be on your toes. And it was almost like remembering how to act again, because there was that general air of spontaneity. Anything could happen at any time. It was such a breath of fresh air. Just so reinvigorating. It really was.

DON S. DAVIS (GEORGE HAMMOND)

The man giving orders at Stargate Command is Lieutenant General George S. Hammond as played by American character actor Don S. Davis, who was born August 4, 1942 in Aurora, Missouri. He graduated from Southwest Missouri State College with a Bachelor of Science degree in theater and art. He served in the military during the time of the Vietnam War, rising to the rank of captain at Fort Leonard Wood in the U.S. Army — seemingly perfect for his later portrayal of military types.

He earned a Master's Degree in Theatre from Southern Illinois University Carbondale. His acting career began getting traction in the 1980s, serving as a stunt double for Dana Elcar on Richard Dean Anderson's MacGyver. *Many other television appearances followed prior to* Stargate SG-1, *including such authority figures as Judge Richard Bartke on* L.A. Law, *a judge and sheriff on* Booker, *Major Sutherland on* Monkey House, *Major Garland Briggs on* Twin Peaks, *Chief Sterling in* Broken Badges, *Sheriff Dan Filcher on* Nightmare Café, *Sergeant Pritchard on* Street Justice, *Judge Gray in* Final Appeal, *Sgt. Brock Thorne in* Cobra, *Admiral Farallon on* M.A.N.T.I.S., *Captain William Scully on* The X-Files, *General Callahan on* The Outer Limits *and General Harlan Ford on* Atomic Train. *There were also two dozen film appearances in that time as well.*

DON S. DAVIS (actor, "Lieutenant General George S. Hammond"): I never really liked science-fiction in film and television, because when I was younger, it was all cardboard and very crude, and it wasn't realistic. And I could read someone like Asimov and envision all of these wonderful things. Or Wells, or whoever, and then I would see it on TV or in a film and — *no.* In fact, my son, when he was about four years old, I guess — or five years old — *Star Wars* came out and he *had* to see *Star Wars.* He really had to make me lots of promises in order to get me to take him to it. And I came out of that movie a *Star Wars* nut. The original *Star Trek* was silly — the crudity of the thing. Even though the actors, a lot of them, now are friends of mine. But I don't like crudity. I'm a painter and a sculptor. I spent 20 years teaching people how to be artists and craftsmen. And then to see something, especially on film, that looks like a [mentally-challenged] two-year old created it in their backyard, is not entertaining to me.

One of my favorite shows on television, for years, was a Canadian production called *Lexx.* It's just magnificent. Within the science fiction realm, *Doctor Who* and *The Hitchhiker's Guide to the Galaxy.* Hell, I've got DVDs of all of them! I'm just saying I came to it late. One of my favorite authors — again, he happens to be Canadian — is named Spider Robinson. If you want to have great fun, read *The Callahan Chronicles.* And his wife is also a wonderful writer. I love detective stories and she has written a sci-fi detective story called "Lady Slings the Booze." And if you can read that — I read that on an airplane and the hostess actually became concerned, because I was alternately laughing and crying and moving around in my seat. Just the imagination of these people! But yeah, I like sci-fi. I was reading Ray Bradbury at the moment that John F. Kennedy was shot. People say you always remember what you were doing, and I happened to be reading Ray Bradbury at the time. See, I grew up with some magnificent science fiction. All the H.G. Wells stories, and Ray Bradbury, and again, Issac Asimov. Just great writers.

Years ago I was brought to Canada to teach at the University of British Columbia and I taught for about 10 years. And I was published. So my summers were pretty much mine, but they insisted that if I *did* work in the summers, it had to be theater related. One of the other faculty wanted to act in film and television. He taught acting and he talked me into meeting his agent. And I wound up doing some extra work, and then, through a fluke, wound up on a film letting some people shoot a mortar full of spaghetti and cottage cheese and food coloring in my face as if the man in front of me had had his brains shot out. And the A.D. on that show — the second A.D. on that show — a couple of years later, wound up being the second A.D. on *MacGyver*. And when they shot *MacGyver*, Richard Dean Anderson's boss was played by an actor named Dana Elcar. They couldn't find a stunt double for Dana who looked anything like him. They were having to put padded suits on these guys, and bald caps, and it just wasn't working. And in a production meeting this guy said, "Well, hell, there's an actor in town that could be his brother! He looks just like him!" And so I wound up becoming his photo double, and then his stunt double. And so Michael Greenburg and Rick got to know me. When *Stargate* came along, they called me in to read for Hammond. That's how I really got that. Not through talent or beating anybody out! They are two very loyal people, and they knew that they could trust me.

BRAD WRIGHT: Jonathan and I had worked with Don Davis, so we wanted him to be the general. And Don is Don. He gives you that incredible, rich Texas voice. I think he's from the Ozarks, but it's a very deep American accent.

JONATHAN GLASSNER: After doing 66 episodes of *The Outer Limits*, we had our favorite actors that we had worked with. Don had played several different parts on *The Outer Limits*. He was just a guest actor, and he had also been on *21 Jump Street* for me way back. So I always loved him and he was the perfect choice for the general. He lived in Canada, but he was American, so he had that sort of Texas/Oklahoma drawl. He was really good for the part.

DON S. DAVIS: I thought Hammond was a two-dimensional figure. I had served in the army in Korea during the Vietnam War. I was an officer; I started out as a Second Lieutenant, got out as a Captain. And I had served under officers that were heroic, certainly. Some who weren't. But who were, as they really *are* in the Army, a cross-section of humanity. I served under guys that were poets and painters and dreamers and schemers. And when I saw Hammond, he was by-the-book. A foil for O'Neill. And it just wasn't true to what the service is really like and they were kind enough to take my suggestions to heart. And they let me, especially as the show [went] on, make him more and more human.

Davis, who had married Ruby Fleming in 2003, was forced to leave SG-1 *at the end of Season 7 due to health issues, although he did appear in several more episodes as a guest star. He would eventually pass away on June 29, 2008 at age 65.*

CHRISTOPHER JUDGE: Every memory about Donny is great. I never made any secrets about how much I loved him, and it's hard to watch episodes and knowing I'll never hear that southern drawl anymore. The great thing, though, is he touched so many people. It's no secret what a beautiful human being he was. I miss Donny every day. I am not kidding. Just the way he conducted himself as a human being. Everything that's wrong about this business, Donny is the opposite of it. Donny was everything that's right about this business. He cared more about other people than he cared about himself. What a great human being. One of the greatest things about *Stargate* for me was that I got to be around Don Davis for 10 years.

MICHAEL SHANKS: I think that moments spent with Don were a plus. I mean, for standout memories, those are the ones that I will probably keep for me, because they were the quieter moments or the more intimate humorous moments that you share when you get to know someone very well over the course of working with him as intimately as we worked together with that group. The greatest moments are not something that the audience will see. The moments of real-life emotion and conversations over a couple of drinks that really are going to be near and dear to my heart that really give me insight into who Don was from the ground up. From a work standpoint, Don was one of those people who every day, along with the rest of our group, we had a good laugh. I'll always remember his desire to get everything right and his constant inability to do so. And how it frustrated him so much, but it became a way for us to blow off steam and have a good laugh.

TONY AMENDOLA (actor, "Master Bra'tac"): Don and I spent some time together in London on an event where we got to see a bunch of plays. He dragged me to all of his favorite art book stores; he was always in search of something and he had such a hunger for the artistic. It's an overused word, except with him, I think. The reason I say that is not only [that] he's an actor, but he painted, he sketched, he did woodwork. He was amazing. And he seemed to have so many other lives, too. He was a teacher. He was in the military. He was born and raised in the States and then landed [as an] immigrant in Canada. There were many, many fond things. We would always gravitate toward having lunch when we were on set together. It was terrific. And to watch him, particularly when he met Ruby — his wife — he changed. She had such a wonderful effect on him.

Now, previous to Ruby, Don was always such a romantic, you know? I always used to call him and we'd go to these events. [We'd] be in London [and] look at all the beautiful women. He was a true appreciator of women. And he was an unassuming actor. A lot of actors, [he] would just tell you "Oh, well, you know I'm not really an actor, and you guys are just lazy." And you go on stage, or on-screen, and he just cleans your clock, because he is the real item. There was something uniquely American about him. His experience. His look. His size. There was just something that was really truthful about what he presented on-screen and in life. So, he *will* be missed.

ANDY MIKITA: Don was very, very dear to me. I can't say enough great things about Don Davis. He was an extraordinary man and I have nothing but the fondest memories of him. I'd known him for many years. He was always just a sweet, kind hearted, gentle but strong man. Every day he would ask about my wife and my children and was genuinely asking. It wasn't just a formality. He really wanted to know, and he had nothing but time for everybody. He was larger than life in his presence and he gave so much to the show. Some of my fondest memories of Don were during the production of "Heroes, Parts 1 and 2," where even in blocking rehearsals, Don would break down with emotion over the subject matter. It was so near and dear to him with his experience in the military. It was a very moving experience. Knowing how emotional Don was and how fragile, really … he was in that situation, so we kind of had to tread a little bit carefully with him. It really allowed us all to see, again, a different side of Don.

BEN BROWDER (CAMERON MITCHELL)

One thing that might make you laugh about actor Ben Browder, formerly of Farscape *and then of* Stargate SG-1, *is his instant reply to the question, "Would you step through a Stargate?"*

BEN BROWDER: It's a basic question and the answer is, yes I would! Hey, I was locked down in L.A. County for a year and a half during COVID — I'm up for pretty much anything that gets me out of here. Someone recently asked me, "Would you go to Mars?" and I said yes without thinking about it. Oh yeah, I'd go. What if it's one way? I'd probably *still* go, which is ridiculous. But if you give me the chance to go into space, I would go in a heartbeat. There are other people who are not into that. You want to go to the North Pole and hang out with polar bears? I'm down. Let's go. I haven't actually fully eradicated my youthful sense of immortality. If you gave me a parachute, I would jump out of a plane. It's a dispositional thing more than anything else; I lack the intelligence and imagination to properly gauge risk.

Robert Benedict Browder was born December 11, 1962 in Memphis, Tennessee. Growing up in Charlotte, North Carolina, he graduated from Furman University in Greenville, South Carolina with a degree in psychology. He decided to study at the Central School of Speech and Drama in London, which is where he met his wife, actress Francesca Buller.

He got his start with small roles in about a dozen films and TV movies prior to his starring role in Farscape, *and made a number of guest star appearances on different TV shows, including a recurring role as Sam Brody on* Party of Five. *From 1999 to 2003 he played John Crichton in the sci-fi series* Farscape, *a role he reprised in the 2004 TV movie* Farscape: The Peacekeeper Wars. *He joined* Stargate SG-1 *as Lt. Colonel Cameron Mitchell in Season 9 and continued playing the part in Season 10 as well as the made-for-DVD movies* Stargate: The Ark of Truth *and* Stargate: Continuum.

JOSEPH MALLOZZI: I think Rick started having the feeling to leave about five seasons into the show, because he was the lead and in a lot of it. *And* he had a very young daughter that he actually wanted to spend time with. He just decided that was the important thing in terms of priorities, so we found ways to lessen the burden in Season 6. I think that was the first season where you saw him begin to appear in fewer episodes, in Season 7 he appeared in even less episodes and then in Season 8 we made him the base commander of the S.G.C. as a way to sort of lessen things even more. And that was it. We missed him, and I think he definitely did begin to miss us, so we had him come back in seasons nine and 10 for guest spots.

PETER DELUISE: One of the things that was causing consternation or a bit of a problem was that Richard Dean Anderson had a custody schedule regarding his daughter. And, being the good father that he is, he wanted to be as emotionally and physically available to his daughter as possible when he had her in his custody, so he didn't want to be away doing our show when he needed to be a dad. What was worked out was that when he didn't have custody, we had access to him. He would come up and he would shoot with us. But that became slightly untenable over time, so what we did was shoot his scenes in advance or behind, wherever they fell on the schedule, and then we'd try to make whole days that he wasn't in. If you noticed, usually the away team would go onto a planet and split themselves in half; two people do this, two people do that. They recon and share information and then the situation is solved. But if Richard Anderson was there, there wasn't enough stuff that he was in to make a day. So, as a result, we were having trouble with the schedule. What we finally fell on was that Richard would just do less overall, until he was replaced by Beau Bridges [as commander of S.G.C.]. Don Davis died, and Richard Dean Anderson was not available to us, so there would be less of him. Then Beau Bridges came in. Beau Bridges? That's fucking awesome. Let's get him in there.

BEN BROWDER: I met Michael Shanks on a plane and we talked about the fact that Claudia Black had been on *Stargate* and then I met Brad Wright and Joe Mallozzi at Comic-Con and we got on really well. At a certain point when Rick was leaving the show, there was a sense of interest in me to take the place of the Jack O'Neill character. When that idea was broached, I watched all eight seasons of the show and I thought, "This would be great." So I went up to do it and tried to figure out how to fit in with the structure of the show.

JOSEPH MALLOZZI: I was a big *Farscape* fan, and I know the Sci-Fi Channel was concerned about the fact that Rick was leaving. I suggested, "They love Ben, why don't we float the idea of getting Ben on the show?" And we did and they loved it so much. We brought Ben on and I remember him watching, like, every episode of *SG-1* before landing on the show. And then, once he was on the show, the crew loved him. He was the guy who would always stay behind and do his lines opposite other actors off camera, which is kind of unheard of in the industry. He was just a great addition to the cast and the *Stargate* world.

BEN BROWDER: Coming in on the ninth season, there are a couple of things to keep in mind. One is that you're not going to replace the most beloved actor on the show, Richard Dean Anderson, or any of those beloved characters. And Rick was the center of the show, which means you're not going to come in and try to do his schtick. You're just going to try and fit in with what they do. One of the things about the military is that it has interchangeable pieces. It's amazing that all of those characters stayed as long as they did, because that wouldn't happen. You'd be moving on to your next assignment in the Air Force; you're going to spend two, three, maybe four years in a really odd situation in the same job, and then you're going to be moved on, particularly officers, who are going to move on to different things.

So you have that structure which invites a new leader. They don't promote from within, they usually promote you and send you somewhere else. That made perfect logical sense from the construct of things, so I didn't have to fight against that. Then the question was, how do I fit in with this group of people? If you're coming in as an officer in command, and there's an existing command structure below you, the first thing you're going to do is look to the people there to see how things are run. You're going to look at the people who have been doing the job before you got there and you're going to look to them for advice. That's what I did as an actor. It's what you do as a person and then you go from there. The other thing is that if the show is called *Stargate*, then that means, in my head, the center of the show was the Stargate.

Andy Mikita was directing the first episode that I'm in and in the script they introduce Cameron Mitchell by having him go into the gate room and he sees the gate. We got to show the gate and there's a push in on Cameron Mitchell and the scene is designed so that this scene ends on Cameron Mitchell's face. I'm talking with Andy and I said, "Look, here's the thing. I think it's a huge mistake to end on a close-up of me. Because I'm new to the show, the fans who have been with it for eight years are now being told that we're supposed to pay attention to this guy. I think that's a mistake, because I'm not what the show is about. The show is about the Stargate. What if we just push towards me and then push *past* me and we focus on the gate?" Which is what ended up happening. So my opinion from day one was, again, that the show wasn't about me, it was about the Stargate and about the team. *That* was my approach.

PETER DELUISE: Without Richard, we were, like, "We need somebody who is a proper leader, who's military." Well, Ben Browder ticked all of these wonderful boxes and was a wonderful "crossover" from *Farscape*. What was bad was, visually, he and Michael Shanks look very similar to each other. They're both white males about the same height with about the same haircut, so that wasn't great. Michael Shanks had glasses and the character was better played with glasses. If you're wearing glasses, you're smart, right?

BEN BROWDER: I need to play characters that are changing. There are actors who do one thing; they do the same thing over and over again and they're great at what they do. And then there are actors who are different every time you see them by either large or small degrees. Or there are actors who you meet and you go, "Oh, yeah, you *are* that character." I'm probably somewhere in between, but I'm definitely *not* John Crichton and I'm not Cameron Mitchell, but when I'm playing them, they exist in a space in my head. And they have a tendency to evolve as I play them. I am not doing a lockdown version of what Ben Browder did, so that makes it harder for me to be episodic in playing characters.

CLAUDIA BLACK (VALA MAL DORAN)

Given the chemistry between Claudia Black and Ben Browder on the Farscape *television series, it was a brilliant idea for the producers of SG-1 to feature them as co-stars on the series' ninth and 10th seasons.*

BRAD WRIGHT: We just embraced that vibe, and it wasn't a view that these were the two characters from *Farscape;* our Vala was very different and Mitchell was very different. Certainly the way Ben and Claudia approach the characters are very different.

They're both serious actors and they wanted to be embodying new characters, so it became less of an issue.

Born Claudia Lee Black on October 11, 1972 in Sydney, Australia, Black studied at Sydney's Angilca Kambala School. Although she appeared in about a dozen films (two of them as a vocal actress), she found a home on television, making appearances on shows like Home and Away, G.P., Police Rescue, A Country Practice, Water Rats, Hercules The Legendary Journeys, Good Guys, Bad Guys *and* A Twist in the Tale. *Additionally, she was a series regular on* City Life *and, of course,* Farscape.

Black made her SG-1 debut on Season 8's "Prometheus Unbound," which resulted in her returning for an arc in Season 9 and then as a series regular the following year. During all of it, she very nicely managed to fit right in.

CLAUDIA BLACK: I was surprised to be able to walk onto a set and feel so comfortable. So just in terms of the social aspects of being in that sort of workplace, I was very grateful that everyone was so kind. And I loved working with Andy and Michael. The other thing was the crew, of course, who were saying, "Your character doesn't die at the end of this — she'll come back for sure!" Not that that matters in science fiction — you can die and they'll find a way to bring you back. At first we didn't think that I'd be able to do the episode. It was just lucky timing that I finished my post-syncs for *Peacekeeper Wars* in time to get on the plane with two days' notice and get the Canadian work permit and get here. Well, it was lucky the Canadian government is very kind to Australians and they expedited the process, because we're part of the commonwealth.

"Prometheus Unbound" was supposed to be a bottle episode: contained budget, nothing off-world, no expensive locations, what have you, just something that was character-based. And I liked that when I first read it, that it was just self-contained story, that I wouldn't have to get used to the whole world straight-away and be overwhelmed by it, potentially. When I spoke to the producers on the phone, and Andy Mikita in advance, they said, "A show that's been running this long, they're going to be a happy set, so I think you'll enjoy it." They were absolutely right. I was sent the first episode, and I got on the phone straight-away and rang Robert Cooper to thank him. I think he was a little surprised, and he was waiting for the "But ..." "It's fabulous ... but!" And he's just waiting. And I think he's not used to compliments, so he quickly and shyly changed the subject. And he was probably busy at the time — I called him probably at a bad time. But I felt very spoiled. And that's when I said to him, "Vala is a treat. You've given her such fantastic things to do and say, and I'm very grateful."

She's a very vibrant, very — hopefully — entertaining character. People responded very, very well — especially on set — immediately to the chemistry between Vala and

Daniel. She's a perfect foil for him, because he is so serious and she's just this wonderful ball of light and energy. And the fact that she's got an edge to her and can't be trusted means, comedically, fantastic scope. And that was the main reason why I took the first role on "Prometheus," because I read the script and thought it was really funny. I just wanted to make sure that they had the same intentions as I had inferred. And so I spoke to Andy Mikita and said to him, "How far can I go with the comedy, because I see some great potential for the character?" And he said, "Oh, go all the way, honey! Do whatever you want." For me to turn that corner from *Farscape*, carrying the huge dramatic heart and soul of that piece as a series, and to be able to flip that and be in a lot of ways responsible for the comedy in our scenes — it's a challenge, it's daunting, but it's a lot of fun.

PETER DELUISE: Originally, I don't think Claudia Black was supposed to participate nearly as much as she did. Her character has a sort of mercenary attitude. An alien who was a mercenary and a female Han Solo, for lack of a better description. Robert Cooper was always super gung-ho about *Star Wars* and anything that had to do with gritty space aliens that were mercenary and looking out for themselves. So Claudia's character was a very self-interested, potentially selfish character who has shades of selfishness sometimes. Also, she was sexy and owned her feminine power. She was elite. And now we had another female in the group as well, which worked well for everybody. Claudia Black and Ben Browder knew each other very well, so they had lovely chemistry and played off of each other wonderfully. It just made really good sense for that to happen.

CLAUDIA BLACK: An opportunity presented itself. Amanda Tapping had personal reasons to be away from work and they asked me to come in and keep her seat warm. Vala was in no way a replacement for any other character. She was just a new, weird element that was as entertaining as she was irritating! But that's what makes her so great, I think. And she's got a bit of a journey to go.

PETER DELUISE: There has to be a balance in everything. You had the science-based discipline, militaristic earthling in Carter, so you needed the opposite of those things with the Claudia Black character. She was alien. She was in it for herself. She was *not* militaristic. And instead of being conservative, she was quite liberal. Her energy was the whole other side of the spectrum.

CLAUDIA BLACK: Rob was very honest with me from the very beginning. He expressed what his desire was and what his intentions were. He said, "You know, I would love ultimately to have you back. I don't know in what exact capacity, but this character has brought something very interesting to the show, and we'd like to workshop some possibilities." They wanted to bring me back again potentially permanently in Season 9, but I had my own personal reasons for not being able to join the show permanently. Then we relocated to do it for a season. It was nice to give it a trial run, to experience Vancouver and the show on a more permanent basis and see if I could still find my smile with the insane hours I'd be doing. I rang the producers and thanked them for everything they did to help acclimatize – or as you guys say, "acclimate." Because they really are a very soft place to land.

Black viewed Vala as a character in denial and someone who tends to sublimate things as a coping mechanism. At the same time, she felt those qualities made her entertaining, irritating and, notably, vulnerable.

CLAUDIA BLACK: I think you start to see the cracks, the chinks in her armor when Daniel tries to bring something up with her and she would make a joke. I think that every time they peeled off a layer, and someone gets a little bit closer to revealing a vulnerability of hers, she ends it with a joke. It became an accepted aspect of her personality — I think they realized that they can't change her. Her journey at the beginning of Season 10, certainly, was to prove that she is willing, able, qualified in some ways and, interestingly enough, able to do things that they can't — in a military environment they're not able to do. She is a renegade who can do all sorts of things on their behalf. And since the Ori were such a dangerous enemy who didn't play by the rules, they probably needed someone on their side who could infiltrate in ways they couldn't. Part of what made her interesting and continuously vulnerable is the fact that she's never belonged anywhere. And if she was going to be at Stargate Command, it was going to be on a short rope. I think they hadn't established nine seasons of a show with the most successful Air Force covert operation to employ someone they think is going to compromise them extensively. So they definitely were going to keep her on a short rope.

You know, I would never expect anyone to be a fan of anything I've done. And the fact that people crossed over and started tuning in to *Stargate* was fantastic. I really appreciate the fact that, from what I heard from people, that they recognize how different the characters are. And I'm glad I was able to do something different for them, and, as always, tried not to insult their intelligence. I'm never thinking of the lowest common denominator when I do my work. So whoever's appreciating it, I'm very grateful that they're entertained by it.

BEAU BRIDGES (HANK LANDRY)

There is so much to the career of Beau Bridges that it would be impossible to reflect on it all in the allotted space. Suffice to say that he was born Lloyd Vernet "Beau" Bridges III on December 9, 1941 in Los Angeles, California. He's part of a showbiz dynasty that includes his father, Lloyd Bridges; and older brother Jeff Bridges. He dreamt of becoming a basketball star, but gradually found himself drawn to the world of acting. He was a student at the University of Hawaii and, beginning in 1959, spent eight years as a part of the United States Coast Guard Reserve.

His first movie role was a small part in 1948's No Minor Vices, *which would be followed by parts in over 80 other films between then and 2020's* One Night in Miami. *His television debut was in a 1960 episode of* My Three Sons. *Many episodic appearances and TV movies would follow, and he would serve as a series regular on* Ensign O'Toole *(1962 to 1963),* United States *(1980), the* Space *miniseries (1985),* Harts of the West *(1993 to 1994),* Maximum Bob *(1998),* The Agency *(2001 to 2003),* My Name is Earl *(seven episodes between 2005 and 2008),* Brothers & Sisters *(five episodes in 2011),* Masters of Sex *(2013 to 2016),* The Millers *(2013 to 2015),* Bloodline *(2016 to 2017) and recurring roles on* Mosaic *(2017 to 2018),* Homeland *(2018 to 2020),* Greenleaf *(2018 to 2019),* Goliath *(2019),* Messiah *(2020) and* Robbie *(2020). Along the way, of course, he appeared in 35 episodes of* SG-1 *and five episodes of* Stargate: Atlantis. *Bridges has won three Emmy Awards (having been nominated 14 times).*

Further on, others involved with Stargate *reflect on working with him, while what follows are the actor's views of having played Landry, in charge of Stargate Command.*

BEAU BRIDGES: Well, I've always been a fan of science-fiction. I've enjoyed it. I think, maybe, they had an idea to come to me because I did the two-hour movie called *The Sandkings*, which kicked off their *Outer Limits* franchise, which ran quite a few years for them and was very successful. I did that with my Dad and my son, Dylan. That was a great experience. I enjoyed doing that show. I've always liked science-fiction, so it was fun to be able to come and do this.

When I was researching generals — which is what I did, and that helped me find the back-story for General Landry — first of all, I was amazed by their education. These guys, a number of them have several Masters degrees. They really come from all walks of life. And as much as the whole challenge of command confronts them, they are people in the end and they have all kinds of human problems just like the rest of us. So I *do* like that, when Landry gets involved in that kind of personal stuff. We didn't really learn about him much more than you do in terms of lead time. It's just like life, kind of.

When you do a character that runs through a whole series, it gives you the opportunity to evolve that person through different kinds of situations that you wouldn't get to in a two-hour movie, or an hour show. General Landry was particularly interesting for me, because when I was hired for the job to play the character, he was basically just a blank page. There was nothing there. So, Robert Cooper invited me to work on the character with him, to flesh him out, and we created a biography between the two of us. I always like to do that with characters that I portray.

He was not a replacement for O'Neill. I think there will only be one Jack O'Neill. Richard Dean did a wonderful job with that character; I like the fact that he was part of the reason I came to *SG-1*. I thought that was clever of them to do that. But right from the get-go, I think General Landry stands on his own. He's his own person. Like I said, I was able to have a hand in creating that with Robert Cooper — that character — so it was fun. And I figured I was really lucky to join such a vastly popular show. I just consider myself lucky. It's like jumping on a moving train. It's a great group, and they welcomed me with open arms.

Like Shakespeare said, "The play's the thing." And I think Robert is certainly one of the best execs in the business. The reason this show was a hit for so many years is because he's writing them and he's watching over the guys that are turning them out — and I like to say the words!

CORIN NEMEC (JONAS QUINN)

When Michael Shanks decided to step away from Stargate SG-1 *at the end of Season 5, Brad Wright and Robert Cooper created a new character, a human from Kelowna on the planet Langara named Jonas Quinn, to join the SG-1 team. He guest-starred in Seasons 5 and 7 and was a regular in season six. He departed after Shanks returned to the show.*

Joseph Charles Nemec IV was born November 5, 1971 in Little Rock, Arkansas. When he was 13, he was inspired to get into acting while watching the young performers in 1985's The Goonies. *He began training at the Centre Stage LA theater company, which led to his getting an agent and, in turn, commercial gigs. He secured a recurring role in the sitcom* Webster *and debuted on the big screen in* Tucker: The Man and His Dream. *Lead roles in the series* What's Alan Watching? *And* Parker Lewis Can't Lose *followed along with a number of guest starring roles prior to his signing on to play Jonas. In recent years he has spent more time working as a producer than an actor.*

CORIN NEMEC: The casting process for me for *Stargate* was really cool, because I didn't have to audition for it, which was surprising. It was a "right place, right time" moment. I was actually at MGM — they don't have studios anymore, [but] where their offices are. And I was auditioning for this little independent film and was out in the courtyard area just rehearsing my dialogue. The casting people from *Stargate* walked by. They knew me from previous stuff. They just stopped and we had a chat for a little bit and they were, like, "God, he looks so much like Heath Ledger." They were looking at each other and said, "We've got this part for a show called *Stargate*. They're going to have a new series regular. You would be awesome for it. You look like you would be perfect." They literally had just got it that day; they were just starting to talk about casting. At the time I was sitting there going to audition for a little independent film that was probably going to pay 100 bucks a day. I'm, like, "Am I interested?" So it was really cool. They sent some tape over, a reel of some work that I'd done to Vancouver. The guys, Brad Wright and all them, checked it out and it worked out great. It was really cool.

Once he was cast, it became evident that, physically, the actor went through quite a change from his first appearance on the show in Season 5 to being a regular in Season 6.

CORIN NEMEC: The physique change, actually, was my idea. When I did the last episode of Season 5, I was much trimmer. But when I worked with Chris Judge — number one, just seeing how big he is, I realized that if I didn't bulk up, I was going to disappear on screen. Richard Dean Anderson is, like, 6'3. He's a really tall guy. I just knew that with the cast being as big and as tall as everybody is … even Amanda Tapping, she's, like, 5'10". So I knew I had to bulk up. I spent the three or so months between when they wrapped that, before they started Season 6, drinking four weight gainer shakes a day. I'd go to the gym twice a day. I'd go in the morning and in the afternoon. I literally was in the gym almost six days a week, practically for the full three months. I put on like close to 25 pounds or something like that. And it's funny, because I bulked up for the show and everything and then it took me a while to finally get it off. Once I trimmed back down to what my weight pretty much was before going on to the show, everybody was, "Are you sick? Are you OK? You look so thin." I'm like, "Check me out in everything I did previous to *Stargate*. I look exactly the same."

Filming the show was an enjoyable experience for Nemec, though there weren't too many people not involved with the show that gave him much of a break for stepping in to replace Michael Shanks.

CORIN NEMEC: It's interesting, because working on *Stargate* is as cool as the show is to watch. The whole adventure of it, all the adventures that you go on, the obstacles you have to get over, the predicaments that you get caught in, the great writing, the dialogue, the different relationships. What I remember is I felt like I was on SG-1. You know what I mean? As silly as that sounds, that's what it feels like. Because you film all those scenes you do; everything you watch on the show, you actually physically get to do. So it's like you lived it, in a weird way, on this show.

PETER DELUISE: You don't want members of your cast to have redundant qualities. It's one of the reasons why Corin Nemec and Michael Shanks couldn't possibly be on the show at the same time, because they serve the same function. People understood that you could only have one or the other, because having both of them wouldn't serve, not even in real life.

CORIN NEMEC: I think the initial backlash came from a very small core, outspoken group of the fandom that had a bit of a volatile reaction to it, which is totally natural. But at the same time, that's not my line of work. I'm an actor and I'm coming in to do my thing, so it wasn't challenging in that respect. Interestingly enough, I'd say 95-plus percent of the fan base grew to like the character and accepted the character overall. Especially by the time Season 6 ended, I think people were pretty much, "Eh, OK — I'm cool with that." For the most part. But coming in on the set and everything, it could have been more difficult, except that everybody is just so cool. All the actors and everybody else were so welcoming and laid back. Also, they wrote the character really well. They gave a nice arc, where the character had to prove himself, and the push and the pull of it all. So they allowed that organic arc to take place, which also assisted in the development of the character relationships.

DARREN SUMNER: When Corin joined in Season 6, there was this ongoing "Save Daniel Jackson" fan campaign that really had a chip on its shoulder. This was not just an ordinary, "Let's rally the fans and tell the studio what we want." This was kind of an angry movement and a quintessential example of fans claiming such ownership over the character that it ended up setting them at odds with the writers.

PAUL MULLIE (co-executive producer, *Stargate SG-1*): Corin Nemec was good. He came in and did what we asked him to do, but he wasn't Michael and I was glad when Michael came back. Unfortunately, we were sort of setting him up to fail. It was a very difficult task to replace that character, because he was such a heart of the show. Like I've often said, Richard Dean Anderson's character was kind of floating above it all and kind of iconic. Michael was more like the audience's door in. Without him, Jonas couldn't be that because he was an alien. Even though he brought a bit of that goofiness to it as a curious guy who was seeing everything for the first time. Maybe that was a door in for some people watching the show, but, ultimately, it was better when Michael came back and I don't think that's a knock on Corin. It just made more sense. The show just made more sense with Daniel Jackson being in the middle of it.

CORIN NEMEC: I did my best to try and approach the character tenderly, in that transition. Just keep the character as not edgy as possible, as likable — that's probably the best word to use — as possible so that there would be an easy transition for an audience to go from being such huge fans of one character to another. I couldn't just go in there and have some too specific, too edgy of a character. You've got to like the guy, you've got to get to know the guy, otherwise it would have never worked. Hopefully, a combination of what the writers were doing and what I was doing is what won over the majority of the fan base during that season.

THE STARGATE

It may seem odd to include an inanimate object as part of the cast, but in the way many Star Trek *fans may consider the starship* Enterprise *a* Star Trek *character, the same could be said about the Stargate, described earlier as one of the great sci-fi story generators. Obviously it was featured in the 1994 original movie version, and was born out of the movie concepts that both Roland Emmerich and Dean Devlin initially brought to the table when they decided to collaborate on the film.*

DEAN DEVLIN: Roland kept telling me about a project that he'd been working on since film school called *Neck Ripple*, and what it was about was a spaceship buried underneath the great pyramid of Giza. He had these great scenes where these children were lured there at night and they vanished. But he never really fleshed it out, though he loved this idea of a spaceship. And I had been working on something that I jokingly referred to as *Lawrence of Arabia in Outer Space*. And in mine, there was a good guy and bad guy who were chasing each other in space. They go through a wormhole, but the good guy hesitates for five seconds before he follows him in. That five seconds ended up being 30 years on the other side when he landed. By then, the villain has taken over those other worlds; there's a time change. We thought maybe there was some way to kind of connect these together into one project. A wonderful production designer named Oliver Scholl was hearing our conversation and he said, "You know, there's a device that's used very often in science-fiction literature, but not that often in science-fiction films." And he said it was a teleportation device. Of course, we saw it in *The Fly* and it was in *Star Trek*, but you didn't see it as often as we see it in literature. And that's when we connected those two movies and the Stargate became the teleportation device. The entire inner circle was done by the physical effects guy, Kit West, who had done the *Raiders of the Lost Ark* movies, so it was a really functioning device on set. The Chevrons clicked in and the inner circle was spinning. That was all practical.

OLIVER SCHOLL (conceptual designer, *Stargate*): In the very first versions that we had, the first ideas, the Stargate was triangular in shape and standing on its tip. Then Roland came up with the idea that you would need some kind of dialing process, so that's when the gate became circular shaped.

HOLGER GROSS (production designer, *Stargate*): A very complicated aspect of the Stargate was that we needed an inner ring that would move and the outer ring would stay in place, it turned out to be a pretty complicated technical piece of equipment.

Emmerich wanted the Stargate to come to life with materials that were real and organic, and so the special effects team started to experiment with water in a large tank.

JEFF OKUN (visual effects supervisor, *Stargate*): When the Stargate erupts into the room, we ended up getting an air cannon and mounting it literally an inch above the surface of the water and fired it off. The first time we did it, we fired it off with 120 pounds of air pressure, which lifted the entire volume of water out as a unit, moved over and landed over on the DP's head, which was my favorite moment of the film. He stirred it up and came up with what's called a stroodle, which was water spinning. If you shoot water, you shoot the underside of it as a perfect mirror. I showed how we could get people into the shots and tests, you turn it up and it becomes magical. To pass through the gate, James Spader had to put his face in the water. I told him we were doing it backwards, so, "Stick your face in the water and we'll wave away all the air bubbles, and when I tap on the tank, act backwards — open your eyes and pull your head out." And he was great.

When it was decided to turn Stargate *into a television series, one could easily have the image in their mind of this huge device being taken out of storage and wheeled over to a new set, but that couldn't have been further from the truth.*

RICHARD HUDOLIN (production designer, *Stargate SG-1*): I was given a pretty free hand to design all these sets. At the beginning, there's usually just myself and maybe a couple of others involved, but in that case it was just me and one other person putting together all of the sets. Then I presented it to the executives and they said, "Yeah, let's do this." The next thing we did was build all of the sets in this one big stage, because the other stage wasn't ready for us yet; they were building as we went. One of the tricky things we had to figure out was making sure that every stage had an "elephant door" — a very large door — to get things in and out of it. We had to make sure that the Stargate, which was *not* going to come apart once it was built, could be moved onto the stage. That was a 19- or 20-foot diameter, and it had to fit through that door once the stage had been built. As I recall, that thing was a real piece of precision, because it locked on every "key" that it had to lock on all of the time I was there, plus more. There were no belts, none of that stuff. It was gears and it worked really well.

BRAD WRIGHT: I don't remember the name of the guy who actually built the Stargate, but I do remember it being a whole wiring thing with the amount of technology that went into it to make it spin accurately. Only the top Chevron ever went "chunk-chunk." Even in the movie, I think they just shot the angle rather than it actually moving. We just actuated one chevron and it was always at the top. That was the *SG-1* gate, which was modeled on the movie. Honestly, because we were going to be on TV, I was the one who pitched the idea of lighting up the triangle of the chevron to make it unique to the television show and to be able to make it pop more on a TV screen and be more distinctive.

JONATHAN GLASSNER: The movie Stargate had been trashed along with most of the props and sets we were hoping to use, so we had to build it from scratch. I insisted that it be very robust mechanically so that it would not be breaking down all the time and holding up production (which made it more expensive, but probably saved money in the long run). I wish I could remember the name of the guy who designed and built the mechanics of it, because he did a heroic job. I can't tell you how relieved I was the first time they demonstrated it for us and it actually worked.

BRAD WRIGHT: Jonathan and I drove out to the desert where they had theoretically stored the Stargate from the movie, but the sun had just eaten away everything. It was just a big metal ring and there was a bit where you could see there had been some plastic. Just completely rotted. I thought I would just go step through the ring, just to see what it feels like, but I looked up and dangling from a thread, kind of coming toward me, was the biggest spider I'd *ever* seen.

RICHARD HUDOLIN: Early on I had gone down to L.A. where they had stored some of the elements from the movie. They had a couple of the key pieces, but the Stargate itself was totally gone. What was left was bits and pieces of different things, which I had loaded into three semis that we could then use to create castings of to recreate the gate, the dial and all of that. But that was all newly created, and lighting it up was a new deal. There was a lot involved in so-called "recreating" something that already existed. It was not just a matter of bringing it in and copying it. There was also the question of, "How are we going to make this work for more than one episode like a movie?"

BRAD WRIGHT: Once they entered the Stargate, we borrowed the feature wormhole footage for the first couple of seasons, because when we tried to do one on our own, it looked like shit. The hard part was going through a wormhole, but also seeing through the wormhole to the rest of what you were going through. The walls of the wormhole had to be translucent so that you'd know we were still traveling. That was apparently harder to do in 1997. And, then, the gate room itself had to be big just to accommodate the Stargate, because we wanted it to be at least the same size as the one in the feature, because going through a little one would be so lame. The reason our "kawoosh" only goes forward and doesn't do that backwards sucking thing is because it would have gone through the back wall of the set. The feature film had a bigger set than we did in terms of the length. We were limited to the size of the studio.

RICHARD HUDOLIN: We also had a portable Stargate that we took on location. It was an exact copy of the one in the studio, except the inner ring didn't move. It took six guys about a day to set it up, because it had to be done in a very specific way, but it was a beautiful piece of engineering.

JAMES TICHENOR (Visual Effects Supervisor, *Stargate SG-1*): The Kawoosh is such a dynamic, turbulent effect it was almost impossible for us to build in CG. We tried to do it a couple of times, because we wanted to do more with it and have different camera angles and what have you, but it never turned out quite as realistic. What we actually did to shoot the kawoosh was prepare a tank of water, modeled on what they did to create the effect in the feature film, and blast it with a little air cannon. The high-powered air cannon had a very focused nozzle exhorting major pounds per square inch of air within a very, very small point. We set that up in the water tank and used gravity to our benefit. We shot the air cannon down and placed the camera shooting straight up at one hundred and twenty frames per second. So we got the effect of this funnel of water coming straight through.

The whole shot took about three days to film. Working in GVFX's model shop in Toronto, they knew exactly which angles they needed, took the camera down, made the environment as black as possible and just started shooting. They ended up with about 10 different angles, which we continued to use. Every time we needed a kawoosh in an episode, we referred back to the ones we shot earlier. We composited them into new shots and always had to very carefully match the perspective angles, so it takes a bit of time to get right.

BRAD WRIGHT: Just going through the Stargate proved challenging financially. This is an interesting fact — you'll be the judge of that — but one person stepping through the Stargate in 1997 in CGI cost $5,000. In 2011, in the last episode of *SGU*, one person stepping through the Stargate cost $5,000. Even though there were all these advances with CGI, it was still a bum in a seat that had to do the work, and there was layer upon layer, upon layer of work that had to be done. So while the mechanical element got cheaper, the person doing the work didn't get cheaper, because it's still somebody's labor, it's still a compositor. All that stuff was still that much money. I don't know how much it would be now, but I bet it would be close. And so, we had all these shots in the pilot, and we eventually had to start cutting them out, because you go through the Stargate half a dozen times, and that's $30,000. That's six people going through the Stargate. It's just because of all the compositing, and nobody predicted it was going to cost that much. You get Richard Dean Anderson drawing his finger through the gate, it was a great effect, but even *that* cost a fortune. And so, we ended up with a pilot where virtually the only visual effects were going through the Stargate and the kawoosh itself, which was kind of cool.... When the Stargate opened up, we called that the kawoosh. When we wrote the scripts, we typed the words, "Kawoosh, the Stargate opens."

CHEVRON III: THE EVOLUTION OF STARGATE SG-1

"You don't understand — this book may contain knowledge of the universe. I mean, this is meaning-of-life stuff."

While the challenge of bringing the right cast together cannot be underestimated in the creation of any television series, it's only one part of the equation. Brad Wright, Jonathan Glassner and the rest of the crew would be tasked with giving life to Stargate SG-1 under what could sometimes be difficult circumstances, yet, thanks to an 88-episode commitment from Showtime, the show's longevity was all but guaranteed. Prior to these arrangements, most television shows had to work their way through season by season with the hope of a pick-up, no genre being more on tenterhooks than sci-fi (including the original Star Trek).

JOHN G. LENIC (producer, *Stargate SG-1*): Those early days, even before we brought in the cast, were really exciting, because *Stargate* was one of the bigger shows to come to Vancouver at the time. It rivaled *The X-Files* and that kind of thing. It was a lot of fun as well with a great sense of everybody working together and trying to make this huge show, but for a budget.

BRAD WRIGHT (co-developer/executive producer): Early on, *Stargate* had a budget of less than a million and a half dollars US per episode. It was a long time ago, so it sounds like a lot of money, but there were so many expenses at the beginning, not the least of which was building a fairly enormous set to serve as home base for the Stargate. But the real kicker was — again, to meet a delivery date — we built that set in a stage, shot the pilot, *tore that set down* and built it again in another stage that was being built for us, but hadn't been completed yet. They had a contractual delivery date for the pilot, but I was saying, "If we hold for just a month, then we'll be able to put so much more money on the screen, and I'll be able to fulfill many more of my writing obligations. We'll get ahead in the scripts." "No, we're backing into this delivery date, deal with it." That was an *enormous* chunk of money coming off the screen for nothing. We got *nothing* out of it.

ROBERT C. COOPER (co-executive producer): Brad and Jon had some ideas about where season one might go and how it might end, but they were in the midst of doing *The Outer Limits* when this started ramping up, and it was *huge*. Probably the biggest thing either of them had ever done. We were flying blind at the beginning and budgets were a huge factor, which is when reality hits the wall. That's where you're, like, "This is a good idea, but it's also completely undoable."

BRAD WRIGHT: For financial reasons, we had to reuse stock shots from the movie. We had the Death Gliders from the feature attacking our people, we had some shots from the movie that we borrowed and footage of the wormhole. We had the god awful symbiote and everything that went along with that, which was expensive as hell and looked like shit. All of that R&D for that stuff was really, really, expensive in season one. We were struggling. We would write, "Let's try to do an alien landscape planet." "No, no, there's nothing like that. We *do* have these trees. How about running through these trees?" We shot and used everything that we could think of; every location that we could find that looked remotely alien. We *did* find an oceanfront in Vancouver with piles of sulfur that were not natural; it was sulfur that had been extracted from natural gas and had piled up. It wasn't really that toxic, so we said, "We could shoot on that, right?" In the episode "Lazarus," where they're walking across the yellow planet with yellow mounds, that's actually mounds of sulfur. We ended up spending quite a lot of money replacing the boots that melted on people's feet, but it *looks* great. Now I think it's illegal to shoot on sulfur, but we were given permission. So we shot it on mountains of sulfur with just the sky behind it. I wrote another episode in season one called "Fire and Water," and we literally shot on a beach in Vancouver and painted out the city on the other side. Again, we were looking for alien landscapes. Instead we got pits, boulders, more pits and lots of trees.

JONATHAN GLASSNER (co-developer/executive producer): We were trying to do feature level work on a TV budget. One fun tidbit is that when we started on the first season of the show, the largest line item in the budget was for visual effects. It was a huge amount of money, but the technology advanced so quickly that by the end of the show, they couldn't spend the money in the visual effects budget. There was so much that had to be accomplished. We had to build a giant wardrobe department; we were literally making our wardrobe. You can't buy alien clothes off the shelf somewhere. The uniforms were real, but everything else had to be built from scratch. When it comes to visual effects, I should point out that when we started *The Outer Limits*, the effects were impossible. But between the first four years of *Outer Limits* and the first three years of *Stargate*, which overlapped, things changed drastically. For instance, for the Asgard on *Stargate*, he started as a puppet we had created for *The Outer Limits*, but he eventually became a CG character. We altered him a little bit and he was used as the face of the Asgard.

MORRIS CHAPDELAINE (puppeteer, *Stargate SG-1*): With the Asgard, there were actually four people to fully run it. There were two on the body — one that does the head and torso, and then one that does the arms and hands. They're both usually in black and tiny and on the floor behind it. They have a real physical, laborious job. It can be a lot of work getting that body to move and articulate its movements properly. And then it would be myself and another puppeteer working the face. I, for example, would do all the eye and brow movements. And each of the Asgard had to have their own personality and expressions. Thor was very different from Kvasir, who was very different from Hermiod, who was very different from Loki — even though it was the same body.

JONATHAN GLASSNER: The other thing is that *Stargate* and *The Outer Limits* sort of built the visual effects community in Vancouver. There was only one house that was there when we started and we needed so much that all these other houses started buying the necessary equipment and training people, and some American houses opened up there as well. And that goes right back to Showtime's commitment, because everyone knew we weren't going anywhere.

Wright continued to try and drive home his position regarding the budget and points to the first episode after the pilot, "The Enemy Within," which set up something that they never really followed up on, which was the idea that a Goa'uld could take over a human exposed to a young symbiote. But the real problem with it was regarding costs. Costs, or keeping an eye on them, also fell to line producer/executive producer N. John Smith.

BRAD WRIGHT: It was written almost entirely to take place on our base, our standing sets. We built one little extra piece that was part of the standing set to the medical lab. That episode had very few visual effects, standing sets only, very few actors and it was *still* almost $100,000 over budget. I had a red flag and I was waving it like crazy, saying, "If we can't do *this* episode, on budget, we're in trouble. I'm just warning you right now. Everybody, when all of you are reacting, *I'm* reacting, because we were doing *Outer Limits* episodes for around the same amount of money, but it just doesn't work that way. It's not there when you drop half a million dollars to move a set from one stage to another and get nothing out of it. You don't have that money, it does not appear on screen."

N. JOHN SMITH (line producer/executive producer, *Stargate SG-1*): My main job as a line producer was being responsible for hiring and firing the crew and making sure we get the film in the can on budget. And the responsibility of making sure the money that was allotted to us to spend over the season was spent and spent judiciously and not over spent. But I'm only as good as the writers. They can write, "We need 50 hot air balloons in this episode and that's what we have got to have." Well, if you can only afford 10, then I'm in trouble. We'd always push for the ultimate limit and try to get as much production value as we could, realizing that if we spent over on this episode, we'd have to save it over the next eight or 10 or whatever. Bottom line is that at the end of the year you had to be on budget. For most years, we *were*. And when we weren't, it was given the grace of MGM who said, "Go ahead, spend the extra money."

Wright recalls that it was about the middle of season one when the studio finally said that they were relenting; that they understood how difficult it was to produce the show at the budget it was at.

BRAD WRIGHT: But that *is* one of the reasons we ran through the trees so much, because it's all we could afford. We weren't capable of building new sets, we didn't even really have the stage space. And the bar was fairly high in terms of the sets, too. I mean, we built the Abydos pyramid set on stage and tore it down to build another one. And when we had to go back to that set, we had to build it again, because we couldn't call *everything* a standing set. The show, budget wise, became this sort of ebb and flow and it ended up saving production, too, because we would start as big as we could at the beginning of the season and try to do some smaller episodes to pay for the ones we just made. That balancing act was something I always had to do. "That's a great idea for an episode; maybe we'll do it next season, because we can't afford to do it this season," or we would build back up to the point where we could have a mid-season two-parter and then we would do another ebb and work up to a finale. So up and down, up and down, and that was a way to control the budget and also not be in a giant hole at the end, because you want to be able to do a fairly large episode at the end.

N. JOHN SMITH: We were always figuring out different ways to do things. There was great collaboration between writing and production and the physical aspect of the construction crew and the painting crew, choreographing what they had to do and then having it finished enough in time so the lighting guys could go in with the director of photography and light the set — all so that when we walked in to shoot for 12 hours, it was all ready to go. It was ideal.

JOHN G. LENIC: When Showtime boosted the order to 88 episodes, that turned into an amazing savings in terms of spreading out the costs. *And* amazing just to be able to chart your own course and know that you have extra money in your pocket. By the time we got to season three, and even season four, our budget was huge on the show. I can't remember what it was, but we'd grown so much. The show itself changed, because we were able to spend more money on construction and special effects. You can see the progression as the episodes go through the first season into the second season, into the third season. Just the amount of time being on location we could do increased. We could shoot outdoors and spend entire episodes on planets and that kind of thing. Or have bigger visual effects battles, which in season one we kept fairly small. Even at the end of season one, we had to do a clip show, which you never hear of anymore. The whole season was basically a bottle show with everything being on the stage. But we got into a rhythm with how we spent money as well. We got to know how Brad was going to write the series and what episodes would be big.

BRAD WRIGHT: And the other thing is John Symes, the President of MGM at the time, had no fear about clip shows. He'd say, "Do a clip show" and I would reply, "I hate clip shows." "*Everybody* hates clip shows." One of my favorite Simpsons jokes is when they actually apologize for their clip show. Who else would do that? The fact that *The Simpsons* made a clip show is even more hilarious. But John thought they were great. He said audiences loved them and they may have. He changed his tune when DVDs became really important, because a clip shown on a DVD set is just a pain in the ass. "I just binged all this; I don't need an episode to remind me of what I just watched." But it became this badge of honor to try to make the best clip show you could. So, "Politics" isn't a terrible clip show. The other one that I made that I'm not ashamed of is "Letters from Pegasus." That's the *Stargate Atlantis* one. And then I think Rob had to do one during Season 7, when I stepped back, because he went over budget. But that's part of the logistics on it.

RONNY COX (actor, "Senator/Vice President Robert Kinsey"): If you go back and look at "Politics," it's a clip show, but for me, personally, it was a *huge* show, because Kinsey had to carry that whole episode. All the other things were just the clips. If you go back and look at it, that's a show that 90 percent of the dialogue and 90 percent of the words going on there were all Kinsey. So in some ways it was a chance for an episodic show to almost be a little *tour de force* thing.

MARTIN WOOD (director, *Stargate SG-1*): I look over some of the episodes I did that were very contained and I think, "Man, there wasn't *any* show that I didn't like doing." You'd think that "Politics" would be, "It's a clip show, so why would it be so much fun?" Well, it *was* fun, because I had to keep thinking of different ways to get into these things, into these clips and stuff like that. Everything was fun, everything was interesting to me.

JOSEPH MALLOZZI (executive producer): I personally hate clip shows. I mean, as a viewer they're just kind of a disappointment. As someone working in production, they're kind of disappointing, too. They're money savers so you can obviously do that big midseason finale, but, like bottle shows, they also offer opportunities to find creative ways to tell a story that has an impact on that world. For instance, *Stargate Atlantis* had an episode written by script coordinator Alex Levine in which the *Atlantis* team was on trial for crimes against humanity in the Pegasus Galaxy. It was a clip show, but it was one that really stepped up and addressed an issue that a lot of fandom had talked about: the question of whether or not the Pegasus Galaxy would have been better off *without* the Atlantis expedition. We never did one for *Stargate Universe*, which is great, but we did a few for *SG-1*. I always kind of dreaded writing those episodes, but, in hindsight, they actually turned out quite good for the most part. I mean, "Disclosure," despite being a clip show, actually turned out pretty well.

BRAD WRIGHT: "Solitudes" was made to save money because we were able to cut a shooting day out of the schedule, but it was a pretty elaborate set, which we actually refrigerated, because there's nothing worse in movies or television shows where they're pretending to shiver, but there's a bit of sweat coming down their face. In this case, you could literally see their breath. And we brought in tons of real ice so that when Carter's chipping away, it's genuine. Some of it was wax, but a lot of it was ice, too. And as I always say, include a helicopter in all your bottle shows. We did a helicopter shoot for that one. We actually flew Amanda up to the glacier and that is her climbing up out of a little sort of crevasse and looking around on the actual North Slope of a real glacier in Vancouver. She thinks it's an alien planet, but it's Antarctica. And by the way, my favorite memory of that episode is reading the *TV Guide* logline that Showtime wrote, which said, "Carter and O'Neill are trapped in Antarctica." *That's* the mystery of the episode. Where are they? Where are they? Where are they? So, I phoned Poncho and I said, "Guys, are you going to get the rights to *The Usual Suspects*?" And he said, "Yeah, probably." "Great, make sure that your logline is Kevin Spacey stars as Keyser Soze in *The Usual Suspects*."

Eventually, though, the two shows [*SG-1* and its first spinoff, *Stargate Atlantis*] would have nine soundstages between Bridge Studios and a whole other studio, which was an old factory with lower ceilings, but still significantly useful free space. It became a lot of space, so we could set up the [starship] *Daedalus* set, which became the *Odyssey* set, which was the *Prometheus* set with a slight variation in the Earth spaceship. They were all on one stage, and we left it up. That became something we had to remain aware of, because we were renting a stage and we better use that bloody set frequently. I'm leaping ahead, but I think we pulled quite a bit off during Season 1 in retrospect, just by keeping our shooting days tight and by creating a corps of directors that learned the rules which we were establishing as we went.

That corps of directors was more important than one might think, given that by having a small pool of people who recognized the strengths of the show and how to achieve them, helped to keep things running smoothly. There would ultimately be 214 hours of Stargate SG-1 *produced, with Peter Deluise directing 56, Martin Wood 47, Andy Mikita 29, William Waring 13, Willigrem Gereghty 12 and David Warry-Smith and Peter F. Woeste 11 each, among others. It also presented a unique situation where they would often actually shoot sequences for each other.*

MARTIN WOOD: *Stargate* made me as a director. I was given a chance to do everything on that show and most directors don't get that kind of time span to experiment in a show that evolves like that. A lot of times when you have a series, it can't evolve in the mega leaps and bounds that *Stargate* did, because we were evolving a technology while we were doing it. We were moving forward at such a massive rate with the way that digital technology was working, the way that special effects and visual effects were advancing. Every year, there was something new for us to try. Every few months, there was something new for us to try. Suddenly we weren't locking off things when we were doing effects shots — suddenly we were panning through it. Then we were running with handheld cameras while Replicators were following us. A lot of what you are seeing today, we were on the cutting edge of that at *Stargate*. Because we were on the air for so long and we were able to [say], "Hey, this is a new lens that is being used." "Hey, this is a new lighting technique that's being used." And for me, as a director, I was able to evolve with that and I learned how to do everything I know how to do on *Stargate*.

ANDY MIKITA (director, ***Stargate SG-1***): There was something special about the group of directors on the show. I would direct shots for their episodes, they would direct shots of mine. Very unusual. But the fact that we had a fairly small roster of directors that were all there long-term — we were able to develop a shorthand with each other. If I was going to be shooting on Stage 4 and Will was going to be in the special effects stage and we each had scenes that we needed from each other's episodes, we would often just either tag team or call each other and say "Hey, listen can you pick this up for me because you're going to be there?" and vice versa. It worked out really well. We were all very close to our own work and it's always hard to give up your own scenes to other people. But at the same time, it's a family operation and we were always there to help each other out and do what it takes. But I'd never seen that before I'd come to *Stargate*. I'd never been witness to that sort of scene-sharing.

PETER DELUISE: Sometimes it was necessary for us to shoot each other's scenes. This was because of actor availability and also sometimes it was because of shared exotic locations where it just made sense to go there once. If you were shooting a scene for a different director, you would try to shoot it the way that they requested as best you could. Subsequently there would be discussions about certain shots and story points which inevitably would end up with us teasing each other, "That's not how *I* would shoot it, but OK."

ANDY MIKITA: We were all pretty attuned to each other's shooting styles. We tried to be as true as possible to those individual styles as we could be. Often we'd just give each other notes as well.

BRAD WRIGHT: So we ended up with this fairly well-oiled machine. We knew we had a 44-episode order coming out of the gate, right? That's unprecedented. But then, before the end of season one, like 10 episodes in, we get a call from John Symes. We put him on speaker and he said Showtime just picked up another 44 episodes. So before the end of season one, we knew we were doing 88 episodes. That, again, helped us make decisions in terms of how we amortize money over seasons. We started buying stuff that you would never buy. It allows you to make longer term deals even with the companies that you're renting from.

ROBERT C. COOPER: We were very lucky to have gotten that long order and to have been a little bit off the radar. Maybe we weren't on the biggest network in the world, but we had a star like Richard Dean Anderson and Showtime was very happy with the debut's ratings, so we were allowed to figure out what the show was over the course of probably the first two seasons. During that time there were great episodes — don't get me wrong — but I would say there were also a bunch you could skip. At the same time, we were building the show and got even luckier that partway through the first season we got that extended order.

BRAD WRIGHT: It was the long order that saved us. And Jon [Glassner] had agreed to stay through season three, but he wanted to go back to Los Angeles after that. Because Robert Cooper had come up and was really proving himself to be super solid, he ended up leaving a bit early. And he wasn't actually writing or producing any of the last bunch anyway, so he went home. But without his executive producing and direct-ing experience in that first year, I think we would have been sunk. And because I was so split focused, it worked out great.

With Stargate SG-1 *airing on* Showtime, *the cable network had requirements of its own that impacted things early on.*

BRAD WRIGHT: MGM always gave notes, but we had creative freedom from Showtime. They called us and said this is or that was great, but something in the deal with MGM wouldn't allow them to give us exclusive notes. So we were very free. Except that John Symes was all over the show at the beginning. He would say, "Why is he shooting in the dark? This is too dark. What's going on? There's not enough color in this set. We need more color. It's too gray." And it was because he had done *Star Trek: The Next Generation* and knew what had worked and how to launch it into syndication. So we just said, "Yes, sir." But it was never the script that was good, you can't do this one or anything like that. Our own standards were pretty high and there would be Jon episodes and Brad episodes in the early years, and then it became Jon episodes, Brad episodes and Rob episodes in subsequent years. And we would actually always fight over Robert's scripts, because they were the easiest to make. Sometimes it might need a polish on the dialogue, but it was structurally creatively solid.

JONATHAN GLASSNER: Showtime was a cable company reliant on subscriptions, so their big thing to us was, "This can't be a show you can get on commercial television, so you've got to break some rules." They wanted nudity and they wanted language and violence, and we fought it all the way. The one thing we caved in on was nudity, so there's full frontal nudity in the pilot. And it turned our stomachs, both Brad and I. We said, "This is a family show. It's just not that kind of show."

BRAD WRIGHT: I didn't want the nudity. I argued heavily against nudity. I said, "I know Showtime wants it, I know that they think it's fine and we should include it, but it's *not* the show we're making. It's just not the show." By then we were writing episodes five, six, seven, and I said, "It just stands out like a sore thumb to me in the pilot." It's like, you're watching a show, laugh, laugh, laugh. Oh, adventure, adventure, adventure. Whoa, full frontal nudity! What the hell? And not even that I'm a prude. It has nothing to do with it. We did *The Outer Limits* with nudity, but there it worked.

JONATHAN GLASSNER: We never did it again, even though there was a little pressure at first.

BRAD WRIGHT: When it came to the nudity, I got in some shit, because my daughter was, I think, five or six at the time. We were going in on the weekend to watch a cut before we locked it and I brought her with me. I said, "I have to take my daughter out during this scene." Not because of the nudity, but because it was the scene where they strip off the clothes of the young Lieutenant, who's the first one to be taken, and then basically the symbiote attacks her. It felt like... sexual violation. And I said, "Guys, it's too far. It's not the show we're making and we're going to get shit for it." And John Symes said, "You know what, we'll pull that back. But we'll keep the first one." And then when we started getting deep fried for it in the press, he said, "Okay, you're right. No more." It just felt tacked on. You know, "It's Showtime, here are some breasts." And not only that, we had to do another version anyway for syndication, so it's not like we didn't have a version that didn't have nudity. That's one of the other reasons I did a recut later on, which is the final cut version of the pilot.

JONATHAN GLASSNER: There reached a point where we started to say, "We're just going to make the show we want to make and not what we're pressured to make or what we think they want." Because Showtime never actually told us we *had* to do nudity. They told us we had to do things that you can't do on network TV, listed a bunch of things and we were uncomfortable doing bloody, gory violence. We didn't think that was okay. For the time of the show, we didn't want everybody using the F word every 15th word, and we had done a lot of nudity on *The Outer Limits*, which worked there, because it was a dark, scary show kids should *not* have been watching.

Despite this hiccup along the way, there was much about the show that was ultimately inspirational — in particular the fact that it presented a core group of heroes that the audience could identify with and/or look up to. One element that allowed it to do so was the fact that the show was aligned fairly closely with the United States Air Force.

BRAD WRIGHT: There were two advantages to working with the Air Force. One, we needed them when we started the show and it's all through the pilot. Things we had no idea about, like simple protocols. For instance, you don't wear your dress blues around the base, people don't constantly salute each other and when they do, they offer the *proper* salute. The other reason we reached out to them is we wanted to shoot second unit at Cheyenne Mountain. We wanted that, because we were looking around locally for a cave entrance, but the only really cool entrance is the actual Cheyenne Mountain. So we sent Martin Wood down for a day with their permission, obviously, and shot the hell out of Cheyenne Mountain, which became our stock footage for years, with those same two guys you see pacing back and forth. Poor guys never got promoted. Martin shot the big steel door closing on the inside for us to use about 10,000 times. And for that, all they really require is that we portray people honorably. That worked for me, because I wanted our characters to behave honorably; at least the military people. And there was always context in terms of what we could or couldn't do.

CATH-ANNE AMBROSE (script coordinator, *Stargate SG-1*): We consulted with the U.S. Air Force entertainment liaison for everything. They did a script review of every episode, for accuracy. They gave us information on props, set decoration, wardrobe and dialogue. We had a liaison who was just great — Captain L'Esperance was a joy to work with. She was quite brilliant. We took their notes seriously, as we wanted to portray every situation as accurately as we could. If we didn't, we would get letters from military folks pointing out any oversights!

BRAD WRIGHT: The Air Force was a little strict at first, and it was getting to be a pain in the ass on some occasions, but Rick wanted it to be accurate. There was the one instance in season one, which I'd mentioned, where we're in an alternate reality. We wanted O'Neill and Carter to kiss before he went off to battle, because they were in a relationship. Well, they said, "Absolutely not." Our solution was really simple: "What if it's *Dr.* Carter, because it's an alternate reality?" And they said, "Fine, no problem." It's because she was no longer a major or captain, but a doctor. As it turned out, a general kissing a captain was completely inappropriate. Initially I thought it was silly, because it was in an alternate reality, but I get it now. It's not like we were changing the uniforms. So as we went forward it became not only a benefit to us, but a benefit to them, because they got to portray Air Force people doing something really cool. To a certain extent, I started feeling conflicted about it, because it was promoting recruitment.

CATH-ANNE AMBROSE: I was fortunate to be invited to a dinner with the chief of the American Air Force, General Jumper [Air Force Chief of Staff], and his wife when they came to the set. It was such an honor to meet Mr. and Mrs. Jumper. He was actually very down to Earth and his wife was quite interesting. I have *huge* amounts of respect for all of the U.S. military folks I've met through the show. Working on *Stargate* taught me a lot about that lifestyle and the dedication these men and women have.

BRAD WRIGHT: The positive portrayal of the Air Force doing something as cool as S.G.C. would lead to people saying, "Is *Stargate* real?" I'm not saying they were telling me people were saying that, but look at how cool it is out there. I mean, the reality is you join the Air Force and you think you're going to fly in a fighter jet, but you're far more likely to be changing the ball bearings of an engine. Very few people in the Air Force actually fly in a jet.

In essence, it's very much like people look at the movie business and think it's so glamorous, but the reality is that if you were to be on set, you'd discover that you're largely standing around day after day watching the same sequences be shot again and again.

BRAD WRIGHT: It is *exactly* like the public perception of Hollywood. We ended up embracing every interaction with the military. We had two chiefs of staff of the Air Force do cameo roles; one was even bigger than a cameo. It was like a full bloody part, and he was good, too. I can't remember his name — Michael was his first name, but I called him Sir — and apparently one of the first things he said when he became chief of staff of the Air Force was, "When do I get to do my *Stargate* cameo?" I'm not sure how true that story is, but because of the positive portrayal of the Air Force, and because they were getting something out of it, too, when we asked for something, it was very easy for them to say yes.

PETER DELUISE: That alliance with the military brought with it a couple of problems. If you remember, early on they wore the official military helmets, but the problem with that, and what a lot of people find out almost immediately, is that they dehumanize the actors, because they make them visually look all the same. That was a problem with the movie *Black Hawk Down* — it was impossible to figure out which actor you were dealing with, because they all looked exactly the same. We were supposed to care about all these people who are getting shot and killed, but in *Black Hawk Down* they all look alike and that's the audience's problem: who's who? It's inevitably part of the problem of people in uniform. Granted that on *Stargate* there were only four of them, and one of them is a blond-haired woman. Originally there were three away team members and then Teal'c ended up joining them as the alien, but my point is when you watch something like *Band of Brothers*, those actors are very quirky and unique. *And* they look very different on purpose. Here's another great example: you're watching a legitimate World War II black and white film, and one guy inevitably cocks his helmet sideways. Why would you *ever* wear your giant combat helmet to the side? Because you want to be a little different.

One of the key elements that allowed Stargate *to survive, and thrive, for as long as it did during its original run and all these years later, is the focus on evolution; of always keeping things in motion rather than allowing the show or its spin-offs to simply stand in place, which obviously would have been a much easier way to go, but simultaneously would not have guaranteed any sort of longevity.*

BEN BROWDER (actor, "Lt. Colonel Cam Mitchell"): In the beginning, when it was on Showtime, *Stargate* started with that episodic feel, much the same way that *Farscape* did. Showtime kind of wanted to push certain things and it found that wasn't the voice of the show, in part because it wasn't Richard Dean Anderson's voice and it was not Amanda's voice, Brad's voice or anyone else's. By the time you're getting into the fifth or sixth season, the show has a distinctive voice which is based around the team. Then Michael Shanks departed for a while and it lost its voice for 15 minutes. When he came back, it felt complete again with the right set of voices. The band was back together and it felt right. Every character found their sense of humor over the course of the show and the characters became more well-rounded human beings over a long period of time. And obviously you have the development of a large body of lore surrounding it, so the internal process of enjoying the show is more rewarding for the long-term viewer.

As a result, the characters in the lore become more fleshed out, which rewards long-term viewing. That's also why it was important to me to watch all the episodes from before I was a part of the show so that it didn't feel like I was plunked in from Hollywood, but more that I was plunked in from the *Stargate* universe. I felt it was a good idea and something that was picked up on by the writers when they realized that I watched every show. They said, "What the fuck is he doing? Nobody watches eight seasons worth of episodes." I was, like, "Yeah, people *do* watch stuff like that and I'm one of those people."

PETER DELUISE: Early on, the writing staff was pretty anemic, and that's where Brad saw that there was enough room for me to come and play. So he invited me in. What would happen is they would come up with a bunch of seasonal ideas, like what they wanted to do for the season, where they wanted to be at mid-season and how they wanted to finish. Who the antagonists would be for the year and what would be the overreaching arcs of the story and directions for the future. Where would we start and end up emotionally? Would our technical abilities improve?

BRAD WRIGHT: Peter Deluise is one of the hardest working people I've ever met, not only as one of our core directors, but as a writer as well. He also found a way to do a cameo in almost every one of his episodes. Sometimes he was just an extra, but some were more subtle than others. One of my favorites was just his initials, PD, laid out in the form of burning candles. We cast both of his brothers, and of course his father, Dom DeLuise, who played Urgo. Watching Peter direct his father, understanding his strengths and sense of humor, was an absolute joy. But Peter understood drama very well, too. I vividly remember him directing one of my favorite early scenes of *SGU* — a lottery scene in the gate room to choose who gets to leave the ship and survive — and pacing it perfectly. One of the most powerful scenes in the series in my view, mainly because of his direction.

JONATHAN GLASSNER: The first show I ever did was *21 Jump Street* and Peter was one of the stars *and* he wanted to direct. I can't tell you how many times I've been on shows where the actors want to direct and they're just horrible, so we were just dreading him directing. But he directed an episode and did such an amazing job that we wanted him to direct a bunch more. And so when I was over on *Stargate*, I said, "I know this really good director who has Canadian citizenship, so he will count towards the show's Canadian content." So we gave him a *Stargate* and he nailed it, *and* all the actors loved him. So we made him the producing director on the show and he ended up as an executive producer on it.

PETER DELUISE: I think of my time on that show very fondly; I was paid to have fun and tell stories. I tried to inject humor whenever I could and the feedback was always very positive. I felt like Brad Wright and, to a lesser extent, Robert Cooper mentored me and gave me an enormous amount of information about how to write a script and how to tell a story. I came on that show just as a director, only then I upgraded to creative consultant and then became a producer/writer in addition to that. I had written some scripts before that, but never the way that I should have. And Brad basically gave me all the tools that I'm still using today. I'm so eternally grateful to both Brad and Robert for helping me through that experience. I had done horror, I'd done comedy, I'd done drama, but never science fiction. It wasn't until that show that I did and dealt with an enormous amount of visual effects.

It's difficult to talk about the evolution of the mythology of Stargate SG-1 *without taking into consideration the contribution of some of its key writers and what they brought to the mix, notably Robert C. Cooper, who joined the show early on; and Joseph Mallozzi and Paul Mullie, the writing team that came aboard in season four.*

JONATHAN GLASSNER: When Brad and I first started setting up *Stargate*, we needed to find a young Canadian writer to work with us and we put the word out. *And* we were getting bad submission after bad submission after bad submission. Then we read something by this kid, Robert Cooper, who was living in Toronto. Robert was very ambitious and flew himself to Vancouver. We didn't ask him to do it and tried to discourage him from doing it, because we didn't want him spending his own money to pitch ideas to us.

ROBERT C. COOPER: I was on the plane and going over my ideas. I had about 10, short two or three-sentence pitches or arenas to sort of talk to them about. Then I wrote down four or five other one-line notions. I got there, we chatted, we had a good few-minute conversation and then they asked me to start pitching. Jon Glassner is sitting at his desk and he's got a pen and a notepad sitting on his desk — he's ready to write down any good ideas that come out of my mouth. I got through all 10 of my first notions and his pen has not moved. So I was, like, "I'm in trouble." I got through a few other notions and then I just basically said, "How about something like *Apocalypse Now?*" *That* he wrote down and I thought, "Thank God, I've got *something*." I just quoted a movie title, but then obviously expanded on it and they had, I guess, enjoyed meeting me. They sent me off to do an outline on that idea, and that was the first episode of the show I ended up writing. It was called "The First Commandment."

BRAD WRIGHT: I was listening and there wasn't an idea that he said that I liked right away, but I knew that I liked *him*. I could see the thought process. I could see that these were good pitches, whether or not they were going to be stories we bought. And then we came upon one, that became "The First Commandment," that was his least fleshed out pitch. We went for a walk and I gave him a tour of the sets and I knew that he was going to write a script and then possibly come on board as a story editor. He had said he was coming to Vancouver and while he was here he wanted to pitch in person. So I said, "What was it that brought you to Vancouver?" and he went, "This meeting." He flew himself out there and that is *exactly* something I would do. That is something I *did* do. He ended up doing a major rewrite on what became "But for the Grace of God," which wasn't just good, it was *really* good. And then "Torment of Tantalus." He did some really great scripts very early on and I knew it would only be a little time before he was naturally able to run with an episode on his own.

JONATHAN GLASSNER: His ideas were great and we said, "Can you move out here and join our staff?" And, of course, he ended up taking my place when I left. The second episode that he ever wrote was a really good one called "The Torment of Tantalus," which I think was one of our first really great ones. I got to direct that one, because it was my choice which one I got to direct and I picked his. Of the ones I wrote, I think the Tok'ra two-parter introducing them as the rebel Goa'uld was one of the best. But Robert got into the whole mythology a lot further, both the backstory and what it was going to lead down the line. The backstory was he brought back Catherine Langford from the movie and we got to do flashbacks. Her boyfriend had gone through the gate, because it had been opened before and nobody knew it. We go to a planet and find him there, and so it was very emotional. And I got to work with those two great older actors who were amazing. We also found this sort of Rosetta Stone there of foreign languages or alien languages that Daniel Jackson got to geek out over, which told us that there were these other alien species other than Goa'uld, which we didn't know until then. It was just a cool story. Everything about it was exciting, *and* it was cool because I got to do flashbacks and period stuff.

Joseph Mallozzi and Paul Mullie had gotten their start writing children's show's for Canadian television, gradually working their way up to tween programming and, of course, the Stargate *franchise. Most recently they co-created the television series* Dark Matter, *based on their comic of the same name and these days are writing separately. Growing up, Mallozzi describes himself as a "huge" comic book fan, which actually raised some concerns with his mother, who in response started to give him sci-fi novels to read. While he continued to love comics, the novels awakened his interest in the science-fiction genre, resulting in his reading the work of Harlan Ellison, Isaac Asimov, Arthur C. Clarke, Ray Bradbury and many others.*

JOSEPH MALLOZZI: In grade five, I wrote my own sci-fi novel; it's something I've always enjoyed and then, ultimately, I always told my mother that I wanted to be a writer. My mother's kind of practical, as most parents are, and she told me, "Well, there's no money in writing. Maybe you'll be a journalist or a lawyer and you can write books on the side." Well, I still made another attempt at writing a novel, which was more of a horror story. My former writing partner, Paul Mullie, said, "Wow! This is terrible, but it would make a good script," so I looked into screenwriting and adapted my first novel into a terrible first script, but I still continued down that path.

When you start off as a kind of a young screenwriter, you have dreams of becoming a famous writer of a film and the truth of the matter is that the chances of you succeeding are infinitesimal. And even if you *do* succeed, more often than not they will totally rewrite you or you will be treated like crap and it's almost impossible to make a living at it. Whereas in television, I did not know this at the time, they're more receptive to writers, there's more opportunity and that is where the power is. Features are a director's game, whereas television is very much a writer's game and if you play your cards right and you're talented, you rise up the ranks and become a showrunner. That was kind of my career path. I started off in animation and then worked my way up to teen live action sitcoms and then action/adventure and eventually landed on *Stargate*. We were supposed to go for two years and we ended up there for 12, so it all worked out.

Now when it came to *Stargate*, when the movie came out they called it a bomb, but I kind of like schlocky sci-fi, so I went to see it. And I was, like, "Well, it's *not* a bomb." I was kind of pleasantly surprised. I hadn't been really familiar with the show, although I did tune in once and watched an episode called "Emancipation," which I thought was atrocious and I felt I couldn't watch any more. Which is kind of unfair, because that just happened to be the episode I watched and it colored my perception of the series. Then our agent reached out and said, "Hey, *Stargate* is looking for writers." He represented, at the time, Robert C. Cooper, who was co-showrunner with Brad. I said, "I don't think I can write the show. I've watched the episode and it's really not for me," but they sent a bunch of scripts and I read the scripts. Afterwards I was, like, "This is a pretty good show." So Paul and I pulled together five pitches and two of them became "Window of Opportunity" and "Scorched Earth." "Window of Opportunity" was our first episode and the script that actually landed us the gig.

Understanding and being able to write in the voice of the show is the challenge. It's why I think Brad and Robert had so much difficulty finding writers for the show and would try out new writers all the time. It's just really tough in that either you get the show and the voice of the characters, or you don't. It's also getting the overall tone of the series and a lot of the time that just didn't have to do with talent, it's just a matter of being in sync with the same kind of humor and sensibilities as the show's creators. What's nice is that when we handed in "Scorched Earth," Brad and Rob were on their way to Hawaii for a golf vacation. They had one script between the two of them and Brad was looking at it. He said to Rob, "I can't read the script, because if it's not good, I'm going to be depressed for the rest of the trip." Rob read it and after he read it, he said to Brad, "You can enjoy your trip." So that was kind of a nice story. And then we auditioned for season four and ended up on staff.

Given the duo's background in children's television, it might not seem like a natural progression to adult science fiction, but as far as Mullie is concerned, it was a smooth segue from one to the other.

PAUL MULLIE: The thing I would say about progressing from animation into science fiction is that animation is all about being visual. The first lesson Joe, who started writing cartoons before I did, gave me was to never write more than three lines of dialogue without some kind of action description; something visual needs to happen. A character's got to fall on his face or something has to happen. Obviously if you're writing cop drama or doctor drama, that's not going to be the case. So while it's not a literal translation, it does train you to think visually for animation, which is very helpful when you're writing science fiction.

When they brought us on *Stargate*, they gave us this gigantic show's bible. We were coming in at the beginning of season four and they'd been building up the mythology for three years and 66 episodes. I've got to admit, we didn't read it. It was impossible. It would have taken months to read, so we got some episodes on tape and just watched them. It didn't take long to get what they were doing. The mythology took me a while to understand, because it's complex, which I think is one of the reasons why people like it, because it's very rich and very deep. Brad and Robert were there to answer any questions, and the biggest problem we always had was pitching something and they'd say, "Yeah, we already did that idea." We were pitching sort of the obvious early episodes of a show like *Stargate*. I remember by the fifth or sixth season, Joe and I were, like, "How come we can't come up with any more ideas? It's crazy; we've done everything." We were sitting in the writers' room, looking at each other saying there was nothing left to do, but, of course, we did five more seasons and then spin-offs, because with science-fiction there are *always* more stories.

What you eventually realize is you have to stop watching science-fiction, because it'll just shut you down since everyone's doing similar things and you've got to not worry about that. You've got to do your own show with its own voice. Even if you do an episode about time travel or something like that, the *Stargate* version is going to be different from the *Star Trek* version. So it's okay to repeat certain ideas as long as you're true to the nature of your own show, basically. And especially the characters. That was a big lesson early on and once we got that, it was just a machine that would keep going.

BRAD WRIGHT: The thing about Paul and Joe that was great is that they were a team and they both had strengths. Joe is a bit of a story engine and Paul was a fabulous rewriter — he would sometimes jump in and help with freelancers or rewrites of new younger writers. That may be frustrating for the young writers on your staff, but it's my responsibility to make the show and not have the actor read a script and say, "What the hell is this dialogue?" It's got to be their voice. Rob and I started writing characters with the same voice and eventually Paul and Joe started writing in the same voice as well. As a team they had unique skills. Paul was very good in the editing room earlier and Joe became good, but Paul took to it more naturally. They worked as a writer-producer team more effectively than any other team. Now they write separately. It's as if they had to go through that journey together to come out so that they *could* work separately, but they were partners for a very long time and are still good friends.

The duo got a crash course in the way that scripts were developed and honed, which would stay with them throughout their careers. And, as a part of the franchise, they and Cooper (all three of whom would be among those that would work on Atlantis *and* Universe *as well) and the rest of the writers were met with a variety of writing challenges, among them fully embracing the possibilities of the science-fiction genre and wrestling with the baby steps that television was taking between episodic and more serialized storytelling.*

JOSEPH MALLOZZI: We would follow Brad and Robert's lead. Every season, we would get together after we had wrapped the previous season, sit down and look ahead to the next season. We'd look at the storylines, we would look at the arcs, we'd see where we were and decide where we wanted to head. And the stories would be arc-related, kind of the ongoing stories of dealing with the different alien races. Occasionally, we'd try to come up with one-off stories. Those are always my favorite, but those were also the hardest to come up with. We came up with quite a few of them in Season 4, and what ultimately dawned on us was that the show, after four seasons, had so much mythology that it provided backstory that you could mine for episodic content. So we found it easier as time went on to come up with stories, which was really the opposite of what we figured would happen.

ROBERT C. COOPER: Brad always said that science fiction isn't one genre; instead, it gives you an opportunity to talk about anything you want. You can address social conscience issues in the somewhat protected veil of other worlds and aliens, but still have something to say. You can do a romantic comedy, you can do a wacky comedy, you can do *Groundhog Day* at the same time that you're doing some other socially conscious important story in the next episode — or even the same episode in some cases.

JONATHAN GLASSNER: In retrospect, I wish we had been a little bolder in talking about issues in our scripts. Science-fiction is a great metaphorical medium to work with. I look back at the original *Star Trek* and think about the episode where the guy is half black/half white and the other guy has it on the opposite side of his face, and it's a metaphor about racism. I wish we had done more of that; I don't know why we didn't.

ROBERT C. COOPER Sci-fi gives you that opportunity to really come in with an idea of something you want to do or something you want to say and then find a way to do it. That's fun; I never saw it as a restrictive genre. What it was, unfortunately, a little bit back when we were doing the show, was a little bit of a ghetto on television.

Science fiction movies were big and had big audiences, but sci-fi on TV was more like syndicated fare. Even if you were trying to do something a little better or aimed a little higher, there was this perception that you were never going to win an Emmy for doing a sci-fi show. That's changed now where you have shows like Marvel's *WandaVision* or *Falcon and the Winter Soldier*. *Battlestar Galactica* is where you had a sci-fi show that was a breakout hit. Back at the time, when we were first doing *Stargate*, the idea of a show having the broad reach that a show like *Game of Thrones* had would have had people laughing at you. With all this audience, and I include myself with this audience, there was this attitude of, "Oh, that's for nerds." But now, the power of that audience has really come to bear and the corporations making the entertainment for those audiences have realized that's actually who we should be making TV for. They watch and they watch repeatedly, and they buy all the products.

JONATHAN GLASSNER: Not doing more of those "message" shows is really my only regret, because we *could* have done them on Showtime. But I think probably the reason we didn't, in retrospect, is the show had a very unique structure from a business perspective. It was aired on Showtime to help pay for the cost of it, and then a certain number of months later, after a window, it went straight into syndication, which is where MGM made its money. So we couldn't do anything too controversial or too "cable." For example, like I said, when we did shoot the one scene with nudity, we also shot a non-nudity version for the syndicated run. But you can't do that with issues. And we were getting pressured to do things that we shouldn't have agreed to. Then we got confident enough to fight them on it and not do it. We did an episode where Amanda was wearing a low cut dress when she was taken as a concubine by this alien. I don't remember the details, but I remember seeing it with my kids — this was a few years ago; they're all grown adults now — and they're going, "Ewww." That was *not* a good one. But about two or three episodes in, we found it. From there on it kind of worked.

BRAD WRIGHT: When it came to episodic and serialized stories, I was probably the one trying to do more standalone episodes. In part, that was because sometimes it was just production, sometimes it was sitting in my line producer's office with a con-struction coordinator, Tom Wells, saying, "I can't build all these sets in time. I need that stage, and you're writing an episode." So, we would have to come up with an episode that didn't require one of our standing sets. Or just use one or two of the sets that we weren't having to screw around with. And basically insert it into the schedule and rush it in. That happened a couple of times, just because the logistics of television are what they are. You can't build everything and you can't expect them to build everything that you want them to like. It takes time, especially since some of our sets are massive. Sometimes we would create a standalone episode, simply because it was the only way to not shut down, to shoot *something*.

JONATHAN GLASSNER: If you were doing the show today, it would be serialized, because that's all they want. Back then, nobody wanted to serialize. They only
wanted episodic so that it could air in any order at any time and it could go either five
nights a week or one day a week. So we couldn't serialize the personal stories and stuff
like that, but we *could* serialize the aliens and the cultures and characterizations, and
have them come back. We kept expanding upon them as the show went on, which
is something that Brad and Rob continued doing. All of that was very much more
developed by the end, which you couldn't have done if we didn't know we had the
commitment from Showtime.

BEN BROWDER: Back in the day, you couldn't take the characters too far away
from who the audience knew they were without people getting confused. Whereas
by the time we were doing *Farscape*, it's on cable and people were using VCRs to tape
shows. *That* changes the types of stories that you can tell. So the magic reset button, to
a certain degree, is part of an antiquated delivery system, but necessary for that system.
People can look down on it, but it's actually kind of really hard to tell a story which
people are going to come back to every week where the characters *don't* develop. It's
the *Murder, She Wrote* paradigm. It's about taking the audience on the Agatha Christie
model of "Gonna solve the crime." That's what they are really into.

ROBERT C. COOPER: We started out as an episodic show and I'd say there was
a good split, maybe even leaning stronger towards the "monster of the week" type
episodes. And by seasons seven or eight, as much as we used to argue with the network
that we weren't making it accessible to new audiences, I don't know how anybody
could have joined in and not known what was going on. Who are they? On what planet? You know, it became a show for the fans. *The X-Files* was the best that I could ever
come up with where they balanced, literally, "monster of the week" with mythology/
alien invasion shows, and I found it the perfect balance at the time. It just hit that sweet
spot. At the same time, the actual mythology episodes made no sense. That was part of
the problem. They didn't have an answer.

It was the precursor to what I called the "*Lost* disease," where the writers are simply
running a con game without any end game. I didn't watch it, because I can sense when
I'm being conned and I don't like that. I don't want to feel manipulated and at the
mercy of some writer god. Particularly one that doesn't know what the hell they're
doing. When it comes to the *Stargate* series, what we frankly did successfully is we
didn't try and sustain one mystery for the run of 14 years. We understood that there's
a certain energy when it comes down to replacing characters sometimes, killing bad

guys, inventing new ones. The greatest shows that are my favorites, like *The Shield* or *The Sopranos*, did that. Yes, there was an arc for Tony Soprano over the course of the entire series, or Mackey from *The Shield*.

BEN BROWDER: *Stargate* is somewhere in between. The audience loves the characters and they love the team. They're attached to the team and what ifs, but the military world sort of caps the personal interactions the fans may want or desire. So you can't put Carter and O'Neill together, because they're in the same chain of command and that's an offense, so you've got the mechanism to prevent certain things from happening — like "The *Moonlighting* Syndrome." The characters *do* develop, they just don't develop in radical ways that you see now. *Stargate* strikes a good balance, I think.

JONATHAN GLASSNER: One thing we did *not* want to do, even if it was episodic, was to ignore what happened to the characters in the different episodes. If something happened to one of them, it stayed in their memories. We didn't just drop it. The best example is Carter's dad. He was dying of cancer and became a Tok'ra. And he kept coming back to the show. We didn't send him off to an alien world and just forgot about him.

BEN BROWDER: Obviously there are soap operas and that paradigm, where characters that have existed forever do kind of evolve. But that was for people who were sitting down and watching every single day. Then you had your *Dallas* and *Dynasty* where there you had the soap opera mechanism being pulled into nighttime. But the merging of those long arcs with the science fiction militarized motif is a later development. And that works, but we have a tendency to look at older forms and judge them. Like, these writers didn't think of this already? Of course they did, but they were constrained by the delivery methods. They're constrained by commercials and all sorts of things. You look at newer shows and think, "Oh my gosh, this show was groundbreaking. How didn't anyone think of this before?" *A lot* of people thought of it and there were people who probably tried to do it.

If we went back and started really plucking through the history of television, take something like *MASH*. If you look at *MASH* from season one to season 11, most of the characters radically change from beginning to the end. So it does exist, it just doesn't exist in large numbers, because at that time you were looking at a show as appointment viewing, which means it has an audience which wants to hit the watercooler after every episode. They were really dedicated to getting to their show and that stopped being the way we delivered television. It started in the eighties with VCRs and then it evolved with cable reruns and syndication with VCRs in conjunction. By the time you get to streaming, we have a completely different mechanism for delivery. It's interesting that *Farscape* was on the early edge of being heavily serialized. Like, "I missed two episodes. What the hell happened? Wait, don't they hate each other? Why are they getting along?"

PAUL MULLIE: Getting serialized is inevitable. If you were doing maybe a really old-fashioned TV show back in the day, they would really do strictly episodic, they'd do a hard reset at the end of every episode. You'd never bring characters back or whatever, but in our case it didn't make any sense to do that. We had this gigantic playground of interesting characters, so why would we forget about this guy or that guy? Bring 'em back. And as soon as you start to bring a character back or an idea back, now you're starting to creep into serialization. The more you do that, the more it builds on itself.

The flip side is you have to be careful, because you want it to be an open door for new people. If you really sort of start gazing at your own navel too much within your own storyline, it can be a barrier to new people coming in. The key to that are the characters. If someone's watching a show and doesn't quite know the mythology, doesn't quite know how the relationships are with the villain, they're not going to connect. But if the characters are interacting in a way that you find interesting and relatable, you've got an in. I think in the streaming era people are obsessed with the idea of serialization. For instance, I tried to watch *Breaking Bad* in the middle of some season and I just didn't get it. But *then*, when I watched it from the beginning, I was obsessed and almost watched it nonstop, because it was so amazing. When we were doing *Stargate*, it was almost a transition thing where that shift started to happen more and more. By the time we got to *Stargate: Universe*, it was much more serialized from the start. This was the early 2000s and *The Sopranos* was just coming up and becoming a big thing *and* was a new way of doing TV.

ROBERT C. COOPER: On *The Sopranos*, every season it would be, like, here's a new bad guy; here's a guy we need to defeat, we would defeat him at the end and the next season we would invent a new bad guy who was maybe better and more sinister in a different way. The reason *Stargate* was able to successfully carry on beyond season eight was because the Ori were just so different from the Goa'uld. We had defeated the Goa'uld so many times. The Replicators really didn't have a personality, so to speak. They were just more of a constant annoyance. So we needed bad guys with a different personality. The old adage is that your good guy is only as good as your bad guys are. You've got to switch it up and not just sort of keep secrets from your audience forever.

As discerned from many of the preceding comments, an undeniable strength of Stargate SG-1 *is the fact that its scope and internal mythology was ever-growing. In terms of the latter, you would certainly have to give the writers credit for continually trying to shake things up when it came to* the team's opponents. Primary among them, of course, was the Goa'uld, the serpent parasites that take human hosts and are driven by a thirst for power and worship who have enslaved millions around the galaxy for thousands of years. From the Goa'uld came individual System Lords (who were constantly at war with each other) and the Tok'ra, a branch of the Goa'uld consisting of those who rebelled against the others. With the Goa'uld came their servants, the Jaffa, who would show up in a variety of ways through the course of the seasons (not the least, of course, was in the form of Teal'c).

The Asgard was initially represented by the character Thor, first in the form of a holographic projection of the Norse god and then as its true self, looking like what we've come to know as the "Roswell Aliens." The GateWorld site describes them as follows: "One of Earth's most powerful allies, the ancient and benevolent Asgard … were once members of an ancient alliance with the Nox, the Furlings and the Ancients. The species was governed by the Asgard High Council, which monitored activity on protected worlds and formed decisions on actions taken against aggressors."

Where the Asgard ran into trouble was with the Replicators, which were all about assimilation and expansion — think of them as insect-like versions of Star Trek: The Next Generation's the Borg. In their initial form they were engineered as nanites by the Ancients in the Pegasus Galaxy as a weapon against the Wraith (as explored on Stargate: Atlantis). They were reborn thousands of years later in the Milky Way Galaxy and part of their evolution was to reach the point where they could replicate human beings.

The Ancients were the beings that created the network of Stargates throughout the universe. Eventually they learned how to ascend to a higher plane of existence, which they would allow Daniel Jackson to eventually do before, then, allowing him to return to his human form (coincidentally at the exact same time that Michael Shanks left and then returned to the series). Then, notably, there was the Ori, for which we turn back to GateWorld: "A race of ascended entities who gained energy through the worship of mortal beings. The Ori were once the same civilization as the Alterans, but (for want of a better term) believed in religion, where their brothers relied more heavily on science. A gap was eventually bridged between the cultures. In consequence, the other Alterans left for the Milky Way Galaxy (to later be known as the Ancients). The Ori used their ascension and knowledge of the universe as justification for praise and worship … The Ori conceived the Origin Faith, one that placed them in the center of creation."

There was also a twist on the Arthurian legends, given an alien connection; and, along the way, of course, there would be individual opponents, including Anubis (a former Goa'uld System Lord who learned the power of ascension), the Replicator Fifth, Goa'uld System Lord Ba'al, Adria the Orisi, Goa'uld System Lord Nirrti, the Ori's Priors, and, of course, their most consistent threat, the Goa'uld Apophis, who has an uncanny ability to come back from defeat, or even death, time after time. Some of that latter point may have something to do with the casting of Peter Williams *in the role.*

PETER WILLIAMS (actor, "Apophis"): I came in with a big ego, that's that. I think that's one of the prerequisites for feeling like you're a god. And *then* they gave me a nice big trailer and then they started calling me "God" … no, not really. He's a false god, so it was easy to play. Mario Azzopardi, who directed "Children of the Gods," had me analyze people with delusions of grandeur. People like Mussolini. He had me look at those people and try to find what it is amongst people who think that they are greater than. That was one of the preparations that I did.

ROBERT C. COOPER: "Torment of Tantalus" looked at Catherine Langford as a young woman, and then later on meeting her in the show — it was about mythology that had already been written to some extent in the backstory of the show, and saying, "Look, why don't we bring these elements from the movie into the show, and then use that to expand the mythology of the series?" Fans sort of point to that episode as being a bit of a mythology firestarter regarding the Four Races.

BRAD WRIGHT: Robert came up with the concepts of the Fifth Race and the concept of Thor turning into a Gray, both of which I really liked. The notion for that came from a conversation where I asked, "Why are we still alive? We must have been protected at some point." It's the idea that all of these dangerous civilizations are out there, yet people on Earth have been allowed to develop as far as they have.

ROBERT C. COOPER: It was also a question early on of the Goa'uld being so much more advanced than us. They had ships, they had cool weapons, they had hand devices — they just seemed godlike and very powerful. And that was a big gap to fill in, in terms of us being able to then stand on some sort of even ground with them. So we needed help. We needed someone who could understand the technology or understand who the Goa'uld were so we could kind of come to understand a little bit more about them. Connecting them to our team and to our world in a personal way was the real trick.

BRAD WRIGHT: All of those conversations turned into solutions. We asked, "Who built the Stargate?" We didn't want it to be the Goa'uld, we wanted it to be something more honorable. Because it's a wonderful thing, a network of Stargates that allow you to go from planet to planet, and it doesn't sound like a device built by conquerors, but it *does* sound like it was something that could have been purloined by an evil race. That makes a lot more sense, hence the Goa'uld. Rob also came up with the Repli- cators. He was big on expanding, and was very good at expanding our mythology. He was also very good at developing the spiritual side of all of these things, like the whole

"Maternal Instinct" storyline, and then the positivity of that followed by the negativity of the Ori. These all come out of spin conversations, which is really one of my favorite things to do.

ROBERT C. COOPER: The Ori was the evolution of the next phase of how religion was being examined within the *Stargate* mythology. The first phase was the Goa'uld and their impersonation of God. So they were false gods and engineered the subjugation of people using the false premise of deities among them. Then we moved ahead in the show and started introducing Ascension and the Ancients and their very much God-like powers. It was interesting to explore the idea that the Goa'uld are very powerful from a scientific technology point of view and are using that technology to impersonate gods. People who are not familiar with that technology believe in it as magic or god-like. The natural extension of that is, "If they're benevolent, then they're just gonna solve all of our problems," which wasn't true of the Ancients who took more of a hands-off approach.

But what came into the conversation was the idea, "What if there are bad ones who took the idea that being worshiped increased your power, so they have a way of *taking* that energy from people?" Well, what's interesting to me is our relationship to those people. How are we affected by them? And so that was the story I wanted to tell: what if there were these bad god-like creatures that were super powerful? It also increases the threat — how *do* you beat them? After beating the Goa'uld so many times, it upped the stakes.

CATH-ANNE AMBROSE: The writers are all really strong, distinctive personalities that complement and blend very well together. It took a while to find the right mix. They all have individual strengths that they bring to the table. They are all total characters. I think that the producers set a really great vibe from the top down that made the crew happy — and that's why many people stayed for so many years.

BRAD WRIGHT: The mythology of *Stargate* that I liked the most was the stuff that came out of or just built on our own storytelling. Meaning we would create a story around a race or group and then that would create an opportunity for more story. The Replicators led to the human form Replicators and the human form Replicators led to a whole arc of stories that were quite cool. And the Goa'uld we're basically Jon and my way of justifying the feature and the idea of multiple transplanted human cultures around the galaxy. If that was the case, then there must be multiple Goa'uld who have all decided, "What a great way to get slaves; we'll pretend to be their God."

ROBERT C. COOPER: Nowadays when you walk in to pitch a show, the network has this expectation that you're going to know exactly what you're doing. Not just for the whole season, but probably the next two or three seasons at least. And they literally want you to walk in with the whole show. And with *Stargate*, that was back in the time of more episodic storytelling where you pitch the engine and *then* you come up with the specifics. And, of course, you had this planned balance of mythology, set up like an arc to keep people interested and coming back week after week. The mythology building was something that was happening kind of on the fly. We had 22 episodes a season to do and there are only so many sci-fi concepts, and if you're using sci-fi concepts as the way in which you're leapfrogging through your episodes, you're going to run out of ideas pretty quickly. I think expanding the world, expanding the mythology, keeping things fresh and new, is the only way to allow a show to have legs.

BRAD WRIGHT: Relatively early on, I guess even when we were talking about breaking the series, I said it can't be just the Goa'uld or we'll run out of stories or it will just get old. It'll be the Goa'uld of the week. I *really* wanted to explore the science or at least try to invent some of the science and the science fiction of the Stargate itself. How long can it stay open? What happens if you dial a black hole? Never thought of stuff like that? Well, that's an episode called "A Matter of Time," which deals with *exactly* that.

ROBERT C. COOPER: When I was coming up with ideas, I often started with a theme or a simple idea that I was really interested in and then tried to figure out what story would allow me to explore it. Or other people would say, "Let's mine this thing that we've already sort of set up in this episode." I would also be, like, "Okay, fine. That's great, but what about something totally new? How do we make this fresh in a way that we hadn't even begun to explore?" Some of that, again, came from stuff that had been previously developed.

BRAD WRIGHT: I think it was Rob who suggested that there should be a fifth column within the Goa'uld — the Tok'ra — who recognized that what they were doing was evil, so basically the good guys within the bad guys and that created an ally which we really quite desperately needed. Once we created that subcategory of the Goa'uld within that mythology, I don't know how many stories we got out of it, but it was a ton.

JONATHAN GLASSNER: We started off by basing most of the aliens on mythologies. We had the Norse gods, which is what the Asgard were. Obviously the Egyptian gods. Then we went away from that, because it got a little repetitive. The theory of the show that Brad and I came up with, which we never really said on the page, is that these so-called gods are the ones that created a lot of our mythology in the past. The

Egyptian gods were based on the Goa'uld, who had visited Earth and the Egyptians thought they were gods. The Asgard were based on the Norse gods. That was just sort of the kernel where we started. I think it's what Dean Devlin and Roland Emmerich intended when they started. Then we kind of veered off of that as we got into hundreds of episodes.

ROBERT C. COOPER: Certainly the movie laid the groundwork for a lot of it, and Brad and Jonathan did an amazing job of laying the groundwork for a ton of the mythology in the pilot and first season. The other thing is that there are always holes, right? There are always issues within your storytelling where it's, like, "Okay we did this, but that created a problem. It seemed like a good idea at the time, but nobody really figured out this big problem." And we would just talk about it.

BRAD WRIGHT: We were very good at sitting in a writer's room and talking all afternoon, and at the end of the day coming up with fairly grand arcs and stories and sometimes entire power structures. The System Lords concept of a bunch of Goa'uld who have a loose alliance and agree not to attack each other constantly; questions like how this universe came about and how it all holds together. What *is* the glue? What are the things tearing it apart? What are the things keeping it together? The Protection Treaty of Earth, the Asgard seeing something in us that's positive and the whole Fifth Race concept. Those are just really strong concepts.

ROBERT C. COOPER: Out of those conversations I would realize, "What we need is another chunk of mythology to solve a particular problem, to explain that issue away. For example, the Asgard, who were just so tremendously powerful that it didn't really make sense why they didn't just come and destroy the Goa'uld. Basically we needed to solve that problem and explain where they are and what they're doing and why they haven't just come in and saved us. So we created the Replicators, which was a way of saying, "Here's the thing you *didn't* know was actually going on." That explains the rationale for why things are happening that we've seen happening. On top of that, I just love basically coming up with new stuff that in some ways felt organic, because it was tied to the old stuff.

JOSEPH MALLOZZI: While we always wanted to come up with episodic storylines, you don't want to have to find a kind of villain of the week. You'd want to create some antagonists, so there was a Goa'uld, but he was built out of the System Lords. So in the two-part episode "Summit," we had Cliff Simon as Ba'al, and he was terrific. He became a villain I always used to love to write for, because he had that sense of style and was a villain with an undercurrent of humor. On another episode, "The Quest," he becomes an unlikely ally with them, but then Carter ends up punching his lights out. Just a lot of fun. And it was all on the strength of Cliff Simon's performance that he became a returning villain.

ROBERT C. COOPER: The Goa'uld attack at the end of season one was interesting, because it felt on the one hand inevitable, but also a very sort of scary and dangerous thing to do. Once you've beaten your bad guys back, it kind of diminishes them to some extent. So opening up the world to the Tok'ra and the Asgard showed you that we were not just a one-trick-pony with just a single bad guy. And the show had very much run its course with the Goa'uld after season eight; we had beaten them and beaten them so badly that they no longer felt like a threat. So if they're no longer a reasonable adversary, what do we do? We create bad Ancients, the Ori, and reinvent the show by reinventing the villains and the mythology.

BRAD WRIGHT: There's nothing more fun than being in a writer's room when stuff is happening. I've said this a million times: I probably laughed more in that situation. You come in, you chat about the day and what's going on, and then you start. "Here's a thought, here's an idea." And I would sometimes throw out a big idea or a big question, "How would we address 'X'?" And Paul or Joe or Rob would turn it into a fun conversation of, "No, we can't do that, because if *that* happened, then *this* would happen."

ROBERT C. COOPER: I was saying recently to someone else not just with the mythology, but with the cast and everything to do with the show, we learned that when you have a successful show, you're very careful with it. It's like a baby; you don't want to break it. Like, "Let's not do anything stupid. Let's not change anything. Let's always make the same thing." But if you never challenge that thing, if you never change it, it will actually fizzle out and die. The only way to grow and to really develop is to push it out there and give it new experiences.

JOSEPH MAZZOLLI: The great thing is you didn't have to come in with a fully formed idea; if you just had kind of an inkling of an idea and you get Brad and Robert started, they would always be able to sort of come up with a great story moment. In fact, I remember a writer pitching an idea and using the wrong word to describe something. Rob kind of turned off, because the story was totally inappropriate for *Stargate,* but then he was, like, "Yeah, that story's not going to work, but you mispronouncing that word gave me another idea." And so Rob, based on this guy mispronouncing something, came up with the idea for what would be an episode. And that's often how it kind of worked. We would have just a germ of an idea and we'd give rise to an episode.

BRAD WRIGHT: And we'd just build and establish rules from there. Then putting a bunch of thoughts up on a whiteboard and realizing, "Wow, this could be really good." Then somebody writes a draft. Joe is always the fastest to read everything; he'd finish reading the script and I'd go, "I'm only on page 20. How can you *possibly* have read the whole thing?" Then we'd sit in my office or Rob's office or eventually we would have a dedicated writers' room and give notes. But that first draft, that still warm script, is a great feeling. It can also be a horrible feeling if you read a script that you had high expectations for that you gave a new person or a freelancer and you're feeling, "This is going to be so much work. I don't even know how I'm going to give notes on this."

CATH-ANNE AMBROSE: Some scripts changed dramatically, and others very little. There are numerous reasons. Some are practical, such as scheduling and availability of actors, and locations. Other changes came after suggestions from RDA or Michael Greenburg. Other times they did a huge rewrite to specifically tailor dialogue to a character after we had cast an actor. "Heroes," parts one and two, was heavily re-written by Robert after Saul Rubineck was cast.

RONNY COX (actor, "Senator/Vice President Robert Kinsey"): Originally when I did Kinsey, it was just going to be a one-shot. It was a clip show, "Politics," to sort of recap the first season and we were never going to see him again. First of all, we had so much fun doing it and the writers and producers loved what I did, and they said, "Ronny, we'd like you to come back for more." And I have to say this: they basically said, "Where do you want the character to go?" I'm not saying I made up where he went. They are certainly in charge of that, but they did call me up and say, "What would you like to do?" And I said, "What about if we did this or this or this?" So about half of the storylines have been from discussions with me and the producers and the writers saying where we'd like to see this guy go. As we all know, playing the bad guy is about twice as much fun as playing the good guys. They're always more interesting.

CLIFF SIMON (actor, "Baal"): I spoke with Peter Deluise and I said, "Look, Peter, this is what I want to do. I want Ba'al to have a few more human qualities. I want him to be angry, I want him to smile, I want him to be happy. I want him to be … whatever. I don't just want him to be mean the whole time, because that's boring as far as I'm concerned." You know, you look at Al Pacino playing a bad guy role and you actually like him, and at the end of the movie you're rooting for him. Even though he's a bad guy you want him to win. And that's actually that's the state I wanted to get Ba'al to. I wanted people to think, "You know, I want Ba'al to go and kill them. That's going to be so cool!"

CATH-ANNE AMBROSE: Sometimes there are clearance issues that come into play which force us to change character names, props, or signage. An example I had was when the name of Carter's love interest in an episode, "Chimera," did not clear with our lawyers, because there is an actual person living in Denver with the same name. Every scene will have to be changed to reflect the new name change. Then, of course, there are the Air Force notes that usually affect minor changes. Most importantly, however, if the actual writing in a script is not as good as it needs to be to go into production, that script will be heavily rewritten by one of the executive producers. Most freelance scripts are heavily rewritten. The person who receives writing credit is not necessarily the person who did the bulk of the actual writing.

JOSEPH MALLOZZI: It's always helpful to be in a room with other like minded, very creative people where someone will throw out a story idea, and then someone else will run with it and it's called spinning. So we would just spin ideas and it was always great, even though we were so incredibly busy. It's hard to believe that in the first few seasons that Paul Mullie and I were there, we were producing 40 episodes of television a year between *SG-1* and *Stargate Atlantis*, which is really astounding when you see that Netflix does eight or 10 episodes of a show a year.

JONATHAN GLASSNER: Delving into those alien cultures was a conscious effort, and the reason it was a conscious effort was because early on we had that order of 44 episodes, so we knew we could spend the time developing them. If you were running the show on ABC and you've got a six-episode order and then another six, you'd be afraid to start going down one of those paths, because you fear that they're just going to cancel you and you'll never be able to finish the story you started. So we said, "This is awesome, let's do this."

JOSEPH MALLOZZI: When we joined in season four, creatively they were really clicking. And, I mean, again, it's not as if the Goa'uld were threatening them every episode, we always kind of found ways to either focus on other threats or basically dug deeper, like dealing with Osiris, who is almost kind of tangentially connected to the ongoing Goa'uld storyline, but offers the opportunity for more or less a standalone episode. "Window of Opportunity" had nothing to do with the Goa'uld and neither did "Scorched Earth." If you have an even balance between the mythology-laden stories and standalone stories. you don't get tired, but after about eight seasons, that's when Brad and Robert decided maybe it's time to sort of wrap up the Goa'uld and find a new villain, which is when they introduced the Ori in season nine.

ROBERT C. COOPER: Change has to be embraced. Like we realized at one point, "Oh my God, Michael Shanks wants to leave. What are we going to do about not having Daniel in the show? Are our fans going to still watch?" We brought in Corin

Nemic to play Jonas and the show kept going; it didn't miss a beat. Not to disrespect Michael or Daniel, and obviously we had a giant lift when he came back, and that's not to in any way disrespect Corin and his performance or Jonas, but it just proved to us that the show itself was bigger than any one element, and that the change actually made a difference. It kept the energy up and it was the dynamic that changed. The conversations were suddenly different between the characters because we changed that element. When the villains are different, everything about how you approach the challenge is different. So the short answer is that changes are good for shows as long as you keep enough of the foundation and enough of what the fans love that it doesn't feel like an entirely new show.

Internally, there would be some significant changes to Stargate SG-1, *in particular the fact that Jonathan Glassner became more of a consultant following season three. On top of that, Showtime elected to stop carrying the series after its fifth season, but due to its popularity in syndication, the Sci-Fi Channel (before changing its moniker to Syfy) decided to pick the show up for what would ultimately be seasons six through 10, and even aired the spinoffs,* Stargate Atlantis *for five seasons and* Stargate Universe *for two.*

JONATHAN GLASSNER: The deal MGM made with me was that if I did *Stargate*, I had to agree to stay for three more years. At that time, my wife was going out of her mind, because her whole life was in California and we were getting older and wanting to start having kids. We had our first child there in Vancouver. At that point my wife said to me, "If we are having any more babies, we are not doing it here." I had to make the hard choice after three years to walk away. And it was a *really* hard decision, but I felt like it was my marriage or my show and I chose my marriage. Luckily I've kept working, but it was a huge risk at the time. And I missed it. I really loved that cast and crew and Robert and Brad and everybody there. It was a great group. I mean, Brad and I put it together, so of course I would. I tried to stay involved with the show; I was a consultant and was being paid as a consultant. Brad and I were still of like minds, though we've kind of grown apart since then. I think it's the first time that he was going to get to run a show by himself, to be the big boss, and he had different opinions of the direction the show should go than I did — and he got to do it, because he was there. I left, so it wasn't my choice.

The one thing that he and I didn't agree on, and I think he would admit this or agree with this, although I'm sure he still thinks he was right and I was wrong, is that what I believe made *Stargate* unique to other sci-fi shows was that although we were traveling to other planets, it was set in the present with today's technology where we didn't have cool things like scanners and shields and all that stuff. We were basically primitive people going in and using an alien technology we didn't fully understand. So we were carrying machine guns and walking through the Stargate not knowing what was going to be on the other side every time. Brad really wanted to be making *Star Trek*, and eventually they captured an alien ship that had scanners and life sensors for planets and all this high tech stuff that didn't exist before. I thought that was taking it away from being *Stargate* toward being *Star Trek*.

BRAD WRIGHT: Jon liked the ancient Egyptian stuff and the Goa'uld more than me. I realized it would get tiring. Obviously the show lasted 10 seasons, so maybe I was proven right. But it evolved even then and it continued to evolve. I was just not so much into the Goa'uld, even though they stuck around for every season and beyond. It was something we inherited from the feature film that I was working to get beyond. I would do stories that had nothing to do with the Goa'uld. I would just do one where, "Oh shit, we dialed the gate where there's a black hole." And a story falls from there.

I had always wanted to write *Star Trek*, but I don't think humanity finding and learning what's out there, and then building on that technology and making it our own, makes it *Star Trek*. In fact, I would argue that what made *Stargate* what it was had less to do with ancient mythology and more to do with the fact that it was people from the here and now with our sensibilities going out into space through the Stargate. And then at that point going, "Holy shit, it's a dangerous universe out there. We better get some of the technology to survive, otherwise we're just going to be relying on the kindness of allies." How long could we count on that? That to me is as much a parable for today as anything else. For better or for worse, humanity's future lies in science and in our ability to conquer the challenges ahead of us *through* science, because we can't go back. To quote *The Martian*, we need to science our way out of this. *That* is where I wanted to take *Stargate*

JONATHAN GLASSNER: Look, the show still was a great show and it kept going for a reason. I always thought it was going to be a success. I didn't know that there'd be spinoffs, but I had a feeling it would run a long time. It was very good. Brad did an amazing job on it. I just think it made it a different show. I don't know that it made it a worse show or a better show, it just made it different. Our people were coming from a place of little knowledge, and in his world, they had a lot more knowledge.

BRAD WRIGHT: Maybe it was *Enterprise* jealousy. But it was also another way to tell the story, because just stepping through the Stargate was getting tiresome and even our performers were getting a little bit of an attitude of, "Here's *another* alien planet," and we would have to say, "Guys, remember: we're going across the galaxy. It's cool *every* time."

JONATHAN GLASSNER: Richard Dean Anderson had a saying he would yell out on set: "LTS," which means "Life's Too Short" and he wasn't having fun. Which is why he eventually left, because he wasn't having fun anymore — *and* he was having back issues and all kinds of problems. But we did have a lot of fun with it and I did miss that, because I was back in the rat race of *CSIs* and networks. But when I did announce I was leaving, Rick couldn't stand to have a talk with me; he was very angry. Once I told him, he pretty much clamped up at that point. He wouldn't even give me the time of day. I think it made him angry, because he was in the exact same situation. He had a kid in L.A. who he wanted to be with. But he was the star of the show and didn't have that option. So I think he really kind of felt like I was deserting him. I don't blame him.

BRAD WRIGHT: Rob's promotion was probably more gradual than he would have liked, because he wants to be in charge. He feels he probably should be, but he wasn't yet, so he was kind of pushing against that ceiling.

ROBERT C. COOPER: Yeah, Jonathan was always wondering what I was doing in his office with a tape measure.

BRAD WRIGHT: It was just a natural moment for him to step up and basically take over Jonathan's role, even though I was sole executive producer for at least a season before he became an executive producer with me. It was no problem for me at all to say he should be an executive producer, too. Because we knew we had a Season 5 on Showtime before the end of season two, there was no doubt that it would go five years at least and I really thought that was going to be it. But then it went over to Sci-Fi for Season 6 and it was a different animal.

THOMAS P. VITALE (former EVP Programming at Syfy Channel and Chiller Network): MGM approached Syfy (then Sci-Fi Channel) about these shows back in 1996, before *Stargate* even premiered on Showtime. That's not uncommon. Studios often try to sell the "back end rights" (the "repeats") for TV shows early in a show's original run. Why? Well, later selling windows — i.e. the repeat runs of a show on different networks — are often where the most profits are generated, especially for shows that run for many years on strong networks and in good time periods. Think of shows like *The Big Bang Theory, Seinfeld, MASH, NCIS*, the *Law & Order* franchise and others — their repeats run for many years in high-profile time periods and generate a ton of revenue. Even classic shows like *I Love Lucy* and *The Twilight Zone* are still running somewhere in the country and around the world every day, meaning they are still earning profits over 50 years later!

In October 1997, it was announced that media mogul Barry Diller would buy USA

Network and Syfy Channel, as well as Universal's television production studio and program distribution business. At around the same time, MGM made us aware that Showtime was potentially going to be moving away from its focus on science fiction programming at some point, and that *Stargate SG-1,* the new *Outer Limits* and *Poltergeist: The Legacy* would be most likely canceled by Showtime. That meant that these three shows were potentially available to Syfy, not only in their "back-end" [repeat] windows, but now as original programs which would premiere on Syfy instead of Showtime. By June 2002, we were finally able to premiere *Stargate* and we had acquired the others. We launched its sixth season and right out of the gate (pun intended), *Stargate SG-1* was a hit for Syfy, and over the years we ordered more new seasons — five seasons in total — as well as two spin-off series. With each renewal deal I did for an additional season of original episodes, I was able to extend Syfy's rights for the older seasons for a further year, which was a huge advantage. On Syfy, we had great success airing older *Stargate* episodes in a four-hour block on Monday nights — a "stack" — from 7pm to 11pm each week. It immediately became our strongest stack ever.

JONATHAN GLASSNER: A lot of the show's extended success is to the credit of John Symes, because when Showtime killed it, he got Sci-Fi to pick it up. And Showtime killed it, by the way, because we weren't doing things that made it a subscription-only show. But there was actually a triple reason for what happened. They kept saying to us every season, "You've got to make this a show that you can't see on network television, because we want to make people want to subscribe to our service." So between the fact that we didn't do that, really, and the fact that it was available however long later in syndication, their research showed it was not getting them more subscribers, so they canceled it. Even though it did well on the network, they didn't think it was getting them *new* subscribers, so they killed it. Plus, a lot of it had to do with the fact that the budget was going up after a certain amount of time.

BRAD WRIGHT: The year that we went to SciFi, there was a person in place we had to take notes from. But then that executive ended up moving on and a guy named Mark Stern took over on Season 7, which I really thought would be the last season. Actually, one of the things I had said to Robert for Season 7 was, "You deserve to be the sole showrunner; I'll still be here, but you'll run things." I had just come off doing a lot of television and my kids were, like, 10 and eight and I wanted to spend some time with them. So I went to our cottage for a month. I was still on the phone all the time with Rob, helping — I hope — and wrote a few episodes, but that changed the dynamic a little bit. We also changed the approach in the sense that we used to prioritize Showtime and then then think about the syndicated version. For Showtime, we worried less about acts for commercial breaks. Then that all flipped around and the order of priority became the syndication version, the Sci-Fi version and the DVD version.

Back to Mark Stern, I had known him for a very long time, because he was an assistant at Trilogy Entertainment Group and then became a producer when I was doing *The Outer Limits*. So he literally phoned me and said, "Hey, Brad, guess what? I'm finally in a position where you have to take my notes." And I said, "Guess what? I'm not running the show this year. Bye." That was very satisfying. He laughed it off, but I have to say, Mark is the kind of guy I'd like to have a beer with at a wrap party, but we were always arguing about *everything*. He was very good at identifying problems, but his solutions were not always the correct solution. About five or six years ago I said to him, "Why don't we add five years to our lives and clear the air a little bit? Get rid of some angst." It was actually a good conversation.

THOMAS P. VITALE: In terms of network oversight of *Stargate SG-1*, even though I dealt with the deal side of the show, and managed the creative side of all our independent productions, studio shows were managed through our west coast group, not by me. That said, I stayed close with the *Stargate* showrunners, Brad Wright and Robert Cooper, and along with MGM's Hank Cohen and Charlie Cohen, we would try to help Brad and Robert navigate any issues with Syfy as much as we could. As with any show, there were always issues which would come up, and Syfy did a ton of audience research on the *Stargate* series that were communicated to the showrunners.

The changes continued behind the scenes with the show. Following Season 5, Michael Shanks decided to leave the series, moving on to what he felt would be greener acting pastures. In his place came Corin Nemec as Jonas Quinn, a human from the planet Langara, essentially filling Daniel Jackson's role on the team. Due to health reasons, after playing Hammond for seven seasons, Don S. Davis became a recurring performer and guest star in the final three years. Richard Dean Anderson, looking to pull back from the show to spend time with his daughter, in season eight, Jack O'Neill essentially took on Hammond's role as he was promoted to brigadier general. From there he would appear in two episodes each of seasons nine and 10, as well as the DVD movie Stargate: Continuum; *plus, four episodes of* Stargate: Atlantis *and five episodes of* Stargate: Universe.

Season nine saw the addition of Ben Browder, more or less filling O'Neill's place as Lieutenant Colonel Cameron Mitchell, which he would play for all of that year and Season 10 and The Ark of Truth *and* Continuum *(in the latter being promoted to the rank of captain); Claudia Black reunited with* Farscape *co-star Browder as space thief (and former Goa'uld host) Vala Mal Doran in one episode of Season 8, eight episodes of Season 9, 10 episodes of Season 10 and the two DVD movies; and Beau Bridges as Stargate Command's General Hank Landry in seasons nine and 10, the two DVD movies and three episodes of* Atlantis.

Also, a new era for humanity began in season six with Earth's first large-scale vessel capable of interstellar travel, equipped with hyperspace engines, able to operate within a planet's atmosphere and land on a planet's surface. For some, as noted, its development and use was controversial in that they felt the show had moved more towards Star Trek territory and away from Stargate. All of this fed into Michael Shanks' observation that in a sense it felt like two different chapters for the show: "I left the show after season five, when I came back it was a different environment."

BRAD WRIGHT: I had said to Michael when he left that we would do it in such a way that he could potentially come back. At the time it was a little contentious, but I think he recognized that, at the end of the day, it was a gift, because he was, like, 25-years-old when he started *Stargate*. He hadn't really tested the waters of anything and working on this show *was* grueling. We were working on a show 22 episodes a year and that *is* grueling. I remember when he came back in Season 6, writing a script that was a really strong episode, because he had meaty stuff to do. And I had to think that maybe I had *not* given him enough before. Maybe he was a young actor in the first few seasons with significant chops, who was always basically the support of Richard Dean Anderson. At the same time, Rick's name *was* above the title. That's where MGM wanted us to focus things and what they were spending the money on. When Michael came back, there was more for him to do, because Rick's role kind of started to get smaller as he pulled back, which is when I pitched the idea of General O'Neill, which meant he wasn't running and jumping and shooting as much and wouldn't be needed as much in front of the camera.

JOSEPH MALLOZZI: Every season was different in its own way; each one had its own distinct character. If I was going to make a distinction, to be honest with you, I would make a distinction between seasons one to eight and then seasons nine to 10. *That's* where the distinction is for me. In my mind, it was the classic team up until Season 6, at which point Michael left and we brought in Corin. But even as of Season 6, that's when Rick started to reduce his time on the show. I can't speak for Michael, but maybe a lot of it had to do with that kind of connection he had with Rick and the Daniel/O'Neill relationship faded a bit with Season 7, but that really had more to do with the fact that Richard Dean Anderson was slowly extricating himself from production. So you had a lot less of that glue, that core relationship, between Jack and Daniel and, for many fans, the heart of the series.

PAUL MULLIE: A big part of the difference between Michael's perception and mine is I missed the first three seasons, so there was probably a much bigger difference between seasons one and 10 than there was between seasons five and 10. I didn't see as much of what he's talking about. For me, it was just a natural progression or evolution of a show that lasted so long that it *had* to change, otherwise it would have just been boring and the audience would have stopped watching. It was never a need to take a different direction, it was just looking for avenues to tell stories. All sorts of new avenues came about with a change in tone. I think the show became maybe a little more serious, a little bit more character-driven and a little less Saturday afternoon syndication. For me, again, it was never a deliberate thing, it was just that we've got these new characters coming in. Some people are leaving, some people are coming in, we've got new devices, new aliens — whatever — and it was a natural evolution.

ROBERT C. COOPER: I would say that Michael's character was a massive part of the fabric of the show and the dynamic between Rick and Michael was great. Plus, Daniel Jackson was a legacy character going back to the original movie and in many ways a character that was the heart and soul of the show. Not taking anything away from O'Neill, Carter or Teal'c, but he was a humanitarian. They were not one-dimensional characters by any means, they all contributed, but at the end of the day Carter was a little more science-leaning; O'Neill was the military guy and Teal'c was our Jaffa ambassador, so to speak, and Daniel really served the role of being the social humanitarian. So aside from losing Michael, we had a hole in the team that we had to fill. And, look, anytime you make those kinds of changes in a situation that's working, you're nervous about it. But the success we had bringing in Jonas, and his ability to sort of blend in, was a testament to the show and the franchise.

CHRISTOPHER JUDGE: There was somewhat of a sense of being sad that Rick and Michael Greenburg and those people had left and kind not knowing what the interpersonal relationships were going to be. All of our fears were allayed very quickly. No disrespect to anyone who was on the show before or those relationships, but I can honestly say that it was the best time I'd had since I'd been on the show. It was great. We had the safety of the *Stargate* franchise, but this really was like an entirely new show. And we were just having a ball. I think the tone of the show was different. Claudia just gave the show something that it never had. It's always had its underlying sense of humor, but with her it wasn't so underlying.

As an actor, let's face it, I'd been doing this for eight years and it was tough to find new challenges or any freshness. So it became that early excitement [again] of trying to find your character and where your character fits into the general diaspora. For as much as it was said to be a team, SG 1 was always "Rick and the other three mooks." You know what I mean? Then in the previous few years it became "the three guys and Rick when he's here." Then it really was a true team, and just like in any group of people, you're always kind of searching to see where you fit in within the group.

JOSEPH MALLOZZI: Many fans, and I, thought the Jack/Sam relationship was equally as important as the Jack/Daniel one. It's interesting, because very much at that time we saw the fandom wars, as they call them, between the Sam/Jack shippers and the Jack/Daniel slashers. What was also interesting is that the fans tended to pick apart every little nuance of the show. For instance, in one episode Daniel and Sam were captured and held in a warehouse. O'Neill and, I think, Teal'c were there to save them and O'Neill went to Sam first. And, of course, the Jack and Daniel slashers were up in arms and the Sam and Jack shippers were elated. And that was not scripted; that was just basically what the actors decided to do with the director in terms of the blocking. The fans tend to read a lot more into those instances than were designed. It's a testament to their love for the show.

DAVID READ (YouTube Channel, *Dial the Gate*): The texture of the show was very different starting in Season 6, beginning with the fact that Rick was not there for as much screen time, and the episodes in which he *was* there, were frequently placing him in a position in the script where he was not as heavily utilized as he had been in previous seasons. Frankly, we were lucky to get him in the show for those last three years in the form that we did, because he always made the scene that he was in dynamite, but, again, the texture of the show was decidedly different. Also in Season 6, there were new writers that brought different textures and in some cases we got a kinder, gentler *Stargate*. So from my perspective, I have to agree with Michael that from season six forward, it was a very different kind of series. And then when season nine came in with Browder and Claudia Black, it was still different.

JOSEPH MALLOZZI: In terms of the types of stories we told, Jonas stepping in for Daniel didn't really impact them, except that Daniel *did* serve a function and Jonas kind of stepped in and pulled up the slack to a certain degree. But it wasn't Daniel Jackson specifically in terms of his archeological background, his knowledge of ancient cultures and the like. At the same time, it's always interesting to bring in a new character, because it kind of opens things up in certain ways. Yet I think with Daniel's departure and Jonas' arrival, it was kind of a wash.

BRAD WRIGHT: Michael was right that an evolution happened, though I'm not 100% sure it was when he left and came back. I mean, there was a natural change in the dynamic when Jonas came onto the show, but when he basically wanted to step back in, it made sense for Jonas to go back to his home world and for Michael to resume his role. And it was seamless; everybody just went, "Yeah, he's back." He and I ended up on good terms. To this day, I love seeing him. We're not friends, but we're definitely friendly and I would love to work with him again.

The changes with Rick were not shocking to me, because I was pre-emptive. Before that became a thing, I literally said, "Look, I want to try and keep you involved in the show as much as you want to be involved with the show, and we're going to try to negotiate a number of episodes. So if you can give me six, that would be great." We'd shoot some different scenes at the same time so that he could be with his daughter. It was so he could help raise her and he needed to be in her life. I got it — I stepped away and handed over the show for a time so I could be with my family. But I also wanted him to be involved because, A, it was important for the show, I thought; and, B, I think it was important for him. He liked working with us and had fun. My arguments, whenever they were about him, it was regarding money with his people. Sometimes it was, like, "Oh, come on, guys, I can't throw that much money at six episodes. I need some help here." So, again, I was pre-emptive and said, "Look, we're going to ask you every year how many you want to do and we'll write the season around that," and that's why he stuck around and why O'Neill showed up every now and then and why he was in the pilot for *Stargate Universe*. And it brought a certain brightness to the show. The other reason is that I didn't want the audience to think of a "post-O'Neill" *Stargate*.

JOHN G. LENIC: Having new actors involved in the show, especially coming into a long-running series, is always new and exciting. Ben Browder and Claudia Black were fantastic. It was a nice fit. Richard Dean Anderson was spectacular all the time, but shooting around his schedule — he would only work three and a half days a week and had every fourth week off — Amanda, Chris and Michael were working to the bone to accommodate his schedule. Going from that to all of a sudden *not* having to deal with that, and yet being able to do a show that was really about taking it in a new direction with the Ori, was exciting.

PAUL MULLIE: In episodic television, everything sets back to zero at the end and stays the same. We'd moved beyond that and were able to evolve and have a new voice as the leader of the team, who's a different kind of dude, and play with that. And then Claudia came in and gave us a whole other element. I guess the show did change for all those reasons, but, for me, it was never anything that I noticed at the moment. I was just making the show and having fun.

JOSEPH MALLOZZI: Rick's pulling back was a bigger change for us than Michael leaving. We missed his sense of humor, and to a certain degree that's what the Cameron Mitchell character brought back. Even though he was capable, he was still a bit of a fish out of water with regard to the Stargate program, so you've got to kind of play catch up and that was fun to explore. Vala, on the other hand, was just a delightfully off-the-wall character that I absolutely loved to write for. The funny thing is we asked for her to be a series regular and Sci-Fi said, "No, just give her six episodes." And then, after they saw the six episodes, they were, like, "Let's make her a series regular," but we said, "At this point, that ship has sailed. If we get a 10ᵗʰ season, we'll make her a series regular," and we did. We had such a great time exploring her backstory; everybody loves a lovable rogue character. The fans certainly do and the writers even more so.

BRAD WRIGHT: Ben had that great attitude of not wanting the camera pushing in on him in his first episode, but to push in on the Stargate and him being in awe of it. Just a great shot that I remember vividly. We needed another general, and that's where Landry came in and we got to work with Beau Bridges, who, by the way, is an amazing actor and a gift to work with. And with Ben and Claudia becoming a part of the show, Robert and I had proposed that we rebrand the show as *Stargate Command* and it would potentially have more legs that way. I suppose MGM was reticent, because they didn't know how many more years Sci-Fi wanted to give us and they thought it would benefit *Atlantis* more to have seasons nine and 10 of *SG-1*.

ROBERT C. COOPER: Ben just came *so* prepared and I will never forget that he was plastered to his couch for two weeks watching *every* episode of the show. He just came into this world with a much more fully-formed idea of what he wanted his character to be.

PAUL MULLIE: Things were definitely different without Richard Dean Anderson. There was a gap there for sure, because he had been such an integral part of it for so long. But I think the show had sort of grown up around him. At first it was Richard Dean Anderson and the rest of the show. Then, over time, the rest of the show grows up and he's, like, "Well, I can leave now and this will stand on its own." I think that's exactly what happened in terms of who made that decision just to keep the show going or how confident they were about it still drawing its audience without him. So the choice would be to create an O'Neill clone, which would have been pointless, shallow and stupid; or take advantage and create a new character and see where that takes the show.

BRAD WRIGHT: There was a bit of an irreverence that Mitchell had that I think O'Neill shared. He called Kassa space corn, because that's what it was, and that's something O'Neill would have said. So he picked up on that vibe and then ran with that while still being much more the physical fighter soldier. I mean, Ben did sword fights, and then he got down and dirty with real hand-to-hand stuff, which he liked doing. He's just a couple of years younger than me and he was in pretty good physical condition to do all that stuff. And, of course, Vala is irreverent and hilarious and doesn't replace anyone. Then you get into the Camelot storylines and the Ori storylines and because they are new, and because the bad guys are new, the dynamic between the team and the enemy also changed.

MICHAEL SHANKS: Obviously Claudia and I had a lot of fun working together and they wrote some great stuff for us to play off of in this kind of antagonistic dynamic that we established in "Prometheus Unbound." It continued on; it was a really nice rapport that brought a nice energy to the show that we hadn't really had on a regular, on-going basis.

ROBERT C. COOPER: It frequently happened where we would bring in a guest character and they would be so exciting and reinvigorating that we'd be, like, "How do we bring them back for more?" That's what made us think Claudia as Vala could be an interesting dynamic to bring into the show. She was irreverent and humorous in a way that still fit into the show, but with an angle that we hadn't had before. But we knew we couldn't just throw Vala on the team. One of the things that we all agreed we loved about her character was the fact that she's a bit of an outsider with an attitude, and that that attitude doesn't necessarily fit right in immediately. And if you just suddenly had her change her personality and join the team and be accepted, it wouldn't feel right. It would probably not be nearly as interesting as keeping her character as a bit of a wildcard.

MICHAEL SHANKS: Ben was very much the sort of stoic colonel that we needed. He's got that Southern twang to his voice, which was a great, different voice for us. And he was a really assertive and specific actor. We had conversations about the scenes all the time. And then, of course, you have Beau Bridges. It was a completely different dynamic in a lot of different ways. They're so professional and they're such nice people. There were no egos in the room. Everybody just sat around in between takes either talking about the scene if necessary or having Beau Bridges tell a few stories about "this happened and that happened" and whatnot. The newness of it felt like a completely different show as well. By the end of Season 8, we solved a lot of threads and it was really good for this new way we were taking the show to really have these new people and these new energies, frankly. And they're great characters, really well fleshed out, very intelligently fleshed out in terms of lots of dynamics between them.

JOSEPH MALLOZZI: Beau Bridges actually filled the void that was left by Don Davis. It was fun having Rick in charge, but Beau as General Landry brought a certain gravitas that we hadn't seen in that role since Don S. Davis. I have to say, I really enjoyed working with Beau, because he and Robert Picardo, another guy who I love working with [on *Atlantis*], had a very similar approach. We had gotten used to actors winging it or changing their lines on set, but Beau and Bob were very particular. They always came up to the office and very respectfully would say, "We wanted to make some changes to the script and just wanted to run it by you to see if it's okay." *Sometimes* it would be the most inconsequential changes, like, "Can we change 'the' to 'an'?" Particularly for Bob, who was on *Star Trek: Voyager* for so many years and they were not allowed to change a single line. And if they ever *did* want to change a line, it would be a big song and dance where they would have to put a call in to the producers who often weren't on set and there would be a whole discussion where, more often than not, the answer would be no. But both of them were very seasoned actors with great instincts.

BRAD WRIGHT: Bringing in Beau Bridges is never going to hurt you and it was damn good. I loved him. Again, he provided a different dynamic to write that was fresh air for us. Ben is a serious actor, too. He has to know what he's saying and why he's saying it. He challenges writers, but doesn't just do it on the day of filming. He's one of those guys who comes into your office and says, "I have a question about this sequence." Sometimes it's *just* a question. All I have to do is answer it, but he's got a good old boy personality and is a thinking actor. He really is. And he brings such integrity to the set and cares about the work. He and Bridges — man, it was a privilege to work with them.

ROBERT C. COOPER: Beau Bridges is Beau Bridges. You knew he was going to *be* that general character. He's just got that star quality, the chemistry and magnetism. He's just one of those actors who looks at what's on the page and asks them, but they also want to bring something to the table that is part of the creative process. You enjoy working with people like that, because they're doing some of your job for you.

As noted, the technical abilities of Stargate Command evolved to the point where the show began to use space vessels, shifting from humanity's take on Goa'uld gliders to starships like Prometheus, Daedalus *and* Odyssey. *Needless to say, their introduction would shake things up story wise.*

BRAD WRIGHT: One of the whole themes of the show was we are primitive in comparison to some of these alien cultures, but we are hungry for all that. That's *why* we go through the Stargate. And we have allies who want to help us and, of course, though we didn't know early on, the Asgard knew they were on their last legs and were hoping that we would basically take their place. And it does explain why they shared so much technology and helped us with stardrives and things. It makes sense: "We want to build our own spaceships. Can you help?" Ultimately, if they knew they were years away from their end, of course they would do that. Sometimes I felt that the mythology we began with was nothing more than just being a trap. We knew we were doing 88 episodes before the end of season one. We knew we had to come up with these other stories, and so I tended to be the one who went outside of that and tried to create the more science fiction-y stories, like what happens when you retrofit a Death Glider? Well, first of all, the Goa'uld thought of that and put in a failsafe to make sure the Jaffa didn't run off on their own to escape. And that led to the episode "Tangent" and a stranded astronauts story that's still within the Goa'uld mythology, because it was Apophis who created this failsafe. But it was a great story that stranded two of our leads and created beautiful visuals of a Death Glider outside, near the orbit of Jupiter. Now, did I fudge the science a little bit between how quickly they got from Earth to Jupiter? Yeah, I did.

DARREN SUMNER (creator, Gateworld.net): Brad wanted the show to evolve and tell different stories, and the ships allow the writers to tell those different kinds of stories they couldn't do before. And there are some *great* stories in there, but it changes the show for sure. Basically the first five seasons or so, the protagonists really have to rely on their own ingenuity, they have to be clever and they have to be lucky. And the second half of the show, once we get ships and beaming technology and so forth, there's less of a demand on the writers to come up with a clever solution to the problem for our heroes. There's less of a requirement for our heroes to be clever to figure their way out of a situation.

PAUL MULLIE: The idea of ships started with the fact that we had this alien technology lying around. It was just a thing that was a consequence of the stories that we had told. So the idea was, "Let's start building ships." First it was fighters or whatever and then it was a big ship with hundreds of humans on board. It would be a natural consequence of what we've been doing for however many years on the show and it was a way for us to start protecting ourselves from alien threats. As soon as you have that option, it's a whole other level of storytelling and for things to happen. I remember the visual effect; I'll never forget that ship rising out of the ground and loving it.

JOSEPH MALLOZZI: I think it was something we could no longer hold back on, simply because after so many years of gaining so much, it just defied credulity that the forces that be would not find ways to implement this technology and create starships, which opened the door for stories and amazing visuals. It was always kind of a fine line, because we had that technology, we had things like the sarcophagus — in case anybody ever died, we just stuff them into it and they come back — which, of course, raises the question of why wasn't Dr. Frazier brought back to life? My assumption was that all of that technology ended up at Area 51, like in that last scene in *Raiders of the Lost Ark* where the Ark is just filed away. But it's really a double-edged sword. Once you introduce the new tech, it gives you more story fodder, but at the same time it makes things a little harder.

ROBERT C. COOPER: The ship had a giant hamstring in that it couldn't get you there instantaneously. It wasn't instant travel across the galaxy. So we were focused on making sure the ships were a *complement* to the show and not allow them to take over.

BRAD WRIGHT: The process within the show started slowly as they naturally try to retrofit a captured glider that doesn't work, but they learn from the technology and they start getting help from the Asgard. Some time passes and we start building other ships, like the *Daedalus* and the *Odyssey*. In a way, that's why there has to be a slightly longer timeline in the story world, because these things would take time to build. Maybe we accelerated that process a little quickly, but it was another way of telling a story. It was another way of movement of people, another way of going to another planet that *isn't* walking through a Stargate, because that was always a little bit annoying to see that every alien culture seems to build all of their culture immediately around their Stargate, which I guess is a little incredible. "You know what? Let's just walk there." I thought part of the natural evolution, possibly accelerated unrealistically, but perhaps realistically, too, because of the Asgard itself, was the introduction of these ships. But it *wasn't* us trying to be *Star Trek*. In fact, I wrote the line, "Sir, we can't call it the *Enterprise*." "Why not?" I mean, I just hung the lantern on that and embraced it. It was fun and funny, but they were military vessels. They were for our defense and we also used them to do fun story things, like flinging a Stargate into a black hole and then dialing in at the same time, so that we could take advantage of the time dilation. All of the sciencey stuff that I like writing helps when you have that extra toy in your toy box in the form of a spaceship.

The other thing is that it was a great standing set. You can only walk around Stargate Command so many times with it being the same gray corridors, so we built a giant spaceship that became all the spaceships, we just changed the name plates. It may not have looked military enough; I would have spent more money on it had I known it was going to become what it became. It started as a few episodes and then became this running set. Then, of course, because it's taking up a whole stage, you say, "We better write something for the set." If you don't, it becomes this stage that's gone fallow and that you're not using, but paying rent on it and lighting it up. Having all that lighting set up is dumb, so you end up doing those shows, too. I like being able to go to a planet that doesn't have a Stargate.

PAUL MULLIE: I remember the set of the *Daedalus*, because it was huge, but it was also interactive. It had a much better human to machine interface than we ever had, because the Goa'uld's aesthetic was very much, "You just touch this thing and you have a mental connection. The ship does what you want it to do." There were no buttons or switches. I know this sounds kind of juvenile to say this, but it became really important to us — important to me — that we have that as an option, because I found the

Goa'uld's spaceship sets really limiting in terms of what types of stories you can tell. That set itself was just big empty rooms. This was part of the aesthetic of the original movie, so we inherited that and did what we could with it. But after a while it was like just sitting there holding a ball and nobody else is doing anything. It's kind of boring, and the *Daedalus* was the opposite of all that. There were, again, buttons and switches, dials and screens and you could pull out the machinery and see the circuitry and all that stuff. For us writing it, it gave us a whole new element to work with.

BRAD WRIGHT: Once you've spent all the money on the set, you take on the control panels, which was a different budget. I loved Earth tech, I loved a button and that you could press a lever and push forward. Paul embraced it, too, which is why the *Destiny* bridge on *Stargate Universe* had all those dials and gauges and stuff. That's why it's so expensive. If you sat in that set, though, you would go, "Holy shit, this looks even better in real life."

CHEVRON IV: SPIN-OFFS, ENDINGS AND LEGACIES

"You are the Fifth Race. Your role is clear. If there is any hope in preserving the future, it lies with you and your people."

Change had become the norm both in front of and behind the cameras on Stargate SG-1 *by the time the show reached its 10th season. Beyond cast changes, there was a spin-off in the form of* Stargate Atlantis, *which could have diluted the brand, but didn't, enjoying a five-season run of its own. There had also been several seasons of those in charge believing that that particular season was the last for the flagship series, only for it to be renewed yet again. But as Robert Cooper explains it, Seasons 9 and 10 were created with a defined goal in mind.*

ROBERT C. COOPER (executive producer): Season 9 was about wiping the slate clean, sort of, and introducing the Ori and preparing us for what was going to happen, which is that they were going to invade and kind of take over. The whole goal from Season 9 moving forward was to bring the series back to where it was when it started in Season 1. And that was to put us at a tremendous disadvantage — wipe the slate clean, make us the underdogs again. Because we had gotten to the point where we won every time. We killed Goa'ulds and Replicators at will. The challenge wasn't there anymore and we wanted to create bad guys that would now be as big a challenge as the Goa'uld were when we first opened the Stargate.

DAVID READ (host, **Dial the Gate** YouTube Channel): The Ori were a very different villain. The franchise was upping the ante in terms of its danger level. We had departed the mustache-twirling villains of the past and were going into a direction that was echoing our society much more politically. That was a fresh approach, and we introduced Mitchell and Vala into the mix. It was a very different series at this point without Rick there and with Amanda off being mom. I think that the Ori were a great addition to the franchise, because, as Daniel says, "I've never been so scared." They managed to find a way to really up the stakes. How can you get more dangerous than the Ancients' arch enemy? From a serious mythological perspective, it was a great stretch to go in that direction to see where the Ancients had come from was a place of a great deal of oppression. That they had made a pilgrimage to our part of the galaxy to get away from that, but they had left evil to continue to fester and their descendants would have to deal with it.

ROBERT C. COOPER: So Season 9 was very much not only just about introducing new members of the team, but also the new bad guys and how that was going to work. And Season 10 was very much about the bad guys executing the plan, the promise — coming through on what they said would come to pass, which is that they were going to come in and take over our galaxy.

In the final episode of Stargate SG-1, *"Unending," the Asgard summon SG-1 to tell them that their experiments to halt their genetic degeneration have failed, meaning they are a dying race. Because of this, the Asgard have decided to give "everything [they] have and know" to the Tau'ri — which is how the Goa'uld and Jaffa refer to humans. Thor tells Colonel Carter that the people of Earth are the Fifth Race, the other four being the Ancients, Nox, Furlings, and the Asgard. When the Ori show up, the Asgard destroy Orilla, and themselves with it, so that their technology will not fall into the hands of the Ori. With the new weapons the Asgard equipped the Odyssey with, they are able to destroy an Ori mothership with ease, but come under repeated assault from two more who chase them wherever they go.*

In a desperate attempt to stop the relentless pursuit, SG-1 and General Landry beam the crew off the ship onto an uninhabited planet and lock the ship in a time-dilation field when they are unable to separate the new upgrades from the hyperdrive. They end up spending between 50 and 60 years trapped on the ship, moments away from death if they ever stop the field. During that time, Landry dies and Daniel and Vala get together. As an old woman, Carter figures out how to reverse time so this never happens, but unless someone stays old, everything will happen the same way. It also requires temporarily allowing the ship to be destroyed to allow an energy blast to power the effect. Due to his greater lifespan, Teal'c volunteers and is able to give Carter what she needs to separate the hyperdrive quickly, and the Odyssey *escapes.*

ROBERT C. COOPER: One of the things the fans have always talked about is that they love when the team is together. And so we put them together for 50 years, just them! And you see the relationships that develop and how they evolve. And then, of course, as science fiction allows you to do, we just undid it all. I think it was kind of a fun way to say goodbye to this era of *SG-1.* We were never going to blow up the S.G.C. and kill everyone. It's apparently quite bad for the reruns! ... We want people to feel as though the Stargate universe is on-going, even though one arm of it is not being produced anymore.

BRAD WRIGHT (executive producer): The story that we came up with is a great, fitting ending to 10 years. It's very moving. ... In a way the final episode of *SG-1* is called "Unending" for a reason. It's got an element of a wrap-up. There's a look into the characters and the personality of the characters fans would never be able to see in any other story.

ROBERT C. COOPER: I know fans don't like to hear the business side of things, but I would have liked to have Richard Dean Anderson in "Unending." Unfortunately, we were over budget as it was and when it comes down to it, what justifies the salary overage from a studio perspective is a potential ratings bump that might help get us picked-up. We were already canceled at that point.

JOSEPH MALLOZZI (executive producer): Word had come down a couple of months earlier that *Stargate SG-1* was finally coming to an end. And, to be honest, despite the countless eleventh-hour reprieves that saw us coming back year after year, the many changes the show had undergone, the fact that we were producing a lofty tenth season of the series, I was genuinely surprised. And disappointed.

ROBERT C. COOPER: It really goes back to the 200th episode party. And I think I've talked about this publicly before, but it was rather unfortunate timing on the part of the network to give us the call that they were not going to renew — I wouldn't say "cancel" — they were going to not renew *SG-1* for the eleventh season. And unfortunately it was one of those good news / bad news calls, where we couldn't be really angry about it, because they were also picking up the fourth season of *Atlantis*, which was very important to us, obviously.

JOSEPH MALOZZI: With the re-shifting of the show two seasons earlier, and the promotion of Claudia Black to series regular that year, I felt the show had been revitalized and could have gone another season – at least. There were still stories to tell and I would have loved nothing better than to get a shot at telling them. And, we almost did. Soon after we got word that the show had been canceled, talks were underway to save it, talks that actually bore fruit. The plan was to produce an eleventh season of *SG-1* as an online exclusive, anticipating a business model that has saved several shows since. All the pieces were falling into place and it looked like we were going to save *SG-1* – and we would have, if not for a contractual obligation that ultimately killed the plan.

ROBERT C. COOPER: It was surprising, because I think we had felt for the first time in a very long time that we were going to do another year. The studio was really looking forward to doing an eleventh season. We had contracts for all the actors, which is usually the biggest stumbling block. And we felt that creatively the show was in good stride, and as strong as it had been in the past. And — I know certain segments of the fans disagree —we felt that it was still a pretty good show. But also, you have to understand that we are well aware of certain internal politics and business decisions and why things get done the way they're done. It wasn't that much of a surprise. Sci-Fi has a budget, and they have to make decisions about how they want to spend that money. And it was obviously still very important to them to have the Stargate franchise on their air. But shows get expensive the more you do. Ten seasons is a lot and *SG-1* was not a cheap show to make anymore.

The end of SG-1, *as these things often do, seemed to come down to a matter of ratings, in particular the fact that the network's block of reruns of the show were starting to decline after staying so strong for several years.*

ROBERT C. COOPER: The cancellation of the series was as much to do with the decline of the ratings of the Monday night rerun pack than it had anything to do with the ratings of the new episodes. What happened was, when they originally acquired *SG-1*, they had a business plan for the third window repeats that saw them getting a particular value out of running the strip for about two years. And they ended up getting four years at a level that they could only have ever dreamed about. So the value was great. And one of the things they didn't expect, but quite clearly saw, was that when there were new episodes on their air, the rerun packs did better. So it was sort of a brand awareness issue, and the fact that people felt that there were always going to be new episodes, so they kept up watching the reruns. But that can only go on for so long. The first signal for people that *SG-1* was in trouble was when the Monday night rerun pack disappeared. When those ratings started to decline, that became the harbinger of the end for the new episodes.

BRAD WRIGHT: Tom Vitale was the guy who understood the numbers at Sci-Fi, who understood how well a show was doing. It's funny, because he and I occasionally butted heads, but he was so frank and open, and his agenda was just the numbers. For example, he's the one who said not to end the show; don't tie it up in a bow, because fans want to believe that they're continuing on these missions even after it's over.

ROBERT C. COOPER: Tom also said that whenever you do things to the series that are huge changes, like killing characters or changing bad guys; things that are somewhat counter-productive to the mythology — the equivalent would be if in the last episode of *Star Trek* they crashed the Enterprise and killed everyone on board. The reruns get significantly hurt by that, because suddenly those people don't exist in the fans' minds anymore. When they're watching the old episodes, suddenly the tragedy lives in their minds, as opposed to the idea that maybe the team is still out there and it's all still really going on.

JOSEPH MALLOZZI: Looking back, I have nothing but fond memories of the show and the many, many individuals who brought it to the small screen, contributing to a series that ran an astounding 10 seasons and produced an incredible 214 episodes. Although I disagreed with the decision to cancel us, putting things in perspective, it's hard to find fault with a network that rescued us halfway through our marathon run. If not for Syfy (formerly known as Sci-Fi), *Stargate SG-1* would have ended with its fifth season on Showtime. There would have been no Mitchell or Vala, no Ori or Anubis, no

Landry, no McKay, and, perhaps most crucial of all, no Teal'c unwittingly attending a reading of *The Vagina Monologues*.

ROBERT C. COOPER: So we had to sort of scramble, because we really were proceeding as though we were going to do an eleventh season. I had a two-parter mapped out, a cliff-hanger ending for Season 10 and we were just right on the edge of when we needed to know. And Sci-Fi was, like, "So, how are you going to wrap everything up and end the series?" And I said, "We're not going to. Just because the ending isn't going to be on your air doesn't mean …"

JOSEPH MALLOZZI: It was a great ride but, like all rides – great or otherwise – it finally came to an end, in this instance with the ironically titled "Unending," episode #214, written, directed, and produced by longtime *Stargate* executive producer Robert Cooper.

ROBERT C. COOPER: The idea for "Unending" was to somehow create something that would be an emotional tribute to the 10 seasons that have come before, and to feel like it was the last chapter in the book — but not necessarily in the series of books. It was a chance to show people, using science fiction, one version of what the future might be like for these characters that they've spent so much time with and loved so much. And I think if there's one thing that fans have always been very vocal about liking about the show, it's the team and liking team episodes, and wanting to spend time where the team is all together. So … "You want a team episode? You want them to be together? I'll give you them together! They'll be together for *50 years!*"

JOSEPH MALLOZZI: "Unending" was clever in that it offered the best of both worlds: a glimpse into the future of the characters viewers had grown to know and love over the show's many years, and the promise that their present-day adventures would continue. Which they did, in two direct-to-video movies: *Ark of Truth* and *Continuum*. You can't please all of the people all of the time and, while many fans loved the series-ender, others took issue with – well, take your pick: the end of the Asgard, the absence of O'Neill, Daniel and Vala finally getting together, Sam and …Teal'c(?!). Still, I loved the way it provided answers and, even if those answers were undone at episode's end, they nevertheless hinted at possible things to come. I was sorry to see the Asgard go (after so many years, I'd come to delight in the antics of those genderless, passive-aggressive know-it-alls), but I was equally sorry to receive their parting gift, the Asgard core that has been consigned to Area 52 for long-term R&D.

Rob saved the shot of the team heading through the gate, one last time, for the very end. From what I hear, they didn't get around to it until well after midnight. I thought it bittersweet that, while everyone behind the scenes was saying their goodbyes that night, the scene that had preceded the farewells not only left the door open to future adventures, but suggested a familiarity and routine that would continue, albeit unseen. Although the fans wouldn't be privy to these future off-world travels, they could take solace in the fact that SG-1 was still out there, doing what it did best: keeping the galaxy safe for the rest of us.

ROBERT C. COOPER: I remember directing the last episode of the series and how emotional that was. We ended up going quite a bit long that day. Being our last day, we had kind of overloaded the schedule. I can't remember whose idea it was, I think it was our assistant director at the time, but we had boarded the day so that the last shot we shot was the team going through the Stargate. That ended up being, I think, around one or two o'clock in the morning and people had gone home who were not on the crew, the office staff or the other people associated with the show, all the producers and writers, and they all came back. Everybody came back at two o'clock in the morning to be there for that last shot. It was pretty emotional. The actors were all very teary in even doing the shot, having trouble holding it together. I remember that as being a sort of nice goodbye.

JOSEPH MALLOZZI: Were there plans to resurrect the Asgard in an eleventh season of *SG-1*? Every season of the show, we went in assuming it would be our last – only to be surprised with a pick-up. Until Season 10 when I was certain we'd be picked up for an 11th season – only to be canceled. Having said that, there were no concrete plans for any Season 11 stories (as we received word of the cancellation early enough that Robert Cooper was able to write a terrific series ender for the show). I think the feeling was that the direction of the series had evolved past the Asgard storylines. Still, the nice thing about science fiction is that nobody really ever stays dead – and especially not an entire alien race.

As things turned out, the Sci-Fi Channel would indeed cancel SG-1 *with the conclusion of the 10th season and rather than season 11, we would get a pair of 2008 made-for-DVD movies that would wrap up various threads from the show. The first,* Stargate: The Ark of Truth, *sees SG-1 traveling to the Ori home galaxy in search of an Ancient device that could stop the war once and for all. But the return of an old enemy — the Replicators — threatens to overrun the ship before they can accomplish their mission. The second is* Stargate: Continuum, *which begins with Teal'c and Vala vanishing during Baal's execution ceremony. The team goes back to Earth to discover that the timeline has been altered and the Stargate program no longer exists. Turns out that Baal himself has traveled to 1939 and altered things, leaving it up to the remnants of SG-1 to put things right.*

In 2009, a second spin-off series, following the successful Stargate Atlantis, *was launched in the form of* Stargate Universe, *a darker, serialized take on the concept that would last two seasons and 40 episodes.*

JOSEPH MALLOZZI: I think *Atlantis* certainly helped *SG-1.* When it premiered, Sci-Fi's Friday night was a powerhouse and the network very much wanted *SG-1* to help launch *Atlantis,* so in that respect it was very helpful. I guess then they felt *Atlantis* was capable of standing on its own two feet and they canceled *SG-1,* which I thought was kind of a mistake. Basically we'd gone 10 seasons and there was no reason we couldn't have kept going, from a creative standpoint, certainly.

BRAD WRIGHT: There was talk of season 11 that came from iTunes, who approached MGM and wanted to talk about the possibility. We recognized that it was very early in iTunes and they would have been there first. It would have been a splash and they would have been the heroes who brought back *Stargate* for one more year. But because of actor deals, writer and producer deals going into season 11, it doesn't get any cheaper and people don't work for any less. The show in general had a pretty healthy budget toward the end. And in terms of what we could and couldn't do, we didn't want to diminish it or do a smaller show. We didn't want to be, "This one we did for the money."

JOSEPH MALLOZZI: iTunes was very excited about it, but then, as talks progressed, Sci-Fi exercised this clause in their contract that didn't allow us to pursue another home. It felt like a version of calling out a game, taking the ball and going home. It was too bad; it would have been very interesting to see what would have come of that.

PAUL MULLIE: The cancellation of *SG-1* was *not* shocking to me. As good as the show was, and I would have kept making it if they'd let me, it *was* 10 seasons. People were, like, "Oh, no, we're canceled," and I was, like, "But we got to do 10 seasons." There's *nothing* to complain about there. Plus, we were still doing *Atlantis* at the time. Then *Universe* came along. So the show was ending, but not *really.*

BRAD WRIGHT: That's when we pitched the idea of the made-for-DVD movies, which became *Ark of Truth* and *Continuum.* To be honest, the goal was to do a couple of them a year and I would have been happy as hell to do that for a while, because it was a lot of fun and it kept the machine going. It would have helped, especially running alongside *Universe* had *Universe* kept going. Or even *Atlantis,* because we were going to do *SG-1* movies and *Atlantis* movies, and it was the collapse of the DVD market that killed it.

With *Atlantis*, the business model, quite frankly, was maxing out after five seasons. I won't get into the deal structure and why that was the case, but the expenses were going to go up significantly while the revenue was not. It was just the way it was structured. Season 6 was going to have to take a huge budget cut, and that show was already struggling. Rob and I got to make two *Stargate* movies, and we really enjoyed that. And the cast really enjoyed being in them. They were quite successful and a big part of MGM's business. So what we proposed was we'd do either two *SG-1* movies a year, or one *SG-1* and one *Atlantis* movie a year for a couple of years, one of each. MGM thought that doing one of each was a great idea and if they were successful, we'd do a couple of years' worth. From there we would do another series and basically be able to combine all the resources. What we had going was this large machine, and all three series were not going to be able to continue. There was no way *SG-1* was going to continue to be on after Season 10, so the thinking was if you're going to continue *SG-1* movies, why not continue *Atlantis* movies? Everyone would make more money and work less hours and it would be fun, plus they'd be able to do other things in between them. So we made *Ark of Truth* and *Continuum*, and we were writing these other movies and doing more budgeting. I think we were developing *Stargate Universe* at the time.

It seemed like the perfect plan and things were proceeding as discussed with development of a third SG-1 *film and a first one focused on* Atlantis ... *until MGM called Wright and asked him to put the brakes on things for a bit and "take a breath," because they were getting odd numbers from their DVD sales.*

BRAD WRIGHT: Long story short, *Ark of Truth* and *Continuum* were among the last two successful made-for-DVD launches. *Period*. Because the bottom fell out of the DVD market and the transition from DVDs to streaming was not anywhere near as financially viable. They knew they were going to make "X" if they put out *Continuum* as a DVD movie and it did great for the studio. Plus, it was a relatively small budget considering we had all the standing sets; it was a $7 million movie that looks like $10 million. I enjoyed making them and would have enjoyed making more, but the DVDs were going away and we were told that we needed to kill them. And that was just three or six months later; we were *so* poised and had left the *Atlantis* set up in order to come back. Then the set got stripped down; it would have been too expensive to keep it standing. The hope was that streaming would really kick in, but there was a gap during which those movies died. And I felt guilty, because I had talked the cast and crew into doing the movies.

Surprisingly, considering how successful and extensive the franchise had been, it all came to an end fairly unceremoniously. Stargate Universe *was in its second season and news of its cancellation was made public while Wright, writer/director Martin Gero and some of the cast and crew of the show were 100 miles out at sea aboard the aircraft carrier* Carl Vincent.

BRAD WRIGHT: We were out of cell phone range. *That* was when Sci-Fi, by Twitter, decided to announce they had canceled the show. We're doing an autograph session on the ship on day two and a young nervous-looking radio operator comes up to me and says, "Excuse me, Mr. Wright. I'm the radio operator from the *Carl Vincent*," and I was, like, "Oh my God, this is bad news of some sort." He goes, "I think they just canceled your show." Somebody had buzzed up and said, "You know those people you've got on the ship? Their show got canceled." And I couldn't do *anything*. I've never felt so helpless away from my cell phone. I'm doing autograph sessions and then we're doing a tour later and I'm on the fantail just doing some Q&A with some crew, while the actual actors are still signing autographs — because, who cares about the writer? So I start pacing around, wondering, "What am I going to do? I've got to figure out how to deal with this." I don't know if it was deliberate, but if it was, it was pretty smart, because I couldn't counter with any sort of statement or come up with anything until that night. Later, I'm at the airport in San Diego calling MGM and asking, "How are we going to deal with this?"

There was a time when it felt like the Stargate *juggernaut would go on forever, but like the pre-Paramount+ Star Trek and "Whedonverse" (*Buffy the Vampire Slayer, Angel, Firefly*), it seemed to have abruptly come to an end — though, in truth, there was hardly anything abrupt about any of them ending.*

PAUL MULLIE: I don't know how it happens. Like I said, I think a lot of it was TV was changing and we did change with it, but the thing that was changing outside of our control was the marketing and selling aspect of TV. *How* you make money on television. We started as a Saturday syndication kind of model and that completely changed, first with cable and then streaming. All of the ownership models of the show changed. You've got Sci-Fi involved, and they're changing how they do business. MGM is involved, and they're changing how they do business. So there was a side of it that we just couldn't control. It was, like, "That model doesn't work for us anymore, so we're canceling the show."

JOSEPH MAZZELLI: I always tell people that when I joined the franchise in Season 4 it was with the understanding that the show would go two more seasons, which would have been the end of Season 5. Then we got the pickup for Season 6 and *that* was to be our last season. And every year I assumed that season would be the last and every year we were surprised by a late season pickup. Until Season 10. I remember being on set talking to Chris Judge — I think we were shooting a two-parter — and he kind of laid out a very compelling, logical argument for why he felt *SG-1* would be picked up for an 11th season, because the two productions were kind of in sync and we were able to realize savings by producing the two shows at the same time. I thought that he was right; that we would probably get an 11th season. And, of course, that was the end and we were canceled.

PAUL MULLIE: And it doesn't matter that you're still popular. It doesn't matter that people still love the show. It's just that things have changed and in our case I was sad for everyone involved with *Universe*, because it should have gone longer. But in the case of *Stargate* as a whole, we had nothing to complain about. Even *Atlantis* with its five seasons, it was, like, yeah, we'd like to keep going, but let's focus on the positive of what we did do as opposed to what we didn't get to do. There was a little bit more of the "what we *didn't* get to do on *Universe*." For me, I would have liked to have seen that show go a little bit longer to tell those stories a little bit better. But what can you do? You make the best show you can make and then other people make those decisions. What it boiled down to is we would have kept making the shows forever if they let us, because it was *that* much fun.

BRAD WRIGHT: People speak of legacies and that *Stargate* is part of ours. Personally, I think of my legacy as having helped build up the television community in Vancouver and helped create careers. Personally, *that's* the legacy I'm most-proud of. I'm talking about showrunners, directors, actors — everyone who has gone on to have amazing careers that began with my show, and I'm proud of that. I'm prouder of that than anything. I'm also proud of *Travelers*, which was uniquely mine and the only thing that was uniquely mine, because I co-created everything else. I mean, MGM made Jonathan and I partners; we both would have done *Stargate* independently, but MGM knew we worked well together and they didn't want to piss off one or the other. When they asked us if we wanted to be partners, Jonathan and I just looked at each other, shrugged and said, "Okay." That's a classy problem, right? Rob, for having done all he did, *deserved* co-creator credit on *Atlantis* and *Universe*. He deserved that 100%, and he's so talented. Paul and Joe never got to create a *Stargate*, but they did get to run the last two seasons of *Atlantis* and probably would have eventually taken over *SGU* had we been lucky enough to continue that.

MICHAEL GREENBURG (executive producer): Richard Dean Anderson and I were there for eight seasons. It was fun! It went by pretty quickly. And what I loved about it is that I got to stay current with the state of the art technology, and composite work, the computer generated stuff that we were tying into live action. To me, it was eight years of a phenomenal grad school where you just stay current with modern technology, which in today's age is so important. If we could keep blowing people's minds week after week, and testing everyone's technical ability as well as the dramatic work that we were doing on the set, that would be amazing. But production challenges just gave us more goals to strive for and accomplish. It was a lot of fun just testing our abilities in filmmaking.

BRAD WRIGHT: We had loyalty in spades, and it went both ways. You have to stick with your people. If you think they're getting screwed financially in a deal, you have to step in and help them out. You know, the cancellation of *Universe* was the only one that hurt. With *Atlantis*, quite frankly, like I said, the business model was maxing out after five seasons. With *SG1*, we did 10 seasons and then we made two movies, with the assumption the door would be open to the future. But the cancellation of *Universe* was a tough one. I *really* wanted that third season. When it was coming to an end and we were keeping the sets up, hopefully to do a *Universe* movie, I got the call that we're not doing it. My next call was to John Lenic and I said to him, "Tear it down." He said, "Do you want to take one last look?" and I said, "I can't." But then, and this was even worse, because it happened so quickly, I decided that I *would* take one last look. I went to see what the progress was or what they had done, but it was an empty stage. They just took it out with bulldozers. It was … gone. Dumpstered. It was, like, "Oh my God, that came down fast." It was a little heartbreaking.

Stargate SG-1 aired its final episode on Sci-Fi June 22, 2007, but, like Star Trek before it, the show has continued to live on, its original fans refusing to allow it to be forgotten and new fans discovering it all the time thanks to it being featured on various streaming services at different times. And the fandom is not some ethereal thing; it's very much happening around us, whether in the form of Darren Sumner's ultimate Stargate online resource at gateworld.net, David Read continuing to interview a vast number of people associated with the franchise on his Dial the Gate YouTube channel, or the multitude of conventions — particularly Gatecon — where fans gather to share their love for the show and interact with its cast and crew. That convention was held annually between 2000 and 2010, and then again in 2016 and 2018 with a return in September 2022.

BRAD WRIGHT: My agent is the one who said, "Don't dis science fiction; it's what we call evergreen." And he's absolutely right.

RICHARD PASCO (Gatecon): The team behind the world's longest-running *Stargate* convention first got together online back in the days of dial-up. UK-based Kathryn Rogers was building a *Stargate* website in 1998 and approached Australian Allan Gowen for some help with her code. Allan had already set up his own *Stargate* site called Ausgate. They both joined another new site for the show called Stargate Command, where fans of the show could join SG teams and take part in games and quizzes. It was the first real *Stargate* fan community. My sister, Kathryn Fryn, invited me to Stargate Command. They all joined the SG8 Diplomatic team where, amongst others, they met

American Sue Seeley. As the S.G.C. community grew ever bigger, it became very clear to all that there was a huge demand for all things *Stargate*. A gathering, or convention was mentioned. Fryn decided to contact The Bridge Studios in Vancouver to tell them about our plans. None of us had ever been to a sci-fi convention before, let alone tried to organize one as we all came from unrelated backgrounds. But, perhaps naively, we didn't think it could be that difficult. Had we known then exactly what was going to be involved, we may have knocked it on the head before it began.

Weeks passed and there was no response from the studio. We came to the conclusion there was no interest from the studio side of things and at this point we almost gave up on the idea. But in a final bid, Fryn sent a new email along the lines of, "How dare you ignore the fans?" And to our surprise, this one *did* get a response, and it was a positive one. The studio told us they would be 100% behind an event, especially as the plan was to hold it in Vancouver where the show was filmed.

FRYN ROGERS (Gatecon): Over the 20 years Gatecon has been running, relationships with the cast and crew have altered considerably as the cast seem to feel at ease with the convention scene, which, for *Stargate SG-1* at least, was very new back in 2000. I, too, have relaxed into my role. These two factors combined makes for a far more casual and fun environment all round. A lot of interaction takes place at our charity auction with the actors doing their best to raise bids. These efforts contribute immensely to raising massive amounts of money for charities such as The Make a Wish Foundation, Cystic Fibrosis and Sea Shepherd. This is due to the efforts of the cast and crew as well as the staggering generosity of our wonderful attendees. And to watch the actors interact with the fans is a complete treat. Gatecon is known for "actor access" and while we try to keep it to a reasonable level, it's impossible to prevent our guests from mingling with the fans in the bar or restaurant come evening. I believe this is one of the aspects that makes Gatecon so popular, both with attendees and guests alike.

RONNY COX: Early in my career, everybody knew that I was the singer/guitar player from New Mexico, but for years I've had such success playing guys primarily in suits and ties that people get really amazed and blown away when I show up with my guitar and then play. One of the things that's been really gratifying is that I've gone to a number of *Stargate* conventions, especially in Europe, where I've done concerts for *Stargate* fans. I play Senator Kinsey/Vice President Kinsey, probably the most hated character on the show. I loved playing that character, by the way, but, first of all, when we went over to England and Germany and Scotland for these shows, I had every reason to think that they didn't really understand what folk music was. I also had every reason to believe that they might just boo us off the stage. And I have to say that the *Stargate* fans — and I'm not using hyperbole here at all — were the best fans for the music that

I ever encountered. They got every nuance of every song, they sat on the edge of their seats. It's a little embarrassing to talk about it. We had six encores. The *Stargate* fans have just been wonderful. They're so supportive of my music. It's been really gratifying to see that. I know this sounds self-aggrandizing, but they always treat me practically like royalty when I go up there. I can't say how enamored I am of all the producers and writers, and of course all the other actors [as well]. I've never been treated better. Ever.

CLIFF SIMON (actor, "Baal"): The whole show was just highlights. It was great, as have been the conventions and traveling around the world and just meeting the people who watch you. I'd probably say the conventions and the fans are the highlights because before I went into *Stargate*, as I said before, I didn't know that this happened. The highlight is actually getting to meet the people who watch you, because, generally, actors never get to meet the people who watch them. You forget people are watching you. And you get feedback — only a stage actor has immediate feedback from the audience, but with film and television, you don't know. You don't know how good you were or how bad you were. But eventually, over time with the fans, you get feedback from them and you realize, "OK, I did a good job."

RICHARD PASCO: The one thing we wanted to do was produce a show for the fans, by fans, but at the same time to make it as professional as we could from the theatrical experience of the on-stage events, including the now infamous *Stargate*-themed stage designs, to the photo shoots, the special convention magazine — that has been a central part of each event, the laminated passes and con merchandise.

JOSEPH MALLOZZI: I started on *Stargate* at a time where fandom was kind of really just getting going online. I actually went online and connected with fans, and it's something that I do to this day. What you gauge is that genre fans are passionate, but it's a double-edged sword. They can be incredibly enthusiastic and supportive, but on the other hand, when you do something they *don't* like, they *will* let you know. As time has gone on and social media has grown, their voices got louder, but sometimes I have to remember that they're kind of a vocal minority. They *will* get a lot of notice usually, but if you're someone who is enjoying the show you either don't say anything or you go on your GateWorld forum. But if you don't like something, you're going to all these other forums and complaining and putting Brad Wright "Wanted" posters online.

ALLAN GOWEN (Gatecon): In the first few seasons of *Stargate SG-1* the internet was a relatively new thing. The likes of Facebook, Twitter and even Google were still a few years away, so fans gravitated towards the early *Stargate* websites and message boards. The start of true *Stargate* communities started to gather on the first *Stargate* websites. It wasn't until the end of Season 3 that *Stargate* conventions started appearing, with a small convention in Sydney, Australia, with only one guest, then the first full blown convention with Gatecon in 2000 with close to 40 actors, directors, writers, behind the scenes staff and even some executives from MGM Television. It was then the *Stargate* fans found the production cast and crew extremely receptive and likewise to the fans, creating an almost instant atmosphere of family and ownership of the show for fans.

DAVID READ: This is not hyperbole. I am always shocked when I look at *Star Trek* fandom online and *Stargate* fandom online and *Star Wars* fandom online. Without a doubt, the *Stargate* fandom has a maturity that the other two do really lack. I think the audience skews older and is really appreciative of the content that they've had. It also benefits from being largely internally consistent and not being mucked with by successive generations. If the online series *Stargate: Origins* had taken over and taken a left turn from canon, then we would be in a different situation more than likely. Largely attributing to that is that *Stargate* has yet to be "blessed" by J.J. Abrams and the like, so there is less divisiveness in our fandom. At this point I host *Dial the Gate* chats every week and everyone is just so happy to be together. A lot of us recognize that *Stargate* is a fraction of the fan base size as some of these other sci-fi shows, so there's a sense of being in the trenches and camaraderie that we're all here together to keep this flame going, which is something that the other franchises just lack.

ALLAN GOWEN: *Stargate* fans are mostly down to earth people from almost every country and race, and everyone accepts each other. Being a show based on the U.S. Air Force, the fan community was popular with a large number of past and present military personnel. *Stargate* didn't seem to attract the "extreme fanatic" that other sci-fi franchises had, with the exception of the "Save Daniel Jackson" (SDJ'ers) campaign in 2002 when Michael Shanks left the series, where some fans showed hostility towards Corin Nemec and the part of Jonas Quinn.

PAUL MULLIE: The fans were interesting. We would have contest winners come in and there was one guy I remember who had tattoos of the patches on his arms. You look at something like that and you're like, "That's crazy." I mean, I'm glad he likes the show, but that seems a bit extreme. But, you know what? Good for him if he's connecting on that level with the show and it's making him feel good and he's getting something good out of it. We'd get fan mail and people would say nice things about how much they loved the show. I appreciated it as well as the life of the show after the fact. The thing that a lot of science-fiction shows — with *Star Trek* being one of the greatest examples of all time — have is that people still watch the show and love it, even though it's so different from the way the genre is made today. That just speaks to the quality of the writing, the quality of the production. There was something there that people could relate to.

JONATHAN GLASSNER: Back in the early days, there weren't that many fans online and they certainly weren't trying to piss people off or fight with each other the way it is now. They were genuine fans, and I'll share a sweet story. I got an email through whatever service I was on in those days — maybe Compuserve — and I received a message from a lady who wanted to thank me. She was in the hospital and suffering from a terminal illness, and had been there for months and months. For her and her husband, the only thing that made their day was watching *Stargate*, and she just wanted to thank me. I had tears in my eyes after I read that, so I immediately went and took one of our posters and went down and had the whole cast sign it for her. Got her name and the hospital room number and sent it to her. You can't do that today, because now there's 50,000 people out there and you get those sorts of emails all the time, and half of 'em aren't even true.

MICHAEL SHANKS (actor, "Daniel Jackson"): Sci-fi fans are probably the most passionate and intelligent group of fans you could ask for. The best thing about them is they kind of keep you honest, because they follow the show so closely. It's important that we have fans that are that reverent, that intelligent and they bring our game up. I think it brings the writers' game up and brings the actors' game up and everybody's obviously paying a lot closer attention to all the details that go into it, which is essentially what leads to making a better show.

PETER WILLIAMS: Science-fiction fans have opened my eyes. They really have. The conventions are a place where there is a distinct lack of judgment of other people, so you can be who you are in a science-fiction crowd. It's not just *Stargate* fans, but science-fiction fans in general. There's a lot of criticism, but *judgments* on who you are as a person aren't there. And there are interpersonal relationships; I've become friends with a lot of fans. They're always impressed for some reason that we talk to them, or even count them as friends. By and large, most of the fans have been considerate and respectful and friendly. That's really why I keep coming back and going to far-flung places.

ERICK AVARI (actor, "Kasuf"): I did a convention a few days after 9/11. That was Gatecon in 2001 in Vancouver. That was a very special one for me. It was the first one I had attended and I wasn't sure what to expect. This terrible thing had happened, the world was in shock and yet people came from all over the world despite the fact that flights were chaotic and the whole world was in panic and turmoil and this convention went on as scheduled. And it was incredibly moving. I was so touched and moved by the fans on that one, that I came back to do a total of about six in all. And I have yet to have a bad [encounter]. A lot of them have been very, very moving personal experiences. I find a lot of *Stargate* fans are handicapped in some ways and in other ways incredibly inspiring. I've always enjoyed talking to them about their lives and their triumphs, their failures, their stumbling blocks. I'm always so touched to see how much what we do as actors and storytellers affects their lives. I'm always very conscious. In fact, it's gotten me into a lot of trouble in the business, because I see very clearly how we have a responsibility to our audience to tell the truth.

DARREN SUMNER (webmaster, Gateworld.net): There are different kinds of fans. I'm sure *Star Trek* is the same way. I have always described myself as a *franchise* fan. I'm a fan of the Stargate as a mechanism of storytelling and the universe that Brad, Rob, Joe, Paul and Jonathan built. So if you give me a live action show and tell me it's canon, then I will find things about it that I like, because it fits into the fabric of the world that I love.

JOSEPH MALLOZZI: After Michael Shanks left, there was the "Save Daniel Jackson" campaign. You see it with *Star Trek* today, you see it with *Star Wars*. Like I said, it's a double-edged sword. I think you've got to be cognizant of what the fans enjoy, but you can't take dictation. It's really tough, because I get fandom. I was a fan of *Star Trek*. I get it. If you're invited to take part in something, let's say, and you do, your support is kind of fueled by the production. And then they make a creative decision that you feel kind of pulls the rug out from under you … That was kind of the Michael thing, even though it was a mutual decision, really, more driven by Michael. For me, I look back at *Star Wars* and I remember watching the first movie and loving it as a kid. I remember seeing it, I think, like 11 times. That first opening was so great; I had scrapbooks and everything. Then I went to see *The Empire Strikes Back* and it just blew my mind, because it was so amazing. And then I saw *Return of the Jedi* and halfway through the Ewoks come out and I'm, like, "What the fuck is going on?" I felt betrayed and George Lucas was, like, "Oh, no, this was always *Star Wars*." And it's, like, "No, it *wasn't*."

And so, I know a lot of people online — a lot of creators and a lot of fans — get upset with fans who basically criticize a show for changing or doing something different, and they will go out there and say, "Don't watch!" You may ask, "How can people take all this time to be so negative about something?" Well, you as a production got these people hooked, got them to support the show and now you're doing something different. Not everybody is going to like it. That's what happened with *Stargate* after Michael left, and not everybody liked it when we did *Stargate Universe*, which was totally different. I think one of the greatest gripes I see is regarding a tonal shift, which I kind of get. Basically if you're shifting tone or contradicting canon, those are the things that I think are a little more egregious. I will say, the fandom is still out there. We recently did a kind of *Stargate* tweetstorm and ended up "trending" in the U.S., Canada and all over Europe. So the fandom is still there.

ALLAN GOWEN: *Stargate* fans started to come alive again with help from Joseph Mallozzi, who began publishing a regular blog with behind the scenes photos, artwork and trivia from the set of *Stargate*. He started a huge movement within *Stargate* fandom with the #WeWantStargate twitter campaign to get MGM and streaming services to notice the popularity of the brand and the passion of the fans. Once again the community was in full voice and united in the cause to get *Stargate* back on television screens

CHRISTOPHER JUDGE (actor, "Teal'c"): One of the things that I'm proudest of, of *Stargate*, is going to conventions or going wherever and having two to three generations of a family attend. They will say, "This is how I bonded with my parents." There's just not much stuff now that families can watch together and all aspects of that family can be entertained. When people ask, "What are you proudest of?" — that's what it is, that all these families found this program to bond over.

PATRICK CURRIE (actor, "Eamon" and "Chaka"): The fans all use the word "family," and after having been to many conventions now — you get it. These people have been together for years. I've seen their relationships grow. And it's hilarious, because they start forming these bonds with us, and we unconsciously do as well. It's just a familiarity, so all of a sudden they find themselves behind the scenes of the profession that we have. And we start to actually appreciate how lucky we are to do what we do.

RICHARD DEAN ANDERSON (actor, "Jack O'Neill"): I've had fans who have been loyal to my career my entire life. I don't quite understand the attraction and that's *not* meant to be self-deprecating in any way. I know I've been lucky and extremely fortunate, and the fact is I do know, pragmatically, that I've made the most out of a limited amount of talent. I've done as much as I can. For some reason people have been attracted to it or were willing to put up with it or tolerate it or be supportive, and the experience in general has been, just as a blanket statement, quite spectacular.

AMANDA TAPPING (actress, "Samantha Carter"): There's just a huge appreciation for the fandom and there's a huge desire to say, "Thank you." And there's a whole new generation who haven't heard the same stories a hundred times, so, yay, fresh ears to listen. I probably do two conventions a year and it's just lovely. I feel so grateful to be able to meet people and thank them for the support, because that's really what it's about. The fandom is great; friendships have been formed from around the globe and they come together to Vancouver from various parts of the world to hang out together. The show is almost ancillary at this point when you see the friendships that have been formed.

For those involved with Stargate, *it's obvious that the continuing interest in the franchise is gratifying, perhaps surprising and is constantly raising the question of why it came to an end when it did, and what it is about the show that allows it to endure the way that it does.*

MICHAEL SHANKS: When we were finally canceled, I *was* surprised, because we'd survived so many years. At our own caution, from season five onwards, there was always the threat of looming cancellation. And for the first time they negotiated a two-year deal instead of the one. I wasn't even aware that cancelation was possible until I heard it. Especially based on the ratings, which weren't that bad. They were pretty good considering most of TV had dropped off 25 or 30 percent across the board. I thought we were doing just fine. And then to hear, it *was* a surprise. We thought for once that we were guaranteed and to find out that we weren't … But at the same time, after doing the show for five years, then not coming back for the sixth year, and then coming back to the show, it's hard to be terribly upset about it, because we had such a wonderful run. I'd been through so much with the show that as much as there are people out there that believed the show could go on forever, there was always the question of, "What territory haven't we discovered? We haven't gone over?" We've gone over so much. Part of me felt strangely satisfied and relieved that we were done.

BEAU BRIDGES (actor, "Hank Landry"): One of my favorite books that I ever read in my life — oh gosh, it must've probably been in my early twenties — by a man named Alan Watts called *The Wisdom of Insecurity*. And what it basically says is that all our lives, our parents and people older than us, our teachers and everyone, keep telling you that to find real happiness in life you must be secure. You want security in a job, security in family, relationships, financial, all of that, you want to be secure, and then you will be truly content. And then Mr. Watts also points out what a pain in the butt that is, because the truth is there is no such thing as security. The only thing you can really count on is that things will change. So if you spend your whole life looking for that secure, unchangeable place, you're going to be pretty frustrated most of your life. You need to just jump into the sea of change and go for it. Change usually isn't easy in the beginning. It wasn't easy for any of us to know that this show was canceled. I'm sure the fans who watched it for 10 years felt the same. But I think change is good, too, because it reinvents life for us when it happens.

BEN BROWDER (actor, "Cameron Mitchell"): The most, I guess, impressive thing about *Stargate* and about being on it and coming on so late, was how warm and welcoming and talented the cast and crew of *SG-1* were. It was a remarkable place and it was a remarkable team that was assembled to put that show together.

ROBERT C. COOPER: This is probably for a bigger, heavier conversation, but I think that *Stargate* was always a show about religion. On the one hand it was a bit of an indictment of religious systems, because of the way they subjugated people, but on the other I feel it embraced spirituality to some extent and what it did was reframe what I felt was the most positive aspects of believing in something. And that thing is believing in bettering yourself and the human race, and bettering in potentially grand ways. I loved the idea of Ascension and the idea of the Ancients and this notion that we were a second evolution of humanity on the same path to discovering how to become something better than what we were. And the Ori were kind of the bastard mutation of that, of how it could go, how ultimate power can corrupt. I do feel those aspects of the show, the races that we explored that were about that human idea of belief in some-thing, in the belief in false things and also the sort of belief in bettering ourselves and humanity, those were the things I was the most intrigued by.

CHRISTOPHER JUDGE: Originally we aired at a time that was perfect. I've always said that good sci-fi is allegory, and that's what *Stargate* was. It was a way of look-ing at our lives and being able to process that without being preached at, without being overly judgmental. It was just a door to open conversations. Another thing I think we were really good at was a sense of humor. We had a great sense of humor about our-selves and I think that really translated. On top of that, we really got along as people. So you combine a sense of humor, the topical nature of the subject matter and sci-fi and you have something. We were going through a period where sci-fi was very bleak with this very dystopian future. For me, when I was young, and to this day, sci-fi has always been about hope and something bigger than yourself, but something you are a part of. It was always very positive to me. There were obstacles, but the tone of it was positive. I really think that the hopeful tone of *Stargate* is why it's so popular now, because we're still in some crazy times and to have a show that resonates with hope, I think is very important.

BRAD WRIGHT: I've had people come up to me and say, "I just want you to know that your show was really important to me, because I had issues with my family" or "I felt alienated at school" or "I felt disenfranchised by 'X,' and your team never let me down. Your show never stabbed me in the back. It never disappointed me and always gave me what I needed emotionally." That's kind of cool, because that's *not* just the actors. That's what we were projecting. That was what the show projected. It was a positive force in a lot of people's lives and you can't *not* be proud of that.

But then there are the fans who are furious that you killed Janet Fraiser or, "Why did you destroy the show when Michael left?" I mailed a picture of me with a target drawn on it. One day I was pacing in the office and Robert said, "Sit down," and I went, "What?" Somebody had what was probably a laser pointer on my face from outside my office. Fans would come and just stare through the gate at Bridge Studios, so I just didn't know. *That* was scary. *And* it's a true story. You've got to take the good with the bad, but I do know that there are people to whom the show was important and I know there are people who saw Carter as a role model and it was a positive force in their lives. There's nothing about that that you can't feel pride in.

DAVID READ: At the end of the day, these are television shows. They are forms of entertainment. But to people like me, they are collections of little Bible stories that give you insight on how to maximize your life. There is something very sacred about that to the human spirit that science fiction really manages to capture. And you're not going to find that in doctor and lawyer shows. You're not going to find that in police procedurals, but you *do* find it in *Stargate*. You find it in nearly every single episode.

JONATHAN GLASSNER: The show was fun for so many different reasons. It was because they gave us the rope to be creative and make what we wanted to make. They ordered those initial 44 episodes so we could take our time with it and had the money to amortize over all those episodes so we could build the giant sets. I have never since been on a show that was so unlimited, and that's such a pleasure. I've directed *CSI* shows that have more money than God, but I've never run a show or written a show since then where I could just write *anything* I wanted. You know, you create a world and six weeks later there's a giant set in a warehouse that *is* that world, with 50 extras in a wardrobe from that world that never existed before. It was *such* a blast.

BRAD WRIGHT: There was such a great relationship with our cast. They say that theater companies always implode because there's too much intimacy; that people are together for too long a period of time and a group can't be together for multiple years. And film crews and casts can be the same way. But on *Stargate* it never grew to the point where I couldn't sit down with one of them and ask, "What are you *really* upset about?" The bottom line is that everybody had that sense of family.

JONATHAN GLASSNER: The cast were a pleasure to be with all the time, and Brad and Robert were always great to hang out with. I honestly can't say anything bad about anybody there. I don't know if you're aware of it, but that feeling is extremely rare.

JOSEPH MAZZOLLI: *Stargate SG-1* taught me that fans initially tune in for the hook, but they stay for the characters. And at the heart of any great sci-fi show is camaraderie and family. Or found family, if you will. So whether it's the rebels of *Star Wars* or the crew of the *Enterprise* on *Star Trek* or team SG-1, fans are tuning in to check in with their second family. They really connect with these characters and that's something I became very aware of and something that I brought to my own show, *Dark Matter* — just kind of this idea of a found family. Whenever I develop a show, it's always in the back of my mind.

MARTIN WOOD (director): What's special about *Stargate* are the four characters that we started with. It was Rick, Amanda, Chris and Michael. And that was what started the propulsion with it. And the fact that it was Brad and Jonathan Glassner, Brad and Robert Cooper, and all the other writers taking these four characters that people loved so much and giving them these amazing stories. So, if *Stargate* is going to come back, it has to come back with that kind of care taken in putting the cast together, and that kind of care taken in putting the stories together — and not just trying to bring *Stargate* back for the sake of bringing it back. Do you know what I mean? There actually has to be that thought put into building a world.

BRAD WRIGHT: When I look back at those early years. There's some really good work in there. But I've got to cut myself a little bit of slack, because it was *1997*. What we did was pretty normal for the day. Go back and watch *Columbo*. Television was made differently. We were hardly cutting edge, but it was pretty good for its time. *And we kept growing*. That's what I'm most proud of: we kept evolving, we kept growing with the times. The characters evolved and became more three dimensional. We acknowledged what came before. It was very much episodic at the start, but we did acknowledge what happened before and carried that forward.

THOMAS T. VITALE (Former EVP Programming at Syfy Channel and Chiller Network): I think the model of being a science fiction series which worked both on an episodic level and a serialized level was perfect for television in the late 1990s and early 2000s. In the genre, *The X-Files* did this, and on Syfy, *Farscape* did this. But most science fiction was purely episodic. And *The X-Files* would alternate between having purely standalone "monster-of-the-week" episodes and "mythology" episodes, but never quite figured out how to combine the two types of storytelling at once. *Farscape* became more and more serialized as the show went on, and was a wonderful TV series, but didn't quite find that balance either and was ultimately a serialized show. *Battlestar Galactica* was purely a serialized show. But *Stargate* perfected the balance between episodic and serialized storytelling throughout its run.

ROBERT C. COOPER: One of the reasons the show resonated is that it was definitely not completely on the vapid, lovey side of the spectrum, but it also wasn't on the serious side of the drama spectrum either. We liked to live in the middle and I think it was that balance that worked for a lot of people. Some people might've looked at certain aspects of the show and thought it was too silly or wacky, but we tried to have a sense of humor about stuff. We also tried to deal with some real stuff. The jokes entertain people, the other stuff is what really bonded them to the show. And what really bonded them to the characters was that they felt there was something more going on.

JOSEPH MAZZOLLI: When I joined the show in Season 4, Brad and Robert had kind of worked out all the kinks and it was a well-oiled machine. *And* the cast and crew were very much family. It was always a very positive working environment. It was always kind of tough, but everyone was happy to be there. That's not always the case on television. I mean, I've been on productions where it's been miserable with people kind of lying or throwing each other under the bus. But on *Stargate*, it was a very supportive atmosphere. Paul and I started off as co-producers and we worked our way up through the ranks to showrunners. Just a great work environment, but also a great show. It's not the type of show you see enough of today, a genre show with a hopeful message and positive characters.

PAUL MULLIE: A TV show is never going to be a nine-to-five job. Maybe it's different now, because they don't make as many episodes or whatever, but I doubt it. They're still cramming their schedule the way they always did and people are working long hours. This is a hard job, especially on the crew. Not so much on the writers and producers; we can always go home if we really want to. You know, "I'm leaving early, guys," and they're still there shooting. Obviously the more responsibility you get as a producer, the more likely you are to be there at the beginning and stay until the end. But the crew doesn't have a choice. These people are putting in the longest hours and I always marveled at them, like, "How do they maintain their energy? Why don't they get burned out?" And they do, but I think you just have to embrace what you're doing. We did the show for so long that the people who weren't really fitting in just kind of naturally fell away. We just all got to know each other so well, because we spent so much time together. And it *is* that family feeling. You're spending a lot of time with these people and you're working really hard together, and if everyone's got a good attitude then it's all about, "All right, let's just do the best we can." You're constantly getting thrown into problems, right? Like, nothing ever works the way you think it will or you show up to a location and things are wrong with it. So it becomes, "How do we fix this?" If everyone had that attitude, it's amazing. And it's a top-down kind of thing.

MICHAEL SHANKS: In the beginning, there was no franchise. We were kind of a fledgling show that didn't know what we wanted to be. We were a spinoff from a big movie, which has got *such* a big track record of working. But there is a franchise now, there is a brand name. The fact that there are so many incarnations of the same thing, whether it be the video game or the merchandising, the various shows, movies and whatever. There's a real entity out there. Obviously it doesn't rival something like *Star*

Trek or *Star Wars* in terms of its size and scope, but that it's a part of pop culture now is something that we never saw coming.

ELIZABETH HOFFMAN (actress, "Catherine Langford"): I think it's marvelous that it lasted as long as it did. And it certainly was a quality show. Everything about it. The scripts were always very exciting and the cast was wonderful. And besides being wonderful actors, they were really nice people. They always had good directors. I'm very pleased they ran that long.

TONY AMENDOLA (actor, "Bra'tac"): To be honest, I have always looked at it in terms of the longevity of the run that they had, which was unheard of for the most part. I think the only thing that could be truly compared would be *Doctor Who*, and even that wasn't consistent, year in and year out. I mean, three shows, 17 seasons, plus the movies they did. I know I was grateful for it.

MICHAEL SHANKS: One of things I always found interesting about watching future incarnations of *Star Trek* is that there was a pursuit of something *bigger* for humanity. Something out *there* — just like we are in life. We're looking for something bigger. We're looking for answers out there. And that's the key about *Stargate* and *Star Trek* that they both bring to the table. They're just regular people like you and me that are relatable to the audience, that are looking for that thing that we're all looking for in our lives. And people can relate to that. Especially if those people care about one another in their pursuit of this goal. With *peril* happening around them. And I think that's what makes a successful *Stargate*.

PAUL MULLIE: The great thing about *Stargate* is that it was contemporary; even though these people were going to other planets, they were also going to the grocery store when they got home. They weren't living in the *Jetsons* era, flying around in space cars or living underground in some kind of post-apocalyptic world. They could drive normal cars and go to the movies or whatever. When they were at work, they went to other planets and that gave the show a different feel from most science-fiction. The space-driven science-fiction was all set in the future based on the *Star Trek* model or *Firefly*.

TONY AMENDOLA: *Stargate*, as all sci-fi, mirrors the modern world. It's not about anything that's out there. It's about everything that's down here [in the heart]. If you look at the world today and you look at the world over the last two millennia, it's a similar thing. That's very exciting.

DAVID READ: With *SG-1*, you had a group of people who loved being together, and that was carried through from Brad Wright, Jonathan Glassner, Robert Cooper and, more specifically on set, Richard Dean Anderson and Michael Greenburg, and all the way down. They were very much of the mind that if we can't have fun while we're doing this, it's not worth doing at all. LTS – life's too short — is something they carried through everything that they did in terms of the people that they selected to work with. How many productions have barbecues on the lot and bring in bouncy castles for birthdays? That is what those people did. They love being together, both on the set and off the set, and it created a genuine family.

AMANDA TAPPING: It's kind of nebulous, but when it was the four of us together, and often when we were on location and the sun was shining and we were just hanging out together waiting for the setups and laughing and being stupid — *those* were my fondest memories of just feeling like a part of the team. And especially as we were starting to get to know each other, just that sort of newness and joy. And then at the very end when we did our last scene, and just that sense of accomplishment of 10 years and all the adventures and the sadness, but also the pride of having done that. And that night we shot the final episode on the final day, we all just hung out, I think we were all together in Ben's trailer and we just hung out. We sat near each other and hugged and cried. It was amazing. So many memories.

CHRISTOPHER JUDGE: Looking back on it, the only time that any of us see each other anymore is now at conventions. Everyone has kind of moved on with our lives and that speaks to the transitory kind of state of the business. You make these great friends and then sometimes you don't see them again for five, 10, 15, 20 years or whatever it is. It's really given me a real kind of perspective on what a great time we had for 10 years.

MICHAEL SHANKS: I felt proud of the show. It wasn't this empty feeling that some shows would get. We knew we were finishing [that last] season. We knew there was a potential for movies, which happened. So we felt pretty good about it overall. We had a nice lovely run and were ready to move forward.

AMANDA TAPPING: The other thing is that Robert Cooper directed the last episode. He set it up so that the very last scene that we shot was all of us going through the gate for the last time, so it was incredibly emotional. And it was a long day; about two in the morning and crew that hadn't been on the show in years, people from the office — *everybody* came to set. The set was packed with people. It was a seminal and emotional moment for all of us.

BRAD WRIGHT: I knew I was unlikely to get a better gig and stay in Canada, and

I felt a very deep, personal connection to everybody. Not just the cast, but the crew and the directors. I wanted to make sure that everybody's careers were going in the right direction and felt that so-and-so deserves a chance to do this or that. You become like a dad, to be honest, of a family or at least a stepdad and you start wanting people to grow and be the best that they can be. Sometimes that means leaving with the knowledge that they can come back. And that wasn't just actors. I mean, people went off and did other shows and they directed for other people, then they would come back and bring new, fresh ideas to us. Like, "You know what I did in this last show?" "Oh, I love that. Let's do it. That would be great!"

THOMAS P. VITALE: The chemistry amongst the actors was so strong and came across on camera. If you were lucky enough to have seen their panels at San Diego Comic-Con, you would see how close these actors were to each other and how great their chemistry together was. I also think the writing was really strong. The shows were funny and full of adventure and suspense. And just as importantly, I think the shows were imaginative. The writers took existing mythologies and spun new stories out of them, so there was an easy familiarity with the mythology of the series, which formed the basis for all the new stories that were being told. And the fact that *Stargate SG-1* and *Stargate Atlantis* worked on two levels, as an episodic adventure that a viewer could watch at any time, and also with continuing story and character arcs which rewarded loyal viewers with an even greater experience, really helped bring in viewers.

AMANDA TAPPING: If *Stargate* returns, it needs to retain a certain sense of humor and not take itself too seriously. That was part of the thing that made *Stargate* so accessible. I think it also needs a great ensemble. You know, that's the one thing that they were always good at putting together; Brad and Joe and Paul and Rob Cooper were always good at putting together ensembles that made sense and worked together. On top of that, science fiction is fast becoming science fact. So much of the technology we were imagining is now actually being used, so I think we can take it so much further, which is cool.

BRAD WRIGHT: The continuing power of *Stargate* is that it's people in a science fiction world that are from the here and now and not from some distant future. It's our sensibilities with all of our mistakes and all of our issues, but also a sense of team, a sense of having each other's back, a sense of never leaving anyone behind. All of those things are the best of military virtues that our team personified. Even with *SGU*, they were the wrong people, but they became the *right* people. They got to *Destiny* by mistake, they were never sent there intentionally and maybe one of the faults of the show is they didn't connect fast enough, but when they *did*, it was powerful and compelling. That's where we were going to go forward had we been allowed to continue.

The third thing is that we never took ourselves too seriously. We allowed the show to be funny. One of my favorite Rob Cooper comments in an interview is when he said, "As far as Brad and I are concerned, we think of the show as a comedy. We always looked for opportunities for humor, just because Richard Dean Anderson as O'Neill had that, but we can't help ourselves. It's part of how we write and part of scenes we write." That also continued in my show *Travelers*. *Travelers* is dramatic, but it's also funny. I think it adds a whole range of interaction and it takes the edge off some of the heavier stuff when we're on a suicide mission. It's not gallows humor, it just comes naturally as part of the team dynamic.

Wright certainly sounds philosophical about much of what went down, and, frustrations and disappointments aside, seems to have rolled with the way things transpired. But that didn't *stop him from recognizing what was perhaps the most personally emotional moment of the entire process and perhaps the one that best represented it all to him as well.*

BRAD WRIGHT: I had to pack up my office at Bridge Studios, which was strange. I had done *The Outer Limits* there and then I did 17 seasons of *Stargate*. All told, almost 20 years, 16 of which were in one office. Even when I stepped away from the show for a time, I said, "Nobody gets my office. I'm keeping my office," because I came back and worked and helped and worked and I would take meetings. When Rob or Paul or Joe were breaking stories, I was there sometimes. So I kept my office knowing I was going to return, but then came the time that the last show was canceled and I had to pack the office. I never imagined giving up, because I thought it would keep going. I mean, that was a pretty arrogant thing to think, but we had reasons to be confident. I'd worked with MGM since 1994; packing that office was very emotional. I was shocked at how emotional it was. My assistant came in and I said, "What are you doing here?" He said, "Helping you." He *wasn't* on the clock. It just blew me away. *Such* loyalty.

CHAPTER V: *STARGATE SG-1* EPISODE GUIDE

"That's why we've come all this way. Why we had to endure all that singing. Get rid of the last bad guy, then there's ... cake."

When Chevrons Locked was first being written, it was being done with a very specific word count in mind and, as a result, there was no intention whatsoever of offering up an episode guide. Things changed, however, and the opportunity came to expand the text. As a result, what follows is a behind-the-scenes guide to all 214 episodes of SG-1 as well as the made-for-DVD movies The Ark of Truth and Continuum. In each instance, at least one person involved with production either in front of or behind the camera offers up commentary. In certain cases, you'll note that episodes have been discussed in the first section of this book, hence there is less here.

Some notes and thanks regarding this guide. Each season begins with a breakdown in bullet point form of highlights of that particular year, which were written by and used with the permission of David Read of Dial the Gate. Additionally, Joseph Mallozzi, who was interviewed in depth for the first section, gave permission to quote him regarding different episodes from his personal blog. On top of that, long after they thought they were done being interviewed, Brad Wright, Robert C. Cooper, Jonathan Glassner and Peter DeLuise generously took the time to talk about episodes, with David and Darren Sumner of GateWorld.net supplementing things. Finally, some quotes from outside sources are credited as such.

SEASON ONE SUMMARY (1997-1998)

★ *Apophis searches the galaxy for new Goa'uld hosts, including one for his queen. He travels to Earth with his forces, unintentionally reactivating Cheyenne Mountain Complex to assess his threat. He also travels to Abydos and abducts Sha're and Skaara as potential hosts. Meanwhile, Daniel Jackson departs to search for Sha're and Skaara (who become unwilling hosts to the Goa'uld Amonet and Klorel, respectively), ordering the Abydonians to bury their Stargate for exactly one Abydonian year.*

★ *Teal'c betrays Apophis and is branded "shol'vah," paving the way for a large-scale Jaffa rebellion and also setting him up to become a member of SG-1, one of nine teams that are formed in response to Apophis' arrival on Earth.*

★ *SG-1 makes contact with the Nox, soon learning just how ancient and advanced the apparently simple people truly are.*

★ *Daniel Jackson destroys Thor's Hammer on Cimmeria, in order to free Teal'c from the Asgard anti-Goa'uld technology.*

* *Having learned about the research on the Stargate in 1945, SG-1 is sent to Heliopolis with Catherine Langford to rescue Ernest Littlefield. There, they discover the ancient meeting place of the four great races, as well as knowledge of their existence.*

* *Teal'c fails in preventing his son, Rya'c, from receiving his first prim'tah. He is forced to leave his son and wife, Drey'auc, on Chulak to fend for themselves.*

* *Nem, still searching for Omaroca, captures Daniel Jackson. Daniel recalls memories of a passage of text which reveal that she was killed by the Goa'uld Belos.*

* *Hathor is released from her Mayan prison by an archaeological expedition and, after making her way to Stargate Command, escapes through the Stargate.*

* *Nirrti wipes out the inhabitants of Hanka to prevent Stargate Command from discovering her hok'taur experiments. Cassandra, the lone survivor, is sent back to Earth as a trojan horse. But an explosive implanted within the child's body breaks down, and she survives. Janet Fraiser adopts Cassandra.*

* *The planet Tollan is destroyed by volcanic eruption, and SG-1 rescues the last evacuation team of Tollan officers. Pursued by the N.I.D., the Tollan instead depart Earth to join the Nox. (Together they will eventually find a way to send the survivors to their people's new home world, Tollana.)*

* *Stargate Command discovers the existence of a second Stargate in Antarctica, used by the Goa'uld to take humans from Earth after the Egypt gate was buried, and takes possession of it.*

* *The last survivor of Altair, Harlan, creates duplicates of SG-1 to help him maintain Hubbald's underground complex.*

* *Senator Robert Kinsey cuts funding to Stargate Command, despite a warning that the enemy may already be on their way.*

* *Having received a warning from an alternate reality (as well as a gate address to a Goa'uld stronghold), Daniel Jackson convinces the rest of SG-1 to defy orders to try and stop the impending attack on Earth. They emerge aboard Klorel's mothership, en route to destroy Earth.*

* *SG-1 and Bra'tac neutralize Apophis and Klorel's motherships.*

* *Funding to Stargate Command is reinstated.*

EPISODE GUIDE: SEASON ONE

Episode 1 & 2 (1.1 and 1.2): "Children of the Gods"
Written by Jonathan Glassner & Brad Wright
Directed by Mario Azzopardi
Guest Starring: Jay Acovone (Major Charles Kowalsky), Vairiare Bandera (Sha're), Peter Williams (Apophis)

Set about a year after the events of the feature film, the Stargate program is revived when Apophis, an alien of the same race as Ra, comes to Earth through the gate seeking hosts. After the attack, Colonel Jack O'Neill and Samantha Carter are sent to Abydos to locate and bring back Daniel Jackson. O'Neill and Daniel befriend Aphopis' first prime, Teal'c, a Jaffa (one who serves as a host to a larval Goa'uld), and he ultimately elects to join with them. He helps SG-1 return to Earth, though they cannot save Daniels wife, Sha're, or her brother, Skaara, who have been taken as hosts.

BRAD WRIGHT (co-developer/executive producer): I remember sitting with Jonathan in the editing after watching a cut of this episode and going, "I don't know how I didn't see this at the script stage," and he actually — correctly — looked at me and said, "Good script note, Brad." But the opening scenes do not feature any of our leads. In fact, it's just this action scene that starts with a really wobbly crane shot and it's just not great from the get go. We should have started the show differently. There was also not really a victory for our people in the episode, except for escape. I suppose escape *is* a victory.

JONATHAN GLASSNER (co-developer/executive producer): I have fairly fond remembrances of that episode, because the cast really gelled. I mean, they *really* became their characters very quickly and it's always such a relief as a showrunner, because you usually expect there to be at least one dog and then you start talking about how you're going to write around that dog. But we didn't have one. Even the smaller players were all really good, so I guess the biggest memory of this one I have is relief.

PETER WILLIAMS (actor, "Apophis"): When I first got the part of Apophis in "Children of the Gods," I had the image of Jay Davison's character, Ra, from the movie in my head. I was a fan of the movie and I sincerely doubted whether they could recreate *Stargate* for the small screen, but it was a gig and I was lucky enough to get cast in this part. And [all these] years later, I'm eating my words. The doubt faded long ago and I'm convinced as to the staying power of the Stargate franchise.

JONATHAN GLASSNER: My only negative on that episode was I was unhappy with the score. The guy who scored the whole rest of the show, Joel Goldsmith, he'd set up a beautiful score for "Children of the Gods" and the studio felt that it was not exciting enough — and *actiony* enough — and they made us rescore it by tracking music from the movie. They cut up pieces of the track from the movie and put it in there. Brad and I argued about it the whole time, but the studio had been so good to us and let us do so many things they didn't agree with, this was the one thing they were not going to give in on.

BRAD WRIGHT: When the opportunity came to create a new cut of "Children of the Gods," MGM asked if there was anything we could think of in terms of extra materials. For some reason I realized I was bothered that Joel Goldsmith's original score from the pilot was used, but it was remixed with David Arnold music from the movie, sometimes inelegantly — which is the polite way to put it. It's hammered all through that episode, so I said I would like to not only go back to Joel's music, but if we're doing that, I'd like to re-dit the episode and cut out a lot of things that just never worked for me, including the nudity and the one line that was worth it to go back in to change all by itself, which is Carter's, "Just because my sex organs are on the inside instead of the outside, doesn't means I can't handle whatever you can handle."

JONATHAN GLASSNER: Amanda *loves* to make fun of that line I wrote. The funny thing is, I didn't even think about the line. The reason I wrote it was to set up a joke where Rick says something to the effect of, "I don't have a problem with women, I have a problem with scientists." Truthfully, I didn't mean it to be misogynist, I meant it to be exactly the opposite, but it comes out that way anyway.

BRAD WRIGHT: I cringed in the editing room at that. Jon tried to take it out and said it was impossible, which we eventually managed to do by cutting out more lines. We brought in a different editor and went back to dailies, and cut a lot of extraneous stuff out. I think we made it a simpler, shorter story and we did a lot of the visual effects, because we'd gotten way better. So there was all of that, but we mostly did it for the score so that it would shine by itself.

DARREN SUMNER (Creator/Webmaster, GateWorld.net): "Children of the Gods" is important, because it has to do two things: set up a TV show, like any other pilot does, but it also has to continue on from and connect to the movie. It has to be credible for people who watch and love the movie, because you want to bring them along into a TV series, but it also has to make the world interesting. If you watch the movie, you know there are dead ends or maybe implied dead ends in the story, like Ra was the last of his race, or every time we go to a planet, we don't know the address home and have to find it to dial back to Earth. So the TV series simplifies all these things while still trying to operate within what the movie set up.

DAVID READ (host, YouTube channel, **Dial the Gate**): "Children of the Gods" is basically the jelly to the feature film's peanut butter; you can't have one without the other, in my opinion, because "Children of the Gods" makes the feature film better. Granted it's not where Dean Devlin and Roland Emmerich would have wanted to go in terms of direction for the characters, but Brad and Jonathan completely got what the movie's potential could be as a TV series.

DARREN SUMNER: Dialing home from wherever we're at is just one illustration of the way that Brad and Jonathan had sort of walked this tightrope of setting up their own thing within an existing universe, while also course-correcting some of that existing universe so that it would work as a weekly TV series.

DAVID READ: It's an exciting two hours; I watched this episode the first time not realizing what it was, *not* having seen the feature film. I thought the first hour was going to be it, but then it went into the second hour and, because I had to get up the next morning, I recorded it on the VCR and kept it going. I watched it the next day and was on board for the next 10 seasons.

Episode 3 (1.3): "The Enemy Within"
Written by Brad Wright
Directed by Dennis Berry
Guest Starring: Jay Acovone (Major Charles Kowalsky), Kevin McNully (Dr. Warner)

Major Charles Kawalsky, who unknowingly by the rest of the SG-1 team was infested with a Goa'uld parasite, begins demonstrating signs of possession. Despite the fact that the Symbiote is removed, the possession of Kawalsky continues, ultimately resulting in his being killed by Teal'c

JONATHAN GLASSNER: One thing we did that we thought you didn't see on network TV at the time, is set up a regular character and then kill him, like we did with Charles Kowalsky. We were trying to be a little more groundbreaking; unexpected, I guess. Later on, of course, *Game of Thrones* did it much better than we did.

BRAD WRIGHT: In the re-editing of "Children of the Gods," we removed the character of Kowalsky from the very end scene to make it more standalone, because that launched a mystery that's really dealt with in "The Enemy Within" with him being possessed by the Goa'uld. I think that change actually helps the whole run, though I got shit from some fans while other fans understood why I did it.

Episode 4 (1.4): "Emancipation"
Written by Katharyn Powers
Directed by Jeff Woolnough
Guest Starring: Cary-Hiroyuki Tagawa (Turghan), Jorge Vargas (Abu), Soon-Tik Oh (Mou-ghal), Crystal Lo (Nya)

The Shavadi, a nomadic tribe descended from the Mongols, view women as property and a tool they control to keep the demons (actually the Goa'uld) away. SG-1 arrives and shortly thereafter Carter finds herself "sold," but she eventually bests a chieftain in hand-to-hand combat, which forces the leaders to begin changing their views.

JONATHAN GLASSNER: This is my least favorite episode — in fact, I'm a bit embarrassed by it. The studio was still pushing for us to make Carter "more sexy," which we were quite resistant to. It just didn't go with her character at all. But Katharyn Powers came up with a story that gave us a way to give the studio a bit of what they wanted without breaking the character. I still remember walking on set and seeing Amanda in that low cut dress and thinking, "This is a mistake." But, of course, it was too late; we were already shooting it by then.

BRAD WRIGHT: Well, this just isn't a very good episode of television and it doesn't hold up well. I am sure it turned off a lot of people.

JONATHAN GLASSNER: We were still finding our feet on this one. If you look at the first half of season one, we had a few dogs in there and Amanda never let me leave this one down; she always blamed me for that. This episode was too preachy and we quickly realized we shouldn't be that preachy. Science fiction is an excellent medium for having little moral tales and subtle messages built into the stories, and that's what we were trying to do, but we just went too far with this one and it wasn't so subtle.

DAVID READ: The show clearly has a lot of stuff going on. It's got the team banter, the high stakes and a historical culture. Tonally the characters are still figuring them-selves out, though. And it's fortunate for us that, unlike something like *Star Trek: The Next Generation* — which took almost three years — *SG-1* doesn't take more than a quarter of a season to do so.

Episode 5 (1.5): "The Broca Divide"
Written by Jonathan Glassner
Directed by William Gereghty
Guest Starring: Teryl Rothery (Dr. Janet Frasier), Gerard Plunkett (Councillor Tuplo), Donny Wattley (Johnson), Roxana Phillip (Melosha)

The planet P3X-797 is divided into two portions, one light and the other dark. The inhabitants of the light side have a Bronze Age culture bearing similarities to the Minoan civilization, while inhabitants on the dark side are infected with a plague that transforms the people into savages. SG-1 find themselves infected and, as a result, are forced to go into lockdown when they return to Earth. Dr. Janet Frasier (the recurring Teryl Rothery) is the one who has to find a cure.

JONATHAN GLASSNER: What was really great was how thrilled we were with Richard Dean Anderson. I had no idea what he was capable of, apart from the straight man stuff he does so well, but here he had to basically play a caveman. Richard did such a fantastic job, it made us start writing more things for him to do that were fun, and stretched him beyond what he's known for.

TERYL ROTHERY (actor, "Dr. Janet Frasier"): I remember thinking, "Oh my gosh, I wonder what it's going to be like to work with Richard Dean Anderson." Sometimes you can be intimidated by certain actors and I have a lot of respect for him. Well, Rick is a delight and he immediately clicked with everyone on the show. There is a touching scene in this episode between O'Neill and Doctor Frasier in which she feels so helpless. He's been transformed into a stone age man and there's a little piece of who the colonel once was that reaches out to Frasier and says, "Experiment on me." I still get goosebumps thinking about it, because Rick did such a great job." (*TV Zone*)

Episode 6 (1.6): "The First Commandment"
Written by Robert C. Cooper
Directed by Dennis Berry
Guest Starring: William Russ (Captain Jonas Hansen), Roger R. Cross (Lieutenant Connor)

SG-1 is sent to find out what happened to SG-9, who had traveled to the plant PSX-513, only to discover that their commander had gone mad and made himself a god there. This is the sort of thing that used to happen quite a bit on the original Star Trek *as well.*

ROBERT C. COOPER: Even though this story idea got me the job on *Stargate* in the first place, I feel there were better choices that could have been made.

JONATHAN GLASSNER: That episode was another example where we were still trying to figure out what the hell sort of show *Stargate SG-1* was.

BRAD WRIGHT: Rob's first episode on staff. First time we tried a crowd duplication shot, which blew me away at the time.
JONATHAN GLASSNER: I was excited to work with William Russ. He has

played so many classic antagonists on TV and in movies and was perfect in the part of Hansen.

DAVID READ: Ask Robert Cooper and he will tell you he really regrets this episode. I think he's being too harsh. Cool technology, the drama is clearly in place, the humor in this episode really expresses the life Robert will be helping to breathe into the rest of the franchise. Sam's former fiancé? Yeah, some stuff definitely wasn't meant to survive, but almost every time I see a beautiful sunset, I still have to fight the urge to say, "When the sky's orange, it's good."

Episode 7 (1.7): "Cold Lazarus"
Written by Jeff F. King
Directed by Kenneth J. Girotti
Guest Starring: Teryl Rothery (Dr. Frasier), Harley Jane Kozak (Sara O'Neill), Kyle Graham (Charlie O'Neill)

O'Neill is replaced by a double when he is struck by an alien crystal, and that double returns to Earth with the rest of SG-1 in order to find the source of O'Neill's private pain, which, of course, is the death of his son. As time goes on, the double is becoming more and more unstable, and the real O'Neill attempts to get home to stop him.

MICHAEL GREENBURG: Rick was really into this episode, because it went back into O'Neill's relationship with his son, and anytime you do something like that, it's going to be emotional and very dramatic. Fortunately, it's a pretty light-hearted set and the director was a jokester, so he kept us going.

BRAD WRIGHT: I have always had a soft spot for this episode. I love Harley Jane Kozac's performance. RDA's, too. It was our way of dealing with the death of O'Neill's son.

JONATHAN GLASSNER: All I remember was that Brad and I teased Jeff King (the writer) incessantly about where the hell he came up with the title. Cold Lazarus usually refers to rising from the dead, not making doppelgangers. He never had an answer — "just thought it was a cool title."

DAVID READ: It was just a matter of time before this episode came along, and it's wonderful that it's sooner rather than later. O'Neill's needs to fully divest himself from the demons of his past in order to completely step out of Kurt Russell's shadow and go in a direction which will be completely different. We tie up the loose ends with Sara O'Neill and the pain of Charlie's death finds a proper place in Jack's heart. We accept this tragedy has been dealt with, and in the few occasions when it comes up later on, it is properly leveraged against Colonel O'Neill's personality.

Episode 8 (1.8): "The Nox"
Written by Hart Hanson
Directed by Charles Correll
Guest Starring: Peter Williams (Apophis), Armin Shimerman (Anteaus), Ray Xifo (Opher)

Things go terribly wrong on a mission, resulting in the deaths of a couple of members of SG-1, but a race known as the Nox — who are devoted to peace — somehow return those people to life. Despite this seeming miracle, O'Neill and others worry about how they're going to be able to defend themselves against the power of the Goa'uld.

PETER WILLIAMS: I remember this episode significantly for one particular line. It's directed towards Jack O'Neill and I yell, "Fool! I will kill you!" Kind of ironic considering what happens a little later on in the series, but I particularly enjoyed delivering that line.

BRAD WRIGHT: This was a fun episode, and Armin Shimerman was very strong. One of my favorites of the first season. I remember seeing lightning approach the location we were shooting from my office window and calling over to warn them.

JONATHAN GLASSNER: When you are just starting up a series, the first episodes are often rough, because you're still trying to figure out the show creatively and in terms of production. "The Nox" was the first episode we did that I thought, "*This* is what we should be doing!" As I recall, that's when we finally cracked what the show was. In fact, along with "Children of the Gods," that was the episode we gave writers as an example of what we wanted to do. And, being a *Star Trek* fan, I was thrilled to get to work with Armin Shimerman, who is such a wonderful actor.

DAVID READ: What an absolutely terrific new species, strongly acted. Great make-up and costumes as well. The Nox are Stargate's answer to *Star Trek's* Organians from a philosophical non-interference perspective and in some respects their powers and abilities. Brad Wright has argued that the Nox are possibly the most powerful of the Four Great Races. I just wish we could've seen more of them beyond Lya's reappearance here and there. But I get it, it's hard to make a great war drama with pacifists.

Episode 9 (1.9): "Brief Candle"
Story by Steven Barnes, Teleplay by Katharyn Powers
Directed by Mario Azzopardi

Guest Starring: Teryl Rothery (Dr. Frasier), Bobbie Phillips (Kynthia), Harrison Coe (Alekos), Gabrielle Miller (Thetys)

O'Neill is seduced by a woman named Kynthia on the planet Argos. The result of the seduction is that O'Neill is only going to live for a hundred days, which is the lifespan of an Argosian. The rest of the team seeks a cure as he continues to get older and frailer.

JAN NEWMAN (makeup artist): It was like trying to hit a moving target to get Richard ready. He didn't like to sit in the chair for very long. I think the longest Richard sat in the makeup chair was in "Brief Candle" when he aged. We never thought he was going to do that, [but] he got really into it after a while. The preparation for that is we had pictures of his father and grandfather. The designers who designed the makeup took some of those aspects and some of O'Neill's physiognomy — that's the right word — to put it together. Richard used to wear contact lenses way back. He hadn't had to wear them for a long time, but one of the things that I really wanted to make sure of is for "Brief Candle" that he had a proper contact lens that looked aging. Because as people age, their eyes change and the color changes. You can have the best makeup in the world, aging makeup, and if the eyes give it away, it doesn't work. So in this instance it did really work for him.

Episode 10 (1.10): "Thor's Hammer"
Written by Katharyn Powers
Directed by Brad Turner
Guest Starring: Gaylyn Gorg (Kendra), Vincent Hammond (Unas), Tamsin Kelsey (Gairwyn), Mark Gibbon (Thor), James Earl Jones (Voice of Unas)

SG-1 finds the descendants of Vikings when they come to the planet Cimmeria in search of allies who can stand up against the Goa'uld. There, O'Neill and Teal'c find themselves trapped in a massive labyrinth, the only escape from which is through the use of Thor's Hammer, which supposedly can destroy the Goa'uld, but keep the wielder of it safe. Additionally, there is the discovery of the original host species for the Goa'ulds, the Unas.

BRAD WRIGHT: This episode created a *ton* of story down the road, introducing the Unas and Thor, too, in a way — just not the Thor that appears in the episode. Can't do much better than James Earl Jones as the voice of the Unas. Pretty great creature make-up, too.

MICHAEL GREENBURG: Steve Johnson in LA did a great job creating the costume for the Unas. We had a ton of talented people in Vancouver to help him out, but Steve is a real pro at making these alien suits look great. The way he applies the prosthetics to their faces really utilizes the expressions of the actors.

DAVID READ: Who knew that fan reaction to the Asgard would be as amazing as it was? We got a lot of mileage out of that race and it all started with "Thor's Hammer." This is a great episode for Jack and Teal'c, and a great episode for Sam and Daniel. It really exemplifies the power of breaking the team up into twos and exploring deeper stories about the franchise through walking and talking.

Episode 11 (1.11): "The Torment of Tantalus"
Written by Robert C. Cooper
Directed by Jonathan Glassner
Guest Starring: Elizabeth Hoffman (Catherine Langford), Keene Curtis (Ernest Littlefield),
Duncan Fraser (Professor Langford), Nancy McClure (Young Catherine), Paul McGillion
(Young Ernest)

Back in 1945, Dr. Ernest Littlefield (wearing a diving helmet) had gone through the Stargate, and arrived on Heliopolis, where he's been ever since. SG-1 finds him there, and they've brought him some unexpected company: Catherine Langford (Elizabeth Hoffman), whose father discovered the Stargate in Giza in 1928 and was Littlefield's fiancé when he disappeared. The character of Langford first appeared in the Stargate *feature film.*

JONATHAN GLASSNER: For starters, this was one of the earlier episodes that Robert wrote that made me say, "This guy is good." And I got to work with two character television actors that I'd always admired and wanted to work with, Elizabeth Hoffman and Keene Curtis. Beyond that, the construction crew built this entire castle set on another planet, supposedly positioned on a ledge. Just a magnificent set. I had so much fun playing with it, because I could go in and swoop around with cranes.

ELIZABETH HOFFMAN (actress, "Catherine Langford"): I thought her sense of adventure was marvelous, as was her curiosity and intelligence.

JONATHAN GLASSNER: The script furthered the mythology of the show a lot. It set up the whole idea of a universal language and a UN sort of place where all the different races and languages were on the wall. Michael Shanks did an amazing job with that scene where he figures that all out. What was also great was shooting the footage from the past where we got to do the old time Stargate, with wood trusses around it, plus you had young Ernest going through the Stargate in a diving helmet. It also rejiggered the history as set up from the feature to say that there was a previous time where attempts had been made to open the Stargate.

BRAD WRIGHT: I think those two guys — Robert and Jon — really hit that one out of the park. Just a good episode of television, and it added so much. It added Catherine Langford, explained what had happened between the Stargate's discovery and the present. It was just really interesting and featured some really good acting, too. A beautiful story. It's one of the really good episodes, but not a huge story; it's much more personal and very much a contributor to the Stargate mythology.

DAVID READ: I loved the idea that Robert had about a universal language that is composed of the literal elements that make us all up, because when you're talking about breaking down barriers between cultures, you can't go any further than the periodic table. That's just genius as a method of communication. On top of that, they went back and mined Catherine Langford from the feature film and brought her into the present. Elizabeth Hoffman did a great job and Keene Curtis was wonderful. Everything just clicked.

DARREN SUMNER: This is when the bigger universe that the show was going to explore started to click into place. Part of the reason it works is because an episode like "The Nox" came before it, so when we discover that there used to be an alliance of four advanced races who got together in this place and communicated with one another, as a sort of United Nations of the Stars, as Daniel put it in the episode, it's important that we already met the Nox, who started to sow the seeds of this alliance.

Episode 12 (1.12): "Bloodlines"
Story by Mark Saraceni, Teleplay by Jeff F. King
Directed by Mario Azzopardi
   Guest Starring: Tony Amendola (Bra'tac), Teryl Rothery (Dr. Frasier), Salli Richardson (Drey-Auc), Neil Denis (Rya'c)

SG-1 attempts to stop the implanting of Teal'c's son, Rya'c, but when the younger man falls ill, the only thing that can save him is a symbiote. Teal'c donates his and obtains another that was stolen. Additionally, the group encounters Teal'c's first teacher, Bra'tac, who opens his eyes to the fact that the Goa'uld are false gods.

TONY AMENDOLA (actor, "Bra'tac"): I've told people before: I often do auditions and they say, "Hey, by the way, this is a recurring character." Inevitably it means, "We'll get you for less money now." It's like a little ploy. The interesting thing about this one is that I was never approached as a recurring character. It was never presented to me that way and I was really happy about that. I did a job, they liked it, they brought me back and kept bringing me back. It was really a pure, instinctual thing. I loved doing the character and they loved writing it. And from that a lot of stuff developed.

Episode 13 (1.13): "Fire and Water"
Story by Brad Wright & Katharyn Powers, Teleplay by Katharyn Powers
Directed by Allan Eastman
Guest Starring: Gerard Plunkett (Nem), Teryl Rothery (Dr. Frasier)

Due to the machinations of an amphibious being named Nem, the SG-1 team leaves PSX-866 with the belief that Daniel was killed, and they're all devastated. Daniel, who's actually alive and well, is being held by Nem, who wants to learn the truth of what happened to his mate, Omoroca, in ancient Babylon. Doing so is the only thing that will garner Daniel his freedom.

BRAD WRIGHT: In this episode, where Daniel Jackson is thought to be off-world, dead on a mission, we called the Air Force and asked how they would do a color guard for a memorial. And they said, "Why don't we send you one?" And that's what you see in the episode: actual U.S. Air Force personnel are folding the flag and doing salutes.

Episode 14 (1.14): "Hathor"
Story by David Bennett Carren & J. Larry Carroll, Teleplay by Jonathan Glassner
Directed by Brad Turner
Guest Starring: Teryl Rothery (Dr. Frasier), Susanne Braun (Hathor), Dave Hurtubise (Dr. Kleinhouse), Amanda O'Leary (Dr. Cole)

"The mother of all Goa'uld," Hathor, uses pheromones to manipulate the men of Stargate Command, and nearly turns O'Neill into a host of a larval. It comes down to the women, none of whom were infected, to rescue the men.

JONATHAN GLASSNER: This is another episode I probably would not have done, though I understand it's a bit of a cult favorite. I'll tell you where it came from. At the time, the studio was pushing us to do sexier stuff. We hadn't done enough sexy stuff and they thought that was important. They were wrong, but they thought that was important. So I sat there and thought, "OK, let me come up with some sort of sexy alien." And Katharyn Powers, she was the expert on all the mythology, said, "So there was this girl, Hathor, and she would be kind of cool." So I read up on Hathor and she *was* very sexy, very involved with sex and seducing human men, so I based a whole script around that idea so that we could satisfy them. We had already decided we weren't going to do nudity or anything, so we didn't really have to do anything sexual. It was just that we cast Susanne Braun, a South African, and she was wonderful. She wore a very sexy costume and to this day she's a big draw at all the conventions.

Episode 15 (1.15): "Singularity"
Written by Robert C. Cooper

Directed by Mario Azzopardi
Guest Starring: Teryl Rothery (Dr. Fraiser), Katie Stuart (Cassandra), Kevin McNulty (Dr. Warner)

The members of SG-7 are killed on the planet Hanka, with the exception of a child name Cassandra within whom the Goa'uld System Lord Nirrti has placed a bomb in her to kill the rescuing SG-1. Dr. Janet Frasier starts to study Cassandra, discovering that the bomb will dissolve on its own if Cassandra is kept away from the Stargate.

ROBERT C. COOPER: I'm usually against putting kids in jeopardy, but this idea was tough to resist. The old adage goes: your good guys are only as good as your bad guys are bad. So how bad are the Goa'uld? Insidious enough to put a Trojan horse bomb in a child. Carter had thus far been largely defined by her role as an Air Force captain and I wanted to humanize her a little more. The ending was debated quite passionately by the writers and cast. Some people thought that the way it was written and being shot meant Carter was committing suicide at the end, and that that was not something Carter would do. I think she had reason to believe there was hope. It was an interesting debate, though there was some precedent given that the Jack O'Neil of the original movie went through the Stargate in the first place knowing he could very well die and was possibly suicidal because he had lost his son.

AMANDA TAPPING: There are obviously defining moments for each of our characters. I think very early on in the series in "Singularity," with the elevator and the little girl — is Carter going to go get Cassie or is she going to go back up the elevator? That was a turning point, I think, for the character.

TERYL ROTHERY (actress, "Dr. Frasier"): I had a really good time doing this story, because it gave old Doc Frasier the chance to lose her lab coat, put on fatigues and carry a machine gun. However, it was the episode "Singularity" that truly served to strengthen [Frasier and Carter's] relationship. Carter became attached to this little girl named Cassandra after she and SG-1 saved her from the Goa'uld. As much as she would like to care for Cassandra, she knows she can't, because of her involvement with SG-1, so Frasier adopts the child. Thanks to the friendships Frasier has made with Sam and the others, she has become a three-dimensional character as opposed to a cardboard cutout spouting off medical jargon. (*Dreamwatch*)

ROBERT C. COOPER: In retrospect, looking back at it now, I would write it differently and maybe less ambiguous and have Carter risk her life to deliver an antidote to Cassandra that she doesn't know for sure will work.

Episode 16 (1.16): "Cor-Ai"
Written by Tom J. Astle
Directed by Mario Azzopardi
Guest Starring: Peter Williams (Apophis), David McNally (Hanno), Paulina Gillis (Byrsa Woman), Michase Armstrong (Shak'l)

Teal'c is sentenced to death by the human government of the planet Cartago, the charge a result of atrocities Teal'c had done while following Apophis. They see him very differently when the Goa'uld attack, and Teal'c fights with *them.*

CHRISTOPHER JUDGE: The episode really cuts to the quick of Teal'c's whole ideology. And that is: "You are ultimately responsible for your actions, and you have to be ready to face the consequences of those actions, no matter what position you later find yourself in. The message to me was that, though anyone can change, you're still held accountable for your actions and it's not enough to say, "Hey, I'm a different person now."

Episode 17 (1.17): "Enigma"
Written by Katharyn Powers
Directed by William Gereghty
Guest Starring: Tobin Bell (Omac), Garwin Sanford (Narim), Tom McBeath (Colonel Maybourne), Gerard Plunkett (Tuplo), Frido Betroni (Lya)

There's a sense of government betrayal after SG-1 rescues a number of highly-advanced Tollan from their world, P3X-7763, which has been experiencing violent volcanic eruptions, only to find the NID is holding them prisoner and demanding advanced technology from them. Daniel hatches a plan to allow the Tollan to find sanctuary with the Nox.

GARWIN SANFORD (actor, "Narim"): I was filming a show in South Africa, and the day before I was flying back, my agent phoned and said "*Stargate*'s phoned. They said they'd like you to guest star in the next episode. But the thing is, you start the day *after* you get back." And I'd been there for six weeks, I guess, so you fly to London, then you fly here. You're already flipping your hours majorly. And then I said, "Well can they get me a script?" But he said "No," because it was three days before. I said "OK. So can they get it to me in London? The airport?" "The London Airport takes no packages." I went, "Oh, right, of course." They'd been suffering under terrorism for a lot longer than everybody else, so they wouldn't take any packages. I said "OK, fine."

So I fly in and that night I pick up the script. Next morning you're in the wardrobe. The next morning you start filming. I was *tired* and kind of jet-lagged. I was trying to get my lines and I didn't know a lot about the show at the time, because I had been working and hadn't seen much of it. So they said, "Amanda Tapping." Again, I had no idea. I said "OK, that's great, whatever." And they said, "You're sort of a love interest for her." So I said "OK." And they'd hired me — Ricky [Dean Anderson] and the producers had used me in a couple of episodes of *MacGyver* years before, so they knew who I was. But they'd looked at my new demo tape to see what I was up to, and apparently that's what they gave Amanda, saying "Here, what do you think?" And she said "Oh, that was kind of neat." Because they'd never asked up to that point. Richard said, "This guy might be your love interest." So she had input. I guess she must've said "Yes," because I was there. I had no idea the experience was going to become working with Amanda. And that's who I worked with almost the whole episode. I didn't have much to do with anybody else.

Episode 18 (1.18): "Solitudes"
Written by Brad Wright
Directed by Martin Wood

Following the malfunction of the Stargate, O'Neill and Carter find themselves stranded on an ice planet within a cave instead of returning to base, where they struggle to survive. Revealed in the end is the fact that there is actually a second Stargate, this one located in Antarctica, which is where they are (a reveal right out of The Twilight Zone*).*

ROBERT C. COOPER: In the story department, Brad was the most famous one for coming in and having an idea, or an image, in his head or a set he wanted to build. He didn't know what the story was quite yet, but he was, like, "I want to do a story where two characters get stuck in an ice cave." Brad tends to build off really interesting imagery, or certain kernels of sci-fi, and then will construct a story around that.

BRAD WRIGHT: My reputation on *The Outer Limits* and other series is that I was always really good at getting back on budget by doing a bottle show that doesn't look like a bottle show when you build an ice cave inside a glacier and refrigerate the stage. In that case you're getting a little beyond bottle show, but it still saves money, because you can shoot it in a shorter time. We actually took a shooting day off the schedule and that's a giant chunk of money at the end of the day. And it was a nice acting opportunity for Rick and Amanda; they both played it really well.

MARTIN WOOD (director): People ask me about my favorite episodes a lot. When people look at the volume of work, it's a very hard question for me to answer. I'd rather say "In this category, *these* are the ones I like." Because, truthfully, the evolution that's happened with me in my directing "skill" has really made a difference in how I like the shows. I look at some of the old shows and I go, "Hoo, hey … I can't believe I did that."

BRAD WRIGHT: This was Martin Wood's second episode directing, and he did a *ton* of it on a crane that was placed on the set, which allowed him a sense of freedom in this set that he otherwise wouldn't have had. Richard Hudolin built a great set, too. I mean, it looked like an ice cave. And there was forced perspective for the Stargate to create the depth of zwoosh that would have created the cave. My other favorite story about "Solitudes" is the moment when O'Neill says to Carter, "I swear, that's my sidearm." Everyone thinks that it was an ad-lib, but it was definitely scripted. It's a great moment in the show and the military asked, "Wait, is that innuendo?" I said, "No, it's his sidearm, what are *you* talking about?"

MARTIN WOOD: One of my favorite shows is still "Solitudes." "Solitudes", "Small Victories" — these are shows that I can watch over and over again and look past the directing and think, "Those are my favorite shows." Things like "Grace Under Pressure" was another one of my favorites. When I'm actually thinking not just how to make it through the day and how to tell the story the best, but what can I add to this story to make it move forward in a way that becomes a more "roundful" story?

DAVID READ: This is the finest example of Brad Wright putting two people in a room and they're just being firecrackers. You can argue that it's Richard Dean Anderson and Amanda Tapping, but I would counter that it doesn't work without Brad. He reads those characters so insanely well and lets them go to places where it's only natural for them to go. He doesn't force them into any corners, and the entire episode is completely gripping despite the fact that they are stuck in their situation. This episode really expresses the commitment that these two have to each other and to their team. And when the chips are down and they feel that they're going to die, Sam calls O'Neill Jack and says that it was an honor to serve with him. There's no greater episode of camaraderie between those two. "Solitudes" is easily one of the Top 10 of the franchise.

DARREN SUMNER: In "Solitudes" you've got a Stargate malfunction story, you have a Sam-Jack story and then the third element of this discovery that the Stargate the wormhole skipped to is not on a nearby planet, it's on Earth. A second Stargate on Earth — just a great, mind-blowing story. That was the show grabbing onto the Stargate mythology and making it its own.

Episode 19 (1.19): "Tin Man"
Written by Jeff F. King
Directed by Jimmy Kaufman
Guest Starring: Teryl Rothery (Dr. Fraiser), Jay Brazeou (Harlan)

In order to survive deadly radiation from the surface, some 11,000 people from the planet Altair migrated underground, where they eventually had their minds transferred into android duplicates of themselves. Now, only one survives, Harlan (Saul Rubinek), who has secretly created android duplicates of the SG-1 team that comes to his world, transferring their memories into those bodies as well. Eventually, SG-1 goes home with the knowledge that exact duplicates of them will remain on Altair.

BRAD WRIGHT: Jon Glassner and I were flying back from LA and we had to solve a problem, because the story had evolved where Jeff King wanted to turn the team into robots, but we didn't know how to end it. Then I came up with the idea that they find their bodies. The whole notion that we were trying to solve through the episode was, "How do we get back into our bodies?" That's what an audience is going to ask. Harlan says it's impossible, but the reason for that is because the bodies are occupied. The brainstorm I had was that SG-1 hadn't been transferred into the robots, they had been *copied*. I thought it was really cool that we weren't even following "our" characters through the episode, but one hundred percent copies of them instead.

Episode 20 (1.20): "There but for the Grace of God"
Story by David Kemper, Teleplay by Robert C. Cooper
Directed by David Warry-Smith
Guest Starring: Elizabeth Hoffman (Catherine Langford), Stuart O'Connell (Marine), Michael Kopsa (News Anchor)

Inadvertently using a quantum mirror on P3R-233, Daniel is transported to an alternate universe, where he finds things are slightly different from his world. But then, when the Goa'uld launch an attack on Earth, he discovers a Stargate address from which the attack began and desperately tries to get home with this information.

ROBERT C. COOPER: Having the Air Force as official advisors was mostly awesome, but occasionally created some hiccups. The AF took issue with the Carter/O'Neill kiss, so I pulled a fast one and said it's an alternate reality; what if she's *not* in the military? Also, MGM was concerned that the script was not enough about "our" people. Who cares about another SGC? They actually wanted to scrap it early on and arguing that Daniel was still our Daniel and in jeopardy didn't satisfy them. That really forced us to further highlight that Daniel was able to get an essential piece of intel in the alternate reality that led to us being able to stop Apophis in ours.

ELIZABETH HOFFMAN: Even though this was an alternate version of Catherine, I went in playing the same lady. They did ask me to do another one, but by that time I was tending my garden and my animals and playing with my grandchildren. I decided enough is enough. I'm sorry I didn't do it. I should have, probably.

Episode 21 (1.21): "Politics"
Teleplay by Brad Wright, Excerpts by Jonathan Glassner, Brad Wright, Hart Hanson, Jeff F. King, Robert C. Cooper, Steven Barnes and Katharyn Powers
Directed by Martin Wood
Guest Starring: Ronny Cox (Senator Kinsey, Robert Wisden (Lieutenant Colonel Samuels)

Thanks to the efforts of Senator Robert Kinsey (Ronny Cox), the Stargate program is shut down for not only the cost of operating it, but because the gate itself is perceived by him to represent a worldwide threat. Of everyone on SG-1, Daniel is the most outraged as he is convinced that Apophis will be attacking Earth, just as his alternate version did in that other universe. Largely a clip show, they nonetheless make it work.

BRAD WRIGHT: One of the things I've learned about doing clip shows is to get a star, and we had a great one in Ronny Cox. And then you have to create a story that stands alone even if you don't see the clips. Before we put the clips in, I edited the show and made a tight little episode. Admittedly it was only 26 minutes long, so the remainder needed to be clips, but I knew what the clips were going to be, because, obviously, I had to set up the example without the story. The goal was to create a good dynamic. The other rule I have is that I don't have a clip in the pre-credits "tease," act one or act five, so the audience doesn't know it's a clip show until they are fully on board.

RONNY COX (actor, "Senator Kinsey"): The producers just called and asked if I would be interested in doing a show that sort of recapped their first season. We did the show and had so much fun that they and I decided we would like to do more together. Brad Wright told me the show was so successful that every time they got a script from an outside writer, Senator Kinsey was in it. I think the great thing about Kinsey, as a character, is that he is absolutely convinced that he is patriotic, good, and doing the morally correct thing. I think that's what makes him more dangerous than any other character on *Stargate SG-1*.

Episode 22 (1.22): "Within the Serpent's Grasp"
Story by James Crocker, Teleplay by Jonathan Glassner
Directed by David Warry-Smith
Guest Starring: Peter Williams (Apophis), Alexis Cruz (Skaara/Klorel), Brent Stait (Major Ferretti)

Daniel discovers an address for the Stargate to reach out to, which leads SG-1 directly to Apophis' ship. There they learn that Skaara has been turned into a host to Klorel, Apophis' son. The vessel reaches Earth orbit as does a true *global threat.*

Alexis Cruz has the distinction of being one of only two actors, along with Erick Avari (Kasuf), who were featured in both the original film and also in the same role on SG-1.

ALEXIS CRUZ (actor, "Skaara"): At the time [of the *Stargate* film], I had been accustomed to working fairly regularly as a young actor. And at that time, I hadn't worked in about a year and I was getting very desperate. I was going nuts and I didn't know what to do. Nowadays, it's a little different. We're used to the ups and downs. But at the time, we weren't. So I was desperate. I was taking anything I could get. And my agent calls me up and he says, "Well, I've got this one part, this audition for a sci-fi movie. It's a low budget sci-fi movie. You would only have three lines and they're not in English. I really don't think it's worth it" — my agent thought very highly of me, and really wanted the best for me, but I said, "I want to do it. I *have* to do it. I'm not doing anything else." There are no small actors … I decided to go anyway. What the heck? I really had nothing to lose. So I think that always ends up freeing you up a little bit creatively. And the whole scene was, really, a mime scene. A lot of physical work. So I just decided to take that route rather than concentrate on, "It's only three lines, let me say these three lines." I tried to work on all of the action, and all of the moments, and all of the life in between those lines. So I did that. And it worked out great.

Once we moved on to *SG-1*, it had already been three years since the film, so not only had I grown up, but I realized, you know, that the character would have to as well. He would have to mature. I had a lot of questions about that to begin with in terms of what the direction was for Skaara. I wanted to go in a darker direction. Heroes are great at the end of the tunnel, after they have been challenged, and this was a very different kind of challenge. This was a very internalized one, rather than an externalized one of rebellion.

I had always had it in my mind that the journey that Skaara had gone through in terms of coming up and being a little shepherd boy to confronting and ultimately destroying his god — that is profound, in and of itself, thematically. So I kind of was pushing with that.

SEASON TWO SUMMARY (1998-1999)

   * *Scientists at Area 51 recover two Goa'uld death gliders and begin to retrofit them for the X-301.*

   * *Samantha Carter is forcibly blended with Jolinar, who is on the run from a Goa'uld ashrak. Jolinar expends all of her energy to preserve Carter's life.*

   * *SG-1 is sentenced by the Taldur to life imprisonment in Hadante. The team works*

with Linea to leave the prison world. Once out, Linea, called "Destroyer of Worlds," escapes.

★ *With Thor's Hammer destroyed, Heru'ur takes Cimmeria for himself. Daniel Jackson breaks the natural cycle of Cimmerian development for the people and reveals the Asgard — their gods — prematurely. Thor arrives in the Asgard mothership Beliskner to wipe out Heru'ur's forces. But Heru'ur himself escapes.*

★ *The P5C-353 Orb is brought back to Earth, where it is opened. Stargate Command agrees to deposit the Orb on P4G-881.*

★ *Apophis takes Rya'c as his pupil. Teal'c receives word and returns to Chulak to rescue his son.*

★ *One Abydonian year to the day, Daniel returns to Abydos and finds Sha're with her father. She is pregnant, and the Goa'uld Amonet is sleeping so that the child will not emerge stillborn.*

★ *Jacob Carter informs his daughter Samantha that he has lymphoma and a terminal diagnosis.*

★ *Shifu, the son of Apophis and Amonet, is born. Heru'ur travels to Abydos to steal him, but Daniel Jackson hides the baby among the Abydonians and makes Amonet think Heru'ur was successful. Apophis, hoping to meet his newborn son, leaves only with Amonet.*

★ *SG-1 meets the Tok'ra and establishes a tentative alliance.*

★ *Selmak, in need of a new host, blends with Jacob Carter and becomes Earth's envoy. Saroosh, Selmak's previous host, dies.*

★ *SG-1 tampers with the natural balance between the Salish and their Spirits, forcing the spirits to reveal their true nature.*

★ *Rogue N.I.D. agents remove the Touchstone from Medrona, plunging the planet into an ice age. SG-1 retrieves the device and returns it to the Medronans before the damage is permanent.*

★ *Jack O'Neill accidentally downloads the entire database of the Ancient repository of knowledge into his mind. The information in his brain allows him to install numerous new Stargate addresses, not known to the Goa'uld, into the dialing computer. O'Neill sends himself to the Ida Galaxy where the Asgard remove the knowledge.*

★ *A black hole causes P3W-451 to succumb to a time dilation field, trapping SG-10 on the planet.*

* *Apophis pleas with SG-1 to protect him from Sokar. He dies of his injuries at Stargate Command. Teal'c sends his body through the Stargate to the waiting hands of Sokar, who reanimates Apophis to repeatedly torture him to death.*

* *Ma'chello tricks Daniel Jackson into transferring bodies. He leaves the base for Colorado Springs, but the authorities soon capture him. Ma'chello is forced to return to his original body, where he dies.*

* *George Hammond notices the same wound on Samantha Carter's hand, and realizes the time has come to write the note to his younger self. After an adventure in 1969 and the distant future, SG-1 returns to their proper time.*

* *Hathor captures SG-1 and stages an elaborate hoax to gain what information they have about the current Goa'uld domain. A Tok'ra agent helps free the team. O'Neill pushes Hathor into a cryogenic soup, killing her.*

EPISODE GUIDE: SEASON TWO

Episode 23 (2.1): "Serpent's Lair"
Written by Brad Wright
Directed by Jonathan Glassner
Guest Starring: Peter Williams (Apophis), Tony Amendola (Bra'tac), Alexis Cruz (Skaara / Klorel), Robert Wisden (Lieutenant Colonel Samuels)

The attempt to save Earth from Apophis' ship is successful thanks to the efforts of Teal'c and Bra'tac, who are planting bombs on the vessel to halt the attacks on the planet. In the end, both ships are destroyed and the two men escape in Death Gliders.

JONATHAN GLASSNER: I directed the season one finale and season two premiere together. For this one, we literally built a ship on a big, giant gimble that we could control and move around. The camera was on a crane, swooping in and out and it was all against the green screen. It cost a fortune to do, but it was fun. Today we do a thousand shots like that in every episode of a show like *The Ark*, which I'm currently producing.

BRAD WRIGHT: The episode where Rick has that great reaction when Daniel shows up and refers to him as a "Space Monkey," which was ad libbed.

JONATHAN GLASSNER: The other thing is that we killed Skaara at the end of part one, but we got such hate mail that we decided *not* to kill him and made it a fake out. We put him in digitally in this episode, so the rings come down and he's standing there. He wasn't actually there, but we were able to save the character's life. We never brought him back again, because we couldn't afford him, frankly. He was asking for too much money, so while we didn't kill the character, there was always the possibility he could return. *There's* an early example of responding to stuff on the Internet.

Episode 24 (2.2): "In the Line of Duty"
Written by Robert C. Cooper
Directed by Martin Wood
Guest Starring: Teryl Rothery (Dr. Fraiser), Katie Stuart (Cassandra), July Norton (Talia), Peter Lacroix (Ashrak)

Carter is possessed by the Goa'uld on the planet Nassya, and when that fact is realized, she claims to be Jolinar, a member of a legendary faction of rebel-Goa'uld who operate in opposition to the System Lords. Carter is actually saved by Jolinar following her assassination.

JONATHAN GLASSNER: The thing about the episode which is important for the series is that it's when we first mention the Tok'ra. It's funny how things develop. The Tok'ra came out of a need in that particular episode to give us a moral and ethical ambiguity on what to do about the Goa'uld that had taken over Sam Carter, but introducing the Tok'ra basically changed the whole series.

ROBERT C. COOPER: When I originally wrote this episode, it had a random SG team member who got infected with a Tok'ra. The script was written and we were about to go into prep with it, and Brad and Jonathan called me into their office and said, "We have a note here that you may not like and is going to require a page one rewrite." I was, like, "Alright, what is it?" And they said, "We want you to make that Carter." I replied, "*Yes*, that *is* a big note, which I would've been good to get at the outline stage." But it actually was a really good note and would make the script better. It turned out to be a *much* better episode. In terms of the Tok'ra as a whole, I don't think we felt we could keep Carter as one of them, but making her dad, Jacob, into a Tok'ra sort of personalized it for the whole team. And Carmen had such a likability, warmth and vulnerability to him that really made the character work. That note ended up adding so much to the show and all of a sudden it opens up all these other things.

Episode 25 (2.3): "Prisoners"
Written by Terry Curtis Fox
Directed by David Warry-Smith

Guest Starring: Bonnie Barlett (Linea), Colin Lawrence (Major Warren), Andrew Whekler (Major Stan Kovacek), Mark Acheson (Vishnor)

After being sentenced to life imprisonment on the planet Hadante, SG-1 escapes with the help of a female inmate named Linea, who has great herbal knowledge. After they set her free, they discover she is known as the "Destroyer of Worlds" for once having deliberately created a vaccine that caused a contagious sickness that killed half the population of a planet.

BRAD WRIGHT: I just remember the set being absolutely *amazing*.

JONATHAN GLASSNER: "Prisoners" was an opportunity to show that our guys don't always get it right. With one character in particular, our people screwed up and let her get away, and she will show up again in some form or another. But in order to keep the mystery, we didn't want to be unrealistic and have the team find her in the next episode, because if she can hide from every species, including the Goa'uld, she can outwit our guys for a time. She got away with some pretty nasty stuff, but we will find her!

Episode 26 (2.4): "The Gamekeeper"
Story by Jonathan Glassner & Brad Wright, Teleplay by Jonathan Glassner
Directed by Martin Wood
Guest Starring: Dwight Schultz (The Keeper), Teryl Rothery (Dr. Fraiser), Jay Acovone (Kawalsky), Michael Rogers (Colonel John Michaels), Lisa Bunting (Claire Jackson), Robert Duncan (Melburn Jackson)

SG-1 arrives on a planet where the people are living in an enclosed virtual reality environment, believing, as they have for many years, that their planet is dead. The team also becomes trapped in this virtual reality, but are able to convince the residents that their planet is not desolate, but is, in reality, beautiful. This results in the people, including SG-1, going free.

JONATHAN GLASSNER: Brad and I came up with the idea for this one while we were on a plane. We were on our way to LA for one of the award shows or something or for a meeting, and one of us said, "What if a whole planet is a game?" It kind of spun off from that, including the notion that they were basically mining our people's brains for more game material.

DARREN SUMNER: The minds of Teal'c and Captain Carter could not be tapped by the virtual reality system for experiences, most likely because of Teal'c's larval Goa'uld and Carter having been joined with a Goa'uld ("In the Line of Duty"). This is the first indication that Carter's experience with the Goa'uld Jolinar of Malkshur will have significant, lasting effects on her.

Episode 27 (2.5): "Need"
Story by Robert C. Cooper & Damian Kindler, Teleplay by Robert C. Cooper
Directed by David Warry-Smith
Guest Starring: Teryl Rotherly (Dr. Fraiser), Heather Hanson (Shyla), George Touliatos (Pyrus)

After he becomes addicted to the effects of the Goa'uld sarcophagus, Daniel Jackson falls in love with planet P3R-636's manipulative princess, the daughter of the planet's ruler, Pyrus the Godslayer, who managed to overthrow the Goa'uld overlord.

DAMIAN KINDLER (writer/creative consultant): I remember pitching ideas to Rob in season two. None of them quite fit with what they were doing, and that was fine. It wasn't the end of the world. I had a lot of other things on the go, but it was really nice that Rob was always keen to take my pitches and present them for me. I never actually had flown out there to discuss anything with Brad or Jonathan or any of those guys; I was just throwing them to Rob, going "What do you think about this?" "What do you think about that?" And then, to my shock and pleasant surprise, he called up one day and said, "By the way, we're going to give you story credit on this one," because there's a pitch that had to do with Daniel and the effects of going through the gate, and addiction, and things like that that really tied in well with another idea. It was the episode "Need." I was very happy about that and thrilled that my name was in some way associated with a really cool show.

Episode 28 (2.6): "Thor's Chariot"
Written by Katharyn Powers
Directed by William Gereghty
Guest Starring: Tamsin Kelsey (Gairwyn), Andrew Kavadas (Olaf), Douglas H. Arthurs (Heru'ur), Mark Gibbon (Thor)

As a follow up to season one's "Thor's Hammer," this is a return to Cimmeria as SG-1 helps defend the planet against invading Goa'uld. They find Thor, who reveals himself to be an Asgard. While dismayed by SG-1's interference, he responds by arriving in person and actually removing the Goa'uld from the planet.

JONATHAN GLASSNER: We had spent a fortune building an animatronic gray alien for *The Outer Limits*, and it was just sitting in storage. I suggested writing an episode that uses it (with its appearance changed a bit) and at the same time, explore who the grays are that UFO enthusiasts talk about so much. Then someone — not sure who — came up with the idea of attaching them to the Norse mythology. So we revisited Thor from "Thor's Hammer."

DAVID READ: This is the episode that really drives home the fact that there exists, somewhere in the cosmos, beings which rival the Goa'uld. Thor may be a bit of a Deus ex machina saving our cookies in the last moments of this show, but when the chips are down, Jack's comments ring true: "Love those guys!" It wasn't long before they had to introduce the Replicators to really give the Asgard a more-or-less permanent distraction.

DARREN SUMNER: The Asgard have been mentioned in past episodes, especially "Thor's Hammer," though we have not seen one until now. They bear a striking resemblance to the Roswell aliens ("Greys") reported by many alleged UFO abductees in the United States. Carter makes this observation, which is later confirmed by the Asgard: they have, in fact, visited Earth many times. They are "a friend to all, protector of all – except the Goa'uld with whom they are at war." The Asgard are at war with the Goa'uld, but it is not yet known *why* the Goa'uld are still such a powerful force in our galaxy. The Asgard are obviously more technologically advanced. It is also possible that the two races are more closely matched, but Heru'ur was sent running because the Asgard mothership caught his ship on the ground.

Episode 29 (2.7): "Message in a Bottle"
Story by Michael Greenburg & Jarrad Paul, Teleplay by Brad Wright
Directed by David Warry-Smith
Guest Starring: Teryl Rothery (Dr. Fraiser), Tobia Mehler (Lt. Graham Simmons), Gary Jones (Harriman), Kevin Conway (SG Leader), Dan Shea (Sergeant Siler)

A sphere brought back by the team from P5C-353 suddenly sprouts rods that impale O'Neill's shoulder, pinning him to the wall. Attempts to remove it reveals that it actually contains microscopic aliens that feed on energy, but are all that remains of their race. Eventually, they agree to relocate to P4G-881, thus saving O'Neill's life.

BRAD WRIGHT: Michael Greenburg came in with an idea and it ended up being a pretty fun episode. I remember pitching it to Rick, because it had to become a major stunt. A ball had these spiky things on it and we're saying, "This thing is dangerous. We need to get it out of here" and it didn't want to leave. It basically locked right onto O'Neill through his shoulder. Just a neat stunt we did, and one of our early face replacement gags. A bottle show where we stayed on the standing sets — again, those are the kind I did to pay for the other, more expensive ones.

MICHAEL GREENBURG: My big "what if" with this episode was, "What if another planet built a time capsule, but instead of a box, it was an orb that actually contained *everything* about that planet? All the information about the people, the technology — even its surviving beings — were somehow put in this orb. The reason? The planet was unfit to live on anymore. So their world is dead and the team finds the orb, brings it back and it likes Earth and wants to stay. That was the seed of the idea.

Episode 30 (2.8): "Family"
Written by Katharyn Powers
Directed by William Gereghty
Guest Starring: Tony Amendola (Bra-tac), Brook Parker (Drey'auc), Teryl Rothery (Dr. Fraiser), Peter Williams (Apophis), Neil Davis (Rya'c), Peter Bryant (Fro'tak), Jano Frandsen (Dj'nor)

Teal'c's son, Rya'c, has been kidnapped by Apophis, according to Bra'tac. SG-1 returns to Chulak, where they find that a brainwashed Rya'c is loyal only to Apophis, who has actually implanted in the younger man a deadly pathogen that, if activated, would have destroyed all life on Earth. To overcome the brainwashing, Rya'c actually needs to be blasted.

JONATHAN GLASSNER: Chris Judge was really wanting some episodes with a little more acting meat for him beyond the stoic Jaffa thing he did so well, so we came up with a real emotional story for him — and he was *awesome* in it.

DAVID READ: "Bloodlines" really left Teal'c's family in a messy situation on Chulak, and it was high time that we saw what happened after Bra'tac took Drey'auc and Rya'c away. What a twist, to turn Rya'c against his father. And we discovered yet another use for the zat gun — it's an electroshock therapy gun! They used that trick once more in "Seth" and then it quietly went away.

Episode 31 (2.9): "Secrets"
Written by Terry Curtis Fox
Directed by Duane Clark
Guest Starring: Carmen Argenziano (Jacob Carter), Vaitiare Bandera (Sha're), Peter Williams (Apophis), Douglas H. Arthurs (Heru'ur), Chris Owens (Armen Selig), Erick Avari (Kasuf), Michael Tiernan (Ryn'tak)

Fulfilling a promise to Kasuf, Sha're's father, Daniel and Teal'c have returned to Abydos, where the evil of Apophis continues to prove to have no bounds: this time Daniel's wife has been captured by the Goa'uld and impregnated by Apophis himself. Meanwhile, a reporter has learned about the Stargate program and is threatening to expose it. We also got to meet Carter's father, Jacob, as played by Carmen Argenziano.

CARMEN ARGENZIANO (actor, "Jacob Carter"): I remember they taped us [for the audition], and there were some wonderful actors I was competing with. And I was totally surprised that I was chosen, because, as I say, this is a very competitive town. Some wonderful actors were up there. Working actors — Charles Cioffi and this and that. And I went on tape and I worked on it a little bit. When I heard the news that I was selected, it was just one of my more memorable times in this business. Very seldom an actor gets a role that affects his life in such a wonderful, dramatic way as this role has. The recognition this role has brought me and the attention, the money, the security, or whatever ... at least the sense of that. Because journeyman actors don't usually have a kind of regular working situation where they're employed on a regular basis. And *Stargate* offered that to me, and I'm forever grateful.

Amanda was there from day one. Amanda is so supportive and so warm. She's such a positive influence on the set. She knows everyone's name. Always up. Always supportive. Always helping. Always contributing. And I remember when I was struggling a little bit with some lines in the first episode. She just held my hand and made a connection. And I've loved her ever since, actually.

An interesting connection to the feature film took place in this episode, with actor Erick Avari reprising his role of Kasuf, though the SG-1 *version offered more possibilities for him.*

ERICK AVARI (actor, "Kasuf"): I was shooting *The Mummy* in Morocco when my agents called and said, "Hey, they're doing this TV series of *Stargate*. It's called *SG-1* and would you like to reprise your role?" I said, 'Let me look into this and see just how they're tackling it." I realized, obviously, that it was all recast and at the time I was the first one off the movie that they had asked, so I was a little trepidation. But I was intrigued by the series. They had rounded off some corners, like Jack O'Neill's character — in the movie, that role would have been unsustainable for a series. But at the end of the movie, his character *does* heal and I think one of the wonderful things about the movie is that a lot of the characters have that arc. There is personal redemption or liberation. So he was able to now go down this other path that was much more ... should we call it TV friendly?

The issue I had was the language. They'd written the role in English and it sounded like it had possibilities. But I had to bridge this hurdle: How do you reconcile the fact that he has learned how to speak English in a matter of three years? Should we then bother with an accent? Then, speaking to the creators and the writers, they were of the opinion that they were more interested in the content rather than staying true to the details of when and how he learned English. And once I came to terms with *that*, then it was removed enough from the movie where I didn't feel like I had to go back and recreate all of the stuff, which is very hard to do, and I think that is one of the reasons why people don't do the series after the movie.

Episode 32 (2.10): "Bane"

Written by Robert C. Cooper
Directed by David Warry-Smith
Guest Starring: Teryl Rothery (Janet Fraiser), Tom McBeath (Colonel May-bourne), Scott Hylands (Dr. Timothy Harlow), Colleen Rennison (Ally), Alonso Oyarzun (Punk Leader), Richard Leacock (Sergeant), Laara Sadiq (Female Technician)

Teal'c begins to undergo a transformation when he's stung by an unknown insect on BP6-3Q1. Upon his return to Earth, his DNA begins to change to match that of the insect's. Confused, he escapes from S.G.C. and befriends a young girl. It's not spoiling anything to say that he gets better.

ROBERT C. COOPER: I always tried to find ways to humanize Teal'c and give Chris a chance to show some range. The idea started with doing *The Fly*. No one likes getting stung by a wasp, so I said to our design team, "What if the alien wasp was *so* big, you couldn't dream of just swatting it away?" Unfortunately, the practical bug ended up looking a little less creepy and scary than I imagined and a little goofy. On a TV schedule, you don't have time to fix it and find yourself saying, "I guess we'll go with that then."

PETER DELUISE: Colleen Rennison made such an impression as the young, street-smart kid, Ally, in this episode that she was cast as another young female character, Cassandra, in the episode "Rite of Passage" in season five.

Episode 33 (2.11): "The Tok'ra: Part 1"
Written by Jonathan Glassner
Directed by Brad Turner
Guest Starring: Carmen Argenziano (Jacob Carter), JR Bourne (Martouf), Sarah Douglas (Garshaw), Winston Rekert (Cordesh), Steve Makaj (Colonel Make-peace), Joy Coghill (Selmak/Saroosh), Laara Sadiq (Technician Davis), Tosca Baggoo (Tok'ra CouncilWoman), Roger Haskett (Doctor), Stephen Tibbetts (Guard)

Due to having been mentally imprinted by Jolinar in the episode "In the Line of Duty," Carter has a dream of a Stargate located on P34-353J at a hidden Tok'ra base. While SG-1 finds and connects with the Tok'ra, their suggestion of an alliance is rejected simply because the Tok'ra don't believe Earth has enough to offer. Meanwhile, Carter's father, Jacob, is dying of cancer.

JONATHAN GLASSNER: The Tok'ra came from me just saying that I was tired of all of these Goa'uld being clichéd bad guys, and the fact that they were getting a little mustache-twirling. There had to be some of them that were good. Even in the

Nazi party there were rebels who were trying to kill Hitler. So we talked about how to personalize it and came up with the idea of Carter's dad having cancer. And thank God Carmen Argenziano, who was such an amazing actor, made it his own so much. That's a good example where we didn't originally plan on doing much else with his character, but he was so good that we said we had to write more for him. And we just kept going with him.

BRAD WRIGHT: That came from an idea that we needed a sort of Fifth Column within the Goa'uld; the fact that not all of the Goa'uld were bad. *Especially* since we introduced the notion that one of the reasons they're *so* evil is their reliance on the sarcophagus to extend their lives. Basically it's a bad thing and, again, it was another smart question from Robert: Why don't we just take one of those things and use them when we need to? From there we spun the idea that maybe it isn't good for you — which was a good idea to kind of rule it out as a fix-all — and so then we realized that that means there could be Goa'uld who are okay, because they share the body. That was interesting and created the Tok'ra. It was necessary in defending ourselves against such a powerful enemy by having an inroad to someone who was equally as powerful.

ROBERT C. COOPER: This goes right back to our desire to evolve the mythology. You walk into the writer's room and you're, like, "Why is it like this? Why are we assuming all Goa'uld are bad? If they're fully-formed personalities, why are they all evil?" And even if it wasn't a question of good and evil, there must be some who disagree with the hierarchy of political standings of the ones who were in charge. So why *not* invent a Goa'uld resistance? That's how we would start many stories.

Episode 34 (2.12): "The Tok'ra: Part 2"
Written by Jonathan Glassner
Directed by Brad Turner
Guest Starring: Carmen Argenziano (Jacob Carter), JR Bourne (Martouf), Sarah Douglas (Garshaw), Winston Rekert (Cordesh), Steve Makaj (Colonel Makepeace), Joy Coghill (Selmak/Saroosh), Laara Sadiq (Technician Davis), Tosca Baggoo (Tok'ra CouncilWoman), Roger Haskett (Doctor), Stephen Tibbetts (Guard)

The previously rejected alliance is suddenly on track when Carter's father, Jacob, offers to serve as the new host to the dying Selmak.

CARMEN ARGENZIANO: This was my favorite episode, where I took the symbiote. The host/hostess of the symbiote is a wonderful Canadian actress, just a lovely lady from the theater. It was such a pleasure to work with her and Amanda that day. I did some of my best work in that scene with Joy Coghill and Amanda. I guess "Tok'ra

2" would be my first episode where I died. Although I think the fishing scene came a little too quickly. I say it at conventions: I think I died and they went fishing. I'm leaving this Earth and I thought there would be more value, more mourning, more something for old Jacob.

DAVID READ: No one can argue that the four SG-1 team members are the core of the show at this stage, but we really didn't get to know a great deal about all of their pasts. We never knew about Jack's parents. Rob Cooper argued that was because there aren't really unresolved issues for him there, but with Sam, we got a great deal of that with Jacob. He was introduced in an episode called "Secrets," where General Carter established so much backstory and tension for Carter. We can see why she joined the military now, and we can see why she is at a distance from her dad, because of how prickly he's been. In Season 3 there's also background information provided about her mother.

JONATHAN GLASSNER: The other thing is we kept saying how talented an actor Amanda was and we weren't letting her show her stuff in a deep emotional story, because it's all action, saving things and figuring things out with astrophysic technobabble. And this was an opportunity for her to have an emotional story with her dad, who she didn't get along with, but she realizes she can save him by putting a Tok'ra in him. Beyond that, it gave us some great future episodes by having this rebel force out there and having Carmen representing them. That was *so* valuable.

DAVID READ: Carmen Argenziano was one of the bright lights of the franchise, and this really is his true introduction — going through his illness and being visited by Hammond. We see that there's a legacy connection between these two, and then on top of that we have the introduction of the Tok'ra as a society, which was only hinted at in the critical episode "In the Line of Duty." It was a great idea that there was this antithesis for the Goa'uld force; that there were conscientious objectors to the Goa'uld philosophy who were also Goa'uld themselves. It was one of those great ideas that exemplifies the coolness of science fiction.

DARREN SUMNER: This was the point in the middle of season two where the show really started to click with me as the type of show that it was: episodic while continuing to pay attention to and honor its mythology, paying things off that viewers will recognize from previous episodes. But it wasn't the old style of completely self-contained, hit the reset button at the end of the episode, because they might air out of order later from the eighties and nineties. This was a show that was respecting its viewers for paying attention and continuing to develop these underlying plot lines and relationships and character dynamics. So when Martouf comes back later in Season 2, when we see Jacob Carter come back in Season 2, when we give the Tok'ra their own GDO with a code to transmit to Stargate Command, those things are all step-by-step extensions of what's set up in this two-parter.

Episode 35 (2.13): "Spirits"
Written by Tor Alexander Valenza
Directed by Martin Wood
Guest Starring: Rodney A. Grant (Tonané), Alex Zahara (Xe'ls), Christina Cox (T'akaya), Kevin McNulty (Dr. Warner), Roger R. Cross (Captain Conner), Chief Leonard George (Elder #1), Byron Chief Moon (Elder #2), Jason Calders (Alien #1), Laara Sadiq (Female Technician)

SG-1 discovers migratory people descended from the Native American Salish tribes on PXY-887. The Salish refuse to allow S.G.C. to mine their planet's large deposits of the valuable mental trinium, believing it would upset the spirits of the natural world. Under pressure from above, General Hammond orders mining to proceed anyway, which naturally incurs the anger of the "spirits," who are actually a highly advanced alien race that had freed the Salish from the Goa'uld long ago. S.G.C. is attacked, but SG-1 convinces them that burying their Stargate would be a better solution than destroying the base.

ALEX ZAHARA (actor, "Xe'ls"): I actually auditioned for an episode of *Stargate* before the first one that I did and got it, but what had happened was casting director Carol Kelsay, who I work with now, apparently there was a mistake in timing. She didn't get back to my agent in time, but it was a good thing because there was another show phoning up just after here. *The Sentinel* TV show said, "We loved Alex. Here's the days. Here's the money. We want him." My agent, Ken Walker, said "That's cool, but *Stargate* has first dibs because he auditioned first and they're interested. I've got to give her [Carol] 24 hours." So he called back, and for whatever reason she didn't get the message, or this or that happened. They didn't get back to him, so we went with the other show.

They [*Stargate*] phoned back the next day and said "OK, here's what we want for Alex." And he said "Look, I'm sorry, I had to let ..." I'm thinking, "Oh, I pissed somebody off." Pardon the language. Anyway, long story short, in the end, I was supposed to be an alien in that with big makeup, but Gillian Barber, I believe, ended up playing the character, and they just put a little veil in front of her face. So here's the deal. Had I got that gig, who knows? Because they would've seen my face the first time! They may have been reluctant to bring me in for anything else. So it was actually a gift that there was a little miss-timing there, because I may have done one episode and you never would have seen me again.

Episode 36 (2.14): "Touchstone"

Written by Sam Egan
Directed by Brad Turner
Guest Starring: Tom McBeath (Maybourne), Matthew Walker (Roham), Jerry Wasserman (Whitlow), Tiffany Knight (Princess La Moor), Eric Breker (Major Reynolds), Conan Graham (N.I.D. Man)

SG-1 is accused by the people of Madrona of having stolen an artifact that's used to control their planet's weather. The claim is that people dressed in S.G.C. uniforms arrived through the Stargate, which causes O'Neill and the others to consider the idea that the Antarctica gate is secretly being used.

Primarily a traveling stage actor, guest star Tom McBeath, who played Colonel Harry Maybourne in nearly a dozen episodes of Stargate, *continues to fondly look back at his time on the show.*

TOM MCBEATH (actor, "Colonel Harry Maybourne"): When I auditioned for it, they said it was possibly recurring, and then the first couple years I think I only did one a year, maybe two. He was just this small, pain in the ass N.I.D. guy and a relatively boring character to play. Luckily, they kept writing stuff and I got to fall out of uniform. It's [actually] a very small part of my life, *Stargate*, and over the six or seven years I've only done 10 episodes. So it does not consume me. I enjoyed going back there as an actor and working with that group of people a lot, and I would have loved to do it more. But the character only raises his ugly head once a year, twice a year. You take what's on the page and you try to make the most of it. You try to find something. You don't look for the easy choices. You try to find the quirky stuff, the fun stuff that really makes it lift off the page and become entertaining. To start wishing that they would write it another way — sometimes you'll get the script and you'll look at it and you'll go, "Oh, God," and you'll wish they had written something else. But there's nothing particular in my mind. As an actor you just take what's there and try to go with it.

Episode 37 (2.15): "The Fifth Race"
Written by Robert C. Cooper
Directed by David Warry-Smith
Guest Starring: Teryl Rothery (Dr. Janet Fraiser), Tobias Mehler (Lieutenant Graham Simmons), Dan Shea (Sergeant Siler), David Adams (Expert)

With SG-1 on P3R-272, O'Neill abruptly finds alien knowledge downloaded into his brain through an Ancient Repository of Knowledge. His mind is threatening to be destroyed by the sheer quantity of information, until somewhere in what he's obtained, he's able to find the address for a Stargate on the Asgard home world. Heading there, they are able to remove the information and save his life.

BRAD WRIGHT: Of the early seasons, I think probably "The Fifth Race" is the closest to the quintessential episode. It's funny, sad, it's got aliens, it's a team episode. Just a good episode of television and most people think it's one of the top five episodes in part because it makes O'Neill special in ways that aren't self-evident. He downplays his intelligence and downplays his heroism, it's his ability to survive that whole thing of having all the Ancient knowledge in his head that's really interesting. And it introduces the Asgard in a bigger way and makes *us* the Fifth Race. It builds, again, upon the mythology of *Stargate*. So there is the Asgard out there and they think we're special, and they think O'Neill is special in particular. So much so that they name a big ship after him. It was just a good, fun, engaging episode that built upon a lot of things.

DAVID READ: An episode that really shows Richard Dean Anderson's breadth as an actor, especially because in most of it he's not even talking, yet he's 100% present throughout. The Asgard were one of those races were Rob was, like, "Fans are either going to love them or hate them," but Rick loved working with the puppet. All of this comes through loud and clear in the show when we get an episode where it deepens the mythology of the four great races, and also really introduces us to the Asgard. This is an episode that is so well-known for its final line about the meaning of life; the idea that we're going to be alright. I think about this episode all the time, because when you watch the news, when I see how awfully people treat each other, I'm reminded of that line and I do believe it. That at the end of the day, we're going to be alright.

ROBERT C. COOPER: The fun behind the scenes aspect of this one was me just trying to have a better relationship with Richard Dean Anderson. He was a tough nut to crack. He kind of came into it with commitment to Brad and Jon, and I was this smart alec young writer who would come on set every now and then. It definitely took him a while to warm up to me. I remember there was a script — I don't remember which one it was — in the second season that I had written and it came back with Rick's notes on it, as they often did. I got a copy and it had check marks all over it. I was, like, "Oh, cool, Rick really likes it." Then I went into Brad's office, which might have been Jonathan's office, and I said, "Oh, this is great news. Rick really likes my script," and he just shook his head. I said, "Check marks are bad, aren't they?" But that was kind of Rick.

I avoided writing a heavily O'Neill-based episode for that reason; I was a little intimidated and shy. I felt like this was my opportunity to do a heavy O'Neill episode, but I was a little afraid Rick would have an issue playing opposite the puppet. I have to say, in some respects I misinterpreted Rick's apparent disdain for the science fiction elements of the show; he would often be the guy who would poke fun at those parts of the show, so I thought he would not want to play those scenes opposite the puppet. I went down to his trailer — it was the first time I had done that — to talk to him about the episode. Well, that was the beginning of our relationship in a way. At the end of the day, he *loved* working with Thor. He loved the puppet. In fact, sometimes he loved acting with the puppet more than he did with people. And then that whole memory issue that went on in that episode kind of got me over the hump of my relationship with Rick, which was pretty good from that point on.

Episode 38 (2.16): "A Matter of Time"
Story by Misha Rashovich, Teleplay by Brad Wright
Directed by Martin Wood
Guest Starring: Marshall Teague (Colonel Frank Cromwell), Teryl Rothery (Dr. Janet Fraiser), Tobias Mehler (Lt. Graham Simmons), Colin Cunningham (Major Davis), Dan Shea (Sergeant Siler), Biski Gugushe (SG Guard), Kurt Max Runte (Major Boyd), Jim Thorburn (Watts)

SG-10 is stranded on planet P3W-451, which is close to a newly-formed black hole. Opening the gate to find out what happened, S.G.C. finds they cannot close it again due to the intense gravity of the black hole, which is resulting in a time dilation. If the Stargate is not shut down, S.G.C. and then Earth itself will be destroyed.

BRAD WRIGHT: Every now and then we used a straight ahead science fiction "high concept." I don't think we could get away with shoot-em-up episodes every week. "A Matter of Time" was one of those stories where we used a sci-fi staple — in this case, a black hole and all the phenomena associated with that — and built the episode around it.

Episode 39 (2.17): "Holiday"
Written by Tor Alexander Valenza
Directed by David Warry-Smith
Guest Starring: Michael Shanks (Ma'chello), Teryl Rothery (Dr. Janet Fraiser), Alvin Sanders (Fred), Melanie Skehar (Waitress), Darryl Scheelar (Cop)

Daniel is manipulated by an elderly man named Ma'chello into switching bodies after being lured in by tales of him being hunted by the Goa'uld as a result of his inventions created to fight them. Now when Machello takes off in Daniel's body, he more or less is leaving Daniel to die.

JONATHAN GLASSNER: That one was fun, because Michael got to play Jackson with Ma'chello in him, Ma'chello himself and Michello with Jackson in him. *And* he nailed all four, including Daniel himself, with subtle differences in each.

Episode 40 (2.18): "Serpent's Song"
Written by Katharyn Powers
Directed by Peter DeLuise
Guest Starring: Peter Williams (Apophis), Teryl Rothery (Dr. Janet Fraiser), JR Bourne (Martouf), Tobias Mehler (Lt. Simmons), Peter Lacroix (Ashrak), Dan Shea (Sergeant Siler)

After Apophis' death glider crashes on PB5-926, he is brought, dying, to S.G.C.. System Lord Sokar (David Palffy) wants him and plans to attack Earth — until S.G.C. hands over the dead body of Apophis. When Sokar leaves, S.G.C. is told that there is no doubt he will use a sarcophagus to revive him and continuously torture him.

PETER DELUISE: When I was invited to direct the episode, first off I was reminded of a movie called *Brian's Song*, which was an ode to a football player who is slowly dying. In "Serpent's Song," I was moved by the title, because I realized we were going to help Apophis die. He'd subjected everyone to a season and a half of arch enemy type things, he was not loved and each member of SG-1 was given an opportunity to have a scene with him to say goodbye. The most interesting thing for me was that it was my first episode and I had to watch pretty much every single one before that to get a real feel for the show and to know exactly how everything was interplaying. It was a challenge, but I was determined to make myself indispensable to the show. I watched all the episodes, which at that time were on videotape, so I had a *stack* of plastic video cassette tapes and I watched them all, making myself super familiar with the episodes.

I followed along in script with the dialogue and I saw over time there was a method to Brad Wright's writing about when he uses the Goa'uld, and they would use the same words every time. The word "Kek" came up, which was death or kill. There would also be subtitles, so I would make a note of those. Over time I collected enough of those and they actually came together to create the Goa'uld bible. It was a great reference just for consistency, and Brad was super keen about that.

Early on I also decided to put myself in my episodes in various little cameos for the sake of fun, not unlike Alfred Hitchcock. I put myself on camera sometimes, or I would put a still frame of my picture in a personnel file or something like that.

DAVID PALFFY (actor, "Sokar"): The preparation in playing a god is the same I suppose as any role I take on. Even with the gods there's a sense of heightened reality that demands a slight reliance on the voice, articulation and body movement that you have to be aware of. But not to the extent of these kinds of externals, which I may say get in the way of what your emotional directives are. The only thing is you first, like anything, go at it from the emotional perspective — to give it justification, emotionally — of why they do what they do. And then, because they are, as I said, characters of heightened reality, you can afford to add a walk or a way that they look. Because the thing is you're dealing with aliens. The fun is finding a certain attribute with them that you can put on what's called an external — a hand movement, the way they look — that sets them apart from the human race. Even though, yes, a lot of the gods have penetrated human form, I find there's something interesting in finding something non-human about the way they move. *That's* basically the difference. I mean, basically you treat it the same as anything, except with playing with these gods you're able to add that extra external onto the character.

DeLuise gives guest star Peter Williams a lot of credit for physical discomfort he had to undergo as Apophis in this episode, who found himself aging thousands of years.

PETER DELUISE: We had to put cataract lenses in his eyes, so he was essentially blind *and* restrained to the bed *and* wearing old age makeup. But he was a really super good sport about that. And, of course, he was speaking in ancient Egyptian, which was thankless in itself. And if he had to pee, I'd never know, because he didn't complain about it.

Episode #41 (2.19): "One False Step"
Written by Michael Kaplan & John Sanborn
Directed by William Corcoran
Guest Starring: Colin Heath (Alien), Teryl Rothery (Janet Fraiser), Daniel Bacon (Technician), David Cameron (Elder), Richard DeKlerk (Joe), Shaun Phillips (Jim)

When an unmanaged aerial vehicle inadvertently kills a large white plant on PJ2-445, SG-1 learns that the inhabitants are dying in large numbers due to their dependency on that plant. A remedy needs to be discovered before the entire civilization is made extinct.

BRAD WRIGHT: We hired a clown performer from Cirque as the lead alien character, and he helped the others to move the same way. It worked nicely.

JONATHAN GLASSNER: Cirque de Soleil was in its infancy at the time, but by hiring some of their acrobats, we were able to utilize that interesting mime-like movement they did.

Episode #42 (2.20): "Show and Tell"
Written by Jonathan Glassner
Directed by Peter DeLuise
Guest Starring: Carmen Argenziano (Jacob Carter), Jeff Gulka (Charlie), Teryl
Rothery (Janet Fraiser), Daniel Bacon (Technician)

*A young boy arrives through the Stargate and warns of a plot by invisible aliens to destroy the
human race in an effort to deny the Goa'uld of potential hosts.*

PETER DELUISE: A fun memory of mine is Jeff Gulka playing Charlie. He was
coming into the gate room and the core cast was in the control room, so there was this
momentary pause where this little kid came out and the entire cast had to physically
move from the control room into the gate room. There was just this wonderful dichotomy of these giant 50 caliber machine guns being pointed at this tiny child. I thought,
"Wouldn't it be great if one of the 'extras' is kind of looking around the shield of his
50-caliber machine gun and is sort of, like, 'Is that a little kid I'm pointing the gun at?'"
For financial reasons I can't direct an extra to perform, so I thought I'd just do it myself,
which was a great excuse for me being the machine gun guard and doing one of my
on-camera cameos. I was thrilled to be able to participate.

JONATHAN GLASSNER: Another example of creativity coming out of necessity.
We were over budget and couldn't afford to create a new creature, yet we needed to
do an invasion show set on Earth so we didn't have to go somewhere. So we came up
with an invisible creature, but the truth is that invisible creatures can be scary. Check
out the Predator film, *Prey*, as an example.

Episode #43 (2.21): "1969"
Written by Brad Wright
Directed by Charles Correll
Guest Starring: Alex Zahara (Michael), Aaron Pearl (Lt. George Hammond), Amber
Rothwell (Jenny), Pamela Perry (Cassandra), Daniel Bacon (Technician), Glynis Da-
vies (Catherine), Fred Henderson (Major Thornbird), Sean Campbell (Sergeant), Efosa
Otuomagie (Security Police)

*A solar flare occurring while they're moving through the Stargate propels SG 1 back in time to
1969 on Earth. There they meet Lieutenant Hammond (the younger version of the general) and
enlist his aid, eventually finding the Stargate in that year and activating it during another solar
fare, resulting in them being sent back home.*

BRAD WRIGHT: What I love about "1969" is that it doesn't take itself too seriously. That's something we consciously tried to avoid with the show. One of the things that made us different from a lot of the other shows on television at the time was our ability to laugh at ourselves and be a little bit off-beat every now and then. At the same time, there was a scene with two young kids going off to war and O'Neill couldn't say anything. *That* was a little powerful.

PETER DELUISE: The puddle passed through from the episode "1969" was used several times after that by me in an effort to save money and, more importantly, time. The visual effects of the Away Team going through the puddle cost rendering time and money and also studio time. All that was required was they be dressed the same and I was able to use the same piece of footage in several episodes.

BRAD WRIGHT: Just a fun episode where it breaks a couple of rules of my own, like having O'Neill start a fire with his zat gun. In my mind, I believe there was already a little fire and he just kind of made the fire a little bigger.

Episode #44 (2.22): "Out of Mind
Story by Jonathan Glassner & Brad Wright, Teleplay by Jonathan Glassner, Excerpts by Hart Hanson, Katharyn Powers, Robert C. Cooper, James Crocker, Jonathan Glassner, Brad Wright, Terry Curtis Fox, David Bennett Carren, J. Larry Carroll, Michael Greenburg & Jarrad Paul
Directed by Martin Wood
Guest Starring: Teryl Rothery (Janet Fraiser), Suanne Braun (Hathor), Tom Butler (Trofsky), Samantha Ferris (Dr. Raully)

O'Neill, Carter and Daniel awakened from stasis in what appears to be the S.G.C. nearly 80 years in the future, but what they discover is that, in reality, it's a Goa'uld hoax initiated by Hathor. In the meantime, Teal'c leaves S.G.C. to find the rest of the team.

DAVID READ: I'll give this for *SG-1*: when they had to do clip shows, they mostly found creative ways to pull them off. And a clip show without Kinsey? OK! I really would've enjoyed the show more if they were actually flung into the future and had to use time travel to undo Hathor's control over Earth. It was an interesting idea for about 25 minutes of the show. Susanne Braun makes an overdue return in this episode. What a class act she was.

SEASON THREE SUMMARY (1999-2000)

★ *Seth is killed by Samantha Carter.*

* *Samantha Carter is promoted to the rank of Major.*

* *The Asgard mediate with the Goa'uld System Lords on Earth and place the planet under the Protected Planets Treaty.*

* *Nirrti is banished by the System Lords and becomes a renegade.*

* *The Orbanians share naquadah reactor technology with Earth.*

* *Amonet/Sha're is killed by Teal'c.*

* *Linea is identified in the body of Ke'ra.*

* *Apophis is branded Na'onak and becomes First Prime to Bynarr, ruler of Ne'tu. Apophis slays Bynarr to gain access to the imprisoned SG-1.*

* *Sokar is killed. Apophis takes his armies for himself.*

* *Klorel/Skaara is recovered by the Tollan people. Humans, Goa'uld and Nox mediate over which entity will take ownership of Skaara's body. The Nox rule in favor of Skaara. Klorel is extracted and sent to a Goa'uld planet of his choice.*

* *Harry Maybourne's off-world rogue N.I.D. operation is halted by Jack O'Neill. Maybourne flees to Siberia.*

* *The Bedrosians excavate their Stargate.*

* *Daniel Jackson discovers Kheb and the location of Shifu. The ascended Oma Desala stops an attack by Apophis and flees with the baby to another world.*

* *Replicators travel to Earth aboard Thor's ship and SG-1 destroys the vessel. One Replicator survives and infests a Russian submarine. The sub is destroyed, and the U.S. military conceals the incident from the Russians.*

EPISODE GUIDE: SEASON THREE

Episode #45 (3.1): "Into the Fire"
Written by Brad Wright
Directed by Martin Wood

Guest Starring: Tony Amendola (Bra'tac), Suanne Braun (Hathor), Tom Butler (Trofsky), Colin Cunningham (Major Davis), Samantha Ferris (Dr. Raully), Gary Jones (Technician), Steve Makaj (Colonel Makepeace), Kelly Dean Sereda (Lieutenant), Oliver Svensson-Tan (Marine), Alicia Thorgrimsson (Jaffa)

Stargate Command sends a rescue mission to Hathor's base to retrieve SG-1, where O'Neill kills Hathor. By utilizing Tok'ra-made tunnels already existing in the world, SG-1 manages to escape and returns home.

BRAD WRIGHT: It's where we're all captured and the guy who's pretending to be a Tok'ra, is not. We had a scene we shot at Stoke's Pit and all these towers erupted out of the ground and started shooting the team that was coming to rescue our team. It was a cool, genuine action sequence that was fun to make. I should point out that shooting at night in February is *not* as much fun as you'd think. I also remember joking with Jon about feeling painted into a corner by part one and having no idea how to get out. I also remember giggling to myself at the time, "*They* are a formidable craft, these shuttles?"

DAVID READ: My big regret about this is we only ever see snippets here and there of Hathor in this episode, and then we push her into liquid nitrogen. The Tok'ra subplot was cool, but the long-term mileage of this episode shows itself in the form of Teal'c trying to rally other Jaffa to his cause. They just aren't ready yet. It makes the payoff in Season 8's "Threads" all the more satisfying. The Jaffa as a race really went on a journey.

DARREN SUMNER: Bra'tac's ship, capable of flying through the Stargate, eventually gained the nickname "needle threader," based on his line of dialogue, "Threading the needle is a skill for the young." In production documents, the ship is identified as a "Prototype Death Glider."

Episode #46 (3.2): "Seth"
Written by Jonathan Glassner
Directed by William Corcoran
Guest Starring: Carmen Argenziano (Jacob/Selmak), Robert Duncan (Seth), Mitchell Kosterman (Special Agent James Hamner), Stuart O'Connell (Tommy Levinson), Lucia Walters (Disciple), Greg Michaels (Jason Levinson), Rob Morton (Sheriff)

The Tok'ra seek a Goa'uld named Seth, who has lived on Earth for thousands of years and now is the leader of a dangerous cult. SG-1 uses zats to overcome the cult members' brainwashing, and in the ensuing rescue, Seth is killed by Carter.

JONATHAN GLASSNER: I have always had an obsession with cults. I'm absolutely fascinated by them. One of the first shows I ever wrote was on *21 Jump Street* and it dealt with a much more realistic cult. In this case I thought it would be cool if the guy who's leading the cult and who claims to be an alien, really is.

PETER DELUISE: In "Legacy," Daniel suffers a major psychological breakdown after picking up one of Ma'chello's anti-Goa'uld devices. Ma'chello was a slightly loony, off-world inventor SG-1 first met in the second season episode 'Holiday,' and he was played under heavy make-up by Michael. One of his inventions is accidentally activated by Daniel and that's the catalyst for this particular story.

Episode #47 (3.3): "Fair Game"
Written by Robert C. Cooper
Directed by Martin Wood
Guest Starring: Michael David Simms (Arthur Simms), Ron Halder (Cronus), Jacqueline Samuda (Nirrti), Vince Crestejo (Yu), Teryl Rothery (Dr. Janet Fraiser), T.M. Sandulak (Sergeant Ziplinski), Laara Sadiq (Technician)

Captain Carter is promoted to the rank of Major, while in the meantime the Asgard warn S.G.C. that the Goa'uld are planning an attack on Earth. With their help, SG-1 negotiates with three Goa'uld System Lords — Cronus, Nirrti and Yu — to bring Earth into the Protected Planets Treaty.

ROBERT C. COOPER: After a rousing and expensive opening two episodes, we knew we'd need a smaller one to keep the studio happy. But big didn't always require budget. Having Goa'uld System Lords come to the SGC was a big deal mythology-wise and kept the budget in check.

DAVID SUMNER: A very important episode where the System Lords come to Earth and the Asgard help to negotiate Earth's inclusion in the Protected Planets Treaty. As a result, the threat of a Goa'uld ship coming and blasting us out of space is temporarily alleviated. That was significant for the show and it gave the writers a chance to showcase some new bad guys; colorful villains that Stargate is famous for. There are a bunch of System Lords out there and they don't like us. They'd conquer our planet if they could, but, fortunately, our alliance with the Asgard is starting to pay off.

Episode #48 (3.4): "Legacy"
Written by Tor Alexander Valenza
Directed by Peter DeLuise

Guest Starring: Kevin McNulty (Dr. Warner), Eric Schneider (Dr. MacKenzie), Teryl Rothery (Dr. Janet Fraiser), Michael Shanks (Ma'chello)

On PY3-948, SG-1 finds the corpses of a number of humans who had clearly once served as hosts to Goa'uld symbiotes. Upon returning, Jackson shows signs of schizophrenia, the cause of which is attributed to a Goa'uld-killer of Machello's, which has a strange effect on non-Goa'uld. Ultimately the device is neutralized.

PETER DELUISE: A tour de force for Michael Shanks as Daniel Jackson, because he loses his mind and has to go into a padded room. I was super excited about it, because Michael is quite an accomplished thespian. If asked, he will chew up any scenery you want, and in that case it's padded walls, so it was nice and chewy. Basically my job was to just get out of his way and he had a great psychotic break from reality. Just a wonderful theatrical opportunity for him.

Episode #49 (3.5): "Learning Curve"
Written by Heather E. Ash
Directed by Martin Wood
Guest Starring: Andrew Airlie (Kalan), Brittney Irvin (Merrin), Lachlan Murdoch (Tomin), Stephanie Shea (Solen), Diane Stapley (Mrs. Struble), Rob Farrell (SF Guard), Sarah Goodwill (Student), Laara Sadiq (Technician)

SG-1 arrives on the planet Orban, where knowledge is harvested through the inhabitants' children, known as Urrone. When a Urrone reaches a certain age, their nanites are harvested and they regress to an infantile state, which is how they remain as the Orbanians have no concept of traditional education.

DAVID READ: This episode is one of the most charming shows *Stargate* ever released. It's an interesting exploration of tolerance and coming face-to-face with a different culture's way of doing things, and the surprising side effects that come out of that. Who ever thought Orbanians would love hopscotch and start up their own Crayola factory?

DARREN SUMNER: Because of the accidental death of his young son Charlie, O'Neill has a special place in his heart for children – especially children who don't get to experience childhood to its fullest. He therefore takes a special liking to Merrin, just as he has to other such kids ("Singularity," "Show and Tell").

Episode #50 (3.6): "Point of View"
Story by Jonathan Glassner, Brad Wright, Robert C. Cooper & Tor Alexander Valenza;

Teleplay by Jonathan Glassner & Brad Wright
   Directed by Peter Deluise
   Guest Starring: Jay Acovone (Charles Kawalsky), Peter Williams (Apophis), Teryl
Rothery (Dr. Janet Fraiser), Ty Olsson (Jaffa #1), Shawn Reis (Jaffa #2), Tracy Wester-
holm (SF Guard)

*Using the mirror from "There but for the Grace of God," an alternate Carter and Charles
Kawalsky come to the S.G.C. from an Earth that has been invaded by the Goa'uld. SG-1 saves
the alternate reality by contacting the Asgard there.*

PETER DELUISE: Alternate reality versions of Kawalsky and Carter! This was a
great opportunity to do "twinning," which I had not done a whole lot of prior to this,
but having alternate Carter and regular Carter be in the same frame was a challenge. At
the same time it was *so* fun, because it was so foreign to everything that we were doing.
And, of course, Amanda Tapping, who's a very accomplished director now, was totally
up to the task of doing this. So she would act opposite a stand-in, and then we would
play back her performance and she would do the other side. Like I said, it was a challenge, but because she was so smart and so adept, she made it very simple. I was glad to
have *her* in the twinning.

On top of that, I love all that alternate reality stuff. "Yesterday's Enterprise" is one
of my favorite *Star Trek: The Next Generation* episodes. In it, Starfleet is at war and the
Enterprise bridge is on fire and Picard jumps over the control board to fire the phasers.
In "Point of View" we stage a mini-war inside the Stargate complex. It's a yard-by-yard,
fight-to-the-death type of battle sequence featuring an all-new lighting scheme and
tons of destruction inside the base.

Episode #51 (3.7): "Deadman Switch"
Written by Robert C. Cooper
Directed by Martin Wood
Guest Starring: Sam J. Jones (Aris Boch), Mark Holden (Korra)

*SG-1 is captured by a bounty hunter (Sam. J. Jones) who uses them to help catch a Tok'ra
named Korra (Mark Holden). The Goa'uld has his people addicted to a drug that can be supplied
only by them, but he repents at the last moment and asks Carter to help free them from the drug.*

ROBERT C. COOPER: I wanted to create a Han Solo-type rogue character who
could recur. Fans seemed to like the episode, but it didn't quite gel as we'd hoped. I
never gave up on the idea. Years later it eventually led to Vala, a more successful version.

PETER DELUISE: I had seen the feature film *Flash Gordon* many times as a kid. Even though I did not direct this episode, I did visit the set and I was thrilled to be able to watch Sam Jones, who played the role of Flash Gordon in the movie, in person. This was also the first episode that did *not* feature a Stargate.

Episode #52 (3.8): "Demons"
Written by Carl Binder
Directed by Peter DeLuise
Guest Starring: David McNally (Simon), Alan C. Peterson (The Canon), Laura Mennell (Mary), Richard Morwich (Unas), John R. Taylor (Elder), Christopher Judge (Voice of Unas)

SG-1 visits a planet ruled by a Goa'uld infested Unas, who uses the persona of the Devil to keep residents ruled by fear. They free the people of the "devil" and instruct them to bury the Stargate.

PETER DELUISE: The outfits of the Unas were inspired by the movie *Predator* with the partial armor and things like that. It was a terribly burdensome outfit and completely covered the performer's body to the point we came close to a medical emergency, because their body couldn't breathe. We learned the lesson early on, cover them with more clothing and *don't* put rubber all over their body. That was a good lesson to learn early on, as well as making an opening so they can pee.

We were also dealing with the fact that the Unas would come with a Goa'uld inside his head and would take sacrificial host bodies as human gifts to the gods. The Unas were the First Ones, the first host bodies to the Goa'uld, which to me meant that they must have occupied the same planet as the Goa'uld. The story delves into the pre-history of the Goa'uld and how the Unas played a key role in their development, so I found that very interesting and informative.

Episode #53 (3.9): "Rules of Engagement"
Written by Terry Curtis Fox
Directed by William Gereghty
Guest Starring: Peter Williams (Apophis), Aaron Craven (Captain Kyle Rogers), Dion Johnstone (Captain Nelson), Jesse Moss (Lieutenant J. Hibbard), Teryl Rothery (Dr. Janet Fraiser), Josh Byer (Sergeant)

SG-1 discovers a world where Apophis was training human slaves to infiltrate Stargate Command. The team shows them footage of Apophis dying and they all renounce him as a false god. Gotta love those simple solutions.

BRAD WRIGHT: "Rules of Engagement" was a script that went through three incarnations. The first, written by Terry Curtis Fox, bears almost no resemblance to what was finally committed to film. Our story editor at the time, Tor Valenza, came up with a spin on Terry's story that finally made it work for me — which is the idea of young soldiers training to infiltrate Tauri and being left behind. I then did a very heavy rewrite on Tor's script and that's what we shot.

Episode #54 (3.10): "Forever in a Day"
Written by Jonathan Glassner
Directed by Peter DeLuise
Guest Starring: Erick Avari (Kasuf), Vaitiare Bandera (Sha're), Teryl Rothery (Dr. Janet Fraiser), Jason Schombing (Rothman)

After being found on P8X-873, Daniel's wife, Sha're, is killed by Teal'c to prevent the Goa'uld controlling her from killing Daniel, who then starts seeing visions of a residual thought transferred to him by Sha're in the last moments: He must find her son, Shifu, who is known to be a Harcesis.

JONATHAN GLASSNER: Michael Shanks came to Brad and I and said, "How long are we going to do this Sha're thing? It's getting old." Brad and I hadn't even thought about it at that time. We looked at each other and we discussed it a little bit and said, "You know, he's right. We're beyond that now. We can get beyond that." So I said, "Well, why don't we kill her? Why don't we get rid of her? If we're going to get rid of her, let's *really* get rid of her." So we did. Let's end that quest for him, because, otherwise, it's always going to be if he left, or if he cured her, or if he rescued her, or any of those things, then you're still stuck with it, really. There just wouldn't be anything left to do.

PETER DELUISE: Vaitiare Bandera was playing Sha're, who was beaming this device into Daniel's head and Michael Shanks was on his knees, succumbing. He was about to die when he had what could only be described as a flash-forward moment or a break with reality. In it, he went off on a massive tangent and had an experience where he was communicating with Sha're, the host body, his ex-lover from the previous show. Now Tim Robbins made a movie called *Jacob's Ladder*, which had the exact structure: they're in the throes of death, then there's a break and you go off and go, "That is what would happen if he lived," but you don't know that. You think he *did* live, but then you come back to the moment and you play it out and you see it's actually his "what if?" hypothetical life flashing before his eyes.

It's that same structure we're using, but I've got to somehow let the audience know that we're coming back to that exact moment in time where things branched off. I didn't know how to do it, but at the 11th hour I had the idea of having Michael Shanks, as he's succumbing to the beam in his head, start to drop his nine-millimeter weapon — I did an insert of that — and then I showed, when we came back from the mental interlude, the gun finally hitting the ground. So the whole thing took less than a second, and that's how I was able to bring the audience back to this moment and show them that only a second had gone by.

Episode #55 (3.11): "Past and Present"
Written by Tor Alexander Valenza
Directed by William Gereghty
Guest Starring: Megan Leitch (Ke'ra), Marya Delver (Layale), Jason Gray-Stanford (Orner), Teryl Rothery (Dr. Janet Fraiser), Luisa Cianni (Woman)

Following the arrival of Linea ("The Destroyer of Worlds" from "Prisoners") the people of the planet Vyus find their memories stricken in an event known as the "Vorlix." SG-1, having failed to stop Linea in the past, feel responsible for what's happened.

PETER DELUISE: When I read the script for this episode, which included an industrial setting in a modern society, I suddenly became intrigued by all the new possibilities of what we might find after walking through the Stargate. Of course I knew anything was possible, but the show had not taken advantage of that kind of setting yet. Most of the stories prior to this had implied that after the Goa'uld had left their human slaves behind on alien planets, they had not advanced very far in technology.

DAVID READ: This episode is maybe the first example of *Stargate* bringing a plotline to a close. We let Linea out and she went to work right away on harming another civilization. Only in this case, she couldn't get out of the way of her own plans fast enough and ended up de-aging not only an entire population, but herself as well, killing God knows how many kids in the process. I'm sorry they never revisited that bad guy again. Friends of mine consider her the best *Stargate* villain out of them all. But she got a satisfying conclusion.

Episode #56 (3.12): "Jolinar's Memories"
Written by Sonny Wareham & Daniel Stashower
Directed by Peter DeLuise
Guest Starring: Carmen Argenziano (Jacob/Selmak), JR Bourne (Martouf), Bob Dawson (Bynarr), Dion Johnstone (Na'onak), Peter Williams (Apophis), Peter H. Kent (Kintac), David Palffy (Sokar), Daniel Bacon (Technician), Eli

Gabay (Jumar), Tanya Reid (Jolinar), Christine Kennedy (Young Carter)

Jacob/Selmak is captured by Sokar, with Jolinar being the only person to escape from Sokar's home moon of Ne'Tu near the planet Delmak. SG-1 is captured and discovers that Apophis controls the moon.

PETER DELUISE: An interesting challenge, because we go to the planet Delmak, where it's basically a volcanic hellscape, dungeon type place where all these poor bastards go to get put away. Then Carter gets put in and she has all of these memories flood her mind as though they're her own — I remember that. And, of course, Amanda Tapping, who was always having to play this semi-stoic military thing, taps into a very passionate place and starts to have a transfer with Jolinar. I remember thinking I was so grateful about the talent of all the core cast, because obviously Amanda Tapping was up for the task.

Director of photography Peter Woeste gave us the smeary dreams look. Smeary dreams is when you shoot at six frames a second instead of twenty-four. What happens is each frame of film is duplicated many times and as there is movement, you get a smear. It looks like the residual image of your hand in its first, second, third, and fourth position, all in one go. It gives a little bit of strobing/smearing effect. If you've ever been on a drug induced hallucination, then I understand that is what you might encounter.

Episode #57 (3.13): "The Devil You Know"
Written by Robert C. Cooper
Directed by Peter DeLuise
Guest Starring: Carmen Argenziano (Jacob/Selmak), JR Bourne (Martouf), William deVry (Aldwin), Peter Williams (Apophis), David Palffy (Sokar), William deVry (Aldwin), Peter H. Kent (Kintac), Eli Gabay (Jumar), Tanya Reid (Jolinar), Bob Dawson (Bynarr), Christine Kennedy (Young Carter), Dillon Moen (Charlie)

SG-1 manages to escape from Ne'tu with Jacob and Selmak and makes it back to Earth. They use a Tok'ra bomb that blows up the moon and destroys Sokar's ship, killing him with it. Apophis, however, escapes and rises again.

PETER DELUISE: The episode begs the question, when ridiculously powerful Overlords are sitting on their thrones, what are they doing? Do they play Parcheesi? Do they play Minefield? Do they play Solitaire? Is someone like Sokar just sitting there doing nothing? *What is he doing?* So I had him playing with a flame, because I couldn't figure out what he would be doing. We had a flame he was putting his finger to — what else is he gonna do?

ROBERT C. COOPER: Some people have wondered why we created this really cool Goa'uld in Sokar, only to kill him off right away. Well, we originally killed Apophis because the character had gotten a little weak. We had beaten him so many times that he was no longer scary. Then we realized we could bring him back in dramatic fashion, and give his character a whole new level by having him rise from the ashes and take over the realm of the scariest Goa'uld we could think of. We built Sokar up exactly for this reason. The more powerful he was, the more powerful Apophis would become when he defeated him.

PETER DELUISE: The second part of a two-part episode where they're still in that same place and have to escape. The big challenge of the episode was that volcanic dungeon-ess area where you had all of these different aliens who had been in various Jaffa and were sent to this prison place. My thought process was it's not unlike Australia when it was a penal colony — the view was, "You're just going to go over *there*." So that was really fun, because you got to see the ragtag version of what was formerly these powerful, well-trained Jaffa and various other aliens, and now they are all sort of stuck as prisoners of war destined for hard labor. *And* they weren't expected to survive. So I always kind of enjoyed that. I also really liked what David Palffy did with the Sokar character, because it was supposed to be over the top and very melodramatic.

DARREN SUMNER: "Jolinar's Memories'' and "The Devil You Know" are more examples of the show honoring its fans and its existing stories, being willing to go back and pick up loose pieces and continuing those stories on. This is a rescue mission to save Jacob Carter from the clutches of Sokar after being imprisoned on his hellish prison moon of Ne'tu, so SG-1 goes to hell. At this point Apophis was long dead for more than half a season and the writers were elevating a new villain in Sokar, but then there's this big reveal at the end of "Jolinar's Memories'' that Apophis is alive again and in charge. *And* he's now in charge of this prison moon and he's got SG-1 right where he wants them. It's very sort of over the top scenery chewing from Peter Williams, and it's just great.

Episode #58 (3.14): "Foothold"
Written by Heather E. Ash
Directed by Andy Mikita
Guest Starring: Tom McBeath (Colonel Harry Maybourne), Colin Cunningham (Major Davis), Teryl Rothery (Dr. Janet Fraiser), Richard Leacock (Colonel Brogen), Colin Lawrence (Sergeant Warren), Dan Shea (Sergeant Siler), Alex Zahara (Alien Leader/Alien #1), Dion Johnstone (Alien #2), Tracy

Westerholm (Surveillance SF), Biski Gugushe (SF Guard)

Stargate Command is under control by aliens originating from P3X-118, using a frequency-based technology that allows them to mimic the appearance of other beings. Carter must ask Colonel Maybourne to help her retake the base.

ANDY MIKITA (director): I'd been a part of the franchise right from day one. I was the first assistant director on "Children of the Gods" with Mario Azzopardi, so I'd been part of the group since its inception. It was actually Jonathan Glassner who was the person directly responsible for having me come on board. From there I worked as a first assistant director for the first season and then as a production manager and second unit director after that. I was doing so much second unit work that basically everybody supported the notion of having me direct an entire episode and felt that I was ready to do so. So "Foothold" was that first opportunity for me. It worked out really well. I thought it was a pretty strong episode and it certainly led to other opportunities for me within the franchise, which was great.

PETER DELUISE: The device Martouf uses to adjust the memory stimulation device is an electric nose hair trimmer! I'm a big fan of nose hair trimmers, not just in my personal life, but I believe they should be included in all sci-fi movies and TV shows as much as the Wilhelm scream.

Episode #59 (3.15): "Pretense"
Written by Katharyn Powers
Directed by David Warry-Smith
Guest Starring: Frida Betrani (Lya), Alexis Cruz (Skaara/Klorel), Kevin Durand (Zipacna), Garwin Sanford (Narim), Marie Stillin (Travell), Bill Nikolai (Technician)

Skaara/Klorel crash land on the Tollans' new homeworld. The Tollan invite SG-1 to represent Skaara in a trial to decide whether Skaara or Klorel has the right to use Skaara's body.

ALEXIS CRUZ: Once again we got to see that struggle between Klorel and Skaara, which I enjoyed playing out. I was free to use my imagination in so many different ways and have some fun with my character. It's one of the reasons I'm drawn to the sci-fi genre. Sci-fi and comedy allow me to experiment with my craft.

Episode #60 (3.16): "Urgo"
Written by Tor Alexander Valenza
Directed by Peter DeLuise
Guest Starring: Dom DeLuise (Urgo / Togar), Teryl Rothery (Dr. Janet

Fraiser), Nickolas Baric (SF Guard), Bill Nikolai (Technician Alberts)

The members of SG-1 are implanted with an AI named Urgo (Dom DeLuise), but they man-age to rectify the problem by visiting Urgo's creator on P4X-884, who implants Urgo in himself instead to improve his personality.

PETER DELUISE: What a great opportunity to work with my dad. The key to that was, again, getting out of his way and I did a lot of two-shots because of the comedy. I would have him and another actor in the shot and I kept shooting close-ups of my dad in case he wanted to do ad libs. So I would shoot a close-up of him in somebody else's shot, but a ton of two-shots because comedy plays better in two shots. The prob-lem with that was my dad would be *so* funny, that his frame partner, the person in the frame with him, would crack up. It was good that I had a cutaway single, so that we got around the cut. You've also got Chris Judge, who is very stoic as Teal'c, who would start to break.

DAVID READ: "Urgo" is an interesting one. There is a subset of fans who just don't like this episode, but I'm firmly in the other camp here. Dom DeLuise is such a gem, and his earnesty and sincerity with the role shines through. I laughed so hard the first time I watched. And you really buy that he is this child-like computer program. You're invested in his mortality and really don't want him to be destroyed when he's removed from SG-1's minds. But Togar probably threw him away five minutes after the team left.

PETER DELUISE: I was thrilled that they wanted my dad to be in there and that I got to work with him. He just showed up and started to play, but I only have a limited time to put together my director's cut, so I put it together as best I could with what I had. But then Brad Wright found alternate takes and the funny lines and injected them. Brad deserves quite the acknowledgment, because he really sat through all the alternate lines and jokes and included most of the funny stuff. The result was this really fun romp with my dad playing not one, but two characters. Twinning again!

DAVID READ: Christopher Judge remembered that they wasted so many hours of film on this episode, because Dom was making them laugh themselves sick. If I ever get the opportunity to go through the dailies on *SG-1*, "Urgo" is the one I'm going to first.

Episode #61 (3.17): "A Hundred Days"
Story by V.C. James, Teleplay by Brad Wright
Directed by David Warry-Smith
Guest Starring: Michele Greene (Laira), Julie Patzwald (Naytha), Gary Jones (Harriman), Shane Meier (Garan), Teryl Rothery (Dr. Janet Fraiser), Marcel

Maillard (Paynan)

SG-1 visits Edora just in time for a meteor shower caused by the planet passing through an asteroid field. Anticipating significant damage from meteorite impact, they attempt to evacuate the inhabitants. O'Neill is left behind while searching for stragglers. After the meteor shower, he cannot find the gate, which has been buried by a meteor strike. It takes Carter and S.G.C. 100 days to develop a means to reestablish contact, using a particle beam inspired by Sokar's attack on Earth in "Serpent's Song."

BRAD WRIGHT: "A Hundred Days' should have been a two-parter. O'Neill wouldn't have given up as fast as he did. Not that it would have been better, I just thought there was too much story for one hour. He does meet a woman, Laira, and it's the closest he came to falling in love again. It's got a couple of nice moments in it. The opening scene is quite good with the near miss of the giant asteroid overhead, and then there's him basically embracing that life. Again, it should have been a two-parter.

Episode #62 (3.18): "Shades of Grey"
Written by Jonathan Glassner
Directed by Martin Wood
Guest Starring: Tom McBeath (Colonel Harry Maybourne), Steve Makaj (Colonel Makepeace), Marie Stillin (High Chancellor Travell), Christian Bocher (Neumann), Teryl Rothery (Dr. Janet Fraiser), Linnea Sharples (Lt. Clare Tobias)

After stealing technology from the Tollan, O'Neill is forced to retire. He joins a rogue SG team dedicated to obtaining advanced technology by any means and then hides them. However, he's actually working as a double agent to find and capture the rogues. He also comes across the Tiernod, a cave-dwelling race on PX3-595 under the protection of the Asgard, who gave them cloaking devices to hide from predators.

JONATHAN GLASSNER: As the title suggests, it was a way to explore shades of gray. You know, if a person steals a weapon to keep that weapon from killing somebody else, but nonetheless he stole the weapon, is it a crime? And how bad is it?

Episode #63 (3.19): "New Ground"
Written by Heather E. Ash
Directed by Chris McMullin
Guest Starring: Richard Ian Cox (Nyan), Daryl Shuttleworth (Rigar), Teryl Rothery (Dr. Janet Fraiser), Desiree Zuroski (Parey), Jennifer Copping (Mallin), Bill Nikolai (Technician), Finn Michael (Soldier)

SG-1 visits a planet designated P2X-416, where the countries of Bedrosia and Optrica are in the middle of a war over the origins of life. The Bedrosians, who believe a Goa'uld created humans on their world, mistake SG-1 (minus Teal'c) for infiltrators and refuse to accept their account that the Stargate is a transportation device as the Optricans have always claimed. Teal'c frees his team with help from Nyan, one of a minority of Bedrosian scientists willing to approach the Optrican position with an open mind.

PETER DELUISE: I'm always entertained by the game "six degrees of Kevin Bacon," so I was especially pleased when Richard Ian Cox, who guest starred in this episode, co starred with Mickey Rooney in a series called *The Adventures of Black Stallion*. Brad Wright had written for that series and my dad knew Mickey Roonery very well and had toured in a play with him and Joan Rivers many years ago called *Luv*.

DARREN SUMNER: An underlying theme of this episode is the ideological war between religion and science. Nyan is a true scientist, who has no unfounded allegiance to abstract belief, but is eager to change what he believes when presented with new evidence. The Bedrosians are dedicated to their faith, and are presented as arrogant and stubborn – unwilling to consider that their beliefs might be wrong, even when presented with hard evidence. This dichotomy is manifested in the characters of Nyan and Rigar.

Episode #64 (3.20): "Maternal Instinct"
Written by Robert C. Cooper
Directed by Peter F. Woeste
Guest Starring: Tony Amendola (Bra'tac), Terry Chen (Monk), Teryl Rothery (Dr. Janet Fraiser), Aaron Douglas (Moac), Steve Bacic (Major Coburn), D. Harlan Cutshall (Jaffa Commander), Carla Boudreau (Oma Desala)

Daniel knows that the Harcesis is on a planet called Kheb; Bra'tac knows how to get there as it is the planet the Jaffa believe to be the destination of their soul after death. They find a Zen monk who teaches Daniel about the ways of Ascension and an ascended being (Oma Desala) saves the child.

DAVID READ: This is a *huge* episode. It makes Robert Cooper look like a genius years later when you can point back at this show and say, "See, the Ancients were set up long in advance!" Bruce Woloshyn of the former Rainmaker Digital said that the ascended beings were extremely difficult to animate. They were the brightest thing in any shot they were in. The animators had to paint out the light rigs and superimpose that flowy creature on top. And someone put a human head on top of that. Just insanely complex.

PETER DELUISE: There are many actors in this episode that qualify for major science fiction crossover casting. Tony Amendola and Terry Chen both went on to do *Continuum* together, Aaron Douglas ended up on *Battlestar Galactica* and Steve Bacic ended up on *Andromeda*.

TONY AMENDOLA: The notion of delegating power, of giving up power — part of the problem when you look at leaders is, again, a Shakespearean theme. "When do you give up power to the young?" Bra'tac is very comfortable with that. As a matter of fact, it's Teal'c who insists that he still stay involved and Bra'tac, right from the beginning, was saying, "No, it's your time. I'm not doing this for me. It's you." And that's why there's such close and really well-written observations of Teal'c's, when we lose our symbiotes, that Teal'c all of a sudden is not himself. Because it's like a mental kind of depression. An absence of this power.

Episode #65 (3.21): "Crystal Skull"
Story by Michael Greenburg & Jarrad Paul, Teleplay by Brad Wright
Directed by Brad Turner
Guest Starring: John Rubez (Nick Ballard), Teryl Rothery (Dr. Janet Fraiser), Jason Schombing (Robert Rothman), Dan Shea (Sergeant Siler), Russel Roberts (Psychiatrist), Jacquie Janzen (Nurse), Daniel Bacon (Technician), Tracy Westerholm (Surveillance SF), Christopher Judge (Voice of Quetzalcoatl)

The team finds a Mayan ziggurat in a lepton-rich environment on planet P7X-377. Inside is a crystal skull that turns Daniel into a ghost. His grandfather, Nicholas Ballard, found a similar skull in Belize and helped out. When they return to the planet, giant aliens who have vaguely humanoid but insubstantial forms appear and return Daniel to normal.

BRAD WRIGHT: I'm not a big fan of the episode, but part of it is my own failure as a writer. I couldn't embrace it very well, although it does have a cool last scene with the giant aliens.

PETER DELUISE: Jason Schombing, a family friend, reprised his role of Dr. Robert Rothman in this episode. When he was first cast in "Forever in a Day," he asked me if the role would recur — a question many actors ponder when deciding to take a role or not. At that time, I told him there was a distinct possibility. He doubted that was true, but reluctantly took my advice to accept the role. Jason ended up getting three episodes in the show and had to admit to me that I was right.

Episode #66 (3.22): "Nemesis"
Written by Robert C. Cooper

Directed by Martin Wood

Guest Starring: Colin Cunningham (Major Davis), Gary Jones (Technician), Guy Lee-Frazier (Technician #2), Michael Shanks (Voice of Thor)

Thor's starship has been infected by Replicators. In order to keep it from landing on Earth, SG-1 disables the deceleration engines so the ship burns up in the atmosphere and crashes in the Pacific. While they attempt to escape to P3X-234, one replicator remains.

ROBERT C. COOPER: I think we made certain mistakes — I wouldn't say they were things that shouldn't have been done, but we created characters and villains that were too powerful. It's the danger of any sci-fi or superhero thing. You make a superhero that's *so* powerful, why doesn't he win every time? I liked when the Asgard ships came down and just obliterated the Goa'uld ships in "Thor's Hammer," but at the same time I was, like, "Ooh, that's a problem." It's the Q phenomenon on *Star Trek*. It's like, he's a god and gods can do anything they want, so the drama literally becomes what does Q want to do and that's not good drama. It's just the character and writers essentially puppeting the godlike character at their will. And you don't feel very satisfied by the resolution of Q just snapping his fingers and undoing the problem. So how do we defy the Asgard? Create something equally as powerful that causes the Asgard a problem, which is how the Replicators came to me. That explained why the Asgard are not saving our asses all the time. They've got their own problems. And then their problems become our problems.

BRAD WRIGHT: Daniel Jackson's surgery was written into the script of "Nemesis" to accommodate Michael Shanks, who came down with appendicitis at the time of filming. I remember coming up with some elaborate reason Daniel wasn't in that morning's scene and pitched it to Rob Cooper. He said, "Why don't we just say Daniel has appendicitis?" I said, "That's *genius!*"

JONATHAN GLASSNER: I love the Replicators. We were actually talking about them for quite a while before I even knew I was leaving the show. They were the enemy of the Asgard, which is why they were created. They were too god-like a race that could do anything, so we needed to make them vulnerable.

DARREN SUMNER: Obviously the Goa'uld and the battle with the System Lords is still going to be an ongoing plot line for many seasons, but here we get our second big bad guy with the introduction of the Replicators. And *they* are going to take us all the way to "Reckoning" in Season 8, when both of those primary antagonists are going to come together and be dealt with.

SEASON FOUR SUMMARY (2000-2001)

* *The Russians recover the Egyptian Stargate from the bottom of the Pacific Ocean and soon establish their own Stargate program in Siberia.*

* *A Russian team is sent to P2X-338 to recover the Eye of Tiamat.*

* *The Rogue N.I.D. begin to experiment with combining human DNA with that of the Goa'uld Sekhmet. ("Resurrection")*

* *Shau'nac is killed by Tanith. Teal'c vows to avenge her death.*

* *Martouf is killed by Samantha Carter. The Tok'ra symbiote Lantash survives in stasis.*

* *Stargate Command begins to transfer Enkaran refugees to a new home world.*

* *SG-1 is sent to Siberia to deactivate their Stargate and investigate the Russians' failed program.*

* *Harry Maybourne is captured in Siberia and imprisoned.*

* *Daniel Jackson establishes peaceful relations with an Unas tribe on P3X-888.*

* *The Enkarans are flown to their original homeworld in a Gadmeer terraformer.*

* *The X-301 is deemed a failure.*

* *Artifacts from the Stuart Expedition are excavated from the ocean floor and sent to the University of Chicago.*

* *Osiris is released from its canopic jar by Sarah Gardner, who is taken as its new host. She kills David Jordan and flees Earth in a hidden ship.*

* *Heru'ur captures Teal'c and offers him as a gift of good faith to Apophis for forming an alliance. Apophis falls for a Tok'ra ruse and destroys Heru'ur, absorbing his fleet. Teal'c escapes with the converted Jaffa, Rak'nor.*

* *George Hammond resigns from Stargate Command. General Bauer takes his place. Jack O'Neill works with Harry Maybourne to uncover Senator Kinsey's involvement and force Hammond to be reinstated.*

* *Robert Kinsey announces his plan to run for President of the United States.*

* *A message from a future Jack O'Neill warns never to travel to P4C-970. Hammond orders the address blocked out of the dialing computer.*

* *SG-1's Altairan duplicates invent power packs and use the Stargate to go on missions. They travel to Juna and are confronted by Cronus. Harlan pleas for the assistance of the original SG-1. Cronus is killed, and all of SG-1's clone duplicates lose power and die.*

* *SG-1 and the Tok'ra detonate Vorash's sun, destroying most of Apophis's fleet.*

EPISODE GUIDE: SEASON FOUR

Episode #67 (4.1): "Small Victories"
Written by Robert C. Cooper
Directed by Martin Wood
Guest Starring: Colin Cunningham (Major Davis), Gary Jones (Technician), Teryl Rothery (Dr. Janet Fraiser), Dan Shea (Sergeant Siler), Yurij Kis (Yuri), Dmitry Chepovetsky (Boris)

The Replicator on Earth has reproduced and taken over a submarine; O'Neill and Teal'c neutralize the threat. Carter goes with Thor to defend the Asgard homeworld from the Replicators. They use the Asgard's newest ship (named the O'Neill) to lure the Replicators into hyperspace, where the ship is blown up.

ROBERT C. COOPER: Here's a case of writing to a set or location that happened to be available. There was a decommissioned submarine parked in Vancouver harbor. Whenever we saw stuff like that, it always quickly became, "How can we use it?" I was super excited to have set up the ominous threat of the replicators and then have them land on Earth so SG-1 would have to stop them.

JOSEPH MALLOZZI: I remember sitting in Brad's office when we first came to Vancouver and having Brad ask Robert how he planned to conclude the season three finale, "Nemesis." Well, Rob knew exactly where he wanted to go with the story and broke it down for us. I remember thinking, "There is no way they're going to be able to pull this off." And yet, he did. *We* did. Again and again. The high point of the episode isn't the Rick Moranis look alike taking a face full of acid in the teaser, or the Russian dialogue that, when translated, reads, "What's that noise?" "Maybe it's that bug from the last episode," or the outtakes — specifically, one depicting a seated Thor requesting a

Mokochino and another with the Asgard reaching up to goose Carter and getting his face slapped as a result.

Episode #68 (4.2): "The Other Side"
Written by Brad Wright
Directed by Peter DeLuise
Guest Starring: Rene Auberjonois (Alar), Anne Marie Loder (Farrell), Gary Jones (Technician), Dan Shea (Sergeant Siler), Stephen Park (Controller), Kyle Cassie (Eurondan Soldier), Kris Keeler (Zombie Pilot)

Humans on the planet Euronda contact Stargate Command for help; they are fighting a losing war against an enemy they call the "Breeders" and have run out of food and fuel supplies. SG-1 travels to Euronda and makes an alliance to trade heavy water for advanced technology to combat the Goa'uld. But SG-1 discovers their new allies are guilty of mass genocide against the "Breeders." In response, SG-1 sabotages and destroys the base.

BRAD WRIGHT: What we were thinking about is that we're always going to a planet and meeting aliens who are the good guys. So what if we gate to a planet and befriend people who are *not* good guys at all? *And* they're at war with the good guys, and so at the end of the episode we end up undermining them. You know, screw the Prime Directive.

PETER DELUISE: I got to work with Rene Auberjonois, who I was familiar with because he had been on *Star Trek: Deep Space Nine*, and that was fun. *And* I got to work with my wife, Anne Marie Loder, who played Ferrell, the pretty blonde lady. So that was great fun to work with her and also Rene.

JOSEPH MALLOZZI: I remember coming away from this episode impressed by Brad and Robert's willingness to take chances, especially with regards to our characters. O'Neill kills someone at episode's end, and I'm not talking in the heat of battle. He gives the order to close the iris and then, seconds later, the Eurondan leader apparently steps through and ends up pasted on the other side. Granted, Jack did warn him not to follow, but, still, it was a calculated move on the part of the usually happy-go-lucky team leader.

PETER DELUISE: That moment at the end where everything's going to hell in a handbasket — it's James Bond having to get out of the villain's headquarters, because it's all coming down and exploding and caving in. I thought it would be nice to know what happened to some of these characters, because we find out Rene's fate: he follows them through the gate, but they close the iris and he gets smushed. And with Farrell, because we didn't know what happened to her, we stacked the lens in a forced perspective and put a huge styrofoam rock above the frame and dropped it. We had her look up and put her hands up as though she could see it falling on her. I was looking at the onboard camera and saw that she played it *so* well, that I became super scared I accidentally hurt her and potentially ruined my chances of marrying her. I'm happy to say that I did *not* crush my future wife's head with a giant Styrofoam rock.

Episode #69 (4.3): "Upgrades"
Written by David Rich
Directed by Martin Wood
Guest Starring: Vanessa Angel (Anise/Freya), Teryl Rothery (Dr. Janet Fraiser), Dan Shea (Sergeant Siler), Kristina Copeland (Waitress), Frank Topol (Big Guy), Bill Nikolai (Technician #1), Laara Sadiq (Technician #2), Daniel Melles (SF #1), Tracy Westerholm (SF #2), Fraser Attcheson (Jaffa Commander), Shawn Reis (Jaffa)

The Tok'ra Anise gives Atanik arm devices to O'Neill, Carter, and Daniel that greatly increase their strength and speed. But the devices rely on a virus that is eventually neutralized by the human immune system, causing the members of SG-1 to lose the strength they gained. However, they don't realize this until they are on a mission on PX9-757, a planet where Apophis builds a new prototype mothership.

JOSEPH MALLOZZI: "Upgrades" was one of my favorite episodes from Season 4. Robert Cooper did an amazing job on the rewrite. A lot of the time, the fans don't realize how much of the "good lines" or even a sizable part of the scripts are actually written by either Brad or Robert. They've done some major rewrites on certain scripts.

BRAD WRIGHT: This was a nice performance piece for our actors. I remember laughing out loud when O'Neill accidentally pushes Siler down the staircase. Siler, of course, was played by our stunt coordinator, Dan Shea.

Episode #70 (4.4): "Crossroads"
Written by Katharyn Powers
Directed by Peter DeLuise
Guest Starring: Vanessa Angel (Anise/Freya), Musetta Vander (Shau'nac), Peter Wingfield (Hebron/Tanith), Gary Jones (Technician), Teryl Rothery (Dr. Janet Fraiser), Ron Halder (Cronus), Sean Millington (Ronac)

The S.G.C. is visited by Shan'auc, a female Jaffa who has discovered how to communicate with her larval Goa'uld symbiote and claims that she has information that could destroy the Goa'uld.

JOSEPH MALLOZZI: In the original version of this script, Teal'c exacts his revenge on Tanith and the episode concludes with, if not exactly a happy ending, then surely a satisfying one. But Brad suggested that, instead, we end the episode with Teal'c restraining himself and Tanith getting away with Shau'nac's murder – at least temporarily. "That's pretty dark," I recall Paul saying. "I like dark," countered Brad. And so did I. The original version of the script also contained a reference to the fact that Teal'c had gotten a (Jaffa) divorce from his wife, freeing him up to pursue that amorous rendezvous with his long lost love. Unfortunately, for some reason it didn't make the final draft and, as a result, Teal'c ended up looking like a big slut to many fans. All that being said, the high point of this episode for me was that damn pointy Tok'ra digs, everything from the porcupine walls to the lethal high-backed chairs. It's a wonder they weren't impaling themselves all the time.

PETER DELUISE: Sean Millington played a character named Ronac and he was a part of the Canadian Football League. A legitimate football star, but because he was Canadian, no Americans knew who he was. So that was quite interesting. The other cool thing was working with Peter Wingfield, who played the Immortal character Methos on *Highlander: The Series*. Then Musetta Vander played Teal'c long lost lover; Christopher Judge came to work a little bit hungover and I remember watching Musetta and Chris and she was reacting to the fact that he was sweating whiskey. He goes, "It's all good, it's all good" and she screams, "Oh!" *And* that was an opportunity to work with Vanessa Angel, who was from the TV version of the film *Weird Science*. So I had all these various people from all different areas converging for this wonderful time.

Episode #71 (4.5): "Divide and Conquer"
Written by Tor Alexander Valenza
Directed by Martin Wood
Guest Starring: Vanessa Angel (Freya/Anise), JR Bourne (Martouf), Kirsten Robek (Lieutenant Astor), Andrew Jackson (Per'sus), Teryl Rothery (Dr. Janet Fraiser), Phillip Mitchell (Major Graham), Bill Nikolai (Technician), Roger Allford (The President)

The Goa'uld can impose subconscious programming on humans, but the Tok'ra have developed a test that's able to detect the programming due to its ability to weed out lies. When it's applied to the staff of Stargate Command, Carter and O'Neill are found to be affected, however they're subconsciously failing the test because of their feelings for each other. Feelings that they try to avoid, and lie about, before realizing what they have to do.

JOSEPH MALLOZZI: Some point to this episode as the genesis of the grand shipper vs. anti-shipper debate as O'Neill and Carter finally admit their feelings for one another – and I suppose it was, except it didn't come as much of a surprise. Shippers rejoiced as, after three years of unspoken mutual attraction, "Sam and Jack" became canon. Anti-shippers, on the other hand, were less than enthused and the forums lit up! And it wasn't just the ship they were referring to. It was also the death of their beloved Martouf and the continuing presence of the Anise character, introduced in response to then President of MGM Television's Hank Cohen's request for "a sexy female alien" (a suggestion he got to repeat on screen when he played himself in "Wormhole X-treme").

DAVID READ: You want to talk about a hard episode to watch? This is one that completely polarized the fan base. You look at the polls and they're *still* 50/50 in terms of people liking and hating the episode, because Martouf is killed. In war, people are always dying and we are in a war for our lives. There are casualties like Martouf and Janet that help remind us that the fight is real and that at the end of the day, not all of us are going to make it.

JOSEPH MALLOZZI: Vanessa Angel was terrific, both in front of the camera and off. I remember watching her audition and coming away very impressed. While most of the other actresses simply said the words, it was clear that Vanessa had actually *learned* the dialogue. There's a big difference. In the end, the decision not to revisit the character had nothing to do with the actress and everything to do with our inability to find a proper, satisfactory storyline for her.

DAVID READ: The Zatar Detector had a great twist in this episode where O'Neill and Carter were considered to be global infiltrators, because they weren't being completely honest about their feelings for each other. And once they do that, they pass the test and then there's this huge sigh of relief. Then Martouf activates and starts on a killing rampage and it becomes a gripping final act.

ROBERT C. COOPER: What makes this an important episode is the attempted summit between the Tok'ra and S.G.C.. It was sort of like a step forward in that relationship. One of the things we definitely did a lot, and it's okay to acknowledge it, is we would take classic tropes or sci-fi ideas and then put the *Stargate* spin on it. This was our *Manchurian Candidate* kind of story.

Episode #72 (4.6): "Window of Opportunity"
Written by Joseph Mallozzi & Paul Mullie
Directed by Peter DeLuise
Guest Starring: Robin Mossley (Malikai), Teryl Rothery (Dr. Janet Fraiser), Dan Shea (Sergeant Siler), Daniel Bacon (Technician), Bill Nikolai (Technician), Cam Cronin (Door Airman)

After an encounter with an Ancient time device on P4X-639, O'Neill and Teal'c get trapped in a time loop that only they know about.

Director Peter DeLuise told Dial the Gate *that he had the props department actually glue Fruit Loops to O'Neill's spoon so that it would look exactly the same at the start of each new time loop.*

CATH-ANNE AMBROSE (script coordinator): I had to get Fruit Loops cleared by Kelloggs, and so the guy calls me back and says, "Well, how do you feel about Eggo Waffles? Would you consider using Eggo Waffles instead of Fruit Loops?" So I go to the writing department and ask, "How do you feel about waffles?" And they're, like, "No! It's Fruit Loops! It's a time loop!"

JOSEPH MALLOZZI: In its earliest form, the pitch for this story was very different, much darker in tone. It involved the team going to a planet and becoming trapped in a seemingly endless time loop orchestrated by a dying race seeking to buy more time to come up with a solution to an impending Armageddon (which became the backstory of the device's genesis mentioned in the episode by Malikai). Rob suggested another spin on the time loop angle and, while I was dubious at first ("Isn't this *Groundhog Day*?" I remember asking. "Yeah," was Rob's counter), I was proven wrong (that happened a lot with regard to some of Rob's ideas those first couple of years).

BRAD WRIGHT: Rob and I said, "If you're going to do *Groundhog Day*, let's embrace it and make it funny. Embrace the humor. I did more of a rewrite on that than anybody remembers, but I certainly do. A great and funny episode. And I remember when we were going to be short, John Smith, our line producer — or maybe our post production guy — coming in and saying the episode was cutting short and that we were going to have to add some stuff, otherwise we'd be three or four minutes short. That's where we came up with things like hitting golf balls through the Stargate and people juggling. Peter DeLuise is an actor and very funny, and he was the director of the episode. He said, "How about doing … *this*?" "Yes, yes, do it; do it!" There was stuff we did that didn't make the cut, and there was so much funny stuff shouted out in the writer's room during lunch that wasn't scripted that we did, like the golf ball thing — which became iconic for the episode. But the ending is quite moving, the fact that this guy did all this as a means of coming up with a solution to save his life without realizing he was affecting the whole universe. The whole universe in that mainly O'Neill and Teal'c were stuck in the same universe he was. Just a very satisfying science fiction version of *Groundhog Day*, with Joe and Paul doing a great job on the script.

PETER DELUISE: Normally when you shoot a scene, you have somebody come into a room and *then* start speaking. In the business that's called "shoe leather," but there's no need for us to have somebody come into a room and *then* begin to speak, we just cut to when they start to speak because it's *Groundhog Day*, so we just reset and go, reset and go. The first time you did it, you walked in the room, but the second, third, fourth and fifth time, you just cut to the first thing you say, because the audience doesn't want to endure having to watch you walk into the room five different times. Because there was no "shoe leather," our script page count didn't make sense anymore. And because we were coming in short, our experimental montage had to be elongated.

JOSEPH MALLOZZI: A lot to love about this episode, but it was the "time off" montage that remains my favorite. And, like the *Groundhog Day* aspects of this episode, it almost didn't happen. The episode was timing short, so several scenes were added (they were all scripted, not improvised as some fans assumed): the juggling, Teal'c's repeated door run-in, Jack riding his bike through the corridors of the S.G.C., Jack trying his hand at pottery, the golfing through the gate and, oh yes, *the kiss*. The latter was Paul's idea and I loved it. Note: We made sure to have Jack tender his official resignation before dipping Carter and planting one on her, just to make sure we didn't catch any flak from our Air Force tech advisors.

PETER DELUISE: If you remember *Groundhog Day*, Bill Murray is trying different ways to kill himself and learning how to play piano and learning how to speak French, and all that wonderful stuff. That was done in a quick cut montage, so we did a quick cut montage. We started to add things like Teal'c and O'Neill learning how to juggle — just so happens that both actors knew how to juggle, so we used that; Richard Dean Anderson riding a bicycle down the hallway for no good reason — fun fact a lot of people don't know about Richard Dean Anderson is that in real life he crossed the entirety of the continental United States on a bicycle as a young person.

ROBERT C. COOPER: This was a good example of the pairing off idea, in this case O'Neill and Teal'c, which you didn't get to see a lot of. Getting the two of them into that type of scenario, not only proved to be very funny, but I think it was good for the show.

DARREN SUMNER: For Rick, "Window of Opportunity" was this amazing storm of his comedic sensibilities, his wit, his groundedness and his dramatic flare. So you get this episode that's just wall-to-wall hilarious, and then in the end the team has to go and confront Malikai, the alien who's doing all this and find out it's because he wants to spend one more day with his dead wife. He tells the team they wouldn't understand and Jack says, "I lost my son," and that's one of the character's best moments.

It's also one of Rick's best performances, because you see that the loss of his son is still an open wound. It's something he's still dealing with — which harkens back to a line early in the first season where Jack says he'll never forgive himself, but sometimes he can forget for a little while.

Episode #73 (4.7): "Watergate"
Written by Robert C. Cooper
Directed by Martin Wood
   Guest Starring: Marina Sirtis (Dr. Svetlana Markov), Tom McBeath (Maybourne), Gary Jones (Technician), Darryl Scheeler (Co-Pilot)

The Russians have been using the second Stargate in secret, but after dialing a world that is completely underwater, they lose contact with their Stargate facility and approach Stargate Command for help. The reason is discovered to be microscopic beings that live in, and control, water. They break free and attempt to return home through the Stargate by controlling human bodies and emitting enough energy to keep a Stargate open indefinitely.

BRAD WRIGHT: Robert Cooper once pitched an underwater story that was technically impossible one season, and became "Watergate" just two years later.

ROBERT C. COOPER: The idea I pitched was like *The Abyss*, but our VFX team said it wasn't doable on a TV budget yet. We were always catching up to the effects movies were capable of. But a year later they came to us and said there had been some breakthrough and it was now possible. I also loved introducing the Russian gate angle of the mythology and, of course, there was also Marina!

MARINA SIRTIS (actress, "Dr. Markov"): I was amazed I got that role. My manager called and said, "They want you to audition for *Stargate*, you have to be Russian. Can you do a Russian accent?" I went, "I don't know." "Well, can you do one by tomorrow?" I went to the audition. There were 19 women and 17 of them were Russian. Well, I had the edge, because the audition was all techno babble. I learned it all, so when I went in I [spoke the lines] and they go, "You got the part." Actually, when I went on the set at *Stargate*, the producer came up after the first scene and goes, "Can you tone down the Russian a little? Tone it down, we can't understand what you are saying."

PETER DELUISE: During the shooting of this episode, Kurt Russell, who played Jack O'Neil in the *Stargate* movie, came to visit the set. He was shooting *3000 Miles to Graceland* on a soundstage next door. Usually a movie set is a buzz of activity. When Kurt Russell stepped onto the set, production came to an absolute standstill. Kurt and Richard Dean Anderson had a lovely chat, and the rest of us snuck pictures of them.

Episode #74 (4.8): "The First Ones"
Written & Directed by Peter DeLuise
Guest Starring: Dion Johnstone (Chaka), Jason Schombing (Dr. Robert Rothman), Vincent Hammond, Gary Jones (Technician), Barry Levy, Steve Bacic (Major Coburn), Russell Ferrier (Captain Griff), Rob Lee (Pierce)

While helping with the excavation of fossilized Goa'ulds on P3X-888, the homeworld of the Goa'uld and the Unas, Daniel Jackson is captured by the Unas named Chaka. The rest of SG-1 tries to find and rescue him.

JOSEPH MELLOZZI: Peter DeLuise kicks off his writers' room stint in fine style with this episode, the first in a string of Unas episodes. Peter's office was located across the hall from mine and, whenever someone would bring their kid to the production office, they would invariably stop to visit with Peter who had a whole routine for the lucky little guests, an act that always started with "Pull my finger" and always ended with an imitation of Barney the Dinosaur. It goes without saying, the kids loved him and stopping by his office was always the high point of any tour. Until years later, when I decorated my office with cool super villain-themed statues.

PETER DELUISE: What I pitched to Brad was the idea of an origin story to see the original Unas planet where the Goa'uld first got blended, which he thought was great. I made it not unlike a reverse of *Robinson Crusoe*, based on what I had known from "Demons," which inspired "The First Ones." I've said with the Unas I would like to see one without a Goa'uld in him, like a raw unpossessed version of that. *And* I would like to see Daniel communicate with it so you get the *Robinson Crusoe* thing. There was this wonderful Australian movie I saw as a child that made a huge impact on me called *Walkabout* [1971], which was a wonderful story about two kids brought out into the woods, but then there was an Australian aborigine on a solo walkabout, which was happening to Chaka at the time. So I borrowed that portion of that story or should I say it inspired it, as well as the fact that he was transitioning from young Unas to adult and had to prove himself on his walkabout.

Episode #75 (4.9): "Scorched Earth"
Written by Joseph Mallozzi & Paul Mullie
Directed by Martin Wood
Guest Starring: Brian Markinson (Lotan), Marilyn Norry (Hedrezar), Alessandro Juliani (Eliam), Rob Court (Caleb), Nikki Smook (Nikka)

Earth resettles a group of Enkaran refugees, a race of humans who have become specifically adapted to their homeworld and thus require exact environmental conditions on another planet, but an alien spaceship is transforming the new planet into a hostile environment.

JOSEPH MALLOZZI: "Scorched Earth" was the very first script Paul and I wrote for the show (even though "Window of Opportunity" was the first produced) and it was what got us our staff positions. While I'd love to take full credit for the character of Lotan, it was Brian Markinson's brilliant performance that really made the episode. As a point of interest (beside the missing Jack and Daniel resolution), the original ending was bittersweet. Rather than the (what I felt was too convenient) solution at the end of the episode, the original script had Lotan deciding to stop the terraforming process, thereby dooming the civilization he had been programmed to seed. The closing scene ended with Daniel in his office, listening to a snippet of alien music, a parting gift from Lotan and the final memory of a distant civilization now extinct.

Episode #76 (4.10): "Beneath the Surface"
Written by Heather E. Ash
Directed by Peter DeLuise
Guest Starring: Alison Matthews (Brenna), Kim Hawthorne (Kegan), Laurie Murdoch (Administrator Caulder), Gary Jones (Technician), Russell Ferrier (Griff), Brian Drummond (Attendant), Jason Griffith (Worker), Bruce Campbell (Worker)

The members of SG-1 have had their memories altered and been put to work in an underground industrial complex. Needless to say, those memories must be recovered if they hope to escape.

PETER DELUISE: Shot in this power station where everyone was slave labor in another hellscape. There were the haves and have-nots, so that was the challenge: converting what was essentially a power station into what looked like an underground alien power source. I think they all had amnesia as well, but they recovered their memories. It was fun to deal with why they had lost their memories and knowing there was something weird going on, which is a bit of a sci-fi touchstone, getting your memory back or the power of your historical relationship with somebody else helps break through whatever the spell was that caused it.

JOSEPH MALLOZZI: I think the script lacked an emotional core – it could have used a Sam/Jack focus. They love one another. It would only make sense for them to be together if they had no recollection of their former lives. The feeling was we had played that particular emotional beat in "Divide and Conquer," and there was a concern if we went that way in "Beneath the Surface," we would be over playing the angle.

Episode #77 (4.11): "Point of No Return"

Written by Joseph Mallozzi & Paul Mullie
Directed by William Gereghty
Guest Starring: Willie Garson (Martin), Robert Lewis (Dr. Tanner), Matthew Bennett, Teryl Rothery (Dr. Janet Fraiser), Mar Andersons (Bob), Francis Boyle (Sgt. Peters)

Martin Lloyd has inexplicable knowledge of the Stargate and claims that he is from outer space, remembering his home address. As things develop it turns out he belongs to a small group of men who deserted their homeworld after losing a war against the Goa'uld. After failing to find anything but more hardship, they chose to desert the rest of their race and hide out on Earth.

JOSEPH MELLOZZI: This episode was borne out of Paul's perusal of several online conspiracy sites that maintained the Stargate program did, in fact, exist and that the TV show was part of a plausible deniability campaign (something we would use in later episodes). Lots of great memories from this episode: Teal'c on the motel bed, the great onscreen chemistry between Rick and Willie Garson (who got along famously off-camera), and some bizarre notes we received at the script stage. In one scene at the military camp, we hear a helicopter fly away. We received the note: "Can we see the helicopter?" Brad responded: "No, we can't see the helicopter, because it doesn't exist. All we have is the sound of the helicopter." Another note was a request to convey the sense of some alien quality in Marty at episode's end, something to let us know how out of this world he truly was. There was a suggestion that, in the final shot of the episode, Marty could wiggle his ears in an other-worldly manner. Suffice it to say, it didn't fly.

Episode #78 (4.12): "Tangent"
Written by Michael Cassutt
Directed by Peter DeLuise
Guest Starring: Carmen Argenziano (Jacob Carter), Colin Cunningham (Major Davis), Peter Williams (Apophis), Steven Williams (General Vidrine)

Teal'c and O'Neill test-fly the first experimental aircraft based on combined Earth and Goa'uld technologies, but soon a hidden trap in the aircraft takes control of the X-301 and propels it to open space. Sam and Daniel enlist Jacob/Selmak's help to rescue them before the life support of X-301 is depleted.

PETER DELUISE: The book *Redshirts* is written by John Scalzi, and he was hired to help write "Tangent." I remember thinking that he was really cool, because we would have good chats with him. He was a voice coming out of the computer, and I believe this was well before he wrote *Redshirts*, which I was a huge fan of. One of the things John came up with was that at one point they're just drifting out in space and are going to use one of the missiles to give them some propulsion, but it doesn't work.

And John says, "No joy on the burn," which means it didn't work. So John had written an enormous amount of stuff, but because of time and because he went off on a major tangent, his contribution to the script came down mostly to, "No joy in the burn," and nothing else. Years later, Corin Nemec and I and a few other people were doing a convention. Corin, five minutes before we're going to go out on stage and start to answer questions, asked for hair gel. The host of the convention in England was, like, "Oh, we've got to get Corin hair gel!" They start running around looking for hair gel and 30 seconds before we're about to be introduced the call came back: "No joy on the hair gel." Which was a reference to "Tangent," which I thought was hilarious.

JOSEPH MALLOZZI: Michael Cassutt was the perfect guy to write this episode. With his heavy science fiction background (having written many short stories and novels in the genre as well as countless non-fiction articles) and hard SF experience, he delivered a first draft that any one of us would have been hard-pressed to match for its authenticity in circumstances and terminology. For months after "No joy on the burn!" became my go-to phrase whenever I was disappointed with something, be it a scripted scene, a production issue, or my lunch order.

Episode #79 (4.13): "The Curse"
Written by Joseph Mallozzi & Paul Mullie
Directed by Andy Mikita
Guest Starring: Anna-Louise Plowman (Sarah Gardner), Ben Bass (Steven Rayner), Teryl Rothery (Dr. Janet Fraiser), David Abbott (Dr. Jordan), Lorena Gale (Curator), Dan Shea (Sgt. Siler)

Daniel's old archaeology professor has died and when he goes to the funeral, he discovers a controversy surrounding the professor's death. SG-1 discovers that a Goa'uld, Osiris, has escaped from an ancient canopic jar the professor's team was studying.

JOSEPH MELLOZZI: I was damn proud of this episode for a number of reasons, the chiefest being its ability to mine an aspect of Daniel Jackson's past that had yet to be fully explored. My inner comic book geek is in full display here as Green Lantern references abound: Professor Jordan, Sarah Gardner, the Stewart Expedition, Steven Raynor – all GL's past and present.

Anna-Louise Plowman's terrific performance ensured she'd be coming back for a return visit, while Ben Bass' performance as Steven Raynor should have done the same except that the follow-up story I had planned for his character never got past the room. The basic premise of the story involved SG-1 heading off-world and discovering they'd been beaten to an incredible archaeological find by another team headed by Steven

Raynor and bankrolled by a wealthy industrialist who had swung a deal to make use of the Russian gate.

After some 3+ seasons, we'd figured the backstories of our team had no doubt been good and mined – which is why it was a delight to come up with a story that explored aspects of Daniel Jackson's life prior to his joining the Stargate Program. It's a fun little mystery with a healthy dose of Egyptian mythology, exploration and discovery, and one megalomaniacal surprise villain.

Episode #80 (4.14): "The Serpent's Venom"
Written by Peter Deluise
Directed by Martin Wood
Guest Starring: Carmen Argenziano (Jacob Carter), Obi Ndefo (Rak'nor), Paul Koslo (Terok), Peter Williams (Apophis), Douglas H. Arthurs (Heru'ur), Art Kitching (Ma'kar), Daniel Bacon (Technician), Wren Robertz (Red Guard), Nicholas Harrison (Red Guard), Kyle Hogg (Jaffa Boy), Chris Duggan (Heru'ur's Jaffa)

The Tok'ra and Stargate Command plan to sabotage a meeting of Heru'ur and Apophis, who want to form an alliance on neutral ground on the homeworld of the extinct Tobin race, descendants of the Phoenicians. The planet is surrounded by a minefield and the team must rig one of the mines to spark a fight between the two System Lords so they destroy each other. SG-1 discovers Heru'ur has captured Teal'c and intends to use him as a peace offering. Jacob/Selmak plans to meet Teal'c and Rak'nor, a supposed friend of Teal'c's on the inside, on the third moon of the planet Tichenor.

PETER DELUISE: There's a torture sequence of Teal'c that was not unlike the torture scene at the end of *Braveheart*, where they take his intestines out and try to get him to ask for mercy, but he doesn't do it. Also, they're in a minefield, which is inspired by *Galaxy Quest*. In the notes phase, somebody said, "This is a very dangerous minefield," and the criticism was, "Aren't all minefields dangerous?" It became a running joke that in this case the mines were especially close to each other, making it *more* dangerous than usual. It was redundant in its redundancy.

JOSEPH MALLOZZI: To be honest, I don't remember much about this episode outside of the Mallozian mines (named after yours truly), the "intercepting the transmission" beat, and the uber-cool pain stick used to torture Teal'c that now resides in my garage.

Episode #81 (4.15): "Chain Reaction"
Written by Joseph Mallozzi & Paul Mullie

Directed by Martin Wood

Guest Starring: Lawrence Dane (Major General Bauer), Tom McBeath (Maybourne), Gary Jones (Technician), Ronny Cox (Senator Kinsey), Dan Shea (Sgt. Siler), Patti Allan (Kinsey's Wife), Gina Stockdale (Maid), Mark Pawson (Reporter), Norma Jean Wick (Reporter), Jacquie Janzen (Aide).

Hammond abruptly resigns as head of the S.G.C., and is replaced by General Bauer. O'Neill suspects there is more to it than Hammond will admit and refuses to let the matter rest. While General Bauer is planning to make a naqahdah bomb and test it, dooming the S.G.C., O'Neill teams up with Harry Maybourne to get Hammond reinstated.

JOSEPH MELLOZZI: The fact that the late Don Davis considered this episode one of his personal favorites makes me exceedingly proud. It was one of those rare episodes that explored Hammond and offered us a peek of the man behind the uniform. Don was his usual brilliant self and the palpable love and respect SG-1 held for their commander reflected the similar love and respect Don commanded, not only from his fellow cast members, but the entire crew as well. Although I got along well with the entire cast, Don was the one I would occasionally go out to dinner with, sharing a love of food with the fine, Southern gent.

Episode #82 (4.16): "2010"
Written by Brad Wright
Directed by Andy Mikita
Guest Starring: Christopher Cousins (Joe), Dion Luther (Mollem), Gary Jones (Walter), Ronny Cox (The President), Teryl Rothery (Dr. Janet Fraiser), David Neale (Dialer), Linnea Johnson (Guide), Bryce Hodgson (Kid), Liza Huget (Waitress).

In an alternate timeline, Earth has defeated the Goa'uld with the help of the Aschen, a bland and humorless advanced people from a world designated P4C-970. Earth discovers too late that the Aschen plan to depopulate the planet by secretly sterilizing much of the population through life-extending drugs. Thus, the former members of SG-1 sacrifice their lives to send a warning back in time to themselves not to contact the Aschen homeworld. The season 5 episode "2001" resumes this story.

BRAD WRIGHT: I probably wrote acts four and five of this episode in a single afternoon; it just came flying out of my fingertips. It was one of those times when I just knew every beat that was going to play, and then Andy shot it like a *Mission: Impossible* show. Just a great little time travel episode, with that note from the future — which I thought was so neat an idea — saying not to go to that planet or it would fuck us up completely.

JOSEPH MALLOZZI: Anytime we can kill off all main characters is an opportunity not to be missed. And they go out in blazing style in the closing moments of this episode, my favorite Brad Wright script of the show's fourth season. This was the first part of what could have been an Aschen trilogy, book-ended by "2001," but that third episode – like many intriguing notions – just never came to fruition.

DARREN SUMNER: Brad introduces the Aschen, another advanced ally to help Earth defeat the Goa'uld, and by the end of it, it's 10 years later when this episode is set and we discover that they're *not* our friends. That they've effectively conquered us and there's nothing we can do about it now, because they're sewn into our society. So the team hatches a crazy plan to send a note back through the Stargate into the past, which is another callback to "1969" when we discovered that if you time it just right and dial a wormhole that is coordinated with a solar flare, the gravity reflects the solar flare back on itself and you go back in time. There's a whole mechanism that the show uses for time travel, like *Star Trek* used slingshotting around the sun. It happens one time accidentally, and then suddenly we're using it to just go back and do field research into 20th century Earth. So in this case the team sends a note to themselves in the past to avert this timeline. And it also gives Brad, as the writer, an excuse to kill everybody off, which is always fun in science fiction.

Episode #83 (4.17): "Absolute Power"
Written by Robert C. Cooper
Directed by Peter DeLuise
Guest Starring: Lane Gates (Shifu), Peter Williams (Apophis), Colin Cunningham (Major Davis), Gary Jones (Technician), William deVry (Aldwin), Erick Avari (Kasuf), Stephen Williams (General Vidrine), Teryl Rothery (Dr. Janet Fraiser), Michelle Harrison (Assistant), Yee Jee Tso (Left Tech), Jenn Forgie (Right Tech), Barbara Fixx (Rear Tech), Coleen Christie (Reporter), June B. Wilde (Maid)

The Harcesis has come to visit the S.G.C. and puts Jackson in a coma-like state. During it, he experiences what it means to have all the knowledge of the Goa'uld.

PETER DELUISE: It's exactly what you think it is: absolute power corrupts absolutely. Another opportunity for Michael Shanks to demonstrate his acting ability as we explore Daniel's Id, where he's super smart and takes over the defense of a planet. And because he's got absolute power, it corrupts his character, absolutely.

ROBERT C. COOPER: We were always looking for ways to have fun with our lead characters. To do something to them that would change them profoundly for an episode — like switching bodies or have them go to the dark side — and then, hopefully, find a way to undo it and, in this case, get our Daniel back having learned something valuable from the experience.

JOSEPH MALLOZZI: Actors love to play bad guys and, in this episode, Michael Shanks delivers a terrific portrayal of our Daniel gone dark side. Destroying Moscow is pretty bad, but one of the most unsettling acts he commits never found its way into the finished version of the episode. In an earlier version, there is mention of the fact that Teal'c inexplicably vanished years ago. The truth about his mysterious disappearance is revealed when Jack stumbles upon his old friend, a prisoner of Daniel who has been experimenting on him, transfusing blood from the Jaffa in an effort to master control of Goa'uld technology.

PETER DELUISE: We shot the episode in a mansion, which is highly recognizable as being a period piece that was also used heavily in season two of *When Calls the Heart*. It's the go-to mansion in Vancouver that everyone ends up… going to. I especially like that, because it was an examination, even though it was fake, even though it never happened in real life, of the internal journey into the mind of Daniel Jackson. I *really* like that.

Episode #84 (4.18): "The Light"
Written by James Phillips
Directed by Peter F. Woeste
Guest Starring: Kristian Ayre (Loran), Gary Jones (Technician), Teryl Rothery (Dr. Janet Fraiser), Link Baker (Lt. Barber)

SG-1 discovers a world abandoned by the Goa'uld where there is a room with a beautiful, mesmerizing light display, but it seems that the light may have an insidious effect.

JOSEPH MALLOZZI: While the final quarter of the show's fourth season delivers some great hits ("Entity," "Exodus"), it also offers up a few misses, this episode being a big one in my book. The beat of Jack rushing Daniel back to the planet aside, the episode never really delivers – surprising given what was, up to this point, a fairly strong season.

Episode #85 (4.19) "Prodigy"
Story by Brad Wright, Joseph Mallozzi & Paul Mullie, Teleplay by Joseph Mallozzi & Paul Mullie
Directed by Peter DeLuise
Guest Starring: Elisabeth Rosen (Jennifer Hailey), Hrothgar Mathews (Dr. Hamilton), Bill

Dow (Dr. Lee), Michael E. Ryan (Himself), Keith Martin Gordey (Professor Monroe), Michael Kopsa (General Kerrigan), Roger Haskett (Dr. Thompson), Russell Ferrier (Major Griff), Ivon R. Bartok (Cadet)

Carter meets a brilliant USAF cadet while lecturing at the Air Force Academy, but the cadet has a problem with authority. Carter decides to show her there are possibilities she isn't aware of. On an off-world mission on M4C-862, a moon 42,000 light-years from Earth, energy-based creatures take a dislike to the Tau'ri and Carter and the cadet must work on a solution to get everyone home. This episode includes a cameo by General Michael E. Ryan, then Chief of Staff of the United States Air Force.

JOSEPH MALLOZZI: This one was another disappointment. I believe I've already mentioned elsewhere how the character of Jennifer Hailey was originally conceived as a younger version of Carter (Samantha, Jr.) but, in the end, came across as petulant and unlikable. Without a doubt, our weakest script of the fourth season, but an episode notable for the very first onscreen appearance of Ivon Bartok, who plays the cadet, in the opening tease, and asks: "Did you say *ten* dimensions?" Brilliant. The role of Hailey came down to two extras, Elizabeth (who eventually won the part) and an actress named Jennifer Halley. It stuck in my head because, in my first draft of the script, the character had been named Jennifer Halley before Paul changed her last name to Hailey. Anyway, Elizabeth was better suited to the role of the young ingenue, but Jennifer would later land the role of Lieutenant Tolinev in Season 5's "The Tomb." The seemingly distant cousins of the alien life forms (zapping bugs) that complicate matters in this episode put in an appearance in *Stargate Atlantis'* "The Defiant One" and *Stargate Universe's* "Water."

PETER DELUISE: There's a Robert A. Heinlein novel called *Space Cadet*, and when I read this script that's what the episode felt like. It's about second generation people who might be a part of the Stargate program, and I was thrilled by that. Also, in this episode Russell Ferrier was playing Major Griff, reprising the role from "The First Ones" and the character was an homage to Samuel Fuller, who directed *The Big Red One*. And we had Grace Park prior to her being on *Battlestar Galactica* and *Hawaii Five-0*.

Episode #86 (4.20): "Entity"
Written by Peter DeLuise
Directed by Allan Lee
Guest Starring: Gary Jones (Technician), Teryl Rothery (Dr. Janet Fraiser), Dan Shea (Sgt. Siler)

Stargate Command sends a probe through the Stargate to P9C-372, a world inhabited by electronic lifeforms. The base computer system is compromised by what is apparently a very advanced computer virus, which eventually displaces Samantha Carter's mind from her body.

PETER DELUISE: I pushed that episode and I think Brad liked the concept, because it is about an artificial intelligence at the base. It was inspired by *Ghost in the Machine*, which had come out in 1993 and there was another one with Jamie Lee Curtis called *Virus*. The same concept was utilized again in *Atlantis*. And because Amanda Tapping was such a big fan of Stephen Hawking, it came to pass that that's how she was going to communicate with this entity, through this little keyboard and having a similar voice to Stephen Hawking; if you recall, that's how she was communicating.

JOSEPH MALLOZZI: The premise was fairly standard but, like most every episode, what set it apart was what made it special for our characters – in this case, Amanda who got to go all Terminator, and Jack who is faced with a very tough call in dealing with the threat. What I found particularly interesting about this episode was that, after many stories in which Jack's military stance conflicts with Daniel's peaceful civilian position, invariably resulting in the latter being proven correct, the results are reversed here. Jack was right. He should have destroyed it when he had the chance rather than allow Daniel and Sam to attempt communication with the entity.

Episode #87 (4.21): "Double Jeopardy
Written by Robert C. Cooper
Directed by Michael Shanks
Guest Starring: Belinda Waymouth (Ja'din), Jay Brazeau (Harlan), Ron Halder (Cronus), Matthew Harrison (Darian), Bill Croft (Sindar), Daniel Bacon (Technician), Tracy Hway (Hira), Michael Jonsson (Juna Warrior), John DeSantis (Jaffa), Paul Stafford (Jaffa)

After Cronus' army captures the android counterparts of SG-1 ("Tin Man") on the planet Juna (P3X-729), the members of the real SG-1 must work with their robot duplicates to free the planet.

ROBERT C. COOPER: Michael Shanks asked to direct an episode, so I gave him one of the most technically complicated shoots we had ever attempted, loaded with motion control and twinning. One of the best twists in the show — Daniel getting his head blown off only to reveal he's a robot — really came about because I needed to get Michael Shanks out of a bunch of scenes so he could focus on the directing part.

MICHAEL SHANKS: We had a lot of fight scenes and a lot of twinning – twinning being character duplication – because of the theme of the episode is that the SG-1 team comes across their old double robot selves that were duplicated in the Season One episode "Tin Man." So that involved a lot of split-screens, photo doubling and things like that. We also did two days on location in a forest somewhere in the lower mainland. (*SFX*)

JOSEPH MALLOZZI: *SG-1*'s fourth season finishes strong with two terrific back to back episodes. This one saw the return of the team robots and offered up one of my favorite act outs ever: Daniel Jackson's apparent decapitation. No, wait! Speaking of D.J., this episode marked Michael Shanks' directorial debut and it was a doozy. With all the twinning and big action sequences, "Double Jeopardy" would have proven a challenge to even the most seasoned of directors, yet Michael stepped up and the result was spectacular.

Episode #80 (4.22): "Exodus"
Written by Joseph Mallozzi & Paul Mullie
Directed by David Warry-Smith
Guest Starring: Carmen Argenziano (Jacob/Selmak), Peter Wingfield (Tanith), Peter Williams (Apophis), Mark McCall (First Guard), Kenton Reid (Red Jaffa), Paul Norman (Apophis' Red Guard), Kirsten Williamson (Tok'ra #1), Anastasia Bandey (Tok'ra #2)

Apophis is on his way to Vorash, the planet the Tok'ra are using as a base. Carter and Jacob/Selmak attempt to wipe out Apophis' fleet by sending a Stargate linked to a black hole into the local sun, in order to make it go supernova.

JOSEPH MALLOZZI: Seriously, how often do you get to blow up a sun? So when the opportunity comes along, you take it! And we did, taking out Apophis' fleet in the process. I loved the sequence of the gate being jettisoned, its thrusters firing as it repositions itself on its way to its fiery end. Another aspect of this episode that I recall was Rick's ad-lib of the line: "We're boned without water," originally "We're screwed without water" in the script. Paul walked into my office after viewing the dailies and asked: 'Can we say "boned" on television?' I remember shrugging back and saying, "Sure, why not?"

We were airing on Showtime, after all, and ultimately boning wouldn't be an issue until the big move to Sci-Fi, a network that would send us its Standards and Practices overview before every season. Amusingly, it would offer up a list of acceptable, unacceptable, and "gray area" words and expressions. The relative permissibility of the latter was entirely dependent on the context in which they were used. For instance, "jerk off" was unacceptable unless, say, as Paul suggested, we used it in a line like, "Somebody push that jerk off that ledge!" Paul and I dedicated an entire afternoon to crafting just the right dialogue context for a host of otherwise improper terms ("Boy, that cock kept me up all night. It just wouldn't stop crowing!" And such.) Time well spent.

SEASON FIVE SUMMARY (2001-2002)

*Apophis dies (again), this time at the hands of the Replicators and a ship crashing into the planet Delmak.

*The ascended being Orlin is forgiven of his wrongdoing and allowed to rejoin the ascended collective.

* SG-1 encounters the Reole and gains access to their chameleon-like chemical.

* Cassandra comes of age and her physiology begins to mutate. Nirrti arrives at Stargate Command to continue her hok'taur experiments. She is discovered and is set free in exchange for saving Cassandra's life.

*The Unas Chaka is captured by Burrock's people. Daniel Jackson and SG-1 manage to free the Unas, but the creatures take the fight back to the villagers.

* SG-1 and a Russian unit investigate the missing team from P2X-338. Marduk retakes a human host. He and the Eye of Tiamat are buried in rubble from a C4 explosion.

*The Tollan Curia form an alliance with Tanith, an envoy of Anubis, to prevent their annihilation, and agree to develop phase-shifting weapons of mass destruction. The Tollan Narim takes matters into his own hands and destroys the manufacturing plant. Anubis's forces destroy the Tollan civilization from orbit.

* SG-1 forms a tentative alliance with the Aschen. When it is discovered that their home world may be P4C-970, Hammond orders the team to investigate further. The Aschen's plan to absorb Earth into their confederation and make humans extinct is thwarted.

*Adrian Conrad is implanted with a Goa'uld. Frank Simmons kidnaps him as a future bargaining chip for the Rogue N.I.D.

*Tanith is killed by Teal'c.

*Anubis reveals his return to the System Lords who (minus Yu) vote him back into their ranks in exchange for destroying Earth. Osiris holds his seat on the council.

* Lantash and Lt. Elliot die.

*Jonas Quinn smuggles naquadria to Earth.

Daniel Jackson ascends with the help of Oma Desala.

Thor's consciousness is downloaded into Osiris' mothership. His clone body lapses into a coma.

EPISODE GUIDE: SEASON FIVE

Episode #89 (5.1): "Enemies"
Story by Brad Wright, Robert C. Cooper, Joseph Mallozzi & Paul Mullie, Teleplay by Robert C. Cooper
Directed by Martin Wood
Guest Starring: Carmen Argenziano (Jacob / Selmak), Peter Williams (Apophis), Jennifer Calvert (Councilwoman Ren'Al), Gary Jones (Technician), Thomas Milburn, Jr. (Jaffa), Dean Moen (Jaffa)

After Apophis has brainwashed Teal'c, SG-1 and Jacob prepare to fight against their foe on board Cronus' ship. A mysterious ship then appears and attacks Apophis' vessel, disabling it and causing them to flee, giving SG-1 the chance to get on board. But danger lurks in the form of an army of Replicator bugs and an auto-destruct program.

BRAD WRIGHT: "Enemies" is a terrific season opener. What I wanted to do was take our two big nemeses of the last two years and put them together, so the episode features Apophis *and* the Replicators with a whole load of twists.

JOE MAZZOLLI: Apophis is dead. That said, this is sci-fi and who knows what the future holds? I just knew what the near future holds.

BRAD WRIGHT: I think it's one of our best episodes ever. At the end of season four, we found ourselves on a ship in another galaxy 120 years away from home, even at top speed, and with our arch enemy Apophis. Another one of our enemies, who has almost wiped us out in the past, ends up inadvertently coming to our aid, and of course, they almost wipe us out, too, but we manage to escape them.

PETER DELUISE: We considered leaving them in Outer Space and doing a year of episodes along the lines of *Star Trek: Voyager*, or even better, *Lost in Space*. However, we didn't think the viewers would buy it, especially since we didn't have Billy Mumy or a robot yelling, "Danger, SG-1! Danger!"

JOE MAZZOLLI: I always found it interesting that, whenever certain fans took issue with a creative decision, they would always blame T.P.T.B. (The Powers That Be) as if we were one giant, multi-headed monster. In truth, we're individual little monsters who have had our share of disagreements over the years on everything from wardrobe decisions to major character arcs. Season Four had seen its share of minor debates, but this episode stands out as the first big blowout. I don't even recall exactly what was being disputed; I only remember it had to do with story structure. That and being really impassioned and, ultimately, very annoyed. In the end, Paul and I handed off the episode to Rob and shifted focus to another script, "The Fifth Man" – and "Enemies" turned out to be a terrific episode.

Episode #90 (5.2): "Threshold"
Written by Brad Wright
Directed by Peter DeLuise
Guest Starring: Tony Amendola (Bra'tac), Brook Parker (Drey'auc), Peter Williams (Apophis), David Lovgren (Va'lar), Teryl Rothery (Dr. Janet Fraiser), Eric Schneider (Dr. McKenzie), Karen van Blankenstein (Nurse)

Teal'c has been saved from dying on Apophis' ship, but remains loyal to his old master. Bra'tac uses an old Jaffa ritual that will either bring Teal'c back or kill him.

CHRISTOPHER JUDGE: The pilot started with Teal'c turning on his people, but why was never addressed. We know that Bra'tac [Tony Amendola] planted the seeds of knowledge, so to speak, of what the goals truly were, but you never saw the journey Teal'c had to make to get to the point where he said, "If I'm ever going to do something to free my people, I've got to do this now." I was very happy to see a whole episode devoted to that. The more we know about Teal'c's past, the more interesting everything else he does is.

BRAD WRIGHT: Loved working with Tony Amendola and Chris in this one. They both got to show off their acting chops.

JOSEPH MAZZOLLI: One of my favorite moments of these early fifth season episodes is the Larry David stare-down Bra'tac gives Teal'c to discern whether he is lying or not. That bug-eyed gawk would always leave me chortling. A great Teal'c episode, though less so for Chris Judge who had to brave the elements on this one. On the day they headed out to shoot the exterior scenes, they discovered a thick blanket of snow on the ground. Oops. It provided what I imagine must have been a somewhat uncomfortable bedding for the shirtless Chris to lie down on.

PETER DELUISE: "Threshold" was set in the snow, so Chris Judge, shirtless, was in the snow, freezing his ass off. He was a good sport about it, but I remember we had to dig out a hole in the shape of his toro and we put cotton bedding in it, so his skin wasn't right on top of the snow. That's my biggest memory of that, next to the fact that the forever training sequence was inspired by the one in *Remo Williams: The Adventure Begins*.

Episode #91 (5.3): "Ascension"
Written by Robert C. Cooper
Directed by Martin Wood
Guest Starring: Sean Patrick Flanery (Orlin), John de Lancie (Colonel Simmons), Teryl Rothery (Dr. Janet Fraiser), Ben Wilkinson (O'Brien), Eric Breker (Reynolds), Rob Fournier (Special Forces Commander)

After falling unconscious, Carter returns from Velona (P3X-636), a planet full of ruins, suffering from suspected exhaustion, though she begins seeing a mysterious young man named Orlin who can walk through solid objects. But everyone believes that she's simply seeing things as a result of that assumed exhaustion.

ROBERT C. COOPER: A big one for me, because it was really kind of galvanizing the core idea that I felt was most interesting and inspirational about *Stargate*, which is we often talked about the fact that the show wasn't necessarily anti-religion, but we definitely were pro-science and were poking holes in false religions that were oppressing people. "Ascension" was the spiritual undertone in a positive way of *Stargate*. It was that sort of Zen idea of self-betterment to the nth degree. And it helped explain the mythology of the Ancients when I first came on the show and I first realized that there was this nugget in the bible for the show about the fact that the Goa'uld were not the creators of the Stargates; that they had usurped the technology and that whoever created it was long gone. I was, like, "Whoa, is no one going to play with that?"

To me that seemed like a big carrot to dangle. So it became a question of where did they go and what's in store for us? Then it became the whole mythology about Earth being the second evolution of humanity and that the first had ascended and reached this non-corporeal state, which you could argue is godlike, but you could also say is just a physiological evolution to some other kind of matter of consciousness. To me, that was the closest to an epiphany in terms of giving us a spiritual dynamic that the show up until that point had kind of lacked. It's not like I created this question, I just said there had to be an answer. It's a little easier when someone kind of lays out the trail for you.

AMANDA TAPPING: This is a huge, huge episode for Carter. We get to see where she lives. I get to wear normal clothes. I drive an amazing car. It's sweet. You know what? I think Carter is very cool. She has a 1940 Indian motorcycle; a 1961 beautiful, mint, vintage Volvo and she's got a Harley in her garage that she's working on, too. How great is that? [And] I have a man. Of course, at first nobody believes he exists; that he's a bit like "my imaginary friend." Actually it's a great episode for me, because everyone thinks I'm crazy and plays into the fact that Carter has no life outside S.G.C.. They play into the fact that she never relaxes, so they keep saying things like "take it easy," "rest" and "go home." So you get to see her house and see that she does have a normal life. It's not like she's a *complete* loser, you know. Well, she might be a little bit of a loser, but not totally.

ROBERT C. COOPER: Sean [Patrick Flanery] did a wonderful job. You have to see the episode, though, to really know what I mean. He and Amanda are just fabulous, so much so that you want to see them in their own little series together. There's a wonderful magic between their characters. The story was well-acted and nicely directed by Martin Wood, who also directed "Enemies." "Ascension" also introduces another new recurring character played by John de Lancie. He's a colonel in the Air Force who has very questionable allegiances. He comes in and poses a threat to General Hammond and Stargate Command by questioning the S.G.C.'s way of doing things. He may or may not be in some way linked to Senator Kinsey, so you're not really sure who's pulling the strings behind his orders or what he's up to.

JOSEPH MAZZOLLI: This was one of those episodes that hadn't sold me at the script stage, but really came together once we started shooting. Sean Patrick Flanery was great and had terrific onscreen chemistry with Amanda. Another perfect example of writer-producer's remorse: an actor who does such a good job that one regrets killing off his character.

Episode #92 (5.4): "The Fifth Man"
Written by Joseph Mallozzi & Paul Mullie
Directed by Peter DeLuise
Guest Starring: Dion Johnstone (Tyler), Gary Jones (Technician), John de Lancie (Colonel Frank Simmons), Teryl Rothery (Dr. Janet Fraiser), Karen van Blankenstein (Nurse), Brad Kelly (Jaffa), Shawn Stewart (Jaffa), Dario DeIaco (Jaffa)

O'Neill remains on a planet designated P7S-441 to protect Lieutenant Tyler, a fifth member of SG-1 whom only the other members of SG-1 can recall. Back on Earth, Hammond informs the team that Tyler doesn't even exist while Col. Simmons returns, seeking to shut the S.G.C. down, citing the latest alien mind games as a possible safety risk.

ROBERT C. COOPER: It's quite a "shoot-em up," because I wanted to put O'Neill in a military situation where he shows his mettle as a one-man force. Rick just eats that stuff up and he does a great job.

PETER DELUISE: In this episode, O'Neill gets stranded behind enemy lines, fighting a new Jaffa faction under an unknown System Lord. In this episode we get the largest number of corpses ever in the show; O'Neill is really trying to outdo the Terminator. We kill everybody – *twice*. We also had Dion Johnstone as Tyler, fooling the others into thinking that he was the fifth member of the group, only to find out that he was, in fact, a humanoid alien who was deceiving them and making them think he was just "the fifth man." That was our first foray into using a CG character with motion capture.

I did a motion capture thing where we had the alien with impossible holes, where you could see *through* the body. It was kind of weird, because we used a bipedal human-oid, but we were going to do a visual effect instead of a costume. Definitely our first experiment in doing a full-blown CG, first person situation.

JOSEPH MAZZOLLI: One of the things I remember about this episode was the hell of a time editing had cutting around all the Jaffa bodies O'Neill had to negotiate on his way to the gate. I mean, holy crap, does he kill a lot of 'em! Apparently, Brad felt the sea of corpses put a damper on an otherwise happy ending.

PETER DELUISE: In that episode we came to the Stargate and there's a bunch of supposedly dead Jaffa on the ground, having been taken care of off-camera, and there was no place on the set where all the actors could get to the Stargate without at least one of them stepping over a Jaffa. And because I was American and they were Canadi-an, when they saw that in the dailies, they were *mortified* that one of them was stepping over a dead body and I caught hell for that. That's why in "Wormhole X-Treme" there was a reference to the dead bodies underneath the frame right there, because silly DeLuise had actors stepping over potentially dead bodies and I was, like, "You don't know they're dead, they could be stunned." In any case, it's all very subjective, isn't it? I was, like, "Okay, I'm sorry." And, of course, I had run out of time during that moment, so I didn't cover it in a way that they could cut around it. So they just pushed in so you couldn't see that he was stepping over a body. They had to fix it up, because the insensi-tive American guy fucked it up.

Episode #93 (5.5): "Red Sky"
Written by Ron Wilkerson
Directed by Martin Wood

Guest Starring: Fred Applegate (Elrad), John Prosky (Malchus), Norman Armour (Dr. MacLaren), Brian Jensen (Freyr)

SG-1 travels to K'Tau and discovers that the sun has been shifted to the infrared end of the spectrum. As a result, all life on the planet is doomed, and SG-1 is responsible. The planet's inhabitants are Norse people and worship the Asgard, believing that the reddening sky is a sign from their Gods. In reality, the event is a solar reaction caused by SG-1's wormhole that spells death for the planet and its people.

JOSEPH MAZZOLLI: Ron Wilkerson's first and best script is a terrific SF tale anchored by one of Richard Dean Anderson's greatest performances. It's a darker side of Jack O'Neill we rarely get to see – angry, intense, and deadly serious. The episode also offers up a side of Carter we rarely glimpse as well: fallible and wrestling with self-doubt. Many layers in this one and it all plays out in very counter-*Star Trek* fashion as the team attempts to force a solution upon the planet's inhabitants.

BRAD WRIGHT: The irony is these people don't want our help and even fight against us, and it's left to Daniel to suggest that maybe there's more to their faith than we can conceive. We had a fantastic time shooting this one, because it's all done in period costume and looks spectacular.

MICHAEL GREENBURG: We had to create an environment with a sky that progressed from blue to red. You can't do that just with filters. We ended up building an exterior set, an Amish-type village, in fact, on a sound stage so that we would have complete control of the lighting. We also shot some live-action footage on location that involved using filters, blue screen and some trick photography. That material then went through what's known as a bleached bypass, which is a neat visual effect. Visually, "Red Sky" is a beautiful show to watch. (*TV Zone Special*)

JOSEPH MAZZOLLI: One of the things we did more in the fifth season than we had before was deal with some darker aspects of storytelling. I mean, "Red Sky" and "Beast of Burden" embody very much the *Stargate* philosophy, which is that we're not perfect. We're humans from the year 2001 who make mistakes and get into situations that can't be solved by snapping your fingers or reversing the polarity of a device on your spaceship. We certainly don't have a Prime Directive. Our heroes will go ahead and poke their noses into things. They do their best to help and/or fix a problem, but they're not always successful. Hey, if you knew things were always going to work out you wouldn't wait around for the end of the story, right?

Episode #94 (5.6): "Rite of Passage"

Written by Heather E. Ash
Directed by Peter DeLuise
Guest Starring: Colleen Rennison (Cassandra), Jacqueline Samuda (Nirrti), Teryl Roth-
ery (Dr. Janet Fraiser), Richard de Klerk (Dominic), Karen van Blankenstein (Nurse)

Dr. Fraiser's adopted daughter, Cassandra, enters puberty and begins developing telekinetic
abilities, but the strain of producing so much energy is causing multiple organ failure. Fraiser and
SG-1 fear that they might not be able to stop the life-threatening changes caused by Goa'uld
Nirrti's genetic experiments.

PETER DELUISE: An example of a girl — Colleen Rennison as Cassandra — getting telekinetic powers and then they were afraid of her, and Colleen was a quite young, talented actress. So she had telekinetic powers and we were dangling a chess piece by invisible thread and it was rotating around as she moved it with her brain. But it was all practical, which meant it was happening in real life. I always remember thinking that if anybody knew how we were achieving this, they would laugh at us. It was so silly in real life, but it looked pretty cool on camera.

JOSEPH MAZZOLLI: This one offered us the rare opportunity to give Dr. Fraiser some screen time and touch on one of Carter's few onscreen non-romantic relationships. The unfortunately monikered Hanka children were named after then MGM studio exec Hank Cohen (who would make a cameo in that season's "Wormhole X-Treme!" as, surprisingly enough, a studio exec).

Episode #95 (5.7): "Beast of Burden"
Written by Peter DeLuise
Directed by Martin Wood
Guest Starring: Larry Drake (Burrock), Dion Johnstone (Chaka), Alex Zahara (Shy
One), Vince Hammond (Big One), Noel Callaghan (Boy), Wycliffe Hartwig (Large
Unas), Herbert Duncanson (Guard #1), Finn Michael (Guard #2), Wycliff Hartwig (Unas
#1), Trevor Jones (Unas #2)

Chaka, the Unas whom Dr. Jackson befriended, has been kidnapped and taken to a planet
where humans use Unases as slaves. On a rescue mission, Jackson is risking not only SG-1's
safety but also an age-old system.

JOSEPH MAZZOLLI: Dion Johnstone reprises his role as Chaka in this follow-up to Season 4's "The First Ones." While Peter DeLuise did the scripting honors on this one, Martin Wood assumed the directing reins. This one is a bit of a blur, but I remember being genuinely surprised by early discussions to offer the role of Burrock to Larry

Drake. His performance as the mentally challenged Benny Stulwicz on *L.A. Law* had been so damn brilliant and convincing, I'd actually assumed they'd hired an intellectually disabled actor to play the part!

PETER DELUISE: We shot in the Western town called Border Town, locally, because *Border Town* was shot there. This was the episode where we had the Unas and the people, and at one point one race was enslaved to the other and then they switched and became the oppressed, not unlike *Planet of the Apes* (which I enjoyed, too). So I wrote and Martin Wood directed, and what was interesting was the combination of the Western town and aliens. Usually we don't have assets like an entire Western town, so that was quite thrilling to me. And because I was such a huge fan of the *Planet of the Apes* movies and TV series as a child, I was thrilled, because this felt like an amazing amount of production value with the combination of special effects and make up in one episode. Also, the dilemma of the oppression of one race and switching, which is obviously stolen from *Planet of the Apes*, but I thought that was a very interesting moral investigation.

Episode #96 (5.8): "The Tomb"
Written by Joseph Mallozzi & Paul Mullie
Directed by Peter DeLuise
  Guest Starring: Earl Pastko (Colonel Zukhov), Alexander Kalugin (Major Vallarin), Jennifer Halley (Lieutenant Tolinev), Vitaliy Kravchenko (Lt. Marchenko), Garry Chalk (Colonel Chekov)

  SG-1 gets trapped in an ancient ziggurat on P2X-338 along with a Russian team. Here they discover the remains of the original Russian team who had gone missing and there's also a Goa'uld on the loose who's willing to kill and inhabit anyone it wants with the sole intention of escaping.

MICHAEL SHANKS: This is a great one for Daniel. As the archaeologist on the show he gets a big charge out of being in his element, and for me as an actor, the character is the most fun to play when he's feeling that way. So this story plays perfectly into that. Our heroes are sent on a mission to investigate an ancient Babylonian temple or ziggurat. In order to uncover the mystery surrounding the tomb, they first must decipher an archaic Earth language. This is where Daniel's problem-solving skills come in handy. Even the door to the place itself is a puzzle and one that my character is able to solve. Of course, once he and the others eventually get inside they find a surprise or two waiting for them. (*TV Zone*)

JOSEPH MAZZOLLI: Vallerin makes mention of their "secret orders" — in this case, to acquire off-world tech (i.e. the Eye of Tiamat). This is why Jack was so mad at episode's end. Regardless of whether Zukhov had the Eye or not, the fact is the Russians were operating under a secret agenda. As for Jack's attitude toward [the Russians] – everyone seems to think that it's a Cold War mentality, but the fact is that in "The Tomb," the other team could well have been British or French and Jack would have reacted much the same way. Essentially, they were shoved down his throat and attempted to override his command. It had nothing to do with any Cold War.

PETER DELUISE: We're basically in a tomb with a sarcophagus in it where we find Goa'uld in canopic jars, so it was whether or not the team could get out without being killed. On top of that, they had to trust Russian partners in order to escape the ziggurat, which we probably would not have even even attempted at this point. Now that Russia has attacked Ukraine, we never would have broached this idea. It's all about timing, I guess.

Episode #97 (5.9): "Between Two Fires"
Written by Ron Wilkerson
Directed by William Gereghty
Guest Starring: Garwin Sanford (Narim), Marie Stillin (Travell), Peter Wing-
field (Tanith), Gary Jones (Technician), Ryan Silverman (Tollan Guard)

The Tollan, in a highly unusual change of policy, agree to share advanced technology with Earth, but Carter's friend, Narim, warns that this might spell great danger for the planet.

JOSEPH MAZZOLLI: Man, this one had all sorts of problems at the outline stage, so much so that it earned the nickname "Between Two Acts." Once the structural problems had been addressed, Ron wrote and delivered a first draft of the script. I remember we were sitting in Rob's office, giving copious notes, when John Lenic's dog hopped up onto the couch and relieved himself on a copy of Ron's script. "That dog pissed on my script!" said Ron. To which Brad replied something along the lines of: "He wasn't the only one." Anyway, in the end, the script came together – as did the episode, which we wound up shooting on the grounds of Simon Fraser University.

PETER DELUISE: Simon Fraser University is a very modern-looking school that doubled well as advanced alien architecture. It was designed by the famous Canadian architect and urban planner, Arthur Erickson.

Episode #98 (5.10): "2001"
Written by Brad Wright
Directed by Peter DeLuise

Guest Starring: Christopher Cousins (Joseph Faxon), Dion Luther (Molum), Robert Moloney (Borren), Gary Jones (Technician), Ronny Cox (Senator Kinsey), Howard Siegel (Keel), Rob Lee (Pierce)

SG-1 visits an agricultural planet inhabited by the Volians, who introduce them to their more technologically advanced allies, the Aschen, who propose an alliance with Earth. After Daniel Jackson and Teal'c discover the Aschen's world to be the gate address they forbade themselves from dialing ("2010"), Earth severs all connect with the Aschen.

BRAD WRIGHT: It's basically the story of what could happen if the events suggested in the earlier episode "2010" went to the worst case scenario and those people weren't just on the planet that we were told not to go to. I feel kind of mean, but Carter has yet another hard choice to make — she leaves the ambassador who was going to be her husband behind — but then, this is television, and if we didn't have hard choices then there would be nothing to watch.

PETER DELUISE: Usually when we tell a story, there's a ticking clock, which is just a clever way of saying that time is short and we have to do something that immediately raises the stakes. This was different in the way that the alien race was overcoming this human population on this alien planet where they had just stopped letting them procreate over time. As a result, they were slowly but surely taking over this planet through a really interesting, weird kind of attrition. They're playing the long game — a *super* long game — which meant that there was no ticking clock. In fact, the ticking clock is inverted, which I really enjoyed.

JOSEPH MAZZOLLI: The sequel to Season Four's "2010" sees the calculating race known as the Aschen make their first (chronological) appearance as seemingly genial, albeit suspicious, emissaries looking to forge a new intergalactic alliance. The episode ends with one major story point unresolved. What of Ambassador Joe Faxon? I'm sure we would have received the answer to that question had the third part of this planned trilogy seen the light of a TV screen. In part three, Brad imagined the remnants of the Aschen race, seeking revenge for the events of "2001," launching a ship-based attack on Earth. Alas, I don't recall why the story never came to fruition, but I have no doubt it would've been great.

Episode #99 (5.11): "Desperate Measures"
Written by Joseph Mallozzi & Paul Mullie
Directed by William Gereghty
Guest Starring: John de Lancie (Colonel Simmons), Tom McBeath (Harry Maybourne), Bill Marchant (Adrian Conrad), Andrew Johnston (Doctor), Ted Cole (Doctor), Carrie

Genzel (Diana Mendez), Teryl Rothery (Dr. Janet Fraiser), Robert Manitopyes (Guard), Jay Kramer (Guard), Frank C. Turner (Homeless Man), Tammy Pentecost (Assistant), Sasha Piltsin (Driver), Raoul Ganeev (Roadblock Soldier), Igor Morozov (Roadblock Soldier)

Carter is kidnapped by a dying millionaire, forcing O'Neill to team up with Harry Maybourne in order to find her.

JOSEPH MAZZOLLI: A couple of things stand out for me about this episode. The first was that ridiculously long search sequence near episode's end that included endless shots of Teal'c and Daniel going up and down stairs. Yes, the episode was short! Another thing was a slight dialogue change in O'Neill's scene with the homeless man. In the original version, O'Neill says, "Yeah, and I've got a closet full of *Playboys* ..." but after some consideration (a.k.a. – getting a note requesting we change it), we elected to go with *National Geographic* instead which, while less Jack O'Neill, was certainly more Richard Dean Anderson. Also, the original draft of the script had a couple of very funny exchanges between the doctors who perform the procedure, but after further consideration (a.k.a. – we received a note that O'Neill provided more than enough comedy for the episode and we didn't need the guest stars delivering as well) we decided to lose them.

Episode #100 (5.12): "Wormhole X-Treme!"
Story by Brad Wright, Joseph Mallozzi & Paul Mullie; Teleplay by Joseph Mallozzi & Paul Mullie
Directed by Peter DeLuise
Guest Starring: Willie Garson (Martin Lloyd), Michael DeLuise (Nick Marlowe / Colonel Danning), Peter DeLuise (Director), Jill Teed (Yolanda Reese / Stacy Monroe), Robert Lewis (Tanner), Benjamin Ratner (Studio Executive), Teryl Rothery (Dr. Janet Fraiser), Christian Bocher (Raymond Gunne / Dr. Levant), Don Thompson (Props Guy), Peter Flemming (Agent Malcolm Barrett), Herbert Duncanson (Douglas Anders / Grell), David Sinclair (Bill the A.D.), Kiara Hunter (Alien Princess), Mar Andersons (Bob), Laura Drummond (Security Guard), Keath Thome (Head SF)

When Stargate Command learns of a television show whose premise closely resembles its operations, SG-1 investigates. They find that alien Martin Lloyd ("Point of No Return") is giving the producers their ideas.

ROBERT C. COOPER: I have this perception that the fans didn't like that episode; that they thought we were laughing at them. That they didn't like us breaking the fourth wall, even though we didn't really *technically* break the fourth wall. But our argument back was, "It's a hundred episodes. We can do whatever we want."

BRAD WRIGHT: I promised a bunch of people, when we started this, that I would make sure we got to a hundred episodes and that we would be healthy when we got there. Well, we did and we were. We kind of said to ourselves that *we* should celebrate the show, too and we were making a little fun of ourselves. Actually, we were making *a lot* of fun of ourselves. Rather than do a heavy, expensive big episode like we normally would do, we did a show that was kind of a *Galaxy Quest* version of *Stargate SG-1*. It allowed one of the characters that we'd already introduced, Willie Garson as Martin Lloyd, to end up doing a parody television series of *Stargate* called *Wormhole X-Treme!* It's very funny.

PETER DELUISE: The premise is that this guy, Martin Lloyd, played by Willie Garson, had a fragmented memory of his experience with the wormhole program, so he pitched a really cheesy sci-fi episode that existed in real life. We were going to have to infiltrate and say, "Oh my God, how does he know so much? What *is* going on?" Then they ultimately came to realize why this TV show so exactly resembles their reality. Even though it was cheesy, it exactly resembled the Stargate program. It was just an opportunity for us to lampoon our own show and *Star Trek* and all sci-fi shows. And then there are a lot of conceits addressed, like, "If you're out of phase with stuff, and you can pass through walls and doors like a ghost, how come you don't fall through the floor?"

JOSEPH MALLOZZI: Oh, boy, where to begin? Over the years, I've referenced the multitude of in-jokes in this episode, from the red spray-painted kiwis (a dig at director Peter DeLuise who used those very alien-looking fruit in "Beneath the Surface") to Hank Cohen's cameo as a studio executive who suggests, "You know, what this show needs is a sexy female alien!" (Art imitating life). There's our faux TV hero trying to negotiate a veritable minefield of corpses (a call back to "The Fifth Man"), someone ridiculing the "one shot stuns, two shots kills, three shots disintegrates" abilities of the alien weapon (hello, zat guns), further ridiculing of doing an episode involving "out of phase" physics (we did plenty), another character's assertion that they'll surely win an Emmy ... for visual effects (the best any sci-fi show can hope for), and much, much more.

PAUL MULLIE: When we were writing it, we knew everyone was going to get their hands on this one. To me, it wasn't even so much a question of the pressure to be funny; but, since everybody had an idea [for the episode] anyway, I thought we'd just write 50 percent of it, and then everybody will come in with an idea for a gag. And that's what happened. Even when we were working on the outline, people were coming by and saying, "You know, you should do this." Everybody pitched ideas involving who they were on the show. It was a big collaboration, with a lot of stuff added to it. It was easy to do all of the spoof elements. It was having an actual *Stargate* story underneath all of the parody that was actually the hard part. But it had to be there, because otherwise the episode wouldn't mean anything.

JOSEPH MALLOZZI: The part of Grell, the Teal'c clone, was actually played by Chris Judge's stand-in, Herbert, while the episode offered a host of cameos from behind-the-scenes personnel including a much heavier yours truly, who demands to know, "Hey, what happened to all the doughnuts?!" I recall director Peter DeLuise making me do three takes, directing me, "You're hungry! You want some doughnuts! But there are none! You're really hungry!" and then, "No doughnuts and you're *really* hungry!" and *then*, "Okay! *Really hungry!*" The day that scene was shot, I found my wardrobe awaiting me in the office: a lime green shirt and a pair of atrocious lime green plants. I wore the shirt but passed on the pants. Apparently, our costume designer did not take the news well. "Writers," she apparently muttered with a roll of her eyes.

ROBERT C. COOPER: I didn't come up with the idea, but I thought the conceit was genius, that there was this television show being created by an alien who we had helped save, who was living on Earth and that the reason that the Air Force let it happen was essentially plausible deniability. That was hilarious. And Peter casting both his brothers on the show, it was just a good time. None of us weren't giggling and having an awesome time casting the other version of the SG-1 team. On top of that, our crew — production designers, costumes designers … everybody — were just, like, "Really? We get to do this and appear in the episode?" Uh, yeah. That's what's fun about it.

PETER DELUISE: We actually photographed *everything*: all of our sets, all of us behind the scenes, all of our equipment — *every* crewmember ended up on camera. We had the back of the sets there, all of the circus — which is our support vehicles, our trucks, all of our mobile dressing rooms … Every single thing that you can photograph, we photographed. My brothers Michael, David and I wrote, produced and directed a movie called *Between the Sheets*, our version of *A Star is Born* where these two people can't stand each other and are having to pretend that they're a couple to strengthen their individual careers, and the plot is whether or not they're really in love. That gave me some prep for this. We had this surrealistic environment on a movie set. And then somebody suggested my brother Michael for the role that would lampoon the O'Neill character.

ROBERT C. COOPER: Every time I think about Willie Garson passing, I get sad, you know? He was so dynamic and delightful in his first episode, so it was great when he came back. One thing I remember … Well, first off, I'm *not* an actor and this episode is the only time I really appeared on screen in this series. Willie and I were sitting together off stage, just shooting the shit and he was complaining about his New York apartment, but also laughing about it. He was such a charming guy. Then I hear the call for the first team, which is when the cast is supposed to come on set. So he gets up, because he follows directions, and I wasn't paying much attention, just doing whatever he was doing. We walk on set and he's still talking. Then Peter yells, "Okay. Action!" and Willie just changed into his character. Instant transformation. I was totally caught off guard, and that look of confusion that I have in the episode was me actually being confused about what was real. I've always had a tremendous amount of respect for actors and that sort of magic they do in becoming something else, but acting feels silly to me. It feels like you're on the playground pretending to be Starsky and Hutch or something.

JOSEPH MALLOZZI: I would love to dig up the outtakes and extra footage on this one. One scene that ended up on the cutting room floor involved the character of Teal'c. SG-1 and Hammond are watching the *Wormhole X-Treme!* trailer at which point we do a pan off the screen, across the briefing room table to Teal'c laughing uproariously and enjoying the hell out of the show – much to the bewilderment of his fellow team members.

BRAD WRIGHT: Like I said, all of us made appearances in the episode. In fact, it ended with Michael Greenburg and I talking and walking away, with him saying, "That's a pretty cool visual effect," and I say, "I've seen better." Michael asks if we can still get 18 holes in and I say, "Yeah, I think so," while the crane's pulling up and those are the last two lines. Oh, and then Michael says, "When do you think we should cut to black?" "Right about now," and then we cut to black.

ROBERT C. COOPER: Maybe now, in retrospect, fans look back on the episode fondly and have a different opinion, but I remember at the time, not a lot of people were too happy with it. The real attraction of science fiction is escapism, and when you pop the bubble and say the world that you're escaping to isn't real, it hurts. You don't want to think that we don't take it incredibly seriously.

Episode #101 (5.13): "Proving Ground"
Written by Ron Wilkerson
Directed by Andy Mikita
  Guest Starring: Courtenay J. Stevens (Elliott), Elisabeth Rosen (Jennifer Hailey), Grace Park (Satterfield), David Kopp (Grogan), Michael Kopsa (General Kerrigan)

  SG-1 is running training simulations for a group of new recruits and, timing being everything, things begin to get more serious when aliens invade.

JOSEPH MALLOZZI: Some episodes you hate at the pitch stage, but end up warming up to once the story has been broken. Others, you hate at the outline stage, but end up actually liking once the script comes in. Still others, you may hate at the script stage, but love once the episode is completed. This is one of those rare episodes that I took issue with from start to finish and, to this day, ranks as one of my least favorites. Why? Because it's not about our characters. That and the all-too predictable late twist that anyone who has ever watched television before will see coming a mile off. On the other hand, the episode was notable for an appearance by a then relatively unknown Grace Park as one of the young cadets.

Episode #102 (5.14): "48 Hours"
Written by Robert C. Cooper
Directed by Peter F. Woeste
Guest Starring: David Hewlett (Dr. McKay), Tom McBeath (Harold Maybourne), Colin Cunningham (Major Davis), Bill Marchant (Goa'uld), Gary Chalk (Russian Colonel), Gary Jones (Technician), John de Lancie (Col. Frank Simmons), Jeff Seymour (Mr. Black), Martin Blatz (NID Guard), Dan Shea (Sgt. Siler), Tracy Westerholm (SF), Ken Phelan (Food Server)

On P3X-116, SG-1 comes under fire from a Goa'uld attack led by Tanith. Teal'c takes the opportunity to shoot down Tanith's Al'kesh, and the ship crashes into the Stargate as Teal'c is in transit to Earth. Teal'c does not re-materialize on Earth, but his pattern is still in the Earth-side gate's data buffer. With a deadline of 48 hours bearing down on them before normal operations resume, SG-1 must work against the clock to find a way to save Teal'c before he is lost forever. As Daniel and Major Paul Davis attempt to make a deal with the Russians, O'Neill finds himself forming an unlikely partnership with rogue agent Harry Maybourne as General Hammond deals with Colonel Frank Simmons. Meanwhile Carter finds herself collaborating with the obnoxious Dr. Rodney McKay (David Hewlett), the world's foremost expert on the Stargate, who has already decided that trying to save Teal'c is a waste of time.

ROBERT C. COOPER: One of the coolest opening sequences we ever did in my humble opinion. I always thought the Joker shooting down the Batwing with a pistol in Tim Burton's *Batman* was ridiculous, but Teal'c shooting down a glider with a staff weapon on the other hand … Also, highlighting a key feature of the gate and turning it into a problem we needed to solve — the fact that you get decomposed, sent through the wormhole as data and then recomposed on the other side.

JOSEPH MALLOZZI: The working title for this episode was "Teal'c Interrupted," but later changed to "48 Hours." I was extremely disappointed. I figured, hey, if you can call an episode "Watergate," you should be able to call another one "Teal'c

Interrupted!" The episode kicks off with the shocking death of Tanith, shocking insofar as he was a mid-major villain who suddenly and all too quickly buys it in spectacularly unspectacular fashion. From what I recall, we were unable to reach a deal with the actor on another episode and, rather than leave the character dangling, elected to write him out instead. This episode also saw the introduction of one Dr. Rodney McKay ("Rodney?" I remember asking Rob at the time. "Is that the name you want to go with?"), an insufferable ass who, over the course of the franchise's run, ended up redeeming himself in surprising fashion.

Episode #103 (5.15): "Summit"
Written by Joseph Mallozzi & Paul Mullie
Directed by Martin Wood
Guest Starring: Carmen Argenziano (Jacob Carter), Anna-Louise Plowman (Osiris), Cliff Simon (Baal), Courtenay J. Stevens (Lt. Elliott), Jennifer Calvert (Ren'al), Gary Jones (Technician), William de Vry (Aldwin), Anthony Ulc (Mansfield), Vince Crestejo (Yu), Kevin Durand (Zipacna), Kwesi Ameyaw (Olokun), Suleka Mathew (Kali), Paul Anthony (Slave), Andrew Kavadas (Zipacna's Jaffa), Simon Hayama (Jarren), Natasha Khadr (Bastet), Bonnie Kilroe (Morrigan)

There is a truce among the Goa'uld and the System Lords meet on a heavily-guarded space station. The Tok'ra plan to kill them all, but require a human who can speak fluent Goa'uld and Daniel is the only qualified candidate. The Tok'ra create a version of the Reol chemical ("The Fifth Man") for the undercover mission. Meanwhile, Anubis attacks an outpost of Kali on the planet Cerador, destroying two motherships. Lord Zipacna, under orders from Anubis, attacks Revanna, the site of the main Tok'ra base after Vorash.

BRAD WRIGHT: There's a bigger, badder Goa'uld beating the you-know-what out of all the other System Lords. The sacrifice of one of the series' favorite characters is the only way to relieve a truly dire situation.

PETER DELUISE: [Apophis] got so powerful that the other System Lords are afraid of a change in the balance of power, and so they decide to band together to solve the problem. In "The Fifth Man" a new System Lord appears, and our heroes have to learn that there are some pretty cool guys out there who they haven't met yet.

JOSEPH MALLOZZI: Boy, the costume department had a field day with this one! This episode was a try-out of sorts, an audition, for future System Lords. I drew on a variety of different cultures, creating a colorful rogues gallery. The hope was that if one popped, we could use him/her in future episodes. Well, one did: the exquisitely evil Baal, played by Cliff Simon.

I remember working on a rewrite of my first draft when we received word that actor JR Bourne would not be able to reprise the role of Martouf due to scheduling conflicts. As a result, my rewrite was a little more extensive. Rather than encountering the Martouf we knew, we encountered his symbiote, Lantash, who had taken a new host. It worked, but, alas, was nowhere near as powerful as it could have been. I publicly toyed with the idea of not using a host body and simply having Carter bid a tearful, smooch-filled farewell to the little rubber snake – but it was more an attempt to irritate my fellow writer-producers than a serious pitch.

Episode #104 (5.16): "Last Stand"
Written by Robert C. Cooper
Directed by Martin Wood
Guest Starring: Carmen Argenziano (Jacob Carter), Anna-Louise Plowman (Osiris), Cliff Simon (Baal), Courtenay J. Stevens (Elliott/Lantash), Vince Crestejo (Yu), Kwesi Amey-aw (Olokun), Suleka Mathew (Kali), Paul Anthony (Slave), Andrew Kavadas (Zipacna's Jaffa), Natasha Khadr (Bastet), Bonnie Kilroe (Morrigan)

A powerful System Lord shows himself for the first time in a thousand years and offers to destroy the Tau'ri and Tok'ra. Meanwhile, SG-1 and Lt. Elliot/Lantash are trying to escape the Tok'ra base.

MARTIN WOOD (director): Goa'uld normally exist in the form of a rubber prop or CGI, but we had to have our actors actually eating something. So we had the eight of them standing around a big vat of bubbling water. As they reached into the vat, a props guy would hand them a burrito. These burritos were filled with noodles, beans and all sorts of things, so as you bit off the "head" of one and a Goa'uld's innards would be hanging out. The CGI wizards later worked their digital magic on the burrito and turned it into a symbiote. I had to shoot coverage of this scene for an hour. The actors kept pulling burrito after burrito out of the vat and biting into them with gusto. The only thing was they couldn't swallow any of this stuff, because it was rather unappealing. So after every take I'd yell, "Cut," and two of our props people, Evil Kenny and his pal Evil Curtis, would rush in with buckets for the System Lords to spit into. Thank God our actors were good sports. (*TV Zone*)

JOSEPH MAZZOLLI: Back in the old days, *SG-1* used to kill Jaffa with gay abandon. They were little more than cannon fodder for our team, nondescript bad guys who deserved everything that was coming to them. Except, as time wore on, knocking off the Goa'uld's foot soldiers wasn't as easy as it used to be, because we started to explore an aspect of the Jaffa that had been glossed over in previous years: the fact that they were essentially pawns. Unlike the ruthless Goa'uld who were motivated by a thirst for power, the Jaffa were misguided and knocking them off grew increasingly problematic. At the end of this episode, we massacre a slew of them with the deadly toxin that targets their symbiotes and, while it may have seemed a smart strategic move at the time, like the food pyramid, asthma cigarettes, and Coca-Cola for kids print ads, it was the sort of thing that eventually went out of style.

Episode #105 (5.17): "Fail Safe"
Written by Joseph Mallozzi & Paul Mullie
Directed by Andy Mikita
Guest Starring: Colin Cunningham (Major Davis), Gary Jones (Technician)

An amateur astronomer discovers a rogue asteroid on a collision course with Earth. SG-1 and a couple of engineers repair the cargo ship that crashed on Revanna and head for Earth. Just before they reach the asteroid, there is a problem with one of the engines. They start heading for the asteroid, but manage to stop at the last moment. Teal'c and O'Neill place a naquadah enhanced nuclear weapon on it, but Carter discovers that the core of the asteroid is composed of naquadah, so exploding the nuke would destroy Earth. They manage to use the ship's hyperspace engines to move the asteroid to the other side of the planet, where it flies off harmlessly.

JOSEPH MALLOZZI: One of the things that I remember about this episode was how uncomfortable Rick and Chris were in those spacesuits (a recurring on-set theme that ran through both shows) – so much so that they simply refused to wear them any longer than they had to. Of course, how long was necessary was open to debate. In one sequence in the episode, they discover Sam and Daniel have managed to save themselves by taking refuge inside a ship's pods. Rather than releasing them immediately, Jack and Teal'c apparently take the time to repressurize the ship *and then* remove their spacesuits (which would take them at least a half an hour) before releasing Sam and Daniel. Nobody else at home seemed to notice, but we sure did.

Episode #106 (5.18): "The Warrior"
Story by Christopher Judge
Written & Directed by Peter DeLuise
Guest Starring: Tony Amendola (Bra'tac), Rick Worthy (Kytano), Vince Crestejo (Yu), Obi Ndefo (Rak'nor), Kirby Morrow (T'arac)

The Jaffa rebellion has a new leader named K'tano, who seems almost too good to be true. SG-1 visits K'tano's Jaffa camp on the planet Cal Mah (meaning "sanctuary") to negotiate an alliance. However, K'tano sends rebel Jaffa on a suicide mission to a stronghold under the control of Nirrti, and when K'tano sends Teal'c on a suicide mission against the Goa'uld system lord Yu, he finds that the new leader isn't what he seems.

PETER DELUISE: I got to work with Rick Worthy, who was amazing. He has the voice of buttered toast [*laughs*]. We incorporated a lot of Capoeira, so I had to come up with words for this special martial arts that the Jaffa knew. As it turned out, I lived down the street from a place where Capoeira was being taught. It's a Brazilian martial art that the slaves did. They were pretending to dance, but they were actually perfecting their fighting skills in a way that their masters wouldn't suspect anything. It is, in fact, a hidden form of martial arts that incorporates what feels like a lot of these spinning, wonderful dance moves. We'd borrowed from all different cultures and things, so I thought, "Wouldn't it be cool if Capoeira was part of what they were doing?" We called it mastaba, an Egyptian word for house.

JOSEPH MALLOZZI: I was awakened at a little past 7:00 a.m. by my ringing cell phone. I got out of bed to answer and discovered I'd already missed two calls from my sister in Montreal. What the hell? I answered. She asked me if I had the TV on. I told her I just got up. She informed me that two planes had flown into the Twin Towers. Another had hit the Pentagon. I was stunned. For a split second, my sci-fi mind assumed some mass mechanical failure, but the truth, far more insidious and disquieting, took hold. I turned on the TV and immediately phoned Paul. "Are you watching?" I asked. "Yeah," he said. "I'm watching."

When I got in to work, the production offices were quiet. Someone had turned on the TV in the conference room (reserved for screening visual effects) and anyone who wasn't on filming was in there, silently watching the horrific events unfold. It was surreal. Down on set, we were finishing up second unit on this episode while main unit photography had started on "Menace." 9/11 is the first thing that comes to mind when I think back to either of these episodes.

Episode #107 (5.19): "Menace"
Story by James Tichenor, Teleplay by Peter Deluise
Directed by Martin Wood
Guest Starring: Danielle Nicolet (Reese), Gary Jones (Technician), Teryl Rothery (Dr. Janet Fraiser), Colin Lawrence (SG-3 Leader), Tracy Westerholm (SF #1), Biski Gugushe (SF #2), Kyle Riefsnyder (SF #3), Dan Shea (Sgt. Siler)

The team finds an android that somehow managed to survive a Replicator attack. They learn she is the mother of all Replicators, but has the mentality of a young child.

JOSEPH MALLOZZI: Danielle Nicolet, who guested as Reese in this episode, delivered such a terrific performance that I started trying to think of a way to bring the character back almost immediately after killing her off. Hey, it happens. Given the events in New York, most flights were grounded and she was unable to fly back to L.A. As a result, she ended up having to stay in town a few extra days. I remember treating her to dinner where the topic of conversation ranged from the music business to the wonderful time she had as a recurring character on *Third Rock from the Sun*. Total sweetheart.

PETER DELUISE: My recollection is that I was covering for Martin Wood on 9/11. We were about to go to work when the Twin Towers were engulfed in flames and we were hearing the details. It was really quite shocking to us. We were trying to stay focused, but it was super hard, because you couldn't stop the news from coming in. This was before everyone had SmartPhones and everything, so people were listening on the radio and I was trying to give direction to my actors. The reason was that it felt like anarchy was just taking over at that moment. It felt like the world was changing in irreparable ways and it was super hard to stay focused. One of my instructions to Danielle Nicolet was, "Not that it matters right now, but I need you to stand here and deliver your lines *this* way." That was just all we could do at the moment. I think we may have taken a day off just to gather our wits, but we weren't really invested in what we were doing at that moment because of 9/11. I just remember that that was what was happening specifically.

Episode #108 (5.20): "The Sentinel"
Written by Ron Wilkerson
Directed by Peter DeLuise
Guest Starring: Henry Gibson (Marul), Frank Cassini (Grieves), Christina Cox (Kershaw), David Kopp (Grogan), Gary Jones (Technician), Colin Lawrence (Major Lawrence), Shawn Reis (Jaffa Commander), Carrie Ann Fleming (Assistant), Chris Newton (Caretaker)

The Latonans are a once-advanced race that abandoned technology to focus on mental development. Their homeworld Latona is defended by a 500-year-old device called the Sentinel, which was inadvertently deactivated by rogue NID operatives seeking to reverse-engineer it. With Latona being invaded by the Goa'uld Svarog, SG-1 brings the NID agents with them to repair the Sentinel and save the Latonans from the Goa'uld.

PETER DELUISE: The episode had Henry Gibson from *Laugh-In*, who used to do a ton of variety shows and also used to work with Ruth Buzzi, a very close family friend. Henry Gibson had gotten the part the regular way and he was soft spoken and lovely. When he showed up, I was, like, "Holy shit, you're Henry Gibson! I grew up watching you, because my dad used to do the variety show circuit on TV when I was a little kid." So getting to work with him was a real treat for me. At one point, I just couldn't help myself and I grabbed his little body by the shoulders and threw him into a dip and said, "I love you, man!" He just giggled like a little school girl. It was really funny.

JOSEPH MALLOZZI: Another misfire in my books, this was one of those episodes I just never got on board with. It was also one of those rare instances where we had to use a little trickery to tell our story, in this case showing newly shot footage in the "Previously On" as a means of introducing (back-selling) some characters who hadn't appeared in the episode being referenced. This episode also marked what I believe was the first appearance of the wonderful Christina Cox, who would later return to the franchise to play the part of Major Anne Teldy in *SGA*'s "Whispers."

PETER DELUISE: We had this idea that we were going to do a *Dirty Dozen* kind of episode, but then we had to keep cutting it down for budgetary reasons until it eventually became the *Dirty Three*.

Episode #109 (5.21): "Meridian"
Written by Robert C. Cooper
Directed by William Waring
Guest Starring: Corin Nemec (Jonas Quinn), Carmen Argenziano (Jacob Carter), Mel Harris (Oma Desala), Gary Jones (Technician), Teryl Rothery (Dr. Janet Fraiser), David Hurtubise (Tomis), Kevin McCrae (Kelownan Scientist)

Daniel incurs lethal radiation exposure when he prevents a potentially cataclysmic accident in a weapons laboratory on the planet Langara, but the mysterious Oma Desala shows him that death can simply be another beginning. While the alien government responsible for the lab accuses him of attempting to sabotage their research, the Kelownan Jonas Quinn tries to negotiate with SG-1.

ROBERT C. COOPER: I knew I was never going to win any fan awards for this one. I also knew, I wouldn't say a hundred percent, that he would come back, but we certainly wanted to leave the door open for Michael Shanks to do so. Having Daniel ascend felt like a really proper and poetic sendoff for a character who was the most spiritual and soulful guy, and the one who was most in tune with that Ascension storyline.

BRAD WRIGHT: We came up with "Meridian" as a way of Michael Shanks leaving the show with the door open for him coming back. Your character is going to move on in a beautiful way, and the ascended version of Daniel eventually became the source of more story. He became very powerful for a period of time and saved O'Neill in "Abyss." I was the one who wanted to bring him back to do the episode and I remember talking to Michael and saying, "Look, I want you to come back; I want to do this episode, but I want to make sure you are open and happy to come back." And he said, "Yeah, let's do it, I just want to read the script." And it was a good part. Really nice, strong, powerful two-hander scenes between him and Rick.

MICHAEL SHANKS: On my very last day I worked only with the actor that was going to be replacing me, which was a bit ironic. The day before, though, was different. It was my last one working with Christopher and Amanda. We spent a lot of time talking about where we had begun, where we'd ended up and the unfortunate circumstances that led to this particular point. So it was a very emotional day. Funnily enough, I felt more like the dying guy who had to make certain that everyone else knew he was going to be OK. I was being more of the comforting person in the situation. There were a number of agendas that had to be solved. Not only did they need to finish off Daniel's journey, if you will, but they also had to introduce a new character. With so many things going on it wasn't really clear why Daniel was being written out in this fashion. I thought there was a bit of chickening out with how it all happened. The big problem, I think, was they were so intent on saying to the audience, "Daniel's not dead!" This was mainly for the benefit of the same viewers who apparently got so upset [the previous] season when Martouf was killed off in "Divide and Conquer." The powers that be wanted to quell any backlash that might take place with the fans concerning Daniel's departure. What they ended up doing lessened the impact of his leaving. They didn't give the viewers a chance to grieve the "passing" of the character.

JOSEPH MALLOZZI: In Season 5, actor Michael Shanks decided to leave the show. When Brad told me, I was shocked. I'd never known him to be unhappy or dissatisfied with the show's creative directions (specifically as it affected his character) but, to be fair, being relatively new to the franchise, I can understand why I wouldn't have been first on his list of people to confide in. I'm sure he'd had many discussions with Brad and Robert, the series showrunners, leading up to what was, no doubt, a very difficult decision for him. Anyway, Brad was clearly disappointed and promised Michael his character would have a memorable farewell. Despite what fans may have thought at the time, there was no ill-will, no bad blood – simply a professional understanding and a desire on both sides to part ways on good, respectful terms. Which is exactly what happened.

MICHAEL SHANKS: The dual storyline involving the new character didn't help. Having said that, I understood why it had to be done, and in all honesty unless I can think of an alternative way of handling something I usually keep my mouth shut and don't gripe. So I didn't really protest and just figured, "OK, fine." I knew it was the end of the road. I didn't mind the story. I just wished there was a better way that it could've been done, but that's neither here nor there at the end of the day. (*Cult TV*)

AMANDA TAPPING: There is a scene where I'm coming out of Daniel's hospital room and Teal'c is about to go in, and the scene is written that Carter and Teal'c pass each other in the hallway and acknowledge a silent glance, and then continue down the hallway. And Chris and I couldn't stop crying for real – and Michael wasn't even in the room anymore, they were just shooting the hallway – so there was this empty bed and it was symbolic and every time I looked at it, I started crying. So I turned to Chris and said, "This is our chance. This is our moment to play something organic where it happens. These characters care about each other and we're losing one of our best friends." So what we did – and the cameras kept rolling, and it was just so beautiful and so spontaneous – is I walked out and he's standing there, and he's like 12 feet tall. I just rested my head on his chest and cried and he put his arms around me and I cried and he did his Teal'c, "I'm about to cry" thing. It's so moving when he does that, and then we released and I kept walking on down the hallway and he steeled himself and then went into the hospital room. And they cut that, for reasons of timing – whatever. I thought that would have been such a crystal clear solidity for that friendship.

JOSEPH MALLOZZI: I remember Michael visiting the production offices to say goodbye and Brad telling him the door would always be open for him to do guest appearances if he was so inclined. Michael voiced his appreciation for the potential opportunity to revisit the Daniel Jackson character. And that, sadly, was that. Until word broke and fandom reacted. To say a lot of fans were displeased would be an under-statement. The boards lit up! The fans were furious! And I didn't blame them. Daniel had been there from the beginning. Hell, he'd been there before the beginning (as a character in the original *Stargate* movie, he pre-dated *SG-1*) and, over his 4+ seasons on the show, had been the team's moral center. Losing him was a huge loss, not only to the fans but the show's creative as well as D.J. had always offered that strong civilian and philosophical counter-balance to SG-1's forceful military approach. More than Teal'c, Daniel was the true fish out of water, braving his strange, often hostile environs in sur-prisingly spectacular fashion. His absence would hurt, not only his fans, but the show as a whole.

ROBERT C. COOPER: Losing Michael was a difficult situation, but, again, when people ask me how did the show go on for as long as it did, I think those changes, as difficult as they were for fans at times, re-energized the dynamic of the show. So you take your four core characters and then take one away and put a new one in, now you have three different pairings that are new, fresh and have a different dynamic to them.

JOSEPH MALLOZZI: Realistically, there was nothing to be done. The decision had been made and we had to live with it. We also had to live with the fan anger directed at us for letting him go and, more pointedly, for creating the circumstances which, in their minds, forced Michael to leave. To say I was surprised by the criticism – well, let's call that another understatement. I wasn't aware of any creative issues surrounding the Daniel Jackson character. I went back and looked over the episodes produced to date and, to my eye, D.J. was well represented in episodes like "Beast of Burden," "Summit" and "Last Stand." And, as the online outrage swelled, it suddenly dawned on me that there was a fundamental difference in the way the Daniel Jackson fans and I saw the show. To them, the relationship between Jack and Daniel was the heart of the series and they felt the show's fourth and fifth seasons greatly lacked this all-important dynamic. To my mind, however, *SG-1* was about the team (although I was always mindful of the print ads for the series that always said: "Richard Dean Anderson in *Stargate SG-1*") and, as a result, I measured the success of each season by its ability to shine the spotlight on all four of our main characters in an equitable manner. Clearly, it was a divide that couldn't be bridged and, as Season 5 ended and work on Season 6 commenced, that divide started to widen.

DARREN SUMNER: Part of the problem is that the fans found out Michael was leaving from the convention stage. Brad Wright was on stage and announced to the crowd that Michael was not coming back for Season 6, and it took a while to get a full answer from all parties involved as to *why* he was leaving the show. Out of respect to the actor, and it being his choice not to sign a new contract, in a sense it was up to him to explain *why* he chose to do that. But, again, it took a while and a lot of people got really mad in the process. A lot of people felt like he was railroaded, being mistreated or wasn't appreciated and, it's my recollection, that it was years before there was a sort of clear understanding among fans as to why he left and the circumstances under which he left.

DAVID READ: I remember bawling my eyes out and falling in love with Mel Harris. I was devastated that Michael left the show. I think Season 6 had been announced at this point and I really didn't know how this was to work. I've always thought that Daniel was the heart and soul of the show, because he was the one not bound by military rules and regulations and is the one who can say, "This is wrong! This is *not* who we are." And when he departed, it was really like the show had had its heart torn out. Not that it couldn't function after that, but regardless of what came next, whatever was next, it was going to be extremely different. Even if they were going to have a character come in who was going to fulfill that role.

MEL HARRIS (actor, "Oma Desala"): For me as an actor, the challenge and reward of playing Oma Desala was that she is not of a world I know. That enabled my creativity and focus to expand in a way I never had before with other characters. The best direction [I was given] was that she was not like others, and was a "being" of her own.

DAVID READ: I think Corin did a great job with what he was given, but I knew Michael was leaving, so I knew by the end of the episode he was going to die. In so many instances in science fiction, characters are killed and are brought back to life in the same hour. But with this one, we knew he wasn't going to come out of it. It really was a different experience, because as he's reviewing his life, we're reviewing with him and we're recognizing his value, not only to the team, but to the galaxy. And Mel Harris as Oma does such a wonderful job of taking him through the moments of his life and trying to get him to realize that the universe is much bigger than him and that he did what he could. That it's okay for him to release the pain of Shar're, release the pain of Sarah and all of the other threads of his life that were left undone. It's a perfect episode and I think it was the first time the show made me cry.

Episode #110 (5.22): "Revelations"
Written by Joseph Mallozzi & Paul Mullie
Directed by Martin Wood
Guest Starring: Anna-Louise Plowman (Osiris), Teryl Rothery (Heimdall), David Palffy (Anubis), P.J. Johal (Jaffa), Shaker Paleja (Jaffa), Martin Sims (Jaffa)

As Jack, Sam and Teal'c struggle to come to terms with losing Daniel, Asgard scientist Heimdall is stranded on Adara II, a planet under attack by the Goa'uld. As the Asgard have no spare ships, they ask Stargate Command, particularly SG-1 to help, using their salvaged Goa'uld cargo ship. Anubis is finally revealed.

BRAD WRIGHT: We introduced a new villain, Anubis, at the end of Season 5, who would become our primary antagonist throughout Season 6. In actual fact, we (SG-1) think he [Anubis] has gone away at one point, but he hasn't. Then, just when we think we're going to see his face in "Summit" – it doesn't pan out the way we expect either. I didn't actually get the idea till we were in prep for the episode, but Anubis is a cloaked figure, kind of like the Emperor in *Star Wars*.

JOSEPH MALLOZZI: We had all assumed that we would end our run on Showtime with a fifth and final season. And we did. On Showtime. But late in the show's fifth season, we received word that *SG-1* had been granted new life. We were moving to Sci-Fi for a sixth and presumably final year. There was much rejoicing, but also a bittersweet farewell to a place we'd called home for those five years. Showtime had been very, very good to us and, as a final thank you, we elected to break tradition and not end the season on a cliffhanger. That way, we figured, our Showtime fans would have some closure, yet also have the option of continuing *SG-1's* adventures elsewhere. Our final farewell to Showtime and Daniel Jackson ends with the suggestion that while D.J. may be physically gone, he'll always be there in spirit. I remember thinking the gust of wind that catches Jack's attention in the final scene (and his subsequent reaction) was perhaps too subtle, but, in retrospect, I guess I was wrong, because all of our fans caught it.

DAVID PALFFY (actor, "Anubis"): Both Sokar and Anubis are unique, I suppose, because they're both villains who, from my point of view, lust for personal power regardless of the consequences of their actions — what their actions have toward any alien race, including their fellow Goa'uld brethren. These two gods, like so many Goa'uld, live by vanquishing those who oppose them for fear they will be vanquishing themselves. Now this is a trait among the Goa'uld, probably stemming from their desperation to survive as a race, but undoubtedly will probably lead to their demise. Because the fact is each one of them is out for their own personal gain. Now comparatively speaking with other aliens or villains I've played, they've been driven by revenge or love. And with both Sokar and Anubis, there's not an ounce of love in any of those people. But when you are playing villains who are driven more by what we would consider more humanly motivated, it sometimes becomes more complicated to play, because of the interpersonal relationships that have been woven into the fabric of these characters.

Now both Sokar and Anubis don't really have these kinds of relationships. They're not seeming to have a series of personal relationships with others that pose a problem for them in making decisions over matters that define them in what we would call humans. And as a result, they are not restrained or affected by human emotion or the morality of, let's say, annihilating an entire race simply with the wave of a gloved hand as with Anubis, or Sokar's penetrating glance. Because I find in playing these kinds of villains that are kind of bigger than life, you always try to find one particular characteristic that sets them apart from each other.

SEASON SIX SUMMARY (2002-2003)

* *The X-302 interceptor is completed.*

* *Teal'c's wife Drey'auc dies.*

* *Naquadria-based hyperspace technology is deemed a failure.*

Anubis destroys the Antarctic Stargate, but fails in destroying Earth.

Jonas Quinn joins SG-1.

Thor's consciousness is transferred into data crystals and sent to the Asgard so that he may be given a new clone body.

Ayiana is unfrozen in Antarctica and spreads the plague to the team. She heals everyone except Jack O'Neill, who is sent to the Tok'ra to be implanted with Kanaan.

Kanaan leaves Jack O'Neill. O'Neill is repeatedly tortured to death and resurrected by Baal.

The Tok'ra locate Egeria on Pangar and set her free before she dies.

The Pangarans share tretonin with Earth.

Frank Simmons and Adrian Conrad steal the X-303 Prometheus. Simmons and Conrad are killed.

SG-1 isolates the entire Replicator civilization inside a time dilation field. The Replicator Fifth is tricked into becoming part of the plan.

The Tok'ra agree to find Harold Maybourne his own planet on which to quietly retire.

Nirrti is killed at the hands of the victims of her genetic experimentation.

The governments of Great Britain, France and China are informed of Stargate Command. Seeds for the International Oversight Advisory are planted.

A Free Jaffa summit at Kresh'ta is ambushed. One hundred eight Jaffa are slaughtered. Both Teal'c and Bra'tac lose their symbiotes and must adapt to the drug tretonin.

The Prometheus is officially launched as Earth's first interstellar vessel, but soon becomes stranded across the galaxy and begins a year-long journey back to Earth.

The Tagrean Stargate is unburied.

The Goa'uld Mot is killed.

* *The System Lords formally disavow Anubis, despite having welcomed him back into their ranks a year earlier.*

* *Oma Desala banishes Daniel Jackson from ascension, leaving him destitute on Vis Uban. She helps the entire Abydonian population to ascend.*

* *Anubis destroys Abydos.*

EPISODE GUIDE: SEASON SIX

Episode #111 (6.1): "Redemption: Part 1"

Written by Robert C. Cooper

Directed by Martin Wood

Guest Starring: Tony Amendola (Bra'tac), Christopher Kennedy (Dr. Larry Murphy), David Hewlett (Dr. McKay), Garry Chalk (Colonel Chekov), Neil Denis (Rya'c), Gary Jones (Sgt. Davis), Tobias Mehler (Lt. Simmons), David Palffy (Anubis), Aleks Paunovic (Shaq'rel), Ivan Cermak (Hagman), Craig McNair (Technician), Carrie Richie (Technician), Dan Shea (Sgt. Siler), Michael Soltis (Medic)

As SG-1 and the S.G.C. struggle to cope with Daniel's departure, they find themselves facing a new threat in the form of System Lord Anubis. Anubis has launched an attack against Earth by using an ancient weapon that will trigger an overload of energy directly into the Stargate which, if the attack is successful, will destroy the entire planet. As the S.G.C. scientists scramble to come up with a solution, Carter finds her abilities as both a scientist and military officer being put to the ultimate test with her struggle increasing as her rival, Dr. Rodney McKay (David Hewlett) later returns to the S.G.C. from Russia, having been ordered to do so by the Pentagon. Teal'c goes off world after learning that his wife is gravely ill, but is left devastated when he learns that she has actually died.

JOSEPH MAZZOLLI: "Redemption" sees Anubis raising the stakes in a big way – and also sees the return of a certain guest character from mid-Season 5. As for Anubis, we wanted to peel the layers on that onion, but for those of you who haven't seen "Revelations" … well, he's not your typical Goa'uld. Appropriately enough, Dr. Rodney McKay also makes a return visit to S.G.C. and takes another giant step toward redemption – a process that would be completed by the time he assumed a lead position in the Atlantis expedition. This episode was also notable for the introduction of the Jaffa Shaq'rel, an otherwise inconsequential character, but for the fact that the part was initially written for a certain NBA star who, according to Chris Judge at the time, was interested in doing the show. Well, that never worked for whatever reason and while I won't reveal the name of the basketball player, it really shouldn't be that hard to figure out.

Episode #112 (6.2): "Redemption: Part 2"
Written by Robert C. Cooper
Directed by Martin Wood
  Guest Starring: Tony Amendola (Bra'tac), Christopher Kennedy (Dr. Larry Murphy), David Hewlett (Dr. McKay), Garry Chalk (Colonel Chekov), Neil Denis (Rya'c), Gary Jones (Technician), Aleks Paunovic (Shaq'rel), Robert Clarke (Scientist #1), Robert Thurston (Scientist #2), Dale Hall (Jaffa Commander), Aaron Douglas (Jaffa #1), Grizz Salzl (Jaffa #2), Dan Shea (Sgt. Siler)

Jack still refuses to let a Russian soldier join SG-1 despite pressure from both Chekov and General Hammond. After learning that Earth is under attack, Teal'c, Bra'tac, and Rya'c embark on a dangerous mission to find and destroy the weapon at any cost. With the plan to contact the Asgard having failed, S.G.C. is left on their own and Carter attempts to find a solution while she continues to deal with McKay's unwelcome presence. Meanwhile, Teal'c, Bra'tac and Rya'c prepare to launch an attack on the planet which houses Anubis' weapon while Jonas later gives Carter an idea to save the planet, but it could result in Earth losing their Stargate and the Stargate Program being shut down for good.

RICHARD DEAN ANDERSON: I think O'Neill feels that Jonas is directly responsible for the demise or at least the damaging of Daniel Jackson. As a result, he harbors some resentment towards Jonas. It's been tempered a little bit over time, primarily because of the fact that he has to be around him. So O'Neill has finally come to the point of accepting Jonas, but not entirely. It's like, "Yes, you can be on our team, but I'm going to be watching you, and, oh, by the way, don't expect me to show any overt signs of friendship towards you."

O'Neill is suspicious of aliens in general. The only exception is Teal'c. He has a wonderfully odd relationship with the Jaffa, who he sometimes forgets is an alien despite the gold patch emblazoned on his forehead. For some reason, though, he refuses to or isn't able to forget that Jonas is an alien. It doesn't help that the guy has become a walking computer. He's memorized everything since coming to the S.G.C.. That immediately makes O'Neill leery, because he has no aptitude or patience for that kind of thing. So he's always socially on-guard around Jonas and consequently deals with him in a somewhat brusque, professional way. (*Interview with Steve Eramo*)

JOSEPH MAZZOLLI: Looking back, this was the episode that cemented David Hewlett as a favorite guest star – so favored, in fact, that years later, when we were trying to cast the part of a medical doctor for the spin-off, *Atlantis*, he immediately came to mind and Brad and Robert decided: "Screw that! Let's put McKay on the team!"

And the rest, as they say, is history. Also in this episode, the role of Shaq'rel was played by Aleks Paunovic, who also returned to the franchise years later, but in a different role – playing Ronon's former Satedan buddy, Rakai, in *SGA*'s "Reunion."

ROBERT C. COOPER: This is one of those lotta balls in the air two-parters where we have many threads involving a lot of mythology elements at play. But the seed of the idea came from a challenge we often set out for ourselves in the writer's room: What if we did something so big and crazy that would make fans yell, "Oh my god!"? Problem was, when the suggestions were made, we often didn't know how to get out of it. In this case, I threw out what if we blow up our gate? Of course everyone asked, how? Why? And then what?! But we then set about trying to make it work and found a cool solution.

Episode #113 (6.3): "Descent"
Written by Joseph Mallozzi & Paul Mullie
Directed by Peter DeLuise
Guest Starring: Carmen Argenziano (Jacob Carter), Colin Cunningham (Major Davis), Gary Jones (Technician), John Shaw (Dr. Friesen), Peter DeLuise (Lieutenant)

SG-1 attempts to salvage a Goa'uld mothership that has been mysteriously abandoned in space near Earth. Unfortunately, the ship crashes in the ocean where SG-1 discovers that Thor's consciousness is still in the central computer.

JOSEPH MAZZOLLI: One sequence had Carter and O'Neill trapped in a chamber that was slowly filling with water. We achieved this by actually doing the opposite. We lowered the specially designed set into a pool, giving the impression that the water was actually rising. We shot at Vancouver's Olympic pool and it was a tough day. Rick and Amanda were very wet and very cold, and had to sport wetsuits underneath their clothing to keep warm.

PETER DELUISE: I tried to work a cameo into every episode I directed, and "Descent" was no exception. I was one of the Navy fellows who came in the pod and waited by the escape tubes for them to return. It's a little hard to read on my uniform, but my name is Dagwood, which was my character from *seaQuest*. It was a fun little inside thing. I still have that Dagwood patch.

Episode #114 (6.4): "Frozen"
Written by Robert C. Cooper
Directed by Martin Wood
Guest Starring: Venus Terzo (Dr. Francine Michaels), Bruce Harwood (Dr. Osbourne), Paul

Perri (Dr. Woods), Dorian Harewood (Thoran), Ona Grauer (Ayiana), Gary Jones (Technician), Teryl Rothery (Dr. Janet Fraiser)

The Antarctic team investigating the site where the second Stargate was found discovers a woman frozen in the ice. When she inexplicably recovers, the team realizes they have finally come face-to-face with an Ancient. The team starts to suffer the effects of a deadly virus and while the woman helps to heal the infected, it becomes clear that it's taking a toll.

ROBERT C. COOPER: I often took inspiration from movies I loved. This episode obviously has a bit of John Carpenter's *The Thing*, but really borrowed much more from a 1984 movie called *Iceman*. The thing about this episode that I like most is the introduction of the idea that present day people are actually the second evolution of humans on Earth. It's the "big reveal" about the Ancients and really kicked the ascension mythology off.

JOSEPH MAZZOLLI: In "Frozen," Jack didn't have a choice. It would either be implanted or die. The fact is, it isn't an easy process — either the implantation or, in particular, the removal. The type of symbiote involved has a lot to do with it. For instance, the reason humans are killed when the symbiote is removed is because the dying symbiote releases a deadly toxin. In the case of Jolinar and Jack's experience, however, this isn't the case. That's because the symbiote can make the conscious decision to kill its host and release the toxin. Early in the episode, one of the scientists claims his grandfather was "one quarter Cherokee." This was an in-joke and poke at actor Chris Judge, who had made the same claim. Also, at one point Jack laments having forgotten to tape *The Simpsons*. This, of course, paralleled RDA's love for the long-running animated series. There were many times he would swing by my office to check out the collection of Simpsons talking figures I kept there. Eventually, Rick's love for the show culminated in a guest appearance by the voice of Homer Simpson himself, Dan Castellaneta [in Season 8's ["Citizen Joe"] – which was soon followed by Rick being asked to guest on *The Simpsons*.

ONA GRAUER (actress, "Ayiana"): The "block of ice" I was in was crazy. Obviously it's light and magic and it's tricks of television, but the block of ice was some sort of plastic that was a little bit hard; it wasn't like jelly. And then they placed some kind of jelly over it and then watered me down, and the first scene that you see in the ice with my arm all cocked up behind my head … We had to do that a couple of times, because it's quite an unnatural position to be in. Half of my body is kind of in this contraption and then just my face and my arm are kind of sticking out. Because they take Polaroids for continuity and stuff, when I saw it for the first time, you kind of go, "Oh my God, what am I doing?" Because you're just in it, you can't see it. And when I first saw the

Polaroid, that's when I just believed in everything that we were doing. I was, like, "This is incredible. This looks like I'm frozen in a block of ice." It was amazing.

Episode #115 (6.5): "Nightwalkers"
Written by Joseph Mallozzi & Paul Mullie
Directed by Peter DeLuise
Guest Starring: Blu Mankuma (Sheriff Knox), Vincent Gale (Agent Cross), Michael Eklund (Dark-haired Man), Peter Anderson (Flemming), Adrian Holmes (Special Ops Sergeant), Scott McNeil (Townsperson), Carin Moffat (Snake Townsperson), Dave "Squatch" Ward (Antagonistic Bar Guy), Sean Tyson (Barkeep / Agent Singer), Christie Wilkes (Delivery Woman)

Carter, Teal'c and Jonas investigate the death of a scientist with connections to the Goa'uld, and find a small town whose citizens harbor a dark secret.

JOSEPH MAZZOLLI: This was one of my favorite episodes of the show's sixth season simply because it was so different from other episodes we'd done – an old-fashioned small-town alien invasion story. Loved the gang all decked out in leather. Vincent Gale, who would later play the part of the cranky Carl Binder Morrison on *Stargate Universe*, appears as Agent Cross. The role of Sheriff Knox is played by the terrific Blu Mankuma, a good friend of the late Don Davis. Blu and I shared an affinity for ribs – lamb ribs in particular. I loved them so much, in fact, that I was "the lamb rib" hotline. Whenever my favorite barbecue joint, The Memphis Blues BBQ Restaurant, made a batch, they would give me a call and I'd drive right over. I remember one night sitting down to a platter of ribs; so wholly focused was I on devouring them, that I didn't even notice Blu until he was standing right beside me. "Breathe," he cautioned.

PETER DELUISE: That was our little tip of the hat and excursion into *The X-Files*. We had a problem with that one in that the story wasn't breaking properly and we were a full act short in the structure of it. The premise is that there are Goa'uld symbiotes taking over these people in a town, so you've got what feels like a combination of *Body Snatchers* and *The X-Files*, because each person was being taken over at night and the secret agenda was to build a spaceship so that they could leave Earth, because they didn't want to be there anymore. That's why our guys were sent to investigate and, of course, Teal'c had to cover his forehead, not unlike Spock covering his ears in the *Star Trek* episode "City on the Edge of Forever."

So it came to pass that there were only four acts and we needed a whole other act, so I suggested in the writing room, "You know what worked in *Predator 2*? There was a secret government agency that was fully aware of what was going on and they were studying the Predators. They were going to create a trap to capture it, only to have the tables turned on them and they all got fucking wiped out." So I said, "As a story structure this works great, because you add this other element of government black op types who are watching, and then they all get wiped out. Wouldn't that be great?" It was agreed on and we incorporated that extra element as an add-on to extend it for an extra act.

Episode #116 (6.6): "Abyss"
Written by Brad Wright
Directed by Martin Wood
Guest Starring: Dorian Harewood (Thoran), Cliff Simon (Baal), Gary Jones (Technician), Michael Shanks (Daniel Jackson), Teryl Rothery (Dr. Janet Fraiser), Ulla Fris (Woman), Patrick Gallagher (Jaffa Commander)

O'Neill has been captured by Baal, but is being held in a fortress too well protected for Stargate Command to help. However, Jonas believes that Lord Yu might be persuaded to lend assistance. Meanwhile, O'Neill is helped through his torturous ordeal by Daniel, who although forbidden from taking action as an ascended being, tries to provide comfort.

RICHARD DEAN ANDERSON: I think out of all the actors, and this is not meant as a slight to anyone else, but rather as a practical comment on the dynamic between Michael and I, he and I had the most fun and trusted each other the most to be able to pull off the kinds of things we did, particularly in "Abyss." The episode has scenes between us that overlap, where we're both going on and the dialogue is fast and intense in content. We were able to pull the scenes off, because we work well together and had had a lot of practice doing it. That's an episode I thoroughly enjoyed doing and it was good to see Michael again. (*Dreamwatch*)

BRAD WRIGHT: The scenes between Rick and Michael are, honestly, as good as we've ever had on *Stargate*. The two immediately gelled again. Michael was a prince and it was terrific to have him there. I do think the episode proved that it wasn't that easy to come up with stories in which Daniel can just come flying back into our midst, but the episode really does cement the powerful nature of Jack and Daniel's friendship.

JOSEPH MAZZOLLI: This was a great episode for all sorts of reasons, but chiefest among them was the terrific onscreen dynamic between RDA and Michael. I know that both of them had a great time, as did Brad Wright who wrote and produced "Abyss." Brad, as the show's co-creator and longtime showrunner, had written some of the best Jack–Daniel scenes in the series, so I was surprised and disappointed when angry fans targeted him. I thought it immensely unfair given all he had done to build the friendship between the two characters, but in this business, it's often less of "Thanks for what you did for us in the past" and more of "What have you done for me lately?"

DAVID READ: I think of "Abyss" as kind of like "Meridian" part two, because now Jack is in a situation where he's being killed again and again, only in this case he's on death's door and he's being brought back. Once again, Brad puts two people in a room and makes some amazing television and Jack has to face some truths he hasn't had to face, really, since Charlie died. What's great about this season is that when the chips are down for a lot of these characters, Daniel comes to be with them. It's Daniel who gets Jack through absolute hell. He's the one who tells Jack, "Just a little longer; hang on as long as you can." Even though there's very little he can do in terms of interference, he keeps Jack from going insane. If Daniel weren't there, there wouldn't have been much of him left for SG-1 to come back for.

JOSEPH MAZZOLLI: One issue I had with the script was the idea of Jack being killed, then brought back from the dead. I thought it opened a can of worms re: memories of the afterlife. I was told the ship had sailed on that particular subject. I don't know if I agree. I always considered ascension a very different matter, an experience specific to an isolated group.

BRAD WRIGHT: Jack was tortured to death, resurrected and then thrown into a cell only to be tortured again. It was a pretty horrific way to go, and then when Daniel says, "You're a better man than that, Jack," and O'Neill says, "That's where you're wrong," it's one of the most powerful acting moments Rick gave on the show. He had a great acting partner in that moment, and it was only Daniel that could save him.

DARREN SUMNER: Just another brilliant two characters in a room script. It becomes one of those crisis situations that peels back the outer layers of the characters and just exposes their core. Jack and Daniel have an argument about who Jack is at his core and it's a *fantastic* hour. This is the episode I point to when people say that *Stargate SG-1* is just popcorn action. The show and its vocabulary was much broader than a lot of casual viewers give it credit for. And this is when *Stargate* was at its best as a serious character drama.

Episode #117 (6.7): "Shadow Play"
Written by Joseph Mallozzi & Paul Mullie
Directed by Peter DeLuise
Guest Starring: Dean Stockwell (Dr. Kieran), Joel Swetow (First Minister Velis), Doug Abrahams (Commander Hale), Gillian Barber (Ambassador Dreylock), Gary Jones (Technician), Teryl Rothery (Dr. Janet Fraiser), Rob Daly (Resistance Leader), Paul Schele (Kelownan

Soldier), Susie Wickstead (Kelownan Aide)

   The Kelownan government contacts the S.G.C., offering to exchange naqahdriah for advanced technology. Jonas' old professor asks him to help a secret resistance group and prevent a world war.

JOSEPH MAZZOLLI: When Dean Stockwell came to Vancouver to guest on the show, Brad took advantage of the gorgeous summer weather to treat him to a round of golf. Apparently they spent their afternoon enjoying the game and chatting about *Married to the Mob*. Most of the *Stargate* producers were avid golfers (Brad, Rob, Paul, John Smith, Michael Greenburg) and so, over the course of my many years on the franchise, I had to put up with endless Monday morning chatter about everything from everyone's weekend scores to re-hashings of recent airings on what I refer to as the Old Golf Channel. It became so annoying for me that I started to follow Japanese Professional Baseball (Pro Yakyu) just so I could interject equally annoying details about teams like the Orix Blue Wave, the Nippon Ham Fighters, and the Yakult Swallows.

PETER DELUISE: We had Dean Stockwell playing Jonas' mentor, and he believes that there is this ultra-secret rebellion going on. In reality, though, it's just the long-term effects of naqahdriah on his sanity and he's just lost it. I thought it was a fun episode in that we don't usually deal with somebody else's psychosis. Dean Stockwell was such a professional and it was a great pleasure working with him.

   Episode #118 (6.8): "The Other Guys"
   Written by Damian Kindler
   Directed by Martin Wood
   Guest Starring: Patrick McKenna (Jay Felger), John Billingsley (Coombs), Adam Harrington (Khonsu), Michael Adamthwaite (Herak), Gary Jones (Technician), Martin Sims (Dolok), Randy Schooley (Meyers), Michael Daingerfield (Big Jaffa)

   Dr. Felger worships SG-1, and when he has the chance to rescue them from a Goa'uld mothership, he does not hesitate.

JOSEPH MAZZOLLI: This was the script that earned Damian Kindler a spot on the writing staff and it was one of my favorites. The episode was tons of fun and our guest stars, John Billingsley and Patrick McKenna, were terrific. One memory I have connected to this episode doesn't have anything to do with this episode at all. While prepping "The Other Guys," a couple of guys from the VFX department came by the office. One was wearing the greatest *Stargate* t-shirt I've ever seen. It had a finger pointing off to the right and, below it, the text: "I'M WITH SHOL'VA."

Early in the episode, O'Neill asks Teal'c who he likes for the cup. Teal'c responds: "I believe the Canucks of Vancouver are superior warriors." During the Vancouver Canucks playoff run of that year, that clip was played several times on the Jumbotron.

DAMIEN KINDLER (producer): I had been coming and going from L.A. to Vancouver and doing lots of work on different shows, and ended up coming in to pitch some ideas to *Stargate* just at the start of Season 6 when it moved from Showtime to Sci-Fi. I pitched four ideas, one of which was "The Other Guys." I came in and worked on the story with them and wrote the script. At the time I was just very happy to have gotten the call to write a script and really enjoyed the characters and process. And the day I delivered the script Rob called and offered me a producer job, which was one of the nicer moments in my career. And that became the next five years of my life.

Episode #119 (6.9): "Allegiance"
Written and Directed by Peter DeLuise
Guest Starring: Carmen Argenziano (Jacob Carter), Tony Amendola (Bra'tac), Obi Ndefo (Rak'nor), Peter Stebbings (Malek), Link Baker (Artok), Rob Lee (Major Pierce), Teryl Rothery (Dr. Janet Fraiser), Kimani Ray Smith (Ocker), Herbert Duncanson (SG Guard), Dan Payne (Ashrak)

The Jaffa rebellion, the Tok'ra and their base commander Malek, and Stargate Command are temporarily forced to share Earth's Alpha Site (a secret refuge) when the Tok'ra are attacked. Suspicion between the Tok'ra and the Jaffa turns hostile when a series of murders occurs.

PETER DELUISE: The intent was to create some sort of peaceful allegiance between the Tok'ra and the Jaffa, and they both had a common enemy, which forced a trust between them. Then we added the element of an invisible assassin that had some of the capabilities of the Predator, because he had an invisibility shield. So there's an uneasy alliance between the Tok'ra and the Jaffa, but a third party comes in and starts killing them, hoping to provoke them into killing each other.

JOSEPH MAZZOLLI: Finally, Peter DeLuise shows off his writing prowess to answer the questions: What is up with the Tok'ra after the events of "Last Stand?" What has happened to the Jaffa after the events of "The Warrior?" "Allegiance" focuses on the relationship between the Tok'ra and the Jaffa. This one's a bit of a blur but for two things: 1) The Rambo-esque sequence of O'Neill's 360-degree machine gun turn that, believe it or not, was at least three times as long in the director's cut; and 2) the hokey ending: "This single blade did what we could not. It has brought us together." Ouch.

PETER DELUISE: There was a great bit with Richard Dean Anderson, who solves the problem of this third race by telling everyone to get down. Then he fires his machine gun in a circle, finally figuring out where the invisible guy is and kills him. That was Dan Payne as Askrak in what was his second kick at the can on our show, the first being in "The Warrior." He later went on to play a ton of different aliens, even the super soldier, for us.

Episode #120 (6.10): "Cure"
Written by Damian Kindler
Directed by Andy Mikita
Guest Starring: Peter Stebbings (Malek), Malcolm Stewart (Dollen), Gwynyth Walsh (Kelmaa), Allison Hossack (Zenna Valk), Daryl Shuttleworth (Tagar), Teryl Rothery (Dr. Janet Fraiser), Trever Havixbeck (Pangar Sentry), Andrew Moxham (Pangar Sentry)

SG-1 visits Pangar, a planet once ruled by Ra. The Pangarans offer a wonder drug called Tretonin in exchange for gate addresses, but fail to mention that the drug is produced by using the progeny of the former Tok'ra queen Egeria. The drug also destroys the user's immune system, causing a crisis when supplies run low. SG-1 calls in help from the Tok'ra Malek and Kelmaa. After Egeria is freed by the Tok'ra Kelmaa, she tells the remorseful Pangarans how to free themselves from the tretonin.

JOSEPH MAZZOLLI: The thing that drove me nuts about this episode was the big Egeria reveal near episode's end that comes about as a result of Jonas *finally*, and conveniently, coming across the text in the underground chamber. Whenever I watched that scene in dailies, all I could think was: "Man, if you could've just started with that particular section instead of saving it for later, things would've gone a whole lot easier."

Episode #121 (6.11): "Prometheus"
Written by Joseph Mallozzi & Paul Mullie
Directed by Peter F. Woeste
Guest Starring: George Wyner (Al Martell), Ian Tracey (Smith), Kendall Cross (Julia), Colin Cunningham (Major Davis), Enid-Raye Adams (Jones), John de Lancie (Col. Frank Simmons), Bill Marchant (Adrian Conrad), Jason Gaffney (Sanderson), Catherine Lough Haggquist (Technical Sergeant), Kyle Cassie (Reynolds), Todd Hann (SF Sergeant Gibson), Colby Johannson (SF Sergeant Finney), Michael Shanks (Voice of Thor)

A reporter has information about the Stargate Program and threatens to broadcast it on television. The S.G.C. offers a deal to allow her access to the Prometheus on the condition that nothing is aired until the Stargate Program is made public. However, the camera crew turns out to be rogue NID agents and take over ships.

DARREN SUMNER: In season six, the show changed in some pretty fundamental ways. It moved to a new network in the form of SciFi, where it got a new and much bigger audience. It had its first major cast change with Corin Nemec coming in as Jonas Quinn, and then by the time we reached the midpoint of the season with this episode, we see that Earth has successfully managed to build an interstellar starship. There had been attempts at this in the past that had gone horribly wrong, as in season four's "Tangent," but "Prometheus" was the first time we had a big spaceship that worked. And in true *Stargate* fashion, it didn't work well and it didn't work all the time. It took a few more seasons for the kinks to be ironed out before we could actually use hyperspace travel and put up a fight if the ship met anybody out in space. This was the first time the show had a vehicle for telling stories that was a literal vehicle for taking the characters off planet or coming to pick them up on another planet in a vehicle that *wasn't* a Stargate. It changed the show in a lot of ways; not right away and not all at once, but by the time we get to Season 9 and we have ships that come in with Asgard beaming technology to rescue our characters just in the nick of time, that's a different show.

JOSEPH MAZZOLLI: Richard Dean Anderson was an executive producer on the show and liked to read and provide notes on all of the scripts. I remember getting a script back from him once and Paul being delighted by how much Rick obviously liked it. "Look at all the check marks!" he pointed out. "Check marks are bad," Rob informed him. Oh. Well, let's just say this script got *a lot* of check marks. Rick greatly objected to the basic premise – that a group could actually steal an Earth ship. As a result, and to spare his character any potential blame, the script was rewritten so that O'Neill wasn't anywhere near the *Prometheus* when it was taken. So passionate was his opinion that, in the scene in which he dresses someone down for allowing the ship to get grabbed, I swore he was actually channeling himself.

Episode #122 (6.12): "Unnatural Selection"
Story by Robert C. Cooper & Brad Wright, Teleplay by Brad Wright, Excerpts Written by Jeff F. King
Directed by Andy Mikita
Guest Starring: Ian Buchanan (First), Patrick Currie (Fifth), Gary Jones (Technician), Kristina Copeland (Second), Tahmoh Penikett (Third), Rebecca Robbins (Fourth), Shannon Powell (Sixth), Dan Shea (Sgt. Siler), Michael Shanks (Voice of Thor)

The Asgard have called all the Replicators in the Asgard galaxy to one planet, Hala, but the time dilation device that was meant to trap them on the planet forever has failed to activate. The Asgard want SG-1 to use the Prometheus to find out why. Unfortunately, what they find is that the Replicators have accelerated time and evolved to human form.

BRAD WRIGHT: Dark ending. Fifth wants to be like us, he wants to leave with us and we fool him into helping us escape. Everybody on the bridge of the *Prometheus* turns to O'Neill and says they're not sure they did the right thing, and he goes, "We did. And I'd do it again." Of course it came back to slap him in the ass, but that's a leader making a decision and sacrificing somebody who was potentially a very harmful enemy.

JOSEPH MAZZOLLI: Although I liked the Replicators when they were first introduced, I felt a little of them went a long way – which was why I loved their evolution into human form. Same villain, but new, improved, and far more dangerous. What made this very good episode great was O'Neill's double-cross of the all-too-trusting Fifth. Was he right to do it? Sure, an argument could be made for the fact that his actions do contain the Replicator threat. Of course, the double-cross comes back to bite us in the ass down the line when Fifth escapes the time dilation bubble. So, would we have been better served taking him with us? Again, hard to say. And that's one of the things I loved about *SG-1*. Sometimes, amid the high adventure and humor, there were situations that offered no easy answers.

BRAD WRIGHT: I pitched the idea of the time dilation device and the Asgard's defense was to gather all the Replicators in one place and then slow time so much that they're harmless to anybody. But it ends up creating another race of super villains all through *Atlantis*, because they had *so* much time to develop relative to everyone else.

PATRICK CURRIE (actor, "Fifth"): In this episode, Fifth is pretty much an adolescent brain. He's just feeling all of these feelings for the first time ever, and I didn't have to be guarded; an adolescent in our world has to feel their feelings, then monitor them and adjust them for the environment that he's in. Whereas Fifth didn't have to do that, he just had to get the information, feel the information, feel the feelings and respond. Which he did and which is why he ends up looking like a villain in some people's eyes. But he really is just responding to our childish inability, I think, to deal with emotion when we're not taught to express it in a way that's healthy

Episode #123 (6.13): "Sight Unseen"
Story by Ron Wilkerson, Teleplay by Damian Kindler
Directed by Peter F. Woeste
Guest Starring: Jody Racicot (Vernon Sharpe), Gary Jones (Technician), Teryl Rothery (Dr. Janet Fraiser), Betty Linde (Mrs. Sharpe), Michael Karl Richards (Guardsman), Raimund Stamm (Hitchhike Driver), Jennifer Steede (Flight Attendant), Jacob Chaos (Ticked Off Passenger), Brad Dryborough (Outta Control Driver), Jacquie Janzen (Commissary Airman)

On a deserted planet designated P9X-391, SG-1 discovers a piece of Ancient technology. When it is moved to Earth for study, people begin to have inexplicable hallucinations.

DAMIAN KINDLER: One I felt I could never get a handle on and have all sorts of regret over is "Sight Unseen." I don't know if I did justice to that at all. That's a little bit of regret.

JOSEPH MAZZOLLI: Boy, did I *not* like this episode, this despite actor Jodi Racicot's brilliant turn as the beleaguered Vernon Sharpe. My note at the script stage was: So what? I mean, okay, people started glimpsing interdimensional creatures that caused them to "Freak out, man!", but when it came down to it, those alien centipedes really weren't much of a threat.

Episode #124 (6.14): "Smoke & Mirrors"
Story by Katharyn Powers, Teleplay by Joseph Mallozzi & Paul Mullie
Directed by Peter DeLuise
Guest Starring: Colin Cunningham (Major Davis), Peter Flemming (Agent Malcolm Barrett), Ronny Cox (Senator Kinsey), Teryl Rothery (Dr. Janet Fraiser), Jon Cuthbert (Agent Devlin), Peter Kelamis (Dr. Langham), John Mann (Luthor), Mi-Jung Lee (Reporter), Chris Harrison (Guard), Simon Egan (SF #1), Daniel Pepper (Hospital SF), Yvonne Myers (Area 51 Technician), Darryl Scheeler (Man), L. Harvey Gold (Committee Member #1), Don MacKay (Committee Member #2), Dale Wilson (Committee Member #3), James Michalopoulos (Leo)

Senator Kinsey is shot, and all the evidence seems to show that O'Neill was the assassin.

CATH-ANNE AMBROSE: We have a situation where we want to use a gun in an episode, so I have to go to the gun manufacturer and say, "We're making reference to your gun, can we get permission?" But they came back to us and said, "Will the Remington model 700 be portrayed in a positive manner and for the purpose that it's intended?" Well, I can't really go back to them and say it's going to be used to assassinate somebody. So we may have to scrap the name. But because everything is fictitious, we don't run into a lot of those problems.

JOSEPH MALLOZZI: See if you can spot Peter Kelamis (*SGU*'s Adam Brody) in one of his first guest spots on the franchise. Yep, that young little guy who gets clotheslined by Teal'c. That's him! This episode also marked the return of one of my favorite characters you love to hate: Senator Kinsey, played by the brilliant Ronny Cox. It was always a pleasure to have him on the show.

PETER DELUISE: I got to work with Ronny Cox as Kinsey and we were telling stories about *Deliverance* and that kind of thing. The assassination attempt took place at the hotel right across the street from Bridge Studio, where we shot. We just walked across the street and started shooting. We got to do a cool metamorphosis thing where the guy had a device that made him look like he was Richard Dean Anderson.

Episode #125 (6.15): "Paradise Lost"
Written by Robert C. Cooper
Directed by William Gereghty
Guest Starring: Tom McBeath (Maybourne), Bill Dow (Dr. Lee), Gary Jones (Technician), Dan Shea (Sgt. Siler)

Maybourne offers to help S.G.C. find a cache of advanced alien weapons, but he is not telling them everything he knows.

ROBERT C. COOPER: A great example of how a guest star role often turned into a rich recurring character. Rick loved playing off Tom McBeath's Maybourne and stranding him and O'Neill together seemed like something that relationship was begging for. Bill Gereghty (the director) had a long history with Rick as well and I think all three had a good time on this one.

AMANDA TAPPING: Maybourne goes along with SG-1 off-world on a mission, and Maybourne and Jack end up getting stuck on the planet, and it's kind of ... my fault, because Maybourne ended up getting my zat. And at first, I said to the writers, "No way, I would never let him get it, and catch me off guard like that! You're making me look stupid!" But they assured me, "Oh, no, we did it in a way that it wasn't your fault." So, anyways, it was my fault, and I couldn't figure out how to solve it, and get rid of the force shield thingy. I start getting really frustrated, and being mean to everyone, so I'm kind of a nasty bitch the whole episode and I'm just so mean and cruel to everyone, because I can't help them. But, in the end, she breaks. She just loses it and completely breaks down and starts crying. Now, during the filming, we were going to do the scene where she breaks, starts crying and everything, and she goes to Teal'c, who's there, and he comforts her, and hugs her. And I think that this was really important, because they don't really show all that much of the friendship between her and Teal'c. There was this scene from "Meridian" where she goes into the hall after her goodbye and she's crying, and her and Teal'c hug. And it was just a nano-second scene and they cut it out.

So I thought it was absolutely necessary that they have this scene, and we kept running out of time. We were supposed to do it one day, and we ran out of time, so they're like, "Oh, well, we'll do it tomorrow." And we ran out of time again, and they said, "Oh, well, we'll do it tomorrow." And they kept putting it off, so I actually went up to them, and was, like, "We have to do this scene! It's important!" And it was one of the few things that I actually fought my heart out for. It was really needed, so we gotta do it in the end. And I think that all her meanness and cruelty to all the scientists and everything was justified in the end, by her breaking down like that. In "Paradise Lost," for example, Jack is lost off-world. As the days pass, Sam grows increasingly agitated. The prospect of losing Jack becomes too much for her and, in a very touching scene, she breaks down and opens up to Teal'c. The feelings are there. They're professionals and can't give in to them for the time being, but they're definitely still there.

Episode #126 (6.16): "Metamorphosis"
Story by Jacqueline Samuda & James Tichenor, Teleplay by James Tichenor
Directed by Peter DeLuise
Guest Starring: Jaqueline Samuda (Nirrti), Alex Zahara (Eggar), Dion John-
stone (Wodan), Raoul Ganeev (Lt. Colonel Sergei Evanov), Gary Jones (Technician), Teryl
Rothery (Dr. Janet Fraiser), Alex Rae (Alebran), Jacquie Janzen (Lt. Rush), Dan Payne (Jaffa
Commander)

The Russian team discovers a planet where Nirrti has been experimenting on the human
population to create the perfect host.

JOSEPH MALLOZZI: And the award for Most Awkward Seduction scene in an episode of Stargate goes to ... Whenever I see the Nirrti's bedchamber scene, I vacillate between squirming and laughing out loud. "Mrs. Nirrti, you're trying to seduce me!" Poor, simple, innocent Jonas. Another thing I recall about this episode was the gratu-itously gory shot of the mutant exploding on the hospital gurney that ended up being cut.

PETER DELUISE: That was our take on *The Island of Dr. Moreau.* Jaqueline Samuda, who's a personal family friend, actually came up with part of the idea for the story. She went to school with Brad Wright, so she was an old friend of Brad's as well, which was kind of cool. We also had several mutant dudes *and* it was the first time an Indian archi-tecture and culture was used. It's something we embraced.

Episode #127 (6.17): "Disclosure"
Teleplay by Joseph Mallozzi & Paul Mullie, Excerpts Written by Heather E. Ash, Michael
Cassutt, Robert C. Cooper, Peter DeLuise, Sam Egan, Jonathan Glassner, Michael Greenburg,
Joseph Mallozzi, Paul Mullie, Jarrad Paul, Misha Rashovich, James Tichenor, Ron Wilkerson

and Brad Wright
  Directed by William Gereghty
  Guest Starring: François Chau (Chinese Ambassador), Colin Cunningham (Major Davis), Garry Chalk (Colonel Chekov), Martin Evans (British Ambassador), Paul Batten (French Ambassador), Ronny Cox (Senator Kinsey), Olga Tot (Russian Aide), Michael Shanks (Voice of Thor)

The Americans and the Russians reveal the existence of the Stargate to the British, Chinese and French governments due to the mounting threat by Anubis. Senator Kinsey tries to use the meeting to hijack the program, but Hammond has a card up his sleeve.

JOSEPH MALLOZZI: When Paul and I learned SG-1 would be doing a clip show in its sixth season, we lobbied hard and eventually won the opportunity to write it! Juuuust kidding. When we were first handed the assignment, we were less than enthusiastic. But, as we started writing, it became, if not exactly fun, then certainly interesting. It's *Stargate 101* as the series deals with an issue that would plague it for years to come: How the hell can the government possibly keep the existence of the Stargate program a secret? Sure, there were past incidents that required some fast-talking ("Exploding spaceships? No, no, no. Those were Cinco de Mayo celebrations. Er, yes, in November."), but the apparent crash of a spaceship into the Pacific Ocean was going to be tough to cover up. And so, rather than even try, we come clean. Of course it stood to reason that our allies would be annoyed at being kept in the dark for so long, so Rob Cooper suggested an appearance by Thor, the ever-affable Asgard, to smooth things over (and put the conniving Kinsey in his place). I love the sequence where Kinsey raises his finger to interrupt only to have Thor trump him by raising his finger (shut up) and continuing.

  Episode #128 (6.18): "Forsaken"
  Written by Damian Kindler
  Directed by Andy Mikita
  Guest Starring: Martin Cummins (Aden Corso), Dion Johnstone (Warrick), Sarah Deakins (Tanis Reynard), David Paetkau (Lyle Pender), Rob Lee (Major Pierce), Trevor Jones (Alien), Bruce Dawson (Crewman)

SG-1 finds a wrecked spacecraft whose crew claims to have been fighting off aggressive aliens ever since they crashed. It later turns out that the crew are in fact prisoners of the Serrakin ship Sebrus. The Serrakin are an advanced race who once helped free the human Hebridans, descendants of the Celts, from the Goa'uld millennia ago. Since then, the two peoples have lived together in a largely harmonious society on the planet Hebridan.

JOSEPH MAZZOLLI: Tiny nitpick but, in the opening scene, O'Neill peers through Carter's telescope and remarks on the fact that he can't see anything. She points out that, no, he wouldn't because it's daytime. Amusing and all if not for the fact that the show had already established Jack as a guy who likes to check out the stars at night through the telescope in his backyard. Was Jack being purposely dense? Perhaps. In fact, as the series went on, O'Neill became increasingly "intellectually relaxed." After some six years of playing the role, I guess Rick wanted to have a little more fun with the character. And that was fine with us, the writers, since it allowed us to do something we always enjoyed doing – bring the funny. Less so some of the fans who began to derisively refer to the new and improved (?) O'Neill as Dumb Jack.

Episode #129 (6.19): "The Changeling"
Written by Christopher Judge
Directed by Martin Wood
Guest Starring: Tony Amendola (Bra'tac), Carmen Argenziano (Jacob Carter), Musetta Vander (Shauna), Peter Williams (Apophis), Michael Shanks (Daniel Jackson), Teryl Rothery (Dr. Janet Fraiser), John Ulmer (Fire Fighter), Gianna Patton (Nurse), Gary Jones (Radio Dispatcher)

Teal'c finds himself jumping between different realities of Earth and the planet Kresh'ta, where a meeting of 108 Jaffa rebel leaders is ambushed by the Goa'uld System Lords. Only Daniel seems to display any understanding of reality.

JOSEPH MAZZOLLI: Actor Chris Judge tries his hand at writing with surprising spectacular results. I say surprising because, while I had no doubt it would be a solid script, I was mighty impressed by how good it turned out (this despite the fact that he neglected to include act breaks in his first draft – "I leave that sh★t up to you, m★th★rf★cker."). From what I remember, Chris really enjoyed the process and was quite proud of the final product.

PETER WILLIAMS: Let me tell you something, Chris is the epitome of the gentle giant, and he's a gentleman as well, despite what we all know about his antics. And his flatulence. He'll forgive me for saying that. Chris has one of the biggest hearts around and I think he deliberately put me in this episode to do me a favor and I'm forever grateful. I mean that sincerely.

Episode #130 (6.20): "Memento"
Written by Damian Kindler
Directed by Peter DeLuise
Guest Starring: Robert Foxworth (Chairman Ashwan), John Novak (Colonel William

Ronson), Miguel Fernandes (Commander Kalfas), Ingrid Kavelaars (Major Erin Gant), Alex Diakun (Tarek Solamun), Ray Galletti (Navigator)

On the maiden flight of the finished Prometheus, the reactor overloads, and SG-1 must find the Stargate buried on the alien planet Tagrea in order to obtain spare parts from Earth. Tagrea was once ruled by the Goa'uld Heru-ur, and the memory of his occupation was so traumatic that the Tagreans buried their Stargate and wiped out all traces of their earlier history, so as to make a new start. Despite opposition from xenophobic elements of the Tagrean military, the progressive Chairman Ashwan assists SG-1 in locating the Stargate and eventually opens relations with Earth.

JOSEPH MALLOZZI: What was this episode about again?

PETER DELUISE: The original premise of the show was that you don't need spaceships, because we've got the Stargate to get us where we want to go. Traditionally spaceships are expensive to build and they can be very limiting as was the case with the original *Trek* series, which was largely on the spaceship. And when they would go down to the planets, the planets would either be forested land or other worldly with cheesy sets and Styrofoam rocks — which we made fun of in "Wormhole X-Treme!" Well, now if we're gonna take on the added expense of these spaceships, if you make a spaceship, you have to *use* the spaceship. The way they would do these enemy spaceships on *Star Trek* was the interior was mostly on screen with one wall behind the alien characters. But the bridge of the *Enterprise* was magnificent and open and had many seats and tons of crew. *Not* the enemy ships. In the *Star Trek* movies, you saw that Klingon ships had bridges and weapons officers and navigation officers, but you never saw that on the TV show.

So having a ship was quite the endeavor and, of course, we wanted to make it as thrilling as possible. Everyone who wrote for the show were fans of *Star Trek* and *Star Wars*, so we really wanted to do it right and not make it too pretty and somewhat industrial. Often Brad will use his knowledge of the military, so that when you're on the bridge of the ship, it's not so different from the guts of an aircraft carrier or a destroyer.

Episode #131 (6.21): "Prophecy"
Written by Joseph Mallozzi & Paul Mullie
Directed by William Waring
Guest Starring: Thomas Kopache (Ellori), Victor Talmadge (Mot), Tom Scholte (Chazen), Gary Jones (Technician), Rob Lee (Major Pierce), Teryl Rothery (Dr. Janet Fraiser), Sarah Edmonson (Natania), Johannah Newmarch (Sina), Karin Konoval (Dr. Van Densen), Karen van Blankenstein (Nurse), Brendan McClarty (Sendear), Dan Shea (Sergeant Siler)

SG-1 finds a planet where the population worship Baal and work in the mines to provide his representative, Lord Mot, with a tribute of naqahdah. SG-1 intends to stop him, but things get complicated when Jonas starts seeing visions that could kill him.

JOSEPH MALLOZZI: This episode turned out to be one of my biggest disappointments of the season. I thought the script was solid, but the entire episode rested on the final twist, the moment in which O'Neill hears the horn and calls out to Pierce. It's meant to be the episode's big, defining moment, but it's so casually underplayed that it loses any dramatic impact.

Episode #132 (6.22): "Full Circle"
Written by Robert C. Cooper
Directed by Martin Wood
Guest Starring: Alexis Cruz (Skaara), Gary Jones (Technician), Michael Shanks (Daniel Jackson), David Palffy (Anubis), Sean Amsing (Tobay), Vince Crestejo (Yu the Great), Michael Adamthwaite (Herak), Veena Sood (Abydonian Leader)

Daniel Jackson contacts Jack and tells him that Anubis has located the Eye of Ra, an enormously powerful weapon. SG-1 heads for Abydos to rally their old friends against Anubis's fleet, while Daniel confronts Anubis and learns the terrifying truth about him. While trying to find the Eye, SG-1 learns that there is a Lost City of the Ancients that may hold the key to defeating Anubis once and for all.

MICHAEL SHANKS: We go back to the beginning of the *Stargate* story and go through a similar battle process with the evil forces of the alien. I always love taking the story back to Abydos, because Daniel has a strong relationship with the people there … I think Daniel knows that [Anubis] won't attack. It was part of my original thought process, too. I was thinking, "Yeah, what is he believing this guy for?" But he's not. I realized that after a second read of the script. He's not trusting Anubis, he's saying that making this deal will allow his friends to escape with the tablet so that they can find the lost city. He's already told the System Lords that Anubis is there. They will come to create a distraction while Daniel tries to get his friends out and save the people on Abydos. Daniel also wants to actually confront Anubis one-on-one. He knows if we find the tablet, it will lead us to the Lost City where the weapons are that can destroy Anubis. I think that he believes in keeping Anubis' trust in that particular moment. Daniel will do whatever it takes to get this Eye that will allow his friends to escape and possibly help the people on Abydos. *(Cyberex Online)*

ROBERT C. COOPER: The first challenge was to bring Daniel back and do so elegantly, as if it was always planned. At the same time, this episode was about how to explore a change up in the Goa'uld, where it's, like, if you think you've seen a bad guy before, you haven't seen one like *this*. We wanted to create some mystery around him and make him feel like something you hadn't seen before. Like any other mythological god that had been supplanted, I feel like our challenge was that when you defeat the bad guys, you need a new bad guy who's even worse. So that was the double challenge of the episode, the bad guy and bringing Daniel back.

JOSEPH MALLOZZI: Ah, another series finale. Executive producer Robert Cooper wraps up *SG-1* in fine style – except that, as we learned late in Season 6, this season would not be the show's last. After six seasons, *SG-1* was still going strong, much to the delight of our new broadcaster, Sci-Fi, who were more than happy to pick up the series for one more year. Which, of course, we assumed would be its last.

DAVID READ: Sci-Fi Channel really gave *SG-1* a second chance for the sixth season. It was something that we as fans really couldn't have dreamt of, but I don't think they were necessarily expecting *SG-1* to be as big a hit as it was. This episode finally gives us a concrete answer as to where the Ancients are now and that we've already encountered them. It's a great return for Daniel, going back to his adopted home and going face to face with Anubis. There's some terrific drama there between Shanks and David Palffy as Anubis.

DARREN SUMNER: *Stargate* does season finales so great. There's lots of build up throughout the season, lots of percolating plot threats and then they all come together and they spend a whole lot of money to do a big season finale. In this case, it's not just a spectacle. Anubis shows up and uses his big new mothership and big new space weapon to obliterate the System Lords' fleet — again, it's not just spectacle, but *Stargate* building on its mythology and expanding its characters. Daniel comes back, we learn more about ascended beings and this is where our long-held suspicion was confirmed that the ascended beings who Daniel has joined *are* the Ancients. *They* are the race that built the Stargates. We as fans have been speculating on that for a couple of seasons at this point, and this is where it was confirmed.

Alexis Cruz' final episode in the role of Skaara came in this episode, in which he and the remaining Abydosians ascend at the end.

ALEXIS CRUZ: Having lived with the character for so long, and then seeing and being a part of the phenomenon of the fandom, and how it reaches people, there's always a part of you that wants it to continue. There's always unfinished business with the character when you've lived with it for so long and know it so well. So there's a little bit of that. But there was a full circle closure. The fandom and the phenomenon was there, and we can now move on from that. And my career could move on a bit, too, in other ways, as well.

SEASON SEVEN SUMMARY

* *Daniel Jackson is located on Vis Uban. After gradually recovering his memories he rejoins SG-1.*

* *Jonas Quinn leaves SG-1 to help rebuild his planet.*

* *Earth's Alpha Site is moved to another planet.*

* *Thor stops Loki from running experiments on humans.*

* *SG-1 rescues the crew of the alien ship Stromos.*

* *Stargate Command establishes a mining treaty with the Unas of P3X-403, which will expedite the construction of BC-303s.*

* *Anubis develops Kull warriors to begin to phase out the increasingly rebellious Jaffa.*

* *Samantha Carter begins seeing Pete Shanahan.*

* *Osiris is removed from Sarah Gardner.*

* *The second Alpha Site is destroyed.*

* *Samantha Carter and Jacob/Selmak develop a technology to combat the Kull warriors.*

* *Emmett Bregman films the Stargate Command documentary.*

* *Janet Fraiser is killed while on an off-world mission, shot down by fire from a Jaffa staff weapon.*

* *Rogue N.I.D. experiments with Sekhmet come to a horrific end.*

* *United States President Henry Hayes takes office with Vice President Robert Kinsey.*

* *Jack O'Neill again downloads the knowledge of the Ancients into his mind, leading SG-1 to Proclarush Taonas to locate a Zero Point Module.*

* *George Hammond is relieved as leader of Stargate Command, and is sent to Washington to advise President Hayes. Elizabeth Weir takes his place.*

* *Anubis takes his battle to Earth.*

* *President Hayes learns of Robert Kinsey's treachery and forces him to resign from the office of vice president.*

* *SG-1 installs the Taonas Zero Point Module into the Atlantus defense system. Jack O'Neill uses it to destroy the 30 Goa'uld ships in orbit. O'Neill, near death, is placed in suspended animation.*

* *Cameron Mitchell, critically injured in the battle over Antarctica, begins a year of rehabilitation.*

EPISODE GUIDE (2003-2004)

Episode #133 (7.1): "Fallen"
  Written by Robert C. Cooper
  Directed by Martin Wood
  Guest Starring: Corin Nemec (Jonas Quinn), George Touliatos (Shamda), Kevan Ohtsji, David Palffy (Anubis), Michael Adamthwaite (Herak), Gary Jones (Technician), Teryl Rothery (Dr. Janet Fraiser), Vince Crestejo (Yu), Eric Breker (Colonel Reynolds), Raahul Singh (Khordib), Johannah Newmarch (Sina), Mary-Jane Baker (SF)

  Daniel is found living on Vis Uban ("place of great power", P4T-3G6), a planet where the Ancients began building their greatest city when they were struck by a plague. Although Daniel has total amnesia, he helps SG-1 destroy Anubis' superweapon.

MICHAEL SHANKS: We've established that [Daniel] had to make a conscious choice. He was confronted with an almost court-like structure, and given an ultimatum: "You either play by our rules and stay, or, if you choose not to, you're out." And Daniel says, "Well, you know what? I don't like the way you do things. I don't think it's the best thing for me, and I'm going back." And when he goes back, he doesn't remember exactly what happened. But over the first five episodes – and one episode specifically, "Orpheus" – he realizes why he came back. He recalls how helpless he felt watching his friends go through these ordeals and not being able to do anything about it. He understands that he's here to do something, and that the Ancients aren't angels. They're just another alien race with their own, separate agenda, and Daniel realizes that if he's going to do something for humanity and for Earth, he has to take a more proactive role.

ROBERT C. COOPER: Daniel really struggled with it and felt like, finally, maybe he had been lied to a little bit, and that what was going on was a bit hypocritical from the other's point of view. And so he decided to get involved, and he got his wrist slapped in a very severe kind of way ... I think fans saw a Season 1 Daniel out of him, and the whole storyline of him being punished and having to start fresh gave him a story reason for going back to that original, slightly less tainted, wide-eyed positive Daniel.

JOSEPH MALLOZZI: Before work began on the show's seventh season, I emailed Rob Cooper a notion I had of an angel cast down from heaven, stripped of his memories and left to start a new life on Earth. Rob ended up taking the whole "stripped" thing literally – much to the delight of Michael's fans. Paul flagged an exchange at the script stage. One off-worlder notes Teal'c's presence with, "He is Jaffa," to which O'Neill replies: "No, but he plays one on TV." Paul felt it broke the fourth wall, but was ultimately overruled. When the episode aired, many fans loved the exchange – while many others followed suit and waved their own red flags. Following the scene in which O'Neill appeals to an amnesiac Daniel, [Daniel] refers to Jack as "Jim." It's a gag that Brad calls back to in *SGA*'s "The Shrine."

ROBERT C. COOPER: Jonas started as a bit of ... I don't want to say anti-hero, but someone who was dealing with the guilt of maybe being responsible for Daniel's departure, and was branded a traitor by his own people. And he gets to go home with the people of his planet seeing that maybe he made the right choice.

Episode #134 (7.2): "Homecoming"
Written by Joseph Mallozzi & Paul Mullie
Directed by Martin Wood
Guest Starring: Corin Nemec (Jonas Quinn), Cliff Simon (Baal), Kevan Ohts-ji (Oshu), David Palffy (Anubis), Michael Adamthwaite (Herak), Gary Jones (Techni-cian), Doug Abrahams (Commander Hale), Adrian Hough, Gillian Barber (Ambassador Dreylock), Glynis Davies (Ambassador Noor), Jan Bos (Ambassador Sevaarin), Daniel Cud-more (Jaffa #1), Aaron Thompson (Jaffa #2)

With knowledge of naquadria, Anubis attacks Kelowna, and SG-1 must come up with a plan to save them. Meanwhile, on Anubis' ship, Daniel attempts to rescue Jonas.

JOSEPH MALLOZZI: Even though the Jonas Quinn character never found firm footing on the show, I was nevertheless sad to see him go. Actor Corin Nemec was a good guy and we got along well, so I wanted to make sure he got a proper, respectful send-off that left the door open for a possible return. And I think we accomplished that in "Homecoming." Corin returned later in Season 7 to guest in an episode for which he received a story credit, "Fallout."

Episode #135 (7.3): "Fragile Balance"
Story by Peter DeLuise & Michael Greenburg, Teleplay by Damian Kindler
Directed by Peter DeLuise
Guest Starring: Carmen Argenziano (Jacob Carter), Michael Welch (Young Jack), Teryl Rothery (Dr. Janet Fraiser), Gregory Bennett (Lt. Col. Harlan Beck), Tom Heaton (Werner), Poppi Reiner (Pamela Ambrose), Ed Hong-Louie (Zyang Wu), Theresa Lee (Interpreter), Ralph Alderman (Shop Owner), Evan Lendrum (Pilot #1), Chris Kramer (Pilot #2), Noah Beggs (Security Force Officer #1), Dan Payne (Security Force Officer #2), Peter DeLuise (Voice of Loki)

O'Neill wakes up one morning to find himself 30 years younger, much to the annoyance of the Colonel. It is soon learned that the same process that caused him to become younger is also causing him to die. The rest of SG-1 discovers that the young O'Neill is a clone and an Asgard is responsible.

MICHAEL GREENBURG: Peter DeLuise and I wrote the original story. It was kind of to attack the Asgard and their obvious physical and intellectual evolution. When you look at these creatures, they have big heads, big brains, and their bodies are kind of genderless. We wanted to examine that and we came up with cloning. They were just cloning themselves and cloning themselves and cloning themselves, with the potential of the vicious cycle that that would create, and then un-create, meaning they reached a point where they couldn't reproduce on their own, so they solely had to resort to cloning and the diminishing returns of that kind of continuation.

So that's what the story was about. And our antagonist in the original story was this character Odin, who was half-human and half-Asgard, and he was out there in this renegade ship in space. Because of this cloning continuum that was showing diminishing returns, he kidnapped O'Neill, who had the mind that they wanted to tap into, and the DNA that they wanted to tap into, to try to abate the diminishing returns of cloning. So that was sort of the foundation and the genesis of that story. And then it completely changed! (*Stargate SG-1 Explorer Unit Official Fan Club*)

JOSEPH MALLOZZI: Actor Michael Welch delivers one of the show's most impressive guest performances in the role of a young, cloned Jack O'Neill. He captures (Rick as) Jack's mannerisms and rhythms perfectly and so wowed us that, in the following months, we tried to spin several different stories that would have seen Young Jack make a return. Unfortunately, none of these stories panned out. I did end up running into Michael Welch at that year's Saturn Awards (Best Award Show Ever!). He told me how much he'd enjoyed his experience on the show while I told him how much we'd enjoyed having him. Interestingly enough, it was the same night I first met actor Ben Browder. We discussed *Farscape*, sci-fi, and the possibility of him doing a guest spot on the show. I ended up writing a part for him as a potential recurring character on *Atlantis,* but a scheduling conflict prevented him from accepting the role – which, in the long run, was a good thing, because it allowed him to accept the more substantial role of *SG-1*'s Cameron Mitchell two years later.

PETER DELUISE: "Fragile Balance" was a great opportunity to lampoon some of Richard Dean Anderson's hijinks, because we had a kid who was a clone of him that was imitating him. So I realized that this was going to be very difficult, especially for a little kid who had never watched the show. So I took him under my wing and I would imitate Richard Dean Anderson and the kid would imitate me doing Richard Dean Anderson. It was his idiosyncratic behavior, including things like putting on his sunglasses. He wouldn't just put on sunglasses, he'd react as though he was adjusting to the change in light. His reason was that he was creating more screen time so that the audience now had registered that he had his sunglasses on, and when he speaks *then*, it feels like his line jumps. So he would make a little bit of a meal out of putting the glasses on, and so, because of the editing process, I would give that to the kid, Michael Welch. And he captured the wry humor and bravado of an adult, confident male. He was just like a sponge and would just imitate him.

JOSEPH MALLOZZI: Having Michael return wasn't the problem. He may be a teenager, but he's still got all the skills and savvy of our Jack. It would have been a simple matter of being faced with a situation that required Jack's expertise – and making the original Jack incapable of offering his assistance. What, exactly, that "situation" was is the question that stumped us.

Episode #136 (7.4): "Orpheus"
Written and Directed by Peter DeLuise
Guest Starring: Tony Amendola (Bra'tac), Obi Ndefo (Rak'nor), Neil Denis (Rya'c), David Richmond-Peck (Jaffa Commander), Gary Jones (Technician), Teryl Rothery (Dr. Janet Fraiser), Sheri Noel (Physiotherapist)

Teal'c is shot by a Jaffa as they retreat through the gate and his self-confidence is greatly shaken. Meanwhile, Daniel remembers that Rya'c and Bra'tac are held prisoner on the planet Erebus, where Jaffa prisoners of war must build Ha'tak ships. Teal'c must regain his confidence if they are to be saved.

PETER DELUISE: The setting was basically a death camp. The Seventh Level of Hell is the most horrifying experience, so I named it "Orpheus" because of Orpheus' descent into Hell. I just thought it would be interesting to show this death camp and these Jaffa who are being punished and worked to death, *and* to show the human spirit in terms of their tenacity and never say die attitude in this most extreme situation. The inspiration for the lead bad guy, played by David Richmond-Peck, was inspired by the bad guy in the film *Cool Hand Luke.*

JOSEPH MALLOZZI: In "Orpheus," the B story is Daniel coming to terms with a return to his life at S.G.C., what he remembers from his past and his time as an ascended being, and what he was able to do as an ascended being and what he wasn't able to do in human form, and vice versa. But it also focuses on Teal'c, and the fact that he is now without a symbiote. He's on tretonin now, which is a substitute for the symbiote in many ways but doesn't offer the Jaffa quite the same protection and, up to a certain point, invulnerability.

MICHAEL SHANKS: This involves the ramifications of Daniel's ascension and the effects of what happened to Teal'c from "The Changeling." The results of these two situations unfold independently and they sort of culminate in a climax that involves a third story. It's very multi-layered and there's a lot of interesting interaction between Teal'c and Daniel. As actors, Christopher and I get to bite into a rather large sandwich, and to see what we do with it is fun. We didn't often get the chance to play off one another. (*Sci-Fi Magazine*)

JOSEPH MALLOZZI: In this particular episode, Teal'c suffers a crisis of conscience because he is not the warrior he once was. It's something he has to come to terms with, and he has a difficult time coming to terms with it until he's faced with a situation in which he must prove himself a warrior. And his story dovetails with Daniel's quite nicely. That's actually a Peter DeLuise episode. It's very nice, much like Peter's many trademark episodes, there's a lot of Jaffa and big battles, and huge expense.

Given that this is one of the episodes that DeLuise both wrote and directed, it does raise the question of what his preference is: helming his own material or capturing somebody else's.

PETER DELUISE: Writing is a tall order and you've got to jump through several hoops to please many people. But the satisfaction that you get about directing your own writing is that there's only so much room on a script page that you can actually write what you were visualizing when you wrote it. So it's not just this story paired with this director and then you get *this*. I think it explodes exponentially where, if the writer and director are the same person, it becomes a much bigger, better deal, because you achieve so much more than you could have written down.

Episode #137 (7.5): "Revisions"
Written by Joseph Mallozzi & Paul Mullie
Directed by Martin Wood
Guest Starring: Christopher Heyerdahl (Pallan), Peter Lacroix (Kendrick), Tiffany Knight (Evalla), Liam Ranger (Nevin), Gary Jones (Technician), Wendy Noel (Councilwoman), Michael Robinson (Councilman #1), Patrick Keating (Councilman #2), Finn Michael (Councilman #3)

Mahg Mar (P3X-289) has a toxic atmosphere, but there is a forcefield dome protecting an idyllic village. That is, idyllic except for the fact that its inhabitants are disappearing one by one, without noticing it themselves.

JOSEPH MALLOZZI: This story started out as a pitch about a town living within a hermetically sealed bubble surrounded by a toxic atmosphere. SG-1 happens upon the scene and discovers its inhabitants are hiding a terrible secret. I hesitate to reveal the shocking conclusion I originally envisioned, because the story we ended up with was so different that I'd love to repurpose it given some future opportunity. Anyway, even though the episode ended up quite different from the way I'd originally envisioned it, I loved it nevertheless. And I wasn't the only one. Then VFX Supervisor James Tichenor really enjoyed the script; it's a great SF standalone episode. And the location we found for the town was perfect in its bizarre cross-cultural architectural weirdness. It is, in reality, a former amusement park, Fantasy Gardens, with a fairly interesting history. We would return there years later to shoot *SGA*'s "Irresponsible."

It was one of those pure SF off-world adventures: no mythology, no ties to previous episodes, simply a cool, SF-themed standalone. To be honest, the original pitch was very different but, over a lunch of dry ribs and spicy maki, Robert Cooper steered us in the direction of what became the eventual story: SG-1 stumbles upon a society living within a hermetically sealed bubble. Members of their community begin to disappear, but no one seems to notice, because their memories are mysteriously altered. This was one of those rare scripts where I knew exactly where I wanted to end up: with a final moment in which one of the characters asks Carter to tell him about the wife he no longer remembers.

Episode #138 (7.6): "Lifeboat"
Written by Brad Wright

Directed by Peter DeLuise

Guest Starring: James Parks (Pharrin), Gary Jones (Technician), Teryl Rothery (Dr. Janet Fraiser), Travis Webster (Tryan), Ryan Drescher (Young Keenin), Kimberly Unger (Infirmary Nurse), Rob Hayter (Orderly), Colin Corrigan (Team Leader)

While exploring P2A-347, SG-1 encounters the crashed alien spaceship Stromos, which contains a plethora of cryogenic pods. The team separates, and Daniel's mind becomes host to many different minds of the ship's crew. When SG-1 investigates the alien ship to find a way to cure Daniel, they discover that the minds of the passengers from the planet Talthus are being saved in the ship's computer.

JOSEPH MALLOZZI: An acting tour-de-force for Michael Shanks, who delivers a multitude of terrific performances in an episode that sees him playing several different characters. Guest star James Park's portrayal of the doomed Pharrin is also incredibly touching and the perfect complement to Michael's multi-layered turn. Brad had the idea for this story back in Season 6 but, since he'd constructed the story for Daniel who had since left this mortal coil, he'd shelved it indefinitely. When Michael came back to the show the following year, however, Brad was able to dust it off and put it back in play.

BRAD WRIGHT: The question I asked was what if a ship storing bodies cryo-genically is failing, and the only way the engineer can save people is by combining consciousnesses into one body and creating multi-personalities in one head that Daniel ends up being the repository for? I don't know how many dozens of minds are fighting to get into the forefront and it's going to kill him. *That* is a great dramatic setup. In order to do an episode like that, you need an actor with the chops to pull it off; some-one who can play 10 characters, sometimes all at once. And there was a neat moment near the end where he's arguing with himself, jumping back and forth between per-sonalities. A great acting opportunity for Mr. Shanks and he pulled it off.

PETER DELUISE: Another Michael Shanks/Daniel Jackson tour de force where he's got a consciousness in his head, which was kind of a cool and great way to save money if you don't want any guest stars. Because Michael had a theater background that Brad was aware of — and Brad himself was an actor — he was trying to tap in as best he could in trying to use Michael's strengths. Whereas Richard Dean Anderson's strengths were wry, witty humor in short spurts, give Michael Shanks a monologue and he would just fucking eat it up *and* would be great.

JOSEPH MALLOZZI: It's one of those self-contained pure SF stories, like "Re-visions" (and the episodes Brad used to produce in his *Outer Limits* days), that always appealed to me in much the same way that I always preferred the stand-alone horror *X-Files* episodes over the arc-driven entries.

Episode #139 (7.7): "Enemy Mine"
Written and Directed by Peter DeLuise
Guest Starring: Michael Rooker (Colonel Edwards), Steven Williams (General Vidrine), Alex Zahara (Iron Shirt), Kavan Smith (Lorne), Patrick Currie (Chaka), Gary Jones (Technician), Michael Shore (Lt. Menard), Dean Redman (Lt. Woeste), Kirk Caouette (Lt. Ritter), Sean Tyson (Unas #1), Wycliff Hartwig (Unas #2)

S.G.C. have found a planet with rich deposits of naquadah, but the local population of Unas do not welcome the mining team. Daniel enlists his Unas friend Chaka to negotiate an agreement.

PETER DELUISE: The title was a nod to the wonderful movie *Enemy Mine* starring Louis Gossett, Jr. and Dennis Quaid. I was so inspired by that that I had to do something to honor that title. This was an example of what we call Aboriginal Unas — they didn't have Goa'uld in them and they had no Goa'uld leaders and they were Goa'uld free. They were tribal and we were experiencing them in large numbers. So it was continuing the saga of the Unas race, not unlike "The First Ones," which was another episode that I wrote. In this case, I thought SG-1 should go to the middle of an Amazon forest and this tribe has never been touched or dealt with, and then there's a misunderstanding and everything turns to shit and gets violent. We had a wonderful actor in the form of Michael Rooker, who ended up in *The Walking Dead* and *Guardians of the Galaxy*. Just an amazing character actor who's been around for a while.

JOSEPH MALLOZZI: "Enemy Mine" was the working title of this episode which, like "Watergate" before it, went from placeholder title to official title before anyone could do anything about it. FYI, past placeholder titles that didn't make it to official status include: "Teal'c Interrupted," "Turn of Events," "Dark Gambit," "Flowers for McKay," "CSI: Atlantis," "Ad Infinitum," "Remember When" and "Beckett Returns." Writer/director Peter DeLuise excelled at stories that, like this one, focused on the show's rich mythology, building upon the races and characters established in previous episodes and developing them in interesting, often surprising, ways.

Episode #140 (7.8): "Space Race"
Written by Damian Kindler
Directed by Andy Mikita
Guest Starring: Scott MacDonald (Golon Jarlath), Alex Zahara (Warrick), Patrick Currie (Eamon), Terence Kelly (Miles Hagan), Allan Lysell (Del Tynan), Hillary

Cooper (Receptionist), Colin Murdock (Ardal Hadraig), Peter Kelamis (Coyle Boron), Ben Ayres (Muirios), Nick Misura (Taupen), Lindsay Maxwell (La'el Montrose)

Carter helps the Serrakin Warrick (season 6's "Forsaken") to enter his spaceship in a dangerous race on his planet Hebridan, the prize for which is a lucrative contract. Carter and Warrick must overcome sabotage caused by one of the participants.

AMANDA TAPPING: I really wanted to find the heart of Carter, and see what makes her tick. What gets her juices flowing and her blood boiling. "Space Race" doesn't show any deep hidden secret about her, but we get to see her having fun. She's an adrenaline junky. She's got a much better sense of humor now.

JOSEPH MALLOZZI: Working on *Stargate* was a writer's dream in that it offered a host of wide-ranging opportunities when it came to scripting an episode. The stories could be arc-driven or standalone, Earth-bound or off-world centered, mythological in nature or purely sci-fi, dramatic or humorous. And every so often, we occasionally did those departure episodes that stood out all the more in the uniqueness of their narrative or execution. "Space Race" was one of those episodes and, as a result and to no one's surprise, was a little divisive when it came to fan opinion. Some fans loved it. Others hated it. Still, whatever negative response it may have received online paled in comparison to the scorn heaped upon "Avenger 2.0."

Episode #141 (7.9): "Avenger 2.0"
Written by Joseph Mallozzi & Paul Mullie
Directed by Martin Wood
Guest Starring: Patrick McKenna (Jay Felger), Jocelyne Loewen (Chloe), Gary Jones (Technician)

Felger ("The Other Guys") is about to be fired, and is desperate to persuade General Hammond to give him another chance. He invents a computer virus able to deactivate a Stargate, and targets one of Baal's principal naquadah mining sites on P5S-117 to test out the virus. However, the virus spreads on its own and the entire network is shut down.

JOSEPH MALLOZZI: Okay, in retrospect the title was one of the best things about this episode. We shot Felger's apartment at the Accent Inn across the street from The Bridge Studios (where we also shot Ronon and Sheppard watching *BSG* on the motel TV, Teal'c enjoying the thousand finger massage in "Point of No Return," and the scene of Kinsey's shooting in "Smoke and Mirrors"). In the original script, Felger is painting his Warhammer figures, but the gang at Warhammer nixed the idea because they felt suggesting a character like him (i.e. brilliant scientist) playing Warhammer would depict the game in an unfavorable light. So we went with *Stargate* action figures instead.

Episode #142 (7.10): "Birthright"
Written by Christopher Judge
Directed by Peter F. Woeste
Guest Starring: Jolene Blalock (Ishta), Christine Adams (Mala), Kathleen Duborg (Neith), Kirsten Prout (Nesa), Teryl Rothery (Dr. Janet Fraiser), Simone Bailly (Ka'lel), Nigel Vonas (Ryk'l), Elizabeth Weinstein (Emta), Julie Hill (Ginra), Nikki Smook (Nictal), Cory Martin (Fallen Jaffa), Kimberly Unger (Nurse)

SG-1 meets a group of all female Jaffa from a planet named Hak'tyl (meaning "liberation"), who have set up their own rebel base. They were rebels against the Goa'uld Moloc who forced his Jaffa to sacrifice their female babies in fire; many of these female Jaffa were rescued as infants by their leader Ishta, (Jolene Blalock).

CHRISTOPHER JUDGE: I actually wrote "Birthright" for Jolene Blalock. They asked me who I saw, and I said, "Well, I kind of wrote it with Jolene Blalock in mind." If we hadn't gotten Jolene, the only two people I really saw doing the role at all were either Jolene or Victoria Pratt. And we were fortunate enough to get Jolene.

JOSEPH MALLOZZI: Actor Chris Judge's second foray into scripting sees him tackle Jaffa cultural constraints, sexism, and uneasy alliances. Thankfully Jolene Blalock was available to play the role. The episode also features a cameo by executive producer Michael Greenburg's wife, Nicky. At one point in the episode, she rides by on a horse and shouts something.

Episode #143 (7.11): "Evolution, Part 1"
Story by Damian Kindler & Michael Shanks, Teleplay by Damian Kindler
Directed by Peter DeLuise
Guest Starring: Carmen Argenziano (Jacob Carter), Tony Amendola (Bra'tac), Frank Roman (Rafael), Bill Dow (Dr. Lee), Zak Santiago (Rogelio Duran), Eric Breker (Colonel Reynolds), Craig Erickson (Adal), Michael Jonsson (Jaffa Guard), Dan Payne (Kull Warrior), Todd Thomson (Ramius's First Prime), Victor Favrin (Chalo), Sean Whale (Ramius)

Teal'c and Bra'tac are attacked by a black armored warrior, impervious to all known weapons, who is found to be an advanced Goa'uld warrior created by Anubis. Daniel visits Honduras to find a hidden artifact which may hold the key to defeating them.

MICHAEL SHANKS: So what ended up happening is that I had about two or three different story ideas that I wanted to be my story originally. I wanted to do a sequel to an episode called "Crystal Skull" from the third season. How Nick, the grandfather, is dying of cancer. Robert Cooper had a similar idea that involved the idea that the Goa'uld get this device that is able to create this brand new enemy designed to replace the Jaffa as our stormtrooper type characters. I got a writer's credit on it, but it's not the idea I originally had. I had more ... pure vision, originally.

JOSEPH MALLOZZI: The first part of our mid-season two-parter (hey, remember the days when the 11th episode was the midway point of the season?) introduced a fearsome new enemy with an equally fearsome codpiece. Yep. Whenever the deadly super soldier strode onto the scene, all I could think was, "I wonder if that's where they keep its battery pack?" The idea of an almost indestructible enemy was a good one and, on paper, it certainly sounded cool – but the finished product was more likely to trigger laughter than any feelings of foreboding. Note: For what it's worth, the Asurans were similarly/mysteriously well-endowed.

Episode #144 (7.12): "Evolution, Part 2"
Story by Damian Kindler & Peter DeLuise, Teleplay by Peter DeLuise
Directed by Peter Deluise
Guest Starring: Carmen Argenziano (Jacob Carter), Tony Amendola (Bra'tac), Frank Roman (Rafael), Bill Dow (Dr. Lee), David Palffy (Anubis), Zak Santiago (Rogelio), Enrico Colantoni (Burke), Victor Favrin (Chalo), Ian Marsh (Thoth), Miguel Castillo (Pedro), Dan Shea (Sgt. Siler), Dan Payne (Kull Warrior)

O'Neill goes to Honduras to rescue Daniel Jackson. In the meantime, Carter, Jacob / Selmak and Teal'c must destroy the facility on the planet Tartarus, where Anubis is creating legions of the new warriors, using a Goa'uld queen to spawn new symbiotes.

JOSEPH MALLOZZI: Enrico Colantoni guests as Burke, a former black ops buddy of O'Neill's, and does such a formidable job that, months later, we were still talking about the fact we have to bring him back and give him his own team. Like so many of the show's creative good intentions, it never comes to pass – but things worked out for Enrico all the same. Also, as much as I didn't love the super-soldier, I was all over the zombies that stalk the jungles of Nicaragua (Vancouver woods with a little help from our Greens Department). Speaking of tearing it up, director Peter DeLuise does a brilliant job here with the action, particularly one shot that sees the Zombie Chalo blown apart. The other guys felt it was too visceral ("Pretty damn goopy!") but I didn't see the problem. It was a zombie after all, not a human being. I mean, it's perfectly acceptable to decapitate robots on screen. I think the same logic would apply. I was overruled.

PETER DELUISE: In a way, this was the origin of the Super Soldier, actually the Kull Warrior, who was almost impossible to kill. This was the Goa'uld super weapon and given that this was an origin, in the process of creating this weapon we needed to stop it. I ended up with the word Kull to convey the idea that you cull the weak and only the strong survive.

Episode #145 (7.13): "Grace"
Written by Damian Kindler
Directed by Peter F. Woeste
Guest Starring: Carmen Argenziano (Jacob), Ingrid Kavelaars (Major Erin Gant), John Novak (Colonel William Ronson), Sasha Pieterse (Grace), Craig Veroni (Weapons Officer)

Carter is on the Prometheus while the ship is on its way to Earth, and is attacked from a spaceship of a type they have never seen before. They try to escape by hiding in a nebula, but all the crew except Carter disappear.

AMANDA TAPPING: "Grace" was such an intense experience. We shot a lot of it in the second unit. In fact, I think we shot most of the show's second unit, so it took us over a month to complete it. As an actor, it was just a real challenge ... Just because you spend so much time alone, so much time inside your head. How to play the head injury without making it over the top, you know what I mean? And it was just an emotional struggle, and I think because we shot the second unit, it was jumping back into that and jumping out of that and jumping back into it. It was a challenge, but it was fun.

JOSEPH MALLOZZI: While I, admittedly, would have liked to see the Sam-Jack arc culminate in their finally settling down together, I wasn't a fan of the dream flash in this episode in which the two lock lips. My problem with it was not so much the content of the sequence as the fact that it was confusing – a hallucination within a greater hallucination. That said, I quite liked the episode that, in its early outlining, jumped back and forth between Carter actually boarding the alien vessel and coming face to face with its crew. In the end, it was decided the story would work better as a self-contained narrative.

AMANDA TAPPING: Who Grace actually was is left open for interpretation – it's left open for my own interpretation, too. I mean, Grace could be Sam's child within. Grace could be Sam's hopes and dreams for having a child. Grace could be the child Sam left behind when she focused all her energy on becoming an Astrophysicist Woman and forgot how to be a kid, forgot how to enjoy life. So she's a bunch of different things. In my mind I chose to make her Sam's potential future. Is she giving up family – which is what "Grace" deals with, what Sam struggles with – is she giving up any chance for a family or a "normal life," because she focuses all her energy on S.G.C. and what she's missing out on in life and if she were to have more of a life, could she bring more to her work? I had sat down with Rob Cooper at the beginning of the season and said, "I think we need to do a show where Sam struggles with her demons and where she questions her life choices and questions what she's missing as a woman and as a contributing member of society. Has she focused too much energy on work? When she lays her head on her pillow at night, what does she think about?" And Rob said, "Well, interestingly enough, there is a show coming up that will deal with that." "Oh, OK!"

Episode #146 (7.14): "Fallout"
Story by Corin Nemec, Teleplay by Joseph Mallozzi & Paul Mullie
Directed by Martin Wood
Guest Starring: Corin Nemec (Jonas Quinn), Emily Holmes (Kianna Cyr), Gillian Barber (Dreylock), Patricia Drake (Lucia Tarthus), Julian Christopher (Vin Eremal), Bill Nikolai (Technician)

Jonas Quinn returns to Earth from Kelowna to enlist S.G.C.'s help. He informs them that naquadria was created in a catalytic reaction and the process is ongoing on Kelowna. If the reaction goes deep enough, heat and pressure will destabilize the naquadria and it will blow the planet apart. Meanwhile, Jonas has been working with the brilliant young scientist Kianna, and they have a mutual romantic attraction, but she is not what she seems.

JOSEPH MALLOZZI: Actor Corin Nemec pitched this story and wrote the original outline for an episode that brings back Jonas Quinn and explores his new life on Langara. The original title of the episode was "Turn of Events," which we couldn't help but note was a title applicable to every episode we'd ever done. It would have been akin to titling an episode "Off-World Adventure" or "Fourth Act Twist!" It was a lot of fun, although one element in the story didn't quite pan out – specifically, Jonas Quinn's love interest, a fellow Langaran named Kianna. On the day the first dailies came in, we were horrified to discover that both actors had unnervingly similar hairstyles that, as a result, made them look like they were related. Which, in turn, made some of the romantic scenes a little ... weird?

Episode #147 (7.15): "Chimera"
Story by Robert C. Cooper, Teleplay by Damian Kindler
Directed by William Waring
Guest Starring: Anna-Louise Plowman (Sarah Gardner/Osiris), David DeLuise (Pete Shanahan), Paul Jarrett (Special Agent Farrity)

Osiris has been visiting Daniel at night and using a mind control device to try to find the Lost City of the Ancients. SG-1 decides to attempt to capture her, but Carter's new boyfriend Pete might get in the way.

AMANDA TAPPING: I think that it's an offshoot of what happened in "Grace." The writers were trying to, A) dispel the "black widow" curse that Carter has, and also to open her up for more experiences and to flesh her out just a little bit more as a human being. And so it's an interesting episode for me, because I felt so out of my element doing these little cutesy-flirty scenes, and of course the kissy-kissy, and it's *so* not a side of Carter that we've ever seen. She really falls hard for this guy, and the fact that he hasn't died yet is a pretty good sign, but I think it's also freaking her out. "Oh, no, he didn't die! Now what do I do? Now I have to have a relationship! How does that work?"

JOSEPH MALLOZZI: This episode also continues Sam's romantic arc with a fellow fandom coined "Stalker Pete." The role was played by David DeLuise, brother of Peter DeLuise. His appearance marked the fourth appearance by a member of the DeLuise family (Dom guested in "Urgo," Michael guested in "Wormhole X-Treme!," David guested in several episodes as Stalker Pete, and, of course, fan favorite Peter DeLuise wrote, directed, produced and had cameos in episodes too numerous to mention).

ROBERT C. COOPER: Poor David, who was so charming and delightful, just got it from the fans who did *not* like Carter having a romantic relationship with anybody else besides O'Neill. I felt really bad for him, because he was so great. I could be remembering this entirely wrong, but I don't feel like we intentionally brought him in, in that capacity to torment the fans. We probably knew *some* of that would come, but I guess we weren't as obsessed with Carter-O'Neill as the fans were. Besides, the bane of any television show is getting your characters together. The tension is so much better than bringing them together.

AMANDA TAPPING: David DeLuise is wonderful. We had instant chemistry. He's very much a DeLuise in that he's utterly charming, has a fantastic sense of humor, but he's a really wonderful actor and we spent a lot of time running scenes and going over different beats and trying to work stuff out. David and I would, you know, after work, go and sit in a coffee shop and run scenes. We went for walks where we were running scenes as if we were the characters. He's wonderful.

The episode didn't address how Carter felt about him essentially stalking her behind her back.

AMANDA TAPPING: I don't think Carter knew to what lengths he was going. She doesn't know that he phoned the FBI. She doesn't know that he ran a background trace on her. She doesn't know that he was doing all these things. The only thing that she knows is at the end of the stake-out, he's there. So yes, he's been following her, but I think she hadn't at that point in the episode had time to assimilate the fact that he'd been following her. And I think the fact that the way the episode ended with the big explosion, and "Oh, my God, he's been hurt," and "Oh, my God, now he's OK," the classified information is no longer classified to this man, because he's seen it, then I can actually tell him what I do for a living. She doesn't even think about the fact that he followed her. At the end of the episode, she's just so relieved that he isn't dead.

JOSEPH MALLOZZI: The thing that stands out for me about this episode was the title, which, over the course of prep, production, and post, was pronounced any one of about a half dozen ways: "Ki-mera," "Kee-mera," "Kee-meera," "Chi-mera," "Chy-mera," "Chy-meera" – and variations thereof. Damian Kindler was the king of the obtuse episode titles and, after following "Ethon" with "Talion," I decided to call my next script "Futtock" (one of the curved timbers that forms a rib in the frame of a ship), but was overruled by my writing partner, Paul, since he'd be sharing onscreen credit with me on this one. Anyway, Damian did a great job on an episode that provides a rarity – actual closure to a storyline! Daniel saves Sarah and, with the help of the Tok'ra, restores her to her former self.

Episode #148 (7.16): "Death Knell"
Written and Directed by Peter DeLuise
Guest Starring: Carmen Argenziano (Jacob Carter), Sebastian Spence (Delek), Mark Gibbon (M'zel), Gary Jones (Technician), Eric Breker (Colonel Reynolds), Nels Lennarson (Major Green), Sam MacMillan (Lt. Glenn), Dan Shea (Sgt. Siler), Dan Payne (Kull Warrior)

The Alpha Site, where a prototype weapon to fight Anubis's supersoldier drones is being created, is attacked by a drone. Carter escapes, but she is on her own and the drone is hunting her.

PETER DELUISE: We found out at the GVRD, which is the mountain where we would always go to shoot our stuff, that we were cutting down all these trees to create a reservoir for drinking water. As a result, the trees had all fallen down, looking like the picture in Russia where the meteor had struck and all the trees there had fallen. I said to Robert Cooper, "Look, all the trees are down and they can't pick them up immediately. We should do an episode where one or our outposts has been blown up and wiped out all these trees, because we'll never have access to that sort of thing again." Robert was inspired, so we moved up the Super Soldier story and said that they had come to wipe out this outpost, and that when the outpost blew up, it blew all of these trees and the only survivor was Carter, who had to fight a Super Soldier.

JOSEPH MALLOZZI: Bit of a nitpick, but if the Alpha Site had been wiped out by the self-destruct, it would have been one massive blast crater instead of a clearing littered with spot fires. Realistically, however, a massive blast crater would have been a huge expense that wouldn't have added much to the episode. Also, the Jaffa M'Zel was a tip of the hat to *Stargate* long time A.D. Bill Mizel, who provided us with many an entertaining concept meeting with his spirited renditions of the scripts – and also showed off some killer dance moves during the shooting of *SGU*'s "Earth."

Episode #149 (7.17): "Heroes, Part 1"
Written by Robert C. Cooper
Directed by Andy Mikita
Guest Starring: Saul Rubinek (Emmett Bregman), Mitchell Kosterman (Colonel Tom Rundell), Gary Jones (Technician), David Lewis (Cameron Balinsky), Tobias Slezak (Dale James), Christopher Redman (Shep Wickenhouse), Adam Baldwin (Colonel Dave Dixon), Ronny Cox (Senator Kinsey), Teryl Rothery (Dr. Janet Fraiser), Julius Chapple (Simon Wells), Christopher Pearce (Jake Bosworth), Bill Dow (Dr. Lee), Dan Shea (Sgt. Siler), Ryan W. Smith (Special Forces Guard)

A film crew arrives at S.G.C. to make a documentary, but find their welcome less than enthusiastic.

ROBERT C. COOPER: This guy is sort of intense, intelligent and a hard-nosed journalist and we're not sure how he is going to portray our heroes. It's all told from the point of view of the camera crew, who are, in fact, not allowed to film any of the ongoing current activities and just end up doing interviews. There is one scene where our journalist really grills Carter about her relationship with Colonel O'Neill. Whether she answers the question or not, just to see Carter squirm in that situation is a lot of fun.

JOSEPH MALLOZZI: *Firefly*'s Adam Baldwin guested on the show. Sitting in the room and watching the dailies, we were blown away by his performance (while Adam was almost literally blown away by the plethora of explosives director Andy Mikita set up for one unbelievable sequence). Word from the set was that Adam loved doing the show. Some fantastic action sequences on the planet's surface. Many guest stars of note in this episode: Adam Baldwin as Colonel Dave Dixon, Saul Rubinek as Bregman, and, of course, Robert Picardo as the pencil-pushing Richard Woolsey, who makes his first *Stargate* appearance in this episode. What a run for Bob who goes from pain-in-the-ass bureaucrat in "Heroes" to the lovable commander of the Atlantis expedition in *SGA*'s fifth season. And speaking of *SGA* and its cast connections to this episode, Adam Baldwin was another actor who so impressed that his name was at the top of our list for possible lead role on *Atlantis*. Sadly, we couldn't make it work, but Adam has (to no one's surprise) kept busy and successful.

ROBERT C. COOPER: I think for me I still very much look back at "Heroes" as one of my favorite episodes. I know everybody who worked on it really enjoyed that episode… for a few reasons beyond even the script and the way it turned out. The fact that it was a bit of a departure for the series. It was also how it was produced. We actually shot an episode that ended up being about 15 minutes too long and I didn't want to cut it down. We edited the show and it was basically finished shooting and I said, "We're going to hold off on putting it where it was supposed to be in the schedule." I ended up writing a whole bunch of new scenes and an entire new subplot that went in-between the scenes that existed. We took a hiatus in the summertime and made a couple of other episodes in the interim and went back and shot these new scenes and then recut the episode to turn it into two-parts.

BRAD WRIGHT: A great idea for a show, but when I looked at the cut I said to Rob, "This is really good, but it's way too long" — probably 15 minutes too long. So we turned one episode into two, which is something we would do a couple of times, because we didn't want to cut anything. So the only thing to do with it was to shoot more and so the rest was picked up catch as catch can over the course of the following month, and then it was put together into a very powerful story.

ROBERT C. COOPER: There's a sequence you probably notice, there's probably a million of these types of fun mistakes in there, but I remember coming back after hiatus and going to shoot some scenes and Richard Dean Anderson walked on the set having gotten this rather extreme haircut. I was like, "What are you doing?" He was like, "What do you mean? I felt like getting a shorter haircut." I'm like, "Yeah, but we're shooting scenes from 'Heroes' today and you're supposed to look like you did two months ago." He was, like, "Oh, well."

Episode #150 (7.18): "Heroes, Part 2"
Written by Robert C. Cooper
Directed by Andy Mikita
  Guest Starring: Saul Rubinek (Emmett Bregman), Robert Picardo (Richard Woolsey), Mitchell Kosterman (Colonel Tom Rundell), Gary Jones (Technician), Tobias Slezak (Dale James), Christopher Redman (Shep Wickenhouse), Julius Chapple (Simon Wells), Adam Baldwin (Colonel Dave Dixon), Teryl Rothery (Dr. Janet Fraiser), Jim Byrnes (Documentary Narrator), Katey Wright (Marci Wells), Christopher Pearce (Jake Bosworth)

SG-1 is called into action while a film crew is documenting the Stargate program, but the S.G.C. comes under investigation after the mission goes terribly wrong.

JOSEPH MALLOZZI: Originally, this script was intended as a fun, different, episode and, along the way, took a very serious turn. This one also resulted in a pretty heavy debate in the writer's room. Suffice it to say, not everyone was in agreement on how this episode should end. That said, I think Robert did a masterful job. It's one of the best scripts he's ever written and is a wonderful salute to the unsung heroes who serve our countries.

ANDY MIKITA: Don Davis was very vocal about the script when it had come out about just how extraordinary it really was, and how close to home it was to him and it really resonated. For those of us in Canada who didn't have to experience the things that the American military service people experienced, we couldn't make that connection the same way that Don could.

AMANDA TAPPING: I would have to say "Heroes" was my favorite episode of Season 7, just because it shows the team at their most vulnerable. It shows the team at their most dire, and I think emotionally for every single one of the actors it was a huge arc for all of us. It just shows what it means to be a part of this team and what it means to be a part of this organization, and how much you're willing to sacrifice, and what the emotional toll is when that happens. It's just a really special episode. It's a departure in a lot of ways, especially the first part with the documentary crew and seeing each of the team members out of their element in front of the cameras and having to talk about what they've kept secret for so long. But then it's got great action and great drama as well. And also what I found appealing for me was Sam Carter on the edge, in the first part being so nervous and so tentative in front of the cameras, and it's just kind of fun to play that sort of angst and that nervousness. And then, of course, in the second half it's just a highly charged emotion the whole time.

TERYL ROTHERY: I feel Robert Cooper did a wonderful job of showing the sacrifices the men and women of the military make. If you have ever attended a con that I have been at, [you know that] I am a huge supporter of the military. And to quote Don S. Davis, it's not the soldiers that start wars, it's the politicians. My character was used as a tool to show that tragedies do happen. Sad, but true.

BRAD WRIGHT: I was also pretty sure this was going to be the last season of *SG-1*, because "Lost City" was supposed to introduce *Atlantis*, which I had been working on. So when Teryl said to me, "What do you think, Brad? They're killing my character.

How should I feel about this?" And I said, "Honestly, Teryl, I think it's the last season, so it's a great way for your character to go out." Then, of course, I had to apologize to her the following season, but we did ask her to play an Asgard, so we did get to bring her back even though she wasn't playing her own character. *Later*, we brought her back as Janet Frasier in an alternate reality.

ANDY MIKITA: Her death was so moving, even at the time when we were shooting the sequence out in the field with a little handheld camcorder, not really seeing it, but hearing it. It was quite something. It was a very moving experience that day.

JOSEPH MALLOZZI: The heartbreaking conclusion to the "Heroes" two-parter sees Stargate Command suffer a huge loss. The writers' room was divided on the death of Janet Fraiser, S.G.C.'s long-time C.M.O., but, after much heated debate, it was decided that since this was going to be the final season anyway (!), it was the perfect time to tell this story – a salute to our armed forces, those who fought, and those who've lost their lives in the service of their country.

DARREN SUMNER: Teryl was never a series regular, she was always a guest star, but she was in it *so much*; like 15 episodes a season. She was the doctor who took care of everyone, the sort of mom who stuck a thermometer in your mouth and put a cold pack on your head and made sure you were gonna feel better. So to pick that character of all characters to kill off was traumatic. And it was traumatic for the actors; it made some of them rather angry that they chose to kill her off. And it was traumatic for the characters. Certainly the trauma of the show is what part two is all about with the characters processing their trauma and then the audience eventually learning what has traumatized them. And then, finally, it was traumatic for the fans to lose such a beloved character.

AMANDA TAPPING: Saul Rubinek brought something to "Heroes" that nobody expected and it was just amazing.

ANDY MIKITA: I have to give kudos to Mr. Saul Rubinek, who did an absolutely extraordinary job as Emmett Breman. He really did bring an awful lot to the table through his wealth of experience as an actor and as a director, too. He's done it all. He was the right guy for the job and I think he was one of the unsung heroes of that episode.

DAVID READ: For a lot of fans, this is the greatest show that the franchise put out. I know for Christopher Judge it's his favorite. Brad always talked about wanting SG-1 to be seen as heroes; people that you could truly aspire to be like, and this show exemplifies that. I'm the son of an emergency medical service helicopter pilot who held that job for 30 years. Every morning that he came home, I was grateful he did so, because he had friends who had died doing the same job. Some mornings he would come home in tears, dealing with the people he helped evacuate out of a bad situation or in some cases literally scraped off the pavement. We watched this episode together and it brought tears to his eyes. Seeing that, beyond my own reaction, I realized that Rob Cooper had really hit a home run, because anyone in that kind of situation can relate to what SG-1 is going through. Davis as Hammond has a magnificent speech with Carter, before we realize that Frasier has lost her life, talking about what it is they have to go through as people. Not only do they have to deal with things that are risky, that put their lives on the line; not only do they have to deal with things that are emotionally taxing, on top of all of that, they can't tell anyone about it.

And then you've got this guy with a camera in their face, working around them, who completely means well, but they're not used to handling this. On top of that, when we lose Frasier, it gets even worse. On top of *that*, you've got the NID snooping around, trying to place blame on whoever is responsible for letting Janet get killed. They have to deal with all of this without relying on anyone, but each other.

Episode #151 (7.19): "Resurrection"
Written by Michael Shanks
Directed by Amanda Tapping
   Guest Starring: Kristen Dalton (Anna), Brad Greenquist (Keffler), Peter Flemming (Agent Malcolm Barrett), Bill Dow (Dr. Lee), Martin Novotny (Interrogation Room Guard)

S.G.C. find the base of a rogue NID operation which has been attempting to mix the DNA of humans and Goa'uld, but all the agents except one have been killed.

MICHAEL SHANKS: It's an N.I.D. story now. I originally had them as a small element in the story, but it's a lot more than I had planned. Now it's about an N.I.D. facility, and they are stealing all these artifacts and are conducting a program which is experimenting with genetic research. They're taking a human host and combining it with a symbiote so that a person would have all the benefits, given the knowledge of the Goa'uld, without having to deal with the Goa'uld. It's a genetics story, where you have this nice, innocent young girl; Daniel, and an evil scientist. And it's about her struggle of treading that fine line between good and evil. It's still mythology-based and still has a backstory, but in this case it's a young girl that Daniel ends up encountering and SG-1 interacts with.

AMANDA TAPPING: Directing was such a phenomenal experience. The crew was behind me a hundred percent. The cast was behind me a hundred percent. The hardest part about directing is making sure that you're prepared. And because I didn't have a lot of prep time, because we were actually shooting our two-parter season finale while I was prepping, it was a lot of homework on the weekends. But ultimately for me, it was sitting down and coming up with an interesting shot list. It's a very talky show, and it's sort of three different episodes in one, so for me it was a matter of trying to assimilate the storylines and trying to give the show movement. And so I chose to make it kind of stylized and was really hoping that that would work, that there would be a lot of movement, so ultimately it was a phenomenal experience.

BRAD GREENQUIST (actor, "Keffler"): I thought Amanda did a wonderful job directing it. She was terrific to work with. As an actor, you always think, "Oh, if another actor is directing something, they may try to manipulate your performance a lot." But actually, what I've found is when actors are directing, they tend to leave the other actors alone out of respect and Amanda did that. Sometimes she'd give me adjustments which were wonderful, but otherwise she wouldn't tamper with it too much, which is something I personally really like.

JOSEPH MALLOZZI: Written by Michael Shanks and directed by Amanda Tapping, this one was all sorts of fun at almost every stage – pre, prep, production, and post. The episode finds the N.I.D. screwing up yet another experiment, leaving Stargate Command to pick up the pieces (and dispose of the bodies). Fans have long speculated on the full name of the nefarious organization and I've read some pretty good guesses: National Intelligence Directorate, National Intelligence Division, Next In Defense. All great. All wrong. What it actually stands for is Not a Real Department. N.I.D. Simple, no? Oh, right. Well, it *was* originally N.R.D., but we changed into N.I.D. because it sounded better.

Episode #152 (7.20): "Inauguration"
Teleplay by Joseph Mallozzi & Paul Mullie, Excerpts Written by Robert C. Cooper, Peter DeLuise, Damian Kindler, Joseph Mallozzi, Paul Mullie, Katharyn Powers, David Rich, Michael Shanks, Ron Wilkerson and Brad Wright
Directed by Peter F. Woeste
Guest Starring: William Devane (President Hayes), Robert Picardo (Agent Woolsey), James McDaniel (General Maynard), Jerry Wasserman (Chief of Staff), Ronny Cox (Vice President Kinsey), Mikka Dargel (Kinsey's Aide), Holly Dignard (President's Aide)

A new President has been elected and must be briefed on the Stargate Program. However, as usual, the new Vice President Kinsey has his own agenda.

JOSEPH MALLOZZI: When Paul and I learned the show was going to be doing another clip show, we lobbied hard for the opportunity ... oh, you've heard this one before. Never mind. Actually, as far as clip shows go, this one was a lot of fun, mainly because it afforded us the opportunity to throw in a twist at episode's end by having company man Richard Woolsey actually demonstrates surprising strength of character by turning his back on the conniving Kinsey and doing the right thing. It's the first step in the rehabilitation of a character who would eventually become one of my favorites to write for. Terrific performances all around by Robert Picardo, Ronny Cox, and William Devane, who had the gals in the production office all a-flutter after taking the time to autograph some pictures for them between scenes.

PETER DELUISE: The Oval Office set that was used in the episode was created for the second *X-Men* film, which opens with Nightcrawler breaking in. It was just an amazing replica that was left over. Every show was writing scripts with scenes set in the Oval Office so they could use that set.

Episode #153 (7.21): "Lost City, Part 1"
Written by Brad Wright & Robert C. Cooper
Directed by Martin Wood
Guest Starring: William Devane (President Hayes), Jessica Steen (Dr. Elizabeth Weir), Tony Amendola (Bra'tac), David Palffy (Anubis), Gary Jones (Technician), Ronny Cox (Vice President Kinsey), Eric Breker (Colonel Reynolds), Jason Howell (Major Harper), Jerr Weddell (Jaffa Commander), Igor Morozov (Russian Man), Mark Pawson (Secret Service Man), Dee Jay Jackson (Cab Driver), Ron Blecker (SG-3 Airman), John Prowse (Colonel Pearson), Holly Dignard (President's Aide), Dan Payne (Kull Warrior)

The S.G.C. locates a Repository of Knowledge on P3X-439 and when Anubis attacks, O'Neill downloads their knowledge into his brain again. Finally, Bra'tac warns SG-1 that Anubis plans an attack on Earth.

JOSEPH MALLOZZI: There was a point in the series when Rick was scaling down his appearances on SG-1, resulting in quite a challenge for the writing department. I remember Don coming up to the production offices one day and volunteering to have his character retire so that O'Neill could take over as the commander of S.G.C. and thus make things easier from a creative standpoint. That was typical Don. Incredibly generous. We didn't take him up on his kind offer, but later on down the line, that more or less became the scenario that was adopted. To my recollection (again, I wasn't privy to these discussions), the call to have Hammond reassigned was a mutual decision on the part of Don and the show's executive producers. He enjoyed a semi-retirement of sorts, focusing on his art, but still finding the time to do the occasional guest spot for us.

BRAD WRIGHT: "Lost City" was the introduction to *Atlantis*, so Rob and I broke that story together. That was a fun one where we had that scene in the Antarctic where Hammond gets to fly the *Prometheus* and come to our aid at the end. But that shot with the ship … I remember the first time seeing that shot finished, with the two armies clashing and flying towards each other as our ship was drilling into the ice, was, at the time, the best shot we'd ever done in *Stargate*. *Love* that shot. Mark Savala was the supervisor of that show and it was just amazing. It was a really cool, powerful way of teeing up *Atlantis*.

JOSEPH MALLOZZI: The plan (actually "plans" since it was fast becoming a habit) was to wrap up the show and then cap it with a movie. "Lost City" was going to be that movie – until we got the eighth season pick-up, at which point it was rewritten and turned into our two-parter season finale. This episode saw the introduction of Dr. Elizabeth Weir. Blonde in "Lost City" I and II, she goes brunette by the time the Atlantis expedition gets underway in "Rising" I and II (in case you failed to notice). One of my favorite moments of this season comes when all of SG-1 gathers for what they think may be the last time. With Jack facing an uncertain future, Sam unexpectedly drops by for a visit. As they sit down for a beer, there's a knock. O'Neill opens the door to discover Daniel at his front door. Not long after, Teal'c comes a-calling. As much as I enjoyed the show's high-adventure, I especially enjoyed these scenes – moments that brought the team together, demonstrating that they weren't just teammates, but good friends as well.

Episode #154 (7.22): "Lost City, Part 2"
Written by Brad Wright & Robert C. Cooper
Directed by Martin Wood
Guest Starring: William Devane (President Hayes), Jessica Steen (Dr. Elizabeth Weir), Tony Amendola (Bra'tac), James McDaniel (General Francis Maynard), Marc Worden (Ronan), David Palffy (Anubis), Michael Adamthwaite (Herak), Ingrid Kave-laars (Major Erin Gant), Gary Jones (Technician), John P. Jumper (Himself), Ronny Cox (Vice President Kinsey), Kurt Max Runte (Colonel Kirkland), Peter Kufluk (Technician), Colleen Winton (National Security Advisor), John Prowse (Colonel Pearson), Dan Payne (Kull Warrior)

Hammond is replaced by Dr. Elizabeth Weir. As Anubis' fleet arrives, SG-1 flies to Proclarush Taonas, a planet with an Ancient outpost and a ZPM. There, SG-1 learns that what they are searching for has been back on Earth the whole time. O'Neill is able to destroy Anubis' fleet using an Ancient weapon buried beneath Antarctica, but the aftermath of the battle reveals a grim situation.

JOSEPH MALLOZZI: Making a special appearance in this episode is General John P. Jumper, former Chief of Staff of the United States Air Force. I remember running into him in the production office the day before he was to shoot his episode and asking whether he had any plans to explore further acting opportunities in the near future. He chuckled and assured me his *Stargate* appearance was a one-time-only thing. "You sure?" I asked. "Next week, I better not turn on the TV and catch you on *Moesha*."

ROBERT C. COOPER: At one point I was told after the fact by one of his aides that when General Jumper took his office, when he actually went into the office, one of the first things he asked was, "When do I get to be on *Stargate*?" So I was, like, "Of course we can figure out a way to work him into the show," and the person who I was speaking to said, "No, you don't understand. He doesn't want a cameo. He wants to be in the show. He wants dialogue. We will send you all of his speeches to show you that he is capable of doing this." If you've seen "Lost City," General Jumper is a full character on the show. At the time he was the Chairman of the Joint Chiefs. What's great is that when he stepped on the Oval Office set, he looked around and said, "Yeah, it's kind of like this."

BRAD WRIGHT: I was actually considering having Atlantis be under the ice in Antarctica, but when we decided to do both shows at once, we realized they couldn't both be based here, which is why we went to the Pegasus Galaxy.

ROBERT C. COOPER: This was originally designed as a feature film that was going to serve as the springboard for *Stargate Atlantis*, essentially the connective tissue between *SG-1* and *Atlantis*. But then we got asked to do both shows at the same time, so we had to pivot and turn that into the two-parter that would launch the show. Then we were told that there's an Oval Office set from *X2* that we could use, would you like that? We wouldn't normally have been able to just snap our fingers and build an Oval Office, so we knew we'd have a whole bunch of scenes set there. Then we had to cast the president and we got William Devane to play him!

DARREN SUMNER: "Lost City" is the perfect two-parter, the perfect *Stargate* episode, the perfect adventure story, the perfect team episode and the perfect mythology builder. It not only pays off years of setup, but it adds new elements, especially with the discovery of the ancient outpost buried in Antarctica that's the setup for the spinoff, *Stargate Atlantis*. It's the biggest story that *Stargate* told up to this point, and I think that's in large part because "Lost City" was conceived to be a feature film.

MICHAEL ADAMTHWAITE (actor, Anubis' First Prime, "Herak"): He's a soldier.

He's a warrior. He's an animal. He doesn't do things thinking, "Oh, this'll get me this, this'll get me that!" He realizes that that may or may not be a byproduct of his actions. He hopes that his actions take him to a positive end for his purposes which are to follow the Goa'uld lords. I mean, I sort of looked at it and I'm, like, "This guy is all or nothing."

SEASON EIGHT SUMMARY (2004-2005)

★ Having survived the destruction of his ship in Earth orbit, Anubis' energy essence transfers into Russian cosmonaut Anatole Konstantinov with the intention of escaping through the S.G.C. Stargate.

★ The System Lords travel to Earth to ask for assistance in destroying Baal.

★ The Replicators are loosed from their time dilation prison. Fifth captures and tortures Samantha Carter.

★ A viable means of combating the Replicators is developed into a weapon.

★ The Asgard once again erase the knowledge of the Ancients from Jack O'Neill's mind in order to save his life.

★ Elizabeth Weir steps down as leader of Stargate Command. Jack O'Neill is promoted to Brigadier General and appointed leader of Stargate Command. Samantha Carter is promoted to Lieutenant Colonel.

★ Fifth fabricates a Replicator duplicate of Samantha Carter.

★ Anubis is imprisoned on KS7-535. He eventually finds a means of escaping.

★ Camulus is captured by Baal.

★ Tegalus nations Rand and Caledonia declare war.

★ Pete Shanahan proposes marriage to Samantha Carter.

★ The Goa'uld Moloc is killed.

★ Teal'c's son Rya'c marries Kar'yn.

* Members of the rogue N.I.D. set off into the galaxy aboard Osiris' abandoned al'kesh vessel.

* Replicator Carter becomes impervious to the Replicator disruptor technology. Fifth is destroyed.

* Vala Mal Doran attempts to sell the Prometheus to the Lucian Alliance.

* The Replicators enter the Milky Way Galaxy and declare war on the Goa'uld. The Goa'uld are all but defeated. The Dakara super-weapon is reconfigured to destroy the Replicators.

* Oma Desala saves Daniel Jackson from death at the hands of Replicator Carter by ascending him.

* With the Goa'uld dynasty in ruins, Baal enters hiding on Earth.

* Jacob Carter and Selmak die.

* Samantha Carter breaks her engagement to Pete Shanahan.

* Realizing Anubis cannot be killed, Oma Desala occupies him in a direct confrontation for all eternity.

* Daniel Jackson returns to Stargate Command.

EPISODE GUIDE: SEASON EIGHT

Episode #144 & 145 (8.1, 8.2): "New Order Parts 1 & 2"
Written by Joseph Mallozzi & Paul Mullie
Directed by Andy Mikita
Guest Starring: Torri Higginson (Dr. Elizabeth Weir), Patrick Currie (Fifth), Kira Clavell (Amaterasu), Steve Bacic (Camulus), Gary Jones (Technician), Vince Crestejo (Yu the Great), Kevan Ohtsji (Oshu), Michael Shanks (Voice of Thor), David DeLuise (Pete Shanahan), Barclay Hope (Colonel Lionel Pendergast), Chelah Horsdal (Com. Officer), James Bamford (Eighth / Replicator)

Three System Lords meet with the S.G.C. after their defeat of Anubis. Carter is abducted by Fifth. The Asgard's new homeworld Orilla is endangered. O'Neill, with the help of the Asgard, is awakened and helps the Asgard in their fight with the Replicators using the knowledge of the Ancients that's still downloaded in his mind. Major Carter is released by Fifth. Jack is promoted *to brigadier general and replaces Weir as commander of S.G.C..*

AMANDA TAPPING: This was an interesting episode for me to film, in more ways than one. As always, it was fun working with the Thor puppet, and I enjoyed the scenes with Teal'c and Sam. Of course, we get O'Neill back, but Sam doesn't find out until almost the end of the story. By that point it was, "Hey, good to see ya," but so much has gone on that "good to see ya" doesn't quite cover it. However, it seems the only appropriate thing to say given the situation. We don't get to interact that much in this story with Daniel, because he's back at the base helping Dr. Weir, who's now played by Torri Higginson.

MICHAEL SHANKS: As a diplomat, Dr. Weir took on a big challenge when she accepted command of the S.G.C. in "Lost City." She was learning as she went along, and that was still the case. Oddly enough, Daniel can identify with that. He was no different when he began his travels through the Stargate. In Dr. Weir, my character sees a version of his younger self, someone who is very idealistic as well as innocent about what's "out there." Daniel has to give Weir almost cynical wisdom in order to help her deal with the Goa'uld. He's like, "The aliens are bad, very bad. They will kill you if they really want to. You can't just walk into the room and expect to start a conversation with them as you might have done in the past with other ambassadors." I think it's a neat way to have Daniel come full circle, if you will. Here's a woman who possesses some of the naive characteristics that he once had. However, before Weir can make the same mistakes as he did, Daniel is able to tell her, "Sorry, but the universe doesn't quite work that way."

JOSEPH MAZZOLLI: Finally, after years of behind the scenes begging and badgering, actor Chris Judge got his wish — and Teal'c got hair. Brad had long-resisted Chris' requests, but finally broke down since it seemed this was going to be it, the show's final season. I didn't think it was such a big deal, especially considering Teal'c had undergone other notable changes over the course of the series' run. Remember that gold tinge his skin possessed, making him look like he was a professional dancer working an all-night rave? Given the fact that certain scenes from this show's first four episodes were shot out of sequence, Teal'c's hair is somewhat inconsistent — but I'm sure Chris will tell you it was a small price to pay for not having to shave his head every morning.

With Brad and Robert looking ahead to *Stargate Atlantis*, a late change was made to the script's first draft. Initially, Richard Woolsey was supposed to take over at Stargate Command, but the decision was made to have Elizabeth Weir step into the role instead. In the second episode, the part of the human-form Replicator that comes out of stasis aboard the *Daniel Jackson* was played by *SGA* stunt coordinator James "BamBam"

Bamford. The episode's final reveal, that Fifth had created a Replicator version of Carter, wasn't part of the story we broke and was included at the draft stage when Robert Cooper was struck by his usual insidiously evil inspiration.

PATRICK CURRIE: Working with Amanda Tapping was unbelievable. I mean, the relationships that you form on set are not "real world." They're real relationships, but they're not real-world relationships. And that's not a negative thing at all. It's just that when you go to work in an office, you're a certain kind of person; and then when you go home, you're a different person. With actors, we're all very much who we are. We're doing our work together. Amanda and I had a great bond, and then we were able to work again. She was my mentor for my first directing gig. I won a contest and they got Amanda to come and be my mentor and we had an amazing four days. There were moments we looked at each other and it was, like, "This feels oddly familiar…" And strange out of context. It was just an incredible artist bonding experience and I've learned a lot from her.

Episode 157 (8.3): "Lockdown"
Written by Joseph Mallozzi & Paul Mullie
Directed by William Waring
Guest Starring: Gavin Hood (Colonel Alexi Vaselov), Alisen Down (Dr. Brightman), Aaron Pearl (Major Kearney), Arvydas Lebeliunas (Anatole Konstantinov), Natalia Vasiluk (Natalia), Holly Ferguson (Lieutenant Evans), Dan Shea (Sergeant Siler)

An outbreak of disease is in fact the effect of possession by the ethereal remains of Anubis. Anubis escapes S.G.C. through the Stargate, though Carter alters his destination to a frozen, barren planet.

JOSEPH MAZZOLLI: The role of Colonel Alexi Vaselov was played by actor Gavin Hood, who went on to win an Academy Award (no, not for his appearance on *Stargate*) in the Best Foreign Language Film category for *Tsotsi*, then later directed *Rendition* and *X-Men Origins: Wolverine*. One of my favorite scenes in this episode comes when Carter visits Daniel in the infirmary. With the ailing and near-death Vaselov lying in his bed only feet away, Carter draws the privacy curtain and proceeds to deliver a dire diagnosis on the suffering Russian. Whenever we watched the scene, one of the writers would invariably pipe up (as Vaselov), "I can hear you! I'm lying right here!" Then, as Carter said to Vaselov, "Don't worry! Hang in there! You're going to pull through this!" Then, as Carter to Daniel, "Not really. He's as good as dead." Then, as Carter returned to Vaselov, "Think positive! You're going to be fine!"

Episode #158 (8.4): "Zero Hour"

Written by Robert C. Cooper
Directed by Peter F. Woeste
    *Guest Starring: David Kaufman (Mark Gilmor), Cliff Simon (Baal), Bill Dow (Dr. Bill
Lee), Eric Breker (Reynolds), Steve Bacic (Camulus), Gary Jones (Walter Harriman), Colin
Cunningham (Major Davis), Pierre Bernard (O'Brien), Dan Shea (Sergeant Siler), Michael
Ryan (John Prior), Jesai Jayhmes (Amra Delegate #1), James Ashcroft (Amra Delegate #2)*

    *When SG-1 goes missing, Baal demands a ransom. After giving S.G.C. a booby-trapped
ZPM, Camulus makes a deal to return to Baal on an assassination mission.*

PETER DELUISE: "Zero Hour" is "A Day in the Life of General O'Neill." It talks
about how hard it is to be the commander of S.G.C.. What the audience will find out
is that General Hammond has been dealing with a whole lot of crap that we never see.
When SG-1 is going off having a grand old time, there's tons of stuff that needs to be
dealt with off-camera with other SG teams that we never actually see. But in "Zero
Hour," we actually do see General O'Neill dealing with stuff that General Hammond
always had to deal with, but we never knew it.

RICHARD DEAN ANDERSON: This story shows audiences what my character
is now being exposed to in his new position. We find out that he happens to be quite
good at what he does as a general. In "Zero Hour," O'Neill is under the scrutiny of the
Secret Service, CIA, or some other U.S. government organization just before a presi-
dential visit to S.G.C. There's a crisis on the base and Jack has to deal with it. His nego-
tiating tactics are no different in that he still gets up in your face to a certain degree. He
also tries to be a little tricky. Of course, in the end O'Neill outsmarts the bad guy and
makes the right decision. So in a quiet way he knows what he's doing, even though all
outward signs would indicate otherwise. (*TV Zone*)

JOSEPH MALLOZZI: It was sad to bid farewell to General Hammond, especially
considering I considered the actor who played him, Don S. Davis, a good friend – but
having O'Neill take over command at S.G.C. opened up a host of welcome new story
possibilities. In this episode, we see the long-time wise-cracking rebel in uniform really
step up and take charge in a big way, maintaining his cool – and trademark humor – as
everything seems to be coming apart around him. S.G.C. Being overrun by alien plant
life was an idea Brad had long wanted to incorporate into a story and, finally, got the
opportunity to see it done here. Chalk Siler's wimpy flamethrower met fire and safety
regulations that prohibited us from using the real thing on set (when used in later episodes of the franchise, like "Cloverdale," the flames were enhanced by our visual effects
department).

ROBERT C. COOPER: The thing I remember most about this episode is that we brought a young man in to be O'Neill's executive assistant. The character was Mark Gilmor, and I wanted to kind of play with what it would be like to work for O'Neill. If O'Neill is going to run S.G.C., what would it be like to work for him? I remember having a lot of fun with that character; he kind of felt like a young Michael J. Fox. You know, what if Alex P. Keaton [from *Family* Ties] was working for O'Neill? Obviously, having gone for so many seasons, we had the room in the show to do this sort of thing.

DARREN SUMNER: Not the greatest episode, but it's really important for Jack's character, because we just follow him as somebody who's now in charge of the base and has to stay behind to deal with all the mundane day-to-day stuff that General Hammond used to do. It's a great Jack O'Neill episode that really kind of set the tone for his new role on the base and Rick's new role on the show. After that, we get a bunch of stories that Jack's just not really terribly involved with, because they didn't have Rick for as many days as they were accustomed to.

Episode #159 (8.5): "Icon"
Written by Damian Kindler
Directed by Peter F. Woeste
Guest Starring: Amy Sloan (Leda), Timothy Webber (Commander Gareth), Matthew Bennett (Jarrod Kane), James Kidnie (Soren), Gary Jones (Walter Harriman), Richard Side (Guide), Leanne Adachi (Rebel Aide), Preston Cook (Radio Man), Charles Zucker-mann (Rebel Soldier)

Tegalus is a world divided between two nations engaged in a cold war: The Rand Protectorate and the Caledonian Federation, both of which possess a large arsenal of ballistic missiles. When S.G.C. sends a MALP to Tegalus, religious fanatics who still worship the Goa'uld start a short-lived coup d'etat in the Rand Protectorate, triggering a war.

JOSEPH MALLOZZI: One of the last things we, as writers, do (and, often not very well) is come up with titles for our damn episodes. Up to the point where the episode gets an official title everybody can be equally unhappy about, it works its way through the notes and rewrite process with a placeholder title. On very rare occasions, usually when everyone is looking the other way, one of those placeholder titles may actually become the official title (see "Watergate" and "Enemy Mine"). If that had happened on this episode, instead of "Icon," your TV listings would have read "English Patient Daniel."

PETER DELUISE: Daniel wakes up in a strange place and he's got a blindfold on, because his face is all messed up. And there's a very pretty girl nursing him back to health. *And* he's on another planet. A lot of the story is told through flashbacks, and it has to do with the idea that the Stargate is, in fact, a religious icon on this one planet. And when it comes to life, and we come through, we set in motion a domino effect whereby religious zealots cause the planet to go on an apocalyptic course of events, where they use their weapons to ensure mutual destruction. And we completely devastated the planet, merely because we opened the Stargate and said hello. We confirmed the idea that their religious icon is in fact a working, living, real, truthful thing. And so the religious zealots sort of screwed everything up for everybody else. And Daniel feels responsible for that, so he stays and tries to make a difference, and tries to set it all right, and therefore gets hurt.

MICHAEL SHANKS: We wanted to address the continuing issue of what happens every time SG-1 walks through the Stargate, arrives on another planet and turns everyone's lives there upside down. We don't mean to, but sometimes the team's mere presence can trigger events. That's what we see in "Icon." Our simply activating this planet's Stargate creates a controversy there and Daniel feels guilty about that. He decides to go back to that world and try to calm things down. As a result, Daniel gets caught in the middle of a Cold War and stranded. While trying to work through his feelings of guilt, he comes to realize that people are going to do what they want. You can't always help those who don't want to be helped. That's a pretty significant discovery for my character. I mean, he constantly finds himself in the middle of these messes that TV always manages to find the right answers to. It was refreshing to see us take a different approach. (*TV Zone*)

JOSEPH MALLOZZI: Two things I remember about this episode (beside the fact that I thought it was one of Damian Kindler's best). During the dailies, we would argue at length about the fact that a bicycle appeared in one of the scenes on this alien world. Some argued that it was "too Earthy" and took us out of the scene, while others (Paul chiefest among them) argued that if aliens were to build a bicycle (or a hammer or a glass or a fork), it would probably look a lot like the ones we had on Earth. Amid all the back and forth on bikes, we completely failed to notice the smoke detector in one of the interior scenes (or, as I later called it, "the alien humidifier"). A lot of debate on that final scene in which bad guy Soren steps out of the room and is shot dead. In the script, he comes out of the bunker, raises his gun – and Carter (I believe) shoots him. The other regulars in the scene argued that they would act just as swiftly and be in on the kill. Then there was a debate over whether or not Soren should raise his weapon and whether our heroes would essentially execute a man who was surrendering. In the end, we solved the problem by having one of the guest stars shoot the villain in cold blood. And, of course, get admonished for it.

Episode #160 (8.6): "Avatar"
Written by Damian Kindler
Directed by Martin Wood
Guest Starring: Bill Dow (Dr. Bill Lee), Andrew Airlie (Dr. Carmichael), Gary Jones (Walter Harriman), Dan Shea (Sergeant Siler), Dan Payne (Kull Warrior)

Teal'c is trapped in a virtual reality training machine that delivers electrical shocks when he fails his objectives. Daniel enters the game in an attempt to save Teal'c from cardiac arrest and together they fight against the increasing difficulty of the game.

MARTIN WOOD: It's a V.R. game. They're using the chairs from "The Game-keeper." And now we're back in those chairs and we've modified them, and they are allowing us to program our own V.R. game to check out how certain scenarios can be played out. In this case, Teal'c gets trapped in a scenario of his own making, because he never gives up and the game is playing until he gives up – and it's not going to happen. It's a very cool episode. "Avatar" repeats and repeats and repeats and repeats, and looks a little bit like *Groundhog Day* or "Window of Opportunity." But it has a twist to it in that it completely resets brand new every time. So it's not like we just start again; Teal'c goes through and resets his game every time he gets killed, but there are subtle differences, because the game is adapting to him.

PETER DELUISE: The V.R. chairs have never left. If you look really closely at "Point of View," you'll see them in the Area 51 lockup. The chairs are on the shelf as we go through Area 51, when we end on the Quantum Mirror, and long-hair Carter and Kawalsky come through. You quite clearly see that the chairs are on the shelf there, because we recovered those chairs from the planet. We took them from Dwight Schultz, who's very upset!

JOSEPH MALLOZZI: I've never been a huge fan of virtual reality episodes as there are only so many ways you can go with them. Still, what makes an episode special isn't so much its premise, but the light it sheds on our main characters — in this case, Teal'c. So, what do we learn about Teal'c in this episode? Well, for starters, we learn he has a really big head. There were two versions of that V.R. helmet he sports in the episode. The first was built prior to any proper head measurement and, as a result, would only fit us mere mortals. The prop department had to come up with a completely different helmet to accommodate Chris', er, roomier head.

Episode #161 (8.7): "Affinity"
Written and Directed by Peter DeLuise
Guest Starring: David DeLuise (Pete Shanahan), Erica Durance (Krista James), Derek

Hamilton (Doug McNair), Gary Jones (Walter Harriman), Lucas Wolf (Jennings), Peter Bryant (Hoskins), Michael Rogers (Col. Richard Kendrick), Christopher Attadia (Eric), Benita Ha (Brooks), Rob Hayter (Sergeant), Adrian Hughes (Paul), Brad Sihvon (Joe), Kate Mitchell (Purse Woman), Judith Berlin (Mrs. Conners), Brad Kelly (Thug Friend #1), Sean Millington (Thug Friend #2)

Teal'c moves into an off-base apartment, where he becomes involved with his neighbor, Krista, who has an abusive boyfriend. Teal'c is accused of murdering the boyfriend and Daniel disappears while trying to prove Teal'c is innocent.

PETER DELUISE: The theme of "Affinity" is Teal'c's and Carter's right to have a life, Carter to have a love life, and Teal'c to have just a life, because he lives on the base, and he's a security risk. And now that he doesn't have a symbiote, you can't just mug him and take his symbiote like they did when the billionaire grabbed him, because he was terminally ill, and they grabbed the symbiote out of that other Jaffa guy. Because he no longer has a symbiote, and he has tretonin in his system, he's not a security risk in that way. So he would like to have something that resembles a normal life, even if it's not normal for a Jaffa to have that kind of life. He wants to interact with other people, and he feels that he has a right to have relationships with women, and go grocery shopping, and watch movies like everybody else. So he goes out in the world, gets an apartment and starts to experience life as an Earthling.

BRAD WRIGHT: It's a great Teal'c story. My favorite part of the story is: Here you have an alien, with capabilities that are fairly incredible and a fairly strong moral code as well. So he's living downtown. If he sees anything happening, he's going to stop it from happening! And I love that. That's actually one of the reasons I love that story so much. He's very capable of just stopping a problem. He's like Batman, living in your neighborhood! Or Spiderman – without the silly mask. And, in fact, it gets him into trouble."

ROBERT C. COOPER: In many ways O'Neill is responsible for getting him the permission to not live on the base anymore. And so now he has to deal with the Powers That Be that are putting pressure on him and saying, "Hey, wait a minute. Teal'c maybe shouldn't be living out in the city." So the story is still about SG-1 – but now that O'Neill is the general, he's in a different situation.

PETER DELUISE: And we forwarded the relationship between Carter and Pete Shanahan. Off camera, as we establish on the show, they meet each other two times a week for lunch, and it's date night, and they're continuing the relationship, just like we suggested in "Chimera," that they had more experience together than just what you saw on camera. It's what would happen if Teal'c and Carter both proactively pursued their right to have a life outside the base. You know, Teal'c has saved the planet a couple times over, and insofar as Carter's sexual tension with O'Neill, she had "Grace" where she made a decision. She says it's very easy to be in love with a man I can't have, so she resolved at that point, even though she was conked in the head, that she would, in fact, investigate her right to have a love life. And because she can't have a love life with the O'Neill character, she has to look for love and affection elsewhere. She has a right to be happy.

JOSEPH MALLOZZI: Believe it or not, actress Claudia Black (who some of you may remember from such seasons as Nine and Ten) was originally considered for the role of Krista, but was busy with the *Peacekeeper Wars* mini-series at the time. Good thing too as, in retrospect, she would have been all wrong for the role (Erica Durance nailed it), but all right for the part of Vala the following year. Around the time this episode was being written, we decided it was silly to always be pinning the blame on the N.I.D. To those who didn't know any better, you'd think they were an evil organization bent on world domination rather than one of the good guys. We squinted, looked the other way, referred to them as "rogue elements of the N.I.D." and eventually came up with a name for a whole new group of bad guys. After much consideration and working our way through a host of possibilities, we decided on one that hadn't been taken on any other show – which was a lot harder than it sounds, because *Alias* went through a slew of them. Anyway, we decided to go with "The Trust," and wrote that into the script. Only to find out during prep that *Alias* had used it in a recent episode.

Episode #162 (8.8): "Covenant"
Story by Ron Wilkerson, Teleplay by Ron Wilkerson & Robert C. Cooper
Directed by Martin Wood
Guest Starring: Charles Shaughnessy (Alec Colson), Tom O'Brien (Brian Vogler), Kendall Cross (Julia Donovan), Chris Shields (Capt. Mike Shefield), Ingrid Torrance (Staffer)

Alec Colson, the powerful leader of aerospace and biotech conglomerates, holds a press conference to announce that aliens exist, that they have already attacked Earth once, and that several governments are aware of this fact. Colson gives the governments involved 24 hours to tell the truth. When the time expires, he shows a living Asgard alien to the media.

BRAD WRIGHT: I asked the Air Force a long time ago what would happen if somebody did find out, and did want to go public. They said, "Well, we would bring them in. We would show them everything, and then say, "Now that you've seen everything, you see why we can't tell the world." Because that happens. I mean, that happens in war. Reporters see stuff they're not supposed to see, and they're asked not to reveal it, and they don't. But in this case, the twist on this story is that they *do* bring him in, and he goes, "Now I want to show the world even more."

JOSEPH MALLOZZI: Not one of my favorites. We really dig ourselves into a hole only to dig our way out and go back to square one. During the big press conference, I wanted one of the reporters to ask, "Hey, does this alien thing have anything to do with that aircraft carrier that mysteriously disappeared last year?" Stargate Command was in a tight spot, with the truth about its entire operation – and alien connections – about to go public. How were we going to get out of this one? Well, while we were brainstorming ideas, someone (won't say who) suggested Thor offer S.G.C. time travel technology that would allow them to go back in time and undo everything. Wha-huh? Does Asgard have time travel technology? Why had Thor been holding out on us? More importantly, with this convenient new technology, S.G.C. could simply go back in time whenever things didn't go their way (i.e. someone got killed, SG-1 didn't save the day, the Nuggets failed to make the playoffs). Needless to say, that idea didn't fly.

ROBERT C. COOPER: I've always loved the part of the mythology about the conspiracy; about the fact that the Stargate program was real and that it was happening now and to us. But there's a certain point at which so much was going on that you have to ask how the world would not figure it out or see what was going on. How did we keep the secret? Well, what if somebody who was rich and powerful and in the know got a clue? What would happen if he kind of figured it out and on the side was trying to make it public? What would happen then? That was just a case of an idea based on the idea that we hadn't really done a big story about all the close calls. So then it became, "Okay, what if we create an interesting character who's at the center of that story?" And so it was an industrialist and this was that story.

Episode #163 (8.9): "Sacrifices"
Written by Christopher Judge
Directed by Andy Mikita
Guest Starring: Jolene Blalock (Ishta), Tony Amendola (Bra'tac), Neil Denis (Rya'c), Mercedes de la Zerda (Kar'yn), Royston Innes (Moloc), Gary Jones (Walter Harriman), Jeff Judge (Aron), Noah Danby (Cha'ra), Steve Lawlor (Cor'ak), Dan Payne (Jaffa), Simone Bailly (Ka'lel), Dan Shea (Sergeant Siler)

Rya'c plans to marry a woman of the Hak'tyl, which makes Teal'c angry. Ishta brings the Hak'tyl to S.G.C., because they believe that their location has been compromised. Carter attempts to find a suitable planet for them. The Goa'uld Moloc captures Ishta on a planet named Goronak. Ultimately Moloc is killed by missiles from S.G.C., but his forces are taken over by Baal.

PETER DELUISE: "Sacrifices" is otherwise known as "My Big Fat Jaffa Wedding." That was the original premise of it, and it's Rya'c who is going to get married. One of the Amazon Jaffa women and he have hit it off. He's been spending time on Hak'tyl with Bra'tac, trying to get them into the rebel movement. And in doing so, he fell in love with this girl. And Ishta wants to stop Moloc. Moloc, as you know, has a crappy attitude, and he has all the women killed because he needs male warriors. And a lot of the priestesses are spiriting the young female Jaffa away, and they've formed their band of Amazon Jaffa. But they have to continuously raid male Jaffa to get the symbiotes, otherwise they'll die. And so Bra'tac and Rya'c are trying to get them into the rebel movement, but Ishta would like to assassinate Moloc, because he continues to kill female Jaffa at birth, which she thinks is reprehensible. But they're saying, for the bigger picture, for the rebel movement, if you kill Moloc, you're just going to get another guy to come in and take over all his troops. What you have to do is, you have to surgically assassinate a bunch of Goa'uld at the same time and create a gigantic power vacuum. That's the only way to really beat them. And so they're at odds with how to properly deal with their problems. She's too close to the Moloc problem to see the bigger picture.

CHRISTOPHER JUDGE: Because "Birthright" went over so well, we started talking immediately about doing a sequel to it. And so I had this idea for what I thought would be a more comical episode, involving a wedding. But as I started writing it, it didn't turn out as funny as I thought it was going to be, because there were serious issues that needed to be addressed as far as their freedom, their goal, the whole Jaffa movement – and as far as the whole Jaffa movement of freedom, and how the Hak'tyl don't necessarily see eye to eye with the bigger movement. And they're going to go about their liberation differently. So I remember giving the draft to Coop, and he said, "Well, how is it?" And I said, "I don't know. It's not funny." And he said, "You know, a lot of times these start out in our minds as what's going to be kind of a lighter episode. But when there are issues that you have to deal with because of an on-going storyline, a lot of times it doesn't end up the way you envisioned it, because you have to address certain issues." So I'm happy with the way it turned out, but it's *so* different from how I envisioned it. I envisioned it just as the power of laughter ... and it's not!

JOSEPH MALLOZZI: What actor and, in this case, writer Christopher Judge planned as a raucous episode ended up being a fairly serious and touching affair. On Screen anyway. Behind the scenes, we were busy regretting the decision to write horses into this script. I mean, it looked like a good idea on paper with the potential for plenty of humor, but we forgot to take one thing into account. Horse shit. Turns out nothing kills comedy like one of your four-legged guest stars dropping a steaming pile in the middle of your gateroom. Lesson learned!

Episode #164 (8.10): "Endgame"
Written by Joseph Mallozzi & Paul Mullie
Directed by Peter DeLuise
Guest Starring: Brandy Ledford (Zarin), Jonathan Holmes (Dr. Bricksdale), Mark Gibbon (M'Zel), Rob Lee (Major Pierce), Gary Jones (Walter Harriman), Peter Bryant (Hoskins), Lucas Wolf (Jennings), Benita Ha (Brooks), Scott Owen (Sgt. Mackenzie), Barclay Hope (Colonel Lionel Pendergast), Rob Hayter (Sergeant), Chelah Horsdal (Comm. Officer), Ryan Booth (Zarin's Jaffa)

Having recently acquired the Tok'ra symbiote poison, the Trust steal the Stargate and start using it to launch symbiote-poison attacks against Goa'uld-occupied planets, killing thousands of Jaffa in the process. Cut off from Earth, Teal'c arranges to be captured by undercover Tok'ra Zarin on P3S-114 to find out if the Tok'ra are behind the attacks. The Trust captures Carter and brings her aboard the Alkesh, where the Stargate is, but she's rescued by Daniel and Teal'c, who beam aboard and use the Stargate respectively. SG-1 and the Stargate are beamed aboard Prometheus. Measures are taken to ensure it never happens again, but the Trust escapes.

PETER DELUISE: "Endgame" is the sequel to "Affinity." "Endgame" is, the Stargate goes missing. It's gone. The game's over. It's an endgame. The storyline for this is, in "Chimera" Osiris was visiting Daniel in his sleep and monitoring his subconscious to try to figure out where the Lost City was. We did a sting operation, and we caught her, but we know that she was operating from a ship, somehow, in orbit, because she was able to beam down and mess with him while he was sleeping. In "Affinity," part of what happens is that Teal'c becomes involved in a murder, and eventually that pays off in "Endgame" when the Stargate is stolen.

JOSEPH MALLOZZI: My writing partner Paul had an idea: the Stargate is heisted from the heart of Stargate Command. *That* was the easy part. The challenge was coming up with a story that explained who took it, why and, most importantly, how? Well, we worked out a nice little Trust / N.I.D. / rogue elements of the N.I.D. angle that worked very well. A fun episode all around, although the one thing I remember about it was the reaction of some fans to the scene in which O'Neill leads the rescue team into the warehouse. He finds both Daniel and Carter bound to chairs and goes to Sam – which outraged some Daniel supporters, because they felt it showed a lack of compassion for Daniel. I'd argue he went to Carter first, because she was the first one to stir and, besides, if he went to Daniel first, would it have necessarily meant a lack of compassion on his part for Sam?

CHRISTOPHER JUDGE: That also was a great episode. I go to this planet for a meeting and see that this whole planet of free Jaffa has been slaughtered. So we think it's the Tok'ra who's doing it.

PETER DELUISE: Peter Bryant, who played Hoskins, was this weird covert agent guy and SWAT comes down on him and he does something really cool. Paul Mullie was, like, "What should he do?" And I said, "Write 'Machine Pistol.'" He said, "What's a machine pistol?" I said it was literally a machine gun in pistol form and he can just be sitting there with a coat and just suddenly start spraying bullets for days." He wrote, "Okay, Machine Pistol" and I took it from there. He was spraying bullets, he chewed up a door and went on from there. Part of that after 9/11 is that it does not take very much for someone to be super lethal. I'd also experienced the birth of my son by then, so human life was very precious. Part of me said, "This looks great, but I don't know if we should romanticize people spraying bullets at people." It seems to me that maybe we should get our entertainment from *not* spraying bullets at people?

Episode #165 (8.11): "Gemini"
Written by Peter DeLuise
Directed by William Waring
Guest Starring: Patrick Currie (Fifth), Gary Jones (Walter Harriman), Jason Emanuel (Tech Sergeant), Dan Shea (Sgt. Siler), Chris Robson (S.F.)

RepliCarter — as many referred to her — informs the S.G.C. that Fifth has made all Replicators immune to O'Neill's disruptor, and promises to help them modify the weapon. In fact, her presence is needed to develop immunity. She destroys Fifth and escapes to lead the replicators.

CHRISTOPHER JUDGE: "Gemini" was great. I was fortunate enough to see Colonel Carter and RepliCarter kind of dueling it out.

PETER DELUISE: "Gemini" was a cool episode, because Amanda Tapping as Carter goes "full Terminator" on the base. Even though Amanda is an amazing and skilled actress, her physicality in the role of Replicator Carter was masterful. She had to remain absolutely stoic and stone-faced while firing a machine gun on full auto.

AMANDA TAPPING: It's actually, for me, probably the hardest episode I've ever shot in eight years, doing the two-character arc. Playing the two of them, trying to find enough differences so that you could see the difference, but [also] making them alike enough that you could believe Fifth created her from the same consciousness as Carter, which was a challenge. I was flipping back and forth – on any given day [I would have to] jump in and out of Replicator Carter four or five times, and Carter four or five times. There are subtle nuances [between them] and that was important to me, because though she has Sam's memories and supposedly Sam's consciousness, she doesn't have Sam's heart. And she comes to Earth with an agenda.

JOSEPH MAZZOLLI: Amanda gives a doubly delicious performance as both Sam Carter and her evil twin in this episode that sees the return of Replicator Carter. It was a very satisfying episode, especially for Amanda who imbued her dual performance with subtle nuances that really set the two characters apart. It was a grueling shoot but, as always, she was a total professional, never once complaining. It's episodes like this one that remind me how terrific Amanda was to work with.

Episode #166 (8.12): "Prometheus Unbound"
Written by Damian Kindler
Directed by Andy Mikita
Guest Starring: Claudia Black (Vala), Don S. Davis (General George Hammond), Ellie Harvie (Dr. Lindsey Novak), Gary Jones (Walter Harriman), Eric Breker (Colonel Reynolds), Morris Chapdelaine (Tenat), Christopher Pierce (Bosworth), Geoff Redknap (Alien #2), Dan Payne (Kull Warrior)

The crew of the Prometheus are incapacitated and removed, except Daniel, when it is hijacked by Vala, a pirate. Vala wishes to trade the ship for Naqahdah, but Daniel succeeds in retaking control of the vessel and, with the help of the crew in an Alkesh, fends off a Goa'uld attack that leaves Prometheus too badly damaged to finish the mission. Vala ultimately escapes in the end.

CHRISTOPHER JUDGE: An episode I wasn't in, "Prometheus Unbound" is just fantastic. It's hilarious. It's one of the more fun – that and "Zero Hour" are probably the two most fun episodes of the year. And Claudia Black is in that one, and her and Shanks just have such a great rapport together.

DAMIAN KINDLER: The *Prometheus* had been part of the *Stargate* universe for three years. Prior to this, we'd done four stories involving the ship. However, Rob Cooper said, "We have the sets, which are spectacular, and loads of VFX shots revolving around the ship. It'd be great to do another *Prometheus* episode." Rob told me the type of episode he was looking for, and I wrote a draft of the script. It was all done very quickly, probably within two weeks. Rob liked the shape the story took and thought the pace was great. At that point, I had to start work on a two-parter ["Reckoning"]. Because of time considerations, Rob took my script and did a polish on it, which bumped up the comedic elements. He did a wonderful job and we were both very pleased with the way it turned out. (*TV Zone*)

JOSEPH MALLOZZI: We finally got the opportunity to cast Claudia Black, and it was in a role that she seemed born to play. Robert Cooper took Damian's solid first draft and injected it with a humorous spin that essentially formed the basis of the Vala character we would come to know and love. To be honest, I wasn't convinced at the script stage as I thought the humor might have been too broad, but all doubt dissolved the moment those dailies started coming in. Wow! As far as eighth season episodes went, this one was probably my favorite for its comic elements and the terrific on-screen chemistry between Claudia and Michael.

Episode #167 (8.13): "It's Good to Be King"
Story by Michael Greenburg & Peter DeLuise & Joseph Mallozzi & Paul Mullie, Teleplay by Joseph Mallozzi & Paul Mullie
Directed by William Gereghty
Guest Starring: Wayne Brady (Trelak), Tom McBeath (Harry Maybourne), Nancy Sorel (Garan), Melanie Blackwell (Servant), Robert Bruce (Local #1), Zak Church (Local #2)

SG-1 finds that Harry Maybourne has become king on the planet where he took forced retirement. The planet is now under a Goa'uld threat, but Maybourne has found writings by a time-traveling Ancient that prophesied SG-1 will defeat the Goa'uld Ares. Ares sends Jaffa to the planet and arrives in his mothership, but his forces are defeated by Daniel and Teal'c and his mothership is destroyed by O'Neill with the time traveling Puddle Jumpers weapons. Afterwards, Maybourne decides to remain on the planet with his people and wives.

PETER DELUISE: This was loosely based on Apocalypse Now where Harry Maybourne is ruler of these people. Everyone liked the Harry character and thought Tom McBeath was amazing as him. It's also when Wayne Brady first came in as Trelak, and he is super fucking talented and incredibly funny, so that was kind of cool. We were using this medieval set, which was cool, too — and it got reused many times over on Stargate Atlantis.

JOSEPH MALLOZZI: I always enjoyed writing the funny episodes and this one was no different. It gave us the opportunity to bring back Harry Maybourne, one of my favorite recurring characters. This episode ran long and, as a result, I had to cut a scene in which Maybourne displays Solomon-like wisdom in a dispute over a duck. When the complainants cannot agree on ownership, Maybourne demands a knife be brought forth so he can cut the duck in half and offer an equal share to each. The men standing before him are shocked at the suggestion and thus, King Maybourne makes his ruling, declaring that neither man is deserving. As the two men head off, Maybourne turns and hands off the duck to one of his assistants with a, "Cook it up. I'll have it for lunch."

Episode #168 (8.14): "Full Alert"
Written by Joseph Mallozzi & Paul Mullie
Directed by Andy Mikita
Guest Starring: Francoise Robertson (Captain Daria Varonakova), Garry Chalk (Colonel Chekov), Gary Jones (Walter Harriman), Ronny Cox (Robert Kinsey), Lucas Wolf (Jennings), Barclay Hope (Colonel Lionel Pendergast), Chelah Horsdal (Comm. Officer), Mike Dopud (Colonel Chernovshev), Joey Aresco (Mr. Parker), Hiro Kanagawa (Mr. Wayne), Allan Gray (Mr. Kent), Dmitry Chepovetsky (Russian Soldier)

Russia and the United States reach DEFCON 1 because the Goa'uld may have compromised both governments via the Trust, which has been entirely assimilated. War is narrowly avoided when O'Neill convinces the Russian President of the truth and the Trust ship is destroyed by Prometheus, but the fate of Robert Kinsey is left unknown as he may or may not have been on the ship when it was destroyed.

MICHAEL GREENBURG: After finishing "It's Good to Be King," we began filming an episode called "Full Alert." It was directed by Andy Mikita and written by Joseph Mallozzi and Paul Mullie. This story is sort of a sci-fi mystery about who is trying to get two nations on Earth worked up to such a fevered pitch that they might blow each other up and the planet as well. Obviously, we've made plenty of enemies over the years, and one of them is masterminding this global plot.

JOSEPH MALLOZZI: There's a point in the episode where Kinsey meets up with three suspicious characters who use the pseudonyms Mr. Kent, Mr. Wayne, and Mr. Parker (the references should be pretty obvious). The scene was shot in an old mansion in Vancouver, presumably the estate of a former game hunter, because one of the rooms was bedecked with animal trophies. This apparently didn't sit well with some of the crew, but especially executive producer Michael Greenburg, an animal lover, who didn't like being surrounded by the stuffed heads.

Episode #169 (8.15): "Citizen Joe"
Story by Robert C. Cooper, Teleplay by Damian Kindler
Directed by Andy Mikita
Guest Starring: Dan Castellaneta (Joe Spencer), Deborah Theaker (Charlene Spencer), Eric Keenleyside (Fred), Louis Chirillo (Bert Simmons), Chad Krowchuk (Gordie Lowe), Alex Ferris (Andy Spencer), Mark Hansen (Older Andy Spencer), Andy Thompson (Calvin), Beatrice Zeilinger (Cindy)

An Indiana barber who carries the ATA Gene has his life ruined when, through an Ancient device, he begins to have visions of SG-1's missions. His life is given back to him when

O'Neill informs his nearly-divorced wife of what had been going on.

JOSEPH MALLOZZI: Richard Dean Anderson's love for *The Simpsons* resulted in him being invited to a table reading of the show – which resulted in him befriending Dan Castellaneta, the voice of Homer Simpson on the show – which in turn result- ed in Dan doing a brilliant guest spot for us in this episode – which resulted in *Star- gate* getting a big shout-out in a later episode of *The Simpsons* guest-starring Richard Dean Anderson. I remember meeting Dan for the first time. I was in the lunch line, standing behind a casually-attired fellow in a baseball cap who seemed distracted by something, when it came his turn to order. "You're up!" I offered helpfully, assuming he was a new crew member. "Joe," said Robert Cooper, standing to my other side, "Have you met Dan?" Oh.

ROBERT C. COOPER: This is on my list of favorite shows. I've never been a big fan of clip shows, but they're budget savers. Any screen time you can take out of pro- ductions means less days shooting, and days of shooting are the most expensive things. So they were a necessary evil, but in this case we even talked about possibly doing the episode without the clips, but the story was so, in a way, brilliantly conceived, in my opinion, you *had* to show the clips. You wanted people to know the things that this character was seeing. And the thing is made to perfection by Dan Castellano.

Rick was a huge fan of *The Simpsons*, and at one point at a charity auction he won the privilege of going to a cast read-through of *The Simpsons*. While there, he kind of befriended Dan, who, it turns out, was a fan of *Stargate*. I believe Dan wrote or partic- ipated in the writing of an episode where the characters go to a sci-fi convention and Richard Dean Anderson is in it as the star of *Stargate*. So they got to be quite good friends, and Dan never really got that many opportunities to play himself on screen, so it became a reciprocal thing where he said, "Hey, I'd love to be on *Stargate*, if that can happen." So it became the opportunity to have him on the show, and I just love the idea of a guy unwittingly being exposed to alien technology.

Episode #170 (8.16): "Reckoning, Part 1"
Written by Damian Kindler
Directed by Peter DeLuise
Guest Starring: Tony Amendola (Bra'tac), Carmen Argenziano (Jacob Carter), Cliff Simon (Baal), Gary Jones (Technician), Samantha Banton (Baal's Lieutenant), Mel Har- ris (Oma Desala), Isaac Hayes (Tolok), Jeff Judge (Aron), Dean Aylesworth (Old Anubis), Rik Kiviaho (New Anubis), Vince Crestejo (Yu the Great), Kevan Ohtsji (Yu's First Prime), Mi- chael Shanks (Voice of Thor)

Teal'c is preparing the Jaffa rebellion to capture the Holy planet Dakara, where the first larval Goa'uld implantation took place. Daniel is abducted by RepliCarter so she can discover the location of the Dakara Superweapon in his subconscious. Baal also moves his forces to Dakara by the order of Anubis.

CHRISTOPHER JUDGE: It's coming close to the climax of the battle for freedom, and this deals with two reckonings. It deals with getting together all the Jaffa, and then trying to take the holy city of Dakara. It's pretty much the climax of this eight-year arc of their quest for freedom. And so Tony [Amendola] is back, and then Isaac [Hayes] is in it, and my brother's in it.

JOSEPH MALLOZZI: The late Isaac Hayes makes a guest appearance as the Jaffa Tolok. He was apparently a huge fan of the show and an utter delight on set – kind and surprisingly soft-spoken.

CHRISTOPHER JUDGE: It was such an honor to work with Isaac Hayes. He's one of the priests that has become a rebel. No one on the planet says "Goa'uld" like Isaac Hayes! But yeah, just a wonderful man.

CLIFF SIMON: I personally tried to bring a little humanity to Baal, so he's not this arbitrary alien guy who's just bad the whole time. He's got to be a three-dimensional character, so that's what I tried to bring in "Reckoning," and it seems to have come across.

AMANDA TAPPING: Actually, when [Carter's Replicator double] comes back, I don't think the two of them are in any scenes together, so that's good! And the differences between them is even more pronounced because Replicator Carter has gone off and followed her own path.

JOSEPH MALLOZZI: This big two-parter was the climax of seven-plus terrific seasons of *SG-1*. We've got SG-1, the Tok'ra, the Jaffa, the Goa'uld, Anubis and the Replicators all involved in the galactic throwdown to end all galactic throwdowns. Although there were three more episodes to go before the season wrapped, "Reckoning" I and II brought things to a head, addressed the major arcs and issues, and tied up most of the loose ends. Of course, there were a few dangling plot threads – which were taken care of in, appropriately enough, an episode titled "Threads."

Episode #171 (8.17): "Reckoning, Part 2"
Teleplay by Damian Kindler, Excerpts Written by Robert C. Cooper
Directed by Peter DeLuise

Guest Starring: Carmen Argenziano (Jacob Carter), Tony Amendola (Bra'tac), Cliff Simon (Baal), Eric Breker (Colonel Reynolds), Gary Jones (Walter Harriman), Isaac Hayes (Tolok), Jeff Judge (Aron), Dan Shea (Siler), Emy Aneke (Baal's Jaffa)

Struggling with RepliCarter, Daniel halts the Replicators long enough for Samantha Carter, Jacob Carter, and Baal to use a combination of the device that dials every Stargate in the galaxy and the Dakara Superweapon to destroy all Replicators. RepliCarter kills Daniel Jackson.

JOSEPH MALLOZZI: Baal, Anubis, the Tok'ra, the Jaffa, the Replicators, uneasy alliances, surprises, death and destruction – this episode has it all, concluding a multitude of outstanding stories in grand style. For all the inter-galactic splendor and ship to ship battles, my favorite moments come when O'Neill and co. blow the door to free Siler and others trapped inside. Seconds after the explosion, Siler pokes his head up out from behind the table he is hiding behind – and discovers an enormous piece of shrapnel embedded in the tabletop only inches from his head. The part of Siler was played by longtime *SG-1* stunt coordinator Dan Shea, who played the occasional background role to an actual speaking part on the show. To this day, he's still doing the con circuit, traveling the world to meet his many, many fans.

PETER DELUISE: Isaac Hayes had that silky smooth voice the whole time; that was kind of neat to work with. It was a thrill to be able to work with him.

Episode #172 (8.18): "Threads"
Teleplay by Robert C. Cooper, Excerpts Written by Damian Kindler
Directed by Andy Mikita
Guest Starring: Carmen Argenziano (Jacob Carter), Tony Amendola (Bra'tac), David DeLuise (Pete Shanahan), Clare Carey (Kerry Johnson), Gary Jones (Walter Harriman), Cliff Simon (Baal), Isaac Hayes (Tolok), Mel Harris (Oma Desala), George Dzundza (Jim), Rik Kiviaho (Anubis)

Daniel Jackson must choose death or powerless Ascension whilst Anubis plans to end all life in the galaxy using the Dakara Superweapon – until Oma Desala stops him. Jacob Carter and Selmak are in trouble. Daniel is returned to human form on Earth.

ROBERT C. COOPER: Obviously a huge episode for Sam/Jack shippers, but it also was pretty huge for the whole *SG* mythology. I felt so lucky having this supporting cast — Carmen, Tony, David, Cliff, Mel Harris and George Dzundza — all in one episode! When the episode came in long, I was sick to my stomach thinking about what I would have to cut to get it down to run time. I asked the studio and network if we could air a 90-minute version. Really 68 minutes with commercial time. They said yes, but then getting the studio to release the extended version on DVD and in syndication proved to be more difficult. I hope people are able to see it. In particular, Teal'c's story line in the cut down version is nowhere near as impactful as it is in the longer one.

DARREN SUMNER: We've got to talk about "Reckoning" and "Threads" to-gether. "Threads" ' is really the denouement for a three-episode arc, and together with the two-part "Reckoning" it tells a really important set of stories, because it's *Stargate SG-1* as it's drawing to a close. "Reckoning" is when the Goa'uld System Lords are dealt with, the Replicators are dealt with, one of the big bads of season eight, replica-tor Carter (or RepliCarter, as fans like to call her) is dealt with, and so it all comes to a head and ends with this beautiful shot of the team. Finally relaxing, finally going fishing together at Jack's cabin at the end of "Threads."

JOSEPH MALLOZZI: And almost every story thread that wasn't wrapped up in the previous episode, gets wrapped up here: Anubis, Oma Desala, the Jaffa quest for freedom, Jacob/Selmak, stalker Pete, and Jack and Sam. Well, sort of in the case of the latter. We know both Jack and Sam end their standing relationships for, presumably, each other – but it's not all that overt which, on the one hand, leaves the door open for future will they/won't they, but on the other hand, is somewhat disappointing given that if there was ever an episode in which to get them together, this would have been it. That aside, it was a terrific episode and Robert Cooper packed so much into the script that the usual 42-minute running time wasn't able to contain it. As a result, a special 90-minute version was released (and later mistakenly omitted when the Season 8 DVD was released, much to the displeasure of most fans).

DARREN SUMNER: In this episode, Jacob Carter got to meet Carter's romantic partner, Pete, played by David DeLuise, triggering her father's reaction to him. It deals with the ongoing storyline of Sam's personal life, her romance and her engagement to Peter Shanahan, and when her dad dies, "Threads" kills off another beloved recurring character in Jacob Carter.

CARMEN ARGENZIANO (actor, "Jacob Carter"): I think Jacob always felt that his daughter could marry someone extremely special. As a character I wasn't terribly impressed — he seemed funny, charming, and goofy. But also, I'm sure as the character I was somewhat preoccupied with my imminent demise and having to break that news to my daughter. I was somewhat conflicted and that scene in the cafeteria where I told her, I just want her to be happy — that was what I really wanted. And I'm learning as a parent right now that we can't dictate to our children as far as personal stuff and attractions and directions they're going. We have so much control over them, and I think Jacob was in the process of letting go of all that. I think Jacob was in the process of letting go of a lot of human values as Selmak. And they, I'm sure, symbiotically got to know each other, and Jacob got to see the universe not from a military American standpoint, but from a more universal, more humane kind of awareness that Selmak employed upon him. I think Jacob was evolving through that, too.

DARREN SUMNER: When her dad dies, Carter is confronted about what she wants out of life and whether or not she's really happy moving on from Jack O'Neill, so "Threads'' is also a very important shipper episode. Sam decides to break off her engagement, Pete's gone and she shows up at Jack's house to kind of put it all out there and tell him how she feels. And just as she's about to, Jack's new girlfriend steps out of the house. So "Reckoning" and "Threads" does everything from the massive scale of the Replicators inside Stargate Command and the fight with the System Lords, the System Lords being wiped out by the Replicators all the way down to these intimate little character scenes of Jacob's death and Jack comforting Sam when he's dying. "Threads" does a little bit of everything.

And we haven't even touched on the Ancients yet, about the whole subplot with Daniel and Oma Desala in the "astral diner," where Daniel finally gets some intel on what happened when he was ascended, why he was sent back, why his memory was wiped, but only partially; why the others haven't stepped in to do anything about Anubis, even though Anubis himself is apparently partially ascended. So "Threads" is full of payoff for those stories that have been going for years at this point.

Episode #173 (8.19): "Moebius, Part 1"

Story by Joseph Mallozzi, Paul Mullie, Brad Wright & Robert C. Cooper, Teleplay by Joseph Mallozzi & Paul Mullie

Directed by Peter DeLuise

Guest Starring: David Hewlett (Dr. Rodney McKay), Don S. Davis (General George Hammond), Robert Wisden (Major Samuels), Colin Cunningham (Major Paul Davis), David Lewis (Cameron Balinsky), James Purcell (Dr. Hirschfield), Alessandro Juliani (Katep), Georgia Craig (Sabrina Gosling), Jay Williams (Ra), Benjamin Easterday (Ra's Jaffa Commander), Neil Schell (Mr. Crandall), Maurico Vasquez (Student)

SG-1 uses an Ancient Puddle Jumper to time-travel back to ancient Egypt to recover a ZPM. However, they cause Ra to take the Stargate at Giza with him when he leaves Earth, altering the future so S.G.C. doesn't exist.

PETER DELUISE: We played things out in the Richmond Sand Dunes, where they make cement, so there's always this deposit of enormous amounts of sand. If you ever see sand on the show, it's all shot in that one place. It was a few sand dunes, and if you looked even an inch to the right, there'd be a giant building there.

JOSEPH MALLOZZI: Whatever happened to all that cool tech SG-1 amassed over the course of their many adventures: the sarcophagus, the healing device, that time–traveling Puddle Jumper from "It's Good To Be King?" Well, glad you asked, because the Jumper makes a return appearance in this episode – before heading back for continued R&D (or, in our timeline, just staying right where it is). Sabrina Gosling, Catherine Langford's niece, is named after Sharon Gosling – author, editor, and freelance writer – who interviewed the cast and crew on numerous occasions over the course of SG-1's lengthy run. Alt. Carter's "Now, just because my reproductive organs are on the inside instead of the outside doesn't ..." is a callback to the SG-1 opener, "Children of the Gods," and what has long been considered one of the most cringe-worthy lines in the history of the franchise.

Episode #174 (8.20): "Moebius, Part 2"
Story by Joseph Mallozzi, Paul Mullie, Brad Wright & Robert C. Cooper, Teleplay by Robert C. Cooper
Directed by Peter DeLuise
Guest Starring: David Hewlett (Dr. Rodney McKay), Don S. Davis (General George Hammond), Peter Williams (Apophis), Alessandro Juliani (Katep), Jay Acovone (Charles Kawalsky), Benjamin Easterday (Ra's Jaffa Commander), Sina Najafi (Egyptian Boy), Christopher Pierce (Bosworth), Rob Fournier (Airman Mansfield)

An alternate-reality SG-1 must go back in time and fix the past to save the future. In the process, the team must re-recruit Teal'c and find the real Daniel Jackson, who is still in ancient Egypt. Alternate-timeline O'Neill and Carter express their love.

JOSEPH MALLOZZI: As for the SG-1 finale – to be honest, "Reckoning" I and II, "Threads" and "Moebius" I and II would make excellent series finales. At the time the scripts were being written (and, later, the episodes produced), we had no idea whether SG-1 would be back or not, but we were satisfied with what would be a terrific series ender. The last half of SG-1 Season Eight offers some huge surprises, adventure, and great character development. The end of an era! Although the series continued, it did so in a radically different fashion. As far as finales go, this one ranks as one of my very favorites. Given that it was a time travel story, there were plenty of arguments in the writers' room on exactly what could and couldn't work within the two-parter's SF constraints, but, in the end, we managed to get it all worked out and my writing partner, Paul, avoided a nervous breakdown.

PETER WILLIAMS: You know how [my reprisals of Apophis] would work? You'd get a rumor. The casting director would call and request details as to the actor's availability. Well, anyone who knows actors, we're always available. Always! Just take it as read, we're *always* available. So you'd get that rumor and the minute you hear that, you *know* something's up. There's a script coming down and I wasn't so much surprised as I was elated.

PETER DELUISE: We were inspired and wondered what if we went back in time and dealt with that and *then*, because it was a time altered universe, we had the big kiss where we *finally* see Carter and O'Neill really go for it in terms of smooching, which was cool. In the alternate timeline, Richard Dean Anderson is a boat owner and takes people on excursions. So the nerdier versions of Carter and Jackson approach him to get some information, but because of regulations they can't be on the boat without life preservers. And because it was a real sailboat, I knew there would be life preservers, so I grabbed them and I said, "Put these on!" They said, "Why? We're only in the slip. It'll look foolish." And I said, "Isn't that hilarious? That Jack made you put life preservers on when you're in the slip?" And then Amanda, who's got a wonderful penchant for comedy, took her life preserver off so roughly that it messed up her hair and she was annoyed at him for it. I always remembered that amongst all the other silly, wonderful things that we did. Just a favorite cheeky moment there.

SEASON NINE SUMMARY (2005–2006)

 * *General Jack O'Neill hand picks Hank Landry to succeed him as leader of Stargate Command. O'Neill relocates to Washington D.C. to lead the newly-formed division of Homeworld Security.*

 * *Vala Mal Doran begins joining SG-1 on missions.*

 * *The Ori become aware of humans living under the protection of the ascended Ancients in the Milky Way Galaxy. Though they cannot confront the Ancients themselves, they begin sending missionaries to persuade the masses.*

 * *The Ori destroy the planet Kallana in an attempt to install a Supergate in the Milky Way Galaxy, but they are thwarted by Vala Mal Doran. Vala herself is accidentally transported back to the Ori Galaxy.*

 * *The Ori cause Vala Mal Doran to conceive a child without a husband. Fearing persecution by Ori followers, she marries Tomin.*

 * *Baal acquires numerous corporations on Earth and funnels their resources into creating clones of himself.*

 * *SG-1 makes contact with the Sodan.*

★ *Anubis' clone son Khalek provides a vital clue for the creation of a Prior inhibitor.*

★ *A Prior plague is unleashed on Earth, killing thousands. The Ancient Orlin retakes human form to create a defense.*

★ *The Prior inhibitor is field-tested and proved largely successful at stopping the powers of the Ori Priors.*

★ *The Ori provide Tegalus with a powerful satellite weapon, but only give it to the Rand Protectorate.*

★ *The Earth ship Prometheus is destroyed in battle over Tegalus.*

★ *A brief truce between Rand and the Caledonian Federation ultimately falls on deaf ears and the two nations destroy each other.*

★ *The Odyssey, a more advanced Earth vessel and the first in a new line of deep space carriers, is launched.*

★ *The Priors release flesh-eating insects on certain worlds which refuse to accept Origin.*

★ *Merlin's anti-Ori research is discovered by SG-1, who begin a search for the weapon he created to defeat them.*

★ *The Sodan civilization is destroyed.*

★ *The Korolev, a new deep-space carrier operated by the Russian military, is launched.*

★ *The Ori construct a Supergate in a hidden location in the Milky Way. Priors pilot ships full of armies prepared to unleash Origin by force. Four Ori warships swiftly defeat the human, Jaffa, Tok'ra, Asgard and Lucian Alliance forces.*

★ *The Korolev is destroyed in battle with the Ori. The ship's new commander, Colonel Chekov, is killed.*

EPISODE GUIDE: SEASON NINE

Episode #175 (9.1): "Avalon, Part 1"
Written by Robert C. Cooper, Excerpts by Robert C. Cooper & Brad Wright

Directed by Andy Mikita

Guest Starring: Claudia Black (Vala), Obi Ndefo (Rak'nor), Gary Jones (Walter Harriman), Bill Dow (Dr. Lee), Matthew Walker (Merlin), Richard Dean Anderson (General Jack O'Neill), Martin Christopher (Lt. Marks), Tyler McClendon (Lt. Banks), Mar Andersons (Air Force Official), Claude Knowlton (Doctor), Wendy Russell (Nurse), Donna White (Crying Mother), Penelope Corrin (Science Candidate #1), Alistair Abell (Science Candidate #2), Robert Clarke (Science Candidate #3), Jason Benson (Military Candidate #1), Sean Arnfinson (Military Candidate #2), Scott Owen (Technician), Michael Jonsson (F-302 Pilot)

Lt. Colonel Cameron Mitchell is recruited by the S.G.C. as leader of SG-1, but finds the original SG-1 has disbanded. Trying to find out how to bring them back together, Vala Mal Doran arrives with an artifact which could reveal an ancient treasure, and Mitchell finds this is his only opportunity to reunite the team.

ROBERT C. COOPER: "Avalon" one and two and "Origin" are the introduction of the Ori mythology; the new sort of take on post-Goa'uld villains and moving on to the Ori as the bad guys of the series. This was obviously also the introduction of Cameron Mitchell and sort of bringing Vala into the storyline on a full-time basis. Their slipping in so easily just shows how talented we all are, although it's hard to convey facetious sarcasm in print, so that might just come off as being arrogant. The truth is, Ben Browder and Claudia Wells had worked together for quite some time on *Farscape* and had a chemistry between them. On top of that, in the week between Ben being signed and starting shooting, he watched all of the previous episodes — a hundred and seventy hours or something — *in a week*. I don't know too many actors that would've done that. And he hadn't just watched them, he *knew* them, so he had a base of reference on day one that was pretty astonishing.

JOSEPH MALLOZZI: One of the things that stood out for me about Ben Browder's first episode was Ben behind the scenes. While he was great onscreen, he was equally great off-screen as well – passing on R&R in his trailer in favor of staying on set to deliver his off-camera lines. He was happy to be on the show and eager to help out in any way he could. The guy was committed.

My only regret with regard to the Cameron Mitchell character was the way he was introduced – specifically, the fact that he was brought in to lead SG-1. Only problem was SG-1 already had a leader in Samantha Carter. Well, theoretically she was except that, by the time Season 9 got underway, SG-1 was no more. With the defeat of the Goa'uld, the team members had gone their separate ways. And so, it fell on Mitchell to get the band back together. My writing partner Paul flagged the potential problem in the writers' room, arguing that giving someone else command of the team (or merely suggesting as much) was disrespectful to the character of Carter. A heated debate ensued and, in the end, a compromise was reached. Carter and Mitchell would share command of the team. Which, in retrospect, did little to quell some of the angry fan response.

Episode #176 (9.2): "Avalon, Part 2"
Written by Robert C. Cooper
Directed by Andy Mikita
Guest Starring: Claudia Black (Vala), Obi Ndefo (Rak'nor), Bill Dow (Dr. Lee), April Amber Telek (Sallis), Mark Houghton, Steven Park (Harrid), Lexa Doig (Dr. Carolyn Lam), Paul Moniz De Sá (Fannis), Martin Christopher (Lt. Kevin Marks), Greg Anderson (Administrator), Brahm Taylor (Villager), Silya Wiggens (Therapist)

After passing all of the tests found in Avalon, the makeshift SG-1 discovers the treasure, along with an Ancient long-range communication device. Hoping to find actual Ancients, Daniel and Vala are given control of the bodies of two people in a distant galaxy, although… it's not what they expected.

JOSEPH MALLOZZI: Claudia Black demonstrated her talent for comedy in previous episodes, but this one showcases her considerable dramatic range as well. I remember watching this episode thinking, "Damn. She *would* make a great series regular!" And the onscreen chemistry between her and Michael was electric. But there was a bit of controversy surrounding this episode's fiery death scene. It was pretty damn horrific – the original edit even more so – and we went back and forth on how much we wanted to show. In the end, I'm surprised that the network allowed us to show as much as we did. It was by far the most unsettling scene in my 11+ years on *Stargate*.

Episode #177 (9.3): "Origin"
Written by Robert C. Cooper
Directed by Brad Turner
Guest Starring: Claudia Black (Vala), Larry Cedar (Prior), Gary Jones (Sergeant Harriman), Bill Dow (Dr. Lee), Mark Houghton, April Amber Telek (Sallis), Steven Park (Harrid), Richard Dean Anderson (General Jack O'Neill), Julian Sands (Doci), Lexa Doig (Dr. Lam), Louis Gossett Jr. (Gerak), Paul Moniz De Sá (Fannis), Greg Anderson (Administrator), Gardiner Millar (Yat'Yir), Penelope Corrin (Dr. Lindsay)

When Daniel and Vala follow a mysterious man to find answers to their questions, they discover the Ori. The Ori, like the Ancients, are ascended beings, but pure evil entities that feel the need to be worshiped and have no rules to restrict themselves. Unknowingly, through Daniel and Vala the Ori know of life in another galaxy created by their long forgotten enemies, so they begin to send their missionaries, Priors, through the Stargate. The first planet visited by a Prior in the Milky Way is P3X-421 and the S.G.C. pays him a visit.

ROBERT C. COOPER: One of the lessons I learned working on this show was that you have to give your seemingly all powerful bad guys some limitations or else why don't they just win right away? In the case of the Ori, evil ascended ancients, we had already built in the fact that even these beings who lived on a higher plane of existence weren't omniscient. They couldn't be everywhere all at once. They still needed the Stargate to get around the galaxy. Another pro tip: Always good to keep the title of the series relevant.

JOSEPH MALLOZZI: With Jack O'Neill transferred to Washington, the S.G.C. found itself under the command of General Hank Landry, played by veteran actor Beau Bridges. Beau reminded me a lot of Robert Picardo (Richard Woolsey) – both were very successful, incredibly experienced, and always made it a point to come by our offices to run prospective dialogue changes by us rather than simply surprising us in the dailies. Like Bob, Beau would always make the time to come up and see us to request even the tiniest of changes. Both of them were class acts and I have nothing but terrific memories of working with them.

DARREN SUMNER: "Avalon" and "Origin" have to set up what is basically a new show, because the Replicators and System Lords have been dealt with, we have new new main cast members in Ben Browder and Beau Bridges; Amanda Tapping is on maternity leave for the first five episodes, so we have a long guest arc for Claudia Black as Vala, and we have to set up the Ori, the new antagonists. Those episodes have *a lot* of heavy lifting to do. And they're done really well.

Episode #178 (9.4): "The Ties That Bind"
Written by Joseph Mallozzi & Paul Mullie
Directed by William Waring
Guest Starring: Claudia Black (Vala), Bruce Gray (Senator Fisher), Gary Jones (Sergeant Harriman), Bill Dow (Dr. Lee), Wallace Shawn (Arlos), Lexa Doig (Dr. Lam), Michael P. Northey (Inago), Malcolm Scott (Caius), Morris Chapdelaine (Tenat), Eileen Pedde (Major Gibson), Darren Moore (Vosh), Geoff Redknap (Jup)

Hoping to disconnect the kor mak bracelets keeping them linked ("Avalon"), Daniel, Teal'c, Mitchell, and Vala try to pry the information out of the person she stole them from in the first place. When he wants something in return, they discover that his request isn't so easy to complete, and they must go on a series of quests to please his demands.

JOSEPH MALLOZZI: This was one of my favorite scripts of my 11+ year *Stargate* run. I loved the opportunity to write an all-out comic episode – and greatly appreciated the fact that I was supported by actors who could deliver the funny. From our series regulars to this episode's guest stars, all did a terrific job on "The Ties That Bind." Another scene that I had to cut at the script stage sought to answer the question many curious fans had been asking for years: "What happens if you need to go to the bathroom on a cargo ship?" In the scene, Jup is at the ship's controls when the door behind him slides open and Tenat enters, pulling up his pants. Tenat "flushes" by initiating the rings that transport away whatever he just left behind in the back. Question answered. And then my fellow producers made me cut it. One of the many amusing memories of this episode concerns guest star Wallace Shawn (Vizzini in *The Princess Bride*. Inconceivable!). Prior to his arrival, I was told he was very excited to be working on the show, because he was, in fact, a huge fan of *SG-1*. So, on the day of his costume fitting, I went downstairs to say hello and welcome him to *Stargate*. "So, you're familiar with the show," I said. "Oh, no, I've never seen it," he informed me. "I don't even own a TV."

CLAUDIA BLACK (actress, "Vala "): In "Ties That Bind," we get a little glimpse of the sort of people Vala deals with, the circles she moves in. Very dodgy, by the way. They cut out a scene where she explains that she *didn't* sleep with that poor guy. She didn't manipulate him that badly. She just got him drunk and made him think they'd had sex— her and Wallace Shawn's character. That makes her a terrible scum bucket, but they cut out the scene. Coop and I were having a conversation about it and I said, "How do you feel about this scene?" and he said, "Yeah, I just don't think she's that much of a cult." And I said, "Neither do I, to be honest." I think that's an absolute last resort and I don't think she's probably ever had to go there. And I don't like the idea that she is *that* sexually manipulative, because that's not a likable character. And while I'm not striving to play someone who is entirely likable, it's great to play someone who's flawed, but everyone has to have redeeming qualities. And I think that's kind of the lowest of the low, really.

JOSEPH MALLOZZI: One of the main reasons I so enjoyed working on those last two seasons of *SG-1* was the cast, and a character by the name of Vala Mal Doran. This episode was an opportunity to examine a little of her (un)professional backstory with a tour de force of the unsavory sorts she did business with over the course of her checkered mercenary past. Claudia had a knack for always delivering a line exactly the way you'd imagined it. Throws in impeccable comic timing, a great onscreen presence and – voila! What more could you ask for? She was surrounded by some equally great talent, in this episode, a wonderful guest cast as well. Vala, Daniel, and Mitchell set out on a scavenger hunt unlike any other.

Episode #179 (9.5): "The Powers That Be"
Written by Martin Gero
Directed by William Waring
Guest Starring: Claudia Black (Vala), Cam Chai (Azdak), Pablo Coffey, Gary Jones (Sergeant Harriman), Lexa Doig (Dr. Lam), Greg Anderson (Prior), Chad Hershler (Villager), Nicola Correia Damude (Play Vala), Matt Johnson (Play Warrior), Mike Coleman (Med Tech)

In order to steer the planet P8X-412 away from Origin, SG-1 is tricked by Vala into going to the planet she previously ruled as a Goa'uld. The inhabitants of the planet know nothing of the downfall of the parasites, and they believe that Vala is still their goddess, until a prior shows up, and attempts to expose her for who she is.

MARTIN GERO (writer): "Powers That Be" is a big Vala episode. I think all of us were sort of chomping at the bit to write a Vala episode before we lost her, so I'm just glad to get one in. I had a blast writing my *SG-1* episode ninth season. I had all of eighth season to get caught up on all my *SG-1* mythology. The new characters are so much fun to write for (not that the old characters aren't) – Vala is like writer candy. You just can't go wrong with that character. I must say, however, that this script owes a lot to the contributions Rob made during his pass. He's (obviously) got a better handle on writing Daniel and Teal'c than I do.

JOSEPH MALLOZZI: Martin Gero's first script for *Stargate SG-1* offers a peek at Vala's dark past, her potentially bright future, and her very colorful present. This episode was actually made up of two different pitches: one about Vala returning to scam a world she once ruled as Qetesh, another involving the healing device and the dilemma it presented. The latter was a notion I'd pitched out, but was going nowhere until we started talking about the first story and realized it made sense to marry the two. As with most every episode, that's the way it worked on *Stargate*. Despite the onscreen credit, everyone in the writers' room participated in the creation of each story – discussing the initial pitch, spinning some ideas, beating out the story, structuring the narrative, and providing notes on the outline(s) and various drafts. If we were going to be precious about our individual ideas, then longtime executive producer Robert Cooper (the master spinner) could have easily laid a co-story credit claim to fully 90 percent of all episodes produced.

Episode 180 (9.6): "Beachhead"
Written & Directed by Brad Turner
Guest Starring: Claudia Black (Vala), Barclay Hope (Colonel Pendergast), Gary Jones (Sergeant Harriman), Maury Chaykin (Nerus), Louis Gossett Jr. (Gerak), Ian Butcher (Ori

Prior), Martin Christopher (Lieutenant Marks), Donald Adams (Latal), Eileen Barrett (Birra), Dan Shea (Sgt. Siler)

Samantha Carter returns to the S.G.C. when the Ori seize control of a planet named Kallana as a foothold in the Milky Way Galaxy. After several attempts to halt the process, they discover that they have been helping the Ori achieve their goal, instead of foiling their efforts. The Ori have been building an enormous Stargate to allow their ships to enter the Milky Way, but they are stopped by Vala, who dies in the process, although there is a possibility that she got trapped in the Ori galaxy.

JOSEPH MALLOZZI: In 'Beachhead,' Carter barely had time to unpack before she was at the frontline, doing what she does best – working on a way to help save the day. Maury Chaykin really tears it up as the Goa'uld , and we love Claudia Black. She was a blast to work with.

Episode #181 (9.7): "Ex Deus Machina"
Written by Joseph Mallozzi & Paul Mullie
Directed by Martin Wood
Guest Starring: Cliff Simon (Baal), Kendall Cross (Julia Donovan), Barclay Hope (Colonel Lionel Pendergast), Gary Jones (Sergeant Harriman), Peter Flemming (Agent Malcolm Barrett), Sonya Salomaa (Charlotte Mayfield), Chilton Crane, Louis Gossett Jr. (Gerak), Gardiner Millar (Yat'Yir), Simone Bailly (Ka'lel), Martin Christopher (Lt. Marks), Ken Dresen (Alex Jameson), David MacInnis (Agent Williams), Diego Klattenhoff (Team Leader), Kevin Blatch (Tobias)

After Baal contacts Stargate Command, they learn he has been living on earth for several months as the head of a major corporation. His demands are that he is allowed to live in peace, or he will blow up a naqahdah bomb somewhere in America. Yet Gerak is determined to capture him… and takes a less "subtle" route. The bomb proves impossible to disarm, so Prometheus beams it into space where it detonates harmlessly, but Baal escapes with many clones at his disposal.

JOSEPH MALLOZZI: While we were spinning this story about Baal hiding out on Earth, I suggested he could be working in a garage under an assumed identity, thus giving us the opportunity to title the episode "Deus Ex Mechanic." Paul pointed out that, given the fact Baal was an ex-Goa'uld "god," an even more appropriate title would be "Ex Deus Machina." Well, when we finished breaking the story, the mechanic idea was out the window, so we settled with "Ex Deus Machina." One of my very favorite titles — made all the greater by those outraged fans who called us out for such an obvious mistake! This episode also gave us the opportunity to see my favorite System Lord, Baal

— played to deliciously evil perfection by actor Cliff Simon — take his overlord act to the environs of planet Earth. And, best of all, dress the part!

CLIFF SIMON: Baal is in Earth clothes. He certainly blended in. He's not hiding out, as in he has a huge estate with bodyguards around him that nobody can get through. He's in plain sight. He's hiding in full view. That's a good way to put it. When you try to hide out, the best place to hide is in your enemy's hideout, if you could. If you're looking at it from that point of view, that's the last place that they're going to look. They've got to look where they think he's going to be most comfortable. And they would never think he's going to be most comfortable on Earth, yet he is. That's what's so great about it.

Episode #182 (9.8): "Babylon"
Written by Damian Kindler
Directed by Peter DeLuise
Guest Starring: Jason George (Jolan), Jarvis George (Volnek), William B. Davis (Prior), Gary Jones (Sergeant Harriman), Tony Todd (Lord Haikon), Lexa Doig (Dr. Lam), Darcy Laurie (Tass'an), Bryan Elliot (Col. Raimi)

A group of legendary Jaffa attacks SG-1 on a planet designated P9G-844 and captures Mitchell. While the rest of the team is forced to retreat, Mitchell is accused of killing one of the Jaffa. As punishment, he must square off against the slain Jaffa's brother, but he could be Mitchell's salvation.

PETER DELUISE: In "Babylon" I got to work with Tony Todd, who played Candyman; Wiliam B. Davis, who played Cigarette Smoking Man on *The X-Files,* and Jason George and Jarvis George, who were brothers playing Sodan Warriors, Jaffa elite fighters with their staffs. That, of course, was the season that Ben Browder came in, which made things a little different. Ben was very physical, not unlike Captain Kirk and whereas Richard Dean Anderson was physical enough, he normally wouldn't do much in the way of hand-to-hand combat stuff. But with Ben, it was a totally different sort of captain, as it was, so you *could* get more physical.

JOSEPH MALLOZZI: Director Peter DeLuise had long lobbied to have Tony Todd on the show and, finally, the perfect opportunity/role presented itself in this episode in the form of Haikon, the leader of the Sodan. Tony's was one of many great performances in this episode, but special mention goes to Ben Browder who went all out, even performing some of his own stunts – with bruising results. After watching one alarming set of dailies, the producers made the executive decision to revoke the lion-share of Ben's stunting privileges!

PETER DELUISE: At one point during shooting, I had this huge container of gum. It was really hot and uncomfortable and I offered pieces to Jason George, Jarvis George, Ben Browder and Amanda Tapping, and it was a little bit of relief from the heat. So we're all standing there chewing gum and Tony Todd was there, but I hadn't realized he was standing behind me, so I didn't offer him any gum. Suddenly I became aware of him and I went, "Oh, hey, Tony. Do you want gum?" And he goes, "Yeah, I want gum. I thought you were deliberately excluding me..." He thought I was trying to help him keep in his ornery and disagreeable character. And I was, like, "No, no, I would never deny you gum. Have all the gum you want, man!" But I thought that was great, that he thought I was deliberately excluding him for the benefit of his character.

Episode #183 (9.9): "Prototype"
Written by Alan McCullough
Directed by Peter DeLuise
Guest Starring: Neil Jackson (Khalek), Robert Picardo (Richard Woolsey), Gary Jones (Sergeant Harriman), Lexa Doig (Dr. Lam), Ivan Cermak (Altman)

SG-1 finds a man frozen in Ancient stasis on P3X-584, and brings him back to the S.G.C. to find out his story. But when Daniel researches the laboratory where the man was found, he discovers that he was grown by Anubis to be a genetically advanced human.

PETER DELUISE: I got to work with Neil Jackson, who's had an extensive career in big movies and some sci-fi. He was Khalek, the badass. This guy was incredibly fit, an Adonis, when he came to play with us. He had just been in a big Oliver Stone movie, *Alexander*, and he was completely ripped. I asked him how he stayed so skinny and he said, "We just didn't eat." So when he came to us, he was a wolf in sheep's clothing. We first get the sheep, then we realize something's going on with this guy and he makes the flip. I said to him, "When you do the flip, I want it to be interesting, because I want the audience not to realize it. I want there to be no indication before that." I had him go nice and slow so that when he became the bad guy, he just *killed* it. It was just such a pleasure to work with him.

ROBERT PICARDO (actor, "Richard Woolsey"): Richard Woolsey's kind of a military think-tank guy, who started out as a villain to threaten the leadership at Stargate Command. If they didn't shape up, they were going to be replaced. The second time I was on, I was involved in this giant scheme engineered by the evil Senator Kinsey. When I realized I was being manipulated, I turned on Kinsey, took a huge risk, and basically spilled the beans on something Kinsey was involved in. So I went from being this hatchet-man jerk to being totally redeemed. That's my stock in trade now. I come back again as sort of the hatchet-man jerk, and I'm redeemed this time in the same episode. I'm hoping to get to the point where I'm so good I can do both extremes in one scene. (*Zap2It*)

JOSEPH MALLOZZI: Alan McCullough scripts his first *Stargate* episode and, based on his efforts here, is invited to join the writing staff. He'll spend two seasons on *SG-1* and four on *Atlantis*, working his way up to supervising producer, displaying not only good story sense but a real affinity for the editing room as well. A great guy and much-appreciated member of the raucous writing room of Carl Binder, Marty G., Paul, and myself that produced *Atlantis'* final two seasons. This episode also marked the first appearance of actor Neil Jackson, who would turn in an equally brilliant performance as the undercover wraith in *Stargate Atlantis'* fifth season episode, "Vegas."

Episode #184 (9.10): "The Fourth Horseman, Part 1"
Written by Damian Kindler
Directed by Andy Mikita
Guest Starring: Cameron Bright (Orlin), Don S. Davis (General Hammond), Tony Amendola (Bra'tac), Gary Jones (Sergeant Harriman), Bill Dow (Dr. Lee), Panou (Lieutenant Fischer), Ty Olsson (Colonel Barnes), Julian Sands (Doci), Lexa Doig (Dr. Lam), Louis Gossett Jr. (Gerak), Greg Anderson (Prior #1), Gardiner Millar (Yat'Yir), Simone Bailly (Ka'lel), Jeff Judge (Aron), Dawn Chubai (News Reporter), Dagmar Midcap (News Reporter), Thomas Milburn Jr. (Hazmat Officer)

When a disease breaks out across America, evidence leads it to be the Ori's doing. Preparing to track down a viable cure, an old friend (Orlin) takes on an unfamiliar human form to help out, but it might not be enough when the team's adverse ally joins the Ori.

JOSEPH MALLOZZI: When we broke this mid-season two-parter, we fully expected to have actor Sean Patrick Flanery reprise the role of Orlin. Unfortunately, it turned out he was unavailable for both episodes. As a result, we were forced to rethink his character's role in the story. In retrospect, it was different but "good" different, offering up some terrific opportunities for both the Orlin character and Samantha Carter. The part ended up being played by Cameron Bright, who has gone on to play the role of Alec in *The Twilight Saga*.

It was great to have Don S. Davis back as General George Hammond. I appreciated the fact that, even though he'd shifted focus to his art and enjoying his retirement, Don still found time to revisit with us. Like most of my friends, we wound up connecting over our mutual appreciation for food and spent many an evening out on the town, bonding over everything from ribs to foie gras.

Episode #185 (9.11): "The Fourth Horseman, Part 2"
Written by Joseph Mallozzi & Paul Mullie
Directed by Andy Mikita
Guest Starring: Cameron Bright (Orlin), Jason George (Jolan), Tony Todd (Lord Haikon), Don S. Davis (General Hammond), Tony Amendola (Bra'tac), William B. Davis (Prior), Garry Chalk (Chekov), Gary Jones (Sergeant Harriman), Lexa Doig (Dr. Lam), Louis Gossett Jr. (Gerak), Noah Danby (Cha'ra), Mark Oliver (French Rep.), Kurt Evans (Col. Johnson), Jeff Judge (Aron), Dawn Chubai (News Reporter), Dagmar Midcap (News Reporter), Simone Bailly (Ka'lel)

While Orlin is working on a cure for the Prior plague, Mitchell and Daniel capture a Prior offworld to further the research of the antidote. Teal'c tries to stop Gerak, now a Prior, from corrupting the entire Jaffa Council towards Origin. Teal'c ultimately convinces Gerak to switch sides. Gerak cures the S.G.C. of the plague, but it costs him his life. Thanks to Gerak's efforts and Orlin's work, a cure is found for everyone else, but Orlin now has brain damage with no memory of who he is and is put in a mental hospital.

JOSEPH MALLOZZI: In this episode, Earth officials attempt to contain an alien virus that spreads from Stargate Command to the United States, then North America and, eventually, the rest of the world. And reporting on the breaking news are – well, news anchors and reporters. And who better to play news anchors and reporters than actual anchors and reporters? Surprisingly, it happens all the time in film and television. We auditioned a bunch of them and, quite frankly, they were all great, but ended up going with local television personalities Dawn Chubai and Dagmar Midcap. The part of the Jaffa Aron is played by Chris Judge's brother, Jeff, with who I was a long-time regular at Chris' notorious poker nights.

Episode #186 (9.12): "Collateral Damage"
Written by Joseph Mallozzi & Paul Mullie
Directed by William Waring
Guest Starring: Anna Galvin (Dr. Reya Varrick), Warren Kimmel (Dr. Marell), Benson Simmonds (Dr. Amuro), Gary Jones (Sergeant Harriman), William Atherton (Emissary Varta), Ian Robison (Mitchell's Father), Maximillian Uhrin (Young Mitchell), Brian Drummond (Security Officer), John Treleaven (Colonel)

SG-1 encounters the Galarans, a civilization that flourished under the umbrella of the Asgard Protected Planets Treaty following centuries of Goa'uld domination. Due to the disengagement of the Asgard from the Milky Way, the Galarans have become concerned for their safety and developed a memory-grafting device, with which they hope to accelerate their technological development. They are eager to trade this technology with Earth in exchange for hyperdrive technology.

After Mitchell's first dose of the memory-grafting device, he is accused of murder. Now the rest of the team must ally themselves with local scientists to prove his innocence.

JOSEPH MALLOZZI: I loved this episode and, as much as I'd like to lay some claim to it, this was all Paul, my writing partner (I was busy working on the next episode, "Ripple Effect"). One of the things I loved about working on *Stargate* was the freedom it gave us as writers. We could tell a variety of stories – standalone, arc-driven, Earth-based, set off-world, SF, fantasy, horror, comedic, or dark. In the case of "Collateral Damage" – standalone, off-world, SF, and dark, and it does all four incredibly well. In the original pitch, it's Teal'c who ends up imprisoned on an alien world, charged with a crime he didn't commit despite the overwhelming evidence to the contrary. Given Teal'c's existing arc that season, we elected to make it a Mitchell story as it allowed us the opportunity to explore his past.

The part of the doomed victim in this episode, Dr. Reya Varrick, is played by the lovely Anna Galvin, who is one of a handful of actors who have appeared in all three *Stargate* series – as the mysterious Vanessa Conrad in one of my fave *Atlantis* episodes, "Remnants," and then as Chloe Armstrong's mother in *Stargate Universe*.

Episode #187 (9.13): "Ripple Effect"
Story by Brad Wright, Joseph Mallozzi & Paul Mullie, Teleplay by Joseph Mallozzi & Paul Mullie
Directed by Peter DeLuise
Guest Starring: Teryl Rothery (Janet Fraiser), JR Bourne (Martouf), Gary Jones (Sergeant Harriman), Bill Dow (Dr. Lee), Lexa Doig (Dr. Lam), Dan Shea (Sgt. Siler), Trevor Devall (Voice of Kvasir)

More than 15 SG-1 teams arrive at Stargate Command, one team at a time, leading the "real" team to conclude that each of the teams have been inadvertently displaced from different parallel realities. One SG-1 team that arrived has Stargate Command's Dr. Janet Fraiser and the Tok'ra leader Martouf as members, both of whom have been dead for two years in the current reality. The events are ultimately revealed to be a plan by the SG-1 team that arrived first to steal Atlantis' ZPM to save their own Earth, but the "real" SG-1 foils them and sends everyone home.

JOSEPH MALLOZZI: Although my head nearly exploded writing the script, I still have nothing but the fondest of memories for this episode, which finds multiple versions of our team creating havoc at Stargate Command. Twin SG-1s team up to close the breach that has created the problem, but it turns out that one of those teams has a hidden agenda. When our SG-1 suddenly finds themselves in trouble, they turn the tables on their captors the only way they can: by thinking like themselves.

PETER DELUISE: That was quite a challenge where we had a room full of Carters. We used this device where we actually moved the camera in the same exact way. It was a device that recorded the motion of the camera and played it back the exact same way every time, so we could have a moving shot rather than a locked shot. But they were very time-consuming; I think we spent the better part of an entire morning duplicating Carters many, many times over. Amanda was so good about lending herself to that. She had already done it, but this was the most. We were going for the record on this one, and she was such a trooper. I'm always grateful to the actor when they realize that the payoff is going to be worth it. I appreciated that.

Episode #188 (9.14): "Stronghold"
Written by Alan McCullough, Excerpts Written by Robert C. Cooper, Martin Gero and Brad Wright
Directed by Peter DeLuise
Guest Starring: Tony Amendola (Bra'tac), Cliff Simon (Baal), Reed Diamond (Major Bryce Ferguson), Dakin Matthews (Maz'rai), Yan Feldman (Til'Vak), Don Thompson, Veena Sood (Dr. Kelly), Eric Breker, , Simone Bailly (Ka'lel), Gardiner Millar (Yat'Yir), Ken Kirzinger (Jaffa Commander), Hugo Steele (Jaffa Guard)

Baal brainwashes members of the Jaffa High Council to thwart their move towards democracy. Cameron Mitchell faces a tough decision when he learns that an old friend is about to die.

PETER DELUISE: Alien politics! At one point I had Mitchell bring Ferguson a video game console and a pizza, and on the pizza box the prop people had written "DeLuise & Son Pizza," along with a picture of my dad and myself on the box. That was kind of fun. *And* it was my cameo for that particular episode.

JOSEPH MALLOZZI: In this episode, a Jaffa undergoes the Rite of M'al Sharran to rid himself of his symbiote – and dies in the process. The rite was performed a grand total of three times before and only one of those instances proved successful (Teal'c being the rare exception). These 25 percent odds are pretty bleak. Compared to the Tok'ra extraction process, which, if the Tok'ra are to be believed, has a better, but still iffy 50 percent success rate. Paul and I called BS on that. Every time we could remember it being performed, it worked beautifully, so it seemed to be more like 100 percent. Which brings to mind one of the many amusing stories from our early days on the show.

Way back when we first started on *Stargate*, Paul and I wanted to know more about this Tok'ra extraction process. Brad suggested we check out an episode called "Pretense." Apparently, all we needed to know about the extraction process was covered in that episode. And so, Paul and I fired up the VCR and sat through 45 minutes of *Stargate's* version of *Boston Legal* and Zipacna walking around with a Carmen Miranda headpiece and, all the while we kept wondering: "When are they going to get around to extraction process?!" Then, as the episode was drawing to an end, the character of Skaara was ordered to undergo the "extraction process." *Finally!* I was all sorts of curious. Would it be a surgical procedure or something much techier and advanced? Would Skaara be awake through the procedure? If so, how would he react? So many questions about to be answered! We watched as the court made its ruling, then watched a time cut to the next scene in which the Tok'ra trot out the Goa'uld symbiote and proclaim the extraction process a success! End episode. WTF?!!!

I'd be remiss if I didn't mention guest star Reed Diamond who plays the part of Mitchell's doomed buddy in the episode. The former *Homicide* lead turns in a brilliant performance and, for the record, was terrific to work with.

Episode #189 (9.15): "Ethon"
Story by Damian Kindler & Robert C. Cooper, Teleplay by Damian Kindler
Directed by Ken Girotti
Guest Starring: John Aylward (President Nadal), Ernie Hudson (Commander Pernaux), Matthew Bennett (Jarrod Kane), Desiree Zurowski (Minister Chaska), Barclay Hope (Colonel Lionel Pendergast), Gary Jones (Walter Harriman), Martin Christopher (Captain Marks), Chelah Horsdal (Lt. Womack), Peter Shinkoda (Caledonian Aide), Sage Brocklebank (Rand Tech)

The Rand Protectorate ("Icon") converts to Origin and is rewarded with the design for a powerful satellite weapon, which they threaten to use against the Caledonians. When Prometheus tries to disable the satellite, it destroys the ship, although most of the crew escape to Caledonia. They are ultimately able to return to Earth through the planet's Stargate, but after doing so, dialogue between Rand and Caledonia breaks down and the two nations annihilate one another.

ROBERT C. COOPER: The important thing worth mentioning is how at this point the ships on *Stargate* became a big part of the show. I mean, we resisted that, obviously, quite a bit early on, because our show was *Stargate* and not *Star Trek*. We didn't want to have a ship show, but as things wore on, and I think people understood quite clearly what our show was and how different it was from *Star Trek*, we started to play with ships having a much bigger role, because they were out there. Like, the Goa'uld had ships, the Asgard had ships, the Replicators had ships, so we needed ships. We couldn't really defend our space with just the Stargate, so building at least one or a couple of ships and then crewing them was kind of fun, because the question became, how can we put a *Stargate* spin on flying a ship using somewhat alien technology. Obviously the warp drive is alien, but how do we put the humans from Earth spin on it that makes it different from *Star Trek*?

JOSEPH MALLOZZI: This episode marked the last episode of the earth ship *Prometheus*, and its unfortunately named commander Pendergast. To be honest, I would have felt a lot worse for him had he been named, say, Evans or Fitzgerald or even Pangbourn – but Pendergast? Whenever his name came up in a script, I would always ask where the name came from. Did some fan win a contest that necessitated we use their name in a script? Close! Apparently, Pendergast was the last name of a friend of one of the writers. With *Stargate* over, I now regret the fact that I didn't name one of my characters Jelly.

Episode #190 (9.16): "Off the Grid"
Written by Alan McCullough
Directed by Peter DeLuise
Guest Starring: Cliff Simon (Baal), Matthew Glave (Colonel Paul Emerson), Vince Corazza (Worrel), Eric Steinberg (Netan), Gary Jones (Sergeant Harriman), Erik Breker (Reynolds), Maury Chaykin (Nerus), Martin Christopher (Captain Kevin Marks), Michael Sunczyk (Vi'tak), Peter New (Farmer)

SG-1 is captured on an alien world after a deal with the Lucian Alliance goes bad ... and the planet's Stargate goes missing. SG-1 is rescued by the new Earth ship Odyssey and they go on a successful mission to retrieve all of the stolen Stargates from Baal.

PETER DELUISE: We had a guest star, Maury Chaykin, from *Dances with Wolves*, as the crazy colonel. He was quite the character. He was the kind of actor where you just get out of his way. I started to direct him and I could see in his face that he was open to *some* information, but not too much. I figured, "Let's see what you come up with." I just let him do what he wanted and he was Maury Chakin and he was *amazing*.

JOSEPH MALLOZZI: Look out! That corn is highly addictive! Ah, sweet sweet Kassa. How you've been mocked, forced to share ignominious conversation company with the likes of explosive tumors, Zipacna's silly hat, and Carter infamous "Just because my reproductive organs are on the inside instead of the outside, doesn't mean I can't handle whatever you can handle" line. Granted, it was one of our sillier episodes that saw the team going undercover decked out as extras from *The Road Warrior* while, back on Earth, Landry matched wits with the gluttonous Goa'uld Nerus (played to pompous perfection by the late Maury Chaykin). At one point during the editing process, Brad objected to the amount of food Nerus had in his cell on the grounds that it was "over the top." In my mind, that ship sailed the second Mitchell uttered the line,

"Get all the population jonesing for space corn."

Speaking of silly – a number of fans complained about the fact that the Lucian Alliance weren't cool enough, that they were a little too silly to be considered a formidable threat to Stargate Command. Well, to be fair, respect was admittedly an uphill climb considering the concept of the Alliance was introduced by these two lovable members [Tenat and Jup].

PETER DELUISE: There's a moment in this where Ben Browder's character is tied up and he's surrounded by guys with guns, and somehow he escapes that situation and he ends up rendezvousing with the other guys later. I said to Robert Cooper, "How does he escape?" And Robert goes, "He always escapes, we don't need to see that." "Really, we're not going to see how he escapes?" "We'll just make a funny line about it afterwards, like, 'It was tough, but I got away like I always do.'" I think Robert thought it would be a funny, light moment. At the time, I was young and immature and I thought, "*No*, you can't have him escape and not explain it." So Robert said, "We don't need to see it, it's fine." I said, "Okay." So the last time we see Ben Browder, he's tied up and *surrounded* by people pointing guns at him. They look more alert than they've ever been and it looks like there's just no fucking way he could possibly escape. So Robert saw the dailies and asked, "Did you do that deliberately to make it look harder for him to have escaped?" And I said, "Yes I did," and he just goes, "Okay. I told you he always escapes."

Episode #191 (9.17): "The Scourge"
Written by Joseph Mallozzi & Paul Mullie
Directed by Ken Girotti
Guest Starring: Robert Picardo (Richard Woolsey), Tamlyn Tomita (Shen Xiaoyi), Mark Oliver (Lapierre), Andy Maton (Chapman), Tony Alcantar (Dr. Myers), Gary Jones (Walter Harriman), Bill Dow (Dr. Lee), John Prowse (Col. Pearson), Guy Fauchon (Pullman), Jason McKinnon (Walker), Sean Hall (SF)

The Ori have engineered a bioweapon of bugs (known as R-75 or "Prior bugs"), asexual, fast-reproducing, omnivorous insects. When given meat, its numbers increase dramatically and they become voracious swarming predators, able to strip a human to the bone in moments. They prefer darkness and spend most of their time underground, where they hunt via echolocation. When a group of Earth diplomats go on a tour on the off-world Gamma Site research base, R-75 overrun the base and consume most of the base personnel. Cut off from the Stargate, SG-1 is forced to flee to a research site and set up a message to alert the Odyssey to rescue them when it arrives. The Odyssey does rescue SG-1 and the delegates and destroys the bugs with a toxin, but the bugs are spreading on other planets and are revealed to be another tactic of the Priors in submitting the people of the galaxy in worshiping the Ori.

ROBERT PICARDO: There's a certain amount of action in this script. We are on the run on the planet, avoiding these, in a sort of a *Starship Troopers* scenario, trying to save ourselves from these ferocious, flesh-eating bugs. So there's a lot of running around. It was fun to be part of the A-plot this time instead of just the sitting-on-a-couch-in-the-President's-office B plot. So I had a good deal of time. Michael and Amanda and Chris and Ben are just great to hang out with. We had a lot of fun together and they're a really cool cast. We had an eating scene and Chris decided to try to crack us up with innovative and interesting ways to eat a corn dog. And I have to tell you, he really put his heart and soul into it.

JOSEPH MALLOZZI: One of my favorite guest stars makes a return in this episode as Robert Picardo reprises his role as the insufferable Richard Woolsey. This, I think, was the first episode I wrote in which I gave the character a little humor – and, as a result, really started to enjoy writing for him. Sure, he was a stuffed shirt, but he also reveals glimpses of vulnerability that make him amusing, even likable up to a point. And Bob, of course, did a terrific job of delivering those subtle and, sometimes, not-so-subtle nuances that – like the point late in the episode where SG-1 and the I.O.A. reps are hurrying away from the bugs, only to have Woolsey speed by them, arms madly pumping.

ROBERT PICARDO: Joe Mallozzi told me when he first mentioned the script to me that he thought we could have a little bit of fun tweaking Woolsey's character, and I think he did. And I certainly did. There's some humorous moments in it. There's some moments where we see a character who's reasonably unflappable and has a very fixed world view and what he's supposed to accomplish in that situation. Suddenly all that goes out the window, and it's a very threatening situation. He has his moments of, shall we say, barely controlled panic.

JOSEPH MALLOZZI: One of the biggest challenges of this episode was the bugs themselves. In the original draft, they buzz along the ground like a giant moving carpet. I limited the cutaways to the swarm figuring that, while expensive, it would not be prohibitively so. The cold reality of the visual effects budget hit me like a punch in the face – followed by three swift kicks to the midsection and the subsequent removal of all the cash in my wallet. We simply couldn't afford sweeping bug swarms. And so, I came up with the idea of having the bugs travel underground which, while not as visually satisfying, lent them a certain creepiness.

Episode #192 (9.18): "Arthur's Mantle"

Written by Alan McCullough
Directed by Peter DeLuise
Guest Starring: Jarvis George (Volnek), Doug Wert (Major Hadden), Bill Dow (Dr. Lee), Gary Jones (Chief Harriman), Eric Breker (Reynolds), Tony Todd (Lord Haikon), Darren Giblin (Conway), Andrew McNee (Technician), Morris Chapdelaine (Prior)

Mitchell and Carter are shifted to another dimension, making them invisible to everyone at the S.G.C.. Teal'c and SG-12 discover that the Sodan have been brutally attacked.

JOSEPH MAZZOLLI: Oh, damn, the whole "out of phase" debate that rears its ugly head whenever we do these types of episodes. As Paul always points out: "Why don't they just phase through the floor?" While we've dealt with some equally far-flung SF notions, Paul always argued that those notions, at the very least, adhered to certain self-contained theoretical laws of physics, but phasing did not. The mechanics of gate travel while "out of phase" was another matter entirely.

PETER DELUISE: We just embraced the out of phase thing, because we had to. The other thing was using Merlin as a real alien being whose wizardry was explained through science fiction. The other thing was scenes where you have other people with you, but you can't acknowledge them.

JOSEPH MALLOZZI: After Carter explains their situation to Mitchell, he responds with: "That was alternate reality, this is alternate dimension. Hell, all I need is a good time travel adventure and I've scored the SG-1 trifecta." He completes the trifecta in the Season 10 series finale, "Unending."

Episode #193 (9.19): "Crusade"
Written & Directed by Robert C. Cooper
Guest Starring: Claudia Black (Vala Mal Doran), Tim Guinee (Tomin), Daniella Evangelista (Denya), Garry Chalk (Chekov), Tamlyn Tomita (Shen Xiaoyi), Michael Ironside (Seevis), Doug Abrahams (Prior), Alex Dafoe (Halstrom), Dan Shea (Sgt. Siler)

Vala Mal Doran makes contact with Stargate Command from the Ori home galaxy, and tells the story of her life undercover in a village of followers building the Ori's invasion fleet and her mysterious pregnancy. She ultimately joins an anti-Ori resistance movement with plans to destroy the fleet, but the plan fails and Vala is nearly killed by her husband, Tomin, before she convinces him to spare her and take her with him to war in the Milky Way galaxy.

ROBERT C. COOPER: Probably notable in my world, because it's my first episode of television I ever directed. It took me a while to hire myself. I guess I was a little suspicious of myself as a director and wanted to make sure I was going to do the job well. It's a clip show, but I tried to give myself something a little easier just to kind of get my feet wet on a set and manage a crew and direct the cast. I was so excited about Claudia and the character of Vala and I wanted to make a show centric to this character who we didn't know if we could trust when she's kind of telling us a story.

JOSEPH MALLOZZI: Actress Claudia Black returns in time for executive producer Robert C. Cooper's directorial debut. An ambitious episode that delivers action, humor, and pathos. It also marks the introduction of the Ori warship. My first reaction to the design: "Uh, it looks like a flying toilet seat." One of the rare instances where my input was *not* appreciated.

ROBERT C. COOPER: There's a sequence where the team is interrogating Vala. I had blocked it in my plan, frankly, quite badly for the sake of coverage. There are ways to block something so that you can shoot it reasonably easily in terms of the number of camera angles that you need to cover the scene. But I did something that I didn't really know any better at the time: Her eyeliner had people on either side and I had doubled my coverage for the scene. I guess I thought it was a bit of a badge of honor, but look-ing back, I don't really see it that way. And neither did anybody else. I did get the most setups in a day that we had done on the show, in the 70s or 80s. On a normal shooting day, it's maybe 30 or 35 setups. I did more than double the number of setups that day, but it was because I had blocked something really badly. I had drawn out this diagram on a piece of paper that just looked like it had been written by a crazy man or a serial killer in his mother's basement.

It was stressful being my first time on set in that capacity. Even though I had a show run for a few years and been on the show for nine years, it's like a different level of re-sponsibility. Like, "Ooh, Mr. Bigshot thinks he's coming down to direct, huh?" Because the grips and gaffers don't really care. They'll take you apart like sharks smelling blood in the water. Being a clip show made it a little bit easier.

Episode #194 (9.20): "Camelot"
Written by Joseph Mallozzi & Paul Mullie
Directed by Martin Wood
Guest Starring: Claudia Black (Vala Mal Doran), John Noble (Meurik), Katharine Isa-belle (Valencia), Matthew Glave (Colonel Paul Emerson), David Thomson (Antonius), Eric Steinberg (Netan), Garry Chalk (Chekov), Matthew Walker (Merlin), Martin Christo-pher (Major Marks), Noah Danby (Cha'ra), Connor Crash Dunn (Ramus), Oleg Palme Feoktistov (Korolev Pilot), Trevor Devall (Voice of Kvasir)

333 Chevrons Locked - Stargate Oral History

SG-1 discovers the village of Camelot on PX1-767 and must face Merlin's security system when they go in search of an Ancient weapon. The Ori invasion begins. A fleet composed of ships from all over the Milky Way made up of the Earth ships Odyssey and Korelev along with ships from the Free Jaffa, Tok'ra, Lucian Alliance as well as one Asgard ship, faces off against four Ori ships and are decimated. The Korelev is destroyed with Daniel and Mitchell on board. Vala, on board one of the ships, can only watch the devastation in horror as she starts to go into labor.

JOSEPH MALLOZZI: On the day we were to shoot the big Mitchell vs. the Black Knight sword fight sequence, it was pouring rain on location. Most any other actor would have complained, but not Ben Browder. He embraced the rain and the mud, going all out — stumbling, slipping, falling, rolling — to outstanding effect. It couldn't have turned out better had we planned it. The sequence was mentioned in a piece done by our old buddy, Ross Hull, for the Weather Channel. This one can earn its slot on the merit of its kick-ass cliffhanger conclusion alone: an all-out space battle that sees Earth and its allies get their asses kicked, Mitchell, Jackson, and Teal'c aboard seemingly doomed ships, Carter free-floating helplessly in space, and a very pregnant Vala watching it all from the relatively safe confines of an enemy vessel where she will soon give birth to the "will of the Ori."

JOHN NOBLE (actor, "Meurik"): I totally understood Meurik. He was a guy who was the governor of a village, entrusted with looking after the people, whilst having this incredible threat over them. I liked him. I thought he was actually a good man. And confronted with these strangers running in with guns and things, no wonder he reacted in a negative way, in some ways. But at the end of it, he sort of was redeemed in the sense that he did what he thought was right, and the right thing for his people. It's just a good, solid, strong character and I was attracted to it.

DAVID READ: The in house visual effects team was responsible for that sequence of the fighting spaceships at the Supergate. They did it all internally and, boy, oh, boy, was that an amazing job they did. It was an extraordinary cap to that season. The threat of the Ori has been looming all season long; there was an episode called "Beachhead" where the Ori invasion was actually supposed to begin, but they postponed it until the end of the season. And Claudia returns at the very end of the episode, very pregnant, and it's a dark note, literally, that Joel Goldsmith ends on musically for that season. The things that are going to come are going to be fought for on a very bloody battlefield. We really got our asses handed to us in that episode.

SEASON TEN SUMMARY (2006-2007)

* Vala Mal Doran gives birth to a daughter, Adria, fathered by the Ori.

★ *Vala Mal Doran becomes a probationary member of Stargate Command.*

★ *SG-1 travels to the Pegasus Galaxy to dial the Milky Way Ori Supergate. In the process an Ori warship and Wraith hive ship are defeated. The ascended Morgan Le Fay provides Daniel Jackson with crucial information before she is whisked away to be punished by the others on her plane.*

★ *Adria destroys the Jaffa settlement on Dakara.*

★ *Vala Mal Doran becomes a full member of SG-1.*

★ *SG-1 joins Baal and Adria on a quest to track down Merlin's weapon, but instead discover Merlin himself. Before dying, Merlin transfers his consciousness into Daniel Jackson so that he may rebuild the weapon once more. Adria kidnaps Jackson.*

★ *Adria transforms Daniel Jackson into a Prior of the Ori. Despite his dramatic change in appearance, the presence of Merlin's consciousness provides him with the protection from her influence. Jackson completes the weapon and sends it through the Ori Supergate aboard one of their ships, killing the ascended beings in their galaxy.*

★ *Baal implants a clone symbiote of himself into Adria to take advantage of her knowledge and power. The Tok'ra remove the symbiote, but not before fatally wounding her. To escape death, she ascends.*

★ *The Asgard genetic degradation problem reaches an irreparable point. The race installs a computer core with an archive of their collected knowledge and technology into the Odyssey and then commits mass suicide, destroying their homeworld and bringing their civilization to an end.*

EPISODE GUIDE: SEASON TEN

Episode #195 (10.1): "Flesh and Blood"
Written by Robert C. Cooper
Directed by William Waring
Guest Starring: Tony Amendola (Bra'tac), Robert Picardo (Richard Woolsey), Matthew Glave (Colonel Paul Emerson), Tim Guinee (Tomin), Eric Steinberg (Netan), Gary Jones (Walter Harriman), Garry Chalk (Chekov), Jodelle Ferland (Adria at 7), Brenna O'Brien (Adria at 12), Martin Christopher (Major Marks), Emma Rose (Adria at 4), Doug Abrahams (Prior), Apollonia Vanova (Russian Weapons Officer), Gwenda Lorenzetti (Nursemaid), Trevor Devall (Voice of Kvasir), Bruno Verdoni (Lucian Alliance Officer)

Following their devastating attack on Milky Way forces, the Ori leave the scene to begin their holy crusade and purify the galaxy of evil. As the remnants of the makeshift Milky Way fleet come together, Vala gives birth to a baby girl, the Orici, genetically altered by the Ori to command their forces. Daniel Jackson has escaped to the Ori flagship, which has just arrived on Chulak to convert the Jaffa into believing in Origin. He pretends to be an Ori warrior while he and Vala attempt to kidnap the Orici, who has been named Adria by Vala. An attempt by SG-1 and Bra'tac to destroy the fleet over Chulak fails and Bra'tac sets a collision course with one of the ships in a futile attempt to destroy it while Daniel is captured by Tomin, Vala's husband. He escapes and knocks out both Adria and Tomin, but is disarmed by a Prior and trapped with Vala in a wall of fire with no way out. In the nick of time, the Odyssey arrives and beams SG-1 off their ship and Daniel out of the Ori warship. As Daniel beams out, he manages to grab Vala and take her with him, but leaves Adria behind.

ROBERT C. COOPER: Adria is sort of a magical being who is an offspring of the Ori. It was kind of one of these immaculate conception scenarios where Vala ended up pregnant, which happened because Claudia was actually pregnant and we needed to come up with a reason why. So we chose an alien god and then the character magically grows from birth to adult within the span of a few days. Vala hasn't seen the child as it was taken away when it was born, and they bring the child back to see her and she thinks they're bringing in an infant, and it turns out to be a three-year-old child. Now we had a fantastic and super cute kid in the audition, but on set she just froze. She got scared by all the lights, the people and all the cameras, and it didn't work out. So we pulled the plug on her.

Will Waring, a camera operator on the show for years who turned into one of our best directors, just couldn't get a performance out of her. But we needed to shoot this at some point, and eventually my now middle daughter, who at the time was my youngest daughter, was about that age. I went home to my wife and said, "Not that I'm trying to put my kids in the show, but she *would* fit the costume." So my daughter, Emma, was the youngest version of the Ori in the show. I actually directed that scene, knowing she would feel more comfortable. And the woman who escorts her in, and you only see her hand on her shoulder, is my wife. Emma still gets a kick out of it; every once in a while somebody she knows will dig up that scene, which is on You-Tube. She thinks it's hilarious.

JOSEPH MALLOZZI: Robert Cooper managed to juggle all of the various storylines and characters in an episode at turns humorous, poignant, thrilling, and shocking, paving the way for the introduction of the season's new Big Bad: Adria, daughter of the Ori (not "oreo," as one actress who auditioned for the role pronounced it). Prior to her reaching adulthood (the ultimate Adria played by the beautiful Morena Baccarin), we glimpsed our villainess in three stages of development: the ages of four, seven and 12. Seven-year-old Adria was played by Jodelle Ferland, who returned to the franchise in *Atlantis'* fourth season as the spoiled princess Harmony in one of my favorite *SGA* episodes. A lot of stuff was going on in this episode and director Will Waring did a terrific job on what I believe was his first big season premiere.

> *Episode #196 (10.2): "Morpheus"*
> *Written by Joseph Mallozzi & Paul Mullie*
> *Directed by Andy Mikita*
> Guest Starring: Robert Picardo (Richard Woolsey), Ben Ratner (Dr. Hutchison), Robin Mossley (Dr. Reimer), Patrick Gilmore (Bernie Ackerman), Toby Berner (Grimsby), Chris Bradford (Medical Technician)

> *Questing for the Sangraal, the team ends up in a mess of trouble when they are struck with a sleeping sickness on Vagonbrei (aka Verus Gen Bree), one of the three planets that the weapon is supposed to be on. Meanwhile, Landry must decide whether or not Vala can be trusted to remain at the S.G.C. as a possible future member of SG-1, but it might not be up to him when the IOA steps in. In the end, Teal'c discovers a lizard (a chuckwalla) immune to the parasite causing the sickness and a cure is reverse engineered from it. Vala is accepted as a provisional member of the S.G.C., though she is not allowed to join SG-1 officially yet.*

JOSEPH MALLOZZI: The original idea for this story was actually ship-based. I pitched out an episode in which the *Odyssey*, on its way back to Earth following an off-world op, encounters a seemingly derelict ship floating in space. SG-1 and some members of the *Odyssey* team investigate and discover the crew long-dead. As they search through the mystery ship's database, they fall victim to the "sleeping sickness." One by one, they drift off until, eventually, only SG-1 remains to put together the pieces before it's too late.

The location was changed to a planet and we ended up using our standing village set in the VFX stage (the sight of such memorable sequences as the interior hive ships, the Atlantis cafeteria balcony, and the big Sheppard/Zelenka space jump in *SGA*'s "Adrift"), shot to creepy effect by the fabulous Andy Mikita. I loved a lot about this episode: Teal'c saving the day, Daniel and Sam slowly succumbing late in the episode, the slow-mo funeral-like montage and, of course, the B-story which focuses on Vala's attempts to cheat her way through a psych evaluation. Claudia Black and Ben Ratner were a joy to watch. Their comic timing was impeccable — quick, restrained, and hilarious.

Episode #197 (10.3): "The Pegasus Project"
Written by Brad Wright
Directed by William Waring
Guest Starring: David Hewlett (Rodney McKay), Joe Flanigan (John Sheppard), Torri Higginson (Elizabeth Weir), Matthew Glave (Paul Emerson), Sarah Strange (Morgan Le Fey), Gary Jones (Walter Harriman), David Nykl (Radek Zelenka), Matthew Walker (Merlin), Chuck Campbell (Atlantis Technician), Chelah Horsdal (Lieutenant)

SG-1 visits Atlantis with two goals: to find new clues about the location of Merlin's superweapon, the Sangraal, and to disable the Supergate by connecting it to a black hole in the hope that they can stop the Ori from sending more ships through. As Dr. Rodney McKay (David Hewlett), Chief Science Officer of the Expedition assists Sam and Mitchell in their elaborate plan to "jump" a wormhole by sending a bomb directly into the Supergate using the Odyssey. Daniel, Vala and Dr. Elizabeth Weir, the head of the Expedition, search the city's databases for information, eventually confronting the Ancient known as Morgan Le Fey. Morgan shows them the address of the two other planets they need to search, but when she tries to tell them something important, she is pulled away by the other Ancients. At the same time, the Odyssey succeeds in its mission, destroying both a Wraith Hive Ship and an Ori warship at the same time, resulting in the S.G.C. achieving their greatest victory to date in the war against the Ori.

"The Pegasus Project" is the first major crossover between Stargate SG-1 *and* Stargate Atlantis, *with the majority of cast members from both shows appearing. Only* Atlantis' *Jason Momoa ("Ronon Dex"), Rachel Luttrell ("Teyla Emmagan"), and Paul McGillion ("Carson Beckett") do not appear.*

BRAD WRIGHT: A fun crossover episode. It was an *SG-1* episode, but they flew to Atlantis in order to solve the problem they had with the Supergate. So there were all of these stories going on: one with the Supergate, one is Daniel's story talking to the ancients and trying to figure out where they are. The problem I had was not remembering what series I was writing for, because we were doing both shows.

JOSEPH MALLOZZI: A crossover fan favorite that I constantly get confused with "Beachhead," another crossover fan favorite. This was the episode in which Mitchell threatens McKay with a lemon – an ad-lib on the day that seemed altogether weird in dailies but, ultimately, ended up making the final cut. McKay's citrus allergy was apparently inspired by a staff writer in the show's early days (before my time anyway) who would always make it a point to proclaim his unique hypersensitivity to anyone who would listen. Whenever they'd go out for lunch, said writer would be very careful to clear all menu items with the server. "I'm very allergic to citrus," he would inform them. "A single drop and I could die!" It wasn't until the end of the season that they discovered the rib sauce their afflicted co-worker had so enjoyed on his bi-weekly lunches at a local rotisserie joint was, in fact, mostly molasses and lemon juice. And Rodney McKay's citrus allergy was born. It was also great to finally get Daniel Jackson to Atlantis. In fact, following *SGA*'s fourth season, there had even been some talk of having Daniel join the Atlantis crew for its fifth season, an idea we unfortunately had to abandon for financial reasons.

DARREN SUMNER: It was an *SG-1* episode where the team finally gets to Atlantis by ship with a really important plan. *And* we get to see the main characters from both shows interacting for the first time. It's great fan service and it's an incredibly entertaining story that's really important, because their mission is to prevent the Ori Supergate from being used again. If you can connect a Stargate to that Supergate, you can keep it "busy." If you can power that wormhole connection with a black hole, then, in theory, it'll last for years or centuries and not shut off. As a result, the Ori won't be able to use it. So this was a really clever kind of story where they have to go to Pegasus, to dial from another galaxy, to dial from the supergate and keep it occupied so that, again, the Ori get a busy signal.

Episode #198 (10.4): "Insiders"
Written by Alan McCullough
Directed by Peter F. Woeste
Guest Starring: Cliff Simon (Baal), Peter Flemming (Malcolm Barrett), Bill Dow (Dr. Lee), Lesley Ewen (S.G.C. Geneticist), Gary Jones (Walter Harriman), Dan Shea (Sgt. Siler), Paul Christie (Major Caffey)

When an Al'kesh crashes only a few miles away from Cheyenne Mountain, the team finds Baal, and he asks them to capture his rebellious clones; in exchange, he offers information about the whereabouts of Merlin's weapon. As the clones are brought in for questioning, SG-1 must determine which Baal is the real one. Eventually the Baals take over the S.G.C. in order to get the S.G.C.'s list of Stargate addresses, which includes addresses known only to the Ancients, in order to find Merlin's weapon. The Baals get the addresses and beam out to a ship in orbit while SG-1 realizes Baal brainwashed Agent Malcolm Barrett to help him escape.

JOSEPH MALLOZZI: Of all the enemies SG-1 faced over the course of their many adventures, Baal remains my favorite. I appreciated his sense of style, his sense of humor, and a megalomania that was at times outrageous and endearing. Cloning him was probably one of the best ideas we've ever had – and by "we" I mean Robert Cooper, who pitched out the final clone reveal in an earlier episode. Suddenly, we had the luxury of multiple Baals, a host of new storylines and, in the case of Brad and Robert, endless pun possibilities.

Cliff Simon, who played the conniving Goa'uld System Lord, was always a pleasure to talk with. He'd swing by the writers' room after his costume fittings and thank us for the work – or, on one occasion, chortle over the "corny lines." So delighted was he by his character's comfortable position on Earth, that he often pitched out the merits of a possible spin-off centered on – who else? – Baal.

Episode #199 (10.5): "Uninvited"
Written by Damian Kindler
Directed by William Waring
Guest Starring: Keegan Connor Tracy (Dr. Redden), Erik Breker (Colonel Reynolds), John Murphy (Sheriff Stokes), Jason Bryden (Trust Operative), Jodie Graham (SG-25 Leader), Biski Gugushe (SG-11 Leader), Brock Johnson (Hunter), James Caldwell (Hunter)

The team discovers several creatures that only appear on worlds where the S.G.C. has used the Sodan cloaking devices. Things get worse when another creature appears in the woods on Earth where Mitchell and Landry are spending some "quality time" at O'Neill's cabin. Coming together, SG-1 and Landry kill the creature and another one that appears and closes off the area even though they're sure they got them all. With the creatures dead, the team and Landry relax together at the cabin.

JOSEPH MALLOZZI: Sadly, this episode will be remembered not for the fun dialogue between host Landry and his unwilling cabin guest Mitchell, or the off-world op involving the rest of the team, but the unintentionally hilarious creature that is revealed at episode's end. Ooof. As far as CG monsters go, it doesn't get much goofier than the thing that comes staggering out of the woods after being shot and expires in spectacular "Ugh, ya got me!" fashion. Without a doubt, the hammiest performance by a computer-generated alien in *Stargate* history.

Episode #200 (10.6): "200"
Written by Brad Wright, Robert C. Cooper, Joseph Mallozzi, Paul Mullie, Carl Binder, Martin Gero & Alan McCullough
Directed by Martin Wood
Guest Starring: Richard Dean Anderson (General Jack O'Neill), Willie Garson (Martin Lloyd), Don S. Davis (Voice of General Hammond), Peter DeLuise (Replacement Actor), Isaac Hayes ("Teal'c, P.I." Narrator), Gary Jones (Walter Harriman), Jill Teed (Yolanda Reese), Christian Bocher (Raymond Gunne), Herbert Duncanson (Grell), Anwar Hasan (Young Teal'c), Cory Monteith (Young Mitchell), Barbara Kottmeier (Young Vala), Jason Coleman (Young Daniel), Julie Johnson (Young Carter), Martin Wood (Director), Dan Shea (Sgt. Siler), Jonathan Hill (Furling), Shirley Hill (Furling), Trevor Devall (Voice of

Asgard), Pierre Bernard (Zombie)

Martin Lloyd contacts the S.G.C., looking for their assistance in writing a feature movie to follow up Wormhole X-treme!, *allowing the audience to see some of the team's most creative fantasies. It also marks Colonel Mitchell's 200th time through the event horizon, and is the 200th episode in the series. In the end, SG-1 go on what appears to be a routine mission and are joined by Generals Landry and O'Neill and Sergeant Walter Harriman. While the* Wormhole X-treme! *The movie is canceled, the series is renewed and survives 10 more years.*

JOSEPH MALLOZZI: *SG-1* was about to attain the loftiest of broadcast heights – its 200th episode – and we wanted to do something special. Something unique. Something everyone on the production would enjoy as much as the longtime fans watching at home. The initial idea pitched out was something called "Remember When ...," a trip down memory lane in which our characters' reflections would form the frames of the varied flashbacks to outrageous missions. While everyone loved the idea of the outrageous missions, the premise of the episode felt too diffuse. We wanted an actual story that would form the heart of the episode. After much discussion, we elected to pay tribute to the franchise by referencing our last milestone – episode 100 – and bringing back Martin Lloyd and the show within a show, *Wormhole X-Treme!* But the fun we poked at the franchise through that spoof production was nothing compared to what we had in store for "200."

Next to *The Simpsons, The Wizard of Oz* was probably the most referenced piece of pop culture over *SG-1's* decade-long run. The fans certainly took notice, which resulted in one particularly memorable piece of artwork being sent to the studio – it depicted the original team as the cinematic classic's adventurous foursome. So, I suppose, it made perfect sense to reference the show by including a little *Wizard of Oz* sequence in the episode as well. Mitchell's line, "Now, how can something work perfectly fine for 10 years, then all of a sudden, it doesn't work anymore?" was an in-story reference to the gate suddenly stopping operations — and, interestingly enough, could have been interpreted as a comment on the show's cancellation.

MARTIN WOOD: I probably did more research for the 200th episode than I've ever done before on *SG-1*, because I wanted to match styles to the TV series and films we were spoofing. For example, if you really know *The Wizard of Oz*, when you see the Goa'uld crushed under the cargo ship in "200" you'll go, "Hey, that's just how it looks when Dorothy's house falls on the Wicked Witch in the original movie." In fact, I even remembered to put a little fern off to the left-hand side of our Goa'uld. For our *Farscape* scene, I watched 10 or 12 episodes of that series in a row to make sure I got the shooting style right. That was so everyone who had ever seen *Farscape* would recognize our efforts to copy it. The same was true of our *Star Trek* spoof. We used seven different shooting styles in this episode, which you don't normally do on a TV show, so that was a huge amount of fun for me. (*Interview with journalist Steve Eramo*)

ROBERT C. COOPER: That's right, people who complained about "Wormhole X-Treme!," we did it again. It's, like, "We've gotten to 200 episodes, so you've got nothing to complain about."

BRAD WRIGHT: The one thing about "200" is that, at the time, I thought it was *so* funny. Then I played the puppet scene for someone and as I watched it I said, "That's not as funny as I thought it was." But it was cool to do it. I talk about going outside the box and we had been such fans of *Team America* and the Chiodo Brothers, who built the puppets for that, built ours. It was our 200th episode and we deserved to have a little fun.

Episode #201 (10.7): "Counterstrike"
Written by Joseph Mallozzi & Paul Mullie
Directed by Andy Mikita
Guest Starring: Morena Baccarin (Adria), Tony Amendola (Bra'tac), Matthew Glave (Colonel Emerson), Richard Whiten (Bo'rel), Gary Jones (Walter Harriman), David Andrews (Se'tak), Martin Christopher (Marks), Peter Nicholas Smyth (Prior), Shiraine Haas (Lieutenant Evans), Sylvesta Stuart (Jaffa), Aleks Holtz (Jaffa)

Deadly battles erupt between the Ori, led by Adria, and the Jaffa, after 100,000 villagers are wiped out by a powerful energy wave which Adria believes was SG-1's doing. She captures Daniel and Vala and uses her powers against them to determine the nature of the weapon. Adria learns about the Dakara superweapon and heads there to destroy it. SG-1 is rescued by the Odyssey, but Dakara and its weapon are decimated, fracturing the Free Jaffa Nation.

JOSEPH MALLOZZI: As I was writing "Counterstrike," I realized that it was a surprisingly sober outing for one particular character and wondered whether it was a little too "down." I honestly can't see how it can't be given the circumstances. Still, we finally get to see the inside of an Ori ship and the story affords a bonding opportunity between two characters with a rocky past.

The second of three scripts I wrote over a 14-day period during one hiatus, I loved this one for the Daniel-Vala moment (something I expand on in the ensuing episode) and the fact that it had all of our team members — and Landry! — in play. I recall actor Ben Browder recommending his friend, actor Mark Dacascos, for the part of the lead Jaffa. I loved Mark Dacascos' work in *Brotherhood of the Wolf* and *The Crow* (and, lately, *Iron Chef America*) but didn't want to cast him only to kill off his character in the episode. I held off and, two years later, cast him as Ronon's former comrade, Tyr, in *SGA*'s "Reunion" – and, the following season, in "Broken Ties." He was one of the nicest people I've ever had the pleasure to work with. Over the course of production on "Broken Ties," I had a half dozen crew members approach me about finding a way to make him recurring. In addition to *Iron Chef America*, you could catch Mark on *Hawaii Five-O* as the villainous Wo Fat and *John Wick Chapter 3* as Zero.

Episode #202 (10.8): "Memento Mori"
Written by Joseph Mallozzi & Paul Mullie
Directed by Peter DeLuise
Guest Starring: Don Stark (Sol), Adrian Holmes (Detective Ryan), Sonya Salomaa (Athena), Brendan Beiser (Weaver), Gary Jones (Walter Harriman), Peter Benson (Devon), Patricia Harras (Fake Carter), Brian Davies (Waiter), Phillip Mitchell (Guy #1), Heather Christie (Waitress), Sean Owen Roberts (Driver), Stephen Powell (Dad), Rachelle Miron (Mother), Rob Hayter (Leader #2), Ian Brown (Kakalios), Rimple Sumer (Restaurant Hostess)

During a dinner out, Vala is captured by the Goa'uld Athena, where she attempts to pry memories out of Vala's subconscious during her time as a host. When things go wrong, Vala develops amnesia and runs away and she must begin to piece herself back together. SG-1 eventually catches up to her and she tries to run again, but Daniel manages to get her to remember him at least and she returns to the S.G.C., where she recovers her entire memory and finally achieves her dream of becoming a fully-fledged member of SG-1.

JOSEPH MALLOZZI: The third script I wrote during those two weeks was a lot of fun – atypical and Vala-centered, but with a nice, emotional pay-off that cements the friendship between Vala and Daniel, suggesting the possibility of much more. I remember one of the scenes I had trouble with was the interrogation of the captured Trust operative. I was wracking my brain, trying to figure out how Teal'c could get him to talk when Rob Cooper – as he often did whenever we reached a creative roadblock – would throw out a suggestion. In this case, simply have Teal'c lean in and whisper something in the operative's ear. Something so terrifying that the operative immediately starts talking. So, what did Teal'c whisper in his ear? Something just too horrible to repeat.

PETER DELUISE: I got to work with Claudia Black, who is always amazing and I *love* her instincts. And the character could say or do *anything*, because she was unscrupulous. I also remember Ben Browder had to be handcuffed to a bed shirtless and he asked me to frame it a certain way because he hadn't manscaped properly that day.

JOSEPH MALLOZZI: In the original version of the script, Vala gets a job at Sal's

Diner. For some reason, it was changed to Sol's Diner. We ended up casting the wonderful Don Stark in the role and director Peter DeLuise suggested we change it back to Sal's Diner, because Don looked Italian. I did. I met Don and told him about the change and he pointed out that he was, in fact, Jewish. Sol's Diner it became. And then I found out he was of German, Jewish and Italian descent. I briefly toyed with Sigi's Diner, but ultimately elected to leave well enough alone at the risk of having the entire Art Department coming after me. Speaking of director Peter DeLuise — the direction of this episode's tease is wonderful – tight, dynamic, and provocative (or, I prefer, WTF?!-inducing).

Episode #203 (10.9): "Company of Thieves"
Written by Alan McCullough
Directed by William Waring
Guest Starring: Eric Steinberg (Netan), Rudolf Martin (Anateo), Matthew Glave (Colonel Paul Emerson), Hawthorne James (Gavos), Adrien Dorval (Borzin), Sean Campbell (Solek), Timothy Paul Perez (Vashin), Gary Jones (Walter Harriman), Scott McNeil (Kefflin), Michael Rogers (Major Escher), Martin Christopher (Major Marks), Morris Chapdelaine (Tenat), Joey Aresco (Slaviash), Geoff Redknap (Alien Lt.), Dean Monroe McKenzie (Henchman)

After the Odyssey, and most of SG-1, are attacked and captured by the Lucian Alliance and the Odyssey is hijacked, Mitchell must infiltrate the organization to save his friends from being caught in the crossfire in a deadly Lucian Alliance civil war, but the situation may quickly go awry. Eventually Vala and Daniel manage to retake the Odyssey and, thanks to Mitchell's efforts, are able to get enough time to repair the hyperdrive and escape after beaming Mitchell and Teal'c aboard. Earth is now officially at war with the Lucian Alliance. But the mission is overwhelmed by the murder of Colonel Paul Emerson.

JOSEPH MALLOZZI: The Lucian Alliance return in fine, occasionally over-the-top fashion — in contrast to their later appearance on Stargate Universe. Major Marks — who was, essentially, first officer aboard Odyssey – was, episodes earlier, promoted to Major. Why? Well, we didn't want the ship's captain calling someone else "Captain,"' so he got the bump and was hitherto referred to as "Major."

In this episode, the Odyssey is forced into a mine field – which became a sort of running joke because, while pitching the scene, either Brad or Robert suggested "a dangerous mine field" (as opposed to, say, any other kind). From that point, whenever someone in the room pitched out a minefield, it was always: "a dangerous minefield ... where the mines are really close together!"

Episode #204 (10.10): "The Quest, Part 1"
Written by Joseph Mallozzi & Paul Mullie
Directed by Andy Mikita
   Guest Starring: Morena Baccarin (Adria), Cliff Simon (Baal), Rod Loomis (Osric), Beverley Breuer (Barkeep), Stephen Holmes (Villager), Doug Abrahams (Ori Prior), Steve Archer (Ori Commander), Kenton Reid (Ori Soldier), Quinn Lord (Child)

   Following a dream Vala has, SG-1 searches a planet whose address is made up of the three addresses that Arthur and his knights searched for Merlin's weapon. On the planet, they discover that Baal is also there and are forced to work with him and Adria to locate the weapon with each group having differing objectives. Together the group passes a series of tests left by Morgan Le Fay, but are confronted by a ... dragon!

   JOSEPH MALLOZZI: I love episodes in which unlikely alliances are formed — and none more unlikely than the ones in The Quest," in which SG-1 must team up with two of their greatest enemies — Baal and Adria — in their quest for the Sangraal. Overall, I liked this episode a lot, but there were a few little things that really, really bugged me. The first was in the scene in which the Ori soldiers descend on the town while SG-1 is hiding in the tavern. In one unscripted beat, an unarmed villager (apparently suicidal unarmed villager) charges toward an Ori soldier and gets blasted. Bad enough, but the blast catches him in the shoulder, initiating a ridiculous backward flip before hitting the dirt.

   Another bump I had with the episode was the time distortion field. I loved the idea — so much, that I didn't heed my writing partner Paul's warning that it would be difficult, if not impossible to pull off. I dismissed his concerns and figured we could cut around any movement on the part of the frozen travelers — which proved easier said than done. A blink here, a waver there, and I found myself pulling my hair out in the editing suite. The final issue I had with the episode was the dragon. Overall, pretty cool, but what was with those gimpy legs? This was also the episode in which the beautiful Morena Baccarin, playing the role of Adria, experienced problems with the colored contacts, necessitating our crack VFX crew touch up her eyes. Did you notice?

Episode #205 (10.11): "The Quest, Part 2"
Written by Joseph Mallozzi & Paul Mullie
Directed by Andy Mikita
   Guest Starring: Morena Baccarin (Adria), Cliff Simon (Baal), Matthew Walker (Merlin), Doug Abrahams (Ori Prior), Steve Archer (Ori Commander)

   After defeating the dragon, SG-1 and Baal are transported to a series of planets where they discover a laboratory and Merlin in stasis. Realizing that the anti-Ori weapon has been destroyed, but that Merlin can rebuild it, the team awakens him and he agrees to build a new weapon, but dies before he can finish. Daniel downloads Merlin's consciousness and continues building the weapon while Carter and Baal work on fixing the Stargate so they can escape. Before Daniel can finish the weapon, Adria, who was left behind, arrives with her forces to stop them. Daniel takes out the soldiers with Merlin's powers and holds Adria off so the rest of SG-1 can escape, but Daniel is captured by Adria and Baal is killed.

JOSEPH MALLOZZI: My many years of playing Dungeons & Dragons finally paid off in this fantasy-themed two-parter — and mom and dad thought I was wasting my time! Again, I loved the double dose of villainy in this one with the indefatigable Adria in dogged pursuit while our team of heroes is saddled with the ever-entertaining Baal. The production did a terrific job, offering up various looks for various planets. My favorite was the snow planet. It was beautiful. And, in retrospect, a pain in the ass, because the stuff they used for the falling snow ended up sticking to the bottom of my dress shoes and just wouldn't come off despite my best attempts. In the end, I ended up having to throw the shoes away.

I recall that, in the first draft, it's Mitchell who races out to take on the dragon with the C4. Executive producer Rob Cooper suggested giving the moment to Teal'c and the script was rewritten. However, on the day, the scene was first up that morning and actor Chris Judge was still feeling the effects of a late-night celebration. Director Andy Mikita took great delight in running Chris through the sequence. *Several times.*

Writing for the Baal character was a lot of fun, because he was such an insufferable ass. I remember writing his scenes with Carter and thinking that, if he'd copped that attitude with anyone else, they would have punched his lights out. And then I thought — why the hell not? Carter slugging Baal was my second favorite beat in the script. My favorite? Baal yelling, "I'll go get help!" and attempting to beat a hasty retreat before getting blasted.

Episode #206 (10.12): "Line in the Sand"
Written by Alan McCullough
Directed by Peter DeLuise
Guest Starring: Tim Guinee (Tomin), Aisha Hinds (Thilana), Eric Breker (Colonel Reynolds), Aaron Craven (Matar), Greg Anderson (Prior), Sean Tyson (Ori Firstman)

In an attempt to utilize Merlin's phase shifting technology, SG-1 answers the cry of a village pressured by Origin, and they attempt to phase shift the entire area. The plan appears to have been successful, until the device fails, and the Ori forces begin their onslaught. Meanwhile, Tomin, ordered to convert Vala to Origin, begins to question his faith in the religion when his views on the Ori's teachings clash with those of the Prior leading the assault, who's using the teachings to justify his actions. In the end, Mitchell and seriously injured Carter manage to bring the entire village out of phase using the power source of an Ori staff weapon, making it seem like the Ori have destroyed it. Tomin helps Vala escape even though he knows it may cost him his life.

JOSEPH MALLOZZI: This episode stands out to me for the great one-on-one character sequences, Vala and Tomin, and Carter and Mitchell. In the original pitch, Mitchell was going to be the injured party and Carter would have had to see to him while scrambling to save the day. Ultimately, it was decided to switch things around since Mitchell had been injured at least twice in recent episodes.

Again, we made effective use of the village set that had been used in previous episodes ("Morpheus" comes to mind) and would be used on both *Stargate Atlantis* and, one last time, in *Ark of Truth*. That enormous set was eventually struck and the stage (VFX Stage, we called it) became the home of the Wraith hive ship set as well various other *Atlantis*-related locations (e.g. the cafeteria balcony looking out on the water).

PETER DELUISE: One of the things about the Ori is that the actors who play them have to wear cataract lenses, so that they're virtually blind. They are absolutely helpless and not enough people on the show appreciated that. When Greg Anderson appeared in this episode, everybody would go off in their own direction and Greg would be completely blind and helpless with this giant staff in his hand. In retrospect, we should have had a designated person whose job was to help them out, but I would say things like, "Do you want some water? Do you have to go to the bathroom?" And then I thought the least I could do was bring them a chair, so it would be, like, "Just bend your knees and sit down where you're standing, 'cause you're fucking blind for fuck's sake." We did have an on-set person whose job was to put the cataracts in and out of his eyes, and I wondered why we didn't give them lenses with little pin holes so they could at least see *something* in the wide shots. But we never did that.

Episode #207 (10.13): "The Road Not Taken"
Written by Alan McCullough
Directed by Andy Mikita
Guest Starring: David Hewlett (Rodney McKay), Don S. Davis (General Hammond), Kavan Smith (Major Lorne), Kendall Cross (Julia Donovan), Bill Dow (Dr. Lee), Michael Chase (Chief of Staff), Billy Mitchell (Senator), Lisa Bayliss (Senator's Wife), Travis Woloshyn (Protestor), Robert Mann (Dr. Bennett), Alexander Boynton (Floor Director)

Carter experiments with Arthur's Mantle even further, but her studies send her to an alternate universe where the Ori are only hours away from obliterating the planet and the Stargate Program has been made public, resulting in martial law being spread across the U.S. In order to return home, Carter must help, but when things finally seem to go her way, President Landry won't allow Carter to return. Carter succeeds in saving the alternate Earth by shifting it out of phase and eventually convinces Landry to let her go by telling him about his counterpart from her world. Carter returns after a two-week absence with the help of Rodney McKay (David Hewlett) and is amused to discover that her team has spent that time talking to an empty room. However, there is still no sign of Daniel.

JOSEPH MALLOZZI: I love AU (alternate universe) stories. I love them so much that I had come up with an AU story late in the show's 10th season. Titled "Yesterday, Today, and Tomorrow," it saw the team jumping back and forth through time, influencing events and being influenced by past actions in a story both ambitious and, admittedly, fairly complex. So complex, in fact, that I took the time to produce a detailed, color-coded outline clearly delineating the different time periods and alternate worlds. Unfortunately, at about the same time I was working on my story, Robert and Alan had spun another AU story involving Carter. There wasn't room for two AU stories in the back half of Season 10, but I wasn't about to give up my story without a fight. Ultimately, it was a conversation with executive producer Carl Binder that put things in perspective for me. After I'd weighed the merits of both pitches, Carl threw me a look and said: "None of that matters. You just do the better story." And, in hindsight, this episode was the better story.

One of the things I love about AU stories is that they allow us to use our pre-established characters in slightly different roles. Or, in some cases, in roles in which we aren't accustomed to seeing them. This episode brought General Hammond and Major Lorne back to the S.G.C. and offered up a more somber take on the Cam Mitchell character. In this reality, Rodney McKay is a millionaire but still a jerk – who ends up doing the right thing. And the President of the United States? Why, none other than Hank Landry. And in universe, fans of the franchise finally got what they'd been asking for: the existence of the Stargate program was finally made public. With predictable results! The decision to reveal the program to the public would have formed the core of the third *SG-1* movie, *Revolution*. After beating out the story with Brad Wright, Carl Binder got as far as completing a first draft before the project was shelved.

Episode #208 (10.14): "The Shroud"
Story by Robert C. Cooper & Brad Wright, Teleplay by Robert C. Cooper
Directed by Andy Mikita
  Guest Starring: Morena Baccarin (Adria), Robert Picardo (Richard Woolsey), Christopher Gaze (Tevaris), Richard Dean Anderson (Jack O'Neill)

When SG-1 discovers a village tempted by Origin without any threats of destruction, they're in for a huge shock when they find out that their own teammate, Daniel Jackson, has been turned into a Prior of the Ori. The team captures Daniel who reveals that he and Merlin have been plotting the destruction of the Ori and need their help to finish the job. The team and O'Neill are skeptical as Daniel's plan calls for reopening the Supergate, which would let through more Ori ships, but decide to do the plan themselves while Daniel is put into stasis. Frustrated, Daniel breaks free, hijacks the Odyssey and kidnaps O'Neill. Daniel and O'Neill arrive to find that Adria and her forces have captured SG-1, but Daniel is able to overpower Adria. With Daniel in command of the Ori ship, O'Neill shuts down the Supergate and Daniel flies the ship through as Vala finishes and activates Merlin's weapon. At the last moment, O'Neill beams the team off the ship, but Adria is left behind. Due to Merlin's modifications to his body, Daniel reverts to his normal self with Merlin gone as well, but it is unclear if the Ori are dead or not. Also, six new Ori warships come through the reopened Supergate.

ROBERT C. COOPER: Where Daniel goes over to the dark side is one of those writers room what ifs, like, "What if one of our characters became the bad guy?" And we did that a lot. We had Carter and the Replicators story, and this was a similar idea. We ended up not making him *too* dark or as dark as we had originally thought.

JOSEPH MALLOZZI: The original plan had been to have Daniel go Dark Side and play out his descent, turn, and ultimate redemption over the course of several episodes. In fact, in its original multi-episode version, this story would have demonstrated a *much* darker Daniel – but it was ultimately decided that making him too dark, regardless of the circumstances, would have damaged the character, so the decision was made to make his turn to the Dark Side a little more uncertain.

ROBERT C. COOPER: Another issue we had was that by then Richard Dean Anderson was on his much more limited schedule. That was an episode where we brought him back and since the Daniel/Jack relationship was always sort of special, this seemed like a good opportunity to kind of reconnect the two.

JOSEPH MALLOZZI: I've always wanted to explore the theme of redemption with these characters, push them to the line — and beyond — and then bring them back and have them suffer the consequences, because, in the end, its their emotional response to these consequences that creates drama and explores hitherto uncharted facets of their personalities.

The reveal of the pale, milk-eyed Daniel stands as one of the top 10 *Stargate* tease-outs ever. Hmmm. Now that I think of it, that could form the basis of a future top ten:

My Top 10 Favorite *Stargate* Tease Outs! File that one away for the future. Anyway, a terrific Daniel Jackson episode that sees the return of Jack O'Neill and one final, glorious in-series reunion between the two best friends.

There's a scene in the episode in which Woolsey (played by the marvelous Robert Picardo) is telekinetically lifted off the ground. Director Andy Mikita dribbled apple juice down Bob's pant leg to suggest Woolsey was so frightened, he'd actually peed himself. Alas, the urine didn't make the final cut. Hmmm. There's one of those lines you rarely see.

Episode #209 (10.15): "Bounty"
Teleplay by Damian Kindler, Excerpts Written by Robert C. Cooper and Ron Wilkerson
Directed by Damian Kindler
Guest Starring: Anne Marie DeLuise (Amy Vanderberg), David Lovgren (Darrell Grimes), Mike Dopud (Odai Ventrell), Eric Steinberg (Netan), Bill Dow (Bill Lee), Gary Jones (Walter Harriman), Timothy Paul Perez (Vashin), Maureen Thomas (Wendy), Ian Robison (Frank), Noah Danby (Cha'ra), Ryan Elm (Gary Walesco), Jody Thompson (Woman), Mark Brandon (Presenter), Jeny Cassady (Alien Bounty Hunter), Brad Proctor (Alien Bounty Hunter), Rob Hayter (Phil), Jackie Blackmore (Female Grad), Ed Anders (Former Football Player), Rob Boyce (Assassin Sniper), Tiffani Timms (Blonde Girl)

After SG-1 destroys a Lucian Alliance shipment of kassa (a crop containing a highly addictive stimulant) shipment near the planet Rolan, the alliance places a bounty on all of the members of the team, threatening national security and lives. Meanwhile, Mitchell returns to his hometown for a high school reunion, accompanied by Vala... and bounty hunters hot on their trail. SG-1 manages to dispatch most of the bounty hunters and convince the last to go after he apparently kills Netan, the leader of Lucian Alliance.

JOSEPH MALLOZZI: The *Stargate* version of *Grosse Pointe Blank* sees Cameron Mitchell going back home for his high school reunion, unlikely date in tow (Vala, natch), and even unlikelier complication lurking in the shadows (an interstellar bounty hunter played with delightful swagger by Mike Dopud). This episode was a lot of fun (one of my favorites of the show's 10th season) and it wasn't just the Cam and Vala fish-out-of-water scenes. Carter and her "hands –on" demonstration at the conference and Daniel's run-in at the Museum of Antiquities all made for a fun and memorable episode. In the latter scenario, Daniel is quietly studying away when a sexy young lady (later revealed to be an alien) comes on to him. Daniel is confoundingly uninterested, suggesting he is either focused on his work, suspicious, or creeped out. Or, perhaps, those Jack/Daniel slashers had it right all along!

This episode marked what I believe was the second in a long line of guest spots actor Mike Dopud has done for us, first as a Russian soldier in *SG-1*'s "Full Alert," then as Bounty Hunter Ventrell in this episode, then as Kiryk the Runner in *SGA*'s "Tracker," then as the Lucian Alliance member Varro in *Stargate Universe* and, most recently, in an episode of *The Transporter*.

Episode #210 (10.16): "Bad Guys"
Story by Ben Browder & Martin Gero, Teleplay by Martin Gero
Directed by Peter DeLuise
Guest Starring: Joshua Malina (Cicero), Alistair Abell (Jayem Saran), Richard
Zeman (Lourdes), Sean Allan (Chancellor), Danielle Kremeniuk (Hesellven), Haley Beau-
champ (Sylvana), Brent O'Connor (Haran), Ron Canada (Quartus)

Searching for a great treasure, the team gates to a planet where they discover that the DHD is a prop in an exhibit; in turn, when they ask for help they appear to have come out of nowhere. Now SG-1 is mistaken for hostage-taking rebels, and they are forced to play the part in order to survive. Things degenerate as the team tries to hold off the authorities long enough for Stargate Command to make contact and send them a power source capable of dialing the Stargate, but Vala discovers a naquadah bomb, which she is able to use to power the Stargate. As the team tries to return to Earth, they are apprehended by the authorities, but Mitchell is able to convince them to let SG-1 go. However, the people of the planet apparently bury the Stargate afterwards.

JOSEPH MALLOZZI: Oof. If "Bounty" was one of my favorite episodes in the show's final season, this one ranked down at the bottom. Daniel just felt out of character. Still, the premise was interesting, a story that formed from an idea Brad once had for a tease: A museum tour on an alien world takes visitors by an ancient artifact, the Stargate, that suddenly comes alive, kawooshing, and introducing SG-1 to the shocked crowd.

I recall sitting in on the auditions for this one and having one of the actors for the role of the museum curator delivering his lines with a French accent. What, exactly, an alien was doing with a French accent, I'm not sure. But, then again, I'm not exactly sure why all the aliens SG-1 encountered spoke English. Oh, right. It was the communication nanites that "infect" all gate travelers, allowing them to understand and be understood in any off-world language. Except Goa'uld, of course.

PETER DELUISE: While filming this episode, we were informed that *Stargate SG-1* had been canceled. It was a terrible feeling. We all had grown so close and spent so much time together. Many people do not realize just how close you can get on a show that spans a decade. Try to imagine being told you're not going to spend any more time with your closest school friends. Most high school relationships have only lasted four years and college is a similar amount of time. Many of us started the show single, had met our spouses, had children and spent many weekends and off seasons together. Now we were being told we did not have a legitimate excuse to hang out all day with each other. We were going to be scattered to the four winds just like on all the other shows we had done before *Stargate*. Every show must come to an end, but this one hurt a little more.

Episode #211 (10.17): "Talion"
Written by Damian Kindler
Directed by Andy Mikita
Guest Starring: Tony Amendola (Bra'tac), Craig Fairbrass (Arkad), Eric Breker (Colonel Reynolds), Peter Kent (Bak'al), Gary Jones (Walter Harriman), Lexa Doig (Carolyn Lam), John Tench (Lizan), Megan Elizabeth (Jaffa Girl), Aaron Brooks (Nisal)

A former foe of Teal'c's has turned to the way of Origin and bombed a Jaffa summit on a Jaffa world named Dar Eshkalon, attempting to rekindle the council. The aftermath appears to have killed many Jaffa, and leaves Bra'tac barely hanging on to life. Enraged at what has happened and seeking revenge, Teal'c now decides to go on a single-minded quest... and it seems that not even SG-1's actions can stop him from achieving his goal. Teal'c ultimately tracks down his old foe and finally kills him, despite being seriously injured in the process.

JOSEPH MALLOZZI: Ah, Damian and his affinity for cryptic titles (see "Chimera" and "Ethon"). For almost the entire duration of the production and post, I kept hearing "Italian" when someone said "Talion." Anyway, bizarre title aside, I thought this was a pretty strong episode, a dark examination of the Teal'c character and one of those instances where the show was fairly on point in exploring a contemporary and controversial subject matter in a sci-fi context. The final showdown between Teal'c and Arkad is mighty gruesome — but nowhere near as gruesome as the director's cut that was so gory it had us wondering whether we'd been overworking director Andy Mikita.

Episode #212 (10.18): "Family Ties"
Written by Joseph Mallozzi & Paul Mullie
Directed by Peter DeLuise
Guest Starring: Fred Willard (Jasec), Gary Jones (Walter Harriman), Bill Dow (Dr. Bill Lee), Lexa Doig (Dr. Carolyn Lam), Martin Christopher (Major Marks), Fulvio Cecere (Colonel Davidson), Paul Wu (De'vir), Lillianne Dieuique-Lee (Kim), Robin Richardson (Trader), Dan Shea (Sgt. Siler), Doreen Ramus (Hazel)

Vala's father, Jacek, makes a deal with the S.G.C. for sanctuary in exchange for helping stop an attack on Earth. As Jacek attempts to repair his relationship with Vala, General Landry is in-spired to reach out to his daughter, Dr Lam, and his ex-wife. With Jacek's information, SG-1 and the Odyssey are able to track down and destroy a fleet of ships poised to bomb Earth, but discover Jacek double-dealing to steal the naquadah on one of the ships already on Earth. SG-1 out con Jacek and captures the ship while Jacek flees in a fake and peddles off the styrofoam peanuts left on the ship instead of naquadah.

PETER DELUISE: Let me start by saying that Fred Willard is fucking hilarious, and he was a natural for Val's crazy dad who is constantly trying to pull a con this way or that way. And also, because at this point we now knew we were canceled, Joe Mallozzi wrote a sequence where Chris Judge goes into a theatrical production of *The Vagina Monologues*. Because the show had been canceled, we had stopped being given notes of any kind. So Joe wrote it as a sort of a dare, like, "What are you gonna do? Cancel us?" So *The Vagina Monologues* stayed, which we were thrilled about. *And* we surrounded Chris with all these wonderful women from the show who were applauding his brav-ery in attending the show.

JOSEPH MALLOZZI: The *SG-1* family had officially learned its fate during pro-duction on "Bad Guys" so, at this point in the season, we already knew we were done. I'd already broken this story, a fun romp that offered up a little back-story into the Vala character (in addition some insight into to Landry and Lam's past), and couldn't really deviate — but since I was in the process of writing the script at the time, a little foresight did give me the opportunity to include a few subtle (?) references to the can-cellation, in addition to one of my favorite endings in *Stargate* history. This episode was also memorable for the hilarious performance of guest star Fred Willard, who played the part of Vala's incorrigible father.

We open with Mitchell and Siler heading down the corridor, catching them mid-conversation. The first words out of Mitchell's mouth: "They canceled it? Really? I didn't even know the new season had started" echoed the online comments of many a fan when they discovered *SG-1* had been canceled. And, later in the episode, Jacec in conversation with Carter: "That's too bad. Because after all your *Stargate* program has accomplished for this network ... of planets, I would think the decision makers would show it the respect it deserves." There were a couple of other references, but I was asked to lose them for the final draft.

Surprisingly, something that no one asked me to lose was the final scene in which Teal'c unwittingly attends a reading of *The Vagina Monologues* (Sorry. *Virginia Dialogues*). I put it in the first draft, fully expecting to be told, "Very funny, but you've got to lose it." Surprisingly, nobody asked me to take it out. Oh, I'm sure some thought about it, or assumed I would make the decision to take it out myself before the episode went to camera, but the scene went over so well with everyone else that I elected to keep it.

Episode #213 (10.19): "Dominion"
Story by Alex Levine, Teleplay by Alan McCullough
Directed by William Waring
Guest Starring: Morena Baccarin (Adria), Cliff Simon (Baal), Peter Flemming (Malcolm Barrett), Eric Breker (Colonel Reynolds), Jonathan Walker (Ta'Seem), Fulvio Cecere (Colonel Davidson), Steven Cree Molison (Player), Paul Lazenby (Jaffa), Derek Versteeg (Jaffa)

In an attempt to capture Adria, the team uses Vala as bait, only to have Baal beam the Orici away in SG-1's time of victory. When they track down the parasite, they discover Baal wants to end the reign of the Ori just as much as the S.G.C., and he's taken a drastic course of action to do so, implanting Adria with one of his cloned symbiotes. The symbiote is ultimately removed and eventually killed, but Baal fatally poisons Adria beforehand and in order to survive she ascends.

MORENA BACCARIN (actress, "Adria"): My character is really trying her hardest to convert the entire galaxy to her religion, sort of like a Nazi. But, she's got a fight ahead of her. It's interesting, the turn it takes at the very end is not what I expected when I was reading it, and I had to ask them, "What does this mean?" (*UGO.com*)

JOSEPH MALLOZZI: Well before this episode aired, I had fans online asking, "What would happen if a Goa'uld symbiote was implanted in an Ori?" Well ... close enough. This episode is packed with back-references (Adria, Baal, ascension, the memory-altering device), jumps back and forth in time (between the present and a past that didn't really happen), pays off long-standing storylines, and propels the show's major arc in a bold, new direction. Which, alas, we wouldn't be able to pick up until the *Ark of Truth* movie. It was a huge cliffhanger. Would Adria be back and under what circumstances? But we took solace in the fact that the plan was to make two movies, at least one of which would allow us to close out the Ori arc. BTW, favorite line: "It's the bad guy equivalent of cordon bleu!"

Episode #214 (10.20): "Unending"
Written & Directed by Robert C. Cooper
Guest Starring: Gary Jones (Walter Harriman), Martin Christopher (Major Marks), Michael Shanks (Voice of Thor)

The Asgard summon SG-1 to tell them that their experiments to halt their genetic degeneration have failed, meaning they are a dying race. Because of this, the Asgard have decided to give "everything [they] have and know" to the Tau'ri. Thor tells Colonel Carter that the people of

Earth are the Fifth Race, the other four being the Ancients, Nox, Furlings, and the Asgard. When the Ori show up, the Asgard destroy Orilla, and themselves with it, so that their technology will not fall into the hands of the Ori. With the new weapons the Asgard equipped the Odyssey with, they are able to destroy an Ori mothership with ease, but come under repeated assault from two more who chase them wherever they go. In a desperate attempt to stop the relentless pursuit, SG-1 and General Landry beam the crew off the ship onto an uninhabited planet and lock the ship in a time-dilation field when they are unable to separate the new upgrades from the hyperdrive. They end up spending between 50 to 60 years trapped on the ship, moments away from death if they ever stop the field. During that time, Landry dies and Daniel and Vala get together. As an old woman, Carter figures out how to reverse time so this never happens, but unless someone stays old, everything will happen the same way. It also requires temporarily allowing the ship to be destroyed to allow an energy blast to power the effect. Due to his greater lifespan, Teal'c volunteers and is able to give Carter what she needs to separate the hyperdrive quickly, and the Odyssey escapes.

DAVID READ: Fans look back to "The Fifth Race" as sort of an epoch-setting moment when O'Neill visits the Asgard. The decision was made to bring that element back in "Unending," with humanity being declared to be the Fifth Race by the Asgard.

ROBERT C. COOPER: I think we were trying to achieve certain things in this episode. You're trying to get a sense of closure even though you're not actually ending the series. You want to feel as though what has come before has had meaning. I think one of the things fans have always appreciated the series for is the fact that we don't reset to zero at the end of every episode, that we've been a part of the show from the beginning and we have a respect for the mythology we've developed — and that it expands. It's there for us to pay tribute to. And that was always going to be a part of that sense of closure — let's finally show a major milestone that something *happens*. Something has to have happened in this episode that people can feel somewhat satisfied: "Hey, I've watched the show since then, since those days, and now I finally get to see the pay-off beat, that we're finally the Fifth Race."

BRAD WRIGHT: Just a great, great hour of television, but this isn't the ending and it was okay to do it that way. Like Tom Vitale from SciFi said, never end a series because it hurts the reruns. But we also knew we were going to be doing the movies that became *Ark of Truth* and *Continuum*.

ROBERT C. COOPER: I think that "Unending" was the emotional ending of 10 seasons of *Stargate SG-1*, whereas the film *Ark of Truth* was the plot resolution of the Ori story.

DVD MOVIES

Stargate: The Ark of Truth (2008)
Written & Directed by Robert C. Cooper
Starring: Ben Browder (Cameron Mitchell), Amanda Tapping (Samantha

Carter), *Christopher Judge (Teal'c), Michael Shanks (Daniel Jackson), Beau Bridges (Hank Landry), Claudia Black (Vala Mal Doran), Currie Graham (James Marrick), Morena Baccarin (Adria), Tim Guinee (Tomin), Julian Sands (Doci), Sarah Strange (Morgan Le Fay), Michael Beach (Abraham Ellis), Gary Jones (Walter Harriman), Martin Christopher (Major Marks), Christopher Gauthier (Hertis), Erik Breker (Reynolds), Matthew Walker (Merlin), Alisen Down (Alteran Woman), Gabrielle Rose (Alteran Woman #2), Fabrice Grover (Amelius), Spencer Maybee (Captain Binder), Simon Bradbury (Alteran Man), Jason Calder (Ori Warrior), Greg Anderson (Prior #1), Doug Abrahams (Prior #2), Morris Chapdelaine (Prior #3), Nicholas Podbrey (Prior #4), Ian Wallace (Prior #5), J. Douglas Stewart (Prior #6)*

SG-1 takes the Odyssey *into the Ori Galaxy to locate the Ark of Truth, a technology originally created by Amelius long ego to forcibly brainwash the opposing Asurans. The ark is unveiled before the Doci, who communicates his knowledge to all other Priors. The ascended Adria is then confronted by Morgan Le Fay and engaged in eternal combat — effectively bringing the Ori threat to an end.*

BRAD WRIGHT: It's the climax of the Ori story line. ...They're not big-budget [films] by any definition, but for us it's pretty good. As we've proven over the years, just give us a little more money and we can make pretty good television or DVDs.

ROBERT C. COOPER: I still look at seasons nine and 10 of *SG-1*, with the Ori mythology and with Cam Mitchell and Vala being part of the show, as almost a different show. And *that* show only ran for two years. The difference is that we really only had two seasons to develop that show and we did build a lot, but then needed to figure out a way to wrap it all up. So I viewed *Ark of Truth* as a bigger episode of the show as opposed to a standalone movie. I think Brad's movie that he wrote, *Continuum*, was a little more standalone. But we had a great time making *Ark of Truth*. Obviously neither one of them is a $200 million Marvel movie, but when you have a little more money, you can do more.

DAVID READ: SG-1 takes the *Odyssey* into enemy territory on a quest to recover that piece of hardware and show it to Dosi, played by Julian Sands, who I would've, frankly, loved to have seen much more of. Along the way we get into another Replicator problem, which was an interesting twist, because we thought that that situation was done. But in terms of a B story, it's a pretty solid one. They would have needed something else going on while they were dealing with what was going on on the ground is Celestis. It's a great end to the arc with Toman, Vala's husband. I think it satisfies Avrias arc as well, Vala's daughter, and the last vestiges of her salvation completely off and resolved things in a pretty satisfactory way.

DARREN SUMNER: They had more money and they didn't have the time constraints or the potential creative constraints of airing on television. It was a great evolution of the show and of the characters. As a payoff to the Ori storyline, it does *exactly* what it sets out to do. We finally get to go to the Ori home galaxy and have a face-to-face confrontation with basically the only Ori left at this point, who is Adria, and the stakes couldn't be higher. For 10 years we've been rescuing planets from oppression and now we're effectively liberating two different galaxies from the oppression of false gods.

Stargate: Continuum (2008)
Written by Brad Wright
Directed by Martin Wood
Starring: Ben Browder (Cameron Mitchell), Amanda Tapping (Samantha Carter), Christopher Judge (Teal'c), Michael Shanks (Daniel Jackson), Beau Bridges (Hank Landry), Claudia Black (Vala Mal Doran), Richard Dean Anderson (Jack O'Neill), William DeVane (Henry Hayes), Cliff Simon (Baal), Don S. Davis (George Hammond), Steve Bacic (Camulus), Gary Jones (Walter Harriman), Jacqueline Samuda (Nirrti), Peter Williams (Apophis), Darcy Cadman (Russian Officer), Peter John Prinsloo (Alex), Jean Daigle (Bosun), Corey Turner (Helmsman), David Ingram (Air Force Major), Dan Shea (Siler), Martin Wood (Wood), Derek Peakman (Tok'ra Elder), Juan Llorens (Cab Driver), Ron Halder (Cronus), Alison Matthews (Interviewer), David Kaye (Interviewer), O.L. Bramble (Jaffa Leader), Reese Alexander (Jaffa Pilot), Mark Pawson (Jaffa Pilot), Tracy Trueman (Neighbor), Jason Benson (Officer), Kirsten Williamson (Officer), Campbell Lane (Older Man), Vince Crestejo (Yu), Jay Williams (Ra), Lebrone Flippin (Baal's Jaffa), Duke Shoebotham (Baal's Jaffa), Mike Roselli (Qetesh's Jaffa), Rob Boyce (Qetesh's Jaffa), Colin Cunningham (Major Davis), Adrian Hughes (Pel'tac Jaffa), Jacqueline Becher (Lady Shopper), Michael Bernacchi (Commanding Officer), Wesley K. Koshoffer (COB), Jason M. Geddes (Officer of the Deck), Alan M. Roche (Officer on Guard), Barry Campbell (Crewman on Sail)

After Teal'c and Vala vanish during Baal's execution ceremony, the team gates back to Earth to discover that the timeline has been altered and the Stargate program no longer exists.

ROBERT C. COOPER: The second movie definitely plays on a lot of the characters and brings back maybe favorites for the fans who have been watching the show. But it's also, as a story, what we call a one-off.

BRAD WRIGHT: *Continuum* is more like *Stargate* of old than it is going forward. It's a good 'ole *Stargate* story made as big as possible. And that, in part, is because Rick is in it. But it's also because it's a time-travel story. Therefore, I was able to bring back a lot of very familiar faces who've been gone for some time.

ROBERT C. COOPER: This is one of those great examples of the tail wagging the dog where something would be presented to us as an opportunity, and in this case Brad would write a movie or an episode about that thing. Like having a version of the Oval Office we could use in previous episodes, or in this case, an admiral from the Navy approached Brad and Martin at some point where they got to fly in T-38s that were taking off of an aircraft carrier, and someone said to them, "Hey, would you like to come up to the Arctic and watch a nuclear submarine come out of the ice?" So immediately Brad's brain went to work and said, "How do we do make that part of a show or an episode or a movie?" That was sort of the genesis of *Continuum*.

BRAD WRIGHT: This is the biggest, best thing I think I've ever done for *Stargate*. I'm very proud of it. You always have some small regret with something that you couldn't pull off. You say, "I wish we could have done this, I wish we could have had that." But there are so few regrets with how *Continuum* turned out that it's not even worth mentioning. Martin Wood did such a good job directing it, and we had such a good time on set together.

The Stargate was at its most vulnerable in history — or at least since it was dug up —when it was being transported from Africa to North America at the outbreak of World War II. So the Stargate is on its way across, Baal is going to sink the ship, [and] somehow a heroic act has to take place to stop the ship from being sunk. And what if the captain of that boat, by cosmic coincidence, happened to be the grandfather of Mitchell?

PETER WILLIAMS: I spent a few sleepless nights on that scene I had in *Continuum*. I came back to do that little vignette — I will call it a cameo, although I don't think that's the strict title of the categorization of the role. I'll say that I was very happy to do it, just to maintain my connection to the *Stargate* franchise.

DARREN SUMNER: I love *Continuum*; it's right up there with "Lost City" for me as one of my favorite *Stargate* stories, in part because *Stargate* felt free. *The Ark of Truth* had to conclude the TV series and wrap up the Ori storyline. Now, with *Continuum*, the second movie, the sky was the limit. The question is, what would you do if you had this bigger canvas to paint on and more money to spend? What a great big sci-fi adventure that you could put your team through. On top of that, I'm a sucker for time travel stories. If I have any complaints, I wish there had been a bigger part for Jack O'Neill.

BRAD WRIGHT: I think about that moment when they arrive in the time altered reality, where Beau Bridges as Landry gives what I call a master class in acting. All of those interviews in the montage sequence were shot in the hangar in one day, and he did *so* many takes. We had four cameras running and he nailed every take every time, and it just blew me away that he did all of that. It's compressed in the episode, because we did several screens and we dissolved back and forth between them. Most people just watch it as a scene in a movie. I watch it and I say, "*God*, Beau Brides is *so good.*" His reading of the line, "The arrogance of what you're asking me to do is mind boggling," where he *yells* it … He bites that word off at the end and that's the only take where he got that angry. I remember seeing it in dailies and starting from there and cutting backwards from that point, because that line reading had to be there. And what he's saying is true: *your* reality's fucked, but ours is fine.

The franchise would continue beyond Continuum *with* Stargate Atlantis *airing original episodes until 2009 and* Stargate Universe *airing for two seasons between 2009 and 2011. What is so odd in some ways is the fact that* Stargate *began as the 1994 feature and once it premiered as* SG-1 *in 1997, new adventures were produced for an incredible 17 seasons over the course of 14 years, but then … it was finished. Certainly not in the hearts of fans or the shows' creators, but one has to imagine that the relative "silence" was deafening.*

At the same time, there also has to be the feeling that this franchise, currently owned by Amazon thanks to its acquisition of MGM, will eventually make a comeback in some form.

JOSEPH MALLOZZI: I went into every season of *SG-1* expecting it to be the last — except for the show's 10th season. By then, I'd finally come around to the show's resilience and honestly believed we'd come back for an 11th season. Sadly, it didn't. With *Atlantis*, I was honestly surprised and disappointed given the ratings were strong and I assumed we'd use *SGA* to pass the torch to *SGU* by programming the shows back to back, much like we'd done with *SG-1* and *SGA*. Finally, the *Universe* cancellation was especially bitter given that we were floated the likelihood of a third and final season to wrap things up — only to have that go away as well.

BRAD WRIGHT: My joke at the time was that I used to get, like, 100 emails a day and I'd have to respond to 50 of them, because they were approvals and so on. I always have the sense that you have something to do or I have to respond to something or approve something. Then your phone buzzes and you go, "Oh … Staples is having a sale." It makes you feel really rough. Then I took too long of a break, because I thought, "I've just created 350 odd hours of television that was quite successful and I should be able to go in and sell another show." But a sci-fi niche is very difficult when basically nobody knows who you are when you reintroduce yourself to the world. So I went out pitching and failing quite a few times, but getting close. And you say to your agent, "Is that everybody?" "That's everybody." Oh, shit. Guess I need to come up with another idea, so you go down and pitch again. My wife was calling me Willy Loman, because I would be going down for my four days of meetings and coming back with all nos. Fortunately I sold *Travelers*, which made me very happy and was great fun. Even if I don't do another one, at least I did another show after *Stargate*.

ROBERT C. COOPER: You just have to look around at all the things that get made from IP that is far less well known than *Stargate*. I mean, that's a valuable piece of IP that was part of the package that Amazon wanted and bought from MGM. Who's going to get to do it and what it will be, I have no idea. But if you offered me a bet, I would take that bet today that at some point in the near future, there *will* be another version of *Stargate*.

MARTIN WOOD: What's special about *Stargate* are the four characters that we started with. That was what really was the propulsion. It was Rick, Amanda, Chris and Michael. And the fact that it was Brad and Jonathan, Brad and Robert and all the other writers taking these four characters that people loved so much and giving them these *amazing* stories. And it's not just four characters, it was also Don, Ben, Claudia, Corin — everybody that stepped into those uniforms. If *Stargate* is going to come back, it has to come back with that kind of care in putting the cast together, and that kind of care taken in putting the stories together — and not just trying to bring *Stargate* back. Do you know what I mean? There actually has to be that thought put into building a world.

PETER DELUISE: It's a cliché, but it's true: when you spend that much time with people, it tends to feel like family. After 10 years of working together, it was painful when the show was finally canceled. We had spent more time with each other than many of our own real family members and I think the general feeling was sadness. It's impossible to work in the entertainment industry and not experience a feeling of loss when the show is finally over, but the optimistic among us knows that our paths will cross again in the future. Vancouver is a small enough town for that to be true. And I believe there is *still* an audience for *Stargate*. The premise of *Stargate* and the story device that it brings, is virtually unbeatable. I believe Brad Wright understands that better than anybody and is the right person to create that show.

BRAD WRIGHT: I suspect that *Stargate* would come back at some point, whether I had anything to do with it or not. And I still do. Whether it's in a year or five years, I strongly believe that *Stargate* will be back.

JOSEPH MALLOZZI: I have no doubt that *Stargate* will be back in time. It's simply too valuable a franchise to shelf indefinitely. Having said that, never underestimate the ability of executives to overlook an obvious great opportunity in favor of something else. By that, I mean that the *Stargate* fandom is still out there and they are hungry for more. A new series by longtime creator Brad Wright would offer the best of both worlds — a perfect jumping on point for new viewers who know nothing about the show and a wonderful continuation for long-suffering fans. I wouldn't be surprised to see TPTB go another way, however, choosing to enlist creatives with no connection to the franchise's past success, alienating the existing fandom and squandering that brilliant opportunity. But I suppose time will tell.

ABOUT THE AUTHOR

EDWARD GROSS is a veteran entertainment journalist (*does that just mean old?*), who began his professional career in the early-1980s, writing articles on film, television and comic books for such publications as *Starlog* (where he would become New York Correspondent), *New York Nightlife, Daredevils, Comics Scene,* and *Fangoria.* He would go on to be Editor-in-Chief of the magazines *Not of This Earth* and *Retro Vision,* as well as Senior Editor of *Cinescape, Femme Fatales* and *Cinefantastique.* Other positions have included Executive Editor of *Life Story, Movie Magic, Film Fantasy, TV Magic* and *Superhero Spectacular,* all from Bauer Publishing; Executive Editor, US for Empireonline.com, Film/TV Editor for closerweekly.com, intouchweekly.com, lifeandstylemag.com and j-14.com; and is currently Contributing Editor to doyouremember.com and Senior Editor of *Geek* magazine. He has written or co-written more than two dozen non-fiction books on film and TV.

Twitter: @EdGross
Instagram: @EdGrossWriter
Facebook: ed.gross.923